Also by Rand Eastwood:

Rand Eastwood | Author
Author & Blogger • Artist & Craftsman
randeastwood.com

Rolling The Bones
12 Tales of Life, Death, Loss, & Redemption
amazon.com/rolling-bones-tales-death-redemption/
dp/0692716203

Woodlands Press
on Amazon
amazon.com/author/randeastwood

OÛSIA Magazine
The Essence of Truth, Wisdom, & Being
Reason • Philosophy • Lifestyle • Culture
ousiamagazine.com

Lifeology Store
Unique & Exclusive Gifts
lifeologystore.com

Typology Mugs
Because Everyone is Unique
lifeologystore.com/collections/typology-mugs

Compass Bookstore
Explore a World of Great Reads
bookshop.org/shop/compassbookstore

EVOLVE: Toward Autarchy
on Substack
Individualism • Consensualism • Free Markets • Stewardship
towardautarchy.substack.com

PRIMEVAL

A NOVEL BY

RAND EASTWOOD

PRIMEVAL

Graphics, Cover Art, and
Interior Design by Rand Eastwood
Author Website: www.randeastwood.com

ISBN-10: 1-7326546-6-2
ISBN-13: 978-1-7326546-6-2

Other Books by Rand Eastwood:
Rolling The Bones: 12 Tales of
Life, Death, Loss, & Redemption
(A Collection of Dark Fiction)

A Quality Publication by

For Lynn

I don't know if this novel would have ever happened if not for you: your kind advice, your enthusiasm—and particularly your constant encouragement—concerning my writing.

As an avid reader, career English teacher, and finally a bookstore manager, you were the first professional with plausible credentials (IMO) to recognize my writing and insist that I pursue it.

And thanks to you, I did—starting with *Rolling The Bones*, which definitely would not have been the book that it is today without your help.

I only regret not having finished *Primeval* in time, and thereby benefiting from your wise and valuable input during its development, too.

But even so, I know—I *felt*—that you were somehow still there, watching over me, guiding me...and more, *believing* in me.

And for that, I thank you. Thank you for *everything*.

May you rest in peace.

"Rand Eastwood is rapidly becoming the thinking man's horror author."

~ Steve Forbes | Saskatchewan, Canada

— Acknowledgements —

Debbie Montgomery
Terry Lyon-McCarthy
Steve Forbes

Many thanks to all of you for reading the first drafts of this novel and providing your valuable feedback. I know it was considerable work, being such a sizable tome, and I really appreciate your help in correcting the text and polishing the narrative.

Thank you!

Joseph A. Eberhardt

The story *Second Chances* — which is told by Chaz to his friends at night around the campfire in *Part II: The Blackjack Club* — was the brainchild of my friend Joseph A. Eberhardt.

Some time ago, I was looking for an idea for a new short story, and so I asked for ideas on Facebook. Several of my friends responded, including Joe, who suggested a company called "Second Chances" that can send you back in time to give you a second chance at something you totally blew the first time around...I liked the idea and ran with it, thought it turned out nicely, and decided to include it in the campfire scene.

Thanks, Joe!

— A Note From The Author —

Anyone who has read my first book, the collection *Rolling The Bones*, will likely recognize Part I of this novel: *The Crossing*.

Originally, *The Crossing* was one of three novellas included in the previous collection; and, being the final piece that I wrote to finish *Bones*, I decided to let myself just run with it—and it turned out to be very fun to write, as well as probably one of the better pieces in the book (or at least one of my favorites!)

But over time, I began to believe there was more to the story...

And as the story further unfolded in my mind, *The Crossing* became Part I of *Primeval*.

However, it's not exactly the same; I went back and reworked the storyline slightly so that it better aligned with *Primeval* as the overarching narrative developed.

But the changes aren't all that substantial; anyone who has already read the novella *The Crossing* could probably bypass that section in *Primeval* and be fine—just be aware that doing so could potentially lead to some slightly confusing inconsistencies in the storyline, or leave a few questions unanswered.

Ultimately, the choice comes down to reader preference...I just wanted to give everyone a heads-up.

Anyway, thanks for taking the chance and giving *Primeval* a shot, and I hope y'all enjoy it!

Cheers!

"This is the kind of music that we want to hear, and nobody's really making this specific combination of elements."

~ Mike Shinoda | LINKIN PARK

"I can do hard things. Doing hard things has intrinsic value, and they will make me a better person, even if I end up failing."

~ Brandon Sanderson | Author

"The old world is dying, and the new world struggles to be born: now is the time of monsters."

~ Antonio Gramsci

PRIMEVAL

Primeval

prī'mēv(ə)l

adjective

1: Of or resembling the earliest ages
   in the history of the world

2: Based on primitive instinct

— Contents —

— Preface —

Approximately 66 million years ago, an asteroid calculated at 6.2 miles in diameter, traveling at an estimated 45,000 MPH, traversed the earth's atmosphere in a few tenths of a second and struck the partially submerged Yucatán Peninsula in the southern portion of what is now the Gulf of Mexico.

The resultant impact crater, 110 miles in diameter and 12 miles deep, lies partially underwater and partially under rain forest near the communities of Chicxulub Puerto & Chicxulub Pueblo, after which the Chicxulub Crater is named.

The kinetic energy of the impact is estimated at 100 million megatons of TNT, or more than 4.5 billion times the energy of the atomic bomb dropped on Hiroshima, Japan—and 10,000 times the explosive energy of the entire world's nuclear arsenal combined.

The seismic jolt would have been 1,000 times stronger than the strongest earthquake ever recorded.

The resultant Tsunamis were likely over 100 meters (330 ft) tall, with the initial wave created by the impact thought to have reached 1.5 km (nearly 1 mile) high, causing massive flooding of the Americas.

With wind speeds of over 600mph, it took less than two weeks for the devastation to envelope the entire planet, with the energy reflected from the atmosphere causing land temperatures to reach up to 750°F, sparking global wildfires and destroying nearly all plant and animal life. Dust, soot, and debris from the impact, along with smoke from the global fires permeated the atmosphere, completely blocking out the sun and plummeting the earth into total darkness for many months, long enough to kill off all the plankton in the oceans, thus collapsing the entire marine food chain and destroying nearly all oceanic life.

And, the combination of blocked sunlight, the nitrous oxide-filled atmosphere, and global acid rain for up to two years also killed off most of the earth's plant life, thus collapsing the land-based food chain as well.

It is estimated that the earth may have been shrouded in darkness for up to two years, and that it took between 500,000 and 1.5 million years for the earth's ecosystem to recover.

And not only has the Chicxulub meteor impact event been determined to cause the demise of the dinosaurs, it is also credited for wiping out 75% of all life on the planet—including oceanic life due to the plankton die-off, and even river-dwelling life due to acid rain runoff, poisoning the rivers and lakes. The only possible survivors were creatures that lived underground.

Paleontologists have identified five such extinction-level events over the past 500 million years, but the Chicxulub event, 66 million years ago, is the only one after which any evidence of humans emerging and evolving has been found: the genus *Homo* appearing around 2.5 to 3 million years ago, but *Homo sapiens* not until around 200,000 to 300,000 years ago.

So: if the human species is as advanced as it is after only a few hundred thousand years of evolution—or 2.5 to 3 million years at the most—how much more advanced would a species be, after *500 million years* of evolution? A species that managed to survive each of those extinction-level events, *because it lived underground?*

Prologue I: The Ritual

**Creswell Crags cave system
on the border of
Derbyshyre & Nottynghamshyre
East Midlands, England
1543**

Father Blakwell was growing impatient.

Standing in the near total darkness of the cave, staring down at the single faltering candle that sat burning on the edge of the large, blood-stained boulder—a makeshift altar—he wondered if he should extinguish the flame until Kyrkham showed up.

After all, the candle had burned nearly halfway down already—and Kyrkham was running late.

The flickering flame threw the tall man's shadow crazily about the rear wall of the cavern, jerking and quivering behind two of the four Servants who were participating in the bloody ritual on this night under a full moon, their shadows joining his in the neurotic dance—only being closer to the cave wall, theirs were slightly smaller, darker, more defined.

The Servants were stationed at each point of a pentangle that was sloppily scrawled in pale chalk on the dusty stone floor, inscribed within a large, somewhat lopsided circle, the center of which was inhabited by the stone altar the priest had ordained for their rituals nearly two decades ago.

Kyrkham, when he returned with tonight's sacrifice, would take position at the fifth, vacant point, which was also the topmost of the pentangle.

This was his reward as the Chosen One this Ritual cycle.

The cave walls surrounding them were covered with symbols, occult-like in appearance, but apotropaic in nature—hundreds, perhaps thousands of them; etched by hand roughly into the limestone, they had amassed over the years into an almost hypnotic tapestry: pentangles (not unlike the one scribed on the stone floor for their ritual), hexafoils, confusing mazes, multiple overlapping diagonal lines, crude crucifixes, all of which were accompanied by smatterings of seemingly random combinations of letters, such as intertwined Vs, and Ps and Ms scratched together.

The Servants all donned black tunics, tied at the waist with old frayed ropes, their faces shrouded and unseen within the pitch-black shadows of the large, drooping hoods, and each grasping their designated items—each representing one of the four elements, according to the requirements of the Ritual, and as assigned to each by Father Blakwell—clutched in both hands against their chests: an athame, representing fire, its blade glinting in the candlelight; a wand, representing air; a pentacle dangling from a bronze chain, representing earth; and a copper chalice, representing water.

Encompassing the priest and altar standing in the center of

the pentangle, they, too, waited in silence.

Though Blakwell also wore a tunic, his hood was thrown back, fully revealing his aging, bespectacled face and a hazard of light gray, nearly white hair. The lenses of his roughly-hewn rivet spectacles reflected the tiny flame before him, making his eyes appear to be aflame, as if evil itself was dancing within the dark and worn wooden frames. An ancient, tattered book lay open on the rugged stone surface before him, glowing under the flickering candle flame: the sacred text he would read aloud during the Ritual, preceding the sacrifice.

And in one hand, hanging by his side: a long, iron dagger.

Before the group, opposite the shadow-dancing wall and below another mosaic of apotropaia, a large crevice opened in the cave floor, marking the deep center of the entire cave system. A hole in the earth the depth of which, they had determined long ago, was immeasurable; their brightest lanterns could not begin to penetrate the blackness, and the cavern seemed to spread in all directions below the cave floor.

Believing it to be a portal of some sort—perhaps a gateway to hell itself—the small sect led by Father Blakwell dreaded what evil entities might visit their village, emerging here from the underworld: be they demons, evil spirits, or terrible beasts of unimaginable origin—perhaps even of primeval origin.

Or perhaps, Satan himself.

Thus, the apotropaia.

And the Ritual.

And the sacrifice.

But then his eyes turned upward, toward the labyrinthine tunnel that led from a hidden opening in the woods into this interior chamber deep within the cave system, as he thought he faintly heard the shuffle of footfalls approaching in the distance.

Or did he?

Without moving his head, eyes only, he glanced around the flickering pentagram, and saw the rest of them were also looking to the tunnel entrance, and was comforted. So they could hear it too, it wasn't his imagination.

Eyes peering into the dark tunnel, he waited.

The sound of hurrying feet neared, growing more distinct, then suddenly stopped, seemingly just outside the cavern entrance. This was disconcerting to Father Blakwell; Kyrkham's hesitance to enter—at such a late hour—most certainly indicated that there was something wrong.

And they didn't have much time.

The man entered the cave slowly, head bowed, hands clasped, the hood of his tunic pulled over his head, hiding his face. He approached Father Blakwell, whose eyes widened in anger as he realized that Kyrkham's arms were empty.

No sacrifice!

"Forgive me, Father," he pleaded in a quiet voice.

"What is the meaning of this?" Blakwell replied sternly. "You didn't bring the sacrifice—and the hour is late!—tell me, where is the child?"

Kyrkham's head fell even lower, and he sighed heavily.

"I don't know...I just couldn't...couldn't...it just—"

—he raised his head to look Father Blakwell in the face—

"—doesn't seem right."

"You all drew lots, fairly—"

—with this, Father Blakwell waved his hand around, signifying the circle of servants, all of whom nodded almost imperceptibly—

"—and you drew the red lot—marked with the blood of the first lamb born this year, the final year of the cycle—meaning your are the chosen one; thus it is God's will, not mine, that you shall do His bidding."

"But…he's just a child!" Kyrkham cried.

"Born to a harlot, a heathen. And some even say a witch! She has bed many in her sinful ways, and I ask you: is it even known who the boy's father is?"

Kyrkham hung his head, and shook it.

"No, Father, it is not known. It could be anyone from the village. Or even a visiting traveler. She herself claims she does not know."

"And tell me, do you believe that she will be fruitful for the Lord, given her sinful, if not outright evil, ways? Do you believe that she will work to advance His kingdom on earth?"

"No, Father, I fear she will not, in all her days."

"And the child…is he not infirm? Will he not be a burden on the entire village, unable to contribute to the common good, due to his deformity? For he can barely walk, no?

"That is true, father. The boy is a cripple, he was deformed at birth."

"Yes…punished by God for the sins of his mother."

Kyrkham just looked down and silently nodded his head in resignation.

"And tonight we will fulfill His will. The child of the sinner has been chosen for this cycle. The entire village will gain from his sacrifice, rather than suffer the loss of one of greater value to the community."

"Well, everyone will gain except his mother…," Kyrkham nearly whispered.

"The mother is nothing but a sinner! A whore! Rumored to be a witch! She contributes nothing of value to the village, to the common good, as God commands! Adultery? Witchcraft? Black Magic? Rampant acts of sin and evil, only to deliver a bastard child—and an invalid at that—that the entire village must tend to and feed, when there's barely enough for the righteous as it is! This is the Devil's work, not God's! So indeed, she will suffer from this sacrifice—but her suffering is just, born from her own evil deeds! And she knows this, for she may be a heathen, and reject God's commandments, but she is far from blind to them! In fact, she is hardly different from Lilith herself—the first woman God created, who rejected the authority of both God and Adam—does not the Apostle Paul write of God's commandment in I Timothy chapter two, 'Let the woman learn in silence with all subjection. But I suffer not a woman to teach, nor to usurp authority over the man, but to be in silence'…? But Lilith would not respectfully accept God's commandment, and instead abandoned Adam and the garden to become the bride of Satan, vengefully sacrificing so many innocent children born of others—except now, for *this* likewise evil and disobedient woman, it will be *her own child* that will be sacrificed!"

Kyrkham looked up again at Father Blakwell.

"Father, all that you say is indeed true of the mother, and yes, the boy may be a burden for the village to bear…but he is also innocent—unlike his mother—and yet is he still deserving of death? He is at fault for nothing!"

At this, Father Blakwell sighed heavily. Then he continued:

"My son, are you not aware that God gives His blessing to rid the world of such blights as those born of sinners? Does He not command, in Isaiah 14: 'prepare to slaughter the sons for the sins of their parents?' And is it not written in Exodus 12: 'and God smote all the firstborn in the land of Egypt, from the firstborn of Pharaoh that sat on his throne unto the firstborn of the captive that was in the dungeon; and all the firstborn of cattle?' And is it not told, in Second Chronicles 15: 'those who would not seek the Lord God would be put to death, whether young or old, man or woman?'"

Then, in a small voice, Kyrkham replied, "But Christ spoke of forgiveness—even of the prostitute who would otherwise have been stoned to death."

"Perhaps so," the priest acknowledged, nodding slightly. "But was that prostitute also a witch, practicing Satan's work?"

Kyrkham just shook his head silently.

Blakwell then continued:

"It is written, in Exodus 22: 'you shall not allow a sorceress to live.' And also, in Leviticus 20: 'anyone who is a medium or spiritist must be put to death by stoning; their death is by their own hand.' So that common whore should be grateful that it is not her life, but that of her invalid and bastard son, that will be sacrificed not only as it is commanded in the scriptures, but for the common good as well. After all, as it is written, his death is by her own hand."

"Yes, Father, I understand the scriptures...but we don't know if the boy's mother is really—"

At this Father Blakwell became angry, raising his voice:

"Would you prefer the Beast select his own sacrifice!? Who knows which innocent and productive villager will be taken? Or if only one? It could be many! The entire village could be devastated with loss! Is that what you wish? Is it not better that God selects the least among us, through the work and sacrifices of we, The Servants, to offer up to the Beast instead?"

Kyrkham lowered his head again, and sighed heavily.

"Yes, Father. This way is better. I shall fulfill my duty as this cycle's Chosen One, and retrieve and deliver the sacrifice as you command."

"As *God* commands," the priest corrected. "Now go and do, for time is short, and we are falling behind in The Ritual."

Kyrkham hesitated, then turned and walked hesitantly toward the cave entrance. But Blakwell called after him, stopping him in his tracks, thought he remained turned away.

"And remember, it is written in Deuteronomy 17: 'the man that doth not hearken unto the priest that standeth to minister there before God, that man shall die."

With this Kyrkham turned his head abruptly and glared in horror at Blakwell for a moment, while the priest—the candle flame still dancing on his spectacles, setting his eyes aflame, and the iron dagger now brandished threateningly—smiled at him; and the smile was not a friendly one, but a sinister one. To Kyrkham the man's grin looked almost evil.

Heeding the not-so implicit warning, he turned back and fled quickly from the cave and toward the woods that bordered the nearby village.

He knew where he would find the boy. Just on the other side of the woods, segregated from the rest of the village, where the heathens and unbelievers and other unwashed outcast lived in their own filth and squalor. And he knew the particular hovel wherein the prostitute—which he had to concede was an unclean sinner, witch or not—lived with her invalid son. And he also knew she would not be home, at this late hour—she would be earning her living out in the streets—and the invalid boy would be alone and helpless until she returned.

Easy pickings…he suddenly realized he should feel lucky being the Chosen One this cycle, with such an easy sacrifice to procure. Very lucky indeed.

Just before entering the woods, he glanced up and saw the huge full moon approaching its pinnacle in the heavens above, nearly directly over the distant village Temple now, and he knew that time was, as Father Blakwell had urged, very short now, with not a moment to waste.

Hard to believe it's been nine years already, he thought.

Turning back to the secret, obscure path that cut through the thick, dark woods to the village, he quickened his pace.

Prologue II: The Storm

Ananias was just finishing carving a series of large letters into the thick wooden pole at the front of the palisade when Manteo, Cooper, and Pratt walked up.

It was getting dark, and the storms brewing on the Atlantic horizon were looking evermore ominous. A constant, silent barrage of distant lightening flickered from beneath the wall of towering storm clouds down to the now churning Atlantic ocean, and what was usually just a sea breeze on the island had picked up noticeably as the storms approached.

Knife in hand, Ananias stood and greeted the men, then they all turned and observed the massive storms obscuring the entire western horizon.

"Look bad," Manteo said.

"*Real* bad," Cooper concurred.

"Might be a hurricane," Ananias said.

"Hard to believe just a little while ago it was clear skies, with a big, beautiful full moon," Pratt said.

As if to emphasize the sudden change, a gust of wind struck them all, forcing squints and cringes.

"Our little huts'll never survive a major storm like that," Cooper surmised.

"And definitely not a hurricane," Ananias said.

Another gust of wind, and they were beginning to hear the rolling thunder. It was getting closer.

"What will we do?" Pratt asked, and they all turned to Ananias.

"I know, we just got settled here, threw up those flimsy huts...but who knows how often we'll get storms like this, and then have to rebuild. Plus, we were too late planting crops, we'll be short of food soon, and especially over the winter, if John doesn't return by then with supplies. And the locals have it out for us—after all, the Secotan slaughtered Grenville's whole company last year, and now most likely killed Howe at the river. It's obviously not safe here."

The others all nodded and voiced agreement.

"And Virginia was just born, and Eleanor is still recovering. They need safe, secure shelter...and I don't know about you fellows, but I'd like to live long enough to see John and Thomasine again some day."

"Me and Pratt have families back home too," Cooper said.

Again, they all nodded in concurrence.

"Okay," Cooper said. "So you don't think we should stay here. But where the hell will we go instead? All one-hundred-plus of us?"

Ananias pointed his knife at Manteo.

"Manteo knows of a cave, over on the other side of the hill. We'll all go there for shelter, wait out the storm, then head out."

"Head out to *where*?" Cooper asked

Ananias tapped the palisade post with his knife, prompting them to look at the engraving.

"What's that?" Pratt asked.

"Manteo's village."

"Where is it?" Cooper asked.

"About fifty miles south of here. Once the storm passes, we'll salvage what we can and take the pinnace and the rest of the boats, head south through the sound."

"Wait...if there's a cave around here, why didn't he tell us before?" Cooper said, eyeing Manteo suspiciously, as another gust of wind blew the native's long dark hair back behind him.

"He told John before he left for England, and John told me. But he wanted it kept secret, because the locals—the Secotan—speak of a legend, evil creatures that live there. They avoid going anywhere near it. So he said only go there in case of emergency. Well, I would call *this* an emergency." Ananias said, nodding toward the approaching storms.

"Fie, White sure enjoys keeping secrets, doesn't he?"

Cooper said, annoyed.

"He said it was need to know—and after all, he *is* the Governor," Ananias responded defensively. Then he turned to Manteo.

"What do you know about the legend?" Ananias asked.

"Dasamonqueponke and Aquascogoc say evil lives in cave…earth shake hard many moon ago, then creatures came from cave…kill many, take others back to cave," Manteo said, exchanging glances with each of the others as he did so.

"Have you seen them?" Ananias asked.

He shrugged again, and shook his head. "I by there many time, never see…beast…creature…only hear talk."

Okay, so it's just an old Indian superstition,." Cooper said, glancing at the others. "Just a tremor, scared them, that's all."

"So we go," Ananias said. "Manteo can lead us there."

Manteo nodded in agreement.

The incessant lightening and thunder was getting louder out across the sea, and the wind was becoming non-stop, rather than merely gusts.

"We need to hurry," Ananias said urgently. "Get everyone together, and tell them to only bring their bare necessities—just what they're able to carry in one trip—and stow any valuables in the storage chests and stash them in the trench. We'll weather the storm in the cave, and once it passes, we'll come back and salvage whatever we can, then load everything onto the boats."

Everyone agreeing, the men broke circle and hurried back toward the huts.

•

The storms were hitting full force—Ananias may have been right, it might have been a hurricane, its winds quickly tearing the huts to shreds as he feared—when the last of the settlers made it to the cave.

Holding up their lanterns for meager light, they inspected the cavernous room, which was plenty big enough to accommodate all of them: well over 100 men, women, and children.

And, they discovered a tunnel in the back of the cave, which was too deep for them to see more than a few feet by lamplight, so they couldn't determine how far back it went, or even in what direction.

So to be safe—a few of them likely recalling the Secotan legend—they decided just to stay in the main cave until the storm had passed.

Around midnight the horrific screaming started, but was short-lived and all but masked by the howling wind and booming thunder of the storm outside.

Then all was silent in the cave.

Prologue III: Lost at Sea

As the 282 ton brigantine danced lightly on the swells, the captain and helmsman stood together at the helm, while a big, beautiful full moon glowed in the night sky. After many days of rain and storms and churning sea, they agreed that the pleasant break in the weather was much-needed and much appreciated. They had finally been able to open the hatches to air out the cargo holds, and the captain had instructed the crewmen to replace a few of the sails that were now in tatters thanks to the stormy weather. The extra sails were now strewn about the deck, ready to put up once the damaged ones were taken down.

The captain was looking through his glass into the darkness on the port side, at the distant black silhouette set sharply against the slightly lighter moonlit sky.

"Almost looks like a big rock," Briggs said. "Or the very tip of a mountain."

"I thought you should know," Richardson explained. "Fortunately, I saw it just in time to maneuver around it."

The captain collapsed and lowered the glass, looking at his helmsman.

"And it's not on the map, you say?"

"No sir," the first mate said. Then he turned and tapped the map that was a spread across a cargo crate. "We're right here, there's no island anywhere near us."

"Can't be one of the Azores, right?" the captain questioned, scanning the map for any land mass even close to the position indicated by Richardson.

"We passed the Azores yesterday, as I notated on the slate. We're a few hundred miles east of there now."

"Ah…thank you for reminding me. I've yet to transcribe the slate to my log, I should do so upon first opportunity."

With that he extended the glass again and surveyed the small island, which was now slowly drifting behind them.

"I don't see any vegetation at all…like solid rock. Do you suppose it's volcanic?"

"Could be, but more likely tectonic. After all, we're right over a major fault line, the Azores-Gibralter Transform—"

"The AGFZ," the captain interrupted.

"Yes," he confirmed with a nod. "Though if there was a tectonic shift, it probably would've triggered a tsunami, that we would've likely seen evidence of somewhere along the Azores archipelago—like what happened with Lisbon—but we didn't."

"Well, we did pass to the north of Santa Maria, between that island and São Miguel to the north. A tsunami emanating from here would likely breach the east or southeast side of Santa Maria, not the north. So even if so, it's doubtful that we would have noticed anything unusual."

"Yes, I suppose you're right."

Again the captain collapsed the glass.

"And you have the coordinates?"

"Yes sir," the helmsman said, handing over a slip of paper, handwritten numbers jotted across it. "But you never know, seismic land formations can disappear as suddenly as they appeared. Could be gone tomorrow, for all we'll know."

"In either case, I'll notate it in my log when I get back to my quarters, along with transcribing the slate while I'm at it. We'll notify the authorities when we dock at Genoa—"

—he held up the slip of paper with the coordinates—

"—they'll need to check it out, and get it on the map, if it's still here by then."

"Especially being so close to the primary shipping lanes," Richardson added.

"Indeed…Gibraltar is very busy these days."

"Yes it is."

"Thank you, Mr. Richardson. And steady as she goes…"

"Yes sir."

Briggs turned to leave the helm, but then stopped and turned back to Richardson.

"Denatured alcohol," he said disappointedly.

"Sir?"

"Our cargo. Unfortunately, it's not the drinkable sort...I could use a stiff one about now," the captain said with a wink and grin.

"I think we all could," the helmsman concurred, smiling back and nodding.

Just then they were interrupted by a woman's horrific scream, the shriek emanating from mid-deck, starboard side.

"That sounds like Mrs. Briggs!" Richardson said, alarmed.

With that the captain bolted across the deck toward the screaming.

"Sarah!"

His wife was standing at the edge of the deck in front of the railing, pointing down toward the water with one arm, a toddler balanced on her hip with the other. Sophie had started crying, frightened by her mother's screams.

"What is it?!" Briggs hollered as he approached.

"I saw a...a...a huge...sea creature! It was wet and slimy, with many tentacles, trying to climb up the side of the ship!"

The captain heard a *splash!* below and looked over the railing, scanning this way and that, in the direction Sarah was pointing. Then he turned back to her.

"Darling," he said softly, "There's nothing down there."

"I'm telling you, I saw something," Sarah said, starting to calm down. "We both heard that splash."

"We're in the middle of the Atlantic. That splash could've been anything," he said. Then: "Why are you up here? And with Sophie, no less?"

"She was crying, seems a bit warm, might be a fever. I

thought the fresh, cool air might do her good."

"Well, take her back down to our quarters," Briggs said. "You shouldn't be up here, it's not safe, especially at night—"

And suddenly, horrific screams behind them…the helm.

The captain turned around just in time to see a great, flying beast swoop down and grab the helmsman by the shoulders with huge black talons.

"Albert!" he yelled, too late.

Screaming again, Richardson grabbed hold of the binnacle, but the creature was too strong, pulling him from it, lifting him into the air, and in one final effort, he clutched the compass on top, but with another great lurch of the beast the compass snapped off, falling to the deck and shattering as the man was carried off into the night sky, his screaming fading into the distance.

Also seeing what Briggs just witnessed, Sarah began screaming again, and now the other six crewmen emerged from below, running and glancing around, wondering what the hell was happening.

"Everyone get back below deck!" The captain hollered, pointing to the stairwell from which they had emerged. Then he turned and grabbed his wife—still screaming, Sophie still crying—by the shoulders and urged her in the same direction. "Get below! And Hur—"

But his command was cut short as two sets of massive black talons ripped though both his shoulders, yanking him screaming from the deck and swiftly into the sky.

The choking blood gurgling up into his throat stopped his

screaming, and as he became light-headed, he gazed down at the ship below, and saw a huge tentacled sea creature scaling up the side of the ship, mounting the life boat—the ties of which begun snapping from the weight—but the creature got hold of the railing above just as the boat broke free and plummeted into the water below. Lifting itself up, the creature snapped off a portion of the railing with some of its tentacles, while climbing up onto the deck with the others.

As Briggs was carried over the ship, on the other side he saw something else—man? Beast? He couldn't make it out very well in the darkness, and at such a distance—walking seemingly awkwardly yet quickly across the deck toward his wife, who was still just standing there motionless against the railing, screaming.

"Sarah," he whispered, helpless, dying himself. Suddenly, he wished like hell that he'd been wearing his sword…

His wife screamed and screamed until he could no longer hear her, and shortly thereafter could no longer even see her.

And just before he lost consciousness, he looked up ahead and saw the tiny, black, mysterious island looming ahead in the night…

Prologue IV: Going Dark

60 Miles West of
Outer Hebrides, Scottland
December 1900

"You're not gonna believe it," he said.

The other two stopped and turned to him.

"It's clear skies out there! If fact, there's still a huge full moon showing, even with the sun rising!"

"About damn time!" Don exclaimed, smiling.

"In over twenty years as a lighthouseman, I don't think I've ever seen a storm as bad as that one," Jim said as he turned back to the sink.

"Scared me, too," Tom agreed. "I actually wrote about it in my journal last night, and even prayed afterward."

"I'm with you," Don said, nodding to Jim. "Worst storm I've seen since I've been working here. But at least it's over now."

"There's another problem though," Tom added.

They other two waited, looking at him with concern.

"From up there, I could see the supply box down by the crane platform is busted up, with ropes and gear strewn everywhere."

"So it really was that bad," Don said, turning to take an armload of dishes to the sink.

"Well, we'll need to fix it, secure the gear, whatever, before the weather turns again." Jim said.

"It's clear skies right now," Tom said, "But there's clouds on the horizon moving this way. Looks like rain soon."

Jim stopped and thought for a minute, then appeared to make a decision.

"Moore and the supply ship are due in four days," he said. "If last night's storm did that much damage to the west bank, we should probably go down and check out the east landing too, make sure everything's in order, so there's no problems when the supplies arrive. We're already running short, last thing we need is a delay restocking."

The others both nodded in agreement.

"And, according to the NLB rules, the lighthouse can't be left vacant, there must always to be someone present to keep watch over things."

Again, the others nodded.

"So I'll stay here, finish cleaning up breakfast. I need to transfer the notes from the slate to the log anyway. Tom, you go down to the east landing and check things out, make sure the Hesperus won't have any problems docking when it arrives in a few days. Don, you go down to the crane platform and see what you can do about the storage box and supplies."

"Why do I have to go to the cliff side?" Don protested, his hot temper starting to flare as usual. "Why can't Tom go there

—after all, he's already seen the damage—and let me go down to the east landing?"

"For one, Tom is a lot younger, and the east landing is a lot further away…he can make it there and back quicker. And for two, you're considerably more experienced, will be better able to ascertain the condition of the crane and equipment, and what will need to be done."

"Ah, bloody hell," Don said shortly. But then he softened a bit: "But I gotta admit you've got a good point…it's just that the cliff side is awful steep, makes me nervous."

"You can handle it. I have faith," Jim said with a smirk.

Just then, thunder rumbled in the distance.

"You guys better put on your slickers," Jim advised. Sounds like rain—maybe even another storm."

•

Don grumbled to himself all the way down the steep steps to the crane platform. There he could see the broken supply box below, with ropes and gear strewn all about. This he had expected, based on Tom's report from up in the lantern room; but what he *hadn't* expected was to find the iron railing damaged, bent, and some sections even wrenched from their concrete bases. And further, he was amazed at seeing a huge boulder lying near the platform with smaller rocks, stones, and dirt scattered around it, apparently dislodged from above.

That thing must weight close to a ton, he thought. *Must've been a helluva storm.*"

At this, he stopped and surveyed the sky. The full moon was almost entirely obscured already, as the storm clouds were fast approaching over the sea. As if on cue, thunder rumbled in the distance as he assessed the weather.

Once he reached the crane platform, he quickly determined that the supply box was damaged beyond repair. It had been torn from its moorings, shattered, the contents strewn everywhere. He figured the best he could do at this point was to collect the ropes and other gear and somehow secure them at the base of the crane until they could figure out what else to do. Maybe order a new storage box on the next supply run?

As he scurried about collecting the scattered supplies— hurrying now as the sky had quickly become overcast and rain drops had begun spitting here and there—he suddenly heard a strange sound from below, like a tarp fluttering in the wind.

Except there wasn't much wind. Yet, anyway.

Stopping with an armload of rope, he peered down the cliff to where he thought the sound had come from.

The cave.

But something was different now.

He'd seen the cave at the base of the cliff countless times since working the lighthouse, and if the sea was rough it could be quite a spectacle, waves rushing in, then exploding outward in a geyser of water and mist.

It took him a minute, but then he saw it: one side of the cave entrance had collapsed, opening it up much larger than it used to be, from a mere crevice to a sizable cavern. He could see the boulders and huge slabs of rock lying on the rocks below, where they had tumbled down from the cave entrance.

He then looked from the cave back to the crane platform

behind him, the huge boulder that had come crashing down from above.

And, of course, the destroyed supply box.

What the hell happened out here last night? Could a storm do this much damage?

Then he looked back down at the cave, and didn't think so.

A tremor? If so, surely we'd have felt it...

But maybe not, if it happened during the storm. Between the wind battering the building and the constant deafening thunder, he supposed there could've been a tremor—just enough to shake that boulder loose and collapse one side of the cave—and they might not've even noticed it during the rest of the calamity.

Then he heard the strange fluttering sound again, except this time above him. But just as he started to look up, something grabbed him from behind by the shoulders, massive talons piercing his body, and he screamed and dropped all the gear as he was lifted quickly into the air.

•

Tom had trotted down to the east landing dock, seeing no noticeable damage the whole way down, and, now standing on the rocks at the edge of the water near the dock, saw nothing amiss there, either.

Though he had still been able to see the moon in the sky as he traveled down from the lighthouse, now the sky was overcast and he could tell it was about to start raining at any moment.

After one last inspection of the dock and deciding all was

fine, he turned to head back—but heard a strange splashing sound behind him.

He turned back to the dock, and, though the water seemed somewhat disturbed around the landing, he saw nothing out of the ordinary.

But just as he was about to turn back and head up the hill, something grabbed him from behind, its huge, wet, slimy tentacles wrapping around him and lifting him from the ground.

He started to scream, but it was cut short as he was plunged into the sea and immediately pulled under.

•

Back at the lighthouse, Jim had finished the dishes, then busied himself cleaning and filling all the oil lamps.

Finished with that, and figuring the guys would be back any minute now. But he was getting concerned, it had been quite a while and neither Tom nor Don had returned yet. He didn't think it should take this long.

And now he could hear the rain starting up outside, and small gusts of wind buffeting the windows above.

But rather than worry, he decided to give them a few more minutes, and sat down in a chair in the kitchen to calm himself, wait for the others, and decide what to do next.

In the silence, he suddenly heard what sounded like a growl or huff, deep and guttural, outside the front door.

Startled, he stood quickly, knocking the chair over in the process, but he ignored it, listening intently.

The pitter patter of light rain, the whistle of cool breeze.

He went to the door and listened, but still nothing.

So he ventured to open the door. Sticking his head out, he looked around, but didn't see anything.

Thinking it might be one of the men, maybe needing help, he stepped outside for a closer look. As he stood surveying the area, a gust of wind blew the door shut behind him.

Shrugging, he turned to go back inside—but something grabbed him from behind, wrapping its huge, hairy arms around him, massive claws sinking into his flesh, and lifted him from the ground.

He screamed and screamed as the beast carried him around the lighthouse and down the west hill toward the cave.

Part I:
The Crossing

The Town of Hope
Old Rope & Black Woods
August 1975

What had been a clear blue sky during the heat of the day was now solidly overcast, clouds heaving and churning like boiling pewter as thunderstorms moved in from the south.

Below the turmoil, Tommy Baker stood motionless near the edge of a rocky canyon cliff high above Hope Creek, his black silhouette cut from the steely glare of the molten sky. Alternating tufts of golden and sun-bleached blonde hair gesticulated atop the young boy's head, grappling with the spectral gusts that swirled about him.

The cooler air, pushing ahead of the approaching storm, rustled its way into the tired tree branches, knotted brush, and waist-high grass of the untamed field that lay behind him, and Hope Creek Canyon yawned up at him from below, deep and cavernous, the stench of death on its breath.

Trying to ignore the raspy, speculative whispering of the audience of weeds and dry grass that anxiously observed him from behind, he contemplated the scene that now played out before him.

The dreaded rope bridge.

Old Rope, the locals called it.

And every kid in town feared it.

But I'm not a kid anymore; I'll be thirteen tomorrow.

Thirteen.

A *teenager*.

And *teenagers* aren't afraid of stupid old rope bridges...

...are they?

He watched as the bridge shuddered, creaked, and groaned in the rising wind, mocking him as he stood there, petrified.

And he knew that the longer he waited, the worse it was going to get.

As if on cue, in that single moment of hesitation the gusts picked up even more, the storm about to unleash its full fury.

Now Old Rope danced in the wind before him, bidding him—no, *daring* him—to come cross. To Tommy, the perpetual creaking and cracking of all the brittle, decaying ropes that snaked throughout the ancient rickety boards sounded as if they were just about to *snap!*, thereby plunging any hapless occupants screaming to their deaths in the rocky canyon far below.

Suspicious, the boy sensed trickery: Old Rope was simply waiting, that's all; waiting for him to venture nervously on board, and—once he had traveled too far across, and was just beyond the point of no return—the evil old bridge would gladly let go, laughing as it happily sent Tommy on an unsolicited ride down, all the way to the bottom of the canyon, where the rushing creek skirted around a gauntlet of deadly obstacles: sharp boulders that jutted up from the water like giant stone teeth; partially submerged logs that lay in wait like so many crocodiles; crowded colonies of dead, broken saplings rising into the air like razor-sharp tribal spear traps.

He also knew that if he *did* go down, and wasn't fortunate enough to be killed instantly on the rocks below—then there were always the turtles and water snakes and carp to finish him off, lurking in hidden cesspools and coves all along the banks of the creek, evil creatures hungrily awaiting just such an opportune feast.

If, that is, he was actually *stupid* enough (or *crazy* enough!) to brave the veritable death trap that dangled haphazardly so high above Hope Creek in the first place.

And in the *wind*, no less…

As the boy contemplated all this, he could barely make out the ominous sound of the rushing creek far below.

Though he was surrounded by the normal sounds of the wilderness—the incessant hiss of cicadas, the birdsong drifting from the woods, the grass and weeds hissing in the wind be hind him—he could hear, just beyond all that, something much more sinister: Hope Creek whispering up the canyon walls, the canyon walls relaying the message to Old Rope, and Old Rope beckoning to Tommy…

It was a conspiracy of murderers.

The boy was kicking himself for being so careless earlier in the day, when the stifling summer heat had coaxed Old Rope into a still and dormant slumber, and it had been so much easier to cross.

Now he was stuck here on the other side, needed to get back across, and was fast running out of time—for nightfall was lurking in the shadows, storm clouds were waltzing in atop the trees, Old Rope was rehearsing its dance of death before him, and the wind was escalating in its intensity with each passing minute.

And he didn't like what he saw.

Not one bit.

•

"Are you ready, Commander Thomas?" Winnie asked, peering intently at his friend through his thick, black plastic-rimmed glasses.

"That's an affirmative, Commander Winston."

Tommy Baker and his best friend Winnie Milhouse were preparing for what had become a month-long mission: arming themselves with their newly-acquired Wrist-Wrocket slingshots, then venturing out into the uncivilized wilderness (otherwise known as the field on the other side of Hope Creek Canyon) to *shoot stuff*.

For the past month, they'd performed this ritual almost daily—ever since they'd acquired the new weapons in town at Hank's Hobbies & Sporting Gear…

It was the summer of '75, and had been the hottest anyone in the town of Hope could remember. Even the old codgers—who'd been around here for what seemed like *forever*, like before the town was really even a town—lamented this fact as they rocked in their old rockers out on their old wooden porches, puffing on their cigarettes or cigars or corncob pipes:

Yes-sir-ree, Bob...this here's the hottest summer I ever seen round these parts...

One day, earlier that summer—end of June, first of July, right in there—the temperature had already hit a hundred degrees by noon, and was threatening to keep right on going, like it was pissed about something and was cranking it up just to get even.

Tommy was over at Winnie's house. They'd gotten bored playing war with their army soldiers and rubber bands, and Winnie's mom had gone to work for the evening (she worked part-time as a cashier at the old *Gas-n-Grub* gas station and convenience store that occupied the busiest corner of *Railroad Pass*, the small retail center located at the big flashing light where the railroad tracks crossed Main Street up on the north side of town; his dad was a truck driver, so was seldom home, and all Winnie knew was that for the past month, he'd been out on the east coast somewhere), so they decided to ride their bikes into town and see if they could score some fireworks for the Fourth—*real* fireworks, not the lame snakes and sparklers and smoke bombs that most the kids their age had to settle for.

The Milhouses lived in a square white clapboard house, one of a whole row of identical square white clapboard houses that ran the entire length of Hillsboro Lane (which Tommy always teasingly referred to as "Hillbilly Lane" in honor of his best friend). Hillsboro Lane was just another crumbling, weed-flanked street in the seedy area of town known as The Flats, a cluster of low-income neighborhoods that were marginalized to the eastern-most edge of town, sectioned off by the industrial rail road tracks that ran along its western boundary.

Or, as Tommy would say with a shrug and a smile: "You know—where the hillbillies live!"

From Hillsboro Lane, the boys rode up to the north end of The Flats and turned left onto Homestretch Avenue, a big four-laner that stretched east-west all the way through the town of Hope, running downtown through Town Square and crossing Main Street smack-dab in the middle of Grande Festival Plaza, where all the best shops were (and where it might be busy enough that they could snatch some Black Cats or M-80s or bottle rockets or Roman candles in all the hustle and bustle without getting caught).

The brand-new, jet-black asphalt of Homestretch—they'd just resurfaced it, bright new yellow and white lines and everything—intensified the already stifling heat of the day; it was like riding their bikes around in a black skillet with the stove cranked.

Feeling like they were melting in the heat by the time they got to Town Square, they decided to cut south onto Fifth Street before they reached the plaza and stop at Hank's, see about picking up a couple of canteens, then filling them at the water fountain out front of the public library, just down Fifth Street and right on Chapel Lane, across from Hope in Christ church (over the years they had found that for some reason, the water always came out cold at that fountain, even in the summer, no matter how hot it got).

When they finally reached Hank's, they parked their bikes out front under the awning and hurried inside, both so soaked with sweat they looked like they'd just come in out of the rain.

Heading across the store for the camping and fishing section in the back, they got sidetracked when they spied the shiny new slingshots in the display case up by the register where they kept the pellet and BB guns (which, unfortunately, were out of the question for them; county ordinance said you had to be sixteen to buy those—fifteen if you took and passed the county's gun safety course and were also fortunate enough to get your parents to sign a waiver, yeah right).

Stopping just short of the first aisle—the model train stuff —they discussed it briefly, and were pretty sure the county's age restriction was just for pellet and BB guns, and not for slingshots. With that decided, they about-faced and beelined up to the glass case by the register.

There were three Wrist-Wrockets on display: a metallic red one, a metallic blue one, and an all-silver one—which gleamed so brightly under the fluorescent lights that it looked white. This deception gave the entire showcase a convincingly patriotic look—quite appropriate for the upcoming Fourth of July holiday.

Huddling together, the boys nearly drooled as they peered though the glass, admiring the finely crafted weaponry.

"You boys just gonna stand there foggin' up the glass, or you gonna buy somethin?"

Startled, the boys simultaneously jerked their eyes up toward the voice. Hank Stevens himself was standing behind the counter, down at the end by the phone. He leaned casually against the wall, big arms across his broad chest, smirking. The office door stood open behind him, revealing an old wooden desk buried under an astonishing array of clutter. Somewhere behind that mess, a smoldering cigarette poured a thin gray stream into the air. Glaring white sunlight from a small window in the back wall cut a white square tube diagonally through the light-blue haze that permeated the entire room.

They were surprised to see him here; finding Hank working the store this early in the day during the summer was unusual. He fished a lot (and, it was rumored, drank a lot) and so his son, Joey—or one of Joey's thug friends from his high school shop class—was usually working, chomping gum at the counter or yakking for hours on the phone or sneaking around the corner for a smoke when business was slow and nobody was looking.

But oddly, Hank was here today.

Probably too hot to fish.

Maybe even too hot to drink.

"They're new," he said as he pushed off the wall with his shoulder and walked over. He was a stocky man, but moved with a smooth, confident gait. Though still solid and muscular, the years had brought on a bit of a beer gut, along with a slightly receded hairline. His remaining hair, mostly gray now, was pulled back into a ponytail, a defiant stand against his own creeping age, which was proving futile; for even with the ponytail, and even with the platinum ear studs he sported in both ears, his accumulating years were starting to show—the inevitable bags and wrinkles moving in uninvited, there goes the neighborhood.

All except his eyes, that is; his bright, piercing blue eyes seemed ageless; youthful, alert—and they helped make him famous for his charming wink. They were his one feature that accurately reflected his perpetually youthful state of mind, regardless of his actual physical age.

An avid outdoorsman, his tanned, leathery complexion was further intensified by a sharply contrasting short-trimmed silver goatee. Numerous tattoos colored his forearms, some of them possibly military.

He was hands-down the coolest adult Tommy and Winnie had ever met.

As he approached, smiling as always, the two reveled in the ashen smell of cigarette smoke and the manly aroma of cheap cologne that always accompanied him to the counter.

Just as he reached the boys, he stooped and disappeared behind the counter. Then, in a muffled voice:

"You're in luck...just got 'em in yesterday, on the truck."

The boys stared into the glass case, watching in anticipation. The sound of keys jingling, followed by a *click!*, then the mirrored door in the back of the case suddenly slid open, almost making the boys dizzy as the optical illusion of depth vanished and the back half of the merchandise before them appeared to break away and angle sideways.

Hank retrieved the silver one, stood, and made a show of properly orienting it and placing it carefully on the glass counter in front of them, handling it gently like some rare, delicate artifact.

The boys stared at it, googly-eyed, Winnie's eyes appearing even bigger behind the thick lenses.

Hank pointed an open hand at each feature, the tips of his fingers following along its smooth contours as he spoke:

"Aircraft-grade aluminum alloy frame…maximum-velocity surgical-grade rubber tubing…genuine cowhide pouch—"

—he paused to looked up at the boys, adding: "Comes with an extra one—and an extra set of rubbers, too," then looked back down and proceeded as the boys giggled at the word—

"—precision-molded handle inlayed with high-impact, all-weather neoprene pistol grips…"

Amazed, the boys looked at each other, then turned back.

Hank held it out to Tommy. "Feel how light it is."

Tommy accepted the weapon carefully, with respect.

"Reach up through the wrist support and hold the grip like a pistol. The wrist support rests up here on your forearm, pad on top, with the uprights angled back toward you."

As Winnie watched with envy, Tommy slid his left arm through the wrist support, gripped the handle firmly, then held the weapon out at arm's length. With his right hand, he gently pulled the pouch back, extending the rubber tubing nearly to his shoulder. He closed one eye, sighted down his arm, and pointed the slingshot toward the open office door. He was amazed at how the forearm support enabled maximum extension of the rubber tubes, without putting too much stress on his wrist. Pivoting upward, he moved his aim from the office door to the corner of the ceiling above the entrance.

As Tommy's arm rose, Winnie noticed something near the bottom of the Wrist-Wrocket's handle, and stooped, hands on knees, to get a better look, squinting up at it through his glasses.

Still stooping, he turned to Hank.

"What's the button at the bottom of the handle for?"

Upon hearing this, Tommy relaxed the stretched rubber tubes and flipped the whole thing over, peering down at the bottom of the handle.

"Ahhh, very observant, young man," Hank commended, relieving Tommy of the now upside-down weapon.

"Watch this."

The boys watched intently as Hank flipped it back to its upright position. They hadn't noticed it before, but they could now see the small domed top of an aluminum button protruding from the backside of the handle just below the grip, centered between the two tubes of the wrist support that extended back toward the user. When he pushed it, a tiny, nearly inaudible *click!* was heard, and Hank folded the wrist support upward against the handle, then pulled the rubber tubes down, hooking the pouch into the crevice that was created by the open hinge.

"Folds for easy storage."

With one hand, he slipped the whole thing casually into his back pocket, then made a show of brushing his hands briskly together, like he had just performed a feat of magic.

"No way!" The boys exclaimed in unison.

"Way," Hank responded quietly, nodding matter-of-factly.

"Now, take a look at this."

As the boys watched, he whisked it out of his pocket, unhooked the pouch, snapped the frame open with a *click!*, then turned it over, placing it upside down on the glass, in much the same way as the boys did with their bicycles whenever they needed to put the chain back on, or fix a flat, or clip some playing cards to the forks along the spokes, or maybe just so they could crank the pedals by hand and shine up some pennies on the spinning tire.

With a flick of his wrist, he spun a quarter-sized aluminum cap off the end of the handle, revealing an empty chamber topped with a gleaming, finely machined thread that screamed of quality craftsmanship.

"Ammo storage."

"Whoa," Tommy said as Winnie let out a low whistle.

"And that's not all."

With one hand, Hank flipped the lid into the air like a coin, caught it in his other hand, then held it out to them, displaying a black rubber gasket installed on the inside.

"Waterproof."

"Keeps the rocks dry," Winnie said, nodding.

"Yeah…very cool," Tommy agreed.

"Not rocks."

The boys looked up with puzzled looks just as Hank turned and pulled a small white cardboard box off a shelf behind him. In a series of deft moves, he turned back, slapped the box on the counter, spun it around to face them, and flipped the top back, revealing rows upon rows of shiny steel balls, layered over an inch deep.

"Precision-ground, high-speed stainless steel ball bearings. Handle holds up to forty rounds. There's two hundred to a box, and each unit comes with a box."

The boys looked at each other and smiled, excited.

"So...how much?" Tommy asked.

"Well, lucky for you guys, they're on sale right now for the Fourth, our annual Independence Day Sale. Normally twenty-five, I'm letting 'em go for twenty. Don't forget, that includes an extra set of rubbers, an extra pouch, and a box of balls—and the balls, bought separately, run four bucks a box, so that's four more dollars you're saving."

Another low whistle from Winnie.

Hank then paused for a moment, leaning with both hands on the counter, tapping one finger on the glass as he looked off into space somewhere, chewing on a thought. Then he looked back to the boys:

"Tell you what—you guys both buy a Wrist-Wrocket, and I'll throw in a coupla boxes of balls, on the house...one extra box for eacha ya."

Hank looked back and forth between the two boys, eyes aglow with youthful enthusiasm—then winked mischievously and clicked his tongue, nodding at them like they were all in on some big secret together.

The boys turned to each other and smiled ear-to-ear.

"That's a good deal," Tommy said pseudo-knowledgeably.

"Yeah—but where will we get the money?" Winnie asked.

Screwing the cap back onto the handle, Hank said:

"Well, you boys think it over, then come back and see me when you decide. And don't worry, if the sale's over, I'll go ahead and hook you up with the discount anyway...*if* I have any of 'em left, that is...I expect they'll sell out pretty quick."

With that, he stooped, set the Wrist-Wrocket back into the glass display case, slid the mirrored back door shut, and locked it with a *click!*

The tiny bell tinkled above the boys as they pushed excitedly out of Hank's Hobbies & Sporting Gear and quickly mounted their bikes, hitting the busy street with just one goal in mind: acquiring their new Wrist-Wrocket sling shots as soon as possible!

It wasn't until they'd pedaled halfway to Grande Festival Plaza in the blazing summer heat that they realized that in their enthusiasm over the Wrist-Wrockets, they had forgotten all about the canteens.

•

Turns out they weren't able to score any real fireworks that day—and they decided not to waste their money buying any of the lame kid's stuff either, so they could instead put it toward the eventual purchase of their Wrist-Wrockets.

In the ensuing weeks, the boys did everything they could think of to raise enough money; they pooled their minuscule allowances, swiped abandoned change off of their parent's dressers, and even sold off part of their comic book collections (but not *Captain America* or *Spiderman*—mostly just the lame ones like *Batman* and *The Incredible Hulk*).

They collected discarded bottles and cans all around town, biking heavy, clinking garbage bags-full all the way out to the recycle center on the edge of town next to the dump, where they exchanged them for a few dollars and pocket change.

By August they finally had enough loot to make the necessary acquisition, and sped eagerly into town to Hank's. Beating the odds, he was there again (what luck!) and made good on his promise, selling them at the sale price even though the sale had ended after the Fourth. Tommy selected the silver one (no brainer), and Winnie the blue one, and they each got two free boxes of ammo.

They were now set for the rest of the summer—which was getting shorter every day, with school starting back up the very next month.

Back at home, their new Wrist-Wrockets easily made their old homemade slingshots look like toys.

Kid's stuff.

Child's play.

Embarrassed, they bid farewell to their old wooden relics, which had served them so faithfully over the years. They actually held a small military-style funeral, revering the toys as veteran soldiers killed in action as they wrapped them in an old newspaper and placed them gently, respectfully, into an empty, discarded shoe box.

Then, pulling down the spring-loaded step ladder, they climbed up into Winnie's attic, and, saluting each other, laid the box to rest inside a large cedar chest, carefully nestling it between piles of old photographs and other memorabilia his family had stored in there over the years.

It was a solemn ceremony, and quite easily justified: arming themselves with mere wood and pebbles simply made them too vulnerable to the enemy.

From here on out, *Commander Thomas* and *Commander Winston* would take to the battle fields armed to the teeth with their new high-tech weaponry, which deployed much faster, more accurate, and highly lethal ammunition.

Real weapons.

Real ammo.

Real soldiers.

●

So today, as always, the boys were operating out of *Command Base One*—otherwise known as Winnie's house, which was the only one even close to their hunting grounds. Tommy lived on a farm out west of town (most days, if he managed to slip away from his dad undetected, Tommy jumped on his bike and headed north on the old County Road 200 that ran past their farm, turned east on Homestretch Avenue, then rode clear across town to Winnie's house. Or, sometimes, he'd walk south about a mile to the train tracks, hop an east-bound freighter across town, and bail on the south end of The Flats, not far from Winnie's house. Either way it was quite a trek, but always worth it to Tommy—especially if his old man was on a binge).

So, out of necessity, Winnie's house was deemed *Command Base One*. From there the boys could easily walk to the field where they hunted, traveling east through the mostly unfenced yards until they came out on an unmarked, single-lane road that skirts the easternmost edge of town. Crumbling and full of potholes, it marked the official town limit—and the beginning of a natural paradise.

Taking the road south a short distance, they again turned east, traversing a narrow swath of woods which quickly gave rise to Silver Hills (the boys guessed it was named for its abundant population of silver maple trees; on windy days, the entire hillside springs to life in waves of silvery swirls).

Climbing up Silver Hills, they eventually came to an elevated clearing, where Hope Creek ran through a deep canyon below. The steep rocky walls shot straight downward, forming a natural barrier to would-be travelers and hikers—and especially young, eager hunters.

Sometime forever ago, the early townsfolk had constructed a rope bridge across the canyon. Looping heavy, stout rope through thick planks of sturdy oak, they lashed it to log anchors planted deep into the ground on either side of the canyon, stretching it across the narrowest point available, where Old Rope dangles high above the creek to this day.

Of course, today there are modern bridges all throughout Hope, stitching the town back together where Hope Creek cuts through as it takes a quick southeastern jaunt through town before turning south again just north of Silver Hills—including a new six-lane steel monstrosity up on the northwest side of town where the highway goes across.

But up there in Silver Hills—where abundant wilderness

begs to be explored, and has yet to be conquered—Old Rope is still the only way to cross Hope Creek Canyon.

On the other side of the dangling rope bridge lay a huge open field, offering fertile hunting grounds for any young, ambitious hunters who just happened to be off school for the summer and were excruciatingly bored and needed something exciting to do, preferably out of the house and away from nosy parents.

The back of the field ended at a nearly solid wall of trees, the forest known in town as Black Woods. The dense, spooky woods were the source of many legends and mysteries that had haunted the town for generations; strange and eerie folklore recounted so convincingly by the old-timers around town that it worried the parents, spooked the teenagers, and scared the total bejeebers out of the kids.

And, right in front of Black Woods, a huge, ancient oak tree stood alone in the field, like a sentinel, a gatekeeper, towering over the boys as they hunted their prey. It almost seemed that in order to pass into the woods—which few dared do anyway —one would have to first gain permission from that massive oak standing guard at the entrance.

Behind that oak, the thick woods that blanketed the east side of Silver Hills were so dark, foggy, and ominous—even said to be impenetrable in some places—that the entire forest was shrouded in mystery.

And the boys discussed the prevailing folklore regularly, especially whenever they got close to Black Woods while they were out hunting.

"So, do you believe any of the stories?" Winnie would ask.

"I've heard all sorts of nonsense," Tommy would answer. "Monsters, giant wild animals, psychopathic serial killers, wood dwellers, witches, ghosts, evil spirits—even UFOs and little gray aliens, believe it or not—but I don't really believe any of it. My ol' man says it's all hogwash. Old wive's tales."

But regardless of what Tommy's dad said, frightening stories abounded around town, scaring or at least intimidating the townsfolk—especially anyone who dared even pass *near* the woods, let alone venture in.

"What about the giant bird?" Winnie asked.

"Nope," Tommy said matter-of-factly.

There had been a few reports over the years of some type of giant bird, or some said it was more like an enormous *bat*—reptilian in nature (many kids like to imagine it's a *dragon*), and at least the size of a man, or even larger—the massive silhouette of which had been glimpsed a time or two swooping over Black Woods just above the treetops and always under a full moon; but those dubious reports were few and far-between, and all of them long ago.

Today, old Vin McCoy is the only one still alive who claims to have seen the thing, decades ago, while out hunting—but now he's ninety-something with no living relatives, mostly deaf and nearly blind too, and a permanent resident of Legacy Assisted Living, Hope's only retirement home—so who knows. They say he's gone totally senile ("crazy ol' coot" is the more technical terminology often used around town) and that the story changes every time he tells it, and half the time can't remember much of it anyway. So that particular, nearly forgotten sighting (a giant bat, bigger than a man? With scales, like a snake? And massive talons? Come on...seriously?) carries about as much credence with the townsfolk as the rest of the worn-out tales of monsters, psycho killers, witchcraft and devil worship, and, of course, the UFOs with their little gray occupants.

"So, what do you think happened to those kids over the years then?" Winnie drilled.

Tommy would just shrug. "Don't know. Could be anything."

They both knew the more popular and credulous of all the stories were those of the mysterious disappearances that have mystified the town for decades—missing pets for one (but who knows really), and even the occasional vanishing adult, especially the elderly (but then again, any of those folks could have simply left town without telling anyone, or, if senile or suffering dementia, without even knowing they were doing so themselves. It happens).

But the one *true* mystery that has gone naggingly unsolved is that of the random children who have gone missing over the years without a trace. Just up and vanished one day, never to be seen again. The town's history was peppered with such disturbing and perplexing reports, going back decades.

So the mystery of the vanishing children has become the real, almost palpable curse in town. Generally considered a rather taboo subject, most people avoided discussing it—and even if they did, they did so quietly, whispering under their breath, so as not to be overheard.

Nobody knows what happened to those missing kids, and nobody can even agree on a plausible theory, so most the time the discussion just trails off, shoulders are shrugged, then the subject gently changed to something more palatable and less ominous.

But there's one thing that most everyone *does* agree on, which is nearly always mentioned whenever the subject comes up: that at night, out near Black Woods, the distant screams of children can supposedly be heard, seemingly coming from all directions at once, yet none discernible. This collective wailing is rumored to be the ghosts of the missing children, forever haunting the dark, eerie, mysterious woods that lurk up on Silver Hills, over on the other side of Hope Creek Canyon.

As a result, many townsfolk have come to believe that Black Woods is genuinely haunted.

And some even claim that the *forest itself* is evil…

But everyone agrees: there are strange goings on in them there Black Woods, and so it's best to keep as far away from that place as possible.

●

Today, the boys casually crossed over Old Rope (there was no wind, so *no problema*) and ventured into the dangerous hunting grounds on the other side of the creek, just like they had done countless times since *The Acquisition*.

Their mission (and oh yeah, you better believe they chose to accept it):

1. Bring order to the world of the untamed;

2. Bring justice to the enemy;

3. Show everyone who is boss;

4. Generally wreak havoc on the lives of any unfortunate creatures—be they fowl, rodentia, or reptilian—that happened to cross their path or carelessly reveal its hiding place.

And they fully intended to accomplish their mission, come hell or high water (and before they got hungry and were forced to abandon their mission, hurrying back to Winnie's house for his mom's famous *beanie-weenies,* or some other righteous meal).

They thought if they were lucky, maybe one day they'd get a shot at the cotton-ball end of a jackrabbit as it ricocheted back and forth ahead of them before disappearing into the brush as quickly as it had burst before them; but so far, no score. It was their dream to bag one of those *waskowy wabbits* someday, and the boys had a running bet as to which of them would be the first to do so.

But success had eluded them all month, despite their new weapons. During their countless missions, they hadn't scored a single hit—no mouse, no rat, no chipmunk, no squirrel, no bird, no snake—no *nothing*.

And they hadn't even *seen* a rabbit.

And today, it was more of the same. Nothing. By noon, all they'd succeeded in doing, really, was scattering hundreds of hardened steel ball-bearings surreptitiously into the ground all throughout the currently undeveloped field.

Perhaps one day, long into the future, some of that secretly planted ammo would finally serve its initial purpose of damage infliction—not via penetration of fur or feather, however, but through the vicious pinging assault of some hapless new home owner's lawnmower blade. Perhaps the future metallic ambush would cause a swearing middle-aged man to miss the first quarter of the game while he dashed off to the hardware store to secure a new blade so he could get the hell back, finish the damn yard, turn on the big game, and start the beer.

After crossing Old Rope, the boys had ventured eastward across the west side of the field, then back again, shooting at random targets, but none of the living variety. Nearing the bridge on their return trip, they stopped, peering east across the field toward Black Woods.

"You wanna try the other side of the field?" Winnie asked.

"Yeah, why not. Maybe there's somethin' over there, since it's closer to the woods. But first I wanna check my ammo, I think I'm gettin' low."

As Winnie watched, Tommy flipped his Wrist-Wrocket over and unscrewed the cap from the bottom of the handle. He was shocked—not a single ball bearing rolled out.

Empty.

How could this be?

Situation Critical...

He summoned his commander voice: "I seem to be out of ammunition—do you have any extra, Commander Winston?"

Winnie unscrewed his handle, and they watched as only two balls rolled out into his hand.

"Last two, then I'm out, Commander Thomas."

He palmed one and handed the other one over.

Desperate, they double-checked all their pockets, plunging and patting themselves all over—but came up empty. Realizing the futility of their situation, they stared earnestly at one another, each hoping the other would think of something.

Tommy shrugged. "C'mon, let's head on back to base—maybe we'll see somethin' on the way," he suggested.

"Yeah," Winnie agreed. "I'm gettin' hungry anyways."

Hearts sinking, they started back to Command Base One.

"After lunch we can ride out to Hank's and get some more ammo."

"Yeah."

They crunched across the field toward the bridge, swinging their empty slingshots at the fluffy dandelion tufts along the way. Swarms of white seeds filled the air around them like tiny paratroopers, swirling wildly about before slowly floating off to explore new lands.

In the dead heat of the day, they again crossed back over Old Rope easily, without incident.

Upon descending Silver Hills, they stepped side-by-side from the woods out onto the old unnamed road. There, they stood in silence for a moment, looking to the south, where the road curved around to the west. There a large, vacant, triangular lot occupied the corner, covered in wild grass, a line of trees running along the back side.

"There it is." Winnie announced with a smile.

"Yep." Tommy concurred with his own smile.

"The very ball field where you homered on that asshole

Eric Brunes…can't believe that was a year ago already."

"Yeah…a whole year, and he's still an asshole!"

They both laughed, then headed towards Winnie's house, reminiscing about Tommy's very first home run…

Tommy's Homer
Summer 1974

When Tommy smacked that baseball clear out of the field —to all his friend's astonishment, and even his own—it wasn't an easy pitch, or blind luck, or even divine intervention.

No, Tommy had *practiced.*

The spring after Tommy's fifth-grade year, when he was eleven, he decided he was going to learn to hit, come hell or high water. He was tired of striking out and being made fun of every time he played with the neighborhood kids in a pickup game.

So, the very first Saturday after school let out, he went to work. Got up early, got dressed, and, with ball and bat in hand, took off out the back door of their farmhouse and headed for the back forty. He tromped through the uncut grass and knee-high weeds all the way out to the old dilapidated barn that leaned precariously to one side just inside the rear fence line, where his dad kept all sorts of old farm equipment and other crap he never used anymore but was afraid to get rid of.

He was going to put that old barn to good use for once: as of today, he had re-commissioned it as the rebound backboard for batting practice.

Standing some twenty feet from the barn, he tossed the

ball, swung, and missed. Tossed the ball, swung, and missed.

When his older brother Will found out what he was doing, he thought he was nuts.

"That's never gonna work," he chided. "In *real* baseball, the ball is *pitched*. You'll never learn to hit it right by tossing it to *yourself*, dipshit."

Of course, Will would never in a million years volunteer to pitch to him, and Tommy knew better than to ask. There's no way he'd do it—especially if there was any chance any of his friends might see them playing together.

And besides, even if he *did* agree to do it, he'd probably just end up throwing the ball *at* him, instead of pitching it *to* him, and he was a pretty good shot, and could throw really hard, and Tommy wasn't about to take that chance.

He knew better.

Will was a mean kid, a bully—just like their dad.

And of course he wasn't about to ask his dad, either. *Especially* in the middle of a binge. His binges came and went, but in the middle, when they peaked, the reeking half-dressed man carried the bottle around with him everywhere he staggered, alternating between fits of rage and bouts of sleep that bordered on unconsciousness. He wouldn't go anywhere —not even to the bathroom—without that seemingly unemptyable bottle clutched in one hand, the brown liquid sloshing.

And about the time Tommy had decided to start practicing out at the barn, was right about the time his old man was carrying that damn bottle around. Not a good time to ask—or say—*anything,* actually. Tommy knew from experience that just as his father's clenched fist could bring that bottle to his lips, his other fist could just as quickly and easily be brought to Tommy's. And worse, he'd be grounded in the house at least a week, to reduce the risk of any one seeing his cuts and bruises before they healed, then asking questions or making phone calls or otherwise butting into old man Baker's private affairs.

And Tommy wasn't sure which was worse—the beatings, or the groundings—and he had no desire to run any experiments to find out.

So he figured he would just have to learn to hit on his own.

Toss, swing, miss. Toss, swing, miss...

After a few dozen tosses, he started occasionally making contact, tipping one behind him or ricocheting it straight into the ground; after a few hundred, he actually started catching some good, solid hits; after a few *thousand*, he was regularly hitting the ball, the *crack!* of the bat and the *thwack!* of the ball striking the wooden slats on the side of the old barn and echoing off into the woods behind the property.

Before long, it was getting pretty easy, so he decided to up the challenge a bit: he began throwing the ball up on the top of the barn and waiting as it bounced haphazardly around on the slanted roof, then dropped down in a totally random place, at a totally random speed.

He learned to quickly gauge the ball as it fell from the edge; and though he only had a split-second to do so, over time he got pretty good at it, successfully hitting the ball more often than not.

And that's what he did. Day after day, toss after toss, swing after swing—for two solid weeks.

Will may have been right—that's not the way to learn to hit a *pitched* ball; but what Tommy *did* learn instead, without really even being aware of it, was even more important: *to keep his eye on the ball.*

Then one Saturday, over at Winnie's house, while the two were lounging around out on the front porch reading and comparing comic books, a gaggle of neighborhood kids came riding by on their bikes, heading for the corner field down on the south end of The Flats for a pickup game. On their way past, Eric Brunes waved the two in, and they readily abandoned their superheroes (the comic books were all old ones anyway), ran inside for their mitts, then jumped on their bikes and peddled ferociously down the street to join up with the gang.

They all parked their bikes on the edge of the street and flooded onto the field. It was a vacant lot, overgrown with wild grass, which the kids had converted into a makeshift ball diamond a few summers ago, using scrap pieces of plywood for bases, which they stashed in the tree line behind the field for safe keeping between games.

After retrieving the wooden bases from hiding and placing them around the diamond, the kids divvied up teams, flipped a coin—and Tommy's team got first bat.

Eric was pitching for the other team (he was a year older, half a foot taller, and a lot stronger (and meaner) than the rest of them, so he always pitched, nobody argued this).

Danny Leer was first up, a decent player, could hit okay, and after one strike he caught one, good connection—but it was a line drive straight into the mitt of Chris McDaniels at short stop.

Winnie was up next. A skinny kid with thick glasses and a pale, freckled complexion, with fine, dark hair that was cut into straight bangs across his forehead—almost a bowl cut, with his small jug-ears sticking out on each side—he was not, by any stretch of the imagination, an athlete. So he looked somewhat comical, standing there intently holding a bat up in the air that was thicker than his own arms.

As usual, Eric easily struck him out, burning three fast balls in a row right by him. Winnie whiffed them all, swinging at the last one so hard his glasses tumbled off and landed right in the middle of home plate, prompting laughing and heckling from both teams as he timidly retrieved them and slumped away.

Then it was Tommy's turn to bat. He stood poised at the plate, bat held high, exactly as he had practiced thousands of times over the past two weeks, ready for the ball to come tumbling down crazy and unpredictable from the barn roof.

Knowing that Tommy couldn't hit—he usually whiffed it, just like Winnie—Eric made the mistake of thinking this would be an easy out. So for show, and probably more just to make Tommy look foolish, Eric performed a wide variety of crazy, gesticulated antics during his windup—prompting laughter from the kids on both teams—then, stepping forward, he at first feigned another fast ball—but at the last second held up and instead tossed a high, slow floater toward home plate.

The ball sailed in high above Tommy's head, then suddenly dropped in front of him just as it reached the plate (pretty much just as it did during his practice sessions).

Keeping his eye on the ball, gauging its speed and distance as it dropped, Tommy swung with everything he had.

CRACK!

The solid impact of bat against ball was so loud and unexpected—like a firecracker suddenly going off—that many of his teammates behind him actually flinched.

But Tommy just stood in disbelief as he watched the ball sail well over everyone's head and into the bright summer sky. Spencer Lewis—who was the youngest and smallest kid in the group, so was always stationed out at center field because no body could usually hit the ball that far anyway—turned and ran across the outfield as the ball sailed over him and toward the trees in the back.

Running as fast as he could, but to no avail, at the last second he threw his mitt into the air in futility as the ball fell and disappeared into the trees, thumping and cracking on its way to the ground somewhere unseen.

Incredulous, Tommy proudly trotted around the bases, his teammates shouting and cheering. As he crossed home, they all crowded around him, whooping, laughing, and patting him on the back, congratulating him on the most awesome homer they'd ever seen.

In the middle of all the ruckus, Tommy heard Eric shout from behind him, "Hey asshole!"

Tommy turned to find Eric staring down at him, pointing his

finger in his face.

"Nobody *ever* homers on me!" he barked. *"EVER!"*

With that, he turned as if to walk away—but then stopped, leaned slightly onto one leg…and launched a roundhouse.

And Tommy never saw it coming; suddenly, he both felt and heard the stinging explosion of Eric's fist as it met his face.

Spinning violently, he landed face-down in the dirt

suddenly, he both felt and heard the stinging explosion of the back of his father's hand as it met his face. Spinning violently, he landed face-down on the hardwood floor.

Arms and legs outstretched, he slid across the smooth floor toward the small bookcase that sat under his bedroom window, his wood desk chair tumbling away behind him and sliding to a stop against the bed.

Rolling painfully over, he saw his dad standing over him, pointing his finger at his face.

"Don't you ever talk back to me!" he barked. "EVER!"

With that he took a swig from the ever-present bottle.

Tommy blinked up at him, wiping the blood from his swelling lips and left nostril. He hadn't talked back, really—he'd merely made an observation. But either way, he should have known better than to say anything at all when his old man was on a binge. During those times, It didn't matter much what he did, what he said—his dad was just as likely to start talking hand to him anyway, soon as something set him off. And just about any little thing could set him off.

This time, he'd been sitting quietly at his desk in his

bedroom, minding his own business, engrossed in the novel The Call of the Wild, *his fifth-grade reading assignment, when his dad had suddenly appeared in the doorway.*

Tommy ignored him, kept his nose in the book.

After looking around the room, he slurred:

"Make sure you clean up this dump fore you go to bed."

Tommy just kept on reading, afraid to speak. Staying under the radar.

Taking a swig, his father finally turned and disappeared down the hallway, prompting a sigh of relief from Tommy.

But a moment later, he was back. This time, he stepped fully into the room, now only a few feet from the boy's desk, looming over him, looking down at him with contempt.

"You ignorin' me?"

A swig.

"No Sir," Tommy said, not looking up from the book.

"Sure LOOKS like you're ignorin' me."

"No, you're just drunk," he mumbled under his breath.

A surge of adrenaline coursed through him when he realized what he just said. He couldn't believe it. Sometimes he suspected he had a trap door located between his brain and his mouth, the way stuff just tumbled out like that sometimes...

Staring down at the book, he hoped the remark would slip by unnoticed. Or with any luck, maybe his dad hadn't even heard it.

Two quick steps toward him, just enough time for Tommy to turn and look up, a quick backhand, and now he was writing on the floor, bleeding.

Again.

Funny, though—all he could think about was how he hoped he hadn't gotten any blood on the book, since it was from the school library and he probably couldn't return it if he had

as the ruckus of shouting and cheering kids immediately stopped, replaced by a morbid silence that quickly spread across the ball field.

Reeling in pain, both hands clenched to his face, Tommy turned over to see Eric standing over him, face flush with anger.

Then, turning, the bully again made as if to leave—walking nonchalantly past Tommy as he lay writhing in the dirt—but suddenly turned and kicked him, hard, in the ribs.

Tommy curled up in a ball, the wind knocked out of him.

Eric turned and stormed off, all the kids stepping out of his way as he barreled through the crowd. Hands shoved into his pockets, mitt clasped under one arm, and not once bothering to look back at the rest of them, he marched to his bike, mounted, and peddled away down the road.

Gasping for air, Tommy watched him go though the drifting clouds of dust, and couldn't help but wonder if maybe Eric's dad sometimes carried a bottle around, too.

Once he'd disappeared around the corner, the rest of the kids gathered around and helped Tommy off the ground, murmuring their condolences and spewing random profanities about Eric.

Tommy brushed himself off, wiped at his bloody nose with his shirttail. The bleeding was already stopping, and the pain in his ribs was already subsiding, and when he finally began regaining his breath, he knew he'd be okay.

After stashing the plywood bases back in the tree line, the kids all rode to Spencer's house, because his mom sometimes made homemade ice cream—and sure enough, there was plenty for them to indulge.

It wasn't long before Eric Brunes and his temper tantrum was forgotten—but the legend of Tommy's awesome homer would live on forever.

Tommy may have spent a few weeks that spring learning how to hit a baseball—but in those few short minutes after scoring that homer, he learned quite a bit about life...

After lunch (double-decker PBJs, groovy potato chips, and Dr Pepper), the boys pretended to watch TV while they waited for Winnie's mom to leave for work. But nothing good was on, and they were just sitting on the floor together, looking at the screen but not really paying attention. Besides, seems it was always just commercials anyway.

That's when Tommy piped up:

"I wrote a story," he said rather timidly.

"Really?" Winnie asked, surprised.

"Yeah…I figured since you're always writing stories—and they're always so good—I should at least *try* to write one. So I was thinking and thinking earlier this spring, trying to come up with an idea. Then I finally got one—during biology class, the last semester before summer break, when we watched a movie about genetics—and spent a bunch of time over the summer writing it down and working on it and rewriting it...and last night I finally finished it, and I think it's pretty good...or at least I *hope* it is...d'you wanna hear it?"

"Of course!" Winnie said, smiling and nodding.

Smiling sheepishly, Tommy looked down, thinking about it for a moment, then, when he had it, he looked back up, donning a more serious expression:

"Okay, so there's this laboratory where they're doing genetic experiments on animals, except there's some kind of accident or cross-pollination or something that mixes things up and they end up accidentally creating some sort of hybrid creature...

...it's called *Carnivores*..."

Carnivores
by Thomas Baker

"What the hell *is* it?" Jason asked the director, a little unnerved.

The two men stood outside the lab's containment room, looking through the wire-infused safety glass window at a large, stainless-steel cage that occupied one rear corner the room. Behind the gleaming bars, a hulking creature sat in the darkness, itself so dark it was difficult to discern among the shadows. Easily the size of a grizzly bear, it's black hide was leathery, scaly, seemingly reptilian in nature, with tuffs of long, course black hair sprouting from its body in random patches. Though sitting upright in the back corner of the cage, it was slumped over, its massive head drooping, as if it was sleeping.

From here Jason could see it had four appendages—but did it walk upright? Or down on all fours?

"Well, we don't know," the director replied. "That's why you're here. I asked the board for the best zoologist in the country, and they sent you."

Jason snapped his head around to look at the man, incredulity in his eyes.

"But you guys *made* it, didn't you?"

"Not intentionally."

At this, Jason's eyes filled with questions, but he just waited for elaboration.

The director sighed, hanging his head. Then he looked back up to Jason:

"Look, all we're working on here is cloning. Nothing complex, relatively simple life forms like rodents. Reptiles. More recently, chickens. But nothing large, exotic or dangerous. Sure, we do a little gene splicing and genetic modification too, but mostly just to eliminate certain genetic markers, to help ensure we develop stable embryos...but that's it."

"Okay...so where did *this* thing come from?" Jason asked, returning his gaze to the beast in the cage.

"We don't know. Best guess is some kind of cross-contamination in the lab. All the embryos start out in petri dishes in the incubation lab. One morning, one of our techs came in and discovered this thing writhing around in a petri dish. It had already eaten the original specimen. But to this day we still don't know how or where it originated."

"In a petri dish? It was that small?"

"Started out that way, yes. About the size of my thumb. Grew pretty fast though. According to the size and weight measurements we were able to take before it got too big and dangerous to safely approach, its growth appeared to be exponential."

"Exponential? So how long did it take to get this big?"

"About two weeks."

"Jesus."

"And we know it's carnivorous. In fact, it *only* eats meat, it totally ignored anything else we gave it. But now, it's getting too big, and too expensive to feed. Yesterday, it went through an entire side of beef. Not all in one sitting, but finished it before lights out. Bones and all. It has a massive jaw full of incisors, bicuspids, and molars—all enormous, like from prehistoric times, think saber-toothed cat. So we need to put it down soon. But first, we're hoping you can help us identify it."

"Do you really think we can get close enough to get a tissue sample?"

"We don't have to. It laid eggs yesterday."

"Eggs?"

Big ones. Like ostrich eggs, only a little bigger, about

the size of footballs. Laid six of them, overnight, we found them the next morning. Harvested them while it slept. Now they're in the incubation lab—"

—he raised his arm, looked at his watch—

"—in fact, Sharon should be tending to them right about now. Let's go take a look."

As they turned to leave, Jason snatched one last glance over his shoulder at the beast, just in time to see it...yawn? Lifting its gigantic head slightly, it opened up, its gaping maw huge, crimson, and loaded with more teeth than he'd ever seen in his life...even as a zoologist. Its long, gray tongue curled upward with the yawn. He also thought he caught a glimpse of one of its eyes open slightly, black and set deep in the side of its head, just before his view was cut of as he exited though the door.

As they walked down the brightly-lit hall to the other end of the facility, a thought occurred to Jason.

"Wait a sec—if it laid eggs, how did it get pregnant? Locked in a cage, no less?"

The director shrugged. "It seems to have been born pregnant. Or, I suppose more accurately, *mutated* that way. Like I said, we had no idea—until suddenly one morning there were eggs."

"How is that possible? I've never heard of that, in any kind of mammal. A few insects, the rare fish or reptile maybe, but not with mammals."

"That's one of the many mysteries that we hope you can solve for us."

Toward the end of the hallway, the last glass door, marked INCUBATION was slightly ajar, beyond which was only a red, heavy steel door capping off the hallway, with FIRE EXIT – ALARM WILL SOUND stenciled across it in large white letters.

As the director pushed into the lab, he called out:

"Sharon, how many times have I told you to keep this door closed—"

—but stopped in his tracks when he saw the lab was vacant.

"Well, I'll deal with her later. For now, let's take a look at those eggs."

Jason followed him into the lab, turning and walking behind the lengthy, solid cabinets and countertop that occupied the center of the room. On the other side of the cabinet unit, the wall was lined with glass cubicles, several of which glowed with orange-yellow heat lamps.

But as the director skirted the end of the cabinets, he stopped dead in his tracks when he saw a pair of feet, donned in women's shoes, protruding from behind.

"Oh my god!" he exclaimed as he rushed around the cabinets to the woman lying on the floor. "Sarah!"

Peering at her from behind the director, Jason wondered how he could possibly identify her; her entire face was gone, leaving only a bloody mass of shredded flesh, gouged and pitted white bones poking through. And her neck was the same tattered mess, and much of her exposed arms and legs, too. Like she was eaten alive.

Blood pooled about her, still fresh, the coppery scent almost overpowering, the floor around her tracked over with tiny red paw prints. A clipboard lay beside her, papers scattered about, a few of them stuck in the blood and soaked through.

"Dear god," the director whispered.

Just then, they both looked up at the wall, and noticed the sliding door of one of the big incubators was open. Inside, the scattered remains of egg shells. Big, *black* egg shells...

"Are those—?" Jason began.

"We need to get out of here, NOW!" The director barked, looking desperately around the room, but seeing nothing. "Lock the lab door before those things—"

Just then a black, leathery creature—smooth, no hair yet, about the size of a small cat—leapt from an overhead cabinet onto the man's head and immediately started ripping shreds of flesh away, biting and tearing at an incredible speed.

The director began screaming and backing away, flailing at the beast, when another leapt onto him from below, latching onto his leg and, like the first, immediately shredding through cloth and into flesh. This caused the man to lose his balance and go down, screaming even louder as he writhed frantically on the floor, blood spilling from both ends.

Horrified, Jason watched the scene for a moment, unsure of what to do. Then he stepped forward and begin kicking at the creatures, trying to get them off the man. But his kicks were doing nothing to dislodge the things. They seemed extremely strong for their size, and were ripping through the director's flesh and muscle, reaching the bone, with astonishing speed.

As the man's screams began to diminish to gasps, Jason looked up just in time to see one of the creatures leap toward him from the end of the long counter. He ducked, and the thing flew over him, landing, slipping, sliding backwards on the slippery tile floor, scurrying with all fours trying to regain its footing to leap again.

"Go!" The director managed in a half scream, half-gasp. "Get out! Lock the door!"

As Jason ran to the open lab door, three more of the creatures emerged and gave chase.

He burst through the door, and, turning to slam it shut, slipped on the tile floor and went down. He quickly regained his feet, but the creatures had already reached the doorway, and all he could do was turn and run for his life toward the fire exit door at the end of the hall, three creatures right on his heels, the other three now joining the chase, their bloody maws hissing their tiny roars, the lab now ominously quiet behind them.

He didn't make it.

Just as he reached the door, the closest three creatures leapt onto his back, pushing him forward as they immediately began tearing his flesh open—his neck, his back, his shoulder—and he lost his balance, screaming and shuffling on the slippery floor, then finally fell forward.

Slamming against the door's bar latch, he shoved the door violently open, activating the fire alarm as he fell through. Rolling into the parking lot outside, he batted at the beasts on his back, trying to dislodge them, to no avail, as the others joined in the attack.

But fortunately, the loud and shrill fire alarm seemed to frighten them, and they relinquished him and darted off together, leaping and hissing down the street until they disappeared, one-by-one, down into an old rusty storm drain...

When Tommy finished, he again smiled sheepishly, watching Winnie for his reaction.

"That was a great story!" Winnie encouraged. "See? You can do it! You should write stories more often, you're good at it!"

"Well, thanks," Tommy said, somewhat embarrassed. "But I'm not as good as you...you always write really great stories, I'll never write one as good as yours."

"Yes you will," Winnie argued. "It just takes practice. You just gotta read a lot, and write a lot. It'll come to you, and you'll get better and better, until you're just as good as me... maybe even better."

"Fat chance...but I'll keep working on it," Tommy promised. "And by the way—do *you* have any new stories? It's been a while, I figure you gotta have a new one by now."

Winnie just smiled—almost menacingly—and Tommy

smiled back, knowing what the answer was.

"Yeah, I've got a new one," Winnie said, nodding. "I was gonna wait until I could brush it up a little more, but it's pretty much done I think."

"Well, I told you mine, now you gotta tell me yours!"

After thinking about it for a moment, Winnie seemed to conclude that he would, in fact, tell the story now:

"Okay," he said, then cleared his throat in preparation.

"So a team of EPA inspectors were sent to do some testing at this big lake. They'd been called in due to a bunch of complaints from locals in the area, that the fish population was way down, and there was an odd smell, and a weird taste to the water in the area. They suspected the nearby chemical plant might be dumping hazardous waste in the lake, and causing all of those problems...but what the team came across was way worse than anything they suspected...I call it *The Harvest*..."

The Harvest
by Winston Milhouse

Ben stood knee-deep in the lake water, black rubber hip-waders glistening wet. He marked each vial of water he collected with a black marker (clumsy with the thick rubber gloves, but he managed best he could), then slid it into a plastic case hanging to one side, its strap looped around his opposite shoulder. The late afternoon had turned increasingly hot and humid, and he wanted badly to wipe the sweat from his forehead, but with his elbow-length gloves dripping with possibly contaminated water, he didn't think it a good idea. So he let the sweat run.

Dana stood on the bank ten or so feet away, taking air samples with an electronic meter, which also hung to her side, its strap also looped around her opposite shoulder. With each sample she took, she jotted notes in a small notebook. And though she had started out wearing a white HAZMAT suit, once she had enough positive air samples to alleviate her fears, she removed her face mask and unzipped the top of the suit, letting it dangle around her waist, revealing a yellow tank top underneath, which was now damp with sweat, clinging to her firm, athletic body like paint...

Once Dana had pronounced it safe, Ben had also removed his face mask, letting it dangle on his chest from the head strap. And now that he could see more clearly, he couldn't help stealing the occasional look over at Dana, watching her in his peripheral vision and timing his covert glances whenever she looked down at her notebook and wouldn't catch him.

There was a white RV parked in a clearing in the distance behind her which was labeled EPA along the sides in big blue lettering next to a circular matching blue water/flower/sun logo.

Somewhere in the surrounding woods, Janice was busy collecting vegetation samples, and Marco was waving about a geiger counter, testing for radiation.

The four would be setting up camp that evening,

staying the night, then finishing up tomorrow before heading back to the lab with their myriad samples for analysis. They had debated getting a hotel room closer to town, but they had all decided it wasn't worth driving all the way back to the city then turn around and drive all the way back here, they would just stay the night on site— build a little campfire for dinner, sleep in the RV, then head out tomorrow once they had finished collecting samples.

Janice was the only one to express reservations, being older (and considerably heavier) than the rest of them, not sure she was all that up to "roughing it" for the night... but she could see the excitement in their faces, heard it in their voices, and quickly relented, just to keep the peace. She was like that, quiet and introverted, avoiding conflict at nearly any cost...but man, she knew her stuff, was one of the best botanists in the country, and they wouldn't consider taking on an assignment like this without her. That would suck.

So they were all relieved when she finally, if hesitantly, agreed to the plan.

However, she had set one condition: she wasn't keen on flying insects—particularly of the biting variety—and so she insisted that they set up a bug zapper when they made camp.

Easy enough, Marco said he had one he could bring, that would plug right into the RV's power.

Or even the emergency generator, if they had to.

Done.

High-fives all around.

•

"Man, they weren't kidding about the smell, huh?" Ben said, wrinkling his nose.

"I'd say, Dana agreed. "Smells...*unnatural*. Chemically. At first I thought I'd get used to it after a while, but so far, no. In fact, it's starting to irritate my sinuses."

"Yeah, throat too." Ben cleared his throat for emphasis.

"Well, if it's any consolation, I'm still not reading anything unusual in the air, seems normal, at least within acceptable parameters." she said, motioning with her chin to her meter. "And when Marco was over here, he said he wasn't picking up any radiation either."

"So sounds like whatever it is, must be in the water." he said, sliding another vial into his case. "So maybe their suspicions were right, about that chemical plant we passed on the way down here—up there on the hill, almost hidden back in the woods, a good ways off the highway, we could just see the top of the main building...and the giant stacks, spewing...*something*. You saw it, too. So what do you suppose they do there?"

"Supposedly just household chemicals, according to the prep file. But that guy back at the gas station said something about a secret government project...some kind of bioweapon," she said with a chuckle.

"That old geezer? He must be in his nineties! You believe him!?" he said sarcastically, smiling.

"No...the guy was obviously a nutjob. Besides, if they *were* doing something like that, the feds would know about it, which means our bosses would probably know too, and so they wouldn't've bothered wasting time and limited discretionary budget funds sending us out here for testing. Just feed a line of BS to the media and have them spread the word and calm everyone down until it blows over and everyone forgets about it."

"Yeah, I suppose you're right," he concurred.

"So it's doubtful there's any secret government project going on, or we wouldn't be out here investigating it. My bet is we'll find trace chemicals in the lake water, then we can order a facility inspection, see if they came from that plant. Probably just the usual illegal dumping, not unusual for big corporations, pay off the right local people, they can get away with it for a while, 'til they get caught and there's enough public outcry to stop it...maybe give them a well-publicized slap on the wrist and a seemingly big fine that in reality a multi-billion-dollar corporation can easily pay, and that's it. But at least it stops. For a while, anyway."

"Maybe. I look forward to analyzing all these samples at the lab tomorrow."

"Me too."

For the next few minutes they both continued collecting samples in silence. And that was when Ben noticed something odd, and started looking all around, up in the trees, up at the sky.

"What?" she asked, noticing his antics.

"Seems awful quiet," he said.

"Of course it's quiet...what do you expect? We're out in the middle of nowhere."

"No, even so...I mean, no birds singing, no critter or insect sounds in the woods...nothing. It's kinda creepy, now that I notice it."

With that, she began looking all around also, listening intently.

"You're right. I don't hear anything either. And it *is* pretty creepy."

"You think that smell is enough to drive everything away? The wildlife?"

Dana considered this, then shrugged. "Doubt it. I mean it's not that strong, I don't think. Just a little irritating. So if something *has* driven all the wildlife away from the lake, it's probably not the smell...it would have to be something else."

"Like what though?"

She shrugged. "Beats me. But that's why we're here, isn't it? Maybe something'll turn up when we compile all the data after analyzing all these samples tomorrow."

"Maybe," he conceded. "I guess we'll see."

Then, motioning over his shoulder with his thumb, he said: "I'm gonna head around to the other side of the lake, get some samples there. That should finish off this case."

"Yeah, I need to move, too. Downwind, I think."

With that she started walking along the bank away

from him to the west, holding the air sampler up in front of her, clear plastic hose dangling, and intermittently glancing down at the monitor.

Ben stood for a moment watching her go (after all, she was *hot*), then began trudging through the shallow water toward the bank, boots sticking in the muddy bottom with each step *thuck splash thuck splash* until he reached solid ground and climbed up.

But when he turned to head east, which would eventually take him around to the south end of the lake, something odd occurred to him, and he stopped and turned back to the water.

Nothing.

He stood silent and motionless for several minutes, alternating between peering left and right out across the lake, and looking down into the green/brown tinted water directly below him, near the bank.

The entire time, he saw nothing.

No fish.

No frogs.

No water bugs.

Nothing.

He never even heard the distant slapping *splash!* of a fish jumping out of the water and back in, a common sound at every lake he had ever been to, and he went all the time as a kid, fishing with his dad.

"Where's all the fish?" he whispered.

He recalled the prep file: the complaints had included

reports from local fishermen claiming that they hadn't caught a single fish in weeks, leading them to believe that the fish population must be way down, in conjunction with the other oddities reported in the area.

Shaking his head, he turned and started east around the lake, thinking he must be imagining things, or he frightened all the fish away with all the ruckus he made trudging back to the bank.

He pulled off the thick rubber gloves as he walked, finally able to wipe the sweat from his brow as he silently considered his thoughts.

There must be a simple explanation...

Or maybe I'm just losing it...

But whatever was going on, he couldn't shake the disconcerting feeling that something was amiss here; first the quiet woods, and now the seemingly lifeless lake.

Suddenly, he was becoming concerned about what they might find here...

•

Around twenty minutes later, Ben stood on the outer rim of a cove he had found on the south side of the lake, holding his shirttail up over his nose and mouth, trying to minimize the stench.

It wasn't working. His throat was catching, and he was fighting the reflex to puke right there in the lake.

Dropping his shirttail, he wrestled the face mask back onto his head, holding his breath as he did so. Once sealed, he exhaled, fogging the mask briefly, then breathed deeply though the filters.

It helped.

A little.

Once the mask cleared, he turned his attention back to the gruesome sight before him:

The entire cove was full of dead fish—had to be *thousands* of them—floating and bobbing, packed together gill to gill, like (no pun) sardines.

"Jesus," he whispered. "Looks like I just found all the missing fish."

But what the hell could cause this?

For an instant that old man's voice entered his head: *some kinda top-secret bioweapon*...but he quickly dismissed the thought, scolding himself.

Pulling the rubber gloves back on, he kneeled and, pushing his thickly gloved hand through the bobbing layer of dead and rotting fish, dipped a single vial into the cove water, capped and labeled it, and slid it into the case.

That would have to do it, he couldn't stay here any longer, the stench was overwhelming, even through the filtered face mask.

And besides, he knew it would be getting dark soon.

When he stood, he realized he was again holding his breath, even with the mask on. But he didn't want to risk breathing, so he turned to head back north to the clearing where they had parked the RV, walking a few steps away before releasing his pent up air with a rush, then breathing slowly at first, testing the air, but with distance the odor dissipated and soon he could breathe normally.

Then he realized: there was a steady breeze blowing due south across the lake...so maybe all these floating dead fish had drifted from the lake into the cove, blown there by the wind?

Possibly.

But then he again stopped in his tracks as something odd occurred to him. Turning back to the cove, he peered intently over the entire stock of dead fish.

He even lifted his face mask, for a clearer view.

He was right: *no flies.*

They should be crawling with flies, he thought.

Then, from the corner of his right eye, he thought he caught movement, out over the lake. Glancing over, he saw what looked like some type of...*shimmering?*...*translucent?*...object floating just above the water's surface. It reminded him of the "flashing lights" he sometimes saw in his peripheral vision during a migraine. He blinked hard a few times, making sure he didn't have something in his eye. But no, it was still out there, a transparent blob just floating there above the lake.

And suddenly, it seemed to flash away out of sight.

Just as quickly as it had appeared, it was gone.

It happened so fast he had to question whether he had seen anything at all.

Maybe it was just the heat.

Or the *smell...*

Shaking his head to clear it (or more likely in

disbelief), he turned and hurried away, his concern growing.

•

Darkness was falling by the time they had all returned to the RV, stashed their samples, notes, and PPE inside, then proceeded to set up camp. The summer heat was dissipating, but the cooler evening air was still heavy with humidity.

Deciding they should collect wood for the fire before it got too dark, the four ventured into the woods on the other side of the clearing, and within twenty minutes they'd amassed a decent pile of both kindling and good-sized firewood just inside the tree line on the edge of the clearing.

Then they proceeded to set up camp.

While Ben and Marco extended the rolling canopy out from the side of the RV and folded down the aluminum legs, Dana hauled a couple of pre-filled coolers out of the back of the RV and placed them strategically underneath, where they'd be in easy reach from the four folding camping chairs, which Janice was positioning in a semi-circle just outside the canopy.

Then Ben and Dana began building the campfire, collecting wood from the pile at the tree line across the clearing and depositing it in front of the chairs, while, as promised, Marco produced a large black bug zapper from inside the RV, hung it from the front edge of the canopy, then ran the cord back inside, plugging it into an outlet near the door. Inside, he looked out the window to be sure it was on. When he saw the blue lights glowing behind the metal mesh screens, he smiled warmly—it was very reminiscent of the black light he had hung above the posters on his bedroom wall back in the day...

When he came back out, he saw that Janice had already taken the third chair (the one nearest the zapper), and he winked at her as he walked around her, heading over to the far chair.

Smiling back, she gave him thumbs-up with one hand, while the other held a paperback book, her index finger marking her place.

Noticing this, he motioned to the book and asked: "Whatcha readin' this time?"

Janice picked the book up and looked at the cover, as if checking the title.

"The Gods Themselves, by Isaac Asimov."

"Really? Sounds interesting. What's it about?"

"Well, long story short," she said, looking back up at him, "It's how technology doesn't always mix well with nature."

"I would agree with that premise," Marco said, nodding. "And hey—how'd you like the one you were reading last week? What was it—"

"The Lathe of Heaven by Ursula K. Le Guin," she interrupted, smiling.

"You like it? What was that one about?"

With that, he turned and sat in the far chair, then

turned his attention back to her.

"Well again, long story short, it takes place after humanity has all but destroyed the world through wars and environmental destruction...and essentially, it makes the point that whenever we try to change the world for the better...it doesn't always work out as intended."

"Boy, you can say *that* again," Marco again agreed, again nodding.

"In fact, the title of the novel—*The Lathe of Heaven*—is taken from a passage in the *Zhuangzi* by the ancient Chinese philosopher and Taoist Zhuang Zhou—"

—she paused to look up into the air dreamily, as if recalling scripture—

"—To let understanding stop at what cannot be understood is a high attainment; those who cannot do it will be destroyed on the lathe of heaven."

She then looked back to Marco for his response.

Marco again nodded, a donning look of understanding.

"So it's a warning: that we shouldn't try to understand *everything*, because *some* things defy our understanding, and we could destroy ourselves—or the whole world—in the process?"

He looked at her for approval of his analysis, and her eyes widened, brows lifted in astonishment.

"Very good!" she said, impressed. "Not bad for a child of your generation!"

He smiled at this, and dismissed the notion with a wave of his hand.

"Janice, you're not *that* much older than us, regardless of what you may think."

"Old enough," she said, returning to her book.

"Old enough to know better, but young enough to do it anyway?" he asked with a mischievous grin.

She looked back up and smiled. "Damn right!"

By then Ben and Dana had finished stacking the wood and lighting the fire, and they stood and took the two remaining chairs to their left.

Once the fire was going strong, Ben stood and entered the RV for a moment, then returned with some long, stainless steel hotdog roasting rods he had brought along. He handed them around, then fished a pack of hot dogs out of one of the coolers and returned to his chair next to Dana, while Marco pulled four bottles of beer wet and dripping from the other cooler.

Dogs and bottles were handed around, relaxing the mood and bringing smiles to faces—even Janice's—and the camping officially commenced.

•

Soon they began discussing the day, what they had found, what they thought.

"Well, the good news is, I didn't find a trace of abnormal radiation, anywhere in the area—and I sampled everywhere around the lake—nada," Marco announced as he roasted his hot dog above the fire—

—he took a swig of his beer—

"—normal levels, everywhere."

The others all nodded and muttered affirmations of the news.

"I didn't see anything unusual, either," Janice added—

—she turned her attention to her roasting rod, turned it to roast the other side of the hotdog, then looked back up at the others—

"—I mean, we won't know for sure until the samples are analyzed in the lab, but I didn't see anything in any of the plant life that looked odd or unusual."

Again, nods and affirmations around the fire.

"But there *is* the odd odor," Dana said.

"Yeah, it was burning my eyes," Janice interjected.

"And my throat," Marco added.

"Us too," Dana acknowledged—

—she motioned between herself and Ben with her now sweating beer bottle—

"—But according to the tests, everything is in the green —some readings were a little high, but they were all within acceptable ranges—leading us to speculate that whatever it is, must be in the water."

"I think it definitely is," Ben stated matter-of-factly.

They all stopped and looked at him.

"You didn't sound so sure earlier," Dana remarked.

He paused a moment, debating what—if anything—he should share of his weird experiences that day. After all, he didn't want them all thinking he was crazy, like that old man at the gas station...

Finally, he proceeded cautiously: "Well, I came across

some...strange things...over on the other side of the lake."

"Strange like how so?" Marco asked, the others just waiting expectantly.

Again Ben paused, unsure of what all to share.

"Well, first of all, I found a cove full of dead fish. *Packed* full, from bank to bank...it must've been damn near all the fish in the lake. And considering I didn't see any fish, or even any *signs* of fish, anywhere else, all day, I'd say it might've been. Plus, the breeze was blowing across the lake right in the direction of that cove, they could've all just drifted in there. Like, all the fish from the lake, dead and floating, now packed in that cove on the far side, rotting in the sun."

no shit
whoa
that had to've stunk BAD

"It did, so I couldn't stay long, the smell was so bad I was about to puke in the lake—even with my face mask on —so I took one water sample and got the hell outta there."

"Okay, so something's in the water, killed the fish," Dana speculated.

"I'd say yes, but we won't know until we run tests on the samples in the lab tomorrow," Ben replied.

But then Marco seemed curious.

"Okay, so you found tons of dead fish in that cove," he reiterated. "But you also said that you came across *some strange things*—"

—he made air quotes with his fingers to accentuate—

"—as in plural. *Things*. Plus you started with *first of all*, suggesting there's at least a *second* thing...so, what else did you encounter out there, that you're not telling us, Benny-boy?" With this he smiled and took a swig of his beer, all in good fun.

yeah
he's right
what else?

"Well, now you're gonna think I'm crazy...but Dana noticed the same thing—"

—he turned to Dana—

"—remember how quiet it was? Not a sound, across the lake or in the woods or anywhere? You commented on it."

"Yeah, I remember...no birdsong, insect sounds, frogs, nothing, it was completely quiet. It was actually kinda creepy, once we noticed it."

"Yes...and as the day wore on, I also noticed that I hadn't seen any fish, nor any *signs* of fish. When I was a kid I used to go fishing all the time with my dad, and you always heard fish jumping from the water and splashing back in. All the time. But today, not a single one."

"Well, you've already speculated all the fish are dead and drifted into that cove," Marco reminded.

"Yes, I did," Ben agreed. "But the next strange thing—I almost didn't notice it at all, but just happened to notice it right before I left—there were no *flies*. None. I scanned the entire area, just to be sure. As bad as those masses of dead fish smelled, they should've been *crawling* with flies...but I didn't see a single one."

"Wait, you're right," Janice now chimed in. "Y'all know I'm rather sensitive about insects, and particularly the *flying* type, right?"

They all nodded in understanding, remembering the bug zapper she'd requested—no, *demanded*—in order for her to participate in this expedition.

"Well, when I was collecting plant samples in the woods, I saw all the usual suspects...the *crawling* types of bugs, just like normal. But now that you mention it, I realize I didn't get a single mosquito bite, or have any flying insects land on me...in fact, I can't rightly remember even seeing any flying insects. *All day!*"

With that they all began looking around in the air, searching for flying insects. And for the first time, they all noticed that there didn't seem to *be* any.

"Not even lightening bugs," Dana noticed.

"And no bugs have hit the zapper, either," Marco mentioned, motioning behind Janice and they all turned to look at the glowing—and dormant—zapper.

"So it would appear," Ben surmised, "that not only are most, or even all, of the fish in the lake dead, but seems everything that flies—birds, and insects—have vanished from this area."

Again they all looked around, up in the air, up in the trees at the edge of the clearing, everywhere.

Nothing.

"Okay, so something in the water killed the fish, and

has some kind of irritating fumes, like maybe chemicals,"
Marco summarized. "But Dana said the air tested okay—"

—he looked across the fire at Dana—

"—right? Some readings were a little high, but
everything was in the green?"

"That's right," Dana concurred, nodding.

"So the air is okay, but something in the water is killing
the fish. But something in the water doesn't explain
what's happened to the airborne creatures."

With that he turned to Ben, next to Dana.

"So what else aren't you telling us?"

Now all eyes were back on Ben, and he realized he was
cornered.

He turned away, looked at the fire, let out a long sigh.

"Is there something else, Ben?" Dana asked, a little
more gently than Marco's interrogation had been.

Ben looked sheepishly up at her, and she raised her
eyebrow expectantly.

"Yes," he finally relented, looking around at them all.
"There's one more thing. But I was afraid if I told you,
you'd all think I was crazy."

"We're listening," Marco said.

"You need to tell us," Janice said. "We need all the
information we can get, in order to figure out what's going
on here."

Ben smiled mischievously. "Of course, I could always
take the *it's a secret, I could tell you, but then I'd have to
kill* you approach."

They all chuckled at this, but then went quiet, waiting.

"Out with it," Dana said. And that seemed to push him off the fence.

"When I was leaving the cove of dead fish, and I'd turned back when I realized there were no flies, and wanted to take another look just to verify that..."

He paused, signing again.

"Yes?" Marco urged him on.

"I saw something. Out on the lake. Or *thought* I saw something. I wasn't sure. I'm *still* not sure."

"Saw something...like what?" Marco pushed further.

"That's just it, I don't know...best I can describe it is, like a migraine."

They all looked around incredulously.

what?
a migraine?
what are you talking about?

"Well, I don't know about you guys, but I occasionally get migraines. Starts with a blind spot, usually in my lower left field of vision, then gradually spreads across the entire field—the classic 'flashing lights' that are often described when referring to migraines."

"I've read about that," Dana said. "They say it's like flashing lights, or blinking lights, in your field of vision— even if the room is dark."

"My sister gets migraines, and she describes it that way, too...like a shiny flashing, or a glimmering, in her vision," Janice added.

"Yes," Ben confirmed. "And that's what it was like today...I saw something out of the corner of my eye, and looked out across the lake, and there was this...like a *shimmering*...a big translucent, gleaming area, that reminded me of the glimmering or flashing visual effect I get during a migraine. And whatever it was, was just floating above the lake."

"What do you think it was?" Marco asked.

"I don't know. In fact, I'm still not sure I saw *anything*. I blinked a few times to be sure there wan't something in my eyes, but about the time I decided there really was something floating out there, it just...vanished."

"Vanished?" Marco asked, incredulity in his voice.

"Vanished, shot away, disappeared...I don't know—"

—he shrugged—

"—just one moment it was there, and the next moment it was gone."

"You were right, I *do* think you're crazy," Marco said, standing. "And while the rest of you decide whether he's crazy and seeing things, or if there's some kind of invisible alien thing floating around out here—I'm gonna go get some more wood for the fire, it's dying out."

With that he strode away from the campfire and into the darkness of the clearing, toward the tree line where they'd piled their gathered wood earlier.

There was a moment of silence around the fire, while the others absorbed what Ben had told them.

Then Dana spoke up:

"It makes sense, in a way..."

Ben and Janice turned to her.

"I mean, we think there's something in the water that's killing the fish, and there's definitely some kind of odor... like a chemical smell...but how do we explain the missing airborne creatures? No birds, no fireflies...no flies, like Ben noticed at that cove where thousands of fish were rotting in the sun..."

"I'm not making the connection," Janice said, perplexed.

"Wait—" Ben said, squinting his eyes at Dana. "Are you suggesting that the floating thing I saw—and remember, I'm not *sure* I actually saw *anything*, it could've been the heat, the chemical smell, the rotting fish stench making me sick, the reduced oxygen through the face mask, *anything*—could actually have scared off the airborne animals and insects in the area? Or even killed them, like some kind of *predator?* And even an *invisible*—or at least *translucent*—predator, at that?"

"How else do you explain it?" she replied matter-of-factly. "On the one hand, it's easy to correlate the dead fish with some kind of toxic contaminate in the water, and the odor correlates too, as some kind of chemical contaminate, and both correlate to the nearby chemical plant that we've suspected since the outset. But none of that explains the lack of airborne wildlife, especially when you consider that the air samples I took were all in the green, so they weren't poisoned like the fish...but on the other hand, you think you saw some sort of airborne... *thing*...floating above the lake—so it's not much of a stretch that, whatever it is, could correlate to the missing airborne wildlife. So short answer, yes. Perhaps even some kind of predator."

"Do you guys think that if the chemical plant is dumping chemical waste—either directly into the lake or close enough that it somehow indirectly ended up here—that some kind of creature could have spawned?" Janice asked excitedly. "Like through chemically-induced genetic mutation of some kind...a new form of life? An aberration? A technological accident?"

With that, she looked around at them, eyes glowing.

"Oh, come on Janice," Ben chided, dismissing her theory with a wave of his hand. He knew what kind of books she liked to read, and motioned to the one now in her lap. "This isn't some crazy science fiction novel!"

"Ben, she has a point," Dana agreed. "We don't know—"

And that's when Marco started screaming.

They all stood and looked into the darkness of the clearing, in the direction of the screaming, in tandem with the sound of an armload of wood dropping to the ground, and could just see Marco's shadowy silhouette flailing about, seeming to be grappling with something.

"Marco!" Ben yelled as he began slowly moving in that direction, wanting to help but tentative, unsure what the hell was going on.

Finally, Marco seemed to break free from whatever

had him, and, screaming violently, began running toward the others, now standing around the campfire. As he approached the firelight, they could see that one of his arms—now motionless at his side, even as he ran as fast as he could—was covered in blood, the sleeve above tattered, and as he drew nearer it became questionable exactly how much of his arm remained attached to his body, *or had it been severed entirely?*

"WHAT IS IT?" Ben yelled, with Dana and Janice both screaming now, too.

But before Marco could reach them, or even answer Ben or say anything at all, he suddenly lurched up into the air, and his screaming went silent.

They all watch in astonishment as he floated several feet above the ground, writhing in silence—the others could see that he was screaming, but could hear nothing—as his flesh began to rip from his body and blood began flooding into... *what, exactly?*

The others watched in horror—and also in silence—not understanding what they were seeing, as Marco writhed and convulsed and was shredded right before them, and his obvious screams could not be heard, and his blood spilled around him, eventually filling what they now could see was a translucent, floating... *something*.

But once it was red with blood inside, its outline—skin, border, whatever it was—became pronounced, and it took on the appearance of an undulating blob, maybe eight feet long, slightly oval or football shaped, about four or five feet in diameter around the middle, floating and silent and pulsing and translucent—until it was filled with Marco's blood, that is—appearing to be totally flexible and objectively shapeless.

And then, right before their eyes, it seemed to...

...*expand?*

Maybe just a few feet bigger, but still—it definitely appeared to grow in size.

"What the fu—" Ben said in a near whisper, too seized with fear to say more, or even to move.

Then Janice began screaming, and Dana grabbed Ben by the arm.

"Let's go!" she yelled, snapping Ben out of his trance, and they both turned and ran toward the RV.

But Janice just kept screaming, hands pressed to her face, and remained bolted to the ground in front of her chair, paperback spread upside down in the grass at her feet, as the...

...*thing...*

...darted quickly across the remaining clearing and engulfed her, moving so fast that Ben and Dana didn't even have time to voice a warning, let alone grab her, and, like Marco, she was immediately yanked up into the air—into the *thing*—and, like Marco, her screams immediately went silent, and the other two, standing just short of the RV's door, Dana's hand on the knob, both yelled "Janice!" in unison, but when their friend was first sucked inside, they could see her writhing and thrashing, and her skin began to shred, just like Marco's had, but then she faded from view within the red-filled blob, and they immediately knew it was too late, and Dana yanked the door open and they both rushed inside, slammed the door shut and locked it, and stepped to the window—the same one Marco had looked out of to make sure the bug zapper was working—and watched in horror, wondering what the hell would happen next... *what the hell that thing was.*

"Janice..." Dana whispered as she watched in horror through the little window. Then she turned to Ben. "We have to do something!"

"It's too late, she's gone," Ben said softly, shaking his head, never taking his eyes off the gruesome scened playing out before them.

Tears welling in her eyes, Dana turned back to the window. She knew he was right, there was nothing they could do. Janice was gone.

And Marco...

But as she watched, the blood-red blob—seemingly having grown bit larger now—began slowly drifting in their direction.

"Ben—" Dana said, fear gripping her.

It moved closer.

"Ben!"

"Shhhhh....." Ben hissed. Then he whispered: "Maybe it can't see us in here...or *sense* us...however it hunts..."

But as they watched in wide-eyed fear, something interesting happened: as the crimson blob floated in their direction, if drifted into the bug zapper hanging from the awning between their window and the chairs where they'd all been sitting, which were now strewn haphazardly about the dwindling campfire.

Sparks flew, with extremely loud zapping sounds echoing across the clearing. As Ben and Dana watched, riveted to the window, the power inside the RV began to fluctuate, the lights pulsing to near dark then back on dimly then to near dark again, while the thing outside jerked and writhed—much like its two victims had, before they were engulfed and cloaked by their own blood—while the zapper started to look like a giant sparkler, electricity popping and arcing, though silently now that it was inside the...*skin?*...of the blob, sparks exploding outward in all directions.

Finally, the RV lights went out completely, and the zapper went dead—and the blob took advantage of the opportunity, freeing itself and darting back across the clearing in a matter of split seconds, and was gone.

Then all was quiet again.

•

They waited a long time inside the dark RV, watching through the window, making sure it was gone, before daring to venture outside again. When they finally decided the coast was clear, Ben retrieved a couple of flashlights from a cabinet drawer, and handed one to Dana. They both clicked them on, making sure they were working, before quietly opening the door, stepping gently into the grass, then easing the door shut as quietly as possible.

The first thing that they both noticed was the smell: somewhat chemically, like what they had smelled around the lake all day, only stronger, and with a definite burned element added.

A quick jaunt around the campsite confirmed that both Marco and Janice were, in fact, gone. Not a trace of either, not even blood—aside from a little in the grass on the far side of the now dead and smoldering campfire, where Marco had emerged from the darkness with one arm mangled, if not missing altogether, before he was snatched back up by the...*thing*.

Tears welled up as Dana picked the paperback book up from the ground near what had been Janice's chair, now overturned in the grass. She noticed it actually *smelled* vaguely of her: that flowery perfume she always wore. Clutching it to her chest with one hand, she continued aiming the flashlight around the area, looking for any other remains or keepsakes of their friends.

She retrieved the four steel hot dog roasting skewers from the ground around the campfire, sliding the half-cooked dogs off into the campfire ashes.

You never know, she thought.

She found nothing else.

Meantime, Ben was maneuvering around the RV, flicking exterior switches and looking into dark windows. Once around the other side, he got into the cab and tried to start the engine, but there was no response. Tried the headlights, nothing.

Giving up, he got out, quietly closed the door, pocketed the keys, and returned to Dana, who stood sobbing by the campfire.

"Best I can tell, the battery's dead," he whispered.

She just looked at him helplessly, eyes wet and frightened.

"But we have the emergency generator. We can use it to charge the battery—assuming it even runs. But it'll take a minute—I don't know how long—so looks like we won't be going anywhere for a while."

"But how do we do that, with that...that...*thing* floating around!?" she cried, her voice elevating with each word.

"Shhhhhhh," Ben hissed, finger to his lips. "Keep it down, will ya?"

He then looked nervously around the clearing, aiming his flashlight all around, hoping she hadn't attracted that thing back.

"That *thing* just killed Marco and Janice, and you want me to *keep it down*!?" she nearly yelled, again her voice rising with each word.

He clamped his free hand over her mouth to shush her, and her eyes widened even more, a single tear streaking down one cheek.

"Look, they were my friends too, okay?" he hissed at her face. "But right now, we gotta figure out how to get outta here, before *we* end up just like *them*."

She nodded in agreement, so he slowly lifted his hand from her mouth, and she mouthed *sorry.*

He then turned toward the rear of the RV, walking quietly in the grass.

She followed, speaking softly:

"So how the *hell* do you think we're gonna be able to set up the generator, get it running—all the commotion *that's* gonna make—and get the RV battery charged enough to start the engine—however long *that's* gonna take—and get the hell outta here, all without that thing showing back up and skinning us alive? Did you see how *fast* it moved? How easily it took them? Like they were just toys...and worse, we can't hear it, and can barely even *see* it— *especially* in the dark!"

Without stopping, Ben responded quietly, "Well, I sorta have a plan."

"*Sorta* have a plan?" Dana whispered. "Well, I hope it's better than defending ourselves with hot dog skewers," she said sarcastically, lifting the skewers up and rattling them like dubious swords.

"Keep an eye," Ben said softly as he opened the back doors of the RV and stepped up inside, shining his flashlight around.

Dana turned and scanned the clearing with her flashlight, peering into the darkness, hoping not to see that thing anywhere—if she even *could* see it, that is...

After some muffled scuffling sounds, Ben returned with the generator, set it down in the doorway, then vanished inside again, returning shortly thereafter with a red gas can and a set of jumper cables. He jumped down, handed the can and cables off to Dana, then turned and heaved the generator out of the doorway.

"Let's set this up under that tree over there, past the RV," he said, jerking his chin in that direction. "Then I'll tell you the plan."

They walked past the RV and Ben set the generator under the tree he had pointed to, then went back and popped the hood of the RV, attached the cables to the battery, then ran the twenty-footers back to the generator, while Dana filled the tank with gas from the can, and spent the rest of the time scanning the clearing with her flashlight—but still saw no sign of the translucent floating predator.

"Let's go back inside where it's safe—I think, anyway—and I'll explain what I have in mind."

With that Dana followed Ben back to the RV and they stepped inside and closed the door. Once inside, they positioned their flashlights on the counter in such a way that they shone onto the back wall, the reflection giving them a little light inside the dark and powerless RV.

"Okay, so what's this big idea?" Dana asked, a little skepticism in her voice.

"Well, you saw what happened when the thing got into the bug zapper, right?"

"Yeah, the zapper went crazy until the power was cut off. So?"

"Not just that...but did you also notice the thing was spazzing out the whole time, and then when the power went out and the zapper died, it got free and took off?"

Dana's eyes lit up.

"Wait—are you saying that the zapper had some kind of affect on the thing?"

"Yes...it seemed to hurt it, and seemed it couldn't get off of it...until the power went out and the zapper died...then it was able to break free and it high-tailed outta here. In fact, we haven't seen it since."

"No shit..." Dana looked out the window, hope in her eyes. Then she turned back to Ben. "Okay, so electricity apparently hurts it...so what? What do you propose we do? What's your plan?"

"A trap," he said matter-of-factly.

She just looked at him, waiting.

Or maybe like he was crazy.

"Look...we have no choice but to start the generator and charge the RV battery, at least enough to get the engine started. But it'll be dangerous in the meantime, we don't know if that thing will return while we're out there, or if we'll even see it if it does."

"So you want to set some kind of trap?"

"A trap...and a diversion."

"Diversion?"

Ben sighed heavily, preparing for the weight of what he was about to say.

"Look, maybe it's just me, but for one, I want revenge...

for Marco and Janice—"

"No," she said forcefully, shaking her head. "Absolutely not. This is not the time for some kind of macho shit. We need to get this piece of shit RV started, and high-tail the fuck outta here—like you said yourself: before *we* end up just like *them*."

She emphasized the last sentence by pointing angrily out the window toward the campsite, which now seemed more like a killing field.

But Ben just ignored her rant, and continued:

"—and for two, I think we have an obligation to make sure this thing doesn't get loose, escape out of here...and to the city...or any populated area. Can you imagine the carnage if it did? We have to end it here. This ends here."

"Are you *serious*?" she almost yelled at him.

"I wish I wasn't," Ben said apologetically. "But think about it: what happens when it runs out of...*food*...here, and moves on? Say, up the river, toward town? How will you feel when people start getting massacred, like we saw happen to Marco and Janice—knowing that we had a chance to stop it here, but we ran away scared instead?"

Dana looked down, pondering this. Ben had a point. Could she live with herself, knowing she'd done nothing? Not even tried? That wasn't like her, she always gave 110% in everything she did. She couldn't back out now, just because she was scared.

"You're right, I couldn't live with myself," she said meekly, returning her eyes to his. "So we need to kill it before we leave. Or at least *try*."

"Yes. And I think we might be able to do that."

"Using electricity? Electrocute it to death?"

"Yes. With the bug zapper."

Again she just stared at him, like he was crazy.

Maybe I am, he thought.

"We lure the thing to the zapper, by hiding it somehow. Unfortunately, that means one of us has to be the bait, draw it in. The other will be positioned at the generator, hit the throttle when the time comes."

He paused.

"I'll be the bait," he finally said with reluctance.

"No, it should be me." Dana protested.

He shook his head and opened his mouth to object, but she cut him off.

"I'm faster. I was in track in high school. And I was *good*. Placed at state all three years. Varsity in college, too. And I still run almost every day, and aerobics—"

—she poked him playfully in his ample gut—

"—when's the last time you ever ran a hundred-yard dash, mister?"

He blushed, couldn't think of anytime he'd run more than a short jaunt in recent years, to catch a bus or get out of the rain or something. And even then he got noticeably winded.

He just shook his head.

"So that settles it. I'm the bait. Between the two of us, I'm the only one with any chance whatsoever to evade that thing when it attacks. I mean, look at Marco...he was in much better shape than you—"

"—and younger," Ben added in his own defense—

"—and that's the whole point I'm making," she said. "All that, and still *he* wasn't even able to outrun it. Do you think *you* could? Probably not...but maybe *I* can."

Ben nodded in resignation. She was right. She was the best hope they had.

He explained the rest of his plan in more detail, to which she agreed, then he retrieved two radios from the charger base on the table, clipped one to his belt and handed the other to her, then unplugged the bug zapper and tossed the power cord out the door. She pulled a kitchen towel from a folded stack in a lower drawer, then they grabbed their flashlights and moved warily outside to start setting up, keeping their lights trained out on the clearing watching for...anything.

It didn't take long for Ben plug the zapper cord into one of the generator outlets, then spin the knobs off of a set of 12v terminals, exposing the brass threaded rods underneath, and clamping the jumper cables to them.

Meantime, Dana retrieved one of the camping chairs by the now dead fire, placing it near the front of the RV, turned around backwards to face the vehicle. She then unhooked the zapper from the awning and set it on the seat of the chair, all the way against the back, all as Ben had instructed.

They both moved quickly and quietly, trying not to

arouse the thing in the process.

Dana returned to the tree where Ben was priming the generator engine, getting ready to pull the rip cord. She carried the kitchen towel in one hand.

"Okay, you know what to do," Ben whispered. "When I get the generator started and the zapper lights up, you take your position. Then all we can do is wait."

She nodded in understanding. Then she had a thought: switching the towel to her other hand with the flashlight, she pulled her radio up and depressed the trigger. "Testing, one-two-three."

Her own staticky voice echoed from Ben's radio, along with some feedback, and Dana quickly release the trigger to silence it.

"Roger that," Ben said softly into his, Dana's radio crackling with the response.

They gave each other a thumbs-up, and Ben grasped hold of the pull cord.

"Ready?" he whispered.

She again gave him a thumbs up, then turned and began walking toward the chair sitting in the grass next to the RV.

As she approached the chair, he yanked the cord. Nothing. He yanked it again, and the generator engine sputtered but died. One more tug, and it fired up, pulsing and belching smoke for a minute, then settling and running smoothly. Both meters bounced to life, one showing twelve volts, the other settling somewhere between one-ten and one-twenty.

He looked up, and the bug zapper began glowing in the chair, softly at first, then strengthening to full bright. Dana draped the towel over it, concealing it, then sat in the chair directly in front of it, pressing her back against it. She clicked off her flashlight and dropped it in the grass next to her. Radio clasped in both hands in her lap, she turned and looked back at him.

They nodded silently at each other.

Then, they waited.

•

The generator droned on, and nothing happened for quite a while. Ten minutes passed. Fifteen. Ben kept scanning the clearing behind Dan with his flashlight, eyes wide, trying to see anything in the darkness.

But so far, nothing.

At least that he could *see*...

It was approaching 20 minutes when Ben thought he saw something back by the trees. Shining his light in the direction, he blinked several times, trying to clear his vision, remembering how hard it was to see the thing in broad daylight, when he encountered it at the lake.

About the time he decided it was nothing, he saw part of the trees...*fluctuate?*...and realized he was looking through the translucent blog, which slightly distorted the objects behind it.

"I see it," he whispered into the radio.

Dana began looking around nervously.

"Try not to move...when it's close, I'll signal you like we discussed. Just be ready."

Dana went rigid, looked front and center, and nodded.

The thing was definitely bigger now. Ben followed it with his flashlight as it floated across the clearing.

Does it grow each time it eats? he wondered.

"It's approaching the campfire site," he whispered into the radio.

Again, she nodded to show she understood, and otherwise remained motionless.

The thing stopped near the fire site—right above where Marco's blood stained the grass, it seemed to Ben—but eventually continued toward Dana.

Ben's eyes widened as he noticed it accelerate, as if finally seeing—*sensing?*—Dana, seated in the chair with her back to it.

"It sees you," he said into the radio. "Remember, be ready to go on my signal."

She nodded, though now Ben could see her trembling.

It floated across the grass in a beeline toward her, and Ben calculated how quickly it was closing in.

"On a three count," he radioed to her.

Closer, and faster.

"Three..."

In striking distance, even faster.

"Two..."

Suddenly, it darted toward her, closing the distance in the blink of an eye!

"One!" he yelled. "Get outta there, NOW!"

With that, she shot out of the chair and began to run toward the RV as fast as her track legs could carry her.

And she made it...*barely*.

The thing landed on the empty chair, lifting it and the zapper into the air, setting the zapper off into wild sparking—which again was silent, now inside the thing.

And like before, the thing began to spasm and writhe as it was being electrocuted from within. But it also seemed stuck there, unable to move away as it battled the zapper, as Dana ran around behind the RV and jumped into the driver's door, slamming it shut.

The generator began to bog down with the load, the zapper dwindling, so Ben turned and levered the throttle, kicking the engine RPMs up, and the zapper lit up again, throwing sparks and arcs throughout the translucent blog, reminding Ben of one of those glass plasma globes like they had in high school science class.

Now the thing was really jerking around, spinning, fluctuating, and Ben could see it was trying to get away, but for whatever reason, was unable to.

He leaned on the throttle, sending the generator engine racing, the zapper glowing now like a hot spotlight, electricity shooting everywhere within the creature like a miniature lightening storm, the creature spastic and convulsing, and now filling with smoke, just as it had filled with blood when it devoured their friends before.

But then, the generator began to bog again, the engine

losing power, sounding like it was about to die! Ben pressed even harder on the throttle, but it was already maxed out. The engine had no more power.

Ben looked up at what now looked like a fireworks show, which continued for the moment, but couldn't help but wonder how long the generator would hold out, running at full throttle.

And as if on cue, the engine dropped substantially and began to sputter.

He jerked the throttle lever up and down, to no avail.

It was dying.

And then, just as he looked back up at the smoke-filled, jerking and writhing blob, it suddenly...*exploded?*

Silently, it dissipated into what seemed like a million little pieces, all of which scattered with lightening speed across the clearing...and vanished into the darkness.

The bug zapper fell to the ground in a burst of sparks and then went dark, just as the generator also sputtered and quit.

The ensuing silence was deafening.

The sound of the RV's starter turning startled Ben so badly he dropped his radio as he spun toward the sound, then realizing it was just Dana starting the RV's engine.

It roared to life.

He ran to the RV, yanked out the starter cables, slammed the hood, then jumped into the passenger side, barely getting the door closed before Dana gunned it, spinning tires throwing rocks and dirt as they bounced and weaved up to the road, and burned rubber turning toward town and got the fuck outta there.

•

Early the next morning, a chipmunk hopped across a flowery field on the other side of the woods that flanked the very road on which Ben and Dana had escaped the area the night before, chasing a bumblebee. When it finally caught the insect with it's front paws, it crouched on its haunches and began eating it, its nose and whiskers twitching in sheer delight.

The tiny rodent never saw the small, baseball-sized translucent blob that shot in from behind it, lifting it into the air and causing it to drop the uneaten half of the bumblebee, its panicked squeals quickly silenced as it was enveloped, then cloaked in its own blood as it was skinned and consumed within the translucent, silent predator.

A bit larger now, it continued across the field, its red filling slowly dissipating as it joined others—countless other small, glimmering blobs, perhaps numbering in the thousands—floating across the field together, consuming every living creature in their path, while the city sat ensconced on the horizon ahead, its inhabitants just now arising to start their day...

"Whoa," Tommy said in amazement. "That was a really good story...might even be your best yet!"

"Maybe...I've been working on it a long time," Winnie concurred. "But yours was good, too. I really like the way you ended it with the creatures escaping into the city's sewer system…what a cliffhanger!"

"Yours, too!" Tommy said excitedly. "The way the creature was scattered into thousands of tiny versions of itself in that field, all of them growing as they eat, and moving toward the city…for a massive harvest! Totally ominous!"

Both smiling now, they began tossing their favorite parts of each other's story back and forth when Winnie's mother came in from the kitchen.

"I'm off to work," she said, then bent down and kissed her son goodbye (which, embarrassed, he made a show of rubbing off in disgust after she left the room). Then she stood.

"You boys behave yourselves," she commanded, throwing a wink at Tommy.

"We will," they both said in unison.

"I'll bring some supper home after work," she said to Winnie. "So you don't have to fix anything. Seeya tonight."

"Bye Mom."

"Bye Mrs. Milhouse."

The boys waited where they were until she closed the front door then trotted down the steps and across the driveway to the car. When the engine started, they moved to the front window and watched as she pulled out of the driveway and drove away down the street. Once her car turned at the end of Hillsboro Lane and was out of view, they ran outside, jumped on their bikes, and headed for town.

•

When they pushed into the cool air conditioning and bright

fluorescent lighting of Hank's Hobbies & Sporting Gear, they couldn't believe their luck: Hank was there again!

They bolted to the counter, where Hank stood with his back to them, clipboard in one hand, jabbing a pen across the various items on the back shelves with the other, apparently counting stuff.

"Hey, Hank!" the boys greeted in unison.

Hank turned around—but instead of looking bright-eyed and peppy like he usually did, he looked rather perturbed, frowning, mouth turned down slightly at the corners.

"How's it goin' kids?" he said quietly, setting his clipboard and pen down and leaning with both hands on the counter.

"What's up?"

Still not smiling, he looked solemnly down at them, waiting, almost like they were bothering him.

"Um...we just need to get another box of ammo for our Wrist-Wrockets," Tommy said.

"Two boxes," Winnie interjected.

"Yeah, two boxes—one each."

Hank sighed, turned around, looked around on the shelves, snatched two white boxes down, then turned and tossed them rather roughly onto the counter before them. The boys turned and looked at each other, wondering why he was acting this way, when he was usually so cheerful and fun to be around.

"Two boxes of balls. Anything else?"

"No sir, that'll do it." Tommy answered.

As Hank was ringing them up, Winnie remembered about the deal they got before, and piped up: "Hey—can you give us a deal, like last time? Like buy two get one free or something?"

Tommy glanced at Winnie than back to Hank, hopeful.

"Yeah, you got any deals like that goin' today?"

Hank sighed again, stopped ringing them up, and just stood glaring down at them.

"You know, you kids are a real piece of work," he grumbled.

The boys looked at each other again, perplexed, then back up at Hank.

"I work hard, all day long, seven days a week, tryin' to make a livin' off this little hole in the wall—"

—he waved his hand over their heads, encompassing the store behind them—

"—and most the time, I just get by. I do alright, yeah, but I ain't rollin', if you know what I mean. And sure, I don't mind helpin' you kids out once in a while, cuz I know you got it hard too—but damned if y'all don't come in here always wantin' free shit now! This stuff don't grow on trees, ya know."

Winnie looked at the floor, embarrassed, and Tommy's eyes widened, apologetic.

"Gee, sorry Hank," he apologized. "That's okay, don't worry about it—we don't need a discount, or anything for free—just thought we'd ask is all."

Without another word, Hank rang up the balls.

"That'll be eight thirty-eight."

The boys dug in their pockets, pooled their money, then slid eight crumpled bills and two quarters across the counter.

Hank snatched them up, flung the register open, tossed the

money in, dug the change out, and slammed the drawer shut.

"Twelve cents," he muttered as he flippantly tossed the coins into Tommy's outstretched hand. Pulling a white plastic bag from behind the counter somewhere, he stuffed the two boxes and the receipt into it and handed it over.

"There ya are."

They both mumbled thank yous as Tommy dragged the bag off the counter and they turned and headed for the door, walking rather quickly to get out of there. But halfway to the door, Hank called them back, his voice softening a bit.

"Hey, kids, wait a sec. Come back over here."

They stopped and looked at each other for a moment, then walked slowly back to the counter, wondering what to expect. Hank was obviously in a bad mood today, and they didn't want to get scolded again.

As they approached him, Hank extended his hand over the counter, motioning for Tommy to surrender the bag.

Tommy handed it up to him, and he set it on the counter, opened the top, turned, grabbed two more boxes of balls, then turned back and dropped them into the bag with the first two.

"Sorry I talked to you guys that way," he said as he was tying the top of the bag. "Havin' a bad day, that's all. Didn't mean to take it out on you."

He handed the bag back to Tommy.

"There. Buy two, get two. And Hank Stevens appreciates your business."

Now he was smiling.

The boys' faces lit up.

"Gee, thanks Hank!" they shouted in unison.

"Now get outta here," he motion to the door with a jerk of his chin. "You boys have fun with those Wrist-Wrockets—and be careful out there!"

The boys thanked him again and bounced toward the door, suddenly feeling on top of the world.

On their way out the door, Hank shouted after them: "And try to stay cool out there, ya hear?"

"Okay!" they chimed in unison as they left the store.

"That was awesome!" Winnie said as they approached their bikes, again parked in the shade under the awning.

"Yeah, Hank's pretty cool. But I wonder what was up? I've never seen him act that way before."

Winnie shrugged. "Me neither."

"Somethin' scared him this morning," someone said, the voice coming from behind them.

The boys stopped under the awning and looked over at the end of the building where the voice had come from. It was Joey Stevens—Hank's son—leaning against the wall, just around the corner, smoking, out of view of the front door. When the boys left the store, they'd unknowingly walked right by him.

"What?" Tommy asked, surprised to see him there.

Joey flicked the butt onto the sidewalk in front of him and snuffed it out with his foot as he walked up to join them under the awning.

Leaning close, he spoke quietly.

"He's actin' all weird like that cuz he saw somethin' this

morning, when he was out fishin'. Scared him pretty bad I think. He doesn't wanna talk about it, but it was bad enough he quit fishin' early and came back. Said he needed to do inventory anyway—which I thought was odd, we usually do inventory the last day of the month—and he's been actin sorta spooked all day."

"Really?" Tommy asked. "What'd he see?"

Joey shrugged. "Don't know. Like I said, he wont talk much about it. A few things, but no details really."

"Where was he fishin?" Winnie asked.

"You ain't gonna believe it," Joey said. He looked around to make sure nobody was within earshot, then leaned back in.

"Blackwater."

The boys' eyes widened.

"No way!" Tommy said, incredulous. "Everyone says to stay away from there, it's dangerous."

"Yeah," Winnie concurred. "That's the worst part of Black Woods—the *scariest* part—nobody goes in there!"

Blackwater was basically a big swamp. Down south of Hope Creek Canyon, on the southern end of Silver Hills where the creek emptied out of the canyon then turned and headed off to the southeast, there was a wide, low-lying area back at the tail end of Black Woods. It was always flooded back in there, a foot or two deep, and since it was at the back side of Black Woods, everyone called it Blackwater.

And true to it's name, it was a dark and spooky swamp; a haven for wild animals, insects, parasites, you name it. And the water was always stagnant, sitting there for weeks or months at a time with little or no circulation, and feared to be full of bacteria and crap that could make you pretty sick. The kids were all warned to stay the hell away from it.

And they did.

"Yeah, well...he usually fishes south of there, where the creek bends back to the east. There's like a big pond there at the bend, shallow along the banks, lots of rocks and boulders, not much current, big shade trees all around. Usually does pretty good there, but not lately—like all summer, really, he hasn't caught shit—so, he worked it north, all the way up to the edge of Blackwater, then decided to go on in, try it out. Figured bein' so shallow, and all that shade of the woods, nice and quiet, and nobody ever fishes there, should be hoppin' with fish. And 'sides, he don't buy the stories anyhow, says they're all BS."

"Even the screaming kids?" Winnie asked. "The ones they say can be heard at night all around Black Woods, supposed to be the ghosts of all those missing kids over the years?"

"That? You don't believe that shit, do you?" Joey chuckled.

Winnie shrugged. "It's just what everyone says."

"My old man says yeah, you can hear what sounds like kids screamin' out there, especially at night—but it's just the wind howling through the canyon, it's not the ghosts of missing kids. In fact, it's not ghosts at *all*, mostly cuz there's no such *thing* as ghosts, dumbass."

Winnie looked down, embarrassed. "Well, I still can't believe he went fishin' in there."

"So what did he see? What scared him?" Tommy asked.

Joey looked behind him, toward the store window. Deciding his dad wasn't looking, he continued.

"Don't really know. All he said was he took the boat in as far as he could, but the water got real shallow and there were too many trees, so he tied it up, put his waders on, and started walkin'. Picked a spot close to one bank, and started casting. But after a while, he started hearing somethin', rustlin' around in the woods behind him."

The boys were riveted. But Joey took his time, milking it. Tapped out another cigarette, lit it. Looked around.

"C'mon! So what did he hear?" Winnie urged, unable to take the suspense any longer.

"Well, that's just it—he don't know. Said it sounded like somethin' big, movin' around on the bank. He kept lookin', but couldn't see nothin'. Just a tree branch movin' here or there, a bush rustlin'. And once, there was a pretty loud *pop!*, and a flock of sparrows got spooked out of a tree above, burst out over him, chirpin' like the devil. Said he glanced back there, thought maybe he caught a glimpse of a big brown furry animal—maybe a bear—but it was too dark back there on the bank, the woods were way too thick back there, so he never did really see it, whatever it was. But it sounded *big*, he'll say that much."

He took a drag, tilted his head back, blew a thin line of blue-gray smoke into the air above him, then continued.

"So after a while he started gettin' pretty spooked, and decided to move somewhere else. Down the bank a little ways, further out from the woods. But didn't matter where he went, this thing just kept followin' him. He could hear it—said he could even *sense* it, getting closer. Finally, he decided that whatever it was, it was stalkin' him, that was for sure."

Winnie let out a low whistle.

"So did he ever see what it was? An animal? Monster? Just somebody followin' him? What?" Tommy pushed.

Joey shrugged. "He won't say. Says he never did see what it was. But y'ask me, I think he really *did* see it, whatever it was, he just don't wanna admit it, cuz he don't wanna talk about it.

All he'll tell me is once he figured out it was stalkin' him—and that he thought he heard it growl once, deep and guttural—he boogied back to the boat and got the fuck outta there."

"Damn," Tommy said. I wonder what it was? You think it really was a bear?"

Joey shrugged. "May never know. But whatever it was, I think it musta been *big*, cuz it scared him pretty bad. I never seen him act like that before. And he won't talk about it, even to me. But he's like that—he don't like to talk about stuff that makes him uncomfortable—but there ain't much out there that makes him uncomfortable, at least not that I know of. Not even bears."

As Joey took another drag, Tommy and Winnie looked at each other.

"You thinkin' what I'm thinkin'?" Tommy asked.

"The shack." Winnie answered.

"Yeah. Maybe whoever—or whatever—is livin' there is what Hank saw—or heard—stalkin' him."

"Maybe." Winnie nodded.

"Shack? What shack? What the fuck are you two dweebs talkin' about?" Joey interrupted.

"Well, a few days ago, I—" Tommy started, but Winnie quickly interrupted him.

"Hey—you're not gonna tell him, are ya? I thought we were keepin' it secret."

"Keepin' *what* secret?" Joey demanded, looking quickly back and forth between them. "Now you *gotta* tell me."

Tommy sighed, looking at the ground. "I don't know…"

Joey flicked his cigarette out into the street, then crossed his arms, towering over them menacingly.

"Okay, howzabout about I kick both your asses unless you tell me?"

Tommy looked at Winnie.

"They'll probably find it anyway," he reasoned. "Since Hank thinks somethin's out there, they'll probably get some guys together and go huntin' for it, like they usually do. And if they find it, or find its tracks and follow it, they'll probably find the shack, too. So it won't really matter, we might as well tell him."

Winnie nodded quietly in agreement.

"You guys got about two seconds to start talkin' before I start swinging."

Tommy looked back at Joey, took a breath, and exhaled.

"Okay. A few days ago, I saw an old shack sittin' way back in the woods behind this hidden cove off Hope Creek, at the last bend before the Canyon. So next day, me and Winnie went back out there to check it out…"

The Haunted Shack
Near A Secret Cove Off Hope Creek
Summer 1975

"I'm tellin' you, it was there," Tommy said. "I *saw* it."

"And *I'm* tellin' *you*, you're crazy, Winnie responded. "You were either just seein' things, or high—or both."

Leaving the end of railroad trestle, they skittered down the embankment toward the creek, scattering loose rocks about.

"I wasn't high. I told you: I swiped this pack of cigarettes from my old man's dresser yesterday, then came and took the boat out on the creek, looking for a safe spot somewhere to have a smoke. Then I remembered that cove we saw a few weeks ago—remember?"

"Yeah, I remember. Down a ways, at that bend, on the left."

"That's right, but we only saw it from out on the creek, we didn't go in. We weren't even sure it was really a cove, with all the branches and stuff in the way. But I thought if it *was*, it'd be a perfect hiding spot, so I went to take a look. And I was right —it's an excellent hiding place...but while I was sittin' in the boat back in there, I looked up and saw it, way back in the woods."

At the bottom of the embankment the ground flattened, the dirt becoming sandy and less rocky. Turning together, the two approached the rotting wood pier that jutted out a short distance into the creek. No longer in use, the old relic was almost entirely obscured by an overgrowth of brush and weeds that had re-claimed the land, creeping out from the woods behind to cloak the pier in a shroud of camouflage along both sides, extending almost to the water's edge.

The pier's outboard posts had sunk into the muddy creek bed long ago, so it ran out at a pronounced incline for about ten feet before disappearing under the murky brown water.

Underneath, a small aluminum rowboat lay upside down on the bank, all but hidden from view.

Without a word, the boys split up, each stepping around opposite ends of the overgrowth and taking positions at each end of the overturned boat. In unison, they bent and hooked their hands under the dirty aluminum edge.

"Watch for snakes."

"Yep."

Together, they pulled the boat out from under the pier, cocked it up at a slight angle, then dragged it over the weeds and brush until they had room to flop it over on an open patch of ground between the pier and the creek.

They'd done it so many times, they now had it down: once they'd traveled back just so far, they stopped simultaneously, lifted the side of the boat to shoulder height, then flopped it over onto the sandy ground with a *thunk!*

They scanned the boat's interior carefully as it rocked back and forth before finally settling.

No snakes.

"Remember that time last summer, when that snake came crawlin' out from under the seat? Pete about shit."

They both chuckled.

"Yeah, scared him so bad he jumped back and fell on his ass in the water."

Both smiling with the memory, they walked back to the pier, crouched behind the weeds, and fetched the oars out of the darkness underneath. Each carrying one, they turned and walked together back to the boat.

"And it was just a water snake—but now he won't even come down here anymore."

"Well, yeah—cuz of his old man."

"Oh, yeah, that's right…almost forgot about that."

While Pete's family was camping out west a few years back, his dad was bit by a snake—a diamondback, one of the most lethal—and nearly died. Fortunately, in preparation for the trip, the entire family had taken a first aid training course together—and their quick action was credited with saving the man's life. But he'd been laid up in the hospital for days, and for a while they didn't know if he was going to make it. Eventually, he pulled through—but now Pete was deathly afraid of any and all snakes, poisonous or not.

After laying the oars in the hull, one along each side, the boys stepped to the rear of the boat, bent, and pushed it toward the water, the empty hull moaning loudly as it scraped across a scattering of rocks imbedded in the mud. The moaning suddenly stopped as the boat glided gently onto the water, and they took turns hopping in.

As if by silent command, they each took their usual positions: Tommy to the front seat, Winnie to the rear. Once the boat stopped rocking, they dropped their oars, one to each side, and guided the boat expertly out onto the quiet water.

They were on the northeast side of town, a large expanse

of largely undeveloped land, acres and acres of rolling fields interrupted occasionally with narrow swaths of woods, a sparsely populated area of town known to the locals as The Meadows. The western edge of The Meadows is marked by the old, rusty steel trestle that carried the railroad tracks over Hope Creek to continue north.

Starting at Winnie's house in The Flats, they could walk the train tracks all the way up to The Meadows, cross over the creek on the trestle, then descend the rocky embankment to the creek below right next to the abandoned pier.

Last summer, when they'd first discovered the pier, they were ecstatic to find the boat hidden underneath. Once they'd pulled it out and tested it for leaks, they'd been using it ever since, unsure of who, if anyone, it belonged to. But every time they returned, there it was, just as they'd left it, under the old pier and camouflaged by the surrounding foliage.

From the pier, they could take the boat down Hope Creek all the way around to the east side of town, then turn back around before Silver Hills began, where the banks on both sides of the creek suddenly shot upward, becoming towering rock walls that eventually created Hope Creek Canyon.

They didn't dare risk going into the canyon; there would be no way out until the other end, and there were jutting ledges, sharp turns, rapids, and boulders all along the way.

At least that's what they'd heard anyway...

So no, they were careful to turn around just as soon as they noticed the banks starting to rise, the emerging rock faces glaring menacingly out at them.

It hadn't rained much lately, so today the creek was moving so slowly it seemed deceptively motionless; but once they got the boat away from the bank and pointed downstream, it continued drifting steadily on its own, they only had to guide it a little with their oars.

As they cleared the first bend and the creek turned south, they immediately took advantage of the seclusion: Tommy pulled the stolen pack of cigarettes from his shirt pocket, shook one to the top, plucked it out with his lips, then shook out another and offered it up to Winnie, who reached out, slid it out, and placed it to his lips.

Tommy then returned the pack to his shirt pocket, pulled a lighter from the back pocket of his jeans, lit up, and handed it to his friend.

Once they were both lit, they relaxed in silence, just smoking and drifting. As they both pretended to inhale, a new demeanor overtook them—an older look, a stronger, more confident look.

Suddenly, they were no longer *boys*; they were *men* now.

As they quietly drifted along, Winnie threw his head back and blew a thin stream of smoke into the air. Watching the smoke dissipate above, he said to the sky:

"I still don't believe you."

"You'll see."

Smoldering cigarette dangling from his lips, Tommy turned and began paddling.

•

Before long they saw the cove approaching on the left, in

the last bend before Silver Hills began to rise and the creek flowed into the canyon.

Dense woods huddled right up to the bank there, and the entire cove was shrouded in long, overhanging tree branches that drooped all the way down to the creeks's surface, effectively camouflaging the entrance. If you didn't know it was there, you'd float right past and never see it. It was only blind luck that they'd spotted it a few weeks earlier—and that was only because they'd been watching a turtle swimming along the bank, its head poking up out of the water, when it turned and disappeared under the branches and into the cove.

Flicking their butts out into the water, they both turned and began paddling the boat toward the nearly hidden cove, then stopped and let their momentum carry them the rest of the way in, the boat gliding silently. Reaching forward with his oar, Tommy lifted a large Sycamore branch up out of the water, its broad leaves wet and dripping. As he did so, Winnie paddled from the rear, and they slipped effortlessly underneath.

When the Sycamore branch came down behind them, they were completely enclosed by the thick shroud of overhanging branches concealing the entrance behind, and the dense foliage crowding the bank around them.

Winnie let out a long, admiring whistle.

"Damn…this is nice."

"Tolja."

They looked around for a moment, then continued inward, occasionally ducking low branches. The cove cut into the bank about twenty feet, then hooked back to the left. Once they rounded the turn, the water was shallow enough they could reach the bottom with their oars.

Shoving their oars into the gravel underneath, they walked the boat into the back leg of the cove—now just wide enough for the boat, but not much wider—until they bottomed out against the bank.

Tommy's head bobbed and weaved as he peered through the woods in front of them, looking for it.

"There!" he pointed deep into the woods.

Winnie tried to follow his arm, peering into the trees.

"I don't see anything."

"See that big oak back there? Look to the left of that, there's a small opening in the pines, and you can see way back there."

Winnie did as instructed, but shrugged.

"I still don't see anything."

"It's behind the pines. See the line of pines back there?"

Winnie squinted deep into the woods, bobbing his head as he tried to see past all the obstructions.

"Okay, I see the pines, I think."

"Keep looking. You'll see it. Just past the pines, through that little opening in the middle. It's dark, so it's kinda hard to see. But keep looking...let your eyes adjust to the darkness for a second."

Suddenly, Winnie's eyes widened behind his glasses.

"There it is! I see it! So you weren't just seeing things!"

"Tolja."

Abandoning their oars in the boat, they stepped out

together onto the bank.

•

Hands on hips, they stood quietly together looking at the old, dilapidated shack. It was small, maybe twenty feet square, and made entirely of wood—warped and split wood slats running along all sides, cracked and rotted wood shingles on the roof, a few missing. And all the wood surfaces were blackened with age, with decay.

The entire structure appeared to be hand-built; leaning slightly to one side, every expanse of wall or roof was bowed like an old swaybacked horse, threatening collapse.

Each of the three visible walls contained one small square window, all of which were broken, exposing ratty cloths hanging inside, makeshift curtains. In the front, the door was also made of thin, rotted wood, split and splintered and blackened. It stood ajar, pushed a foot or so inward from its warped frame, revealing a brief section of dirty wood floor within, which disappeared into darkness.

Winnie let out a low whistle.

"Do you think anyone lives here?" he whispered.

"Sure doesn't look like it, with the door standing open like that," Tommy said. "And all the windows are broken."

The boys crept quietly first to one side of the shack, then around to the other, craning their necks trying to see into the dark interior through the broken windows and tattered curtains, and listening for any sounds emanating from within.

"I don't hear anything inside," Tommy muttered.

"Me neither…but I don't know…"

Finally, Tommy crept up to the front of the shack, tip-toeing up onto the cracked and faded wood porch, doing his best to step quietly around all the dead, dry leaves. Winnie stayed behind, watching his friend from a distance.

Once he reached the doorway, he leaned in just far enough to peer around the door and into the darkness. After a moment, looking and listening, he turned back to Winnie and shrugged.

In response, Winnie ventured up onto the porch, stopping close behind Tommy.

"I don't think anyone's here." Tommy whispered.

Just then a breeze blew through the woods, rustling the trees around them and initiating a low, hollow moan as it coursed its way through the shack, pushing the frayed curtains inward from the glassless window frames, then exiting the open front door, blowing the dead leaves at their feet away across the front porch—and reinforcing the notion of emptiness within.

"Hello?" Tommy called through the door. "Anyone home?"

Nothing. A few birds chirping, leaves rustling in the breeze in surrounding trees.

Looking at each other, they shrugged and shook their heads.

Turning back to the crumbling door, Tommy gently pushed it open, squeaking it back on rusty hinges. They both leaned in and glanced around inside, then stood back and looked at each other, shrugging again.

Then they turned and ventured inside.

Empty, the shack comprised just a single large room, with one small square window on each wall except the back one, allowing just a bit of sunlight in. The wood floor was covered with dirt and leaves, and the entire skeletal framework of the structure was exposed on the inside, the single-ply walls consisting of planks mounted to the outside, but no interior walls were added. And no ceiling either, the room extending upward ten or twelve feet, angled on both sides by the roof, myriad seams and holes brightly aglow with sunlight. Spiderwebs and cobwebs occupied nearly every available corner, and the place stank of mold, rotted wood, and... something else...a strange odor...perhaps somewhat gamey, like an animal's den or dog cage.

Stopping just inside the door, the boys looked around in the semi-darkness. Though there was no furniture, there *were* all sorts of odds and ends lying about, mostly along the walls, which at first glance appeared to simply be discarded trash. But upon closer inspection, almost all of it was dishes, or food-related: plastic cups, soiled and molding paper plates, fast-food and deli-food pack ages, open and discarded cans (beans, soup, corn, etc), plastic eating utensils, wadded napkins, empty to-go drink cups capped with lids and straws.

"Looks like someone's been living here," Tommy said.

"Or some *thing*, anyway," Winnie corrected.

At this, Tommy turned and looked at him in disbelief.

"Well, it could be anything," Winnie tried to explain, while pushing his glasses back up on his nose. "Could be a person —a homeless person, a crazy person, a hermit, who knows—

or it could be an animal. Like raccoons. They dig in trash cans all the time. Or a mountain lion, or coyote, or even just a dog. Or maybe even a *monster*, like the one in all those stories they tell around town. *Anything* could be carrying food in here an eating it."

Tommy rolled his eyes. "A monster. Eating fast food?" he asked in an incredulous tone, pointing down to an empty Big Mac container on the floor. "Fountain sodas with lids and straws? Plastic forks? And when's the last time you heard of a monster using a can opener? Or an animal, for that matter?"

"Just sayin', jeez."

"No, whatever's been living here has to be smart enough to open tin cans, drink out of straws, and clean up with napkins. So either it's a person, or it's the smartest animal—"

"Or monster."

—it's not a monster!"

Looking around the room, Tommy spotted something in the corner, and headed over.

"See? Look right here," he said as approached the right rear corner of the room. There, he set to kicking around a pile of old clothing, rags, a tattered blanket, that was all lying there in an elongated fashion.

"Looks like a bed."

"Man, I didn't even *see* that, with all the trash. I bet it is."

"And there's a candle right here next to it—"

—he nudged the candle with his toe—

"—probably for light."

"Could be," Winnie had to admit.

They scanned around the room again, taking a closer look.

"What's *that?*" Winnie asked, pointing to the opposite, left rear corner of the room. "See that square black thing there in the other corner?"

The sun, at its southwest angle, only shone in from the front door and the window on the right side of the shack, so the rear and left portions of the room were darker and shadowed. And with no window at all in the back wall, the left rear corner was the darkest of all.

"I don't know," Tommy said, walking over.

Winnie followed.

Closer now, they saw that the square black thing wasn't a *thing* at all—but a hole in the floor.

"No shit," Tommy said, dipping one toe into the hole, verifying there was nothing there but air and darkness.

About two feet wide, the opening ran right up against both walls, the hole disappearing down into the earth. Winnie shifted to the side, while Tommy stood in front, and they both crouched, hands on knees, peering down into the darkness.

"Can you see anything?" Winnie asked.

"No, it's too dark in here. I can't see shit."

They both dropped to their knees, hands gripping the edges of the flooring, looking in, trying to see something down there.

"I think I see the bottom," Tommy said. "Looks like it's about five or six feet deep, then goes back that way." As he described it, he pointed to the rear of the house.

With that, he hooked one hand on the ledge, and swung

himself down into the hole.

"Hey, don't—!" Winnie began to protest, but it was too late.

Tommy landed in the soft dirt at the bottom with a *thump!,* stood and peered into the darkness for a moment, then turned and looked back up at Winnie.

"Looks like it goes back a ways, like a tunnel. I think I see light down at the other end, maybe thirty or forty feet away."

"Really? It's a tunnel out to the woods?" Winnie asked.

"Looks like it."

With that, Winnie turned, dangled his feet into the hole, then dropped in. Turning, he examined the dirt wall behind him. Starting about halfway up, a series of deep divots were dug into the dirt, stringy roots dangling from them.

"Look, they're like steps," Winnie said.

Tommy stepped closer, ran his hand into a few of the elongated holes.

"Yep. For climbing back up into the shack."

"Uh-huh."

When they turned from the wall, they heard strange, hollow clacking sounds at their feet, and the both stopped to look— but it was too dark. Tommy knelt, feeling with his hands and straining to see. From this close, he could just make them out.

"Bones!"

Winnie knelt beside him, running his hands all around. There were dry, hollow bones everywhere, scattered around on the floor and piled all along the corners against walls.

"What kind do you think they are?" Winnie asked.

"Don't know. They're pretty small, probably too small to be

human. So some kind of animal I guess."

"Weird. So whoever—or whatever—lives here must hunt small animals, brings them back here to eat, then tosses the bones down here you think?"

Tommy shrugged. "Could be. Or maybe some animal—like you say, a mountain lion, a coyote, or even a dog—lives in the woods and just uses this tunnel, comes down here to eat, where it's quiet and protected. Hard tellin', really."

They stood and peered down the long dirt tunnel. The far end glowed slightly where it opened back up into the woods.

"So, let's see where it goes," Tommy said, starting forward.

Winnie grabbed his arm. "I don't know…who knows what's down at the other end? What if it *is* an animal? And what if it's hangin' out in the woods down on that end? Sleepin', or huntin' or something? We just gonna walk right up to it, like hey there, Mr. Mountain Lion, how's it—"

—but he stopped short, as they heard a thump above them.

"What was tha—" Winnie started.

"Shhhh!" Tommy cut him off.

Another thump, some shuffling sounds.

"Somebody's up there!" Winnie whispered.

"Probably just the wind," Tommy whispered back.

Then the clang and rattle of an empty tin can hitting the floor, bouncing and rolling.

"Let's get out of here!" Tommy hissed, and they both darted down the tunnel toward the growing light at the other end.

That end was angled upward, and they were able to scamper up the inclined wall on hands and knees, spewing dirt and pebbles behind them as they went. Bursting to the surface, they flopped themselves onto the ground among the trees some thirty feet or so behind the shack. To their relief, there were no wild animals lying in wait, ready to devour them; just a flock of sparrows, which burst from a tree above when the boys emerged from the tunnel, and twittered away into the woods.

Crouching in the brush, they quietly peered back at the shack, but didn't see or hear anything, or anyone.

Then Winnie had a thought; turning, he scoured the woods behind them. His eyes widened as he turned back to Tommy.

"Hey—is this Black Woods?" he nervously whispered.

Tommy turned and looked for a moment, then shrugged.

"I don't think so. Black Woods is downstream a ways, up on the back of Silver Hills. We're probably pretty close, though."

After a minute of silence ticked by and they hadn't seen or heard anything, Tommy signaled with an outstretched arm to go around the other way, far clear of the shack, to return to the boat. Winnie nodded in understanding. Remaining crouched, they slinked off through the woods, glancing at the shack as they circled it, but seeing nothing.

•

Back in the boat, they shoved off as quickly as they could, exited the cove, and started paddling upstream. It wasn't until they were far from the cove that they dared break their silence.

"So what do you think it was?" Winnie finally asked.

"Probably just the wind, like I said," Tommy answered with a shrug. "Wind came in through the broken windows, blew some stuff around. An empty can rolled across the floor."

"I don't know," Winnie was skeptical. "That can sounded like it was *tossed* onto the floor. I think whoever's living there—or *what*ever's living there—came back, and we're just lucky we were already down in that tunnel when it did."

Tommy fetched the pack of cigarettes, slid one out with his lips, offered the pack up to Winnie.

"I think you're imagining things, chicken shit."

Winnie took one.

"Then who dug that tunnel, Mr. Smartypants?"

Digging his lighter from his pocket, Tommy lit Winnie's cigarette, then his own.

"Who knows?" Tommy shrugged, then leaned back and blew smoke into the air. "Probably always been there, since the shack was built, like maybe a century ago. An escape route, or secret entrance, somethin' like that."

"A *century* ago? Winnie repeated, incredulous. "Fast food? Fountain sodas with lids and straws? Plastic forks?" he parroted, mocking Tommy's previous words. As he did so, he was smiling hugely, reveling in the payback.

"Okay, asshole," Tommy retorted, smiling back. "I'm talkin' a century ago that it was *built*. Hell, *anyone* could've stayed in there, or ate in there, over the last few years and left all that crap laying around everywhere—hikers, campers, a homeless guy, people partyin', whatever."

"Well, maybe. But I don't like it. And it's fine with me if we never go back." Winnie said, now blowing his own smoke.

"Like I said: chicken shit."

They paddled a while in silence. Then Winnie spoke up:

"Think we should tell anyone?"

Tommy stopped paddling, held the dripping oar motionless in the air, and looked back at Winnie.

"Probably not. They'll either think we're lyin', or crazy, or we might even get in trouble cuz they'll wonder what in the world we were doin' all the way out here. And besides, we'd have to tell 'em bout this boat, and then they'd probably take it away or think we stole it or somethin', and that would suck. So no, we should probably just keep it to ourselves."

With that, he turned and continued paddling.

Winnie smiled. "So it'll be our little secret, huh?"

Without turning, Tommy smiled too.

"Yep. One of many."

•

"So that's it," Tommy concluded. "Nothin' much to tell, really, seein' as we never actually *saw* anything there. But we *heard* somethin', like your dad did. And I wonder if whatever *we* heard is the same thing your dad heard, too. Somethin' that lives out in Black Woods. Or maybe lives in that shack in the woods by the creek, and just hunts in Black Woods. Like in all the stories."

"Well I'll be damned." Joey said, finally uncrossing his arms. "You two might have just had the first sighting around Black Woods in years. You'll be famous, you lucky bastards!"

Winnie's eyes widened. "You really think so?"

Joey turned and walked toward the door of the shop.

"I'm gonna go tell my dad right now," he said without

looking back. "And you can bet by mornin he'll have a huntin' party together, he and his buddies will go out lookin' for that shack, and for whatever you heard while you were there…and for whatever *he* heard stalkin' him in Blackwater Swamp. And word'll spread, you know how this town is, can't keep somethin' like this a secret, no way. You guys'll probably get in all the papers—even that stupid tabloid everyone reads, *Hope To Tell*—they thrive on this kinda shit."

"But I thought you said he won't talk about it," Tommy asked.

Joey opened the door, but stopped and looked back.

"That was when it was just him. Probably just didn't wanna sound like a fool, or especially that he was scared. But now that somebody *else* heard the same thing out there, and saw some weird shit, too—well…that's different. Now he's got an excuse to go back out there lookin' for it, and can take his hunting pals with him, cuz now they won't think he's so crazy."

And with that, Joey disappeared inside.

As the boys mounted their bikes, Winnie asked, his voice hopeful: "You think he's right? We'll get in all the papers? Even *Hope To Tell?"*

Tommy shook his head. "Doubt it. I think he's full of crap."

"Too bad…it'd be so cool to get in the papers."

Ammo in hand, the boys peddled up Fifth Street, hooked a right on Homestretch, and headed…well, home.

•

By mid-afternoon, they were back up in their hunting field,

fully ammo'd up.

But as usual, their hunt was disappointing. Winnie had a shot at a bluejay sitting in a sapling, but missed, prompting the bird to dart across the field and into the woods, scolding them the whole way.

They started to give chase, but couldn't catch up with it, so they stopped short of the woods, resting beneath the big oak. But just as they turned away to head back out into the field, a squirrel began chattering at them from above, perched high on a branch that dangled out from the tree line.

The boys quickly pulled and aimed, but the quick little critter scurried down the branch and disappeared to the backside of the tree before they could release. The boys ran toward it, Wrist-Wrockets stretched tight and at the ready—but then they slowed to a stop at the tree line.

There they stood looking up at the forbidding wall of trees, taking it in.

The thick woods loomed ominously before them like a gargantuan creature lying in wait. At the tree line, the bright summer sunshine suddenly ended—as if somehow simply chopped off—and a gloomy darkness began. Inside, old gnarled tree trunks huddled closely together, ghoulish and angry, their ancient branches intertwining high above, creating a nearly solid canopy. What little sunlight managed to penetrated the shroud of secrecy only added to the overall spookiness of the woods, slanting down in razor-thin blades that swirled with mist and dust and a host of tiny, creepy-looking flying insects.

As the two stood peering into the dark depths, an eerie hush seemed to fall over not only the woods before them, but the entire field behind them as well. It was almost as if the boys were being watched, and all of nature was collectively holding its breath, waiting to see what horrific thing was about to happen.

The boys turned to one another, trepidation in their eyes.

"I'm gonna go get that squirrel," Tommy finally announced, turning to enter the woods.

But Winnie grabbed his arm.

"We can't go in there," he whispered. "That's Black Woods."

"Yeah? So?"

"What about the monster?" Winnie reminded.

"Jeez, Winnie!" Tommy scolded. "There is no monster! Just get over it!

"But we don't know!" Winnie cried back. "Nobody knows!"

"Look, my old man says it's all bullshit, says the old codgers around town just make that stuff up to scare everyone —especially kids. And if you think about it, Mister Scaredy-Cat, it's probably just a clever way to keep kids like us from wandering into Black Woods, that's all."

A little embarrassed, Winnie looked down, absently pushing a rock around with his foot. Then, in a small voice:

"But what about...you know...all those sightings? All those people who say they've seen it?

"I don't know...they probably just saw a bear or something. Except we don't really have bears around here, either, so who knows what they saw."

"Well, all those people must have seen *something*," Winnie protested. "And people say they saw it walkin' *upright* too, like a man…or like Bigfoot! And some say it can even *fly!*"

"Dude, I'm tellin' ya, it's all just talk. There's no monster livin' in there. My dad says so. And so does Hank, Joey just said so, remember? And besides, there's no such thing as Bigfoot. Or a giant bird, as big as a man."

"Bat," Winnie corrected. "They say it's a giant bat."

"Okay, giant bat, whatever. There's still no such thing."

With that he continued toward the tree line.

Winnie fell in behind him.

"Still, they've never found it—so they don't know *what* it is! And what if—*whatever it is*—is hidin' in there right now, just waitin' for some kids like us to go in there, and—"

Winnie stopped in his tracks, riveted with fear.

Becoming impatient, Tommy stopped and turned back.

"I told you, there's no monster!" he chided. "There's not even any such *thing* as monsters! Jeez, I stopped believin' in monsters when I was like four—about the same time I stopped believin' in Santa Claus, and the Tooth Fairy, and the Easter Bunny. You tellin' me you still believe in all that crap?"

Winnie stared at Tommy, pushed his glasses up.

"No, not really I guess."

"Okay. So let's go."

Tommy turned back to the woods, but Winnie didn't move.

"Okay, so what if it's *not* a monster, like you say? What if it's a *man?* Like a serial killer, or a kidnapper, or a child molester or something? Some crazy guy or homeless guy, that's living in the woods, starving, looking for something to eat—like *us?*" What if it's whoever's stayin' in that old shack we found?"

Tommy turned back around.

"Well, if there *is* a man somewhere in there—and I'd say he'd pretty much *have* to be crazy, to be livin' in these woods, or even in that old shack—"

—he held up his Wrist-Wrocket, smiling in confidence—

"—then we'll just shoot him if he comes anywhere near us!"

Finally resigned, Winnie joined his friend at the tree line.

"Well, I suppose we could do that—but I doubt these little ball bearings will do much to stop a *crazy* guy. In the movies, they shoot 'em with *guns*, and half the time that still doesn't stop 'em!"

"Dude, that's just in the movies. That's not real."

"Okay, then, what about Jimmy Walsh? He always carried that switchblade around with him—and he was *sixteen*—and he still disappeared! So if it was a crazy guy in the woods that got him, then even that big knife of his must not've done him much good, huh?"

"What? Jimmy Walsh? You really think he was attacked or kidnapped by a crazy guy living in the woods? Come on."

Winnie shrugged. "I don't know. But *nobody* knows what happened to him, he just disappeared that one day, and been missing ever since."

"I think Jimmy ran away is all. He got caught smokin' pot at school under the football bleachers, remember? He probably knew he was in super-big trouble, since his ol' man's a big-wig on the school board and all. Figured he was in for a real hidin', probably get grounded for life—and for sure would be kicked off the football team, and he was supposed to *start* next season. So he split. Took off. Plain and simple."

Just then, thunder rumbled far off in the distance.

"Shit, a storm's coming," Winnie said.

They both stepped a few feet away from the trees, and peered across the field into the southern sky. Sure enough, dark storm clouds loomed on the horizon, bruised and swollen.

Winnie let out a low whistle.

"Damn, looks like serious business," Tommy observed.

"Yeah, we better head back," Winnie suggested, trying his best to sound disappointed rather than relieved.

Cupping his hands around his mouth, Tommy shouted into the woods: "Lucky squirrel! Next time, you're mine!"

As he hollered, a flock of sparrows burst from the treetops, startling the boys. Snapping their eyes upward, they watched as the birds scattered and disappeared further into the woods.

"Weird. I didn't even see them up there," Winnie said.

"Or *hear* them, either. *That's* what's *really* weird. Like they were just sittin' up there all that time, watchin' us."

"Yeah. And I wonder why we're seeing them everywhere all of a sudden? Flocks of sparrows, I mean."

"That's right—there was a flock of sparrows at the shack we found, remember? Down at the other end of the tunnel? They took off when we came out."

"Yeah—and Joey said a flock of sparrows got flushed from

a tree down in Blackwater, when that thing—whatever it was—was stalking Hank, too."

"Yeah...pretty weird, huh?"

"Sparrows, sparrows, everywhere," Winnie jingled, as he peered all about into the treetops above.

With that, the boys turned and trudged back toward the bridge. And as they went, the strange silence suddenly lifted, and the normal sounds of nature—the birdsong, the cicadas, the chatter of squirrels—returned to the field.

As they approached Old Rope, they stopped about twenty yards short and simultaneously clicked the buttons on the bottoms of their Wrist-Wrockets, folded them in half, secured the rubber tubes, and slipped them into their back pockets before continuing toward the bridge in silence.

But then, they again stopped in their tracks, this time at what they heard: off in the distance, a happy, bouncy tune—vague, nearly imperceptible—wafting to them from across the canyon.

Could it be....?

As the two stood motionless, the light melody danced across Hope Creek Canyon from the town side—at first piecemeal, as it wrapped itself around the clustered houses, weaved through the cars parked in driveways and the pickup trucks parked in the streets, growing stronger as it neared, the many dispersed fragments melding back together, again solidifying into one before traveling up Silver Hills, across the canyon, and to their ears.

The boys listened intently, and yes! It was indeed that

magical melody that always enchanted and delighted children everywhere: the unmistakable, happy little tune of…

…*the ice-cream truck!*

Upon confirming the sound, the boys looked at each other in googly-eyed excitement.

"It's gotta be in The Flats," Tommy guessed.

"Yep. Sounds like it's pretty close, too!"

Not another word needed to be said, for it was understood: *If they didn't hurry, they were gonna miss it!*

With the day's fruitless hunt already forgotten—*mission accomplished*—they ran full-bore the rest of the way to the bridge, tripping and stumbling over the rough terrain. And, being a hot, windless day, Old Rope lay idle before them—so without hesitation, they ventured on.

After quickly trotting across the rickety bridge, they hurried down Silver Hills towards civilization, visions of *dreampops* and *fudgesicles* dancing in their heads.

•

When they burst from the brush onto the old nameless road on the edge of town, they couldn't believe their luck: the ice cream truck was *right there*, on the north end of the street, facing them, music blaring, a handful of kids gathered at its side waiting to order.

It must have just stopped, because the driver—an old man who all the adults in town simply referred to as "Wilson" (and none of the kids knew whether that was his first or last name) —was still in the driver's seat. He threw a lever, triggering the big reflective yellow sign to swing out from the side of the van:

CAUTION:
CHILDREN
CROSSING

The boys waved at him from down the road, and he waved back through the windshield as he stood. Reaching up, he flipped an overhead switch to turn off the blaring music, then turned and worked his way between the cab's bucket seats and back to the order window, where he sat down on an upside-down five-gallon bucket and slid the window open.

The boys hurried up the street as the other kids crowded in around the side of the van, money in hand. A makeshift, jumbled line eventually formed, and business commenced.

The kids in front of them turned and dispersed one at a time as they received their treats, leaving Tommy and Winnie alone at the window when it was finally their turn.

After scanning the old chipped and paint-flaked menu off to the side, Tommy ordered his usual *Bomb Pop*, and Winnie of course ordered an ice cream sandwich, always his favorite.

After rummaging around in the chest freezer behind him, Wilson turned back to the window, treats in hand.

"These together or separate?"

The boys looked at each other, then shrugged.

"Might as well be together," Tommy said, as they dumped their pocket change together onto the small wooden counter that protruded from under the window.

"Okay, two-eighteen then."

Tommy counted out the proper coins, then slid them across as Winnie plucked his unused coins off the counter.

Tilting his head back so he could see through the bottom of his bifocals, the old man scrutinized the coins in his opened hand, nodded in satisfaction, then began dropping them into the register drawer, expertly sifting them by denomination with his thumb before they slid out of his hand and into the proper sections of the drawer.

"Perfect," he announced, closing the drawer with one hand while holding the ice cream in the window with the other. "And there ya go, boys," he said cheerily as he handed the treats over.

"Thanks, Wilson!" the boys said in unison, each taking their respective treat. But as they turned from the window to leave, the old man stopped them.

"Say, uh…I noticed you boys came outta them woods up the street there."

The boys stopped and looked at each other, wondering what was up, if maybe they were in trouble or something, then turned back to the window.

"Yeah, so?" Tommy said, frowning.

"Well, I was just wondering if you guys been up in Sliver Hills? Up by the canyon? You guy's ain't been playin' around up there, have ya?"

Winnie clammed up, afraid now, but Tommy answered:

"Well, we don't play right around the canyon, no sir. We go across the rope bridge to the field on the other side. That's where we go to hunt."

At that, Winnie jabbed him in the ribs with his elbow.

"With our slingshots," he added, to clarify.

"Old Rope?" The man gasped. "You two been goin' across Old Rope? That's mighty dangerous, y'ask me. They shoulda took that old rickety thing down years ago!"

Winnie piped up: "It's no big deal, really. Specially on a day like today, when it's calm, no wind or anything."

As if to refute this, thunder rumbled again, closer now, and a breeze kicked up, noticeably cooler than the hot, heavy air that had stifled the day up until now.

Wilson looked up at the dark storm clouds building on the horizon.

"Shame it's cloudin' up...there's supposed to be a super moon tonight, I was looking forward to it. Don't get a chance to see 'em very often."

"Super moon?" the boys said in unison.

"It's a huge full moon, when the moon is closest to the earth in its orbit. They're rather rare, and always amazing to see."

"Wow, I've never heard of that," Tommy said.

"Me neither," Winnie chimed in. "I sure hope I get to see one sometime."

"Well, you probably will some day, if it's not hidden by the clouds, like it will be tonight," Wilson promised.

"Cool," Tommy said, and the the two boys looked at each other, smiling eagerly.

"Anyway, you boys shouldn't be playin' around up there around Old Rope. That old rickety thing is dangerous, and besides, it's too close to Black Woods. And plus, there's an old abandoned mine back in them woods somewhere, and that's *definitely* too dangerous to be playing in—might even be a wild animal or somethin' livin' in there."

"A mine?" Tommy asked. "Really?"

"Used to be a silver mine, decades ago. But they closed it down, been vacant ever since. That's why it's called Silver Hills. You boys didn't know that?"

"We always thought it was because of all the silver maples," Winnie said.

"Yeah," Tommy agreed. "That's what my ol' man told us."

"Nope, it's cuz of the silver mine up there. But regardless of the mine, you should stay away from them woods anyway... they're evil. Dangerous. You never know what could happen."

"It's okay, Tommy shrugged. "My dad says there isn't—"

"I lost my daughter to them woods," the old man interrupted. "Many long years ago, back when she was just a little girl. It's true you know, what they say, the stories about the missin' kids. I know it, first hand, cuz my little Charlotte was one of 'em that went missin'. Black Woods is haunted, y'ask me. Somethin' evil livin' in there. Or maybe the woods themselves is evil."

Eyes wide, the boys turned and looked at each other.

"You lost your daughter in Black Woods? She's one of the missing kids?" Winnie asked. "Did the *monster* get her?"

With that, Tommy sighed and gave Winnie an impatient sideways look.

"Hang on a sec," the old man replied, holding up an index finger. Turning, he shuffled to the front of the van. Reaching over the driver seat, he turned the key, killing the engine with a sputter and shake, then returned to the window and sat down.

"I don't like to talk about it—fact is, I *haven't* talked about it for years, try to forget about it, but it don't matter, I can't never forget what happened—but if it'll help keep you kids from goin' back up there, make you understand that the stories are true, that the danger is real—then I'll tell ya what happened to me and my little girl Charlotte so many years ago, God bless her soul."

The boys stood transfixed, unopened ice cream in hand.

Wilson crossed his arms in the window, then just sat there for a moment with a blank stare, as if thinking it over. After a long silence, he let out a resolute sigh. He then turned and opened the chest freezer behind him, pulled out a *Big Dipper* ice cream cone, turned back to the window, zipped the wrapper off in one pull, and took a bite, tiny bits of crushed peanuts sprinkling down onto the counter. Chewing slowly, he looked back up at them over his glasses, and began:

"It happened way back in the spring of thirty-nine…"

Charlie Vanishes
Spring 1939

Spring had arrived early, and a wonderful Saturday was in the making, following a big, beautiful full moon the night before. Now it was warm and breezy, with puffy white clouds drifting across the sky. The world was finally coming back to life, after hibernating through a long, harsh winter.

That morning, the Women's Literary Club was holding its monthly Book Talk at the public library, so Liz Wilson had headed out directly after breakfast, her tabbed and notated copy of John Steinbeck's *The Grapes of Wrath* clamped confidently under her arm. Since Claire Atkinson was picking her up—who was not only the president of the club, but also an influential member of both the Town Council and the School Board—Liz wore her best hat.

That left Lornell (he was named after his grandfather, who immigrated to the States from Scotland in the late nineteenth century, though today most everyone just called him Wilson) to tend to their daughter Charlotte until late afternoon sometime. So he needed to come up with some ideas of what they could do together to pass the time.

She was only eight, so his options were limited.

First, he enlisted her to help in doing the breakfast dishes. Mostly, she stacked them in the drainer as he washed and rinsed them and handed them off.

When they were finished, he stood in the kitchen looking down at her, while drying his hands with a dishtowel.

She looked up at him, blinking expectantly.

"Well, what are we gonna do now, Charlie?" he asked as he draped the towel on the front of the sink.

Shrugging, she walked to the dining table, slid out a chair, climbed up into it, and sat there fidgeting with her curly blonde hair, again just looking at him.

"Well, we need to do *something*," he said. "You plan to just sit there playing with your hair all day?"

"No," she said.

"Well then, what would you like to do? It's up to you, kiddo.

It's Saturday, I'm off work till Monday, and we got all day to do what ever we want, at least till your mother gets home. You got any ideas?"

"We could go fishing," she muttered, looking sheepishly down at the table.

"Fishing?" he asked, incredulous.

"You go fishing all the time, and I never get to go with you," she mumbled, still avoiding his eyes.

"You wanna go fishin' with me?" he asked, still not believing his ears. "Since when?"

She shrugged. "I dunno. Lately."

"Well I'll be...looks like you're a Wilson after all! Fishin's probably in your blood! Definitely runs in the family!"

"So...can we go? Just this once? *Pleeeeaaaase* Daddy?"

"Huh. You're serious, aren't you?"

She nodded vigorously, blonde curls bouncing.

He shrugged. "Well, I don't see why not. Let's go fishin'! And afterward, for lunch, how about we have ourselves a nice little picnic? Perfect day for it!"

"Yaaaaay!" Charlotte threw her arms into the air in victory.

"But first, I suppose we should get you some fishin' gear."

"Okay!"

Then he looked her over. She was wearing a pink dress.

"Well, first off, you can't be fishin' in a pink dress, can ya? No, I don't think so. So why don't you go change—put on somethin' don't matter if it gets dirty, or wet—while I fix us some lunch to take with us?"

"Okay." She slid off the chair and hurried down the hall.

Just as he finished packing the picnic basket with peanut butter sandwiches cut into triangles, four bottles of soda, and paper lunch bag full of Liz's special home-made chocolate chip cookies, she emerged from the hall re-clad in an older, faded denim knee-length dress, and the cutest little pink and white sunhat he'd ever seen.

"Where'd you get that hat?" he asked.

"Mommy got it for me last summer for when we go to the park. So I don't get sunburned."

"Huh," he said. "First I've seen it. Looks awful cute on ya."

"That's what Mom always says."

He had her carry the basket and a folded-up blanket outside and put it in the cab of the truck (which he always called "Ol' Double-A", but she didn't know why) while he fetched his fishing hat from the top shelf in the coat closet and the rest of his gear from the storage area in the back of the laundry room.

Outside, he loaded the gear into the back of the truck. As an after thought, he went to the side of the house and grabbed a bucket from under the spigot, dumped what little water was in it out on the grass, and set it in the back too.

"What's that for?"

"You'll see."

They smiled at each other as they climbed into opposite sides of the cab. Then he started her up, backed excitedly out of the drive, and headed out to Jason's.

•

The bell above the door jingled as they pushed into *Jason's*

Jigs Bait & Tackle Shoppe, Lornell holding the door open and Charlotte slipping in under him.

"Mr. Wilson!" Jason greeted from back behind the counter. "Good to see ya! Been a while!" Looking down at the little girl approaching the counter, he smiled.

"And who might this be?"

Lornell strolled up behind her. "Charlie, say hello to Jason. He owns the place."

The little girl blushed, but timidly complied.

"Hello."

"Well hello there, Charlie! Nice to meet you. And that's a mighty pretty hat you're wearin', Miss Wilson!"

He then looked up at her dad, eyes wide. "This is Charlotte?" he asked, incredulous. "She was still in diapers, suckin' her thumb last time I saw her! Sure growin' like a weed, ain't she?"

"And already too big for her britches, y'ask me."

"Oh, Daddy!"

Jason chuckled.

"So what can I do ya for?" he asked.

"Well, Charlie here needs a new setup…somethin' her size. Maybe a little bigger, somethin' she can grow into."

"Alright. Cane or reel?"

"I think reel should work—but somethin' simple, she can handle easy."

"Okay, I got just the thing I think, about her size. And what about tackle?"

"Nah, already got everything I need in my box. Could use a

tub of red worms, though."

"Ahhh, goin' out today, huh? Nice day for it, finally."

"Yep. Liz is out gabbin' with her girlfriends in the literary club about books and such, so me and the little tyke here are gonna take advantage, go out to the creek and do our best to haul in a few—"

—he looked down at the top of Charlie's head—

"—ain't we, sweetie?"

"Haul in a *bunch!*" she corrected.

Her dad chuckled, then looked back up at Jason.

"She's definitely a Wilson," Jason observed as he smiled down at the little girl, then looked back up at Lornell.

"Cocky, just like her dad."

He winked, and the two men smiled at each other.

•

After leaving Jason's, they drove through town to the north side of Hope Creek, crossing over on Caboose Lane, which ran parallel to the railroad tracks. As they crossed the skinny two-lane bridge, he pointed out the big steel trestle off to the right, telling her that's where the train goes across.

"It's *huge!*" she exclaimed.

Chuckling, he pulled off the road and parked in a grassy area under the shade of a towering white-barked American Sycamore.

Before getting out, he turned and dug two sodas out of the basket between them, and handed one to her. Then they hopped out, fetched the gear out of the back, and headed down the rocky embankment toward the creek. Aside from rock and gravel, it was mostly just clumps of wild grass, and some scattered tall weeds—so it was pretty easy going really.

Once they reached the bottom, they stopped on the bank of the creek, and he pointed downstream.

"See that wood pier sticking out into the creek down there, on the other side of the train trestle?"

"Uh-huh."

"That's where we'll be fishin' from. Go ahead, you walk in front of me. And be careful, it can get pretty slick through here. Don't want ya fallin' in."

"Okay."

Together, they walked carefully along the creek. Soon they passed under the trestle, then in short time stepped up onto the pier, where they set their sodas down and relieved themselves of their gear.

"This is pretty neat," she said, looking around at the pier.

"An old buddy of mine built it—Earl Richards, lives right up the hill there—we used to work together, at the shop. Put it in a few summers back during the drought. Creek damn near dried up, to where it was just a narrow stream out there in the middle, so he took advantage and put this pier in before the thing filled back up when the rain came in the fall. Pretty smart, that's what I think. Says he plans to get a rowboat someday, too, but I don't know. He ain't around much anymore, since he retired. Hear he bought a place down in Florida, spends most his time down there now. But the way I see it, there ain't no sense lettin' a perfectly good pier go to waste, is there? We might as well put it to good use, right?"

She shrugged. "Might as well."

"Now, let's see your rod there, I'll show ya how to set it up."

Settling to his knees before her, he slid his tackle box over, opened it up, and fishing lessons officially commenced.

•

Along about noon, they decided they were getting hungry.

"I've got the perfect spot in mind for our picnic," he told her.

"Okay."

They packed up their gear, he hauled a full stringer of fish out of the creek—loaded with several bluegill of varying sizes, and one good-sized bass—and they headed back to the truck.

First thing he did was drop the two empty soda bottles into the bucket in the back, followed by the dripping line of fish.

"So *that's* what it's for!" she exclaimed.

"Catch on fast, don't ya?"

"Of course. I'm a Wilson," she said with a shrug.

Smiling, they loaded the rest of the gear.

Once he drove them back across the Caboose Lane bridge, he came to a large wooden sign, dark brown with *The Lookout* carved in the front of it and painted yellow, with a long yellow arrow underneath pointing to the left. Turning there, he headed west on Lookout Lane, a narrow two-laner that hooked south as it snaked its way up the north side of Silver Hills, terminating in a roundabout near the top, where a large circular clearing had been cut from the woods.

From The Lookout, you could see nearly the entire town of Hope spread below.

Parking spaces lined the outer ring of the roundabout, one

of which was occupied. As Lornell approached, his eyes widened at the sight of the all-white Packard Convertible sitting there, shiny and clean, with the top down.

A smattering of picnic tables sat around in the grass, and a family of three was occupying the table nearest the Packard. A nicely-dressed couple—the man in a white long-sleeve button-up, tan slacks, and a white fedora, the woman in a lovely white and yellow flowered dress and a white wide-brimmed sun hat —with a little red-headed boy dressed in coveralls who looked to be about Charlotte's age, maybe a year or so older. They appeared to have just finished eating, and were packing everything up to leave.

He pulled in behind the Packard, leaving an empty space between them, giving the family plenty of room to access their trunk. He killed the engine, picked up the picnic basket, and smiled at his daughter.

"Oh, I see!" Charlotte said, sitting up and looking through the windshield. "Picnic tables!"

"Oh, no, no," he said, shaking his head. "We can't have a real picnic if we sit and eat at a *table*, now can we? How's that any differ'nt than eatin' at the table at home?"

She thought about this for a moment.

"Guess it's not."

"Here, take the blanket. I know a better spot, up top."

When they got out of the truck, Lornell lifted a hand to the couple in greeting, approaching them as they loaded their picnic gear into the trunk of their car.

"How you folks?"

The man waved back.

"Just fine, thanks. How 'bout yourself?"

"Good, thanks."

Seeing Charlotte approaching, the young boy walked right up to her and introduced himself.

"Hi, I'm Ted. What's your name?"

"Charlie."

"But Charlie's a boy's name," he said, looking perplexed.

"My real name is Charlotte. Charlie's just my nickname."

"I have a nickname, too. It's Red...cuz of my hair."

Charlie looked at his crop of thick, red hair.

"I like your hair."

"Red, leave her alone and come back here, help your mother load the rest of our things!" the man ordered.

"Yes, sir," the boy answered, and immediately returned to the rear of the car and started handing stuff up to his mom.

The two men shook hands.

"Lornell Wilson. That's my daughter, Charlie."

Charlotte waved timidly.

"Raymond Kelly. Or just Ray, really. My wife Nicole, and our son Ted."

The three nodded to each other as Nicole closed the trunk, then walked around to the passenger side and opened the door, allowing Ted to climb into the back seat of the car.

"Hafta say, that's the most red hair I've ever seen on a lad."

"Yeah, he gets it from his granddad. Dad was a full-blooded Irishman, came to the States when I was just a baby. Kid's got the same exact hair as pop. Didn't get it from me—"

—he lifted his hat for a moment, exposing his sandy blonde hair, a shock in front pasted to his forehead with sweat—

"—mine's blonde, like my mom's—"

—then he placed it back.

With that, they both looked down at the boy, who was sitting quietly in the back seat.

"Ted, say hello to Mr. Wilson."

"Hello, sir."

"Hello, son," Lornell greeted.

He looked back to Ray. "Mighty well behaved, too."

"We got lucky," Nicole said as she sat down and closed the door. Then, donning a devilish grin: "He's a good boy...nothing at all like his father."

"She's right about that," Ray concurred with a nod. "You know, they say our genes skip a generation, and I think they're right—thank God for miracles!"

They all chuckled at this.

"That's a real nice car," Charlie said from below. Shading her eyes with her hand, she was looking it over from end to end. This also turned her dad's attention to the convertible gleaming before him in the sun.

"It sure is, Charlie," he said, looking it over himself, then up to Ray. "What year is it?"

"Thirty-one. Deluxe Eight Roadster. Love it."

"She's a beaut, that's for sure. I knew soon as I saw it you folks ain't from around here."

"Iowa," Ray said, opening his door to get in. "Mill Springs. Just spent a couple weeks out on the west coast, see the

Pacific. On our way back home now. Stopped in town to gas up, saw the sign for The Lookout on our way back out, thought it'd be a good place to stop for lunch."

"It is."

"Yes, it is," Ray agreed as he sat down. "Beautiful view. Nice little town." With that, he closed the door.

"Well, it was nice meetin' you folks," Lornell said, tipping his hat as he stepped away from the car, guiding Charlotte with his hand to do the same."Have a safe trip home."

Ray started the car, the in-line eight-cylinder engine bursting to life then purring like a big cat. He put it in gear, did one loop around the circle, then they all waved as the car headed back down the hill.

"So you ready to eat?" Lornell asked, looking down at Charlie.

"Yeah, I'm starving!"

He twitched his head in the direction of the woods.

"Follow me then."

She fell in behind him as they traversed the clearing uphill toward the woods, basket and blanket in hand. As if on auto-pilot, he drifted to his left, and stopped at the tree line directly in front of an almost invisible path that cut into the woods. If you didn't know it was there, you'd never see it.

"I used to bring your mother up here once in a while for nice, quiet little picnics, back in the day," he said.

"Why'd you stop?" she asked.

This took him aback. He stood for a moment, considering.

"Now that's a good question," he finally said, as if stumped.

"Don't rightly know I guess. Maybe we just got too busy." Then he shrugged. "And 'sides, she's never been too fond of gettin' her shoes dirty."

"Is that why she stays inside and reads all the time?"

He chuckled at this.

"Probably."

Bowing slightly, he gestured toward the path with his arm and open hand.

"Ladies first."

It was a short expedition through the patch of woods that separated the picnic area from the open fields atop the hill. After just a few minutes crunching through the under brush, they stepped out into the grassy clearing that ran along the west side of the canyon.

She followed him as he walked up close to the drop-off, where they could look right down into the canyon and see the shimmering creek water tumbling through the rocks hundreds of feet below.

"Wow!" she exclaimed. "We're WAY up here!"

"Yep. Beautiful view, ain't it?"

"Sure is!"

Turning, she noticed the rope bridge dangling across the canyon down at the far end of the clearing. She pointed at it.

"Can we go across the bridge?"

"No, honey, that's probably not a good idea. Dangerous."

Then she spotted the gigantic oak, standing alone in the field just in front of the woods on the other side of the canyon, offering a huge, shady area beneath.

She pointed across the canyon at it.

"Let's have our picnic over there, under that big tree!"

"Honey, the only way over there is the bridge, and I don't—"

"PUH-LEEEEAASE, Daddy? Just this once? It's so pretty and shady over there. And that great big tree looks so lonely, standing there all by itself."

He considered it a moment, looking up at the sky as if he could actually see the wind, then scrutinizing the bridge, see how much it was swaying or bouncing as a result. But besides a light breeze, all was calm, the bridge motionless. Apparently what little breeze there was wasn't enough to sway the bridge.

"Well, I suppose that's as good a spot as any," he said. Then he looked down, pointed a finger at her. "But don't you *dare* tell your mother we went across that rope bridge, you hear me?"

"Okay, Daddy, I won't—I promise!"

"Hold my hand, and don't let go till we get across."

Hand-in-hand, they walked to the bridge, crossed over the canyon, and headed over to the big oak, ducking around its thick trunk to the other side, closer to the woods. There, he let go of her hand and motioned to the ground.

"Spread the blanket out right here."

Together they pulled and smoothed the blanket, working the kinks and creases out. Then they sat, divvied up the lunch from the basket, and commenced picnicking.

The sound of the creek far below wafted up the canyon walls with the warm, springtime breeze. By the time it reached them where they sat, it sounded like just a tiny, babbling brook, blending with the light breeze and gentle birdsong that drifted from the woods behind them.

About halfway into their lunch, Charlotte looked at her dad.

"Tell me a story!" she demanded.

"A story?" he said. "Well, alright...so what story do you want me to tell?"

"Kip The Kangaroo!" she exclaimed.

"Really? You wanna hear that one again? You've probably heard it a hundred times."

"It's my favorite!" she said.

"Well, okay...you're the boss. You want Kip the Kangaroo, then Kip the Kangaroo it is!"

With that he stood, then crouched down with his hands curled in front of him, imitating a kangaroo...

Kip the Kangaroo
by Lornell Wilson

"Kip the kangaroo got loose in the zoo—"
—Wilson curled his arms in front of him and started
hopping around, Charlotte giggling—
"He hopped up to an animal and asked, who are you?"

"I'm Edward the elephant," the animal replied,
"and I can use my trunk like a hand—"
—he pressed his shoulder to his face and hung one arm,
swinging it like a trunk, opening and closing his hand—
"—I'm the biggest animal there is
That walks upon the land."

"Hi, Edward the elephant!" Kip said with a smile and a wave,
"I'm Kip the kangaroo!"
Then Kip hopped up to the next animal he saw
and asked, "Who are you?"

"I'm Billy the bear," the animal replied,
"and I'm very big and strong—"
—Wilson stood up straight and curled his arms up,
flexing his biceps like a strongman—
"—in the summer I eat fish, berries, and nuts,
and I sleep all winter long."
—with that, he laid his face down on his hands, clasped
together as in prayer, and closed his eyes—

"Hi, Billy the Bear!" Kip said with a smile and a wave,
"I'm Kip the kangaroo!"
Then Kip hopped up to the next animal he saw
and asked, "Who are you?"

"I'm Gina the giraffe," the animal replied,
"and my neck is very very long.
I can reach fruit at the top of the trees,
when the fruit at the bottom is gone."
With this, Wilson craned his arm way up in the air,
pretending to eat with his hand, like a hand puppet, then
back down to crouching, kangaroo arms curled.

"Hi, Gina the giraffe!" Kip said with a smile and a wave,
"I'm Kip the kangaroo!"
Then Kip hopped up to the next animal he saw
and asked, "Who are you?"

"I'm Mike the monkey, the animal replied—"

"—He's my favorite!" Charlotte exclaimed,
smiling ear to ear—
"—and I live in the tops of the trees," he continued.
"I have four hands and a very long tail—"
—standing on one foot, he held out both hands and
his other foot, shaking them in unison—
"—so I can climb up there with ease."

"Hi, Mike the monkey!" Kip said with a smile and a wave,
"I'm Kip the kangaroo!
Then Kip hopped up to the next animal he saw
and asked, "Who are you?"

"I'm Sammy the snake," the animal replied,
"and I have no arms, or legs either.
When I want to get from one place to the next,
I get down on my belly and sleeeeether."
He pronounced the final word long and sarcastically,
weaving one arm back and forth like a snake,
to which Charlotte laughed hysterically.

"Hi, Sammy the snake," Kip said with a smile and a wave,
"I'm Kip the kangaroo!
Then Kip hopped up to a person he saw
and asked, "Who are you?"

"I'm Zeb the zookeeper," the person replied.
"Get back to your pen right away!—"
—he turned and pointed to his right,
a stern look on his face—
"—and Kip hopped back a happy kangaroo—"
—he finished by hoping a short distance away, then

turning to say the last line over his shoulder—

"—for he'd made many friends that day."

"Yaaay!" Charlotte cheered, clapping with her tiny hands.

But just as Wilson returned to the blanket and sat down, a loud *pop!* emanated from the woods, off to their left, not far from where they sat under the tree.

They both stopped and stared into the trees, listening.

It was quiet for a moment; then they heard rustling sounds, bushes or tree branches, something.

Lornell put his soda down and hollered "Who's there?" in the direction of the woods. They both looked all around, trying to see or hear something, anything.

Nothing.

"What do you think it was?" Charlie asked.

He shrugged. "Don't know. Squirrel climbing around in the trees or something."

They continued eating, but then heard the rustling sound again, this time louder, closer, in the woods directly behind them. Whatever it was, it was obviously moving.

He put his soda down again, stood, took one step closer to the tree line, and cupped his mouth.

"Hello? Who's there? Anyone? We can hear you, so you might as well come on out! No sense sneaking around, you ain't foolin' anyone!"

Nothing.

Breeze blowing through the leaves above them.

Turning, he looked down at her, and she looked back up at him, worry on her face.

He placed his finger to his lips, signaling her to be quiet.

Stooping, he plucked a good-sized rock from the ground, and threw it into the woods, in the direction of the sounds. It snapped and cracked through the brush, leaves floating down behind it.

"I know you're in there! Come out, before you get hurt!"

Then, a really loud *crack!*—like a branch snapping—but this time, further to the right, as if whoever it was—or *what*ever it was—was circling them.

He turned and pointed at Charlie.

"You stay right there, don't move. I'm gonna check it out."

"Don't go!" she begged. "Daddy, I'm scared—don't leave!"

"I'm not gonna leave," he reassured her. Bending, he picked up another rock. "I'm just gonna step inside the trees—"

—he pointed behind him with his empty hand—

"—so I can see in there better, make sure everything's okay. Then I'll come right back. So don't you move, you hear?"

"Okay. But hurry, okay?"

"I'll be right back. It's probably nothing anyway, just a squirrel or somethin'. But I wanna check it out, make sure."

With that, he tip-toed across the grass, hesitated at the tree line for a moment, peering in, bobbing his head this way and that trying to see inside—then disappeared into the trees.

She waited on the blanket under the big tree, eyes wide, soda bottle clutched to her chest.

He had only taken two or three steps into the woods, but it was already so dark he could barely see any distance at all. The canopy of tree branches was so thick and interlaced it blocked nearly all the sunlight.

He peered in as far as he could, slowly scanning the area

he thought the last sounds had come from. He saw nothing.

Heard nothing.

Then, he realized how truly strange that was; he actually *heard nothing*—no cicadas, no crickets, no birdsong, no scurrying or flying critters, *nothing*.

The silence was mesmerizing; he just stood, entranced.

Until Charlie screamed, that is.

High-pitched, blood-curdling, terrified.

Followed by a low, guttural grunt.

From something *big*.

Breaking from his trance, he spun and sprinted the few steps before bursting from the woods, his daughter's name on his lips.

"Charlie—"

He stopped in his tracks.

The blanket, the basket, the food, all of it was there—but his daughter was gone. Her soda bottle lay beside the blanket, a brown fizzing puddle spreading in the grass.

"CHARLIE!!" he yelled as loud as he could. Horrified, he glanced all around the area—the blanket, the field, even up in the tree—she was nowhere to be seen.

"CHARLIE!" he yelled again, as he started running along the edge of the woods, looking in at every possible opportunity. First one way, then the next, yelling his daughter's name into the woods with every few steps.

"CHAR—"

He stopped dead in his tracks. There, in front of him, right on the edge of the woods, in the tall grass.

Her pink and white sun hat.

Dropping the rock, he snatched up the hat, examined it. No dirt, no blood, just a hat. He put it to his nose, inhaled deeply, taking in her sweet aroma.

He tore into the woods directly at the point where her hat lay, and spent the next hour searching everywhere throughout the dense, dark trees and brush for his daughter—calling her name, over and over and over, as loud as he could, until he had no more voice with which to call.

But it was all for naught.

She was gone...

Winnie let out a low whistle.

"Eventually, I went into town fast as I could drive, and got the sheriff—it was Rudy back then, Rudy Shelton—and he and a young Deputy, kid by the name of Adam, I think—Adam, or Adams, don't rightly recall—came up and searched around, but they didn't find anything either, and soon it got too dark out anyways. So next day they organized a search party, police and townsfolk both, and they searched the entire area for two days. Even called in a dive team to search the creek below, maybe she'd fallen and drowned. But I knew better."

With tears welling in his eyes now, the old man popped the last of the cone into his mouth, brushed his hands together, then wadded up the wrapper and brushed the crumbs off the counter.

"Know how I knew they wouldn't find her?" he asked. "That she was gone for good?"

Too riveted to answer, the boys just shook their heads.

"The sparrows."

They both frowned, perplexed.

"See, after I searched the woods all that time, and decided to go into town and get the sheriff, that's when I seen 'em—up in that big oak tree."

"Sparrows?" Tommy asked.

"Sparrows. Whole flock of 'em, just sittin' up there lookin' down at me. I stopped and was looking back up at them, when they all of a sudden burst from the tree and flew off into woods. And not a peep from 'em, either. Just all quiet-like. It was real creepy. But that's when I knew."

"Knew what?" Winnie asked, still perplexed.

"Oh—I don't suppose you boys know what's special about sparrows, do ya?"

They looked at each other, shrugged, looked back.

"Guess not," Tommy said.

With that, Wilson leaned closer into the window, lowering his voice.

"You see, legend has it, sparrows can catch the souls of the recently departed. So I suspected that flock I seen was carrying the soul of my little girl. I *sensed* it."

The boys again looked at each other, eyes wide.

"Wow," they whispered, then turned back.

"And they *know*, too. That's what's really special about 'em. They know when it's about to happen, when someone's about to give up their soul. So they wait nearby. So if you ever see a whole flock of sparrows just sittin' around somewhere, like they're waitin' for somethin', that's probably exactly what they're doin'—waitin' for someone's soul, that they know is about to die."

With that, he sat back up out of the window, wiped his eyes quickly with the back of his arm, then turned and tossed the wadded wrapper back into the van somewhere.

As he did so, the boys once again turned to each other.

"You thinkin' what I'm thinkin'?" Tommy asked quietly.

"Sparrows, sparrows, everywhere," Winnie jingled softly.

Apparently not having heard them, the old man turned back and continued:

"So I knew, when I seen them sparrows, they weren't ever gonna find my Charlotte. She was gone, whatever evil beast lurks in them Black Woods took her from me, and I've never seen her since. Just hear her voice at night."

"You hear her voice?" Tommy asked.

"Yep, at night. No doubt about it, it's her. That same scream that I heard when I was in the woods that day and she disappeared. For forty years now, I been hearin' her scream, over and over, like a nightmare I can't wake up from."

The boys looked at each other, eyes wide, then back.

"So it's true what they say?" Winnie asked. "The screams of the missing kids can be heard at night, around Black Woods? It's their ghosts or something?"

"Oh, absolutely. For a long time, it was just Charlie. That's cuz she was the first—I wish she wasn't, cuz if others had disappeared before, and I'da known the danger, then I'da known better than to take her anywheres near them evil Black Woods. But over the years—seems to be about every eight or ten years, I reckon—another soul disappears, and another voice joins the chorus. I lost track, but it's been a few now. And you can hear their ghosts—or their souls, or whatever they are —screamin' at night...all through the woods, even down the hill some times."

The boys just looked at each other, wide-eyed.

"You boys ever hear about Nicholas Hughes? Went by Nicky? He was the next one to go, after Charlie. Vanished about—he stopped and thought for a moment, looking up at the ceiling of the van, than back at them—well, I'd say it was in the mid to late forties I think."

They told him they'd heard some stories, but were way too young back then to actually remember anything.

"Well, he was about your age, and he and a friend were messin' around up there by Old Rope. Ends up, Nicky went across, but his friend—Douglas something or other, or maybe Douglas was his last name, I don't rightly recall, he don't live here no more anyways, went in the military right out of high school—anyway, he was scared to cross. What I hear, Nicky stood on the other side—the Black Woods side—taunting his friend, calling him all manner of names trying to get him to cross over. But he just ended up crying at Nicky's bullying and left, went home. But Nicky never made it back home, and nobody's seen the boy since. Disappeared, just like the rest. Just like my little Charlotte. Just up and vanished."

"Wow. I haven't heard about that." Tommy mumbled.

"Me either." Winnie added.

"And then there was that sweet little girl back in the fifties

—don't recall her name…Tracy maybe? Lived in The Flats?—and then those hippies in the sixties."

"Hippies?" the boys said in unison.

"Yeah, a young couple—societal dropouts—campin' up in the hills, up and vanished, like all the others."

The boys just turned and looked at each other, shocked.

"So that's why I'm tellin' ya, you two shouldn't be messin' around up there. In fact, you shouldn't be goin' anywhere *near* Black Woods. *Especially* now."

"Why not now?" Tommy asked.

"You boys don't listen very well, do ya? Typical kids. I just got done tellin' ya, seems about once every decade someone goes missin', didn't I? Well, last time—those campers that vanished—was nine years ago…that means it's prolly close to time for the next one. Neither of you wants to be next, do ya?"

"No sir," they both chimed in unison.

"Well then, you stay away from them woods, you hear?"

"Yes sir," they again chimed in unison.

The man stood up from his bucket.

"Now, go eat your ice cream 'fore it melts all over ya."

The boys had forgotten all about their ice cream, and looking now, were surprised to see the packages in their hands dripping in the street. They both started quickly unwrapping their treats, holding them out at a distance so they wouldn't drip on their shirts. Too much, anyway…

As they did so, thunder again rumbled in the distance.

"Ya know, it's too bad that storm's movin' in," Wilson said, peering off into the horizon. "Tonight's super moon. But we won't be able to see it, blasted weather."

"Super moon? What's that?" Tommy asked, with Winnie turning to listen too.

"It's a full moon like usual, 'cept it happens to also be at the point in its orbit when it's closest to the earth. Makes it look a lot bigger than usual. Don't happen all that often, so I always like to see it when it does…but not tonight, I reckon."

Both Tommy and Winnie turned to look up in the sky, and Winnie said: "Yeah, that's too bad. I'd like to see a super moon."

"Me too," Tommy muttered.

But the sky was quickly filling with clouds as the storm moved in, blocking any possible view of the moon.

Then they turned back to Wilson, and Tommy shrugged.

"Maybe next time."

"Maybe," Wilson replied. "Now you two best head home, 'fore ya get rained on."

"Yeah, that's where we're headed," Tommy said. "Winnie lives right over on Hillsboro."

"Alright then. Guess I'll see you boys next time I'm in the neighborhood."

The old man turned away from the window to leave, but Winnie called after him.

"Hey—can I ask you a question?"

Tommy just looked at his friend, curious.

Inside the van, the man turned back. "Sure. What is it?"

"Why does everyone call you Wilson?"

The old man looked stunned. Giving Winnie a perplexed

look, he replied: "Why, cuz that's my name! Why else?"

He then smiled, winked, and without another word headed up to the front of the van and climbed into the driver's seat.

The boys looked at each other, shrugged, and walked away smiling as the van started up, the caution sign folded in, and the ice cream truck did a grinding U-turn in the old crumbled road and headed back into the neighborhood.

Once it turned the corner, the music started back up, the happy jingle echoing all around the small clapboard houses and fading away.

•

The boys stood on the side of the road, eating their ice cream in silence, thinking about what Wilson had told them.

Thunder rumbled in the sky, a little closer this time.

"That's weird, what he said about the sparrows," Winnie said. "After we were just talkin' about seein' so many lately."

"Yeah…but you know what really gets me? That that Nicky kid was playin' up there in the same field where we hunt when he disappeared," Tommy said.

"Yeah, and he was our age, too," Winnie added.

Walking over to the closest driveway, they dropped their wrappers into a trash can that stood awaiting collection.

Then Winnie froze, as a thought occurred to him.

"Hey—"

Tommy gave his friend an inquisitive look.

"Speaking of our age—isn't tomorrow your birthday?"

Tommy sighed dejectedly as he stooped and picked a small rock up from edge of the road. "Yeah…"

He flung the rock side-armed into the woods across the street, the boys listening as it tore through the foliage.

Then Winnie bent and selected a rock of his own.

"What's the matter? You don't act very excited."

"That's because I'm not."

Winnie stopped mid-throw, his arm raised up behind him, and looked over at Tommy.

"C'mon, it's your birthday…that's a *good* thing."

He turned and flung the rock high and hard. They both watched the small, spinning silhouette soar into the bright sky, then descend into the tops of the trees, where it disappeared with a falling sequence of soft thuds. A perturbed blackbird burst from somewhere within, twittering loudly as it flew off to find refuge elsewhere.

"Nice one."

"Thanks."

They turned and started toward Winnie's house.

"Well normally, it *would* be a good thing…problem is, it's my *thirteenth* birthday—and at my house, every thing changes when you turn thirteen."

"Oh, that's right—the farm."

"Uh-huh."

•

At Tommy's house, the standing rule was that once you turned thirteen, you were no longer considered a *child*, but a *teenager*—the first stage toward manhood—and that meant you started working the family farm. Not that Tommy and his older brother Will didn't already help out; they did, performing many chores: collecting eggs, milking cows, the typical yard work, house work, helping their dad with the machinery, etc.

But once the boys reached that dreaded age of thirteen, the farm became their full-time job.

Hard work.

In the fields.

All day.

Edgar Baker was a poor farmer (in both senses); a stingy penny-pincher, he always claimed he couldn't afford to hire farmhands—not even the seasonal migrant workers— although he somehow managed to afford a seemingly endless supply of booze and cigarettes.

So, on the Baker farm, slave labor it was.

And, he had no problem cracking the whip when needed— or even when not; Edgar Baker was not only a poor farmer, but a poor father as well.

And on top of all that, he was also a poor husband; in his countless drunken fits, he'd harassed and beaten his wife to the point she'd up and left them all in the middle of the night, back when Tommy and Will were just toddlers. They'd not seen or heard from her since.

Though the boys were devastated when she left, their dad wasn't; instead, he actually seemed *glad* she was gone.

"At least now a man can get some peace and quiet 'round here," he said. "Woman couldn't cook worth a shit anyhow."

And that was it; life on the Baker farm went on.

Then, three years ago, Tommy's older brother Will suffered

the misfortune of turning thirteen. And to this day Tommy remembered their father's threatening words the night of Will's ill-fated birthday:

"Bill, startin' tomorrow, there'll be no more free-loadin' around here. Uh-huh, ya heard me right, I called ya Bill, cuz that's your name, here on out. Will is a boy's name, and you ain't a boy no more, you're a man. And come tomorrow, Bill Baker, you're to start actin' like one—and workin' like one."

And from that point on, their father not only stubbornly refused to call his son *Will*, but even prohibited Tommy from addressing his brother by any name other than *Bill*, so hell-bent was he to demonstrate to both boys that Will was no longer a child, but a man, and must therefore work.

And work hard.

When they were alone together, Tommy still called his brother *Will*—but it wasn't long before Tommy figured out that *Will* had pretty much gone away anyway; someplace far away, someplace deep on the *inside*—and left behind an empty husk called *Bill*.

And this saddened Tommy tremendously.

His missed his big brother.

The farm work was grueling, and unrewarding. Sunup to sundown, in the heat, in the rain—even in the snow, if winter came on and harvest was running late—which it usually was.

And, to make things worse, the Baker farm possessed very little modern equipment. Most of their equipment was rusty, or in disrepair, or just plain inoperable—so *Bill* was forced to make up for much of their father's lack of proper maintenance and preparation through long, hard manual labor.

And Tommy had witnessed first-hand what happened to his brother, once he started working the farm.

Will changed, withdrew—and slowly became this new *Bill*.

And he didn't like what he saw.

Not one bit.

But after that first season, his big brother seemed to surface for a while, became the old *Will* again—only with a wary, nervous aspect about him that Tommy thought was strange and not like *Will* at all. He noticed his brother's eyes darting about the room while he constantly tapped his foot or jiggled his leg, like he'd developed some kind of nervous tic. He couldn't seem to sit still.

Edgy.

Skittish.

Like a long-tailed cat in a rocking chair factory.

Then, during the second season, *Will* seemed to go under for good...

...and never resurfaced.

So for the last two years, *Bill* was completely withdrawn, nearly catatonic. And he had also started sneaking cigarettes and booze from their father, even sometimes getting caught. And whenever he got caught, the punishments were severe.

Will called them *whippings*;

Tommy called them *beatings*;

The old man called them *lessons*;

And *Bill* called them *worth it*.

Whatever you wanted to called them, they were nearly

unbearable for Tommy to watch; he couldn't even imagine how *Will* was able to take them, over and over and over.

Eventually, *Bill* started acquiring his cigarettes and booze elsewhere (Tommy never knew where and didn't ask). Late at night, he lay in bed and watched in silent awe as his brother disappeared out the bedroom window, then returned in the wee hours reeking of smoke and liquor. Sometimes he came back beat up, bruised and bleeding; again, Tommy never asked—and *Will* never bothered to explain.

Surprisingly, their father never remarked about *Bill's* occasional black eye, split lip, or facial abrasions; maybe he thought he'd inflicted it on the boy himself, during one of their *lessons*. Or maybe when he was on a binge.

And, to make things worse, over time the old man had started doing a lot more drinking and smoking himself—his binges were becoming evermore frequent—and a lot less working, now that *Bill* was taking up some (actually *most*) of the slack.

And all this had been a *lesson* for Tommy; he knew that it would one day be *his* turn, and he already dreaded hearing his father's words:

"Tom, startin' tomorrow, there'll be no more free-loadin' around here. Uh-huh, ya heard me right, I called ya Tom, cuz that's your name, here on out. Tommy is a boy's name, and you ain't a boy no more, you're a man. And come tomorrow, Tom Baker, you're to start actin' like one—and workin' like one."

And now, it was here. Tomorrow, Tommy turned thirteen.

And he didn't like what he saw coming.

Not one bit.

●

"Well, at least you'll get paid, right?"

"Shit. You kidding?" He refuses to even hire the immigrant workers—even for harvest. Don't wanna pay 'em, says they're all a bunch of lazy, good-for-nothin' mooches. So he's sure as hell not gonna pay *us*—we're supposed to be *earnin'* our keep."

"Wow. That sucks."

"Tell me about it."

Cutting through the nearest yard, they both jumped as a rabbit suddenly exploded from under a bush near the house and darted past them and across the street, heading for the woods on the other side.

Turning, they both reached back for their Wrist-Wrockets simultaneously, like two gunfighters racing to the draw (Winnie with his left hand, Tommy with his right), when Tommy suddenly stopped in horror at what he felt (or *didn't* feel) behind him: *his Wrist-Wrocket was gone!*

Winnie already had his shot loaded and was stretched to maximum extension, gently pivoting back and forth as he targeted the darting prey ahead of him—while Tommy spun around like a dog chasing his own tail, grappling at both of his rear pockets in disbelief.

Winnie let go, but his shot skipped off the asphalt behind the rabbit just before it disappeared into the woods.

Finally noticing the antics of his friend, Winnie turned to him with a quizzical look on his face.

"What're you *doing?*" he asked. "You didn't shoot at it!"

"It's *gone!*" Tommy yelled. He was bent around awkwardly, trying to see his backside as he searched for the sling shot.

"What's gone?" Winnie asked, not understanding. Then his eyes widened. "You mean your Wrist-Wrocket? What do you mean it's gone?"

"I don't know!" Tommy yelled back, in horror. "I put it in my back pocket, same as you did, before we left the field—but now it's gone!"

A panicked scouring of the ground immediately around them followed, but their search did not reveal the errant Wrist-Wrocket.

Tommy was devastated.

Then, he looked squarely at Winnie.

"I gotta go back," he said matter-of-factly.

He turned to go, but Winnie grabbed his arm.

"You can't go back now—it's gettin' dark—"

—he pointed up to the sky, which was not only darkening, but rumbling with thunder too—

"—and plus, the storm's almost here!"

Tommy shook his arm free, and continued walking. "That's exactly why I gotta go back *now*—so I can find it before it gets too dark, then try get back here before the storm hits."

With that he turned and ran down the street, to the point where they cut off into the woods and headed up the hill.

Winnie ran to catch up, concern building in his voice.

"But you don't even know where you lost it! Why don't you just wait, and we'll go back up and look for it tomorrow, when it's light out and there's not a big-ass storm comin?"

Tommy stopped and turned to his friend.

"I won't be able to come over tomorrow, today's my last day before I gotta start workin' the farm. So I gotta go back *now*, if I ever wanna get my Wrist Wrocket back. Stop worrying. I'll get there and back before the storm hits."

As if to refute this statement, the sky flashed brilliant white, thunder roared directly above them, and the wind picked up.

As he looked into the woods, and up the hill he was about to climb, Tommy suddenly realized that their paths were about to physically split—Winnie cutting west across the open yards to his house on Hillsboro Lane, and Tommy cutting east through the thin swath of woods, then up Silver Hills and across the rope bridge to the field, where he thought he must have dropped his Wrist-Wrocket, probably when they were running toward the bridge in all their excitement over hearing the ice cream truck—and also realized that they were about to split emotionally, too.

"You better get going, then. And *hurry*," Winnie warned.

"No sweat. I'll go find it, that way I'll have it for next time."

But Tommy knew, deep down inside, there wouldn't be a next time. Not after today, not after he turned thirteen. Starting tomorrow, everything was going to change—even his very name, from Tommy to Tom—and he was already preparing himself for it, bracing for it, both mentally and emotionally.

As he stood looking into the eyes of his best friend, Tommy suddenly felt strangely distant. As thunder rumbled overhead, filling the silence, he felt a change coming over him.

A hardening of the heart.

"So I guess this is it," he finally said, shrugging. "Don't know when I'll be able to go out huntin' with you again, Commander Winston."

"But we'll still have Saturdays, right? The weekend?" Winnie asked, hope filling his voice.

But Tommy shook his head. "Farmin's seven days a week."

There was another silence, and Tommy felt himself growing even more distant, more indifferent. In a way, he was glad—it all seemed much easier that way.

"So...seeya when school starts?"

"Yup. When school starts."

But Tommy knew that this, too, was a lie; that everything would be different then.

He and Winnie had been best friends for years; Winnie was a few months younger than him, and that never made any difference before. But now, even though nothing much *seemed* to be changing—in reality, *everything* was changing.

Tommy knew that their friendship—at least the fun, youthful, unguarded intimacy that they had shared until now —was over.

Tomorrow, Tommy had to start being a man.

And working like one.

And Winnie didn't.

Winnie was lucky; he lived in town, in a normal house. His parents worked normal jobs, lived normal lives. Winnie would get to remain in the utopia of childhood for a few more years; a few more summers of romping in the fields, boating on the creek, chasing rabbits; a few more summers of playing pick-up basketball games in one of his friend's driveways, or pickup baseball games down in the corner ball field; a few more summers of cookouts with their neighbors or family friends, of playing with his friends. Because Winnie could still *have* friends...he could even make *new* friends...maybe even a new a *best* friend...

Tommy suddenly wished he could stay twelve, could remain a boy, even if for just one more year; but he quickly dismissed the fleeting thought as reality moved in and took hold of his mind. Tomorrow he was to become a *man*, and everything he knew as a *boy* would come to an end, whether he liked it or not.

So he might as well learn to like it.

Resolving himself to this, he held out his fist.

"Seeya then."

When Winnie bumped his fist, Tommy felt his love for his best friend vacate him, as if rushing down his arm and into Winnie's, for him to take home and keep forever, like a photo.

Or a memory.

Without further words, Winnie turned, stuffed his hands in his pockets, and silently walked away across the yard, his Wrist-Wrocket riding along in his back pocket. Tommy just stood and watched him go, distancing himself from his former friend; no longer knowing him, no longer loving him, no longer allowing himself to be twelve and have a best friend.

And now, suddenly, he hated him; hated him with a passion, and never wanted to see him again. He didn't really know why, or where this sudden rage came from, but that was fine; he sensed it was better this way.

Easier.

Must just be part of becoming a man, he decided.

Nodding in acceptance of this, he turned from Winnie and started into the woods. As he did so, the sky lit up in a series of flashes, and thunder boomed above him.

Suddenly, he felt scared; not so much scared of going back up to the field with it getting darker by the minute and a furious storm bearing down—but of the life he faced upon returning home later that evening. Scared of leaving his bright, sunny childhood behind and forging onward into the dark, lonely mysteries of manhood.

Scared of turning out like his brother.

Or worse—like their father.

As if on cue, lightening flashed again, burning everything a brilliant white, and thunder roared all around him—and Tommy broke into a run.

He raced through the woods, tree branches whipping his face and neck, underbrush scraping past his knees and shins, the trees swaying in the wind behind him as if urging him on, faster and faster.

Through the woods, up the hill, out into the clearing, and across the rope bridge, which was just beginning to sway in the rising wind.

Didn't take long, either. There it was, the shiny silver frame gleaming at him from the green grass and weeds not ten feet from the other end of the bridge. He was right, it had fallen out of his back pocket when they were running toward the bridge to catch the ice cream truck.

Smiling, he picked it up, brushed it off, and returned it to his back pocket, pushing it down hard to make sure it stayed put this time. But then, as he turned back to the bridge, he stopped in his tracks as lightening once again lit the darkening sky, and thunder rolled across the canyon to him as he looked at the rope bridge in front of him.

And he didn't like what he saw.

Not one bit.

He watched as the bridge shuddered, creaked, and groaned in the rising wind, mocking him as he stood there, petrified.

And he knew that the longer he waited, the worse it was going to get.

As if on cue, in that single moment of hesitation the gusts picked up even more, the storm about to unleash its full fury.

Now Old Rope danced in the wind before him, bidding him—no, *daring* him—to come cross. To Tommy, the perpetual creaking and cracking of all the brittle, decaying ropes that snaked throughout the ancient rickety boards sounded as if they were about to *snap!*, thereby plunging any hapless occupants screaming to their deaths in the rocky canyon below.

Running out of time, he knew he had a decision to make.

He needed to cross, and *quickly*. If he waited much longer, it would be too dark to see, or it would begin raining, or the bridge itself could collapse—maybe even with him on it.

But then, he again heard his father's voice:

"Come tomorrow, Tommy Baker, you're to start actin' like a man—and workin' like one."

The words echoed in his head—and suddenly, he wasn't so sure he wanted to cross Old Rope after all.

Why? What's the point? he thought.

Instead, maybe he could stay in paradise forever...

That's it! Just stay here, in this field, hunting, exploring, playing! Winnie could even come up and visit him once in a while. If he stayed here, maybe he could stay twelve forever, never have to grow up, never have to work the farm.

For all he cared, dad and Will could work themselves to death on the farm if they wanted to.

But not Tommy.

No sir.

As he considered all this, he suddenly heard a *pop!* from a distance behind him, and turned to look back at the woods on the back side of the field.

Black Woods.

What was that? The wind? An animal? The....monster?

Now he really *was* scared...

Get a grip, he scolded himself. *There is no monster!*

He turned back to Old Rope, watching as the ancient, flimsy bridge danced and thrashed in the growing wind—and that scared him too.

But neither the monster in the woods behind him nor the flailing bridge before him scared him as much as the life he faced on the farm, starting tomorrow. Or even as much as leaving his childhood and venturing into manhood, scared and unprepared and alone.

Is that what he really wanted? To give up everything he loved and resort to a miserable life of hard work on a failing farm? To risk be coming a zombie like his brother, or a drunken loser like his dad? To ultimately end up with no friends, no wife, no future?

More rustling sounds came from behind, along with a deep, guttural growl. He turned and looked again, just in time to see branches snapping back into place within the dense foliage, as if pushed gruffly aside while something— something *big*—passed through them.

And that's when he noticed them.

Above the oscillating branches, up in that giant oak tree that stood alone in the field, the faithful sentinel forever guard ing the entrance to the mysterious Black Woods: sparrows.

Hundreds of them…

A huge flock, scattered among the branches, motionless.

It was the oddest thing, too: they weren't skittering about, or ruffling their feathers in the wind, or flying in and out of the tree; instead, they were all just perched solidly on the wind-swayed branches, unmoving and silent.

Like they were watching him.

Waiting…

Really scared now, Tommy turned his attention back to the flailing bridge.

Back to his future.

And he knew it was now or never…

Then, suddenly, he realized: when you grow up, come of

age, become an adult, there is a transition, a crossing over; but the child that you were before the crossing stays behind in childhood, and the adult that you become after the crossing moves on into adulthood.

And once you make that transition, once you cross over, there is another element—a tiny piece of you—that is cast off; and that tiny piece of you dies.

And from that point on, neither the child nor the adult are ever completely whole again.

And he didn't like the thought of that.

Not one bit.

And so now he wondered: is the crossing inevitable?

Or is it a *choice?*

Perhaps there's some way around it, some way he could refuse to participate, to say no to growing up, and yes to staying twelve forever; or, perhaps there was a third option— one that would neither force him to cross into adulthood, nor force him to stay forever a child.

And then, suddenly, he realized there *was* another option.

An easier way.

And so he made his choice.

Just as rain began to fall, he lowered his head and charged toward Old Rope, which was now undulating wildly in the grip of the impending storm.

But he was not alone.

Something was behind him, closer now; he could hear its heavy breathing.

But he was determined not to turn around and look, or to

slow down for any reason whatsoever.

Head down, he ran.

Ran to beat the devil.

But whatever was behind him was gaining on him, and quickly—for now he not only heard it, but *sensed* it, its closing heaviness picked up by the rising hairs on the back of his neck.

Would it catch him before he made it?

He hoped not.

As he ran, the rain intensified, now coming down angry and with a vengeance, and the wind increasing to near gale force, accentuated by the lightening and thunder now constantly ripping at the sky.

Determined, lashed by wind and rain, he stayed the course, his head down, a low growl slowly rising from his throat and quickly escalating into a rebel yell as he ran with all his might, the unknown before him drawing ever nearer, the unknown behind him now right on his heels.

Tommy's valiant cry echoed forever throughout the canyon's rocky cliffs, inflicting the small town of Hope with yet another sorrowed mystery, haunting Black Woods with yet an other mournful voice, a young boy's rebellious yell forever awash in the cleansing rain that fell that evening deep into the heart of Hope Creek Canyon.

— Interlude —

It was late September, and the ice cream season was ending.

But before parking his ice cream truck in the barn for the winter, Wilson waited until night twilight, then quietly drove back to The Flats and parked it behind some trees flanking the old unnamed road.

Opening the back doors, he slid out an axe, then quietly clicked the doors shut.

Heading up Silver Hills, he vanished into the darkness.

Before long he was up in the field, standing before Old Rope. Looking down, he could just see the creek far below, lightly shimmering in the moonlight.

A quick scan of the thick base ropes lashed to the log anchors on the side of the cliff revealed precisely where he needed to cut.

With one foot up on the log, he began swinging the axe, well over his head, coming down hard on the stout rope, now hardened with time and elements. He was surprised at how much it resembled a heavy wood branch, the way the axe chipped away at it rather than cutting through with just a few swings as expected.

Once he penetrated the first rope and that side of the bridge began to dangle and twist, that rope no longer being taut, he then made quick work of the hand ropes above, which where a little thinner.

Then he turned opposite and began chopping at the far base rope, which was a little more difficult as he was now facing the opposite way and had to swing left-handed to cut the rope at an angle toward the canyon. To better stabilize himself, he anchored his right foot atop the rope, so it didn't feel like he was about to tumble off the cliff and into the canyon with every awkward swing.

A few more chopping swings, and the final rope began to loosen from the anchoring log, the weight of the bridge stretching the cut apart, revealing fewer and thinner strands to be cut.

Pausing to catch his breath, he wiped the sweat from his forehead, tightened his grip on the axe handle, set his jaw for the final swing, raised the axe over is head—but the final strands of rope suddenly snapped from the weight of the bridge, before he brought the axe down to do the deed.

POP!!

The rope sounded like a shotgun when it snapped, and it was so unexpected he didn't have time to move his foot, and the long, loose strands of rope lassoed his ankle as they whipped past it, yanking his entire leg out from under him before he even knew what was happening.

He was yanked off the cliff with such force he threw the axe up into the air, before screaming all the way down and across the creek.

The cliff was higher than the creek was wide, so he didn't even have the fortunate benefit of landing in the water, his best hope of surviving the fall. Instead, he slammed into the opposite cliff at near free-fall speed, shattering bones and cracking his skull against the solid rock, immediately knocking him unconscious.

And there he hung, dangling upside down by his noosed foot, until he eventually bled to death.

It was days before someone discovered Wilson's ice cream truck hidden in the trees out on the edge of town, and a search party soon found his body, still hanging from Old Rope on the far side of the creek, his skeleton picked clean of flesh by the countless birds that still perched in the massive oak that towered above, watching quietly, as if waiting for more of the rare delicacy.

Part II:
The Blackjack Club

The Town of Hope
Hope Creek &
Blackwater Swamp
August 1985

"Hit me," Chaz said.

His eyes looked comical, rendered huge by the thick lenses of his black plastic-rimmed glasses, like those of an alien or some kind of giant insect. However, while unfortunate, this visual effect did not deter the boy's ability to maintain a fairly good poker face—even for an eleven-year-old.

"You sure?" Jackie prodded, facing down his opponent with his own piercing blue eyes.

"Did I stuh-stuh-stutter? *Hit me!*" Chaz demanded.

The boys were playing blackjack—well, their own made-up version of the game anyway, which turned out to be more like a combination of blackjack and Texas hold 'em—inside an old vacant barn that they had quickly commandeered after Jackie had discovered it earlier that summer, back near the overgrown fields of the long-abandoned Baker farm, nearly hidden from view behind a thick row of pine trees that traversed the back half of the property.

Two other young boys were watching the drama unfold as the four sat in a circle on the dusty wood floor: Nick (who, at thirteen, was the eldest of the group by a year and the largest by at least thirty pounds) and Ryan (he and Jackie were both twelve, and over the years had naturally befriended each other, since they had been sitting next to each other in their homeroom at Hope Elementary since the first grade).

Over time, Nick and Ryan had gotten accustomed to Jackie and Chaz squaring off this way—with Jackie being the charismatic leader of their group and Chaz being the brains of the operation. Always fascinating scenarios, they were well worth observing until they played out, the outcome typically elusive until the end (and somehow, they *both* usually won, each in his own way).

Jackie had paused, intentionally antagonizing Chaz with the delay. Slowly, he lifted a smoldering cigarette to his lips, sucked it to a living neon red, then lowered it again. Head back, he blew the gray smoke up into the rafters above. It snaked upward, bouncing from board to board like an upside-down waterfall, until finally collecting in a roiling pool against the cracked and rotting roof.

Jackie was a black boy, twelve years old with ebony skin. Extremely handsome—some even called him *pretty*—he was also blessed with what many claimed to be the biggest, brightest, most stunning smile they'd ever seen on anyone in the small town of Hope.

He had a silver crown on one of his front teeth—the second

to the left—which always seemed to flash, almost electrically, whenever he smiled. He would simply smile, and tilt his head back a little, and *flash!*—there goes the silver tooth, like a tiny flash bulb. It was extremely captivating to anyone who witnessed it. His rare, stunning blue eyes, set into his beautiful, dark face, only enhanced his smile. He was well aware of the mesmerizing power his looks gave him and often used this God-given gift toward persuasion to his advantage. Add a heaping helping of charm, and you had a very lucky boy who could manage to get pretty much whatever he wanted from pretty much anyone he wanted (at least within reason).

Looking back to Chaz, Jackie intensified his glare, hoping to dissuade his friend from taking another card.

Nick and Ryan watched the confrontation in silence.

But Chaz didn't break; he merely returned the icy glare over the top of his hole cards, which he held tightly up against his chin.

Finally realizing that his hypnotic looks were not going to pay off this time, Jackie tried logic instead.

"You SURE you wanna hit?" he said, his voice taking on an air of caution. "You already got thirteen showin—"

—he waved his extended finger over the three cards the were laying face-up on the floor in front of Chaz: five of clubs, six of spades, two of hearts—

"—plus add in your hole cards—"

—he gestured at the two cards in his opponent's hand—

"—you take another card, you'll bust for sure."

"C'mon, just hit me, will ya?" Chaz said impatiently, rubbing his eyes under his glasses with one hand as if exhausted.

"Do it", Nick ordered, giving Jackie a stern, "or else" glare. Nick Gardner was not only best friends with Chaz, and thus felt a fraternal obligation to protect him like a little brother, but he was also considerably bigger than the rest of the group. Even though he was only a year older than Jackie and Ryan, he towered over them, a full head taller, and his overall size and weight was rather intimidating.

"Alright, alright!" Jackie relented. Then, sighing in resolution, he tossed a card on the floor next to the others in front of Chaz.

Five of diamonds.

"That's eighteen showin'," Jackie announced.

"No shit, Sherlock. I *can* add, you know," Chaz answered sarcastically.

"Well then? What're you waitin' for?" Jackie fired back.

"Stay", Chaz said confidently. Placing his hole cards face-down on the floor, he picked up his own smoldering cigarette and took a drag through his grin, overemphasizing his decision to stay. He couldn't help but cough a little as he blew out the smoke (he never actually inhaled it, just pretended to), his own smoke blending with Jackie's among the ancient pine boards above.

One of the double-doors in the front of the barn stood agape, pushed outward and stuck forever that way. Sometime over the years the decaying barn had shifted, leaning precariously to one side and wedging the bottom of the door into the ground, binding it permanently in that position. (In fact, the boys had surmised, that was probably the only thing keeping the barn from collapsing altogether).

Somewhat obscured by a substantial overgrowth of weeds, the eternally open door was the only source of light inside the barn, aside from the two tiny broken windows on either end, and the slivers of brilliant white summer sunlight that slashed through the multitude of cracks and splits in the roof of the dilapidated old barn, shooting down in razor-thin streaks that sliced the drifting clouds of cigarette smoke into paper-thin spiraling tentacles, bringing them to life momentarily before they vanished back into the shadows.

Overall, there was just enough light inside during the day for them to be able to see what they were doing, but that was about it. So in the evenings, when it got too dark in the barn to see at all, candles were employed. Over the summer they had all scrounged a plethora of candles of various sizes and colors from wherever they could find them and placed them strategically about the interior of the barn, adding a spooky ambiance to the place—*especially* on story night...

Incredulous at Chaz's dubious decision to stay on eighteen, Jackie called him out.

"Nuh-uh!" he blurted. "You busted, didn't you? You gotta go out if you busted!"

"Nope, didn't bust. I stay." With this, he pushed his glasses up on his nose (a constant necessity, which over the years had become an unconscious habit, whether needed or not, that they all seemed to notice except Chaz himself) and, glaring through the thick lenses, he locked eyes with Jackie while discarding the smoldering butt in the ashtray and folding his arms triumphantly across his chest.

Shaking his head in disbelief, Jackie muttered under his breath, "No way you didn't bust on eighteen," and then turned to Ryan, sitting across from him, and gestured with the deck. Ryan tapped his face-down hole cards with one finger, signifying that he wanted a card. Jackie dealt one, face up. Six of clubs. Ryan double-checked his hole cards, bending the corners up slightly so only he could see them, then waved his hand over the cards.

"Stay."

Jackie then turned to Nick, the final player, who was seated to his right.

"Stay," Nick blurted, before Jackie could ask.

"Oooh…big man stays on two," Jackie said admiringly. "Must be good ones."

Nick just smiled, and folded his hands in his lap, waiting.

"Dealer stays," Jackie said matter-of-factly, leaving his two hole cards face-down on the floor and placing the remainder of the deck off to the side, out of play.

"You're staying on two cards?" Chaz cried in disbelief. "Don't tell me you dealt yourself a blackjack on the final hand! There's *no way*—you must be *cheating—he's cheating!"*

He was pointing at Jackie, but looking at the other two boys for support. Neither of them was even looking at Chaz, for they had long ago learned to ignore him and his wild rants.

Instead, they just continued looking at Jackie, waiting.

Seeing the futility of his pleas, Chaz sighed in resolution and picked his hole cards back up, glaring at them as he impatiently awaited the outcome of the hand.

Lying in the center of the four boys was a haphazard pile of coins—mostly pennies, nickels, and dimes, but a few quarters were hiding in there, too. It was all the money the four boys possessed among them, and it was a considerable pot for the times. After hours of play, it had all been bet on this final hand. The pile was also strewn with other valuable goodies, such as marbles, firecrackers, and army soldiers. In the minds of the boys, these treasures were just as valuable—if not more so—than the coins in which they were buried.

Nick had even tossed in his lighter—an old Zippo he'd swiped off his dad's work bench sometime back. The others were so envious, as the lighter was extremely cool—entirely chrome-plated, with a black lucky horseshoe engraved into one side, and a black dragon engraved in the other—and now that shiny little treasure, lying amongst the rest of the tarnished coins and other odds and ends, was the granddaddy prize of them all. When Nick had tossed it in, the other boys all stared wide-eyed at each other in disbelief, and the game heated up, each of them desperately hoping to win that sucker.

"Well, whatcha got?" Jackie asked Chaz expectantly.

Suddenly grinning ear to ear, Chaz placed one of his hole cards face-up next to the line of cards on the floor.

"Two, and—"

—he delayed, holding the final card up in the air and out of everyone's view, building the suspense—

"That's twenty," Jackie said. So all that can save your ass now is an—"

"Ace!" Chaz cried, slapping the ace of hearts down in front of him. "Twenty-one!" he announced. "I win!" He then reached out with both hands and began raking the pile of coins and other prizes toward him.

"Hold on a minute there, bud." It was Ryan, sitting to Chaz's left. They all looked at him, with Chaz stopping abruptly, poised in the raking position like a statue.

Ryan turned up his hole cards behind the six of clubs showing before him. "Nine, and another six, for a pair of sixes…that's twenty-one! So it's a tie—we split the pot!"

"Crap." Chaz muttered as he sat back, disappointed. Then he bolted upright again, as a thought struck him. "Okay, so we split the pot—but who gets the lighter?" At that moment, he wanted that Zippo lighter more than anything else in the world. He looked around the group with pleading eyes.

Ryan opened his mouth to answer—

"I do." Nick interrupted. They all looked at him, puzzled.

"You can't take it back, it's part of the pot!" Chaz exclaimed.

"Read 'em and weep!" Nick turned over his hole cards in one swipe: ace of diamonds, jack of clubs. "Blackjack! So *I* win the pot—including my lighter!"

They all stared at the blackjack lying on the dusty floor before them.

"*Jeez-Loueez!* Chaz shouted. "I can't *even* believe this bool-shit! How lucky can you get? He won his own lighter back!"

Smiling, Nick began raking the pile in. Squinting one eye, and opening one side of his mouth, he did a fairly decent impression of Popeye: "Ya wins some, ya loses some. Ug ug ug ug ug."

"Not so fast," Jackie warned in a stern voice.

Again, everyone stopped—this time looking at Jackie.

Jackie slowly turned one hole card: ace of spades.

"No way!" Chaz said. "Cheater—"

—he looked around at the others—

"—I toldja he was cheating—"

—then back at Jackie—

"—don't even tell me that you dealt yourself a—"

"Blackjack!" Jackie cried, smiling huge, as he turned over the jack of spades with a slap. "I win—!"

"No, it's a tie," Nick corrected. "We both have blackjacks."

"Yeah, that's right!" Chaz agreed. "It's a tie! But *now* who gets the lighter?"

"No, mine is suited," Jackie said calmly, pointing at the two matching spades lying before him. "Suited blackjack beats a regular blackjack, remember?"

"That's right," Ryan concurred. "Suited blackjack always wins over an unsuited one. That's the rule."

As Jackie smiled, his silver tooth flashed as if to confirm the victory, and, chuckling mischievously, he leaned over and began raking the pile toward himself.

"AAAAAHHHHHHH!" Chaz shrieked in total disbelief. "I can't *believe* I drew a six-card twenty-one—and LOST! What's up with that SHIT? Scooping the line of cards up from the floor, he stood up and threw them across the barn as hard as he could, but they only traveled a few feet before bursting apart in mid-air and fluttering everywhere, diminishing the desired effect. "FUCK!" he screamed at the top of his lungs, accentuated by a few drops of spittle that sprayed from his mouth as he plopped back down on the floor, again rubbing his eyes under his glasses.

Chaz was like that, particularly when he was losing a game —and he lost a *lot*. The other boys had mostly learned to ignore him when he flew off the handle, especially since he did it so often. And you never knew when he would just up and lose it, either. Everything would be going along just fine, then some little thing would happen, some tiny little annoyance, and BAM—he'd snap like an old dried-up rubber band. It was annoying, sure—but they tolerated it, simply because the benefits of having him around far outweighed the occasional temper tantrum he was prone to.

At eleven he was the youngest of the group, and by far the smallest—the stereotypical wiry little geek who carried books with him everywhere and had a penchant for conducting his own little science experiments.

Even with those thick black plastic-rimmed glasses, complete with white tape wrapped around one hinge or the other where he constantly broke them, his geeky persona never seemed to bother him—he was always too busy inventing cool stuff, or fixing things, or learning something new that would knock his friends back a step or two in open-mouthed awe, to really care much about what anyone thought of him or his ridiculous glasses.

He'd lived next door to Nick his entire life, and, with neither having any siblings with which to play, over the years they'd become the best of friends.

Nick, Chaz, and Jackie all lived in the same neighborhood —Edgewood, a cozy little neighborhood located down on the south end of County Road 200, on the other side of the railroad tracks that ran along the south side of town.

Shrouded by woods on its south and west sides, Edgewood marked the southwest town limits of Hope. (Ryan was the odd man out, living in town, but at least somewhat close on the southwest side, so it wasn't too long of a bike ride down to Edgewood).

Once Jackie and Ryan had befriended each other in home room, they started visiting each other at their homes after school, on the weekends, and over the summer, riding their bikes back and forth between their neighborhoods. So it was only natural that Ryan, while visiting Jackie one day, also met and befriended Jackie's neighborhood friend Nick, who'd happened to swing by, and the three of them began hanging out together. And before long, Nick suggested that they let Chaz hang out with them too.

At first Jackie and Ryan were leery of letting that weird little geek join their group, but when Nick became insistent— almost threatening—they relented and reluctantly agreed.

But before long they were glad the kid was around.

Sure, Chaz was a very strange cookie—but he was also a very *smart* cookie. He was, in essence, the quintessential nerd.

The Coke-bottle glasses with black plastic frames and white tape was just the beginning; he also always wore plaid, short-sleeve button-up shirts, complete with pocket protector, and his pant legs were always at least an inch or so too short, showing a stripe of white socks above his shoes.

His pocket protector was always loaded with a mechanical pencil, a pen or two, a pocket ruler, and sometimes some other gizmo or gadget that the rest of the boys weren't really sure *what* it was, or what it could possibly be used for.

Occasionally, one of them would ask about some strange item he was carrying in his pocket protector, and Chaz would pull it out and begin explaining the proper function of the tool. But halfway into it he'd lose them all and they would have to just sit there and wait for him to finish, and when he finally did they would all nod as if they understood. It didn't take long for them to finally learn to stop asking—or risk looking like complete fools.

He was also the only one of the four with blonde hair. Blonde, like almost white blonde. The extreme blonde that many kids in school made fun of, often calling him *tow-head*.

Between his light blonde hair and his extremely pale complexion, the kid almost looked albino.

Another odd thing about Chaz was his name. His real name was Charles David Miller. But he insisted (*demanded,* in fact) that they call him "Chaz", and refused to be called by anything else, not even anything just a *smidgen* more normal. It was Chaz—not Charles, not Chuck, not Charlie—not even the optional Dave or David, using his middle name as many people do who are cursed with first names that are obviously selected by their parents purely in revenge for them coming along and ruining everything.

Nope. It was "Chaz", and only "Chaz"—or else you got to listen to another of his high-pitched rants for ten minutes.

So Chaz it was.

But talk about *smart*...he had brains coming out his ears.

Chaz taught them things that made their days much more fun and interesting than they would have been otherwise. On any given day, a day that the boys probably would have just ended up in a mud fight for lack of innovation or creativity— or, if they were lucky, maybe terrorizing a hapless cat that wondered into the yard—Chaz would show up with something really cool to do instead.

One day he showed them how to make parachutes for their G.I. Joes. He instructed them, step by step, to cut open one of those big green plastic lawn bags, then use a string and marker to scribe a huge circle on it. Cut out the circle, poke eight small holes around the edge, the first four opposite each other like a cross, the next four exactly in-between the first four, then tie strings to the holes and to the G.I. Joe. Fold up the parachute, then wrap the strings first around the parachute, then around the G. I. Joe, then throw him as high into the air as you could, and as he dropped—*poof!*—the big chute would open, and old Joe came floating down just like a real paratrooper.

That little trick kept the boys happily occupied for nearly two weeks.

Over various summers, they'd built miniature boats to float

down Hope Creek, home-made kites, tennis-ball cannons, toy rocket cars using model rocket engines, and one time a bowling-ball catapult (they could shoot that sucker clear across the street), and a multitude of other really cool things—all at the direction of Chaz. Seemed like each week he came up with a new project—and it always ended up being cool and fun and sometimes a little bit dangerous.

Eventually, they dubbed the launch of these new projects under his direction "Miller Time." And whenever they commended him on one of his latest amazing inventions, he'd simply shrug, push his glasses up, and say matter-of-factly: "Piece-uh-cake."

Chaz may have been a skinny little nerd, with a bad temper that exploded a little too often—but the guys loved having him around. He kept things interesting.

On the other hand, he couldn't win a game to save his life. It was weird, really—as smart as he was, with all the things he knew, all the things he could do—the kid couldn't win a board game or card game or even a simple game of Horse to save his life. He just couldn't do it. Couldn't figure it out for some reason. Maybe that was just it—he tried too hard, or thought too much, or something. After all, it's just a game, not a Science Fair project or extra-credit math problem. Or perhaps it was because games always require some degree of luck. It varies, of course—some games are pure luck, and some require mostly skill and strategy and just a little luck. But ALL games include some level, however small, of that crucial element: Pure, dumb luck. No amount of pure calculation or scientific method will ever completely suffice, produce a consistent win. Consistent winning requires consistent good luck. Chaz may have been a genius when it came to science, math, chemistry, and calculations and design—but he had the worst luck in the world—like drawing a six-card twenty-one in a game of blackjack…and *losing*.

•

"Fuck me," Chaz muttered, sulking in disbelief. One of the cards he'd thrown was still fluttering about in the air, and slowly floated down and came to rest on his knee, as if mocking him.

Seeing this, the other boys burst into a gale of laughter.

Embarrassed, he quickly brushed it off in disgust.

"Jackie ALWAYS wins….it's not fair!"

He was right, too. Jackie seldom lost, at any game they played, especially if there was any luck involved whatsoever. He seemed to be the antithesis of Chaz, when it came to luck. Whether it be the toss of the dice or draw of a card, he always seemed to get exactly what he needed to pull off a win. The others were convinced he must be the luckiest kid alive. Luck seemed to follow him everywhere. They were all amazed at some of the stories he told them from his past, and how luck had played a huge roll in keeping him alive when he could've (or even *should've*) been killed, or keeping all his teeth or all his fingers when anyone else would have lost some or all of them if they had gotten themselves into a similar predicament.

But not Jackie.

As the saying goes, some people are so lucky they could

fall into a pile of shit and come up smelling like roses.

And the boys believed that to be true of Jackie.

From the floor, Chaz looked up and glared at Jackie, just in time to see him *(flick!)* his newly-won Zippo to life, and light a brand-new cigarette that dangled from his lips.

Chaz's eyes widened at the sight.

"Gimme one!" Chaz jumped from the floor and leaned toward Jackie, already forgetting his unfortunate loss of the card game.

Nick and Ryan chimed in together. "I want one."

"Me too."

Jackie pointed the pack of Marlboro Reds around the group, each of the boys sliding one out.

While the rest of them stood, brushed off their fannies, and began dispersing from the makeshift circle into other areas of the barn, Jackie slipped the Zippo into his back pocket, then began sorting through the rest of his winnings.

•

It was August of 1985, nearing the end of their summer vacation, and the four boys were playing inside the hot, dusty barn that sat on the now vacant farm that ran along old County Road 200 out on the western outskirts of Hope. At one time it was the Baker farm, run by Ed Baker and his sons Will and Tommy, but it was abandoned years ago, and was now just acres and acres of wild and overgrown fields that spread westward from the barn, which sat in the back forty between the farmhouse and the crop fields.

As far as why the farm is now vacant, the story goes that

some years ago—sometime back in the seventies—Will's younger brother Tommy had mysteriously disappeared.

His best friend Winnie—who was reportedly the last one to see Tommy alive—told authorities that after spending the day together hunting in the field up near Black Woods with their slingshots, they were heading home to Winnie's house when Tommy suddenly realized his slingshot was gone out of his back pocket, he'd apparently dropped it somewhere up in the field, and the last he'd seen of Tommy was when he'd headed back up Silver Hills to go look for it in the field on the other side of Old Rope. A huge storm was rolling in, and Tommy was going to try to hurry up the hill, across Old Rope, look for (and hopefully retrieve) his slingshot, then try to get back before the storm let loose.

But he had never made it back.

And nobody had seen the boy since.

Search parties were organized, divers were brought in to check all along Hope Creek, they'd even summoned a police helicopter down from Northridge, which not only carried a huge 1600-watt search light—its intense beam slicing up the night over the entire area for three days—but had infrared search capabilities too, which supposedly could detect someone even in total darkness.

That is, if that someone was still *alive*…

But nothing.

Tommy was never found, dead *or* alive.

Eventually, the search had petered out, and Tommy Baker's picture and personal stats were unceremoniously filed along with the hundreds of thousands of other forgotten files that filled the cabinets at the National Center for Missing Children.

And over time, the town seemed to return to normal.

Business as usual.

But then, a couple years later, there was a freak accident out in the fields on the Baker farm. Seems Ed had been out driving his tractor, pulling a baler, when apparently a problem developed with the equipment and he'd stopped in the middle of the field to investigate. With the tractor and equipment still running, he'd dismounted the tractor and stepped between it and the baler to inspect the equipment, and at some point had evidently gotten his glove or sleeve caught in the tractor's PTO shaft, which was still turning full-tilt. Not only did it tear his arm clean off, but the top portion of his overalls got wound up around the shaft, binding him up into the equipment, trapping him there while he was losing copious amounts of blood from his tattered stump—all that remained of his left arm.

According to reports, Baker's oldest son Will had been home at the time, and told investigators that when his dad hadn't returned to the house by nightfall, he went out to see what was up, make sure he was okay.

After first checking the garage, then the front and back yards, he went out and checked inside the barn out on the back forty. Finding no sign of his dad there, Will grabbed a flashlight and headed out into the fields, where he discovered Ed's corpse still hanging there in the equipment. Once he'd determined that his dad was, in fact, dead, he'd returned to the house and called 911.

Thing about it is, witnesses noted that Will seemed distant while telling his story to the police and paramedics, and had not cried, not shed a single tear, the entire time. And, he'd been filthy head to toe, his hands blackened with dirt and grease—like he'd been working out in the fields all day with his dad...

Nothing nefarious on Will's part could be proven, of course, but many speculated—knowing the man, his penchant for drinking, his strained relationships with his sons, the rumors of abuse (which many suspected was why his wife had left him years before), and with Will's friends reporting that Will had been acting awfully strange lately—detached, a loner, almost catatonic sometimes, and many wondered if he'd gotten involved with drugs—it'd been easy to speculate that the boy had actually been out in that field working with his dad when the accident happened, and had simply stood and watched his old man hang there and bleed to death, maybe even strolled back to the house for a tall glass of iced tea and a smoke, while Ed Baker died a slow and lonely death out there in the field.

But Will got the benefit of the doubt.

No charges were ever filed.

Life went on.

Shortly thereafter, the boy had up and disappeared, along with his old man's Ford F250 dually pickup truck. Just packed up and left, looked like. At eighteen, he was considered a legal adult, and upon his dad's death had inherited the entire farm, the house, the out buildings, all the equipment, the vehicles, everything, so there was no call for the authorities to look for him, he'd broken no law; but he'd vanished without a trace, no notice to anyone, no nothing.

Just gone.

It wasn't until months later that Sheriff Collins got to thinking more about Ed Baker's accident, and one afternoon he'd approached Deputy Bailey about it when the young man arrived at the station for shift change:

"You know, once the investigation was over, on account of the boy's poor mental and emotional state, I moved that tractor myself, drove it out of the field and parked it inside the barn, out of the weather, since it was supposed to rain that night."

"Yeah, I remember that," Bailey concurred.

"Well, I also remember wondering, having run all day, and bein' way out in the field like that, if there'd be enough gas in the tank to get it all the way back to the barn, even took a full gas can out there with me just in case. But turns out it had plenty of gas in it, over three-quarter full."

The deputy shrugged. "So?"

"Well, think about it: if it was running when Ed got caught up in the PTO, and Will didn't go out to check on him until hours later, after dark—when he noticed his old man hadn't returned to the house, like he claimed—then that tractor would've been sitting out there in the field running all damn day. It would've run out of gas—or close to. But no. It was damn near full."

The deputy's eyes suddenly lit up with understanding, and he nodded. "I see where you're going with this...so in other words—"

"—in other words, somebody must've turned that tractor off earlier in the day—*way* before sundown, when the boy claimed he found his ol' man out there dead."

They looked at each other solemnly for a silent moment, both suddenly understanding what had probably *really* transpired out there on the Baker farm that day.

"So what now?" Bailey asked. "You gonna do anything?"

Sighing, the sheriff thought about it for a long moment, then shrugged.

"Nah. Too late now, anyway. Nothin' I *can* do, really. The boy's done flew the coop, and that asshole dad of his is already long dead and buried. 'Besides, you know what they say: what comes around, goes around." Then he winked. "That Karma's a real bitch."

With that he flipped his Stetson up onto his head, turned, and walked out of the office, the sound of his boots echoing down the hallway as he clomped his way to the front door.

The deputy watched him through the office window as he drove off—turning left toward town, instead of his usual right, the direction of his home—and suspected he might be heading for Mason's Tavern for a cold one (or two or three) instead—and he smiled.

He didn't blame him.

Not one bit.

•

So, long story short, first the younger Baker boy Tommy had mysteriously vanished, then a couple years later their father Ed was killed in a grisly farming "accident", after which the older boy Will had just up and left, not to be seen again.

And the farm had fallen to ruins in the years since.

Eventually, the farmhouse was condemned; since it sat on the front of the property up near the road, and was falling into such disrepair, it was finally deemed a safety hazard by local authorities and subsequently boarded up. And over time, the townsfolk pretty much forgot all about it—except the local teenagers, that is; once word got out that the house was officially vacant, some of the more venturous kids had snuck around back, pried the boards off the door, and jimmied the lock open. Now they all had a safe place to party, way out there in the country with no threat of getting caught—by parents or the police.

And you know how kids are…

Though many of the townsfolk suspected the old farmhouse had become a nighttime and weekend hangout for teenagers to do all the illicit things teenagers do in the absence of parents, nobody cared all that much, there didn't seem to be any trouble out there, and anyway, who the hell wants to drive all the way out there just to check on a vacant house, looking for delinquent teenagers (who might turn out to be your friend's or neighbor's kids, how awkward would *that* be?) —all based on mere rumors?

Besides, *Dallas* was on…

Then one night the farmhouse had mysteriously caught fire and burned to the ground. By the time the firefighters arrived, there was nobody to be found anywhere near the place (of course), and the old, rotting wood-sided structure was completely engulfed in a raging inferno. By that point, it was mostly a matter of containment, keep it from spreading into the bone-dry fields and the woods beyond. The cause of the blaze was never determined, but a combination of booze, cigarettes (and probably weed), and drunk, careless teenagers was suspected.

Damn kids…

Next day, bulldozers razed what was left of the house, and portable dumpsters filled with burned rubble and charred debris were hauled off to the town dump, leaving nothing but a scorched and cracked concrete slab littered with the smaller junk and burned refuse that nobody bothered cleaning up and hauling away.

The barn, however, sat out on the property's back forty, close to the woods to the south and the fields to the west; mostly secluded by a thick row of close-knit pines standing midway between the barn and the house, the town's teenage party crowd had apparently never noticed it sitting back there.

But Jackie had, while roaming around the farm one day earlier that summer simply because he had nothing else better to do.

Though Chaz and Nick lived on the south side Edgewood, Jackie lived up on Northwood Drive, the northernmost street, which entered the neighborhood directly off of CR 200. So it wasn't uncommon for Jackie—whenever he got really bored at home and there was nothing good to watch on TV, and none of his friends were available to hook up, and he *really* wanted to get out of the house and *do* something—to jump on his bike and ride up CR 200 just for the heck of it; but that particular day was the first time he'd ridden so far; he made it all the way up to the Baker farm, which was probably half the distance to Homestretch, the main east-west drag through town.

When he crested the final hill and the old abandoned farm came into view, he quickly recalled the rumors about the older kids breaking in and vandalizing the house, and probably burning it down too, and about the boy who'd vanished years ago (Bobby? Lonnie? No, it was *Tommy*, that's right), and about the father who'd been butchered in a gruesome tractor accident out in the field, and how his older son had just stood and watched him bleed to death while mangled and trapped in the equipment (or so the rumor went), and how shortly thereafter he'd jumped in the old man's truck and vanished without a trace…

As he neared the farm, all those mysterious stories tantalized him; excited, no longer bored, he decided to stop and check the place out.

Why not?

Turning left off the road, he pedaled up into the now weed-infested gravel drive that ran clear to the back yard, stopping in the shade of a huge, billowing maple tree that stood in the side yard.

Quickly dismounting, he leaned his bike against the ancient, gnarled trunk. Glancing around briefly, he decided that he didn't need to bother with the bike lock, there was nobody around for miles.

Turning, he ventured toward the house.

Or where the house *used* to be…

First he meandered around the blackened slab, kicking through the refuse that still littered the property. On one end, he found charred bits and pieces of what looked like bedroom furniture—melted plastic knobs on burned bits of dresser drawers, a wooden chair leg scorched at one end, a half-burned pillow—then he spotted a book poking out from beneath a pile of rubble. Curious, he stooped, pulled it out, and brushed it off.

An old library book, from the school library:

The Call of the Wild.

He kept it, intent on reading it (and he did, later that evening, until he got to page 27, which had what looked to him like spots and streaks of dried blood on it…a little freaked out, he took the book out to the trash can that his dad had set in the driveway for pickup the next morning, pushed it way down into the depths of the can, and then the next day, just to be sure, watched from his bedroom window as the trash guy emptied the can into the big rumbling truck, then jumped up and rode the truck down the street, stopping and belching smoke as the guy jumped of and emptied cans along the way, until they finally turned the corner and were gone).

Circling the rest of the foundation, book in hand, he found nothing else of any interest. Needing to pee, he headed across the back yard to the dense row of pines that offered a little privacy for him to relieve himself, and, stepping through to the other side, happened to see the old barn sitting back there by the woods, just in front of the vast fields that stretched off to the west.

Leaning precariously to one side, the ancient barn looked to be untouched: no plywood covers nailed across the broken windows, no boarded-up doors with PROPERTY CONDEMNED or NO TRESPASSING signs posted on them.

In fact, one of the two wide double-doors in the front of the barn was actually hanging open, angling haphazardly down to the ground as if coming off its hinges.

After quickly relieving himself behind the trees, Jackie ventured cautiously across the backyard to the barn, stopping just outside the open door.

Peering into the darkness, he found it to be, well, a farmer's barn. Off to the right was a tractor, with some kind of farming machinery attached to it, both covered in mud and dust; old, rusty equipment sat everywhere, all of it covered in dust and cobwebs; hay bales were stacked against the back side, blackened with age, and a workbench sat just to the left of the doors, laden with rusty tools (and a few empty liquor bottles), and just general farm-looking stuff sat all about the place, all sitting undisturbed for what must have been years.

It was *very* cool.

He couldn't wait to show the guys!

Turning to leave, he spied an old, tattered baseball lying just inside the line of weeds that ran along the open wall of the barn—the only wall that was not secluded by trees—and he snatched that up, too, before racing his bike back down County Road 200 to Edgewood, eager to tell his friends what he had found!

It wasn't long before the old barn was christened as the boys' own private clubhouse, where they met regularly all summer while school was out. And so far, they'd not seen anyone else out there, not a single soul, ever.

Just them.

It was their little secret.

And before long, The Blackjack Club began to take shape…

The four boys had inadvertently started the club earlier that summer. Being years before the explosion of video gaming and decades before the proliferation of the Internet, physical games ruled the day: card games and board games and army soldiers and comic books indoors if it was raining or cold out, and cowboys-n-indians and hide-n-seek and cops-n-robbers and G.I. Joes (or whatever new idea Chaz came up with) outdoors, if the weather cooperated. (Though Nick and Jackie both had Atari 2600 Game Systems, all four of them couldn't play at the same time, and besides, there was no power in the barn where they now met regularly, and they'd much rather meet there than at any of their respective homes, which unfortunately usually included the watchful eye of an adult).

Then one day, shortly after school had let out for the summer, old Harvey Crocker—everyone called him Harv—taught Jackie a card game called *blackjack* at Tony's Barber Shoppe while they were both waiting for a cut and Tony was full-up and running behind, as usual (some of the regulars often remarked that if Tony worked his scissors as fast as he worked his jaw, well, then, things might just move along at a slightly faster clip (no pun)...but the guys didn't really mind—they were all there just as much for the socializing (especially without their wives around) as they were for the haircut).

Harv had to be a hundred years old, or so it seemed to Jackie, and rumor had it that he knew every card game in the book—and even a few that *weren't*.

After moving the stacks of magazines, they spent probably forty minutes or so facing each other over the small table that sat between their chairs in the waiting area, old Harv shuffling and dealing out cards, Jackie drawing or staying and learning to quickly add the cards up to twenty-one without going over (the whole ace thing confused him at first—with it being either a one or an eleven, or sometimes both, starting out as an eleven but changing to a one as the cards were dealt—but eventually, he got the hang of it. Sort of, anyway...)

When Harv was called up for his cut, Jackie continued to practice by himself, and by the time he was called up, he had it down. And to his glee, ol' Harv waved at him on his way out, and told him he could *"keep that deck of old wore-out cards, I got plenty more laying around the house."*

The next day, Jackie showed the rest of the boys how to play, and the game was an instant hit. Soon they were playing several times a week, and after some time they even started changing it up and inventing their own rules, to keep the game fun and interesting.

The current game included an element of poker, with each player betting into a pot after being dealt their first two "hole" cards—and then, consistent with blackjack, the rest of their cards being dealt face-up for all to see, with the end goal of getting as close to 21 as possible without going over—or, of course, to actually be dealt a blackjack on the first two cards.

Their evolved game was great fun for the boys, and they tried to play whenever they could—especially if they could all manage to elude their parents and play unhindered, for they appeared to be somehow cursed: whenever there were adults around, it seemed the boys couldn't stay out of trouble for very long.

So they quickly learned that hey—without any adults around, everything was just fine and dandy, they could play to their heart's content without causing any problems or getting into any trouble.

Weird.

So when Jackie'd had the good fortune (he was always so lucky!) of discovering the secluded barn on the abandoned Baker farm—where they were now playing—obviously, they'd immediately started hanging out there.

It was a no-brainer.

And after a few weeks, Nick just happened to call their group, as they were planning their next secret meeting out at the barn, *"The Blackjack Club"*—and the name stuck.

The Blackjack Club was born.

When Jackie had finished stuffing the loot he'd just won into his pockets, he turned to the others, who were just idly standing around holding their unlit cigarettes, waiting for a light from Jackie and his newly-won Zippo.

But instead of offering them a light, he said:

"By the way, I wanna show you guys somethin' I found."

And with that, he turned and strolled out of the barn, a trail of smoke streaming behind him.

Puzzled, the other boys just stood and looked at each other for a moment. Jackie was like that sometimes—the boy always seemed to have something up his sleeve—and once again they wondered what was up. Then finally, as if on cue, they all broke formation and ran out together, chuckling and calling out to Jackie.

Besides, he had the lighter…

Outside, Jackie was already halfway across the weed-infested back yard. He was walking slowly, but deliberately—a boy on a mission, but not in a hurry. With the smoldering cigarette pinched between two fingers of one hand, he was swinging a stick he had picked up somewhere along the way with the other, batting the tall grass and weeds as he went.

When the rest of them caught up, the four stopped and passed the lighter around. Puffs of smoke rose above the group, and trailed them as they continued on.

Soon they could tell where Jackie was probably headed: the big trash heap.

In the other corner of the property, a few hundred feet away from the barn, was a huge trash heap, which was somewhat concealed by the woods that flanked the north side of the property. Rising about eight feet high, and spanning twenty to thirty feet in diameter, it had apparently been the Baker family's catch-all back in the day: all kinds of leftover wood scraps, old rotted furniture, broken window panes, countless bottles, jugs, and other cracked and/or broken containers, old rusted bins and buckets, lamps and other household junk, and even an old stove off to one side, which had sunk a few inches into the mud over the years.

Of course, the boys had already picked over the heap back when they'd first commandeered the barn—spent half a Saturday rummaging through the junk—but decided that it was just that: old junk, nothing worth salvaging. So after that, they'd pretty much left it be.

But apparently Jackie had found something there that he thought was worth showing them, and they were excited to see what it was.

For several minutes they all quietly followed Jackie across the yard.

Then Ryan finally piped up:

"What're you gonna show us?"

"Something cool."

That's all Jackie said, and it hung in the air for a few moments, while they all walked and awaited further explanation.

But he offered none.

Instead, he took a final drag of his cigarette, then flicked the butt ahead of him and stepped on it on his way by, twisting it into the ground with one quick motion, never breaking stride.

"What is it?" Chaz asked from behind.

"You'll see."

Jackie didn't stop, or even slow down, or even look back at

them—he just kept walking, smiling mischievously.

"Race ya!" Nick suddenly shouted, flicking his own cigarette butt to the ground—and was off running toward the trash heap.

Accepting the challenge (of course), Chaz and Ryan both dropped their cigarette butts and the four boys burst into a foot-race, tearing through the overgrown grass and weeds, whooping and laughing, swinging their sticks wildly above their heads as they ran. Ryan and Jackie quickly left the bigger Nick and smaller Chaz behind, running side-by-side all the way to the heap, full sprint. Reaching it together they turned and stood, leaning on their sticks, gasping for breath. Throats hot with the exertion, they spit into the grass between breaths as they awaited their friends.

Nick and Chaz joined them moments later, also winded, and after they all caught their breath, Jackie led them around the back side of trash pile and toward the woods beyond.

The rest of them followed, glancing at each other with wonder and trepidation. *Where is he taking us?*

Upon breaching the woods, Jackie started beating his way through the underbrush with his stick. The others entered behind him, ducking one-by-one under the low-hanging branches.

Once engulfed by the trees, they all stood there for a moment, looking around and blinking, waiting for their eyes to adjust to the relative darkness of the woods. Adding to the eeriness, the chorus of birdsong that had permeated the woods only a moment prior had abruptly stopped, and now countless birds flitted silently about in the trees above, cautiously watching these unexpected intruders.

As their eyes adjusted to the shadows and things began to take shape, Jackie ventured forward. The rest stood and watched as he stepped behind a huge tree trunk and into a small clearing. Then his head poked back around and looked at them.

"Back here."

His head then disappeared back behind the tree.

The rest of the boys followed in single file, curious. None of them spoke as each stepped behind the tree and into the clearing.

"Ta-dah!" Jackie sang, waving his hand over a small group of large black cylindrical objects that were huddled together before them, almost hidden in the shadows.

Sticks resting at their sides, Nick, Chaz, and Ryan stood there staring at them, frowning, trying to figure why Jackie thought this was such a big deal.

Finally recognizing them, Chad shrugged.

"Okay, so it's some old barrels," he said. With that, they all looked from the barrels to Jackie.

"That's right!" Jackie confirmed, smiling. Amazingly, you could still see his silver tooth flash, even in the dim lighting.

"Fifty-five gallon barrels!"

They all looked back at the barrels. There were four of them, leaning together in the middle of the clearing.

"I found 'em back here earlier today, before the rest of you got here. I got here kinda early, and was rummaging around on the trash heap while I was waiting for you guys—but this time went down the back side of the pile, by the woods, instead of the front side like before—and that's when I saw these sittin' back here."

"Why didn't you tell us earlier?" Ryan asked.

Jackie smiled. "I wanted it to be a surprise...thought I'd wait till after the game, then show you guys straight-up, steada tellin' you about it beforehand. That woulda took all the fun out of it."

"Well, this is real fun, that's for sure," Chaz said sarcastically.

"So what's in 'em?" Nick asked.

"I don't know what *used* to be in 'em," Jackie replied, "But they're all empty now." He swatted the side of the closest one with his stick, and the resulting *thoooom!* indicated that it was, indeed, empty.

Jackie was still smiling big, like this was some great find.

"So why do you suppose they're back *here*?" Nick asked, perplexed, looking around at the surrounding woods. "You know...in the woods. Steada on the trash heap, with the resta the junk?"

Jackie shrugged. "Who knows...maybe they were keeping 'em for some reason...you know, just in case they needed 'em. Never know when a fifty-five gallon barrel might come in handy, right? So maybe, steada tossing 'em on the trash heap once they were empty, they stashed 'em back here where they're outta the way, but they could get 'em back out if they needed one for somethin', like fertilizer, herbicide, pesticide—"

—he shrugged—

—who knows?"

"Okay, so there's some big ol' empty barrels sittin' back here," Ryan said. "So what?"

"C'mon, guys, use yer 'magination!" Jackie chided. "Think… what could *we* use 'em for? What could we make with four big-ass barrels like this, that would be really cool?"

While the rest of them chewed on this for a moment, Jackie stared at Chaz, waiting…

Suddenly, Chaz's face lit up. "A raft!" he shouted, beaming with excitement.

"Exactly—a raft," Jackie confirmed, nodding. Then he jerked his stick up to his face like a microphone: *"Ding ding ding ding!"* he sang in a high-pitched bell imitation, then announced "Tell him what he's won, Johnny!" in a mock game-show host voice, while turning and pointing his stick at Chaz.

"Wow, a raft! That *would* be cool!" Nick concurred.

"You think we can really build a raft? I mean, one that actually *floats?*" Ryan asked, excited now too, but skeptical.

As if on cue, they all looked at Chaz.

The young whiz smiled, and began slowly nodding his head. You could see him already designing it in his head.

"Of course," he shrugged. "Piece-uh-cake."

So it was decided.

Manning one barrel each, the boys dragged them out of the woods, then turned them over on their sides and rolled them across the yard to the barn, standing them back up in a row along the wall next to the door, where they could inspect them in the sunlight for seaworthiness.

They were all lidded, each with a screw-in plug about 3" in diameter located to one side, near the edge. The caps were all present, but were rusted in place and couldn't be removed. The boys decided that was good, they wouldn't have to worry about them coming loose and the barrels leaking once the raft was out on the water.

After inspection, the barrels were moved into the barn and placed together in a cluster, forming a table of sorts. Then they went to work on a plan.

Using their blackjack scoring notebook and Chaz's ready supply of pens and pencils, they stood in a circle around the barrels, making a list of supplies for their new project. The raft was going to be their best gig yet!

"The main thing we're gonna need is boards for the deck," Chaz said.

"I already got that part figgered out," Jackie said. "Allied Construction Company, down at the bottom of the hill, by the railroad tracks. There's piles of scrap boards in the lumber yard behind the building. And the yard runs right up to the bank of the creek. It's perfect."

"Yeah, but it's fenced," Nick reminded them. "And it's a *tall* fuckin' fence, too."

"You ain't never climbed a fence, fat boy?" Jackie chided.

"But what if we get caught?" Ryan interjected.

"We can climb over after dark, right?" Chaz asked.

"And besides, how're we gonna get the barrels *there*, genius?" Nick chided back.

"That's right," Jackie confirmed, nodding at Chaz. "It'll be dark time we get there." Then he turned to Nick. "And to answer your question, we'll just roll 'em." He smiled at the prospect, silver tooth flashing.

"Roll them?" Ryan asked, incredulous. "All the way down to the construction company? That's pretty far."

"Yeah, but it's downhill the whole way," Chaz said. "Should be doable."

"Might even be *fun*," Jackie added, smiling.

"I don't know," Nick was shaking his head. "Ryan's right, it's pretty far. Probably like ten miles. Maybe more."

"Like Chaz said, it's down hill the whole way from here. Should be doable. Ten miles ain't nothin—specially downhill."

The boys all looked around at each other, nodding in tentative acceptance.

"As far as gettin' caught," Jackie looked at Ryan, "If we meet here at the barn tomorrow morning, and park our bikes inside, then we can roll the barrels down the hill, along the road all the way down to the creek, get there tomorrow late afternoon or evening. We'll stash 'em in the woods there, then cross over on the bridge. By then it'll be dark, and two of us can climb the fence—"

"I'll climb it!" Chaz blurted out, raising his hand.

"—yeah, so me 'n Chaz will climb over, and toss the boards over to you guys. When we got enough, we'll climb back over, and we all carry the wood back over the bridge to the woods, however many trips it takes. Then we camp there for the night, and build the raft on Saturday."

"Wait," Ryan said, concern in his voice. "Wouldn't that be...you know...*stealing*?"

"It's scrap," Jackie said, shrugging. "Junk. They probably gotta *pay* someone to haul it away now and then. Fact is, we'll probably be doing them a *favor*, taking some of it away for free. Save 'em some money."

He smiled, like a true salesman.

This logic seemed to assuage Ryan's concern, as he nodded quietly in acceptance.

"Okay, so we got wood for the deck," Chaz checked off the first line on the list he'd made. "We'll need a couple hammers, a saw, and a bunch of nails. And rope."

"I can bring the hammers, nails, and saw from my dad's workshop in the garage," Nick said. "But why rope?"

"First we'll build a frame, and lash it to the barrels using rope. Then we'll nail boards across the top of the frame to make the deck," Chaz explained.

"I can bring the rope," Jackie said.

"Needs to be nylon. Water-proof. Regular rope could start to deteriorate once it gets wet."

"Got it. Pretty sure my dad's got a roll of that in the shed. It's blue I think."

"If it's blue, it's probably nylon," Chaz agreed.

"I can't believe it, we're gonna make our own *raft!*" Nick shouted, excited. To this they all cheered, and high-fived each other around the table (barrels).

They were all getting more and more excited with every passing minute.

Once they calmed back down, they made a list of what each of them was to bring, including raft-building supplies, camping gear, and food. Nick and Jackie both had backpacks with built-in cooler compartments that held re-freezable ice packs in which they could pack perishables. The other two just had regular backpacks, so could only bring dry goods of the non-perishable variety. But between the four of them, and the two cooler-backpacks, Jackie figured they could bring plenty of food for a three-day weekend.

"That long?" Ryan asked, again concern in his voice.

"I figure we meet here tomorrow morning, spend the day rollin' the barrels down to the creek, then swipe the wood from Allied's scrap pile tomorrow night, like we said. Then we camp out in the woods overnight, then build the raft Saturday morning, and start down the creek."

"What about the canyon? The rapids?" Nick asked.

"Well, we definitely don't wanna go into the canyon, it's too dangerous," Jackie responded. "Rapids and big rocks and shit, from what I hear."

"I've heard that too," Chaz said, Nick concurring with a "Yeah, me too," and Ryan just nodded in agreement.

"So somewhere before we get to the canyon," Jackie continued, "we'll dock the raft, and camp for the night."

The all looked around and nodded in agreement.

"Then Sunday morning, we head back upstream. Once we dock, we can stow the raft in the woods somewhere for safekeeping, then hike back here to the barn. Should be back here by late afternoon—it'll be faster coming back, without the barrels—then we all bike home, should all of us be home in time for dinner Sunday."

"And school Monday morning," Nick lamented.

They all groaned.

"But what a great way to end summer vacation, huh?" Jackie said triumphantly, beaming. "Go out with a bang!"

This prompted another round of cheers and high-fives.

Now that the food, gear, and plans for the trip was all decided, they then got down to the serious business of…their parents.

"Okay, now we gotta clear things with our parents," Jackie said conspiratorially. "From tomorrow morning till Sunday evening."

"So how the hell do you think we're gonna be able to work all this out with our parents?" Nick said, his voice taking on a defeated tone. "For three whole fucking days?"

"I might have a way," Ryan said softly.

They all looked at him with widened eyes.

"My parents are going to this big Christian convention out of town somewhere—I think in Colorado Springs? Yeah, Colorado Springs—anyway, I begged them to let me stay home, since it's the last weekend of the summer before school starts—and, cuz of the carnival. I always go to the carnival, every year."

"That's right!" Jackie exclaimed. "The carnival is this weekend! I forgot all about it!"

"Yeah, it starts Friday night and runs until Sunday night," Nick confirmed.

Again, a chorus of excitement went around the group, then they all focused back on Ryan, who continued.

"They didn't want to let me stay home by myself, but I talked them into making Denise come down from Northridge to check on me over the weekend. She hates doin' that, but as long as mom and dad are payin' her tuition and shit, she's pretty much gotta do what they say. So she's comin' down on Saturday to check on me."

Ryan's older sister was in college at Mountain Springs School of Medicine up in Northridge; after spending her first year living in the dorm, then returning home for the summer, this year she had moved in with some friends who had their own apartment (though Ryan suspected it was really a *boy*friend, and that she was really *shacking up*), and was spending the summer there instead.

"Even with Denise agreeing to check on me, they were still reluctant—but then I promised I'd read somethin' from the bible each day while they're gone, and they finally agreed. So I've got the house all to myself all weekend."

He looked around at the others, waiting for someone to come up with an idea how this could work in their favor.

And of course, it was Jackie.

"Ryan my man, you just bought us the whole weekend."

Ryan looked at Jackie, perplexed. "How's that?"

All the boys were now staring at Jackie, waiting.

"You live in town, close to Grande Festival Plaza in Town Square, right? Where they hold the big carnival every year?"

"That's right, it's just a couple miles from my house."

"Well, the rest of us live in BFE, all the way down there in Edgewood. Really inconvenient if we wanna go to the annual carnival all the way up there in the middle of town, wouldn't ya say?"

Ryan's eyes lit up, as it dawned on him where Jackie was going with this, and Jackie continued.

"So, here's what we do: tomorrow, you leave a note for your sister for when she comes by on Saturday to check on you, saying you went fishing with me, and then we're going to the carnival later. Make sure to write my parent's phone number on it too, so it looks legit. I'll tell my folks I'm going fishing with you, and then we're going to the carnival, and I'm staying at your house for the weekend."

He then looked up at Nick and Chaz. "You guys do the same—tell your folks you're going fishing with me and Ryan during the days, then we're all going to the carnival in the evenings, and we'll be staying at Ryan's for the weekend, since it's right down the street from the carnival."

"But what if someone calls Ryan's house?" Nick asked.

"Easy peasy," Jackie answered. "Ryan, you leave a message on your answering machine that nobody's home because you all went to the carnival."

Looking around at all of them, he continued.

"So if any of our parents call Ryan's house, the answering machine will verify our story, we're all at the carnival. If Ryan's sister calls my house to check on him, my folks'll tell her we went fishing, and are going to the carnival afterward. As far as anyone will know, we're all out fishing during the day, then going to the carnival in the evenings, and we're all staying at Ryan's house for the weekend, which makes sense since it's so close—except Ryan's folks are out of town, but they're trusting Ryan's sister to check on him, so they won't have to."

"Okay," Chaz interjected. "But what if Ryan's parents call, get the answering machine, and find out that Ryan changed the message? Won't that raise the alarm? Make them wonder why he changed it? They'll know somethin's up, and Ryan'll probably get in trouble when they get home."

Ryan shrugged. "I'll just tell 'em I didn't want 'em to worry about me if they called and I wasn't home, so I let them know in the message that I was at the carnival with you guys. 'Sides, by the time they get home and ask me about it, it'll be too late anyway. We'll still get to go rafting, right? If they're a little worried cuz I changed the message on the answering machine, once they get home and see everything's okay, they'll calm down. No biggie."

They all looked at each other and nodded in recognition of the brilliance of the plan.

"And you don't think your sister will be a problem?" Nick asked Ryan. "When she has to come all the way down from Northridge to check on you?"

"Shit, she really doesn't want to come all the way home just to check on me. But she has to, my parents said. And when she does, I bet she'll bring her boyfriend along. So when she sees the note, and realizes she doesn't have to do shit now cuz I'm out fishing with Jackie, she'll probably be glad and turn right around and head back to Northridge. At most, she might call Jackie's house—but that's it. I doubt she even does *that*. Like I said, she doesn't wanna do *any* of it."

"And even if she *does* call my house to check on you," Jackie added, "My folks will verify the story: you went fishing with me, and we're going to the carnival later."

They all once again looked around at each other, nodding in approval. Smiles broke out across all their faces as they anticipated the fun adventure they were going to have that weekend. Then Jackie looked at Nick.

"Nick?" he asked, a dubious look on his face.

"I don't know," he sighed. "Dad's been drinking a lot lately, and sometimes that makes him mean, sometimes easy-going. You never know. With any luck, he'll be in the easy-going mood this time."

"Let's hope so," Jackie concurred.

Nick shrugged again. "Either way, I'm coming. I'll figure sumpm out, don't worry. I always do."

"Cool," Jackie said, nodding. He then turned to Chaz.

As the group looked at Chaz, quietly awaiting his response, his face widened into a mischievous grin.

"Piece-uh-cake," he said, sealing their fate.

And so it was on.

They spent the next half-hour double-checking the list of everything they would need and what each of them was to bring, and planned to meet back at the barn in the morning, usual time.

Then, just as they all started to leave the barn and head

home for dinner, Nick stopped in his tracks, remembering something.

"Hey—what about story night?" he asked the group. "That was supposed to be tonight, and I've got a pretty good one this time…but I forgot all about it, with the rafting trip and all."

Thursdays had traditionally become "story night" for the club, wherein they all took turns telling scary stories by candlelight in the darkness of the barn. It became somewhat of a contest, to see who could come up with the best story each week, and they each had their fair share of victories.

Chaz and Ryan both chimed in that they, too, had forgotten all about it, in all the excitement about the raft, but Jackie just smiled devilishly.

"I already got that planned," he explained. We're gonna save 'em for the trip, and tell 'em Saturday night, while we're *really* campin', *really* in the woods, *really* in the dark, around a *real* campfire—not just sittin' here with a few candles burnin' in this ol' barn, pretendin' we're scared."

That got Chaz to thinking, and he asked Jackie: "Hey—if we raft down Hope Creek all day Saturday, how far you think we'll get by Saturday night, when we stop to camp? All the way to Black Woods you think?"

Realizing this possibility, Ryan, Chaz, and Nick all looked at Jackie with trepidation. After all, Black Woods was rumored to be *haunted*…

"I don't think we'll get *that* far," Jackie said. "Probably pretty close though."

They all looked around at each other, wide-eyed and

smiling, excited at the prospect.

"So think up some good ones, boys," Jackie said. "It's the last weekend of the summer before school starts, so this coming story night, around the campfire, out there in the dark woods, will be the grand finale!"

With this, he smiled so big his tooth flashed.

"Well, mine's really good," Nick said confidently. "I think you guys'll like it."

"Mine too," Chaz chimed in. "I been working mine up all week, I think it's pretty good."

"We'll see," Ryan said. I've got a doozy in mind myself."

"Ha!" Jackie scoffed. "Mine will top all yours, hands down. I guarantee it!"

Laughing and cajoling, high-fiving and slapping each other's backs, the boys exited the barn, mounted their bikes, and headed home for dinner.

And to lie their asses off to their parents.

And to a man (or boy), their plan worked.

By bedtime, they were all in the clear until the following Sunday evening.

They met at the barn early the next morning, sure to leave their houses before their parents were up. Dawn was just breaking as Jackie, Nick, and Chaz quietly met up in their neighborhood and began biking up CR 200 together. Ryan was the straggler, as usual, coming from town, and the others stashed their bikes and fishing poles inside the barn while they waited for him to show up. Each of them wore a backpack with bedroll, and canteens slung to their sides, their packs loaded with the supplies they'd all agreed on, some for the raft, some for camping.

It was full light by the time they started hauling the barrels outside, and that's when Ryan rode up, pack and roll bouncing along the pitted gravel drive and across the weed-infested back yard toward the barn.

"You got the rope?" Chaz asked Jackie.

"Yep. Nylon, like you said. Grabbed the whole roll."

"Cool." Then he looked at Nick. "Tools?"

"Two hammers, saw, hatchet, tape measure, and a whole box of sixteen-penny nails," Nick confirmed. As he spoke, he absently rubbed the side of his right eye, where Chaz noticed he had a welt.

"Hey—is that a *shiner?*" Chaz asked, prompting Jackie to turn and look too.

"It's nothing," Nick said. "Old man didn't take too kindly to me telling him I was spending the weekend with you guys. He immediately said no, had a list of chores for me to do, but I insisted, and he didn't like that too much I guess. He's been drinkin' lately, under a lot of stress at the station, long hours and shit. I woulda asked Mom first, but she was working, as usual." He shrugged. "No biggie—I'm here, aren't I?"

Nick's father was a hot-tempered cop, big burly guy known for picking on people, and this kind of thing wasn't new to the boys. Every now and then, a new welt or bruise showed up somewhere on Nick, and he always blamed it his old man's job —the hours, the stress, the responsibility. Or, sometimes, maybe the booze.

His mother, the rare times she was home during such abuse—she worked at a florist in town, and was always busy with church events and all sorts of community activities—always stayed out of it, turning a blind eye and quickly finding something else to focus her attention on, usually in another room. And every once in a while, she sported a bruise or two of her own—just visible under the thick makeup she tried to hide it under, if you knew to look.

"But you said your dad said *no*," Jackie ventured.

"He did, at first. But after our...*discussion*, and I kept on insisting I was going—even after he clubbed me (a helluva backhand, but I got right back up)—he finally just said "whatever, do what you want, you always do anyway" and turned and walked away, back to his TV in the living room, that cop show he likes was on, Charlie's Angels—I think he's got the hots for that Farrah chick—though I can't say as I blame him, she *is* pretty hot—"

—at this, the boys all heartily agreed—

"Well, I like Kate Jackson better, she's the smartest one," Chaz said.

"No way, Jaclyn Smith's the best, she's got that sultry, girl-next-door look," Ryan said.

"Nope. Cheryl Ladd," Jackie interjected.

At this, they all looked at him.

"Even better than *Farrah*?" Nick said, incredulous.

"*I* think so," Jack confirmed, nodding and smiling. "But then, I've always had a thing for blue-eyed blondes."

Then the boys all began talking at once, arguing over which

of the women were their favorite and why, and why the others were obviously crazy.

Finally, after the debate died down, Nick continued:

"So anyway, I guess he fell asleep watching TV, cuz he was still there on the couch this morning, snoring his ass off, empty beer cans all over the coffee table, and their bedroom door was closed so I knew Mom was still asleep, too—she usually gets home pretty late—so I slipped out the back door without waking them."

With that, Nick squinted his welted eye and did a Popeye laugh out of the corner of his mouth: "Ug, ug ug ug ug."

"Nice move," Jackie approved, smiling.

But Ryan was concerned. "You don't think he'll be pissed at you when you get home?"

Nick shrugged. "Yeah, I'll probably get a good hiding," he said sadly. But then he looked around at all of them, smiling ear to ear. But hell—it's WORTH a hiding!"

They all heartily agreed and praised him for his courage, high-fiving him and slapping him on the back and shoulders.

Then, Chaz turned back to his list and got down to business.

"Okay, so we have everything we need to build the raft," he said. "Now just need to go get the wood."

As he spoke, Ryan was rolling his barrel out of the barn, having stashed his bike and fishing pole inside.

"So, how're we gonna do this?" Nick asked Jackie. "I hope you've got a plan."

"First, let's take a look," Jackie said. With that, he started across the yard toward the road, and the others followed.

Standing on the edge of County Road 200, they looked to the north, the direction of Hope Creek.

"It's pretty flat the whole way from here to Homestretch. That'll be the hardest part. But it's all downhill after that."

"Whadaya think? Coupla miles probably?" Nick asked.

"At least," Ryan answered. "I rode my bike that way one time, coming to you guys's neighborhood. Thought I'd try going up to Homestretch, then taking Homestretch to 200, then down 200 to Edgewood, and boy was I sorry. It took *forever*. Now I always just cut across Dover to Cottonwood, and come down through town. It's a lot faster."

They all stood in silence, staring down the road.

"Okay," Jackie finally said. "So we roll the barrels a few hours to Homestretch. Should be there around lunchtime. We break for lunch, then start the downhill part. It'll go a lot faster then, should reach the creek by dusk. We break for supper, wait for it to get dark enough—then cross the bridge to the construction yard, climb the fence, and swipe the wood from the scrap pile."

They were all nodding in agreement as they continued gazing down the road, the rasp of cicadas and chirps of birdsong drifting about the surrounding trees.

"Well, let's hit it," Jackie said, turning back and walking toward the barn.

Again they all followed silently, resigned to their task.

The trek was an arduous one.

The day quickly heated up, with the humidity rising right

along with it, and there wasn't so much as a light breeze to bring them any relief whatsoever along the way. Soon they had all shed their shirts and tied them around their waists, but there was nothing they could do about their backpacks, so they all sweated profusely under them as they rolled the barrels along the cracked and broken asphalt of the old, unkempt country road, nursing their canteens of water. Though they'd started out cracking jokes, yucking it up, and bantering back and forth as childhood friends will do, after about an hour they went silent, all of their energy focused on rolling the barrels before them at an excruciatingly slow pace, while they seemingly got bigger and heavier with each passing minute.

Whenever the occasional car or truck approached, they'd hustle off the road, abandon the barrels in the weeds and tall grass, and hunker down at the edge of the woods, out of sight until it passed by and was long gone. Last thing they needed was for someone to see them and stop and start asking questions. Or worse, have someone recognize any or all of them and start calling parents when they got home.

No, they didn't need any of that; so they stayed out of sight of all passing vehicles. Better safe than sorry.

Finally, about the time they were beginning to think they'd never make it, and were actually tossing around the idea of stopping and turning back (or better, just abandoning the barrels right there in the weeds, heading back, and finding something else to do all weekend—like, say, go to the carnival, which at this point wasn't sounding too bad)—they saw the bright red three-way stop sign at Homestretch off in the distance, wavering in the heat rising from the sun-baked asphalt.

"There it is!" Jackie called, pointing at the tiny red octagon gleaming in the sun, around a hundred yards away.

"Yesssssss!" Chaz hissed, pumping his fist.

"So we're gonna make it after all," Ryan said quietly, wiping a sweaty arm across his equally sweaty brow.

Nick just stood there panting as he stared at the distant sign, sweat running down the sides of his face, dripping from his nose, his chin. Then he turned to Chaz.

"What time is it?"

Chaz was the only one who ever wore a watch. And he *always* wore a watch, rain or shine. He had one of those oversized, multi-button gizmos with all the bells and whistles, stuff the rest of them would never be able to figure out how to use anyway.

"Almost one."

"Perfect," Jackie said. "We'll be at the top of the hill by one, and can break for lunch, then head down to the creek. We'll have our wind back, and be rested, and the rest of the way is downhill."

With sighs of relief, they all agreed, and with renewed vigor, they began rolling the barrels as quickly as they could toward the blazing red sign in the distance.

After crossing the T-intersection at Homestretch (waiting until there were no vehicles visible in any of the three directions before crossing, again to avoid being seen), they approached the break in the terrain where it started downhill. Only one car had passed through the intersection while they were there, and they easily avoided it, dashing behind a huge boulder that sat ensconced in the southwest corner of the intersection, thick weeds sprouting all around it. Once the coast was clear, they spied a nice copse of pine trees slightly to the northwest, about halfway between Homestretch and the break downhill, and headed over behind them for lunch.

Ryan unpacked a cellophane-wrapped stack of peanut butter and jelly sandwiches and handed them out, and they all shared a small bag of barbecue potato chips from Chaz, passing it around as they ate their sandwiches between steady swigs from their canteens, all of them plenty thirsty after their long, hot, and sweaty trek.

Once they had finished lunch, they ventured out from behind the pines and stood at the top of the hill, looking down the slope. It was a steep embankment, mostly covered in thick wild grass.

The road, to their right, angled sharply downward, and was full of potholes as far as they could see. Apparently, it had not fared well over time, the old asphalt eroded by years of rainwater washing down the embankment.

"Whoa...that's a lot steeper than I remembered," Nick said cautiously.

"Way I figger it, the steeper the better," Jackie said.

"We get them started, the barrels'll probably roll all the way to the creek by themselves," Ryan said.

"No, just this first part is steep," Chaz said, pointing down the embankment. "Maybe fifty yards or so, steep like this—"

—he then pointed out toward the north—

"—then it levels out some, the rest of the way to the creek. Still runs downhill, though. It'll sure be a lot easier the rest of the way than it's been so far."

The boys nodded in agreement. Then they all looked at each other, waiting for someone to signal that they should proceed. But nobody moved. Instead, they all turned and once again peered silently down the grassy slope.

And suddenly, Jackie looked at the others sideways, smiling mischievously.

"I got an idea," he said. "First, lets get the barrels."

Retrieving the barrels from near the road, they rolled them up to the edge of the incline and stopped there, all of them turning to Jackie, wondering what trick he had up his sleeve this time.

Stooping, he carefully positioned his barrel right on the edge of the drop-off, then stood behind it. Then, holding his arms out to his sides for balance, he stepped carefully up onto the barrel, to the gasps of the others. They all looked at each other wide-eyed, not believing what their friend was doing.

The barrel wobbled back and forth, Jackie bending his knees and throwing his arms this way and that to maintain his balance, until finally the boy and the barrel settled as one. He slowly straightened, then turned his head, smiling ear-to-ear, and looked at the rest of them, standing in awe behind him.

"You're not really gonna—" Nick started, but too late.

Suddenly shuffling his feet, Jackie launched the barrel off

the ridge and down the embankment, pumping his legs like a mad dog as the barrel rolled under him. Down, down, down he flew, shuffling atop the barrel, his laughter echoing up to the other boys, who stood watching and smiling, still not believing it.

Then, partway down, he called back to the others, "Last one down's a rotten egg!"

Accepting the challenge, the other three quickly positioned their barrels along the ridge as Jackie had done, and began trying to step up and balance on them. Ryan was up quickly, but Nick and Chaz both took a couple of tries before they managed to maintain their balance.

All three barrels aligned side by side, all three boys holding their arms out to their sides for balance, Nick yelled *Go!*, and they were off to the races, shuffling their feet as fast as they could, riding the barrels downhill at lightening speed, while laughing, whooping, hollering, and shrieking all the way.

Chaz was the first to go down. Having no athletic inclination whatsoever, he only made it a quarter of the way down when his feet flew out from under him, and he came down on his backpack on top of the barrel. He and the barrel both bounced up into the air, then tumbled together a few times before the barrel broke free and sped on down the hill, leaving Chaz behind, rolling and sliding, unhurt and still laughing, a trail of glasses, pens, and other pocket gadgets littering the grass behind him.

Further down, Ryan was moving at a pretty good clip, but Nick soon took the lead, surprisingly—maybe it was his strength, or maybe it was his size, and sheer gravity was working to his advantage—but either way, he was making an impressive show of speed and agility as he gained on Jackie below.

Then, Ryan's barrel struck a rock hidden in the tall grass, sending the barrel bouncing into the air with Ryan cartwheeling above it. Like Chaz, boy and barrel tumbled together a few times before the barrel settled and resumed its downward trek, leaving Ryan summersaulting in the soft grass, cursing his luck between gales of laughter.

Continuing down the hill, the two rogue barrels angled away from each other to either side of the incline, finally rolling to a stop halfway down, coming to rest in the tall, thick weeds that lined both sides of the hill.

Now the race was on between Jackie and Nick. Jackie was beginning to tire, huffing for air as he shuffled his feet as fast as he could, glancing over his shoulder at the larger boy gaining on him at a surprising pace.

Ahead, where the steep incline broke and the ground leveled out somewhat, an old fallen tree lay across the field directly in their path, like the finish line on a race track.

Time was short.

Nick was right on his ass.

Jackie could hear him huffing, could almost feel the low, hollow echo of the barrel running along the ground under Nick's heavy feet.

With renewed vigor, Jackie lowered his head in concentration and gave it all he had, the log looming before him approaching with frightening speed.

But Nick caught up to him, and pulled alongside.

Now they both had their heads down, working their barrels as hard as they could, with only a short distance to go before reaching the downed tree ahead, the unspoken finish line. Shouts of encouragement floated down from above, as Ryan and Chaz cheered them on from the hillside, anxious to see who would win the race and claim victory.

Then, the boy's cheers fell off as they realized that the other two were about to slam full-speed into the tree, which was now only a few yards away. They watched in horror, grimacing, hands to their heads, bracing themselves for the imminent impact.

Running neck-and-neck, Jackie and Nick both began straining forward, reaching out to the finish line to claim the slimmest of victory—but just before they reached the tree, they both lost their balance and flew forward off their barrels just as the barrels struck the tree with a double *thoom-thooooom!*, bouncing off to the sides while the boys sailed up and over and out of sight.

Ryan and Chaz then heard a giant *splash!*

Looking at each other wide-eyed, they took off running down the hill to see what had happened to their friends. They reached the fallen log together and looked over it, winded from their run.

Ends up, there was a drainage ditch on the other side of the log, running along the bottom of the hill. It was full of stagnant water, a few feet deep, probably from the last good rain. After half-falling, half-diving from their barrels, Jackie and Nick had landed in the green slimy water, and were now hauling themselves out, soaked to the bone but unhurt.

Upon seeing them and realizing they weren't hurt, Chaz and Ryan began laughing hysterically as their friends climbed out of the ditch soaking wet with strings of green slime hanging from their backpacks, muddy wet leaves stuck in their hair.

"That was totally *awesome!*" Chaz managed between fits of laughter.

Finally out of the water and back on dry land, Jackie and Nick stood and looked at each other, wet and slimy and pathetic, and they both began laughing, too.

The four boys' gales of laughter drifted up the hill, mingling with birdsong from the surrounding woods before dissipating into the clear blue summer sky.

•

The boys reached Hope Creek in the early evening, just as they'd hoped. And man, were they wiped. The rest of the journey had been downhill, yes—but after that first steep hill, it was only a slight downhill grade that ran for miles, and the barrels were still a job to roll, even out in the road.

But nevertheless, they made it.

Luckily for Jackie and Nick, the day had been hot enough that they'd mostly dried off from their little swim in the drainage ditch during their trek. And since their backpacks were water-resistant, their supplies hadn't gotten wet at all.

Just shy of the bridge that took CR 200 over the creek, the

four boys cut to the west, rolling the barrels across a narrow clearing, finally stopping near the edge of the woods. There they all collapsed in the grass, completely exhausted and drenched with sweat.

Once they stopped panting, they stood, righted their barrels, and, leaning casually on them, randomly tipped their canteens back with muffled metallic sloshes as they peered to the north.

Across the way, on the other side of the creek, the eight-foot chain-link fence was just visible, jutting above the brush and weeds, guarding the equipment yard of Allied Construction Company. Filthy, rusting NO TRESPASSING signs hung on every other section of the fence, centered between the poles.

The huge, faded white warehouse-style building loomed off in the distance, silent and ominous, a few hundred feet inside the perimeter fence. Various types of pale yellow heavy construction equipment—bulldozers, dump trucks, earth movers, backhoes, you name it, every one dusty and rusty and caked in dried mud—sat motionless around the yard like a crew of exhausted workers.

"Thar she blows," Nick said in his Popeye voice.

Bending, Chaz dropped his backpack to the ground, turned it, opened an exterior pouch, and pulled out a small pair of camo-green binoculars. Placing them right up against his glasses, he scoped the distant construction yard.

"Are you sure there's scrap wood in there we can use?" Ryan asked.

"It's there," Jackie ensured them. "You just can't see it from here. It's just inside the corner of the fence there, behind those trees. See? You can see the top of the sawmill sticking up right there. That's where they cut the wood to size, and they pile the scraps off to the side."

He was pointing to a line of small, thin, scraggly trees that had gown along the fence line, obscuring the view inside—but the upright orange frame of the sawmill was just visible, protruding a foot or two above the foliage.

"Well, I still don't see any wood," Ryan said, remaining skeptical.

"Don't worry, I seen it a million times, whenever we drive up here."

"Why in the world do you guys drive all the way up *here*?" Chaz asked, lowering his binoculars. "There's nothing up here, 'cept the construction company...and the rail yard, but that's on up a little ways from here...not exactly tourist attractions."

"My parents like to go on Sunday drives sometimes, take the convertible and drive through the country, along this road," Jackie explained, pointing back up the county road they'd traveled to get here. Placing a fist against his chest, he said in a deep mocking voice, "One with nature!"

They all began chuckling.

"No shit? Your dad really says that?" Nick asked, smiling in disbelief.

"Yep. Pretty much every single time. He loves the great outdoors."

Eventually their chuckling subsided, and they started

planning their next move.

"Okay, we got some time to kill before it gets dark enough," Jackie said.

With this, Chaz lifted his arm and looked at his oversized multi-function watch, pushing a series of buttons on the sides. Looking up at everyone through his glasses, he announced: "An hour and ten minutes to sunset, to be exact."

"Cool," Jackie said. "We can rest up for a while—"

"And break for grub!" Nick finished. "I'm starving!"

A chorus of agreement went around the group as the rest of them began relieving themselves of their backpacks.

Looking around, they spotted a somewhat clear, rocky area nearby where the grass and weeds were relatively thin, dragged their packs over, and plopped themselves down in a circle to eat.

•

Soon dusk relented, dissolving to full dark. A symphony of crickets, frogs, and other unseen nocturnal creatures filled the air, while swarms of fireflies dotted the entire area with slow, streaking yellow flashes.

Leaving the backpacks and barrels clustered at the edge of the woods, the boys hurried silently across the bridge in a crouching gallop, then, once across, they huddled together at the corner of the fence.

The yard was nearly completely dark, just a few outdoor halogen security lights that ran along the back of the warehouse, each swarming with moths and other tiny flying insects. They cast a cold, fluorescent glow up near the building, while above, a half-moon, set in the cloudless night sky, cast a pale, ghostly hue on the yard, the equipment now inky and full of shadows.

"Okay, you guys know the plan," Jackie whispered. "Me and Chaz climb over, and toss boards over to you guys.

"How will we know when we have enough?" Nick asked.

"I know how much we need," Chaz answered. Then, looking at Jackie: "Biggest we want is two-by-fours. Anything bigger'll be too hard to cut. So one-by-fours and two-by-fours. And if we can find any long pieces, that'll help a lot, specially for the frame. Just remember, the longer they are, the fewer we need. So go for the longest pieces first."

"Got it," Jackie confirmed. Then he looked at Ryan and Nick. "You guys carry as much as you can on each trip across the bridge, and as soon as Chaz thinks we got enough, we'll climb back over and help carry the rest."

Jackie looked up at the fence for a moment, then back.

"And remember, everyone be *quiet!* Who knows if they have any guards on duty, or if anyone's inside…let's not take any chances."

Ryan and Nick nodded in understanding.

The fence rattled and clinked softly as the two boys scaled quickly up and over, landing with thuds on the inside. Then Nick and Ryan backed away, allowing enough room for the boards to land.

The two small silhouettes slinked away into the darkness, and the gentle sliding and clapping of wood boards could be heard as they began shuffling through the scrap pile.

Jackie was the first to return to the fence. He heaved one long board up and over, which landed and rolled quietly in the grass in front of Ryan, who without a word quietly picked it up and carried it over toward the road.

As Jackie turned and disappeared, Chaz showed up, carrying two shorter boards. He flung them over one at a time, and after they landed quietly in the soft grass and weeds, Nick stealthily shouldered them and slinked out to the road.

Soon, they had accrued enough on the roadside for Ryan and Nick to take a load back across the bridge.

This process went on for nearly half an hour, smooth and quiet, like a well-oiled machine. Eventually, Chaz and Jackie met at the fence together, and after tossing their boards, Chaz whispered, "Okay, one more trip, and that should be enough. I think I saw a really long one down underneath the stack, I'm gonna try to get that one out."

Jackie nodded, and they returned together to the wood pile. As Chaz stooped over and began tugging on the long board that protruded out from under a bunch of smaller scrap pieces near the ground, Jackie gathered a few shorter pieces from his side of the pile and headed back toward the fence.

Meanwhile, Nick and Ryan, having once more returned from the bridge, quietly gathered the remaining wood and moved it out to the roadside, then stood at the fence waiting for the next load.

But suddenly, a very loud *BANG!* echoed from the scrap heap behind Jackie, followed by an extended, noisy ruckus—sounding to Jackie like a bunch of boards sliding and skidding down the sides of the pile like a wood avalanche.

Apparently, Chaz had lost his grip on that really long board he was wrestling with, and, loaded down with so much scrap, it had slapped down really hard on the boards beneath it, and caused all the smaller pieces on top to scatter, sliding and tumbling down the pile, making all kinds of racket in the process.

And that's when they heard it.

Way off in the distance, up near the building, a dog started barking. And not just *any* dog, you could tell by the sound of it —deep and ferocious, it obviously meant business—but a *guard dog!*

And it was getting louder by the second, apparently running full speed toward them!

"Oh, shit!" Jackie hissed under his breath, darting the rest of the way to the fence and tossing the boards over quickly as the barking drew closer.

Turning, he cupped his hands around his mouth and hissed "Come on, Chaz!" as loudly as he could into the darkness behind him, then turned and flung himself onto the fence, scrambling up as fast as he could. Up and over he flew, Ryan and Nick stabilizing him as he dropped to the ground on the other side.

Then they all turned back to the fence, expecting Chaz.

But Chaz wasn't there.

And the dog had easily cleared half the distance from the building already, barking its head off as it it neared.

All three began shouting under their breaths for Chaz,

whose ghostly silhouette they could just barely see in the dim moonlight, still at the woodpile, bent over, vigorously yanking on that long board with everything he had.

The dog was now getting dangerously close, so close that they could hear the deep growling in its chest between barks as it weaved between the machinery and toward them.

Finally, the long board suddenly broke loose and slid quickly out, throwing Chaz outward and to the ground. Now the boys were hollering for him to get the hell out of there, forget the board, just get up and get out—

But unbelievably, Chaz jumped to his feet, grabbed the board by one end, and, barely able to lift the far end off the ground, swung it around as he turned, then began running toward the fence, the board swaying before him.

Luckily, the dog's direct path was blocked by the sawmill's conveyer table, which stuck out a ninety degree angle from the machine, over on the far side of the wood pile. Reaching it, and not being able to duck under due to the array of legs, support rails, and undercarriage struts, the dog was forced to detour around the end of it, buying perhaps an extra five seconds for Chaz.

The kids were all yelling now, rooting for Chaz to make it to the fence before he became dog food, and Chaz was halfway to the fence, running awkwardly with the length of the board flailing ahead of him, its end bouncing up and down just above the ground as he ran.

Suddenly, the dog bolted around the end of the conveyer, and intensified its barking as it pursued the boy to the fence, hunching its back tightly, straining to run as fast as it could.

Now the boys could see it, and were horrified: it was a huge, mostly black German Shepherd, the biggest dog they'd ever seen.

Their yelling escalated.

With his friends all screaming at him in an incoherent jumble of panicked voices, and sensing the dog bearing down on him, a rebel yell emerged from Chaz's throat as he approached the fence:

"EeeeaaaaaaahhhhhhhhhhhhhhHHHHHHH!!!!"

And just as the dog was about to overtake him, the far end of the board dug into the ground at the base of the fence, flinging Chaz up into the air like a pole-vaulter. Screaming all the way, he catapulted in a wide arch toward the fence, the dog running under him as he went, barking up at him.

He struck the fence near the top, and quickly scrambled over, his glasses tumbling off in the process and falling into the grass below. But then he just hung there, gripping the top of the board that was sticking a foot or so above the top rail of the fence.

The dog began leaping up onto the fence and sliding back down, barking furiously, but was coming far short of the boy as he hung near the top.

Then, to the horror of the boys: back at the building, random lights began flicking on, first inside, then outside.

At this, they all went silent, knowing what it meant.

Someone was coming.

Someone…like a *security guard!*

Returning to hissing whispers, the boys once again looked up at Chaz, assailing him with a jumble of pleas and commands to let go, come down, come on so they could all get the hell out of there—but Chaz would not let go. He hung there, clinging to the end of his prize board. He obviously wasn't going to give it up.

The dog continued its barking and jumping, and now a tiny bouncing light could be seen off in the distance, working its way from the building through the yard toward them, weaving this way and that through the equipment: a man approaching with a flashlight.

Finally understanding what Chaz was doing, Nick jumped onto the fence and scurried up as fast as he could, until he was next to Chaz. Then he, too, grabbed the end of the board, then kicked his feet from the fence, adding his own falling weight to the cause.

And it was just enough.

Inside the fence, the board began swinging slowly upward, pivoting on the top rail of the fence as it lowered the boys on the other side.

"Maverick!" the security guard hollered just before vanishing momentarily in the darkness behind a bulldozer, which sat maybe halfway across the yard from the building.

As the board swung outward from the fence, the dog yelped and skittered backward, unsure of what was happening, a little guarded, then began barking again.

Once the board broke the plane and angled downward to the outside of the fence, it began sliding quickly across and down, sending Nick and Chaz tumbling to the ground.

"Quick, grab the wood!" Jackie instructed, just as the man emerged from behind the bulldozer in the distance. They could now hear him hollering at the dog, which was still barking its head off at them, now also flinging itself against the fence with reckless abandon.

The boys quickly and quietly scooped all the boards up from the grass (Chaz first plucking his glasses from the grass and shoving them into his shirt pocket, then manning the long board that had nearly cost him his life), then, following Jackie's lead, they all crouched low and headed down the weed-filled creek embankment toward the creek, then darted to their left and ducked under the bridge. Once underneath, Chaz walked quickly backward, dragging his lengthy board out of sight.

Sweat running down their faces and panting as quietly as they could, they huddled under the steel girders, listening.

The dog had stopped barking, and was now just yipping and whining as the man approached.

"What's the matter, Mav?" The man's voice floated down from the yard. "What's out there?"

With that, the boys watched the white beam of the flashlight sweep around on the ground before them, across the creek, then back up the embankment and back to the yard, all in quick, jerky motions.

"There ain't nobody out here," the man said to the dog in a ridiculing tone. "What was it, a coon or something?"

The dog barked playfully.

"Probably just another fuckin' feral cat, wasn't it? "

The dog yipped, as if in confirmation.

"Ya know the yard's full of 'em, but ya just can't leave 'em alone, can ya? C'mon ya knucklehead, let's get back inside 'fore we get ate up by mosquiters out here!"

As the man spoke, the dog's tags jingled incessantly, sounding as if it was hopping and frolicking around the man, all the while happily yipping and whimpering. Then, as the two retreated back toward the building, the dog turned its head over its shoulder and barked one last time in the general direction of the boys, a warning broadcast into the night.

Now barely breathing, the boys waited a couple more minutes—until all was silent for a good while, indicating that the coast was finally clear—then they all exhaled in relief, wiping their sweaty foreheads and shaking their heads at the close call.

Without a word, they emerged from hiding, gathered the remaining boards, climbed quietly up the embankment, and stole back across the bridge and into the night.

•

Once they reached the edge of the woods where they'd been stashing the boards, Nick shoved Chaz gently from behind, causing him to stumble forward a step.

"What're you trying to do, get us *shot?*" he asked gruffly.

"Hey!" Chaz barked, turning and glaring up at Nick. "We needed some long boards, I told you that! Fuck off!" With that he slammed the board down onto the ground, as if for emphasis, while still staring up at Nick, jaw set.

"Shit, what good is a raft, if we're all fuckin' dead? Or in jail?" Nick retorted, his voice escalating.

"So when'd you learn to pole-vault?" Jackie interjected, trying to distract them, cool them down a little. "Pretty awesome, y'ask me!"

With that, Ryan and Jackie both began chuckling.

Nick suddenly smiled. "Yeah, I gotta admit, that *was* pretty awesome." As he spoke, he gave Chaz a little friendly jab to the shoulder, and began chuckling himself.

"And what was that rebel yell you did?" Ryan asked. "Some kind of ninja shit, or what?"

With that, all three began to laugh.

"EeeeeaaaaaaaaahhhhhhhHHHHH!!!!" Jackie mocked, sending the other two into hysterics.

"Hey, fuck you guys!" Chaz said, crossing his arms and scowling. Then he just stood there glaring at them while they laughed. But try as he might, he couldn't stay mad, and soon he was laughing right along with them.

•

Because they'd almost gotten caught, and were afraid the guard and his dog were now on the alert, they decided to retreat further up the road a bit, try to find a clearing back further in the woods to make camp, where they wouldn't risk the campfire being visible from the building.

Leaving the boards and barrels at the edge of the woods, they carried their backpacks back south along the road until they spied what looked like a narrow path that cut into the woods on the right. Deciding that it looked promising, they ventured in. A short time later, the path opened into a small clearing: sparse rocky ground strewn with small boulders.

Perfect.

Didn't take long for the four of them to gather enough old tree limbs and rotted timber from the surrounding woods to get a small campfire going, and the rocky terrain helped ensure it would stay contained and under control.

Chaz pulled his multi-purpose tool from its holster on his belt, extracted a sizable knife blade, and went to work sharpening some long, thin branches he'd harvested from a small tree on the edge of the clearing.

As he did so, Nick opened the cooler section of his backpack and broke out a package of hotdogs, then pulled a package of buns from the main compartment on top. He'd even thought to bring a handful of ketchup packets (he always grabbed extras in the school cafeteria, just in case), which he now handed around to everyone.

Soon they were grilling hotdogs over the fire, and the aroma was absolutely righteous.

Famished, they ate dinner in silence, wolfing the dogs down as soon as they were even remotely warm—they were too hungry to wait for them to cook through properly—and even so, they were still delicious.

When they finished, Jackie offered his pack of Reds all around (luckily they'd stayed dry when he took is little unexpected dip, tucked deep inside his backpack). They each slid one out, and lit them with various burning or smoldering sticks from the campfire.

Then they all sat back and smoked quietly, each pretending

to inhale, then blowing mouthfuls of smoke into the air, watching as it blended with the smoke from the campfire then drifted upward into the dark, star-speckled sky above.

As the fire began to wane, casting flickering orange glows onto their faces, they began discussing their adventure in the construction yard: the ruckus Chaz made, the dog, the guard, their antics and cutthroat escape; and as they relived the events, each building on the excited recollection of the others, the story became more and more exaggerated, as if the whole incident grew a little in their minds as they recounted it.

First, the dog got bigger—growing to near monstrous size by the time they finished; then the guard turned out to be armed to the teeth; and finally, Chaz mentioned thinking he'd heard a helicopter circling overhead....and that got them all laughing, the absurdity of it.

Finally they began hunkering down for sleep, rolling out their bedrolls and reclining slowly onto them, as if not wanting to let go of the splendid evening in exchange for mere sleep. As they did so, Ryan pulled a bible from his backpack.

The other three boys stared at him, incredulous.

Noticing this, he stopped, bible clutched in front of him.

"What?" He looked around the group. "I promised my parents, remember?"

The others glanced around at each other, then shrugged and began bedding down, leaving Ryan to his reading.

Ignoring them, he shimmied up against the tree at the head of his bedroll, brought a flashlight up in front of the opened bible, and clicked it on. The reflecting light revealed a smattering of multi-colored bookmarks—what appeared to be a bunch of sticky-notes—protruding from the top of the book, faded and crumpled.

Noticing these, Jackie said, "Wow…you read that a lot?"

Ryan looked at him and blinked. "Of course."

"That's a lot of bookmarks."

"I bookmark the important verses. The stuff about life. About being a good person."

Then, with a teasing smirk, he looked around at all of them. "You guys should try it sometime."

A chorus of moans and chuckles and fuck-yous emanated from around the group.

"So, is there a lot about life, about being a good person in there?" Jackie asked. "Because I thought it was all just stories—what do they call 'em? "Pairbles" or something?—and all these commandments we gotta follow or we go to hell when we die, and that Jesus did miracles, and died for our sins. You know, stuff like that."

Ryan shrugged. "That's all in there, sure. But there's also a lot of stuff about life, how to live life so you're happy and fulfilled. You know, like philosophy and self-help and stuff. After all, religion and personal spirituality are the keys to success in life."

This prompted a round of scoffs from the others.

"What, you guys don't believe me?" he asked them in an incredulous tone. Holding the bible up as if displaying it to an audience, he said matter-of-factly, "It's all in here."

"Okay, give us an example," Jackie said.

Ryan looked at him for a moment, as if trying to determine if he was serious or making fun of him. Finally, nodding, he complied.

"Alright."

Pulling the bible back to his chest, he began flipping through it with one hand, beaming the flashlight onto the pages with the other. Now he had the attention of Nick and Chaz as well, who sat up on their bedrolls and waited.

After reviewing a couple of the bookmarked passages, but rejecting each with a quick shake of his head, he finally found one he liked.

"Okay, here's one—"

—he looked up at the others—

"—this is about anxiety, or worrying—"

—then back down at the book.

"Matthew six, verse twenty-five," he began.

"For this reason I say to you, do not be worried about your life, as to what you will eat or what you will drink; nor for your body, as to what you will put on. Is not life more than food, and the body more than clothing? Look at the birds of the air, that they do not sow, nor reap nor gather into barns, and *yet* your heavenly Father feeds them. Are you not worth much more than they? And who of you by being worried can add a single hour to his life? And why are you worried about clothing? Observe how the lilies of the field grow; they do not toil nor do they spin, yet I say to you that not even Solomon in all his glory clothed himself like one of these. But if God so clothes the grass of the field, which is alive today and tomorrow is thrown into the furnace, will He not much more clothe you? You of little faith! Do not worry then, saying, 'What will we eat?' or 'What will we drink?' or 'What will we wear for clothing?' For the Gentiles eagerly seek all these things; for your heavenly Father knows that you need all these things. But seek first His kingdom and His righteousness, and all these things will be added to you. So do not worry about tomorrow; for tomorrow will care for itself. Each day has enough trouble of its own."

The boys all nodded in understanding, glancing at each other with mild surprise.

"That sounded like regular talk," Nick remarked, somewhat astonished. "I like that. Our bible is full of *thees* and *thous* and *shalts* and stuff...makes it hard to understand. But yours sounds normal."

The others voiced their agreement.

Ryan turned the book around, facing out the cover. "New American Standard. My favorite translation, cuz it's easy to read and understand."

"Cool," Nick said, nodding. "I like it."

"Okay, give us another one," Jackie said.

Ryan again flipped through his plethora of bookmarks, until he found another to share. Again, he looked up—

"—this one's about being a good person—"

—then back down again.

"Galatians five, verse twenty-two," he began.

"But the fruit of the Spirit is love, joy, peace, patience, kindness, goodness, faithfulness, gentleness, self-control;

against such things there is no law. Now those who belong to Christ Jesus have crucified the flesh with its passions and desires. If we live by the Spirit, let us also walk by the Spirit. Let us not become boastful, challenging one another, envying one another."

Again, the boys all nodded in understanding.

"Wow, that *is* good stuff," Jackie remarked.

Ryan again held up the book for all to see. "Like I said, the key to success in life."

With this, Chaz spoke up.

"I hate to break it to ya, but there's a new way to success these day, I think you may of heard of it—it's called *science*."

The others chuckled at this.

"When the bible was written," Chaz continued, "they still thought the world was flat, and that the sun revolved around the earth, steada the other way around. Science debunked all that centuries ago. And plus, when we sent men to the moon? The Apollo spacecraft didn't travel through heaven, pissing off God and the angels on its way, either. So that proved that there's no heaven up there somewhere—"

—he waved his arms sarcastically in the air above him—

"—and so there's no hell down there, either—"

—he lowered his gesticulations to reference the ground—

"—and so I think all that stuff you're reading is hocus-pocus. Superstition. I'll take science over religion any day of the week…I mean hell, they didn't even know how to make a light bulb back then."

"What's any of that got to do with being a good person?

Living a good life?" Ryan asked, rather defensively.

"That's not what you said," Chaz quickly retorted. "You said *the key to success in life*. And I say the key to success isn't religion, it's science."

He looked around, and they were all just looking at him, like they expected him to elaborate. So he continued, first pointing to Jackie.

"That lighter?" he asked. "That you used to start the campfire? Science." He then turned to Ryan. "That book you hold in your hands? Science. Gutenberg's movable-type press. The first book he printed *was* the bible, in fact. And not to mention the flashlight you're using to read it with." He then looked around at all of them.

"All our backpacks?—"

—he then pointed off into the trees—

"—even those barrels? And the raft we're gonna build—"

—he returned his hands to his lap—

"—Science." He then shrugged. "If not for science, we'd all still be livin' in caves, huntin' wild animals with rocks and spears, gatherin' fruit and nuts, tryin' to survive the weather, especially winter—and dyin' at the ripe-old age of thirty."

"That's all fine and dandy, but I think it misses the point."

It was Nick who spoke now, and they all turned to him as he was tugging off his shoes in preparation for bed.

"Ryan was talking about succeeding in life by being a good person, doing the right thing. And by trusting in God. Right?"

"That's right," Ryan said, glad to have someone else on board to back him up. "Like I said, religion—"

—he held up the bible, then down again—

"—and spirituality. Pursuing a personal relationship with the Divine."

"Okay, but Chaz is talking about our *quality* of life, through scientific discoveries, or, basically, advances in technology—all of which has improved human life for centuries, and continues to improve life for everyone, right?"

He looked over to Chaz then, who nodded in agreement.

"But say we all went to church, and read the bible, and tried to be good, as Ryan does. And say science enables us to easily start a campfire out here in the woods, and to have flashlights, and backpacks, and to build a raft, or any of the nice things we enjoy in modern civilization. Does any of that make any one of us more successful than the others?"

There was silence for a moment, as they all looked around at each other, but nobody could answer. Nick had a pretty good point.

"So you're both wrong, because neither science or religion will necessarily make any one of us more *successful* than the others, assuming we all start out equal, read the same bible, and have access to the same technology."

"Okay, I'll bite," Chaz said. "So what's *your* answer? What to *you* think the key to success in life is?"

"Power."

"Power?" Chaz said.

Nick then stood, rising above the rest of his reclined friends, the fire throwing undulating red and yellow glows and black shadows over his hulking figure in the night.

He stepped over to Chaz, and looked down at him.

"If I were to beat the living shit outta you right now, and take all your stuff, what could you do to stop me?"

The others whistled and wooed at the threat.

"Nothing, I guess." Chaz said in a small, nervous voice.

"That's right. Nothing."

He then turned to Ryan.

"And how about you? Your bible gonna stop me from kicking your ass, and taking your stuff?"

Ryan just looked quietly down and away, not wanting to answer.

"That's what I thought."

Turning, Nick returned to his bedroll and plopped down.

"Power. Strength. You gotta force your way, take what you want, stand up for yourself—or just be a weak little victim." He shrugged. "Survival of the fittest."

"That's your ol' man talking," Jackie said. "And we all know he's a power-freak."

Agreement echoed around the fire.

"Maybe so, but I think he's right. Seems to work for *him*. He gets awards at work all the time, and raises and bonuses. Officer of the year, the most citations, shit like that. And now he's even up for a promotion."

"So in other words, to be successful, you gotta be an asshole? A bully?" Ryan challenged.

"Hey, watch it," Nick warned, pointing a threatening finger at Ryan. "That's my ol' man you're talkin' about...he may take some of his stress out on me and mom once in a while, but he's still my dad."

"Sorry," Ryan said sheepishly.

But then Nick shrugged. "But yeah, maybe you're right, too. Maybe ya gotta be an asshole, or a bully. But then again, it's not just assholes, or bullies, or cops, that win by using strength or power. It's kings. Heroes. Politicians. Athletes. Corporate CEOs—"

—he looked at Ryan, gestured to his bible—

"—the Pharaoh. King of Egypt. Had all those slaves— "

—then he looked back at Chaz—

"—the *scientists* that made the atomic bomb that killed thousands of people…and chemical weapons—"

—then he pointed into the woods in the direction of the distant lumber yard—

"—that security guard, with the gun, and that big dog—"

—he returned his hands to his lap—

"—even my dad, when he's workin' the beat—"

—the others glanced quickly at each other, the unspoken truth shared silently between them—

"—they all have *power*, and they all use it to their own advantage. Power over others. Power over companies, over towns, even over entire *nations*. That guard back there had power over us, so we were helpless to do anything but to run and hide from him. So it's not just assholes, it's *everyone*."

Then he shrugged at the sheer simplicity of it all, and continued:

"I say, you wanna be more successful in life, the key is power. Strength. Brute force. No such thing as a free lunch.

Everyone's out for themselves, so ya gotta beat 'em all at the game, or be the loser. Like I said, survival of the fittest."

Looking around at all of them, he continued: "Like in our case, either I kick all your asses and take your stuff—making me the most successful—or you all gang up on me, kick my ass, and take my stuff, split it between you. And the leader of your little group—whoever has the most power among you—would then be the most successful of all of us, and on down the line to me, who would be least successful."

He then looked mischievously around the group, and took on a tone of arrogance: "Of course, that'd never happen, cuz I'd kick all your asses before you had a chance to do *shit* to me."

They all laughed and chided, Chaz throwing a tuft of plucked grass at him, which he ducked, grinning.

But then silence ensued, while they all contemplated Nick's point. It was difficult to disagree with it.

Then Jackie suddenly spoke up: "You may be right Nick, but there's one factor you're not considering."

They all looked at him, waiting.

"Yeah, what's that?" Nick responded.

"Luck."

"Luck?" Nick echoed. "What do you mean, luck?"

"You know, like being in the right place, at the right time. That stroke of luck that comes outta nowhere, like a bolt of lightening, and changes everything. Some people call it serendipity. Like the guy who invented the Slinky. He was a navy engineer, trying to design a spring that could be used to stabilize the sensitive instruments on ships while at sea. He accidentally knocked one of his prototypes off the table, and watched it "slink" to the floor, and that gave him the idea for the Slinky. Ended up selling millions."

"Really?" Chaz remarked. "I didn't know that!"

The others agreed, that was news to them.

"Or like, a musician just happens to run into a bigwig from a recording studio in a bar, and they hit it off, and gets a recording contract and gets rich and famous...sorta like Harrison Ford—you know, Han Solo in Star Wars?—he met director George Lucas when he was installing cabinets in Lucas's house. Lucas liked him, and the rest is history."

"No way! Really?" Nick said, excited. He was a big fan of Star Wars and especially liked Han Solo (though his favorite was, secretly, Princess Leia).

"Or like Steve Perry, the singer for Journey. He got lucky, just happened to be born with one of the most amazing voices in rock 'n roll history. Or like someone winning the lottery. Pure luck. Happen to buy a ticket one day at the gas station, with your gas and a soda—and BAM! You're a multi-millionaire, and everything changes. Or like, a guy gets on a plane for a business trip, and happens to sit next to a woman, a total stranger, and they get to talking. They end up falling in love, and get married. You can't plan that shit. It's just pure, dumb luck. And I think that's the key to success in life—if you can call it a *key*—luck. That's it. I don't think there's any rhyme or reason to things that happens in the world—"

—and then turned to Ryan—

"—not even Divine intervention—"

—he looked at Chaz—

"—and everything that happens can't be calculated, or confined to the physical laws of science—"

—he then looked at Nick—

"—and you can't force *everything* to happen, no matter how much power you think you have—"

"—it's all just random, blind luck. And there's nothing any of us can do about it, either—you either got luck, or you don't. Highly successful people are just *luckier* than the rest of us, that's all."

He smiled then, his silver tooth glinting dimly in the firelight—because he was well aware that he, himself, was pretty lucky, and he hoped that luck would bring success in his own future.

They were all nodding and contemplating this when suddenly a voice emanated from the woods behind them.

"You're all wrong!" It was a girl's voice, and, startled, they all jerked their heads toward the direction from which it came, Ryan pointing his flashlight.

To their astonishment, from the direction of the road, a young girl stepped from the woods and started walking toward them. She wore jeans, sneakers, and a long white tee shirt, untucked. Mounds of blonde hair bounced on her shoulders as she walked. As she neared, the glow cast by Ryan's flashlight revealed her to be about their age, maybe a tad older—and rather tomboyish.

"It's love," she said, matter-of-factly, as she plopped down on the ground between Ryan and Jackie and crossed her legs, then turned and smiled at Jackie.

Stunned, the boys all glanced around at each other, not believing what was happening, not knowing what to do.

"Um...who are *you?*" Nick finally ventured.

"Casey," she again said matter-of-factly. As she turned and looked around at the group, Ryan's flashlight illuminated the side of her face, which sported a large bruise. Seeing this, the boys all looked around at each other, wide-eyed. Then, when she turned back toward Ryan, they saw that her nose had been bleeding a little too, but seemed to be dried now, just a small, dark red circle under her nostril, and a few dried feathers of blood nearby on her cheek, as if she'd been wiping it away.

"Jeez, what the hell happened to you?" Ryan asked, unable to contain himself. "Somebody hit you?"

"Actually, it's Casandra, but I go by Casey," she said, seemingly ignoring Ryan's question. "Only my stepdad calls me Casandra, and I *hate* it. I hate *him*. But everyone else calls me Casey. I like that name a lot better. And it's Casey *Wells*, after my *real* dad, not *Sanders*, after my mom's new piece-uh-shit husband...even though that's supposed to be my legal name now."

"Did your stepdad do that to you?" Jackie pushed the issue, motioning toward her face.

She looked down, looking ashamed, but didn't answer.

They all looked around at each other again, nobody knowing what to say or do. Jackie shrugged, letting it go.

"Where you from?" he asked, changing subject. "And how'd you get all the way out here?"

"I live with my mom in town. Neighborhood called Valley View, on the northwest side, off Sunset and Westcreek."

"That's up just a few miles north of me," Ryan said. "I live near Town Square."

"So that'd be east of the county road, right?" Jackie asked her, twitching his chin in that direction. "Way over on the other side of those woods somewhere?"

"Yes. Way over on the other side of the woods somewhere," she confirmed, nodding.

"That's pretty far...how'd you end up here?" Chaz asked.

"Mom wasn't home today, she was working. She's *always* working, says we need the money, and she makes good tips at the pub. So I was home alone with Jake—he *was* just her boyfriend, which wasn't so bad, wasn't around all the time, but they got married last month, and it's been hell ever since he moved in. So he's her husband now, my stepdad, a real asshole, *God* I hate him, I don't know what mom sees in him, 'cept he helps pay the bills I guess—and he was drinking (of course), and ordering me around doing chores. Finally I got fed up and told him to go to hell, he's not my dad."

"Good for you!" Nick cheered, and all the boys concurred, praising her and chuckling at her audacity.

That's when he..." she trailed off, looking down, then looked up and resumed: "...well, you know. Then he sent me to bed without dinner. Then later, when he opened the door to check on me, I was in bed, faking that I was asleep. When he closed the door, I got up, got dressed, and climbed out my bedroom window. Ran across the street and into the woods, then just kept walking. Anywhere, I didn't care…*anything* to get away from him, away from…" she trailed off again, looking down at her hands.

"And you walked from way over there all the way *here?*" Jackie asked her, incredulous.

She shrugged. "Guess so. I walked for hours, didn't really know how far I'd gone, or where I even *was*. Then, when I came out on the road back there, I smelled food cooking, and followed the smell across the road and into the woods on this side, and saw you guys back here eating around the campfire."

"So you'r saying you've been spying on us this whole time?" Chaz accused.

Again, she looked down, ashamed.

"Sorry. But I was real hungry."

With this, Nick turned and began rummaging through his backpack. Soon he produced the hotdogs and buns. "We got some left over, if you want 'em."

"Hey—you think we should be helping her?" Ryan objected. "She's a runaway. We'll get in trouble, won't we?"

"And what the fuck are *we*, dumbass?" Nick responded.

The others laughed at this.

"Well…with *us* it's different," Ryan continued. "Our parents *know* we're out, they just don't know *where*—"

—he turned to Casey to explain—

"—our parents think we went fishing all day, and then went to the carnival this evening, and that we're all staying at my house for the weekend, because I live down the street from Grande Festival Plaza—"

"—where the carnival is," Nick added—

"—Ryan's parents are out of town, so they don't know we're not really there," Chaz explained—

"—so worst that could happen to *us*," Ryan finished, "is we get grounded when we get back, or a simple hidin', something like that—*if* our parents even find out what we *really* did all weekend."

—he then looked from her to the group, pointing a thumb in her direction—

"—but *she* really ran away, and her parent's don't—"

"Parent. Just my mom," she corrected. "That asshole isn't my dad. Never will be, as far as I'm concerned."

"Okay, so her mom doesn't even know she's gone—"

—he turned back to her—

"—I mean, how old are you, anyway? Eleven? Twelve?"

"I'll be thirteen next month," she answered proudly.

"Okay, she's almost thirteen—"

—he turned back to the others—

"—so she may be almost a teenager, but she's still a minor, and a runaway. Shit like that can get her, or her mom, or even *us*, arrested. Or they could take her away, put her in a foster home or something. All kinds of serious shit can go down—and we'll all be right in the middle of it, in serious trouble right along with her. And that's a lot worse than just some kids—*boys*, mind you, not *girls*, which would be *way* different—lying to their folks and spending the weekend rafting."

At this, Casey's eyes lit up. "You guys are *rafting*? How cool!" She started looking around their small camp, and into the outskirts of the woods. "Where's your raft? Can I see it?"

"We haven't built it yet," Chaz said. "We're gonna build it tomorrow morning, then float it down the creek. Stuff to build it's sitting down there at the edge of the woods, by that little clearing before the bridge."

"Great! I can't wait!" Casey exclaimed.

"Wait, wait, wait," Ryan said, holding his hands out, becoming annoyed now. "You aren't going with us." He then looked around at the guys. "She's not going with us, right?"

Nick turned the stick he was working on around and handed the end of it to the girl. A hot dog was stuck on the other end, and she held it over the fire.

"Thanks!" she said, smiling.

Looking at Ryan, Nick shrugged. "I don't see why not. You're just being paranoid. If nothing else, she can help us build the raft."

"Well, we don't have any extra tools for her," Chaz said. "But she could help in other ways. Holding the boards while we nail them together. Carry supplies. You know, a gopher."

"Gopher?" she asked. "What's a gopher?"

"Just a helper," Chaz explained. "You know: go-fer this, go-fer that..."

The others chuckled at this around the fire.

"Ah, I see. Okay, I'll be the gopher!" she exclaimed, smiling eagerly at the prospect.

Ryan sighed heavily and looked up at the night sky, exasperated.

"Sheee's not go-iiiing," he sang quietly to the stars.

The others watched in silent awe as this pretty young blond-haired girl, bathed in the golden glow of the campfire like a little angel, watched her hotdog intently, turning it slowly on the stick as it began to sizzle and pop.

"So, love?" Jackie asked, remembering what she'd said during the spectacle of her grand entrance.

She looked up, a surprised smile on her face. "What did you call me?"

Smiling at the misunderstanding, he shook his head. "I mean when you first showed up, when we were talkin' about the key to success in life, and you said we were all wrong, that it's love."

Her smile waned, and she looked almost disappointed. "Oh. That's right. Love. Love makes the world go 'round. That's what mom says anyway. And I think so too. Love is what makes life worth living."

Then her smile returned, and Jackie smiled back, and the two locked eyes warmly for a moment.

Then she continued: "So you all might think that religion and spirituality, or science and technology, or strength and power— "

—she looked from one boy to the next as she spoke—

"—or even luck—"

—with that, she returned her gaze to Jackie—

"—is the key to success in life. But what's any of it worth, without love? That special someone to share it all with? Without love, no amount of success would be worth the effort, seems to me." She shrugged. "I mean, without love, why bother? You might be *successful*, sure—but there's *no way* you'd be happy."

The boys all looked at each other, unable to refute this.

"Here," Nick said, handing her a hotdog bun.

Taking the bun, she pulled her stick forward, wrapped the bun around the cooked dog, slipped it off the stick with a short sizzle, then began eating voraciously as they all watched, dumbfounded.

When she finished, Nick began introducing everyone around the fire.

"By the way, I'm Nick," he started. Then, pointing around to his right, that's Chaz, Ryan, and Jackie.

"Jackie? Isn't that a girl's name?" she said, teasing.

"Jackson," he responded. My name's really Jackson, but everyone calls me Jackie. Sorta like how your real name is Cassandra, but you go by Casey—which can also be a boy's name. Fits you good, though," he finished with a nod of approval and a smile.

"Jackie...I like it! And by the way, has anyone ever told you you've got an amazing smile?" she asked, smiling back.

"All the time, actually," he said, still smiling. He felt himself blush at the compliment, and suddenly felt all warm and fuzzy inside...he was starting to like this strange, pretty girl, just a little...

Suddenly Nick spoke up, apparently wanting to horn in on their little moment and capture Casey's attention for himself:

"Just like I'm Nicholas, but go by Nick," he said, pointing to himself. Then he pointed over to Chaz, "And he's Charles, but goes by Chaz—"

"—HEY!" Chaz protested, but Nick ignored him, instead pointing to Ryan—

"—and Ryan is…well, just Ryan I guess, whatever—"

—at this, Ryan held his both hands up in wide-eyed bewilderment, like WTF?—

—and then Nick just sort of trailed off, before looking back at Casey and grinning, face flushed.

During the introductions, Casey had followed Nick's gestures and nodded at each boy, and when he was finished, she looked at Nick with an appreciative smile, but then turned back to Jackie, widening her smile.

"I think they're *all* cool names," she said, smiling then turning to Jackie. "*Especially* Jackie."

The two again locked eyes, quietly smiling at each other.

Seeing the obvious, Nick let go an audible sigh, his face collapsing into disappointment, and he turned away and started straightening his bedroll, preparing to lie down.

Soon they all bedded down. Turning back to Casey, Nick offered to share his bedroll with her, but she declined, said she'd be alright sleeping on a small patch of grass—which happened to be right next to Jackie, to Nick's chagrin.

"Suit yourself," he said flippantly while rolling roughly away, his back to the group.

Ryan, finally too exhausted to keep arguing about the girl sticking around, was the first to fall asleep.

The rest followed.

Sometime in the middle of the night, Casey quietly rolled

over and cuddled against Jackie, pressing herself to his back.

And Jackie didn't mind.

Not one bit.

•

The next morning, Ryan ceased his objections to Casey going with them, outvoted as he was by his friends. He still didn't like the idea, but he also didn't want to ruin the day for everyone, himself included—so for now he'd decided to keep his thoughts to himself.

Being Saturday, they knew the construction company was closed for the weekend, and nobody would be in the lumber yard (at least as long as the security guard didn't come out of the building—and it would probably be way too hot outside to worry about that). And besides, the construction building was clear over on the other side of the creek, hundreds of feet away, with plenty of trees, shrubs, and weeds between here and there, so they should be able to work on the raft in peace, nobody the wiser.

So they moved the wood and barrels out to a clearing next to the creek, which was also far enough away from the road that even if a car or truck did come along—which they thought was doubtful, this far out in the boonies—they wouldn't be all that visible from the road. Worse case, a quick stash of the tools in the weeds and dash to the woods would prevent any unwelcome intrusions.

Once everything was moved, they all stood in a circle, taking a breather, wiping their arms across their foreheads. Even though it was still morning, they were already sweating heavily in the stifling heat and humidity.

After a minute, Jackie rousted everyone from their break. "Miller Time," he announced, taking a bow and gesturing toward Chaz, as was their custom. Over time, it had become their way of indicating it was time to let Chaz take over the operation, whatever it may be.

And with that, construction commenced.

Chaz had already sketched out the raft, and, blueprint in hand, began walking briskly about, instructing the others what to do.

Nick manned the saw and tape measure, and began measuring and cutting boards to Chaz's specifications, using a somewhat flat, knee-height boulder as a cutting bench.

Jackie commandeered one of the hammers, and, as it turns out, Casey was pretty deft at swinging a hammer too, to all the boys' surprise (and, secretly, admiration).

So Ryan and Chaz helped hold the boards in place while Jackie and Casey hammered the nails in.

First, using some of the shorter lengths of two-by-fours, they built four rectangles—or "saddles," as Chaz called them—each just the right size to fit snuggly onto an overturned barrel, nesting just far enough that the barrels couldn't slide all the way through. These they lashed onto each of the barrels using the nylon rope that Jackie brought, the rest of them pulling it as tight as they could before Chaz secured it using some kind of sailor's knot that baffled the rest of them as he looped and yanked, looped and yanked.

Once all four barrels were "saddled," they built an outer

frame using the longer two-by-fours, nailing it to the sides of the four smaller saddles, stitching the shorter pieces together with a small patch nailed inside, straddling the seams where needed.

Once the outer frame was complete, they ran a strut down the center, front to back, then built the deck on top by nailing a patchwork of one-by-four boards across the frame and center strut.

As the morning wore on it quickly heated up, the humidity even worse than it was the day before. They all began to sweat profusely, and all the boys except Nick peeled their shirts, piling them in the grass off to the side. Nick left his on, apparently self-conscious about his size when around Casey.

And speaking of Casey, soon the boys were all stealing glances at her—especially Nick, who had seemed particularly smitten with her ever since she showed up the night before— not only admiring her handiwork, but her good looks—her gorgeous blonde hair, her glowing blue eyes—now that they could actually see her in the sunlight, instead of shrouded in darkness and shadows around the campfire. Plus, the dried blood under her nose was gone now, and the bruise on her face had faded considerably.

But aside from all that, they had also noticed, for the first time, her tiny budding breasts—which her white tee-shirt, dampened with sweat, clung to occasionally.

After a series of covert, wide-eyed glances at one another, soon they were all well aware of the unexpected sideshow, which seemed to motivate them all to work at a feverish pace, an unspoken (maybe even subconscious?) attempt to outdo each other in the girl's presence.

But Casey never seemed to notice the silent distraction she was causing, just kept working alongside them, focused on getting the raft finished.

A few hours later, they all stood, streaming with sweat and covered in dirt, looking at an eight-foot by eight-foot wooden raft, standing nearly two feet high atop the four overturned barrels.

Turns out, the project not only went smoothly, but much faster than any of them had anticipated: they actually finished before noon!

Lifting one leg, Ryan pushed on the corner of the raft with his foot, shoving it hard. It didn't budge.

"Seems awful heavy," he said. "You sure it'll float, with all of us on it?" With that, he shot a sideways glance at Nick.

"Hey, fuck you, okay?" Nick said, grinning. "I saw that!"

This summoned a chorus of chuckles from the others.

Jackie looked at Chaz. "Yeah, you sure it'll float?"

Chaz shrugged. "Sure. As long as the total weight of the raft is less than the total weight of the water it displaces, then it'll float."

They all looked at each other wide-eyed, impressed.

"So with four fifty-five gallon barrels, that's two-hundred and twenty gallons of water. I'd estimate about two-thirds of the barrels would have to submerge before the deck even touches the surface of the creek. So that's roughly one-hundred and fifty gallons...and at eight-point-five pounds per gallon—"

—yanking a mechanical pencil from his shirt pocket, he slapped the now mangled blueprint down on the deck of the raft and did some quick math—

"—that's a total of twelve hundred and seventy-five pounds she'll carry before the deck goes under."

The others again looked around at each other, this time nodding as if they agreed with Chaz's speedy math (the reality is, they had no clue, and had to trust him).

"Now, I weigh about seventy-five pounds," Chaz said as he jotted the number down. Ryan?"

"About ninety."

"Jackie?"

"About a hundred, I think."

Chaz wrote the corresponding numbers down in a neat column on the pad.

Then they all looked at Nick.

"One-twenty," he said with a straight face.

They just glared at him.

He threw his hands out. "What?"

"C'mon, Nick, we all know you weigh more than that," Jackie prodded.

"Okay, one-thirty."

They continued staring at him.

He sighed, relenting, and said in a meek voice, "Alright, one thirty-five…and that's the God's-honest truth, okay?"

"You sure?" Jackie said, squinting at him skeptically.

"Yes, I'm sure. They weighed me at the doctor's office just last week during my checkup, so I know it's right, no matter what y'all think. Damn—you guys are brutal!"

"And I weigh about eighty-five," Casey chimed in.

"Except you're not going," Ryan said under his breath.

"She's going! Get over it!" Nick hollered back at him, surprisingly angry.

"Alright, alright, keep your panties on, will ya?…sheesh!" Ryan conceded, hands in the air in a calming gesture.

They were all looking at Nick now, surprised at his angry outburst. Cheeks flushed, he smiled sheepishly at Casey.

"That's right, I'm going!" Casey asserted, matter-of-factly. "Besides, I helped build the raft—so damn straight I'm going!" Then, looking over at Chaz: "And by the way, awesome design work, Charles. Brilliant, you ask me."

"Don't call me that!" he blurted back, his eyebrows furrowed above his glasses as he pointed at her with his mechanical pencil. "It's *Chaz!*"

"Sorrr-rrie!" she apologized, wide-eyed. "Chaz, then. Nice work, Chaz."

"Thanks," he said rather sheepishly, dropping the threatening pencil, torn between the compliment and the perceived insult. "Just don't call me Charles, okay?"

"You got it!" She nodded in agreement, before turning, walking over to Jackie, and looping arms with him. She looked back at the others.

"I'm going," she said, matter-of-factly. Then, looking up at the side of Jackie's face, her face only inches away, she asked quietly, "Aren't I, Jackson?"

After only knowing the boys for one day, she had quickly

discerned who the leader of their little gang was.

Jackie smiled ear to ear, his silver tooth flashing over and over as he nodded in affirmation. "Yeah, you can go," he managed, even though he was obviously embarrassed. Then he looked around at the others. "I say she can go…"

With this, Ryan turned in a huff, and walked over to their pile of shirts, fetching his out and gruffly pulling it over his head, obviously irritated.

Nick just stared for a moment at Casey and Jackie standing there, arms interlocked and beaming, then he tore his eyes away and walked over to the raft, plopping dejectedly down on the edge of it.

Chaz didn't seem to care one way or the other, was back to his blueprint on the deck, reviewing his calculations and jotting notes.

"…under one condition," Jackie continued.

"Condition? What condition?" Casey asked, arm still locked with Jackie's.

"Look," Jackie started cautiously. "Ryan's right, we could all get into some serious trouble if you get caught with us, you being a runaway."

"That's right," Ryan confirmed confidently as he returned to the group, bolstered now that someone else was finally agreeing with him.

"I just won't get caught," Casey said, shrugging.

"That's right…because you're gonna turn yourself in."

At this, everyone turned and looked at Jackie.

Letting go of Jackie's arm, Casey took a quick step back.

"Turn myself in? Are you *crazy?*" she cried, incredulous.

"It's for your own good," Jackie said insistently. "And you know it. Your mom is gonna be goin' crazy, worried sick, wonderin' what happened to you. Before long, the cops will be lookin' for you too. Hell, they might even put a search party together, everybody in town will be on the hunt. And when they find you with us, we'll all be in some serious shit!"

Casey sighed and looked down, appearing to relent.

"Yeah, you're probably right...so what the hell am I supposed to do?"

Jackie shrugged. "Easy. You come rafting with us—we're gonna camp downstream tonight, then raft back up here tomorrow, then hike back to the barn—"

"Barn?" she interrupted, a confused look on her face.

"We meet at this old barn we found on an abandoned farm down the road there—"

—he twitched his chin toward the road—

"—toward the south end of town."

"It's the old Baker farm," Nick added.

"I've heard of that," Casey nodded in recognition.

"Anyway," Jackie continued, "It's sorta like our secret clubhouse. We meet there a lot during the summer. We stashed our bikes there on Friday, before rolling those barrels down here."

"Secret clubhouse! That sounds really cool!" she said, smiling now.

"So, you can go with us all the way down the creek and back, and hike with us all the way back to the barn, but only if you agree turn yourself in after that, when we all go home from there."

"She can go home with me," Nick said with authority.

Everyone turned to Nick.

"What?" Jackie asked, perplexed.

"My dad's a cop, remember? She can ride home with me on my bike, and we'll tell him she got lost in the woods, and I happened to run into her on my way home from Ryan's house, where he thinks we were staying after going to the carnival…I mean, if I really *did* ride my bike home from Ryan's, I'd take Homestretch out to the County Road, then head south to Edgewood…there's a good mile or two of woods along there, we can say that's where she was lost, and I saw her and gave her a ride to my house, hoping dad could help her get back home. He'll know exactly what to do."

They all nodded in agreement.

As much as any of them might hate to admit it, Nick's plan was absolutely brilliant.

"Good thinking, Nicko!" Chaz suddenly cheered, and the group voiced their agreement in a chorus of praise.

Nick's cheeks were again flushed, and he was looking at her, smiling, hoping she now considered him her hero.

Then Jackie turned from Nick to Casey.

"So, deal?"

She nodded. "Sounds good to me—especially since we can just say I was lost, and not really a runaway…shouldn't be in too much trouble then! And I really don't want my mom worrying. So, deal!"

She stuck her hand out, and Jackie shook it, one big lurching shake, then they let go—but she continued to smile at him, eyes twinkling, face flushing...

Again embarrassed, he finally made himself look away, smiling sheepishly. Then everyone turned back to Chaz, who turned his attention back to his rumpled and dirty blueprint.

"Okay, so we add Casey's eight-five pounds..."

He gashed a quick line below the rough column of numbers and added them quickly, jotting the total down faster than any of them could have, even if they used a calculator.

"See?" he said, holding the sheet up for all to see. "That's only four hundred and eighty-five pounds. Then of course, there's the wood frame and deck, and our backpacks, and any other supplies we take onboard, but that should only be a few hundred pounds at the most. So we'll be way under the max load of twelve hundred or so."

He looked up at the group. "She'll float, piece-uh-cake."

"Okay, so she'll float," Jackie said. "But what about oars? How we gonna steer it?"

"Good question, and I've already got it figured out," Chaz replied, holding one index finger in the air.

Folding the paper and shoving it into his shirt pocket, he jumped up and walked over to the few boards that remained, laying in the grass next to the raft. Picking out two of the longer one-by-fours, he marked each quickly in two spots with his pencil, then had Nick cut them out. The result was two notches roughly six inches long in opposite sides of the board, about eighteen inches apart.

Chaz took one from Nick and, holding it up in front of the others, he demonstrated how the notches made the boards easy to grip, one hand at each notch.

"So there's our oars," he said, tossing it onto the deck of the raft, and Nick tossing the other along with it.

The others nodded in agreement.

Problem solved.

After a quick water break, Jackie and Chaz retrieved their shirts and pulled them on. Then the boys repacked their backpacks, refilled their canteens from the creek, and loaded everything onto the raft.

Excited, the five of them stood shoulder-to-shoulder and pushed the raft slowly down the embankment—the barrels thrumming on the hard dirt and rocks like big timpani drums —and out onto the water.

As the front barrels began to float, lifting the rear barrels from the grass and weeds that lined the creek, they jumped aboard. One final shove from Nick with one of the oars, and they were afloat.

The creek was moving slowly, almost imperceptibly. They floated silently outward from the bank, then began drifting with the current, the raft bobbing gently. Nick manned an oar on one side, and Jackie on the other, and together they easily guided the raft out to the middle of the creek.

Then they all looked around at each other, smiling.

"See?" Chaz said. "Piece-uh-cake!"

•

Soon they calmed down and settled in to enjoy the peaceful

trek down the creek. It was warm, breezy, quiet, and serene, the thick woods that now enveloped the creek on both sides sliding slowly past like plush, dark green walls.

"Hey—got any of those reds left?" Chaz asked Jackie, holding his hand out in expectation.

"Sure," Jackie responded, turning to dig the pack out of his backpack. "But we gotta go easy—pack's gettin' empty, and they gotta last us two days."

"That's okay, I brought a pack too," Nick announced. "But they're lights, not reds. Dad switched a while back." He shrugged. "But still. It's a full pack, swiped it outta his carton on top of the fridge while he was passed out on the couch. He'll never notice they're missing."

An approving chorus of *good jobs* and *way-to-goes* went around the group.

Chaz and Jackie both took reds, while Ryan and Nick took lights. Then Nick offered his pack up to Casey, who was sitting across from him between Jackie and Chaz. He was smiling shyly again, face flush again.

But Casey shook her head, and waved him off. "No thanks. My mom doesn't smoke, so I never tried it, either. But my stepdad does, like a chimney. And It's *so* gross! *He's* so gross! So I'll *never* start smoking!"

Nick was obviously disappointed, but he masked it by shrugging it off. "Suit yourself," he muttered as he stuffed the pack back into his backpack.

Jackie sent the Zippo lighter around, and they all lit up.

It was quiet for a moment, as the boys smoked and relaxed,

the raft gliding smoothly down the creek, no parents, no school...nothing but the sounds of nature all around them.

Casey broke the silence.

"I'm getting hungry," she muttered, looking timidly around at them. "I hate to ask, specially since you fed me last night..."

"Oh, shit!" Nick exclaimed. "We shoulda ate lunch before we launched the raft! We coulda built a fire! I didn't even think of that!"

"Great...now what're we gonna do?" Ryan said futilely.

"Not to worry!" Chaz said triumphantly, gleaming at them through his thick glasses, again holding one index finger up in the air.

He then turned and began rummaging through his backpack, finally pulling out a small, flat blue metal box, and a green metal cylinder. He opened the metal lid on the box, exposing a round burner. Folding down two collapsable wire legs on each side, he set the tiny portable grill down on the deck, and began screwing the green propane cylinder into it from underneath.

"No way!" Jackie cried in disbelief. "You brought a little portable grill?"

Chaz just stopped and looked at him incredulously.

"Of course," he said, matter-of-factly. Then he shrugged. "You never know...what if we couldn't start a fire? Like if it was raining or something?" With that, he went back to screwing the propane cylinder into the bottom of the grill.

The others began looking at each other and chuckling. It was so absurd, but so like Chaz. And they were all glad he'd thought of it, even if it did seem a little overkill.

"Well, what else you got in there that might come in handy in an emergency, Mr. Paranoid Prepper?" Nick asked jokingly.

Chaz stopped and just stared at him over his glasses, obviously perturbed. "Okay, since you asked, smart ass," he said curtly. Then he turned and dug deep into his backpack. "First, I have…candles." He pulled a rubber-banded bundle of long white candles out of his pack and held them up in the air.

They all looked around at each other, grinning.

"Actually, that's a pretty good idea," Jackie said.

"Yes, it is," Chaz concurred matter-of-factly. Setting them aside on the raft, he then dug deep in his pack again, and pulled out another rubber-banded bundle of long, tubular things, similar the candles, only these were dark red, and looked to be made of paper or cardboard.

"Looks like dynamite!" Nick exclaimed.

Again, Chaz looked at him like he was an idiot.

"Flares," he corrected, still not amused.

"Cool!" Casey said, smiling.

"Where'd you get flares?" Ryan asked.

"They sell 'em in town at Hank's," Chaz explained. "In the camping section."

"Wait—don't you gotta be eighteen to buy flares? Jackie asked, perplexed.

"I think you do," Nick agreed.

"So how the hell did *you* manage to get 'em?" Jackie asked Chaz in a suspicious tone.

Everyone looked at Chaz, waiting for an explanation.

"Well, you're right, you gotta be eighteen to buy 'em, and Hank would've never sold 'em to me in a million years," Chaz said. "But I got 'em from Joey last summer—you know, his son that works there? We traded. I fixed his boombox for him—it was real easy, just had a loose connection inside, I re-soldered it in like ten seconds, wham bam thankya ma'am—and in exchange he snuck me some flares out back, while he was on a smoke break. Ever since then, I've been saving 'em for...*just such an emuh-jenseh—*"

—managing a decent southern drawl, he said the final words in a mock FogHorn LegHorn voice—

—and the rest of the group broke into a round of cheers around the raft:

No way!
Cool!
Good thinking!
Great trade!

Then Jackie prodded once more:

"What else you got in there, genius?"

Chaz shrugged. "A roll of duct tape...some waterproof matches..."

"Waterproof matches?" Casey interrupted. "There's actually such a thing as waterproof matches? How is that even possible?"

She looked around the group, amazed.

"I've heard of those, but never seen 'em," Nick said. "But yeah, you can buy 'em."

"Actually, I made these myself," Chaz said.

They all turned again to look at Chaz, dumbfounded.

He shrugged. "It's real easy. Just get those strike-anywhere matches—you know, with the wooden sticks—and dip the head in melted wax, like from the pool at the top of a candle that's been burning, and let it harden. Then, when you go to light the thing, the first strike scrapes off the wax, the second strike ignites the match head."

As the rest of them looked around at each other nodding at the common sense answer, Chaz plucked out a small roll of nylon line, with a red-and white ball dangling from it, and a small plastic container taped to the side.

"Fishing line, bobber, and pack of hooks," he said.

Again, they nodded in appreciation. You never know when you might need to fish for food, in an emergency.

Next he pulled a chrome-plated tool out of his pack, and held it up for them to see, a plier-looking gizmo with some some small gears visible inside it and a big winged handle on one side.

"Can opener."

"That's great, but what the hell we gonna need a can opener for?" Nick said sarcastically. He then looked obnoxiously around at the trees surrounding the raft on all sides, and threw up his hands. "It's not like there's any stores around here."

Another quick pluck, and Chaz held up a large can, clad in a red-and-white label. "Ravioli, of course," he said, donning a shit-eating grin. Then another pluck from his pack, with his other hand, and he held up another red-and-white labeled can, side-by-side with the first.

"And Spaghettios!"

Another round of cheers:

Spaghettios!
I LOVE Ravioli!
Awesome!
Yes!

After returning the cans and opener to his pack, he stuffed the candle, flares, and matches back in, too. Then, rummaging around in there a little more, he next produced a tiny black metal skillet, that couldn't've been more than six inches in diameter, with a fold-out handle. He snapped the handle out with a *click!*, then held it up for his friends to admire.

"How cute is *that?*" Casey exclaimed.

"Pretty cool," Nick agreed.

Chaz then turned and placed the tiny skillet on top of the equally tiny grill, then turned to the others and said, "Okay... whadowegot?"

"I've got a few hotdogs left, but not many," Nick said, dragging his own backpack around from behind him.

"Wait, I got just the thing," Jackie said, turning to his backpack. "In the cooler part," he explained as he zipped open a large pocket about halfway down on the back. From it he pulled a dripping blue plastic re-freezable ice pack, followed by a chilled package of hamburger, which he held up before them.

"Ta dah!"

"Alight!" Nick exclaimed, the others chiming in likewise around the raft.

Opening the top of his backpack, Jackie rummaged around and pulled out a large zip-lock bag with four hamburger buns and four slices of cheese inside. He held it up too, staring to celebrate, but then it hit him.

"Um...." He looked around at the others apologetically. "I only brought enough for four of us."

"That's okay, Casey can have mine," Nick offered valiantly, shrugging. "I'll have a hot dog."

"No, I'm not gonna eat your hamburger," Casey protested. "I'll be happy with another hot dog. You know what they say, beggars can't be choosers."

"Look, we still got hotdog buns, right?" Jackie interjected. "So we'll just split the hamburger and cheese five ways, and then one of us can use a hotdog bun instead of a hamburger bun. Okay?"

They all agreed to this, and Casey volunteered for the hotdog bun, grinning at Jackie all the while, again impressed. She thought he was the wisest of the boys, and a natural leader —and she really liked that.

Using his pocket rule, Chaz measured and divided the hamburger into five exactly equal portions (of course), formed them into patties, then started cooking them one at time in the tiny skillet.

Thin clouds of blue-white smoke drifted over the calm green-brown creek water and vanished into the surrounding woods, as five young friends and their homemade raft drifted further and further down Hope Creek, and the summer sun drifted further and further toward the mountains that buckled the western horizon.

•

"It'll just take a minute," Denise said as Andy gently pulled his black Mustang into her parent's driveway.

"You don't want me to come in?"

"You don't have to," she said. "I just gotta check on Ryan real quick, and then we're outta here." She opened her door, and as she got out of the car, her boyfriend turned the engine off and opened his own door.

"I'm coming with you."

"Okay. Whatever."

He followed her up the sidewalk and stood behind her on the porch, hands in pockets, scoping the neighborhood behind them while she fished her keys out of her purse and unlocked the front door.

The note was on the entryway table, next to the answering machine.

"That little fuck," she muttered.

"What?" he asked.

"He's not here," she said, turning and holding the note up. "Says he went fishing with—"

—she snatched the paper back down to read it again—

"—a friend of his named Jackie."

He shrugged. "So?"

"So?" she said incredulously, looking back up at him. "So he's *supposed* to be here, and I'm *supposed* to be checking up on him. But he's *not* here, so now what the fuck am I supposed to do? Mom and dad will be pissed! And we wasted our time coming all the way down here to check on the little turd!"

"Not to mention the gas," he said, nodding.

She looked down at the note again. "Wait—he wrote a phone number at the bottom, Jackie's house I guess."

"So call it. That way you can tell your parents you checked up on him, and he was fine."

With that, he started glancing up the stairs.

"Your bedroom upstairs?" he asked expectantly.

"They're all upstairs," she said, distracted, not catching his tone. Instead, she walked briskly over to the cordless phone on the end table in the living room. Reviewing the note again, she dialed the number.

Andy's attention was now focused on the hallway at the top of the stairs. Straining his neck, he looked this way and that, trying to identify Denise's bedroom.

"Hello, I'm sorry to bother you. This is Denise Harris, Ryan's sister? He left a note here saying he was with—"

—another quick glance at the paper—

"—Jackie? He wrote down this phone number, so I'm just calling to check on him. He's there? With Jackie?

Andy walked over, stepped up behind her, put his arms around her in a bear hug, and started nibbling her ear.

"I see. So they went fishing early this morning, and then they're going—"

—she pulled the phone from her ear and covered the mouthpiece—

"—stop it," she whispered, smiling and raising her shoulder to block his advances, then brought the phone back up—

"—going to the carnival tonight?"

He ran his hands across her belly and then upward, cupping her breasts, while kissing her on the back of her neck.

She leaned forward, smiling, hunching her shoulders, trying to concentrate on what the voice on the other end of the line was saying.

"I see...and do you know what time they'll be back from the carnival?"

Andy suddenly plucked the phone from her hand, pushed the END button with his thumb, and tossed it onto the couch.

"Andrew!" she protested. "I can't believe you did that! I need to check up on Ryan, like I promised my parents!"

"He's fine," he said as he kissed her. "They already told you," another kiss. "Stop worrying so much."

"But—"

"Look, I told you—I'm meeting the guys at Eddie's Eight Ball later, try to make my gas money back at the tables. So we don't got much time."

With that, he grabbed her by the hand and pulled her toward the stairs. Giggling, she looked back at the phone one last time, then set the note on the entryway table as they passed by it and hurried up the stairs.

•

They all looked above as the raft floated first under the Caboose Lane bridge, then under the railroad trestle.

"That was pretty cool," Casey said. "I've never seen the underside of a bridge that close-up before. Or a railroad trestle, either."

"Me neither," Ryan said.

The others concurred, it was a first for all of them.

As the trestle drifted away to the west, they turned their attention to the east, the miles of brown water stretching before them. The afternoon was waning, and a breeze was kicking up. It felt good.

"What's that?" Nick suddenly asked, peering toward the north shore, clutching the oar in his elbow, one hand shading his eyes, the other pointing at a large, dark object in the water, twenty or thirty feet from the raft.

Everyone turned and looked in the direction Nick pointed, also shading their eyes from the sun.

There were two round wooden posts protruding upward from the bank, then a wood deck of some sort stretching out into the creek, the entire length submerged.

"Looks like an old dock or pier," Jackie guessed.

"Yeah, a long time ago maybe," Chaz concurred. "But it's sunk now."

They silently gazed at the sunken, rotted structure, covered in algae and a host of underwater plants, as the raft floated gently by.

Then Jackie looked up at Chaz. "What time is it?"

"Almost six."

Jackie peered ahead at the creek, which was beginning a slow bend to the south.

"Looks like this is where the creek turns south," he told the others. "That means the canyon's probably not too far after that. And it's gettin' late. We should plan on findin' a place to stop and camp for the night. Don't wanna risk gettin' caught in the canyon."

"Why not?" Casey asked, curious.

"Rapids," the boys all said in unison.

"Oh," she said, nodding her head in understanding.

As they floated around the bend, everyone kept an eye out for a good stopping point. But the thick woods crowded right up to the creek's edge, offering little in the way of safe harbor.

Now that the grill had cooled, Chaz began packing it and the cooking supplies back into his backpack in preparation for landfall. Casey told the others she had to pee. Half in jest, Ryan prayed aloud for a safe place to land the raft, eyes closed, hands raised to the heavens. Nick continued quietly guiding the raft from behind with his oar, stealing whatever glances he could get away with at Casey as she lay glistening in the sun. Meanwhile, Jackie scouted the banks, turning back and forth, eyes shaded as he scoured both sides of the creek.

Then he saw it.

"There!" he shouted, pointing to what was now the east bank, the creek having turned to the south.

The rest of them looked, but nobody could see whatever it was that Jackie was pointing at.

"See?"

He was pointing on an oblique, ahead and to the left.

"Those branches hanging out over the water? I think that's a cove!"

Then Nick saw it. "I think you're right," he concurred. You can tell by how it gets darker back there than the woods around it."

He swung the oar around to the side of the raft, began guiding it in that direction.

"I don't see anything," Casey said.

"Okay, now I see it," Ryan announced. He pointed down low, showing Casey. "You can just see the opening, under those branches. See? It's not solid woods back in there, like the rest of the bank. Kinda dark and hollow-looking."

"Okay, I think I see it now," she said, nodding her head.

Chaz removed his glasses and squinted hard across the creek, then replaced them, shrugging. "I can't see shit," he said. "I just hope you guys are right."

As the raft approached the low-hanging branches, Jackie poked the other oar under them and lifted them up to make way. Creek water dripped from sodden leaves as they drifted underneath, splattering on the raft's deck like rain.

Soon they saw that Jackie was right, it was a cove, nearly concealed by the thick foliage.

Once they were inside, Jackie eased the branches back down behind them. The raft just fit! Then Jackie turned and peered ahead, analyzing the layout.

"Looks like it goes in about twenty feet or so," he said, pointing into the depths of the inlet. "Then it hooks to the left. Real narrow back there, though, I don't think we'll fit."

Digging the oar into the creek bed, Nick pushed the raft deeper into the cove, until they could hear the barrels scrapping on the dirt and rocks below, and the raft ground to a halt, the front edge bumping the bank where the inlet turned to the left.

"Perfect!" Jackie exclaimed, as they all began collecting their gear, strapping on their backpacks, and traversing the raft toward the bank.

Jackie jumped off first, then turned and took Casey's hand to steady her as she jumped off. A quick glance up at Nick—who was at the rear of the line—told him that his big friend had definitely noticed the gesture, and also that Casey held onto his hand just a moment longer than necessary once she was standing on the bank next to him. Nick immediately looked away, attempting to hide his resentment—but Jackie saw it.

Then, one by one, Ryan, Chaz, and Nick also leapt from the raft and onto the densely shrouded bank next to Jackie and Casey. Once everyone had deboarded, they turned together toward the woods.

The chorus of birdsong that permeated the solid green canopy above halted abruptly as the kids ventured into the woods, the five of them ducking under branches and stepping around thick tree trunks. Once beyond the tree line, they stood in silence, peering into the gloomy depths of the woods.

"Now what?" Ryan asked.

Jackie shrugged. "Now we just gotta find a clearing big enough to set up camp."

"Looks awful thick," Nick said, peering into the dense foliage. "And it's pretty dark back in there, too."

"Speaking of dark," Chaz added, looking at his watch while punching a series of buttons on the side, then looking back up at the others. "We have exactly two hours and two minutes before sunset."

"Sounds like plenty of time," Casey said casually.

"Yeah—*if* we can find a good spot pretty quick," Jackie cautioned.

They again stood silently for a moment, scouring the woods in all directions, looking for anything that looked like it might offer a promising direction in which to start.

As they searched in silence, the birdsong gradually started back up, once again enveloping them.

"I don't see shit," Chaz muttered.

"Me neither," Ryan concurred.

"Maybe we should just pick a direction and start walking that way, see if we find a good spot," Nick suggested.

"You guys see that row of pines way back there?" Jackie asked the group, pointing forward ahead of them. "Just past that big oak tree?"

With that, Casey squeezed in against Jackie, looking over his shoulder feigning trying to see what he was pointing at. Jackie didn't mind, he just smiled and acted casual, like nothing out of the ordinary was happening, all the while hoping Nick didn't notice.

After a moment of craning their necks and squinting into the woods, one by one the others finally concurred that they could see the row of pines Jackie was pointing out to them.

"Well, I see a gap in those pines, right in the middle there, and looks like there might be a clearing on the other side."

"Could be," Nick agreed.

Chaz shrugged. "Well, as usual I can't see that far, but I also don't see any other options…so we might as well try it."

They all agreed, so Jackie began working his way through the thick brush, and the others followed.

Once again, the birds fell silent, flittering quietly above, wary of these unwelcome intruders.

•

Once inside the row of pines, they stood looking at the charred rubble of what apparently used to be a small hut or shack—before it had burned to the ground, that is. Hard to tell what it had been, as not much remained. It had collapsed on itself as it burned, leaving only a couple of the corner sections of the wood-shingled roof unburned—though old and rotted.

But there was a large clearing around it, which would suffice nicely as their campsite for the night. And they might even be able to scrounge up some unburned wood from the old shack to use for firewood.

"How the hell'd a hut, or shed, or shack—whatever it use to be—get out here?" Nick asked, bewildered. "In the middle of the fuckin' woods?"

"Maybe it was built by a fur trader, like back before the town was here. Used the creek to travel, and built hisself a little hut out here to stay in while he was trapping," Jackie speculated.

"But why is it burned down?" Chaz asked, looking around at the surrounding trees. "Doesn't look like there was a forest fire or anything."

With this, they all glanced around at the trees, which were

lush and green, with no sign of any fire damage.

"Good question," Nick concurred.

"Somebody must've burned it down," Ryan said.

"Maybe it was the Indians, a long time ago," Casey reasoned. "If it was a fur trader's hut, maybe it was back when there were still Indians here, and maybe they didn't like the White Man invading their land, their woods, poaching their furs. So they burned his hut down—but were careful not to start a forest fire, because this is their hunting grounds." She shrugged, and looked around at the others for their opinion of her theory.

"Could be, but I doubt it's that old," Chaz surmised, picking up an unburned piece of wood from the edge of the rubble and holding it up for closer inspection. He then tossed it back to the ground. "Looks like the whole thing was made of wood, which probably would've rotted a lot more since then, if it was *that* old."

The group nodded at his theory, gazing down at the pile of burned rubble.

"Who knows," Nick muttered, shrugging.

"Well, anyway, doesn't really matter, this is our camp for the night," Jackie announced. Then, turning and waving his hand over the ground, "This area in front looks like the biggest clearing, so we'll set up here. Alls we need now is some firewood. We can prolly scrounge some usable wood from this old shack, and get any more we might need from the surrounding woods."

Dropping their backpacks in a circle in the center of the

front clearing, they went to work collecting wood, Nick and Ryan rummaging through the burned debris of the shack, the others splitting up and searching through the woods around the perimeter.

As Jackie entered the woods behind the burned shack, a flock of sparrows burst from a tree above him and silently dispersed into the surrounding treetops, not a peep. He stopped in his tracks, looking up, watching them them scatter in total silence.

"Weird," he whispered.

Still looking up at the treetops, he continued walking forward into the woods, and as he took another step suddenly there was nothing there, just a big hole in the ground, and he let out a startled yell as he fell into darkness.

•

Hearing Jackie's scream, the others dropped whatever wood they'd collected and came running.

Soon they were looking down into a shallow hole—maybe five or six feet deep, the bottom of which descended at a steep incline. Jackie lay at the bottom of the incline, covered in leaves, grass, and dirt.

"Are you okay?" Casey shouted down at him.

"Yeah, I'm okay," Jackie hollered up at them as he stood up and began brushing himself off. "Just startled me when I stepped, and there was nothing there and I fell. I never saw the hole, I was looking up at the trees, a flock of birds—sparrows, I think—and stepped right in it. Luckily, it's not a straight drop, I just rolled down this incline."

"Dude, you're lucky you didn't break a leg," Nick said. "Or worse, your neck."

"What's down there?" Chaz asked, noticing the darkness behind Jackie. "Can you see anything back in there?"

Jackie turned and peered into the shadows behind him for a moment, then looked back up and shrugged. "Not sure, it's too dark. But looks like a tunnel."

"I'll get my flashlight!" Chaz said excitedly, then turn and ran toward camp, where their backpacks were lying.

"Me too!"

"Great idea!"

As Jackie watched from below, his friend's faces—all except for Casey's—disappeared from around the hole.

"Somebody get mine, too!" he yelled.

"I'll get yours," Casey called down to him, smiling happily as she turned and disappeared.

•

"How far do you think it goes?" Ryan asked.

They stood together at the bottom of the hole, peering into the darkness of the tunnel, the four blue-white beams of their flashlights swinging all about but not revealing much, other than the nearly black dirt walls and floor, all of which were impregnated with stones and gnarled and dangling roots. It reeked of damp dirt and rock down there, the musky smell of mold, mildew, moss...

"It goes in the direction of the shack, or whatever it was that burned down," Jackie said.

"Cool! Like a secret tunnel from the shack to the woods?"

Casey asked, excited.

"Could be," Jackie said.

"Boy, that *would* be cool, wouldn't it?" Nick agreed, smiling at Casey. But Casey was squinting into the darkness ahead, leaning against Jackie, following the beam from his flashlight.

Meantime, Chaz was examining some of the roots that stuck out from the wall, the thicker ones cut off short and ragged, the thinner ones long and dangling like threadbare strings.

"Most of these roots are dead," he said, breaking one of them off in his hand, the wood dry and brittle. "Looks like this tunnel was dug a long time ago."

"Well, it does look like it might go to the shack," Jackie surmised, peering into the darkness. "Let's see if it does."

Is if on cue, they all began walking that way together, flashlight beams dancing around them as they went.

Before long the tunnel ended abruptly, and their flashlights revealed an opening above that apparently breached the floor of the burned-down shack—but it was completely covered in charred wood and other debris, sealing off access to the structure above.

"Steps," Chaz said, shining his light on a series of divots that were cut into the end of the tunnel, leading up to the opening. He turned to Casey. "Hold this," he said, shoving his flashlight into her hands. But, as he stepped toward the wall, a hollow clinking sound was heard around his feet, and he stopped, looking down.

They all shined their lights at his feet, and saw that Chaz

was standing among a collection of small bones which littered the ground around him.

"Bones?" he said, perplexed. He stooped and picked one up, then held it up in the glow of multiple flashlights. It was short, flat, and slightly curved, broken at both ends, tarnished and dirty.

"Are they human?" Casey asked nervously.

Chaz shrugged. "Don't know. They seem kinda small to be human—unless it's, like, little kids or something. I'd say probably more like some type of animals. But as old and broke up as they are, it's hard to tell *what* they are."

He tossed it on the ground with the others, the four flashlight beams following it. Jackie shone his light over the immediate area, looking at the bones, then slowly turned it down the tunnel, the way they'd come, but the rest of it was just plain dirt.

"They seem to be just here," he observed, returning his light to the smattering of bones lying about their feet. "Right below the opening to the shack."

"Almost like some animal uses this tunnel as its den," Nick suggested. "Drags its prey in here to eat it...then all that's left is bones. Maybe it hunts the woods around here."

"You know, maybe we should get the hell outta here," Ryan suggested, now sounding pretty scared. "Before *our* bones are added to this mess, by...who knows *what's* livin' down here."

"Nothin's livin' down here," Nick reassured him. "This end is boarded up— "

—he pointed to the opening above, covered with charred

rubble and thus impassable—

"—and the other end opens up into the woods—"

—he turned and pointed to the far end of the tunnel, where the waning sunlight glowed in the distance, then dropped his arm and shrugged—

"—and we've walked through the whole thing. It's just an empty tunnel."

"He's right," Jackie agreed, looking at Ryan, nodding. "They're ain't nothin' livin' down here, or we'da seen it by now. So just calm down, we'll be outta here soon anyway."

With that, Chaz turned and began carefully scaling the dirt wall, alternating his hands and feet into the roughly hewn divots, bits of dirt and pebbles tumbling down from them as he did so.

Once he could reach the floor of the shack, he reached up with one hand and shoved against the charred boards and debris that covered the hatch. After trying a few different spots, none of which even budged, he hopped back down to the floor, brushing the dirt from his hands.

"No go," he said, retrieving his flashlight from Casey. "Stuff's not gonna budge."

"Let me try," Nick said, stepping past the others and handing Chaz his flashlight. In just a couple of quick steps he was high enough to reach the opening—but, just like Chaz, he shoved as hard as he could against the rubble, trying multiple spots, before hopping down and concurring with Chaz that the hatch was, indeed, covered for good.

"Well, so much for that," Jackie said. "Nothin' down here to see, after all. Might as well head back to camp, and finish collecting firewood."

"Amen to that," Ryan agreed wholeheartedly.

"Yeah, and I'm gettin' hungry anyway," Casey added.

"Me too," Nick agreed.

Chaz handed Nick's flashlight back to him, then looked at his watch, pushing a series of buttons.

"We're down to an hour and twenty minutes before sunset," he reported.

"Okay, let's get a move on," Jackie said, turning to head back in the direction of the entrance in the woods. Casey walked with him, and then followed by Ryan and Nick, with Chaz falling in behind the group. The opening in the far end of the tunnel glowed softly with a lazy, golden sunlight, and even from such a distance, it was evident to all of them that evening was setting in.

•

Once they'd scampered back up the embankment at the opening of the tunnel, Casey turned to the others and said, "I gotta go."

"Go where?" Chaz said, confused.

"You know," she answered, twitching her head toward the woods. "To…the lady's room?"

"Ah," Chaz said, blushing.

"I gotta go too," Jackie added.

"Me too," said Nick.

"Okay, restroom break!" Jackie called out, and the four boys began trudging into the woods. But Casey didn't move.

"Um...I gotta go...number two." She was looking at the ground now, pushing a rock around with her toe, and looked to be blushing, though her hair dangled in front of her face, hiding it.

The boys stopped and turned back to her. Then Nick said with a sigh, "Me too..."

Then Ryan raised his hand, nodding in concurrence.

"Okay," Jackie said. "So we each head out in separate directions, find a private place to do our business, then meet back at the burned shack, and we'll make camp."

With a chorus of agreements, the boys all fanned out into the woods. Casey watched them go for a minute, then turned and headed off in the opposite direction of the others, to make sure she had plenty of privacy.

•

After a while, the boys met back at the rubble site, and were setting up camp and collecting wood for the fire, when Jackie realized Casey wasn't back yet.

"Where's Casey?" he asked, peering into the woods.

"Maybe girls take longer," Chaz suggested, shrugging.

"Or maybe she went further away for a little more privacy," Ryan offered.

"Maybe," Jackie agreed skeptically, then went back to stacking the firewood in the middle of the clearing.

Finally, once they'd collected enough firewood, Jackie again stopped and stood looking into the woods.

"She definitely shoulda been back by now," he said, growing concerned.

The others joined him, peering into the shadowy forest.

"You think she got lost?" Chaz wondered aloud.

"Maybe she ran away again," Ryan said sarcastically, prompting a quick elbowing from Nick.

"Think we should go look for her?" Nick asked Jackie, now concern rising in his voice, too.

Jackie nodded in confirmation. "Yeah, let's go," he said as Ryan sighed heavily.

With that, they trudged together into the woods, heading in the direction of the tunnel opening where they'd last seen her, and started calling her name.

Just as they reached the tunnel, they heard her answering their calls off in the distance. Within a few moments she reappeared from the woods, out of breath and noticeably dirty.

"We were worried," Jackie said.

"Yeah, where'ya been?" Nick asked, concerned.

"I found a cave!" Casey gasped, still out of breath. "Thought I'd check it out!"

"A cave?" Jackie repeated, incredulous, as the others chimed in with a chorus of astonished remarks.

"Where?" Chaz asked.

"Did you go in it?" Ryan inquired.

"Are you sure? I never heard of any caves out here," Nick said, skeptical.

"It's over there, around a bend—"

—she turned and pointed into the woods, then back—

"—I decided to go around the bend for more privacy, and when I finished and stood up, there it was, in the other side of the hill! I just went in a little ways though, it was too dark inside...definitely need a flashlight...but I thought I saw another opening—a BIG one—way in the back...I started toward it, but it got so dark I ended up tripping over a pretty big rock—"

—she raised a dirty arm, revealing a large bloody scrape on her elbow—

"—so I got outta there and came to get you guys. Who knows how deep it goes!"

With that, they eagerly hurried back to camp to retrieve their flashlights, then headed back into the woods toward the hill, Casey leading the way, everyone jabbering excitedly.

•

Once inside the cave, they stood shining their flashlights into the pitch-blackness beyond the massive hole that opened in the back wall like a giant throat. It was huge—at least eight feet in diameter—and even with all of them shining their lights into the blackness, they could see nothing, the light just faded away into the depths.

"Looks like a big tunnel," Nick observed. "But a lot bigger than that other one."

"So where do you think *this* one goes?" Ryan whispered, sounding somewhat nervous.

"Well, it sure doesn't look like it goes in the direction of the shack," Jackie said.

"I don't think we better go in this one," Casey warned, taking a step back. "It's awful big...and looks deep. We could get lost."

Nick stooped and picked up a rock. "Stand back," he announced.

The others stepped aside, and Nick heaved the rock into the darkness, while they all stood silently, listening.

They heard the rock land on the ground some distance away, then bounce a few times and roll to a stop..

But nothing more.

Nick shrugged. "Sounds level and dry. We should be able to go a little ways in…at least as far as that rock…it'll probably be okay."

"Alright, but you first," Ryan said.

"Sure." With that, Nick stepped to the front of the group, and ventured forward into the gaping mouth of the tunnel. The rest of them looked nervously around at each other, then Chaz turned and followed behind him.

"Hold my hand," Casey told Jackie, who turned and just looked at her. "So we don't get separated in there," she explained, pointing into the tunnel. "I mean, it's awful dark back in there."

Ryan heaved another impatient sigh, an obvious reminder that he never wanted the girl to go with them in the first place.

Finally, Jackie took Casey's outstretched hand and followed, pulling Casey through behind him.

Turning away, Ryan took one last look at the sunlit opening of the cave behind them—taking note that the sunlight was definitely fading as evening set in—then turned and shone his flashlight toward the tunnel, hesitating.

"Come on, Ryan!" Nick urged, stopping and shining his

light back toward his friend. Now in the tunnel, his voice echoed all around.

"Yeah, we don't got much time!" Chaz reminded, also turning and shining his light at Ryan as his voice echoed at a higher pitch.

Jackie and Casey stopped and turned too, waiting.

"Alright, alright, keep your panties on," Ryan muttered as he hesitantly ventured into the blackness of this new and uncharted tunnel.

•

Flashlights leading the way, the kids walked a short distance, looking for the rock Nick had thrown. Unfortunately, the tunnel was strewn with rocks, and there was no way to identify which one it was...so they stopped, shining their lights this way and that, trying to decide what to do.

Shrugging, Nick turned back to the others.

"It seems fi—"

—he stopped short, noticing Jackie and Casey holding hands, then turned quickly away to hide his jealousy, instead shining his light off into the darkness—

"—fine so far," he continued, lowering his voice to keep the echoing to a minimum. And then, without turning back around: "I think we should keep going."

" I *would* like to see how far it goes," Jackie agreed. He looked to Casey for her response, and she nodded in agreement.

"Okay", she said.

Chaz shrugged. "Fine by me."

Then the three of them turned to Ryan, shining their lights on his face. He looked a little scared.

"Ryan?" They all said in unison.

He sighed in resolution, knowing he was out-voted.

"Okay, as long as it seems safe," he said. "But if it starts getting dangerous, or anything weird happens, we get out."

"Of course," Jackie said, while the rest chimed in their agreement.

With that, Nick continued forward, followed by Jackie and Casey—still holding hands—then Chaz, who was looking down at his watch, pushing buttons with tiny beeps, and Ryan following the rest tentatively, nervously shining his flashlight all around.

They walked for quite a while, maybe twenty minutes or so, meandering this way and that with the sweeps and turns of the tunnel. Though they saw nothing unusual in this tunnel— it was very much like the other one, only bigger—they could tell they were traveling slightly downhill, because the semi-dirt walls gradually gave way to solid rock, and the temperature was dropping noticeably. The dampness also increased the further they went, and the wet, musty odor from the cave gradually dissipated, replaced with a slight sulfury smell, and…water?

"Smells sorta like a pond or lake," Chaz noted.

"Yeah, weird," Jackie concurred.

Suddenly, Nick stopped in front of the line, and Jackie and Casey bumped into him, then Chaz and Ryan bumped into them, like a collapsing accordion.

"Hey, why'd you—" Jackie began, but then he saw why. Releasing Casey's hand, he stepped up next to Nick and pointed his flashlight downward..

They were standing on a precipice, and here the tunnel dipped suddenly downward at a steep angle, eventually disappearing into an inky blackness below.

"Damn!" Chaz exclaimed, stepping up and shining his flashlight down the incline too.

"Holy shit," Ryan whispered, joining the others, all four flashlights now aimed down the deepening tunnel but revealing nothing but pitch-black abyss.

"Looks like this is the end of the tour, ladies and gentlemen," Nick announced in a mock tour guide voice, holding the end of his flashlight to his mouth like a microphone.

"Where does it go?" Ryan whispered, frightened at the prospect.

Nick suddenly turned to the others, shining his flashlight up under his face, making himself look shadowy and spooky.

"All the way down to *hell*," he said eerily, looking directly at Ryan.

As the others chuckled at this, Ryan just glared back.

Still chuckling, Nick turned back and aimed his light back down into the darkness. Then Chaz clamped his flashlight under one arm and started digging in his pocket, finally pulling out his compass. Shining his light on it, he turned it this way and that, watching the needle, then he frowned. Looking up now, he glanced around at the inside of the tunnel, as if getting his bearings, first pointing behind them, then to the right, apparently figuring out where the entrance was located in the back of the cave, and then the woods where they had started.

By now the rest of them were watching him, training their flashlights on him, wondering what he was doing, waiting for an explanation.

"Weird," he finally said, again pivoting in all directions, eyes glued to the face of the compass. "Based on where we started, at the cave around that bend in the side of the hill, and the general direction we've been walking, I would've swore this tunnel heads almost due south," he explained, finally looking up at the others. "But what's weird is, my compass—"

—he held it out under his flashlight, for them see—

"—just keeps spinning around, it won't settle on a direction. The needle should always point to magnetic north, but it's not...it's just spinning and oscillating, like it's caught in some kind of weird magnetic field or something."

The group watched as the needle on the compass spun quickly around in one direction, slowed, stopped, then spun around in the opposite direction, slowing and stopping again before repeating the strange gyration.

Seeing this, Jackie turned and looked behind them, tracing their journey in his mind the way Chaz had.

"I think you're right, Chaz, this tunnel should be heading south...your compass is just fucked up."

"And if *does* go south, then this part must go directly under Silver Hills," Chaz added.

"That can't be right," Nick disagreed. "Silver Hills is over on the other side of the creek, isn't it?"

"The *front* half is, yes," Chaz agreed. "But creek runs down the middle, basically dividing the hill. This tunnel goes under the *back* half—I bet we're under Black Woods."

"Black Woods, holy shit! If that's true, we need to get the hell outta here!" Ryan exclaimed, his voice echoing away into the depths below.

"Hang on a sec," Jackie said, raising his hand up to Ryan in a calming gesture. Then he turned to Chaz. "Are you sure? I mean, our camp ain't in Black Woods."

"No, it's not. But it's close. Once Hope Creek turns south—right before it enters the canyon—that's pretty much where Black Woods starts. And remember, we've been walking down this tunnel, heading south—meaning in the direction of Black Woods—for—"

—he shone his flashlight onto his watch—

"—wait, that's weird."

"What? Jackie asked, frowning at Chaz.

Chaz looked up. "Remember back when I checked the time and said we had an hour and twenty minutes before dark?"

They all nodded and agreed.

"Well, that had to be at least twenty minutes ago, right?"

Again they concurred, with Nick adding "At least, maybe even longer."

Light back to watch: "Well, my watch says it's only been like five minutes."

"So your battery's dyin', so what?" Nick suggested.

"No, I put a new battery in before I met you guys at the barn," he said while pushing a few buttons with tiny beeps.

"Secret clubhouse," Nick corrected, winking at Casey, then stealing a glance down, relieved to see that they were no longer holding hands.

"Maybe the same magnetic field that's messin' up your compass is messin' up your watch, too," Jackie offered.

"Could be," Chaz agreed, looking up and dropping his arm to his side. "Anyway, if we been walking south around twenty minutes now, maybe close to a half hour, that probably puts us really close to Black Woods—if not directly under it."

"Maybe this part of the tunnel—where it heads so steep downhill like that—is the beginning of Black Woods," Casey suggested.

"Hey—maybe this is one of the reasons they say Black Woods is haunted!" Nick said, excited now. "Or that there's a monster livin' in there somewhere! Because of this secret tunnel! Who knows what might be down there! Or what lives in these tunnels…like a monster?"

"And the weird magnetic field here—or whatever it is that's messing up my compass, and my watch, and maybe even any other electronic devices brought near this area—probably adds another unexplained element to all the mysterious stories," Chaz added.

"And on the other end of Black Woods, where Hope Creek comes out of the canyon, is Blackwater Swamp," Jackie added. "Maybe that's where this tunnel comes out, on the other side of the hill. Somewhere in the swamp."

"Maybe that's why it smells like pond water in here," Nick guessed. "Cuz this part of the tunnel goes down and the end comes out in Blackwater Swamp."

Jackie and Chaz both nodded at the possibility.

"And Blackwater Swamp is supposedly haunted too," Ryan said. "So maybe Nick and Chaz are right: the cave, these tunnels, the strange magnetic field in here, and anything that might be living or hiding in here, all tie into the stories…the hauntings…*the monster*."

"I bet they are," Nick agreed. "I wonder if anyone else knows about these tunnels?"

"Somebody must know," Jackie said. "I mean, the cave isn't very far from that shack, and especially from that other tunnel that runs from the shack to the woods."

"Maybe that's why someone burned it down," Chaz suggested. "To keep anyone from snooping around there, then wandering over here and finding *this* tunnel—the same way *we* did."

"You mean the way *I* did," Casey corrected, wanting the credit for the discovery.

"Whoever," Chaz responded flippantly. "The point is, *somebody* must know about all this…and thus the rumors, the stories, the tales that probably just kept growing taller and taller over time."

The rest of them nodded at the logic of this.

"Well, obviously, we can't go down there," Jackie said, pointing his light back down into the unseeable depths. "And even if we did, we'd never be able to get back out, at that steep angle—especially on solid, smooth, and probably damp rock like that. And 'sides, we really need to get back and get the campfire going before it gets dark."

Just then, a deep roar echoed up the tunnel from the depths, long and rumbling. They could actually *feel* it through their shoes, standing on the rock floor, while tiny bits of rock and dirt rained down on them from above, the kids looking up and around and shining their flashlights everywhere, trying to see what was happening.

But then as soon as it started, the rumbling faded away.

"Holy shit!" Chaz barked. "What was *that?*"

"Damn…I've never heard anything like that," Nick said quietly, as they all looked around at each other, eyes wide.

"Think it was the monster?" Casey asked nervously.

"That didn't sound like some *animal*, it sounded *evil*," Ryan whispered, peering back down into the tunnel. Then he looked around at the others, fear contorting his face. "Like *Satan himself*…maybe this place really *is* haunted!"

"That didn't sound like *any* kind of living creature," Jackie said rationally. "Sounded way too big. 'Less it was a dinosaur, an' there aren't any dinosaurs livin' around here, last I heard. But an animal? Even a monster or demon? I don't think so."

He then shone his light at the floor of the tunnel, moving it all around their feet.

"I don't know about you guys, but I could *feel* it…the ground itself was vibrating beneath us…like a tremor."

"Do we have tremors here?" Casey asked.

"I don't know…I don't remember any," Jackie shrugged.

"It was the devil," Ryan reiterated.

"Will you knock it off with the devil shit?" Nick said sternly, shining his light into Ryan's face.

"And besides, there's no such thing as the devil," Chaz said matter-of-factly.

Nick dropped his light from Ryan's face and turned his attention to Chaz, who was once again tinkering with his watch. Without looking up, he continued: "I'd say Jackie's onto something...it *did* feel like a tremor, or like these tunnels were shifting somehow."

"That's great," Nick sighed. "We're about get buried alive."

Just as Ryan turned to Chaz to refute his atheistic claim, Chaz let out an *oh shit!*, then looked up at the others, eyes wide, looking buggish through his thick glasses.

That stifled Ryan, while the rest of them turned their flashlights onto Chaz.

"I just realized: if we've been in this tunnel for twenty to thirty minutes, that means we have less than an hour before it gets dark—and it'll take us even longer to get back to camp!"

"You heard the man," Jackie responded, looking around at the others. "Gotta hustle! Assholes and elbows!"

With that, they turned and hurried back the way they had come, talking excitedly about where they thought the tunnel might go, and what monsters might be dwelling deep under Black Woods, and down in Blackwater Swamp—where they were now certain that the tunnel must re-emerge.

•

It was getting dark by the time they backtracked out of the

tunnel, through the woods, and back to the camp area; but between the salvageable wood from the burned-down shack, and the abundance of branches and deadwood available in the surrounding woods, they were able to build a fire in no time, and arrange their bedrolls around it just as full dark set in.

For dinner, it was Spaghettios and Ravioli all-round, heated right in the open cans over the fire then divvied out in metal camping plates and cups, with plastic spoons and forks, an odd assortment assembled from various supplies each of the four boys had brought along.

Famished from the long day, and from all the excitement over the cave tunnels they had found, they sat around the fire and ate silently.

Once they had finished, they hunkered down on their bedrolls, again Casey sharing one side of Jackie's.

Jackie broke out his smokes, and offered them around. "Last ones, boys. Enjoy them while you can."

Each of the boys took one, then Nick pulled his lights out of his backpack and shook the pack, peering inside, inspecting the contents.

"No worry, I have enough to get us back home," he said.

He again offered them up to Casey with a *you sure?* look on his face, and she again declined, waving her hand and wrinkling her nose at the prospect, and Nick shrugged and returned the pack to his backpack.

The boys smoked in silence, each of them staring into the fire, enjoying the mesmerizing symphony of crickets, frogs, and countless nocturnal creatures that permeated the woods around them. Casey leaned in against Jackie, then slid her hand into his. They interlocked fingers, both smiling in the glow of the campfire.

Seeing this, Nick sighed and sulked a little, but he was starting to get used to the reality. And, deep down inside, he really couldn't blame her. Jackie was good-looking, smart, charismatic, and a born leader. Nick was just a big lug. Nice guy, maybe—but what did he have to offer a girl like Casey?

Hot dogs?

He suddenly guffawed at the thought, but quickly stifled himself, looking sheepishly around to see if anyone had noticed. Nobody seemed to, everyone was off in their own little world.

He just smiled and shook his head. *What a loser...*

A few more quiet moments drifted by when suddenly Jackie sat up excitedly and looked around at the others.

"Hey—tonight's story night, remember?"

A chorus of *that's rights* and *oh yeahs* from the others.

"Story night?" Casey asked, perplexed.

Jackie turned to Casey to explain.

"Yeah, on Thursday nights, after we play our usual round of blackjack in the barn—"

"Secret clubhouse," Nick corrected.

"—yeah, our secret clubhouse," Jackie amended, "We tell scary stories, by candlelight."

"Well, they're not *always* scary stories," Ryan interjected. "Sometimes they're just weird or spooky, sad, or sometimes even funny."

"Yeah, but they're *usually* scary," Jackie said. "At least that's the whole point—that's why we tell 'em at night, in the darkness of the barn—"

—he glanced over at Nick—

"—I mean *clubhouse*—"

—then back to Casey—

"—by candlelight."

"Then we vote for the best story," Chaz added.

"Yeah," Jackie concurred. "But this week, since we were plannin' this rafting and camping trip, we decided to wait and tell our stories tonight—out here in the *real* woods, around this *real* campfire!"

"And, since this is the last weekend 'fore school starts back up, we decided tonight will be the *grand finale!*" Ryan exclaimed.

Again, an excited chorus of *yeahs* and *that's rights* echoed around the group.

"Cool. Can I play too? I like to make up stories, and I write little stories all the time. I could tell you guys a new one I came up with earlier this summer."

Jackie looked around at the others and shrugged.

"I don't see why not. How bout you guys?"

The others agreed, no problem.

"Okay, so who wants to start?" Jackie invited, looking expectantly around.

"I've got a pretty scary one," Ryan said softly, staring at the ground between himself and the campfire. He was always very timid with his storytelling, and it was very unusual for him to volunteer to go first.

Jackie nodded at him, impressed. "Ryan, my man…"

"Oooooh, the religious guy wants to tell scary story…this should be good!" Nick said in anticipation.

"I gotta here this!" Chaz chimed in.

With that, they all turned their attention to Ryan.

"I call this story…*IT.*"

The rest of them looked around at each other smiling and nodding, already liking the title, and anticipating the story, before turning back to Ryan, rapt:

"So there's this woman…she's a reporter, and she's been sent to this town to check on a possible story. The news station where she works has been running this series of stories on nuclear power plants, how dangerous they are and stuff, and they'd heard rumors that this one nuclear power station had mysteriously shut down, plunging the whole town into darkness, with no electricity. It sounded like a perfect addition to their series, so they sent her there in a company car. She drove all evening to get there, so she could be the first to break the story—but on the way into town, she got lost on the backroads up in the hills out on the edge of town, because it was storming real bad that night, raining like crazy, and the road she was taking was flooded over, so she tried to detour around and then she got stuck because there was a big tree laying across the road in front of her, that the wind had knocked down in the storm…and now there's something stalking her in the woods, some kind of monster…"

IT

by Ryan Harris

Jen jumped slightly when her car phone rang, the Pulsar II's backlit number pad casting its dim green light into the dark interior of her car from its base mounted on the console between the seats.

"Thank God," she whispered as she snatched it up and pressed it to her ear. She had abandoned all hope of using it in this storm—

"—Wait, she has a *car phone?*" Nick interrupted, a look of incredulity on his face.

The others mumbled in agreement to the protest.

"I said she's a reporter," Ryan said, almost indignant. "Reporters have car phones. Don't you guys watch TV?"

"Car phones are real expensive," Chaz said.

"The news station where she works bought it. It's a company car. That way their reporters can stay in touch when they're traveling. You know, call in the big stories, get the hot tips, stuff like that."

They all nodded at this, looking around at each other as if in consensus that it was an acceptable explanation.

"Now, like I was sayin', she answered the *car phone*—"

—"Hello?"

"Jen, it's Matt."

"Hey, Matt. Sorry, I keep losing phone service out here in BFE. This storm—"

She winced as a brilliant flash of lightening and shriek of thunder cut her off. Glancing down at her dash, she saw the LOW BATTERY light was still on, bright red.

"Jen, where the hell *are* you?"

I'm fucked, that's where I am, she thought.

"I'm...not sure, really. I was on the highway, but after I took the exit into town the road was flooded over, all this rain, so I detoured onto this side road that headed uphill, figuring higher ground—"

"I've been trying to reach you all evening—*Jesus*, you were supposed to report in *two hours ago!*"

She could barely hear his voice crackling from the phone as a new wave of pounding rain viciously assaulted her car—a herd of tiny horses stampeding across the roof above her—with the *slap-slap, slap-slap* of her windshield wipers running on high adding to the chaotic din.

She stared through her windshield at the huge tree that lay across the road in front of her. It basked, gnarled and wet, in the slowly fading circles of her headlights, then vanished into the darkness to either side of the road.

"I know, I know—look, Matt, I don't know how long I'll have service, so I need you to listen to me. I've got a problem...I'm out here in the middle of nowhere, in this storm, and there's this tree down across the road, and my car battery—"

Noticing the phone was dead silent now, she yanked it from her ear and looked at it.

The keypad was dark.

"DAMMIT!", she yelled, slamming the handset down on its base.

Sitting quietly in the rain and thunder and the *slap-slap, slap-slap* of her wipers, she stared through her windshield at the monstrous tree that blocked her path, trying to think.

She peered to the left, then the right, trying to see a way around. It was so dark up here, no streetlights, she couldn't even see to the sides of the road; just the small circle in front of her cast by her headlights, which were fading fast, along with her dying battery. She tried switching to high beam to see better, but it didn't help much, so she switched it back to conserve battery.

Even the flashes of lightening were too brief (and too blinding) for her to see anything beyond that short portion of the massive tree trunk that lay directly in front of her headlights, its tangle of now errant leafy branches whipping about in the gusty wind.

Suddenly, she had a thought; she leaned over, banged the glove box open, and rummaged blindly within.

It's here, I know it's here, as she pulled piles of papers and other knickknacks from the dark compartment, discarding them onto the floorboard. Finally, she produced a small flashlight.

Aiming it out the window, toward the edge of the road where the tree dissolved into the darkness, she slide the tiny switch to ON.

Nothing.

"DAMMIT!"

She shook it, slapped it furiously against her palm—but knew the batteries were dead; it had barely worked the last time she'd used it, which was one night months ago (coincidentally, the last time the car battery had died, in the darkness of the parking garage at the station, and she'd had to get a jump), and though she'd reported the problem, of course the company had apparently never managed to replace the batteries (in either—the car, or the flashlight).

Frustrated, she roughly discarded it onto the passenger seat, where it bounced a few times before rolling back toward her and stopping against the base of the car phone.

She was thinking about trying to back up—try a three-point u-turn on this tight, wet, country road flanked by mud and filling culverts (easy to get stuck in), and surrounded by woods and darkness (easy to get lost in)—when she happened to glanced up at the rearview mirror and noticed a pair of headlights slowly approaching off in the distance.

Relief swept over her.

•

The distant headlights eventually materialized into an old pickup truck rumbling loudly as it pulled to a stop on the side of the road, just a short distance behind her car.

Peering into her rearview mirror, she watched through rivulets of rain streaking down her back window as the driver's door creaked open and a dark figure emerged, then the door *creaked!* and *banged!* shut, old and stout and hollow-sounding. Then a beam of bluish-white light snapped on, pointed in her direction, and began a bouncy approach.

As the silhouette drew closer in the darkness, a flash of lightening momentarily revealed an older man, donning overalls over a plain white t-shirt, a trucker-style ball cap sitting slightly askew on his head. He was getting drenched in the downpour.

Gotta be a local farmer...

As he drew nearer, she switched her eyes to her side mirror, and noticed that the beam of light was emanating from a very long, black flashlight—that to her looked more like a club than a light—and a mild uneasiness began building in her gut. She sat, eyes glued to the mirror, clutching her steering wheel, holding her breath...

With one hand he shined the light in the window at her, quickly pointed it around inside the rest of the car, then rapped on the glass with one knuckle. She bumped the button, lowering the window just enough to peer out over it. He bent down, touched the bill of his cap in salutation.

"Howdy, ma'am...you okay?" he asked in a deep, grandfatherly voice, laced with genuine concern.

"I'm okay—just can't get around this damn tree...was about to try turning around—"

—she then pointed to her dash—

"—and my low battery light is on, too."

Rainwater dripped from the bill of his cap as he peered in at her dash, then stood and looked her car up and down. Turning, he pointed the flashlight at the culverts—first to one side of the road, then the other. Both were now raging with muddy water, and beginning to spill out onto the edges of the pavement.

"You ain't goin' nowhere in *this* (he stroked her car with a beam of light)...road's half-mud as it is, and'll be flooded over soon. And fog, too, once it cools off a bit... prolly be pea soup 'fore long."

He stood in the downpour, hands on hips, looking back up the road in the direction he had come. Then he turned and shone the flashlight up and down the tree lying in front of them, then back to her. "Power's out up at my house...happens a lot up here, specially in these big ones. Thought I'd get down to Eddie's for the night. That's my son, lives couple miles further down, toward town—house is newer, better service, power don't go out so much, like at my old place—but it don't look like I'm gonna make it that far."

As if on cue, lightening flashed, burning him white, and a clap of thunder rumbled off into the night.

He bent over again, peering at her through the small space above her window. Rainwater dripped from his hat, his nose.

"You can come back with me in the truck if you want. Wait out the storm up at my place. Don't wanna stay here, do ya? In all this rain? With yer bat-tree dyin?"

Her apprehension must have shown in her eyes, because he quickly shrugged, looked back toward his truck, and offered up another plan:

"Or, I got a CB radio in the truck...could try callin' someone, maybe...come get ya. Maybe get a tow?"

He turned back to her, and waited patiently in the pouring rain.

"That would be wonderful, thank you." She forced a smile as she hit the button, raising the window. But before it closed all the way, he signaled to her and she stopped it.

"Best kill yer lights, save what bat-tree ya got left."

"Thanks. I'll do that."

She finished closing the window, then flicked the headlights off. The resulting darkness startled her—she didn't realize how much light her headlights were actually providing, reflecting off the wet tree and shining all around her. Now, without them, it was pitch-black in front of her. The tiny orange Low Battery light glowed menacingly up at her from the darkness, and the old man's truck headlights behind her cast the entire interior of her car in a strange, shadowy glow.

She watched in her side mirror as the man sloshed purposefully back to his truck, which was now nearly obscured in the rain, thickening fog, and near pitch-black darkness. It was reduced to two bright headlights piercing the black backdrop, and that was about it.

By the time he got back to his truck, she could barely make him out either, just a dark, blurry silhouette as he opened the door to get in. Pausing for a moment, he switched off the flashlight and tossed it into the cab.

Then she saw it.

•

At first, it simply looked like the fog swirling around behind the man, tinged red by the truck's taillights—only with a vague silhouette lurking within, blending into the darkness behind. But as she studied it, intrigued, the shadow within seemed to coalesce, take shape, grow, darken—as if *gathering* itself. It did not take on a distinct shape, however—not like an animal, or a human—but something bigger, monstrously bigger, wide as the old truck, and nearly entirely cloaked from view in the rain and fog and darkness.

Still not sure what she was seeing (if anything), she turned around and looked through her rear window, straining for a better view, throwing one arm over the back of the seat.

Her eyes widened as the dark, indistinct form within the fog suddenly narrowed at the base and rose into the air, some ten, now fifteen feet, now more, until it was towering above the old man—who must have sensed something behind him, because just then he turned around and looked—

—and screamed.

His cap tumbled off as he was suddenly seized and lifted off the ground, screaming and writhing, caught in the powerful grip of something unseen, something unfathomably huge, its hulking mass shrouded in the dense and swirling mist.

His scream ended abruptly when he was flung violently over his truck, striking a large tree on the side of the road with such velocity that Jen heard the bone-shattering impact inside her car. She stifled a scream, clamping her hands over her mouth and watching in horror as the man's lifeless body slowly peeled from the tree trunk and flopped face-first into the flooded culvert behind his truck with a splash.

Riveted, she watched as the shadow in the fog shifted again—lowering and spreading to its original form—then glide fluidly behind the truck to where the man's body had landed, the fog swirling all around it, disturbed by its movement, yet at the same time cloaking it.

A sudden shriek and burst of green light inside her car scared the shit out of her, forcing a tiny yelp from her as she jumped, jerking her attention down to the phone nested on the console between the seats. It rang again, the backlit keypad throwing its dim green light up into the darkness, giving her face a sickly luminescent glow.

Alarmed, she snatched the receiver off the cradle and slammed it back down again, cutting off the call and silencing the phone. Glancing back up at the rear window, her fear was confirmed: the monstrous shadow in the fog stopped abruptly beside the truck, just short of where she figured the old man must be lying in the flooded ditch—and began shifting again, this time flowing quietly in her direction, pulling the fog along with it as it seemingly floated—or *slithered*—along the side of the road.

She froze, watching in horror as it—whatever *it* was—approached her in the misty darkness.

•

Sheriff Ray "Mac" McCormick was just hanging up the phone on his desk when Deputy Wallace walked into his office. The young man stopped in the doorway, leaning a shoulder on the jamb. With one hand, he jabbed the front brim of his cowboy hat, knocking it back an inch or two on his head—a much practiced move, very cool—and it also made him look younger, very boyish—and he knew damn well the ladies *loved* it.

Matched his baby-blue eyes.

"Any news?"

The sheriff swiveled his chair back and swung his feet up onto the desk, crossing his boots in the same motion. He wrapped his big hands around the back of his neck, tilting his cowboy hat forward over his own blue eyes (although his were more faded and bloodshot, more years) and heaved a sigh.

This was also a much-practiced move. It seemed the two lawmen were having a private little "coolness" contest that only they were privy to—and it was possible that even *they* weren't fully aware of it.

The power had blinked out a short time ago, leaving only the building's emergency lights glowing, and in the relative dimness Mac jerked his chin in the general direction of the phone sitting amongst the piles of rubble on his desk. As he did so, the window glowed white momentarily, and thunder rumbled overhead.

"That was the NRC. They're already on their way. The power plant called right 'fore they did. And they already talked to Jacksonville."

"So it IS the plant." Wallace pushed off the door frame and walked toward the desk, his boots knocking across the hardwood floor. Nearing the front of the desk, he quickly spun an empty chair around backwards and straddled it, facing the sheriff. He dropped his hat onto one knee and crossed his arms over the back of the chair.

Another much-practiced move. And also very cool.

And it put him up over Mac, two to one.

"Figgered it prolly was, whole town goin' out at once like that."

Wallace raised an arm to wipe the sweat from his forehead. No power meant no air conditioning, either. It was getting warm in there, and the humidity hung in the air like a blanket—typical summer evening in the south—and the storm that had been raging outside all evening sure wasn't helping.

"So what happened? They know?"

"Seems it's some sorta problem with the cooling system. Like a leak somewhere. They said the system's been losing pressure all day, and they been monitoring it close. But when routine system checks didn't turn up anything, and the pressure kept droppin', then the boys suited up and went inside."

"Those guys are nuts, goin inside a nuclear reactor core like that. Hell, just *workin'* there's crazy. Not me, no way." Wallace shook his head at the prospect, eyes wide.

Mac stopped, searching over his cluttered desk. In a moment he spotted a white styrofoam cup off to the side. He bent forward just enough to fetch it, his old spring-back chair squeaking in protest, then leaned back again, a look of satisfaction materializing across his face.

He sipped the already cold coffee and grimaced slightly.

"Well, they checked the whole core, head to toe—pressure readings, temp readings, even Geiger counters—and still didn't find anything." As he spoke, he raised his cup high, then lowered it again, illustrating the inspection for the deputy. Then, with a quick bottoms-up, he finished the coffee in one gulp, and continued, looking serious.

"But the system pressure kept droppin', and when it finally dropped below a certain point, why, the system shut *itself* down. Automatically. Guess these days they're programmed to do that."

He turned and tossed the cup across the room and into the trash by the door—another cool move, which also rather artfully added to the finality of the story.

Now they were even: two up.

"And the lights went out." Wallace finished.

"Yup. Whole damn town. Bang. Just like that." The sheriff snapped his fingers sharply for emphasis.

"So when's it supposed to be back up?"

Mac shrugged. "Don't know." Then he pointed out the window in the general direction of the power plant—and as if on cue, the window again lit up with a flash of lightening, a little less intense this time, and thunder rumbled off in the distance.

"But if the NRC boys are gonna be snoopin' around at the plant", he turned now to point at Wallace, "I can guaran-damn-teeya that it won't be till *they* say so." He accentuated each word with his finger in the air—and the Deputy could almost feel it thumping his chest.

He then dropped his hand to his lap and looked out the window again, frowning and perturbed. Quietly, almost to himself, he added:

"And I'm sure the feds'll take their own sweet time, like always." He looked back to Wallace, his face suddenly taking on a flippant look.

"So to answer your question—it'll prolly be a while."

"So...Jacksonville," Wallace said, nodding slightly in understanding.

"Jacksonville." Mac nodded in confirmation, then dropped his feet to the wood floor with a bang. The sheriff stood, and the deputy followed suit, putting his hat back on as he did so. While they both hitched and adjusted their police belts, Mac explained.

"Forunately, they're only runnin' about eighty percent right now. So they're gonna bump it up to ninety and change, and pipe the extra juice down here to us."

They both stretched, revealing dark, wet rings around their armpits. Mac yawned big enough to catch bugs in, so Wallace waited, then spoke when the sheriff's face came back into view.

"Is that gonna be enough?" Wallace asked, sounding skeptical.

"Gonna hafta be, that's all we get. But I'll take it. Should be enough to keep the emergency grid on, anyways. Outsida that, we're prolly just lookin' at the downtown area, not much more. And that's good, cuz last thing I wanna be doin' is cruisin' the streets downtown in total darkness—no streetlights, no *nothin'*. That's just askin' for trouble."

"Tell me about it."

Mac walked toward the door, and Wallace started to follow, but then stopped, pondering something.

"Say, isn't this, like, the second time lately? Third?"

Mac stopped in the doorway and turned to Wallace, pulling a wad of chewing tobacco from a round flat tin in his hand and stuffing it under his bottom lip. He pocketed the tin, and now it was his turn to wipe the sweat from his forehead: lift the hat with one hand, wipe the forehead with the opposing forearm, and replace the hat—all in one quick, smooth motion.

"Fourth, actually," he replied, his words fuzzy through the chew. "First three were just safety violations, though. NRC shut'm down till they got things back up to code, usually less than a day. No real danger, just typical government reg'lations. This is the first time there's actually been a *problem*, at least that I know of."

"You think there could be a radiation leak?" Wallace sounded nervous. Wallace *looked* nervous.

Mac chuckled, shrugged flippantly, and turned to leave the office.

"I dunno," he answered.

As they left the office, Mac explained: "Cooling system's a sealed system. See, they pressurize the water first 'fore they send it through—that way it can absorb more heat without boiling."

Wallace followed him down the short hall, through reception, and to the front door, listening intently.

The stifling heat hit them hard as Mack opened the door. They stopped and faced each other before heading out into the rain.

"So the water doesn't absorb any of the radiation?"

The sheriff turned and spit a brown load at an angle into the grass beside the front porch, then continued.

"Water stays clean, supposably. But y'ask me, I say a pipe that water can find its way *out* of, causin' the pressure to drop—like they say it was tonight—well, that there's a pipe that radiation might just as easily find its way *into*, dontcha think?"

He spit again.

"Seems like," the young deputy agreed.

With that, they hurried down the quick four steps in the rain, their boots sounding like distant machine guns rat-a-tatting on the concrete, then dashed across the asphalt lot toward the cruiser.

Once inside the car and doors slammed quickly shut, Wallace continued: "But they still don't know where the leak is?"

"Not yet," Mack said. "But seein' as they couldn't find anything anywhere inside the plant, they're guessin' it might be somewhere tween there and the river."

"The river?"

"Yup."

"Why the river?" The Deputy queried, looking perplexed.

"See, they pump the heated water from the plant out to the river, couple miles north of the lake, so it can cool off before it gets back to the lake. Then they pipe it from the lake back through the reactor again. One big re-cycling system. I remember when they was buildin' it, back 'fore you was even born. Big-ass concrete pipe runs through the woods way up there in the hills, then dumps out in the river—"

—he pointed into the darkness to the west, where they both knew the power plant, hills, and river were located—

"—and I remember the locals picketin' and protestin' the whole time they was buildin' the damn thing. Specially the natives."

"The natives? What was *their* beef?"

The sheriff shrugged. "Apparently, they ran that big cement pipe right over some kind of old sacred Indian burial ground up there in the hills somewhere—I don't know where, I ain't never seen it myself—but man, those ol' boys weren't too happy bout that, not at all. I didn't think they was ever gonna settle down."

"But seems they must have, huh? I've never heard any complaints about it. So what happened?"

"What I hear, the company offered 'em some... *restitution*—I guess that's a fancy way of sayin' *hush money*—and that settled 'em down right quick." Then he smiled. "Amazing what a little wampum'll do."

"Yep, 'tis indeed," Wallace agreed, smiling back.

"Wampum do cure many ills."

"Yes it do," Mac agreed with a smiling nod.

Then Wallace's face turned to concern—

"—Wait, wampum? What the heck is Wampum?" Chaz asked, confused.

"Yeah, I've never heard of that either," Nick joined in.

"Isn't it some kind of money?" Jackie offered. "Like, Indian money?"

"Yes," Ryan confirmed. "Wampum was shell beads, strung together. Some Indians used it for money," he explained.

"Really?" Chaz responded, incredulous. "They could use shells for money?"

"Yeah." Ryan then elaborated: "Tubular beads made from special shells. They'd string them together to make ornaments or belts, or put them in leather or cowhide bags called wampum bags, that they carried around with them. To the

Indians, wampum was sorta like jewelry is to us—so it would be like us trading gems or jewelry for stuff, instead of using what we call money."

"Oh, okay," Chaz said, nodding. "I just never heard of wampum before. So it's basically money."

"Indian money, yes."

The rest of them nodded in understanding, and Ryan continued his story—

"—so like I was sayin', the deputy started lookin' pretty nervous…"

"—So if what they suspect is true," the deputy conjectured, "that there might be a leak in that cooling water pipe, somewhere 'tween the plant and the river, then don't that mean that radiation is prolly leakin' out too? Like maybe somewhere up in the hills?"

Wallace turned and peered in that direction, as if he actually expected to see some kind of neon green cloud glowing out there in the distant darkness.

Mac looked down and chuckled again, shaking his head, almost scoffing. He was obviously unconcerned.

"Son, I hope not—and I surely doubt it. I sure as hell hope they wouldn't be dumbass enough to be pumping radioactive water into the river, anyway. And 'sides, the government wouldn't never allow that anyhow. So stop worryin' that little head of yours…let them do their jobs—find that leak and fix it, and get the power back on—while we do ours, which is patrolling the streets during this blackout, make sure the town stays quiet and safe."

Then, as an afterthought:

"And stop thinkin' so damn much, *Einstein*," the name pronounced with mild sarcasm. "That's prolly why ya worry so much, cuz ya think too much. Did you ever think of that?"

He rolled the window halfway down, spit a brown glob out, then rolled it back up and started the car.

"Well, if we ain't careful," Wallace mumbled as he settled in and secured his seatbelt, "we're all gonna end up glowin' green one day."

"Maybe we will," Mack agreed. "But till then, we got a job to do."

With that, he swung the squad car around and headed out of the parking lot and into the darkened streets, the rain intensifying.

•

Thinking quickly, Jen pushed the master button on her armrest, locking all four doors simultaneously with a unified *click!*

She then watched in silence as the fog enveloped her car, first wrapping around the rear, then sliding along both sides. About the time the front edge of the fog was crawling across the front door windows, the rear window grew suddenly dark—as if something solid had moved in very close to it—and then shattered with a great *crash!*, a shower of pebbled safety glass spraying and bouncing across the back seat.

Screaming, she unlocked her door and burst from the car. At first she ran straight ahead, just trying to get away from....*it*...whatever *it* was...but stopped short when she realized she had nowhere to go in that direction, thanks to the huge tree lying across the road. Turning momentarily, she saw the entire car now cloaked in the fog, the dark shadow of the creature—or creatures, she didn't know if it was one, or many, or *what the hell it was*—moving around the car and toward her within the approaching thick murk.

She screamed again, and turned toward the woods. Between the front edge of the fog and the downed tree, she saw she only had an opening of a few feet—and closing quickly—before the fog would cut off her escape.

There was no time for thought, no time to decide. Screaming again, she bolted between the fog and the tree, across the front of her car and into the trees that lined the other side of the road. Oddly, she felt a cold patch of air brush across her skin as she dodged the leading edge of the fog just before making the tree line.

She ran in blind panic and rain through the darkest woods she had ever seen, which angled steeply down the hillside from the road. She stumbled downward, downward, the woods seeming to close in around her.

As she fled, she no longer saw the lightening, heard the thunder, or felt the pounding rain; she was no longer aware of anything save her own labored breathing, her own grunts and puffs as she tore through the undergrowth and endured the sting of endless whippings by unseen brush and tree branches that grappled for her in the darkness.

Finally, at the bottom of the embankment, bleeding from countless cuts and scrapes all along her exposed arms, face, and neck, she stopped suddenly, plastered herself wetly behind a huge tree, and listened. She swallowed hard, trying to stay her breathing, trying to hear...*it*—whatever *it* was—without *it* hearing *her*.

It was definitely behind her.

She could not hear it, for the way it moved—silently shifting in the darkness, like the very fog that cloaked it—was soundless.

No, she *sensed* it.

And she knew it was closing in on her.

What the hell is it?

She thought about what she had seen: just a huge, obscure form—at best a silhouette in the fog, nearly one with the darkness itself—rising above the old man, taller than his truck—

The truck.

She thought back, rewound the horrific scene in her mind. From what she remembered, the old man's truck had been left untouched—and was still running!

That was her way out!

She had to go back; she had to somehow elude *it*, somehow get past that evil thing cloaked in fog, somehow stay alive long enough to get back up to the road, throw herself into that truck, turn around and get the fuck out of there!

Sounded crazy, but she sensed it was the only way she would get out of these woods alive.

Just then, cold tendrils of fog began curling around the massive tree trunk from behind, and she screamed, pushing off the tree and heading to the right, now running along the wooded bank, parallel to the road above.

At least here, at the bottom of the embankment, the ground was flat, and relatively clear. She ran along the tree line, trying to gauge the distance she needed to go before heading back up the hill, hoping to reach the road up top as close to the truck as possible, all the while the pouring rain drenching her to the bone.

But right when she was about to turn back up the hill, her foot caught an exposed root, sending her flying forward and splashing face-down into standing rainwater, sliding a few feet in the wet, slippery mud before slowing to a stop.

Pulling herself to her knees, she scampered through water and mud toward another huge, gnarled tree, then scurried behind it and slapped herself against it, her back pressed to the rough bark. With one quick swipe of her arm, she wiped the mud and water from her face, ignoring the slathering of mud that now coated the front of her blouse, running down with the rain.

Once again, while attempting to squelch her heavy breathing, she tried to listen, tried to determine exactly where...*it*...was.

But then, what she saw before her caught her full attention, and she exhaled long and hard, and gazed silently at the scene, squinting through the downpour:

A large rectangular clearing, starting at the tree line at the bottom of the embankment and continuing south, maybe fifty feet wide. It stretched away, a hundred feet or so, before the forest took up again.

And scattered haphazardly, all throughout that clearing: holes in the ground, elongated, each a couple feet wide, and perhaps four or five feet long. To Jen, they looked freshly dug—roughly hewn, piles of rocky dirt and mud piled around them. They were all nearly full to the brim with water now, as the entire clearing was becoming flooded with the rain.

But then, a flash of lightening lit up the sky, and she saw what she'd been unable to see in the darkness: there, twenty or thirty feet in front of her, elevated eight or ten feet into the air, running at a diagonal above the clearing: a massive concrete pipe, six feet in diameter, maybe more. As the lightening dissipated across the sky, she followed the huge black silhouette set against the fading glow of the clouds with her eyes, to where it emerged from the woods at the bottom of the hill—when another flash of lightening lit up the scene, and her eyes widened at what she now saw: a massive tree had fallen from the edge of the woods, landing across the concrete pipe, cracking it from top to bottom. The tree lay across the pipe at an angle, its roots ripped from the ground, the pipe stopping its fall before completion.

At the bottom of the pipe, from the split in the concrete, water poured in a solid stream, flooding the entire area.

She followed the gushing water from the bottom of the huge concrete pipe down to the ground, and flowing in, out, and around the multitude of holes scattered all throughout the clearing.

Her eyes then returned to the pipe, and she followed it to the left this time, to where it once again disappeared into the woods and out of site. Lightening flashed again, and that's when she saw it, mounted on the pipe, just before it re-entered the woods: a yellow triangular sign, with a black, three-pronged circular symbol inscribed within. She recognized it immediately, for she'd seen it at all the nuclear power plants she's visited, covering stories in this series for the news station: Radiation Hazard.

She looked again at all the holes in the ground, the water pouring from the pipe, flooding the area, and wondered...

Leaning forward, she crawled on hands and knees straight out from the tree, careful to keep the massive trunk between herself and...*it*...until she reached the nearest hole in the ground. Another flash of lightening lit the entire area just long enough for her to see not only piles of dirt, rocks, and mud encompassing the oblong hole in the ground, but also...

...footprints?

Glancing around, she determined that yes, the mud was riddled with footprints all around the hole, which seemed to be joined by others before they all seemed to trail off into the nearby woods.

She looked past this hole to some of the others that were close enough for her to see in the darkness, and saw the same: scores of footprints, of all different sizes, pockmarking the ground around all the holes, as if crowds of people had been walking around and between them.

Or had they dug them? And if so, why?

As she hovered over the nearly water-filled opening in the ground, examining the prints that she now saw were everywhere, hands and knees sinking in the mud rainwater, she realized she felt something odd under her right hand, something that at first she thought must be a little pile of pebbles or something, but then it slid slightly in the mud, and she realized it was some kind of flat object lying on the ground.

Clutching her hand into a fist, the object bunched up in her grasp, and she plucked it out of the mud, held it up close to her face so she could see it in the darkness.

It was some kind of remnant, like thick, course leather or cowhide, torn on both ends, tatters hanging, and as the mud washed off in the pouring rain, she could see it was strung with...

...beads?

The beads were of myriad colors, strung together to

make some sort of design or diagram along the length of the material, ending in tatters on either side where the remnant was either torn off—no, more like worn to shreds, the material seeming to be deteriorated or rotted.

It looked to be (or was, long ago) part of a belt or sash, or possibly a bag, woven from leather or cowhide or some such material, and decorated across its face with beads.

Definitely some sort of old Indian artifact.

But how did it get here? In the middle of the woods?

Shrugging, she tossed it back to the ground next to the hole with a tiny *splash!*, and her thoughts returned to the truck. She needed to get out of there, get back up the hill to the road and the truck, make her escape, before...*it*... caught up to her. She could investigate the rest later, see if it was in some way linked to the nuclear power plant, and the rumored problems she was sent here to cover.

Then again, she sensed its presence.

Sensed it growing closer.

It was almost upon her now, she just *knew*.

What was it?

Suddenly, her journalist nature kicked in; she needed to *know*...

And she was instantly overwhelmed with the urge to *look*...to turn and look behind her, around the tree...to look at *it*...get one good look before turning and fleeing with all her might, as fast as her legs could carry her, back into the woods and up the embankment to the road, the truck, and her escape from this God-forsaken place.

Her skin began to prickle, the hair stood up on the back of her neck, as she sensed it drawing ever closer, probably nearly within her reach, just on the other side of the tree now.

She knew she should run...

Run *now*...

But she wanted to *look*...

Needed to look...

Using both hands, she wiped the rainwater from her face, then exhaled deeply, gathering herself, preparing herself for the horror she knew she would see, when she stared that monstrosity in the face.

Then, in one quick motion, she snapped her head around the side of the tree, peering directly at the massive shadow that stood cloaked within the heavy, almost glowing fog that was now swirling and heaving directly before her—

—and screamed.

Ryan stopped, then smiled at everyone, sitting wide-eyed around the fire.

"So then what happened?" Casey asked excitedly.

"That's the end," Ryan said. "You'll have to use your imagination for the rest."

"Wow...that was a pretty good story," Nick complimented, nodding in approval.

The others echoed the sentiment around the campfire.

"Good one, Ryan," Jackie congratulated. "Your best yet!"

"Thanks!" Ryan said, leaning back and gloating.

"Radioactive contamination of an ancient Indian burial ground," Chad said, nodding. "Cool idea…I love it!"

"And, it just goes to show ya," Ryan summarized, "what could happen if you don't give the dead a proper Christian burial."

Nodding sounds of assent echoed around the group.

"Okay, who's next?" Jackie asked, looking with eager eyes around the group, his silver tooth shining slightly in the firelight.

"I'll go," Chaz volunteered. Then he turned to Ryan.

"That was a great story, Ryan…but I don't know, mine just might have ya beat!"

"I doubt it!" Ryan replied with confidence.

"I've been working on this one for a while…and I think it's pretty good…"

Smiling, he pushed his glasses up on his nose, then rubbed his hands briskly together as if preparing to tackle a big job. Then he looked around at the rest of them, the flames reflecting off his lenses giving him a devilish look.

"Ready?"

Everyone confirmed, anxious to hear his new tale.

"Okay…so…there's this new company that uses advanced technology—like the stuff they got on *Star Trek*—to send people back in time and give them another chance to hook up with a love from their past, who they somehow blew it with the first time around, and have always regretted it—you know, the "one that got away—"

—he punctuated the term with air quotes—

"—and the company is called *Second Chances…*"

Second Chances

by Charles "Chaz" Miller

"So, how much does it cost?" Jack asked, as one of the sales guys pointed a tiny remote control at the huge projection-screen TV that sat against the facing wall and turned it off, a barely audible, staticky *pop!* emanating from its speakers as the screen went dark.

Jack was sitting in the overly-bright presentation room at the posh offices of *Second Chances*, a new company he had seen advertisements for while riding the subway to and from work lately.

"Well, everything you own, of course," the other sales guy said matter-of-factly, as he leaned casually against the end of the polished walnut conference table to Jack's right, slightly bent, jacket hanging open, tie tangling before him.

Jack snapped to his right, staring wide-eyed at the guy. *"Everything I own?!"* he cried, incredulous.

The other sales guy set the remote control down on a glass coffee table that sat between the sofa—where Jack was sitting—and the projection TV, then stood and looked down at Jack, a friendly smile on his face.

"Don't worry, Mr. Lewis…Jack…may I call you Jack?"

Jack shrugged. "Sure…everyone else does."

Well, Jack, I know it sounds like a lot, and it's always upsetting at first. Trust me, all of our clients react the same way in the beginning, even after watching the highly persuasive demo video that you just did. But you gotta remember—if it works, you won't be back. Ever. Everything you own now will mean nothing to you, because it will never have existed in the first place...at least not in your new life."

Jack heaved a sigh and stared down at the expensive-looking, plush burgundy carpet, shaking his head slightly as he contemplated the weighty decision. Then he caught something the man had just said, and looked back up, shifting his eyes back and forth between the two salesmen standing before him in their expensive suits.

"Okay, that makes sense I guess—but you just said *if it works*...but what if it *doesn't* work?"

The two men looked at each other, but said nothing.

•

Jack was just hanging up the phone on his desk when his boss stepped into his office.

Looking up, he greeted him casually: "Hey Bill,"

"Jack, I need to see you in my office."

Jack glanced down at his Day-Timer, which was open on his desk.

"Sure—looks like I've got a three o'clock open—"

"I mean *now*, Jack."

At this Jack's stomach tightened, but he kept his smile intact, and shrugged flippantly.

"Okay."

He stood, clicked his pen closed, slid it into in his shirt pocket, and followed his boss out into the hall.

They took the elevator up to the executive offices. During the quiet ride upward, Bill said nothing, just stared at the number display above the doors, hands clasped in front of him. The silence was deafening; for the first time in all the years he had worked there, Jack actually wished there was elevator music to listen to...

The ding of the bell, the soft slide of the elevator door, the silent walk down the brightly-lit hall on the bouncy new carpet all the way to Bill's office down at the end.

"Look, Jack," Bill began after he shut his office door behind Jack and was walking past him and around the end of his desk, not even waiting to sit down first.

Once behind his desk, he stopped and waved a hand at one of the two shiny leather chairs that sat facing him. "Have a seat."

Reluctantly, Jack sat down, never taking his eyes off his boss. He had a bad feeling about this, and it showed in the trepidatious look on his face.

Bill finally pulled his own chair out and sat down. He folded his hands together on the desk in front of him, looked up at Jack, and sighed heavily.

"You've been with the company for a pretty long time," he started.

"Going on twenty years," Jack responded.

"And you and me, we go way back."

Jack nodded. "Damn near as long. Since Roberts left."

Bill sighed again, looking down at his desk with the weight of his thoughts.

"What is it Bill?" Jack prodded. "Just say it."

Bill looked back up. "It's your numbers, Jack. They're down. *Way* down. And have been for a while now. And they're getting *worse*, instead of *better*."

"Bill, you know what I've been going through— "

"Yes, I do," Bill cut him off. "Divorce is never easy. I've been through it myself. And that's exactly why you've lasted *this* long with the company—I've been playing defense for you, keeping the Board off your ass. They'da shit-canned you months ago, they had their way—but I've been holding 'em off, telling 'em you'll come back around... but Jesus, Jack—it's been what? Six months now?"

"About that, yes. A little less. Five and change."

"So almost six months, and you've yet to turn your numbers around...in fact, they've consistently declined, even just last week! Not only are you not pulling your weight around here, but you're actually *costing* the company money! And you've become a liability to the rest of the team, and they're starting to complain. In this business, there's no place to hide—everybody knows who's slacking, not pulling their weight. It shows up in their paychecks, in the quarterly profit sharing bonus. They don't like it, all they gotta do is take a minute to look at the sales chart in the conference room to see why...or, I suppose, *who*. Before you know it, everyone's complaining to brass, and brass doesn't like that. Keeps up, they start looking for a fall guy. And to be honest, I just can't cover for you anymore—"

—with that he sat back in his chair, folded his hands over his chest—

"—do you know what yesterday was, Jack?"

Feeling helpless now, Jack just shook his head and shrugged.

"The quarterly board meeting. When they review all the numbers, from everyone, all the way down the line. And, though the pretense is for doling out the quarterly bonuses—assuming it's been a profitable quarter, of course —it's also to see where they need to cut. And whoever's numbers aren't there, that's the first place they cut. And this is the *second* quarter your numbers haven't been there, Jack. Last quarter, you were on the cut list, but I talked them out of it, especially since you passed the first month with flying colors—before your marriage went on the rocks, I guess—but then the next two months went down the toilet. I pointed that out, told them you were having some personal problems, promised them you'd turn it around. I showed them your history, going back years, how you always came through, always got the numbers, rain or shine. And *Outstanding* numbers, most the time. So they bought my story...*last time*..."

"Look," Jack said anxiously. "I'm turning it around. I am. When Linda left, I was devastated, sure. But we didn't have a good marriage anyway, I fell out of love with her a long time ago...if I ever even *was* in love with her, which now I doubt...we were too young...*I* was too young, I didn't know what I was doing. Hell, I didn't even know who I *was* back then. But even so, it's not just the marriage, it's the *finances*. She brought in close to half our income."

"Look, Jack, I don't need to know your personal—"

"I almost lost my house, Bill," Jack interrupted. "You know that. It was all I could do to stay out of bankruptcy. I got so far behind on everything, my credit went to hell, and I had to sell practically everything I own, including my car, to make ends meet. And I've still got creditors calling and harassing me, but I'm getting caught up, making deals, buying time. And I could still lose the house —I've finally got the mortgage caught up, but I don't know how long I can keep it that way. And without a car, I had to start taking the subway to work, which took me a while to figure out, the maps, the schedules, made me late to work a few times, 'til I got a handle on it. And the lack of a car makes it really hard for me to meet with my leads—"

Bill held his hands out in a stopping gesture. "Jack, I know...you've been giving me that same sad story for months."

"But it's true!"

Bill returned his hands to his desk, looked down, hung his head, and heaved another heavy sigh, shaking his head slightly in remorse...

•

Jack would have never thought all his stuff from his

office would fit into one lidded printer paper box.

But it did.

And that box now sat in his lap as he quietly rode the subway home.

As he watched the underground world go by in a blur, he thought about his life—or the life he *used* to have. It seemed surreal, how things seemed to be going along just fine, and suddenly it all went to shit, almost in the blink of an eye. First, Linda walks out on him.

Just like that.

Then, over the ensuing months, he'd worked his ass off trying to keep from losing everything—and right when he thought he was succeeding, right when he was on the cusp of turning it all around, making it work—he loses his job... of *twenty years*.

Just like that.

But you know what was *really* surprising? The fact that deep down inside, he didn't really care. Here he was, having lost everything, and was riding the subway home— a home that was now as good as gone too, like every thing else—and he

Just.

Didn't.

Care.

Because for the first time in decades, he realized how little it all meant to him, how he never really was all that happy...

Suddenly, he threw his head back and laughed out

loud, breaking the morbid silence and prompting brief, perturbed looks from the other passengers.

And then, his thoughts wandered off, as they so often did, to the girl he had *really* loved, so long ago...

Wendy.

The one that got away...

If he'd been with *her*, instead of Linda—who he felt he had never really loved quite like he thought he would have loved Wendy—well...things would be different...a *lot* different...a lot *better*, he thought.

Man, what I wouldn't give for another chance with her...but hell, does she even live here anymore? I haven't seen her since high school, so maybe not...on the other hand, I still live here...so maybe she still does, too...but who knows...

And then he saw that ad again.

As the subway was slowing to a stop, he peered through the window at the poster outside, encased in the glass advertising box mounted on the wall next to a row of worn, beat-up steel benches.

Second Chances: reuniting you with your long-lost love, the one who got away...here's your chance to live the life you've always dreamed of!

Upon deboarding, he walked directly over to the ad, the box of office supplies rattling in his arms as he trotted along. After a quick review, he set the box down on the bench, flipped the lid off, dug out his Day-Timer, flipped it open, slid out the pen, and jotted down the phone number from the poster.

•

"Well, actually, that's never happened," one of the two suited sales guys answered.

"It can't, really—not the way our process works...it's fail-safe," the other chimed in.

But then Jack's attention was captured by a gorgeous brunette that he spied through the glass wall as she was leaving the adjacent office with two other suits, shaking hands and smiling as she did so. For an instant he thought she looked familiar—perhaps maybe he'd seen her on the subway?—but she quickly turned away and headed down the hall toward the front doors, the sales guys following, and he dismissed the thought.

Both of his sales guys noticed him gawking, glanced up at the woman, then smiled at him.

"She's one of our clients," one of them said. "She was reluctant at first, just like you—but she finally signed on yesterday, and came in today for her preflight. See? She's not afraid to live the life she's always dreamed of—and you shouldn't be, either. If that pretty little lady can do it, certainly you can do it."

"Preflight?" Jack asked.

The guys both chuckled.

"That's just what we call it," the other sales guy explained, smiling. "Sort of a preliminary meeting, an orientation if you will. After the client signs all the papers, then we do a briefing—our *preflight*—how it all works, what to expect during the process, that kind of thing. Then we schedule the actual *flight*, usually the following morning. Gives them a chance to say their goodbyes, but then return before all the legalities kick in—you know, the asset transfers, legal procedures, all that. That's all scheduled to happen afterward, so our clients don't have to worry about any of it."

"And moving that quickly also helps prevent them from getting cold feet and changing their mind," the other added. "No time for second thoughts—after all, we have a strict no-refund policy, all sales are final."

He grinned at Jack like a true salesman.

"So how, exactly, *does* it work?" Jack asked.

With this, one guy gave the other a cautionary look, shaking his head ever so slightly.

"Well, thing is, we can't reveal the actual process yet, until you've signed the contract and all the legal paperwork—there are patents, proprietary methods, intellectual property, those sorts of things to consider, to protect—so what we do instead is give our potential clients kind of an *overview*."

"Overview?" Jack asked.

"That's right," the other continued. "An overview, a general synopsis. We'll go over it in more detail once you sign on—assuming that you do—during your preflight. But for now, all we can give you the basic concept."

"Alright," Jack said, nodding. "So what's the basic concept?"

With that, the two positioned themselves next to each other before him, on the other side the coffee table, obviously a rehearsed move.

Then the guy on the left began:

"See, there's actually no such thing as *time,*" he offered. "Time is just a human construct, one that we came up with in order to better organize ourselves as society evolved."

"This is what Einstein proposed," the other jumped in, "That time isn't consistent, only the speed of light is consistent. *Time* is actually flexible. That's why time stands still—or even *regresses*—the faster you travel, the closer you get to reaching the speed of light."

The two salesmen then began what seemed like a dialog between them, each taking the next line, tossing it back and forth, again obviously rehearsed:

"And what is light? It's a *wave*. Essentially, a type of motion."

"That's right—so that's all time really is: motion. All that actually exists, in the entire universe, is *motion*—which, at its smallest manifestation, is *vibration*. Everything that exists—from light, to seemingly solid matter—are just different frequencies of vibration."

"And get this: *brain waves* are vibrations, too."

"And you've probably heard the saying, perception is reality? Well, it's true. Our entire reality is right here—"

—he tapped on his temple with his forefinger—

"—and that means our entire reality is nothing but... *vibrations*."

"And just like we have memories of the past, we also have memories of the *future*—when we visualize it. The images we see when we visualize the future are no different than the images we see when we remember the past...which means in a way, we can see the future, because we envision what we hope to do, the things we make and invent, how events will turn out, before it actually becomes reality."

"So it's potential reality in here first—"

—he again tapped his temple with his index finger—

"—before it becomes reality out here—"

—he finished by extending his arms out to encompass the entire room.

"So what does that make your memories? Even the ones that never really happened, we only fantasize that they did, or could have?"

"Potential reality?" Jack guessed.

"Bingo!" The two sales guys said in unison, both looking exceedingly pleased that he got it. Then one of them continued:

"Now, there's a school of philosophical thought—which more recent discoveries in quantum physics are starting to support—that says without consciousness, nothing in the universe would exist."

Jack frowned at this, looking totally confused, and so the other guy jumped in.

"It's like the old saying, if a tree falls in the woods, but there's nobody there to hear it—does it make a sound?"

"I've heard that one," Jack said, nodding.

"Okay—so now look at the entire universe that way: if there was no conscious being to perceive it, would any of it exist?"

Jack shook his head and shrugged. "I don't know. I suppose not."

"That's right! It wouldn't."

"Now let's reverse that idea," the other offered. "If nothing exists unless someone consciously perceives it, then what if someone consciously perceives something that doesn't exist?"

"It exists?" Jack tentatively guessed.

"It manifests!" They both said in unison.

Jack's face lit up as he grasped the concept. And at that moment of Jack's apparent understanding, the two sales guys began volleying between them again:

"So once again, we're proposing that our perception *becomes* our reality—and not just in our heads, but even in the physical realm!"

"Whatever we perceive, is."

Jack began slowly nodding now, thinking he understood. A little, anyway...

"Now, the rest of the process is quite a bit more complicated, and we're not at liberty to divulge the specifics to you yet anyway, but suffice it to say, you're put under deep hypnosis—and don't worry, we use only professionals in the psychiatric field for this—during which we have you recall that very moment when you missed the love of your life—the one that got away—while we record your brainwaves—in other words, the *vibrations*—of that moment, as it exists in your mind."

"Then it's a simple matter of duplicating those waves electronically—sort of like recording music, or any other sound, really, only much more complicated, obviously—and then re-inserting the recorded vibrations into the frontal cortex, the hippocampus, and both amygdalas simultaneously."

"The hippocampus is the part of the brain that stores old memories—retaining facts, data, context, and such—but the amygdalas are the critical parts, because they store our more *emotional* memories...you know, those that involve intense feelings like love, fear, passion, and the like...plus, they're more quickly accessed by the frontal cortex than the hippocampus is...and being more intense and more quickly accessed is why we tend to remember emotional events so much more vividly. And not only is the frontal cortex involved in retrieving our *old* memories as well as creating *new* ones, but also in envisioning "memories" that *haven't happened yet.*"

"By inserting the reproduced vibrational coding into all four of those sections of the brain simultaneously, we manage to trick the brain into believing—*perceiving*—that it's really happening, in the current reality."

"And since our perception *is* our reality—well then your reality changes, and becomes the new, inserted reality, based on the reproduced brainwaves...and your life starts over, at that point. And from that point, you have the opportunity to change everything."

"Then everything else is forgotten, because it never happens."

"Remember: perception *is* reality."

"And you, Mr. Lewis, can have the reality you've always dreamed of, with that special person you've always dreamed of—you know, the one who got away—all you have to do is *perceive* it. And we're here to help you do that...and then to make it *your reality*."

"You can do all that?" Jack asked them in wide-eyed incredulity.

"Absolutely!" One of them said, as the other nodded vigorously.

Then, again as if rehearsed, they both said in unison:

"We can give you a Second Chance!"

•

After signing all the company's required contract and release forms and scheduling his preflight and recording session, Jack then spent the rest of the day—

"—wait, wait, wait," Nick interrupted. Everyone else just stared at him, waiting. Noticing their perturbed looks, he looked around at each of them like they were all crazy.

"What the hell was all *that* mumbo jumbo about?" he asked. "Perception is reality, full frontal something, hippopotamus, caligula…? What the fuck?"

"It's frontal *cortex*, hippo*campus*, and *amygdala*, not *caligula*, dumbass," Chaz reiterated.

"Whatever...so what the hell does all that even mean? I thought this story was about *time travel*, not *psycho-babble*."

"Look, it doesn't really matter," Jackie said, shrugging.

"That's right," Chaz agreed. "It doesn't really matter *how* they're sending him back in time, just that they *are*. The *real* story is what happens to him *after* that, not how they do it, how he gets there—"

—he shrugged—

"—he just does. Can't you just roll with it for now? We're coming to the time-travel part."

The others muttered their agreement, wanting Nick to calm down and shut up so Chaz could continue his story.

"Well, alright. I'll just roll with it, I guess. But get to the time-travel part soon, will ya? And try not to use so many big words, okay?"

Chaz just sighed and rolled his eyes, then continued:

"So, like I was saying: after signing the company's requisite contract and release forms, and scheduling his preflight and recording session, Jack then spent the rest of the day—"

—spent the rest of day working down a laundry-list of legalities and related paperwork that the Second Chances agents had issued to him to complete, in preparation for his upcoming "flight": power of attorney forms, along with instructions concerning property deeds, assets, insurance policies, bank accounts, investments, debt obligations, the whole nine yards.

He signed it all over to the company, had everything notarized and filed with the appropriate authorities as per the instructions.

He was finished by the end of the day.

And he was excited, for the first time in years.

•

Two days later, at 10am, Jack was in deep hypnosis, lying on a rolling platform bed with what looked like a big metal colander engulfing his entire head, the doctor on a rolling stool, crouching near his face. Scores of electrodes ran from all over the dubious helmet, coalescing into a ribbon cable at the head of the bed that ran to a sprawling bank of computers that covered the entirety of the wall behind him.

There were two techs in scrubs monitoring the equipment, scores of tiny lights blinking, multiple computer monitors either displaying green flowing graphs or scrolling data, a soft beeping sound emanating from somewhere.

After some time, one of the techs turned from the equipment and approached the bed.

"Doc?"

The doctor turned and looked up at him.

"He's reached stage four, ready for launch. You can proceed now."

Nodding, the doctor turned back to Jack.

The tech then turned and signaled to the other, who turned and began flipping switches and pressing buttons. More tiny lights came on while others went dark, and the monitors all changed, showing different images and data now, and in blue instead of green, and the beeping sound suddenly increased in both volume and frequency—all of which only the techs could interpret.

But then the tech stopped, hand resting on the last switch, and looked over at the other for final confirmation —who provided it with a single, silent nod—then turned back and emphatically flipped it on—and watched as two huge spool-to-spool tape reels began slowly and silently rotating below.

The other tech then looked back at the doctor, and signaled with his hand to begin.

The doctor leaned in close to Jack's ear.

"Jack, are you still there? Can you hear me?"

"I'm here, doc," Jack mumbled quietly. "Can hear you just fine..."

"Do you remember Wendy? The girl you told me about? From high school?"

"Wendy...of course I remember her...sweet, beautiful Wendy..."

"Jack, can you tell me what happened? How you met her? Then what went wrong?"

"I've already told you all that..."

"I know, Jack. You have. But humor me, will you? Tell me about it again. It's an interesting story."

Jack sighed.

"Jack, I know it's hard, it's a bad memory, and it upsets you. But you've got to keep talking about it, if you ever want to get over it. So tell me again, Jack. It'll make you feel better the more you talk about it."

Jack sighed again, heavier this time.

"Come on, Jack. You can do it. Tell me about Wendy, from your high school days. You said you met her in math class? And then what happened?"

Jack sighed one last time, but relented.

"Yes...Wendy was in my math class...Mrs. Pearson... GOD I hated that old bitch...but I noticed Wendy the first day, and fell in love with her...love at first sight...and as the semester wore on, I fell more and more in love with her...and one day, during the last week of the school year, I decided I needed to ask her out before school let out for the summer and I might not ever see her again...

•

Jack was waiting impatiently for Wendy to enter the classroom. The bell hadn't rung yet, and Mrs. Pearson hadn't even arrived yet, and students were still trickling in and taking their seat, so Jack decided to take advantage and go up to the front of the classroom to feign sharpening his pencils before class began.

Standing there grinding each one to a fine point, he kept his eye on the door, waiting...and nervous...in fact, he felt a little strange, almost dizzy, and he suddenly realized that he couldn't really recall coming to class, like he just woke up in here, and for some reason everything seemed a bit surreal...but he chocked it up to his own extreme nervousness...after all, today was the *big day*...

Finally Wendy walked in, her beautiful dark hair bouncing with each step. She headed around the back of the room to the last row of desks that ran along the windows, then turned and started forward, toward her desk up in front.

Jack pulled his pencil from the sharpener, feigned inspection of his sharpening job, nodded in approval, then headed down the same row of desks that Wendy was heading up.

Meeting halfway, they stopped face to face, Jack smiling down at her, Wendy smiling up at him, her big brown eyes melting him.

"Hi," he said sheepishly.

"Hi," she answered, still smiling at him.

He took a deep breath. It was now or never...and he could feel his face turning beet red.

"Listen...I was wondering—"

"Hey dork, get your ass outta my face," a burly voice

from behind him suddenly demanded, cutting him off.

As Jack turned around to see who was barking at him, Wendy dropped her head in embarrassment and brushed quickly past him, shyly proceeding up the aisle to her desk, where she slipped into the chair and opened her math book without looking back up.

"What the fuck? Now get your crotch outta my face before I put you down, asshole! Jesus!"

It was Matt Colburn, quarterback of the football team. He was big, athletic, and very muscular—and was also well-known for being lewd, rude, and pretty much a dick to everyone (except the hot girls, that is...and they seemed to be mindlessly attracted to him like moths to a porch light...)

"Sor-ree!" Jack exclaimed, hands held up in a calming gesture as he backed away from the jock. As he continued to back down the aisle toward his desk in the rear, he glanced up at Wendy, who had buried her nose in the math book now lying open on her desk, ignoring everyone else in the room.

Especially him...

Heaving a heavy sign, he turned and headed back to his own desk in the back of the room, sitting down gruffly just as the class bell began ringing out in the hallway, and Mrs. Pearson entered the room, gently closing the door behind her.

For the rest of the week, he'd couldn't muster the courage to even approach her again—let alone ask her out

—he was just too embarrassed at the fool he'd been made of that day.

Soon after, school let out for the summer...and he had blown it.

And he had regretted it for the rest of his life.

•

"That's good, Jack, you did good."

The doctor then turned to the techs at the equipment, one of which nodded back while the other gave a thumbs up. Then one began throwing switches again while the other hit a lever with a *clunk!*, stopping the reel-to-reel, then another *clunk!* and they began quickly rewinding.

Once the tape finished rewinding, the tech pulled the reel off the spindle, walked to the other end of the computer bank, and snapped it onto a spindle there, then fed the end of the tape into a tray protruding from one of the computers, fed it into an empty reel on the other side, wound it a bit, then closed the lid on the tray with a *click!*, trapping the tape between the two readers. Once the computer indicated that the tape was properly engaged, he began once again throwing switches along the front, which once again changed the light patterns and monitor activities, but this time all in red, and the beeping sound ceased altogether.

As the tech did all this, the doctor stood, flipped through a few pages on his clipboard, scribbled something down, then turned back to the techs.

"All good?" he asked.

"Perfect. We got everything we need," on of them responded, the other nodding in agreement as he continued surveilling the monitors. "Thank you. We'll take it from here."

"Very well," the doctor said as he turned and walked to the door. As he opened the door and exited the room, he muttered *I need a cigarette* under his breath, then was gone, the door gently clicking shut behind him.

With the tape engaged and the computers set, the tech placed one hand on a key that dangled from a cylinder next to the tape reel, then turned and looked at the other tech who, with one last glance at all the monitors and blinking lights, walked over and placed his hand on an identical key in an identical cylinder down on the other end of the bank, then looked back over at the other.

"Three, two, one..." the other said aloud, displaying the count with the fingers of his other hand, "*...launch.*"

They both turned their keys simultaneously with a loud *clunk!*, and the entire bank lit up into a multi-colored constellation of flashing lights, various images and columns of data streaming and scrolling at lightening speed across all the monitors, the beeping sound returning as a loud, constant tone—and the tape reels began slowly turning, feeding Jack's recorded memory into the computers...

A few minutes passed as each tech walked along their respective ends of the bank, quickly reviewing all of the lights, switches, monitors, data, etc. Meeting in the middle, they nodded to each other indicating success, then turned together to look at the bed—

—the empty electrode helmet was now lying dormant on the now equally empty bed—

—then turned back to each other smiling, bumped fists, and returned their attention to the equipment.

The piercing tone faded until it ceased altogether, and the dancing lights all began to slow, the monitors all flatlining one by one.

One of the techs threw a lever with a *clunk!* and the tape stopped.

As the other retrieved a clipboard from a hook on the wall next to the computer bank and started scribbling on it, the other began throwing a series of switches, shutting the equipment down in proper sequential order.

•

Jack was waiting impatiently for Wendy to enter the classroom. The bell hadn't rung yet, and Mrs. Pearson hadn't even arrived yet, and students were still trickling in and taking their seat, so Jack decided to take advantage and go up to the front of the classroom to feign sharpening his pencils before class began.

Standing there grinding each one to a fine point, he kept his eye on the door, waiting...and nervous...in fact, he felt a little strange, almost dizzy, and he suddenly realized that he couldn't really recall coming to class, like he just woke up in here, and for some reason everything seemed a bit surreal...but he chocked it off to his own extreme nervousness...after all, today was the *big day*...

Finally, Wendy walked in, her beautiful dark hair bouncing with each step. She headed around the back of the room to the last row of desks that ran along the windows, then turned and started forward toward her desk up in front.

Jack pulled his pencil from the sharpener, feigned inspection of the the sharpening job, nodded in approval, then headed down the same row of desks that Wendy was heading up.

Meeting halfway, they stopped face to face, Jack smiling down at her, Wendy smiling up at him, her big brown eyes melting him.

"Hi," he said sheepishly.

"Hi," she answered. Then, glancing quickly around the room, she whispered, seemingly to herself, and nearly inaudibly: "Thank you, second chances."

This triggered something in the back of Jack's mind... *second chances...why did that sound familiar?*

And with it, an image flashed through his mind: a beautiful dark-haired woman walking with two men in suits down a fancy hallway...

"What did you just say?" Jack asked her. "Second chances?"

"What...?" she frowned, looking and sounding confused. "I...I was just thinking about something...maybe it was a dream I had last night....but now I don't remember."

And just as quickly as they had manifested, the

strange image and familiar words vanished from Jack's mind too, fading forever from his memory like a dream fades within moments of waking.

Refocusing on the task at hand, he took a deep breath. It was now or never...and he could feel his face turning beet red.

"Listen...I was wondering—"

"Hey dork, get your ass outta my face," a burly voice from behind him suddenly demanded, cutting him off.

Jack somehow resisted the urge to turn around and see who was barking at him. Somehow he knew he needed to do this, or he would regret it for the rest of his life. So, ignoring the asshole behind him, he willed himself to continue.—but just as he opened his mouth to do so, she dropped her head and pushed forward.

"Excuse me," she muttered as she brushed past him.

Jack watched in incredulity as she slipped into an empty desk in front of Matt Colburn, who was sitting behind him, apparently the one who had been barking at him. Matt was quarterback of the football team. He was big, athletic, and very muscular—and was also well-known for being lewd, rude, and pretty much a dick to everyone (except for the hot girls, that is...and they seemed to be mindlessly attracted to him like moths to a porch light...)

Abandoning her math book on the desktop, she quickly turned to Matt, her big brown eyes glowing, and began...

...*flirting* with him? *Seriously?*

And worse, Matt began flirting right back, smiling his

bright, perfect smile, while she giggled and fawned, then reached out and put her dainty hand on his muscular arm as she leaned forward to whisper something...

Heaving a heavy sigh, Jack turned and headed back to his own desk in the back of the room, sitting down gruffly just as the class bell began ringing out in the hallway, and Mrs. Pearson entered the room, gently closing the door behind her.

As he sat there fuming, he noticed the room was starting to tighten up, becoming sharper, the strange surrealness fading, as well as his mild dizziness...along with, of course, all of his hopes and dreams...

Turns out Jack heard nothing the teacher said during class that day, was totally oblivious to the lesson, because instead he had become thoroughly obsessed...angrily plotting his plan for sweet revenge...

•

He awoke with a start.

He knew it was early in the morning, for the sun was shining through the small east window of his cell, casting elongated shadows on the cinderblock wall above his cot, exaggerating the bars over the window, reminding him, as they did every morning.

He had been dreaming, though it was fading fast from his memory: a girl he loved long ago; a boy who stole her from him; and his sweet revenge...

Then it was gone.

But it was no dream.

Just a long-lost memory.

He pondered: if I had the chance to do it over—to go back in time, to that fateful moment that changed my life forever—would I still do it?

He shrugged.

Hard to say.

And besides, there ARE no second chances...life is what it is...

Reaching out to the nightstand, he picked up the pencil lying next to his journal.

Turning over on the cot, he reached up and scratched onto the rough wall above him:

"I have nothing but time."

Then, reconsidering, he crossed that out and scrawled beneath it:

"There's no such thing as time."

He wasn't sure what that meant, where he had gotten that notion—but it seemed true.

Chuckling at his own hopelessness, he rolled back over, tossed the pencil back onto the nightstand, then lay back, hands behind his head, staring at the same dirty plaster ceiling he had been staring at for so many years. With any luck, he would drift off again...

...perhaps this time to another time, another place...

Finished, Chaz sat back, awaiting his friends' response.

All was quiet, as they apparently had to think about it for a minute. Then Nick spoke up:

"Whoa...dude, that's messin' with my head!"

"Yeah, time travel does that," Chaz said matter-of-factly.

The others agreed, it was a somewhat complicated story, but they all liked it.

"So they both went back, but for different reasons," Casey said slowly, puzzling it out. "Just happened to be to the same exact moment?"

"You got it," Chaz confirmed.

"And so Jack's life actually turned out worse, instead of better." Ryan figured.

"Cuz you never know how you're gonna affect the past, or the future, if you could go back in time." Chaz added. "You can't just assume you'll be able to fix what you want...cuz *everything* changes."

Another round of *whoas* and *cools*.

"Chaz, my man, you may have just topped my story IT!" Ryan commended.

"Maybe...I guess we'll see." Chaz feigned skepticism, but sound pretty confident.

"Okay, so who wants to go next?" Jackie asked, glancing around at the remaining three.

"I'll go," Nick said.

"Nick, you have the stage," Jackie said, gesturing to his friend that he was up.

"I call my story *Process of Elimination*," Nick said, casting an ominous glare around at everyone, invoking dread.

"Okay, so there's this guy—I couldn't think of a cool name, so we'll just call him Bob—out shopping for his wife's birthday, and stops into a pawn shop called *Ron's Pawns*...

Process of Elimination

by Nicholas Gardner

"This is a nice one."

As he spoke, the salesman plucked the shining piece from inside the glass case and laid it on top, the silver and pearl glinting under the fluorescent lighting.

Bob watched, wondering if he was Ron, or if he just worked there.

"That's genuine pearl," he said, squinting through the column of smoke that drizzled up from the cigarette hanging from his lips.

They both stared down at it in silent admiration, the salesman waiting patiently.

Bob liked it, but decided it wasn't "the one." He just didn't think something so small would do...after all, this was his *wife* they were talking about—it was her birthday, and this year she said she wanted something special, something that would make her stop feeling like she was just getting old.

Bob sighed heavily. He'd been there a while now, and looked at several items already—but none of them seemed like the right one. And there were so many to choose from! He had no idea the process of elimination could be so difficult...

"I like it," he said. "Really, it's beautiful...but I think I'm looking for something a little bigger."

"I see," the man said, nodding.. "Something with a little more *flash?*" He obviously knew all the right buzz words.

So Bob decided he probably *was* Ron, not just a clerk.

Because he *knew*.

Bob nodded in agreement.

The man moved down a bit, fumbled with some keys, then snapped the back of the display case open.

"This one is very popular."

As he reached into the back of the display case, a dead ash floated down from his cigarette and exploded into a dime-sized black mess on the old, scratched glass countertop. As if in response, he sucked the cigarette back to life with a glow, a cloud of blue-grey smoke bursting from his nose and floated to the ceiling.

"It's bigger, but not *too* big...might be just what you're looking for. And the brushed finish gives it a unique look...sort of high-tech." The glowing end of the cigarette danced with his words, a bouncing ball along the bottom of the screen in a sing-along.

He lay it expertly on the glass for Bob to admire, so much silver flashing under the lights. He had to agree—it was awesome. Even with all the smoke dimming the lighting, it glistened like new. It was beautiful.

The man finally plucked the cigarette from his lips and held it to his side, behind the counter. "Waddya think?" He beamed, excited. He obviously loved his job.

Had to be Ron.

"I like it," Bob said, gently picking it up. It felt heavy. He liked that—felt like *quality*—didn't feel cheap.

"Can't go wrong with this one." He took another drag, then crossed his arms, the cigarette casting a smoke trail to the ceiling above him.

Again, he quietly waited, smiling.

Such a pro.

Bob wanted to get something big, but not *too* big; just big enough to show her that he was serious.

This one could do the trick.

"If you like it, we can do the paperwork right here." He turned, opened a file cabinet, yanked out a folder, and slapped it on the counter.

Bob was taken a little aback; he hadn't expected this..

Not at Ron's Pawns, anyway.

He gingerly placed the piece back onto the glass, the sliver gleaming under the lights.

"Yes, I like it. Actually, I *love* it. But..."

Ron waited. No attitude, no expression. Just waiting, listening, ready to try to change his customer's mind. Ready to do whatever it took to make the sale.

Bob turned and looked around. At the moment, there was nobody else in the pawn shop. Just himself and ol' Ron. Bob, with his expensive pleated slacks and sleek black designer button-up, boasting a Rolex on his wrist and an expensive Blackberry on his belt...and Ron, with his short-sleeved plaid shirt, faded blue jeans, black steel-toed boots, and wire-rim bifocals. And, of course, the ever-present cigarette, smoldering by his side.

Leaning forward, Bob lowered his voice to a near-whisper: "You got anything with less..." he stopped and frowned, looking down at the counter, searching for the right word, then back up at the man behind the counter. "You know...*paperwork?*" I mean...that can't be traced to...well, that shows that I bought it *here?*"

With this, they locked eyes—and Ron caught his meaning.

Again, he knew.

"I can pay cash," Bob added quickly, hoping to sway him. "I've been saving up for this."

Ron glanced nervously around. Seeing nobody else in the shop, he relaxed a little.

"I close at eight", he said rather gruffly. "Come back then. Anything comes in, you can take a look before it's processed." He yanked the shining piece off the counter, bent, placed it back into the case, closed and locked the door, then stood up.

"It'll cost you, though. I don't like buyin' and sellin' stuff under the table—I get enough harassment from the government as it is, just the nature of the beast—but right now I need the business. Thing's've been tight lately, economy bad as it's been."

"Money isn't an issue," Bob said. "Like I said, I've been saving. How much should I bring?"

Ron glanced around the room again, then back at Bob, staring at him while deftly crunching his cigarette out in the ashtray to his right.

"All of it."

•

And that's exactly what he did. Went home, retrieved his entire stash of cash from his home safe (it was her monthly euchre night with her friends from the office, so she wouldn't be home until late), waited anxiously until it was time, then returned to Ron's Pawns, arriving just after eight.

Ron met him at the front door, opening it just far enough to talk to him as he stood outside in the darkness.

"You're in luck," he said quietly. "Something came in about an hour ago, I think you'll like it." He twitched his head to the right. "Meet me around back."

Without another word, he closed and locked the door.

Bob drove around to the back alley behind the pawn shop, which was almost completely dark, just one lamppost on the far end of the building casting just enough dim florescent light to see, barely. Ron opened the thick, windowless steel door, and waved him over.

Leaving the car running, Bob got out, left the car door hanging open, and approached the tiny concrete porch, where Ron stood waiting like a ghost in the dark doorway.

He showed him the new arrival, and sure enough, it was the one. It was perfect. Bob nodded, and Ron turned and place it gently back into a small white box sitting on a table just inside the door.

They did the deal right there, Bob handing over a thick

roll of hundred dollar bills. Ron didn't even bother counting it, just stuffed it into his pocket. Turning inside to the table, he picked up the box and handed it over.

He started to close the door, and Bob turned to walk back to his car, but Ron stopped the door just far enough to stick his head out.

"And remember—you didn't get it here. Anyone asks, I know nothin' about it."

Bob nodded in agreement. "Absolutely. And thanks!"

Without responding he slammed the door shut, and the lock clicked from within.

Returning to his car, Bob drove down the alley to the back corner of the building, and stopped under that one dim lamp post. Excited, he wanted to take one more look at his new purchase before heading home and letting his wife have it.

He slowly opened the box, and smiled ear to ear. It was beautiful—and definitely the one! Ron sure called it...

The silver and gold glinted slightly, even in the dim light cast down from the lamp post; the silver shine of the polished stainless-steel .38 Special revolver, alongside the gold color of the six brass shells Ron had included in the box, unbeknownst to him...a nice little bonus!

Still smiling, he slapped opened the cylinder, and began sliding the shells into the chambers, one by one...

With that Nick stopped and looked around, grinning sheepishly.

"No way!" Chaz cried. "I thought he was shopping for jewelry! Totally faked me out!"

"Me too," Ryan admitted, smiling. "You had me, hook-line-and-sinker!"

"I was starting to wonder," Jackie said. "But I wasn't sure until the end...and, I really like the title's double-meaning: process of elimination...very clever!"

"Thanks!" Nick beamed. Then he turned to Casey. "So what'd you think?

Casey was frowning. "I don't know...I think it was sad."

At this, the boys looked around at each other, shrugging perplexedly.

"Well, not all stories have happy endings," Nick said.

"And 'sides, you don't know Bob's wife," Jackie posited. "I mean, what if she was a bitch, or was cheating on him and deserved what was coming?"

A chorus of *yeahs* and *good points* from the others.

"You know...sorta like your step-father," Nick cautiously ventured.

Casey glared at him for a moment, but then softened. "Well, okay. You're right. So maybe she deserved it." Then she smiled at him and nodded her approval. "It *was* a good story… it probably just bothered me a little because I'm a girl, like his wife...and hope to be married some day."

The others voiced their understanding.

Then, after a moment of silence, Jackie spoke up.

"Alright, who's next?"

"Why don't *you* go now?" Casey suggested. "I wanna here

your story!"

The rest chimed in, so Jackie relented.

"Well, I do have a pretty good one this week."

This got their interest piqued, and they egged him on.

So he sat up, cleared his throat, waited until he had everyone's rapt attention, then began:

"Okay, so there's this couple that just got married, and they're planning to spend their honeymoon in a cabin at a local ski resort up in the mountains...but there's a big snowstorm blowing in, so they're racing out of town and up the mountain ahead of it, trying to get to the cabin before the storm shuts everything down...I call it *The Wedding Gift*..."

The Wedding Gift
by Jackson Riggins

It was dusk, nearing the close of another cold, wet December day in Montana. Soft feathers of snow drifted lazily from a solid pewter sky, silently pelting the windshield of Steve Cole's speeding Jag, quivering momentarily, only to be casually whisked away by the nearly inaudible *flick-flick* of the windshield wipers in delay mode.

What was left of the soft, misty shroud of daylight was departing, slipping silently out the back door to the west. It ushered in nightfall in its stead, to take watch over the mountainside and all that resided there, under what promised to be a cold, moonless sky. The transition was smooth, seamless; rehearsed to perfection over millennia.

As inconspicuous as it was, Cole noticed this shift-change of nature—every second of it—in his seemingly vain attempt to stay within the daylight and leave the night behind him. Pressing the accelerator a little harder —a thought more than a motion—he coaxed his Jaguar XK6 to just under sixty. *"Come on, baby. . ."* he whispered under his breath. *". . just get us there."*

He had to be careful; these mountain roads were treacherous even when bone dry and the asphalt warmed to mild adhesion by the summer sun, let alone when wet and freezing during an impending snow storm such as this. But Steve also knew there were plenty of blind curves and pull-offs that cops liked to hide in up here in Big Belt, *and* it was Saturday night, when the drunks were out and the odds were up. Like shooting fish in a barrel. Anything over sixty would be a ticket, sure as shit. Under sixty, and he could probably weasel out with just a warning...

He doubted the cops would be out in this weather, though. But why take the chance?

It's my honeymoon, that's why, he thought.

Another deft urge, and the dial rose further....sixty-two...sixty-five—

"Wait, wait, wait—"

—it was Ryan this time—

"—what the heck is *Big Belt?*"

"I was wondering the same thing," Nick concurred.

Chaz nodded in agreement, and they all looked at Jackie, waiting for an explanation.

"It's a mountain range in Montana," Jackie said matter-of-factly, shrugging.

"You sure?" Nick grilled. "Ive never heard of it."

The others agreed, none of them had heard of Big Belt Mountains.

"Yeah, I looked it up in my dad's Road Atlas. It's just south of Great Falls."

He looked around at all of them convincingly, and since adding the city name to his explanation seemed to solidify it, the others looked around at each other and nodded in acceptance.

"Well, okay, if you say so…" Ryan relented. "Continue…"

"So anyway," Jackie continued, "Cole was speeding up the mountain in his Jag…"

—speed was essential, as Cole was in a three-way race: racing the darkness of night; racing the storm; and racing his own dark and stormy libido. He was well aware that the few scattered snowflakes that dotted the landscape ahead of him were mere messengers, dashing about, warning all in their path that the rest of their army was on its way up the mountain. An army of countless soldiers, soldiers that would soon overtake the road, the woods, and eventually the entire mountain, relentless, overpowering by sheer numbers. They would obscure the landscape, blind all spectators, and bury everything in their path in a white fury.

In preparation for the assault, snowstorm warnings had been issued for the entire area. Channel Five *(Five At Five Coming To You Live!)* was predicting six to ten inches, with wind gusts of thirty to fifty—which meant it would be blowing and drifting, and generally making life miserable for everyone.

The road up Big Belt was already wet with melted snow, but the sleek silver sports car handled it well. Steve sank deeper into his leather bucket seat, and sighed. Relaxing a little, confidence overtook him. He was certain they would make it to the cabin before the storm hit. He turned and smiled at the beautiful blonde that occupied the passenger seat. Leaning over the console that separated the front seats, she lay against him, her head resting on his shoulder.

Angela had now been his wife for nearly two hours.

"I can't wait," she whispered in his ear. "The cabin, the skiing, the time away from the rest of the world..."

"That's right, honey," he agreed. "Just you and me for two whole weeks."

She purred contentedly, and lifted her head just enough to kiss his cheek, then returned to rest on his shoulder. The unmistakable aroma of expensive champaign wafted about her, making him smile.

Steve and his new bride were racing the storm eastward, heading up the mountainside to Big Belt Ski

Resort, where they had rented a small, cozy cabin hidden away up in the mountain wilderness. There they would spend their honeymoon—two full weeks of newly-wedded bliss—before heading down the mountain and returning home just in time for Christmas.

Lofty pines and breathtaking oaks cloaked the mountain road on the outer side. Blurring by, the massive wall of green and brown streaks were quickly fading to so many shades of black and gray as the night set in, interrupted only by the occasional faded yellow traffic sign warning of tight curves or treacherous grades ahead. Inside the road's curves, cliffs huddled right up to the pavement and halted abruptly, where men, machines and explosives had chiseled out the cold angry rock, pouring warm friendly asphalt in its place.

As the darkness thickened, the snowfall thickened with it, as if encouraged by it, somehow braver hiding within the shadows. Snow was beginning to stick to the rock face above the road, softening its jagged complexion with gentle fuzzy white lines, each spreading toward the other, soon to meet, inevitably to completely envelop the cliff—as well as the road it embraced.

Noticing this ominous progression, Angela suddenly sat up, peering anxiously out her side window.

"It's snowing harder," she said, concerned. She turned to look ahead, into the dwindling twilight, the two white tunnels of blowing snow that were brightly illuminated by the piercing headlights. She turned to him, eyes strained with worry. Her eyes more resembled two big pools of chocolate than actual human anatomy—and the look she now gave him enhanced that feature, mocking reality, almost cartoonish.

Cartoon puppy-dog eyes.

He returned the look with one of strength and reassurance, his piercing blue eyes glowing, even in the diminished daylight, as if they themselves were plugged into the dash along with all the other multi-colored lights. A haphazard shock of dark hair dangled between them. He smiled, his pearly-whites glowing even more than his electric eyes.

"Don't worry, we're gonna make it...no problem," he reassured her. "Another ten or fifteen minutes and we'll be out from under this storm...leave it behind us...it'll be clear skies the rest of the way, you'll see."

She nodded slightly, then he returned his attention to the road—quietly coaxing it to sixty-five, hoping she didn't notice.

Fuck the ticket, he thought. He wasn't going to let this snowstorm—or some damn road pirate, for that matter—ruin his honeymoon.

Sighing heavily, she returned to his shoulder. "Just hurry, okay?"

Her hand wandered up his right leg, coming to rest against his crotch.

"I am," he whispered. He glanced down at the speedometer and watched it rise, as he was now rising, in response to her provocation.

•

Behind Cole's racing jag, some twenty miles to the west, the mountain suddenly kneeled down and succumbed to the city limits of Brenton, Montana. At that point, the natural wilderness stopped and concrete and steel began.

North of town, Brenton Way connected with Highway 12, which then headed up Big Belt Mountain, meandering this way and that over the rugged terrain. Highway 12 stretched clear across the entire state of Montana, hitting all of the best ski resorts and their glamorous 5-star hotels along the way.

The newlyweds had made it out of town directly after their wedding and reception at Brenton Baptist—as the first few flakes of snow began to waft down from the ominously darkening sky—and directly before the storm unleashed its fury on the town.

Knowing what was coming, they had thrown their luggage into the trunk, which was now full to the brim.

But then, upon further consideration, they decided to bring a few of their wedding gifts along, that they thought might possibly come in handy during their honeymoon at the cabin.

As they were loading them into the back seat, they happened to come face-to-face, ducking simultaneous into the opposite doors, prompting them to stop and smile at each other.

He looked down at all the gifts, then looked back up and said: "Ya know, *you're* the *best* gift."

With this he smiled, while she donned a sarcastic look and responded:

"Damn straight...I mean, how would you *ever* survive without me?"

He shrugged in a *who knows?* manner, she smiled and nodded in agreement, then they both backed out of the car and closed the doors.

Shortly thereafter, they hit the road.

•

Now the snowstorm was in full swing, the snow coming down *hard*. So hard, in fact, that Sheriff Strom Bennett had already declared a snow emergency and closed off most of the streets in town. The only two still open were Brenton Way and Washington Boulevard, the two main drags that crossed each other in the center of town, with town hall on the northwest corner and the police headquarters poised opposite. All six of the town's big smoke-belching snowplows were noisily working these two four-lane thoroughfares non-stop, trying their best to keep them passable for what little traffic remained—mostly people trying to get home from work or Walmart or Brenton Way Discount Liquor.

The National Weather Service had warned of the storm, monitoring it as it left the Rockies and trekked across Helena National Forest en route to Brenton and Big Belt Mountain. But the "experts" had severely misjudged the storm, underestimating its potential to worsen. Secretly, the storm had sucked up extra energy and moisture as it passed over Canyon Lake, just west of Brenton. On radar it still appeared to be a mere Category Two, prompting storm warnings in its path and not more than casual alertness from the citizens of Brenton. In reality, however, it had quietly grown past Category Two, and even surpassed Category Three entirely undetected—and exploded into a Category Four just as it reached Brenton, unable to contain itself any longer, dumping tons of Canyon Lake water down on the town in the form of snow. Not just snow—but an angry, furious attack of snow, ice, wind, and freezing temperatures.

The town was quickly buried in the wrath of the storm, and even the bravest of the brave succumbed to its harsh whipping and chaffing and freezing. Final light witnessed them all running, tails tucked, collars flipped up or hoods tied, abandoning luxuries for mere necessities, running for the warmth and safety of their homes and families—and hiding from The Beast behind brick and mortar and double-pained windows, and in front of warm fireplaces and space heaters.

Finally, at Brenton and Washington, futility set in. The massive, bloated storm clouds completely masked what was left of the sunset, prematurely painting the sky pitch black. The snow was blinding, coming in sideways, riding on brisk forty and fifty mile-per-hour winds—with even higher gusts whipping the millions of little bastards into a sharp, angry fury, slicing the frozen air, stinging the face, lashing the eyes, making it nearly impossible to see. The snowplow drivers could no longer see what they were plowing, and one had scraped the paint and side-view mirrors off of more than one of the half-buried line of cars that were still parked along Washington Boulevard, abandoned to the storm, with little red EXPIRED flags tattling from atop the old meters that stitched the sidewalk all the way west to Brenton Square and east to Brenton Park.

The temperature had plummeted into the teens, and was still dropping—threatening to give the snowplow drivers a memorable case of frostbite and windburn if they persisted. Besides, the snow was coming down so fast that even the plows were struggling to maneuver, occasionally getting stuck in the ever growing drifts or on nearly invisible patches of ice hiding under the snow. Finally, the plows were sent back to base before it was too late and even *they* got stranded in the storm. The snow had built to eight inches already, with drifts reaching over a foot—and it had been snowing for less than an hour.

•

Sheriff Bennett pulled his white Ford Bronco, police lights flashing, into the interchange of Brenton Way and Highway 12, on the northern edge of Brenton, just before the highway began its ascent into the Big Belt Mountains, the storm lashing his vehicle as if punishing it for daring to venture into its territory.

The overheads sent rhythmical stripes of red and blue through the waves of white fury and off into the blackness beyond. His windshield was covered in a thick blanket of snow, with little slanted eyes of blackness cut out by the windshield wipers whisking madly to keep up, making the Bronco appear to be sneering.

The sheriff had ordered the highway entrance closed to traffic due to the weather emergency, and in response road crews had set up barricades—big orange and white-striped sawhorses with bold black letters stenciled onto the crossbeams: ROAD CLOSED, each topped with a battery-powered flashing yellow light—across the entrance to the onramp onto Highway 12.

But as he was heading to the station to monitor the snow emergency, a route that took him past the highway interchange, he had noticed that the wind had blown the barricades over, and they were now buried nearly out of sight in the snow, their angled legs on one side sticking up in the air like a dead, stiff animal—and he certainly didn't want anyone trying to get on the highway in this mess.

Fighting the wind and snow, Strom got out, slipping, nearly falling, both hands gripping the door for support. Once stabilized, he closed the door and turned toward the ramp.

Head lowered against the wind, one hand holding his Stetson in place, the other arm held outward for balance on the snow and ice, he slowly worked his way over to the downed barricades. Once there, he was surprised that he had made it without either tripping in the snow or slipping on the ice underneath and falling face-first into the bitter cold drifts.

Heaving the first barricade out of the snow, he reset it onto the road, brushing the snow from the stenciled words on the front and the light on top. Fortunately, the light was still working, flashing a dull light that caused the snowflakes flurrying around it to pulse yellow.

After doing the same with the second barricade, he noticed they both had sandbags straddling the lower crossmembers, as they should. But apparently, it wasn't enough, the gale-force wind had blown them over anyway. So to help stabilize them, he kicked thick mounds of snow around each of the legs, stomping and packing it until they were both anchored firmly in place.

"Should hold 'em for a while, anyway," he said softly to himself.

He then turned from the flashing yellow lights atop the barricades to the flashing red and blue lights atop his vehicle, and started back.

It was even more of a struggle to return to his Bronco than it had been to reach the barricades; the snow had deepened noticeably even in the short time he had worked. The wind had also picked up, and he could tell that the temperature was still dropping. Nevertheless he fought his way back to his truck, and managed to climb in and quickly shut the door—leaving The Beast outside, wreaking its havoc.

Tossing his snow-coated hat onto the passenger seat with one hand, he yanked the radio mic off the receiver with the other.

"Bennett to base," he announced with authority.

"Base here....Jeez, where the hell *are* you, Strom?" the worried voice came back, crackling and garbled from the storm. It was Mike Mason, a young Deputy who just started last month. Being the rookie, he was cursed to work all the shit shifts, of course—like Saturday nights during snowstorms.

"Highway Twelve at Brenton. Had a problem with the barricades, but the situation is resolved."

"Highway's closed now, right?"

"Yep. Looks like nobody's gonna be skiing this weekend. Twelve'll prolly be closed at least a week after this baby is over...maybe longer. Till then, nobody'll be able to get up Big Belt without a helicopter."

"Strom, you better get back here right quick...it's gettin' bad out there...*real* bad."

Tell me about it...

"Damn Weather Service—"

—then the radio suddenly hissed and crackled with static, coinciding with a blast of wind that rocked Bennett's Bronco, rattling the windows—

"—some warning, huh?"

"Roger that...but after all these years, I've gotten used to their...*ineptitude.*"

"Well *I* haven't...this storm has me worried."

"Don't worry, Mike, I'm on my way back. I'll be there in a few. Over."

"Copy. We'll keep the lights on for ya. Base out."

Hanging the mic back on the radio, Bennett floored it, spraying high arches of snow into the air as he did a half-donut in the intersection. Once straightened out, he paused to turn the overheads off, then began creeping slowly through the snow, which was now at least ten inches deep.

The four-wheel-drive Bronco moved steadily down Brenton toward headquarters, the big all-terrains spinning intermittently but holding their own, his tire tracks quickly fading under fresh snow as Bennett and his Bronco slowly faded into the night.

•

The buck was perched high above Highway 12, on a point known to the locals as Pine Ridge. A majestic bull elk, twenty-two pointer, sleek, as powerful as he was beautiful, balanced with both front hooves on the edge of the rock face that plummeted downward nearly one hundred feet to meet the road below. The cliff here did not drop straight down, like the others; rather, it offered a mild grade, just enough so that a few shrubs and seedlings had taken root here and there along the numerous ledges, trying to eek out a living on the small amount of soil that had collected there over time.

Among these brave and stubborn plants was a snowberry bush, huddled against the cliff just below the ledge where the large animal stood. Although much of the plant was withered with the cold of winter, there were still a few ripened berries on the downward side, dangling out over the cliff, tantalizing the beast. The tiny, glistening white berries were just beyond his reach, and he inched further out onto the cliff's edge, craning his neck as far as he could downward, reaching out over the ledge and down the rock wall, mere inches from the glistening white berries. He was so close he could smell them—their sweet wintergreen flavor radiating its scent around them—which made him crave them even more.

Leaning out, shifting his massive weight forward to his front hooves, he came within striking distance of the berries. The wind had picked up, along with the snow, which was coating one side of his fur white, and adding a thin glaze of moisture to the rock ledge on which he carefully balanced himself. The wind and plummeting temperatures began to freeze the glaze on the rocks. Likewise, snow and ice was building on his hooves, and the wet fur above them was hardening into icicles. Just one more inch, and the luscious berries would be his, then he would quickly retreat back into the shelter of the woods to weather the storm. He strained as far out as he was able, shifting so much of his weight forward that his rear hooves were barely touching the ground. It required all of the buck's strength and balance to keep him from falling forward and tumbling down the cliff.

Finally, within reach, he began plucking the berries

one by one from the dangling branches, quickly devouring them, barely bothering to chew. Each successive berry pulled the beast incrementally further and further over the edge of the rocks, closer and closer to the point of no return. If he ventured out much further, his own weight could suddenly shift, catapulting the huge animal over the ledge and plummeting down the snow- and ice-covered cliff to the highway below.

Just as he finished the last cluster of berries, straining to his absolute limit to reach them, balanced ever so precariously on the edge of rock, the wind shifted—and a sudden gust struck him from behind, momentarily rocking him slightly forward.

The gust nudged the beast barely an inch, but it was just enough to tip the scales. His rear hooves left the ground, forcing his weight forward beyond the fulcrum created by his front hooves on the edge of the cliff. Then, his front hooves broke free from the icy rock, suddenly sliding downward. For an instant, the buck struggled to recapture his balance, all four hooves scampering for a hold on the icy rock ledge, but it was too late, and too slippery.

Quickly abandoning all hope of regaining his balance, the six-hundred pound bull elk began a half-running, half-tumbling descent down the rock face. There was just enough grade to keep him from free-falling, and he instead entered into a mostly uncontrolled gallop, sloppily jumping from ledge to ledge as he fell. He was all hooves;

slipping, scampering, jumping, falling, galloping down the slope, one moment in control and the next totally out of it, emitting bursts of frightened bawls along the way.

A mini avalanche of snow, rocks, dirt, and broken limbs began rolling with him, making it even harder for the animal to maintain his skirmish and avoid an all-out plummet down the cliff. But the buck was strong and agile, and was able to right itself upon each tumble; to leap, even for only a moment, onto the smallest of footholds. With muscles rippling under fur, the beast managed to more or less gallop his way down the rock face rather than fall to a certain death on the asphalt below. His sheer strength and agility turned certain death into a fighting chance to live.

•

Christopher Cole was muttering softly to himself as he hung another ornament on the brightly decorated Christmas tree.

"I sure wish Daddy was here to help."

"Come now, you're doing a fine job on your own," Abby Cole commended. "Your father will be proud of you when he sees how well you decorated the tree."

Abby was Christopher's grandmother. He was staying with Steve's parents during his honeymoon with Angela, who as of today was now his step-mother (and that was okay with him, he liked Angie...not as much as his *real* mother, of course, but she was gone and he understood that she was no longer an option...so Angie it was).

He looked forward to their return, so that Christmas could start!

Suddenly the back door burst open, and a bitter gust of wind and snow swirled into the kitchen, blowing a flock of papers and magnets off the front of the refrigerator. As the magnets rattled across the white linoleum floor and coupons, sticky notes, and a scribbled grocery list fluttered about in the air, a man emerged from the flurry of snowflakes into the open doorway, burdened with an armful of split wood logs.

Bundled in coat, gloves, scarf, and hat, Victor Cole stumbled in, head held down against the wind. A second angry gust lashed him from behind, pushing him forward as he stepped across the threshold, slamming the door open against the kitchen wall with a *bang!* The old man's hat took flight, blowing off his nearly bald head, joining the myriad of hapless magnets on the floor. The newly escaped notes and photos from the fridge rode the second wave of wind across the kitchen floor, easily sliding over the old worn surface—and a few of them disappearing under the stove.

The second blast caused Christopher's grandpa to stumble, nearly fall, as more snow rushed in behind him. Finally, he turned and pulled the door away from the wall with one foot, then pushed it shut with his shoulder, and all was quiet again. The Beast raged outside, a muffled fury that rattled the doors and windows, moaning as it worked its way through the pines and around the eaves.

"Looks like it's turned into real hum-dinger," he speculated as Abby and Christopher rushed into the kitchen from the living room on account of all the ruckus..

"I don't understand," Abby said, shaking her head in wonder as she retrieved her husband's hat from the floor. "They only issued a mild warning....something like six to ten inches, with some drifting...not a severe winter storm like this."

She strolled to the window, pulled back the curtain on one side, and peered out, assessing the brutality of the storm that raged outside while clutching her husband's hat tightly to her chest.

Suddenly the lights began flickering, threatening to go out and leave the three standing in the darkness of the old kitchen. They buzzed and fluctuated wildly for a few seconds, then came on strong again. Victor chuckled.

"Now don't you worry your little head, Abs.....we got enough firewood downstairs to last into next week, if we hafta hunker down that long—and Lord willin' we won't—and even if we do, we got enough'uh your cannin' in the basement to feed us to spring."

He grinned at this, stretching his thick grey (and now snow-coated) mustache from ear to ear. Some of the embedded frosty powder floated to the floor, released by the smile. He winked, and proceeded across the kitchen to the basement door.

"Let me put this kindlin' up, then I'll come help finish the tree."

"Gramma said maybe I could light the tree this year!" Christopher announced, excited at the prospect. Grinning ear to ear, he looked up at Abby, beaming, awaiting his grandfather's approval.

The old man stopped in the stairwell, and turned. "Is that right?" He glanced from the boy to his wife.

"Whaddya say, Vic?" Abby asked. "I think he's old enough....besides, Steve's not here to do it....." Then she, too, then awaited her husband's nod.

"Well...I do think it's about time Steve handed that old tradition down to the new man in the family."

He turned and disappeared into the darkness of the basement, the creaking stairs following his heavy footsteps.

Christopher looked up his grandmother. "Does he really mean it?" he asked, not wanting to get his hopes up too soon.

"Well, you heard him, same as me."

"YES!" Christopher exclaimed, pumping his fist in victory. He turned and ran back into the living room, eager to finish the tree.

The lights flickered again, and they could hear Grampa shouting something in the basement. But as always, the old house persevered, and the three of them were able to finish decorating the tree without the use of flashlights or candles. Soon fire roared in the fireplace, warming the living room and smelling of the outdoors, winter, pine trees, and family.

Christmas was in the air.

The tree finally finished, Victor ran the thick orange extension cord around the edges of the living room from the tree to the outlet on the other wall, then handed the plug end to Christopher. "Lighting the tree" consisted of the simple act of plugging the cord into the outlet, and watching as the multitude of lights—some blinking, some solid, all in an array of colors—came to life, officially kicking off the Christmas season. It was a simple act, but an important and symbolic one. Christopher was elated; this would now be his privileged duty, for which he had waited his entire life—and it would probably be his until he had children of his own some day.

Christopher, Abby, and Vic gathered on the far side of the living room. Arm-in-arm, the elder couple donned a solemn air of seriousness, preparing for the all-important ceremony.

Christopher proudly held the all-important plug up with one hand, awaiting orders from his grandparents to plug it in...

•

In total darkness and near blinding snowfall, Steve Cole continued his race up Big Belt. He had been forced to slow a bit, as the snow and ice began building on the pavement, but was still hovering around fifty-five. The curves were becoming treacherous, and he had almost kissed the outer guardrail more than once—being offered a glancing view down the mountain he didn't much care for, before regaining control of the car and returning to a safer section of the road...

...*like between the lines*, he thought, scolding himself.

Luckily, Angela had dozed off, so Steve was able to drive a little faster than she probably would have been comfortable with, in what was quickly looking to be a vain attempt to leave the storm behind them and reach the warmth and safety of the cabin before it caught back up with them.

Soon, he thought. *Just a little further...*

He still hoped that he could beat the storm, that soon the snowfall would begin to thin, signifying his approach to the leading edge of the storm—followed by his escape out from under it. An hour later he and his new wife would be cuddling together warmly in the cabin, sipping champagne in front of the roaring fireplace, listening to the storm howling harmlessly outside. And after it passed, they would enjoy two weeks of wonderful skiing on the fresh snow the storm left behind.

He looked up at the small plastic photo holder that dangled from his rear-view mirror. A snapshot, sloppily trimmed with children's scissors, displayed Steve sitting in a rowboat, holding an oar high over his head with both hands. Between his legs, sharing the same small seat, was Christopher, his five-year-old son. The boy was grinning ear to ear, showing a gap of missing teeth, and holding up a stringer of fish they had caught that day out on the lake. His hat was on backwards, with crazy tuffs of golden hair poking out here and there, and his forehead was red with sun, nearly matching the bright red life jacket tied around his tiny body. He had Steve's ice-blue eyes, but they were tempered a bit with a smattering of freckles that crossed his nose between them. The freckles could only have come from his mother, Linda—Steve's first wife.

Linda had snapped the photo from the dock as the two returned from the annual Father & Son Fishing Contest held at Brenton Lake every July. The pair had won the competition that year, catching more than three dozen, fully ten more than the second place winners—and former champions three years running—Sheriff Bennett and his boy Ollie.

The Duo had credited the feat to Steve's "secret bait", which was really just baby crickets, but it was fun to witness the entire town wondering what miracle recipe they had concocted that seemed to make the fish practically jump into their boat. To this day people still asked him what he used that year, and he would just adopt a mysterious look, glancing around for eavesdroppers, and whisper "Secret Bait. I could tell you, but then I'd have to kill you."

That was two years ago, one month before Linda was diagnosed with Hodgkin's, and six months before she died during an intense chemotherapy treatment. Christopher was seven now, and seemed to be recovering from his mother's sudden death fairly well. When Steve met Angela a year later, Christopher took to her immediately, and the three of them got along wonderfully. When Steve and Angela decided to marry, they sat down with Christopher and literally asked his permission, assuring him they would not marry without his approval. Fortunately, he wholeheartedly approved, and the three of them hugged and cheered and laughed the rest of the evening. They were all truly happy together.

"Don't worry, big guy—I'll be back before Christmas," he whispered from behind the wheel as he gazed at his son smiling up at him from the boat. "I promise."

And in that moment, his love for his son became almost overwhelming, bringing tears to his eyes...

•

"Well, go ahead son," his grandfather beckoned, as his grandmother watched the dark tree in anticipation.

That was exactly what he had been waiting for, he didn't have to be told twice. Bending, he lined the plug up with the outlet, then, looking back over his shoulder at the tree, shoved the plug into the outlet, and watching with an excited smile as the tree lit up in bright, glorious flashing colors.

It was beautiful! But then, he felt something...a warm, loving feeling, deep inside...a *presence*. Looking up at his grandparents, he said, in a surprised voice:

"Daddy's here."

They both looked from the tree down to Christopher.

"What was that?" Abby asked, not sure she had heard him right.

"Daddy's here...I feel him...he's here!" he said, smiling ear to ear, now both hands clutched to his chest.

Abby and Victor looked at each other and smiled, Vic shrugging.

"Of course he is, honey!" she answered in a loving tone. "He's always here in spirit. We all are, and always will be! Because we're family!"

"That's right," Victor agreed, nodding.

With that, they turned back to the tree, basking in the lights and the warmth of the fireplace...and of *family*.

Beaming, Christopher also stared at the tree, the lights twinkling and flashing all over, bringing it to life...

•

Steve's gaze turned from Christopher's photo down to Angela, still asleep with her head resting on his shoulder. He turned back to the road, which he could now barely see through the raging snow. Gipping the steering wheel in concentration, he desperately tried to strike a balance: drive fast enough to get out from under the storm, while still driving safely enough to get them up to the cabin in one piece.

He recognized the curve ahead. It was a wide curve, wrapping around a high rocky cliff that towered above the road—some called it Pine Ridge—a mildly graded incline marked with sparse vegetation that set it apart from the other rock faces, which were merely harsh jagged rock rising straight into the air with no signs of life whatsoever. It was a mental landmark to him, one that he passed countless times en route to the resort. He also knew that it marked exactly half an hour to go, half an hour to reach the resort, and their cabin—half an hour, that is, at *normal speeds*. He would never make it that soon at his present rate. Excited at the prospect of finally reaching his destination and getting out of this storm, he again lightly coaxed the accelerator...*sixty...sixty five...*

•

The buck made it all the way down the cliff without actually falling, deftly hopping and jumping and stumbling and bawling from ledge to ledge, until he reached the final outcropping of rock, about eight feet above the highway, and decided that was close enough, and with a final, massive effort, leapt out and away from the face of the cliff and down to the highway below.

And right then, Steve Cole's speeding Jag came flying around the curve from out of sight behind the cliff.

The buck landed on the asphalt directly in front of the car, and Steve hadn't seen it until that moment.

"Oh sh—!" was all he managed before slamming on the brakes and yanking the wheel to the right, trying to dodge the massive beast and continue on.

And he might have made it, too, except that was the same direction the buck was moving, with way too much momentum from the jump to stop or change directions. The huge animal continued scampering forward, trying to catch his balance, hooves slipping everywhere on the wet and icy road, his one visible eye wide with terror in the

Jag's headlights.

Angela awoke with a start, jerking up and staring out the windshield, just as Steve yanked the wheel even harder, desperate to pass the buck on the right, but then the rear tires broke free, and the rear of the car began to slide forward on the left. And though the front end did, just barely, miss the buck, the rear end, spinning forward now, struck it.

The impact was bone-jarring.

The windows along the left side of the car exploded in shredded glass, the rear window spider-webbing.

The elk bawled loudly upon impact—the rear of the car striking his rear flank, spinning him around and sending his head into the windshield, shattering it. And though the impact detonated the front airbags, the buck's antler ripped into the one on the driver side as it punched momentarily through the glass then back out, pulling much of the tattered airbag remains out with it.

The intense impact also launched the car into an uncontrolled spin in the opposite direction now, the rear end having glanced off the massive elk.

Wearing no seatbelt, Angela was thrown screaming back across the passenger seat, her head striking the window sharply before she sank back against the seat, unconscious.

The car spun end-for-end across the wet and icy road, careening toward the drop-off on the outside of the curve. Unfortunately, the outer guardrail didn't start for another ten feet or so, so there was nothing to keep the car on the road. Its front wheels reached the edge first, and the Jag careened forward and plummeted down the wooded embankment.

The buck was badly injured and knocked into a state of shock, but his momentum from the downhill run and eight-foot leap kept his body spinning and sliding across the wet and icy road behind the Jag, until it too plunged over the edge and onto the embankment, where it lay concealed in the brush and bushes, twisting and writhing and bawling momentarily before going still.

Steve had no control of the vehicle at this point, all he could do was stay on the brake and hope for the best, grasping the steering wheel for dear life as the Jag bounced down the embankment, wedding gifts from the back seat now flying and tumbling all over the inside of the car.

On its way down the car happened to miss several standing trees, but there was an enormous fallen tree lying across its path at the bottom of the embankment, it's dead and gnarled branches sticking out in all directions.

Just before the car struck headlong into the massive fallen tree, a thick branch protruding from the middle of the trunk punched through the broken windshield on the passenger side, spearing Angela through her neck, killing her instantly, just before the car slammed into the trunk of the tree, stopping it with a jolt.

Upon impact with the tree, Steve's head struck the

steering wheel violently, knocking him unconscious, while the floorboard above the pedals buckled with the impact, first breaking his ankle then collapsing altogether, gripping his leg like a sprung steel bear trap.

And just like that, all was quiet.

As Steve, Angela, the Jag, and the dying buck all lay motionless, the ever-thickening snowfall silently blanketed them.

•

As Christopher,, and his grandparents stood admiring the twinkling tree, the power suddenly went out, plunging the entire house into darkness. And just as suddenly Christopher had another feeling, this time a bad one. In the darkness, his grandparents heard him say softly, "Daddy's gone now."

•

Before long, the power went out across the whole town, plunging Brenton into a stifling darkness, and then the phone lines went down as well.

Sheriff Bennett's Bronco was the last vehicle to brave the storm in Brenton that night. He barely made it back to Headquarters, where he and Mason decided to hole up for the night and weather the storm.

Now all that any of them could do was wait...

•

Steve was starting to lose track of how many days had passed.

When he had first regained consciousness, deep in the

night, he had found he was unable to escape the car, as his mangled leg was trapped within the buckled floorboard. He gave it everything he had, screaming and screaming with the searing pain, but he never came even close to freeing his trapped leg.

He had also quickly determined that Angela was dead, having been nearly decapitated by a stout branch that had stabbed through the windshield upon impact with the tree, pinning her to the passenger seat, one arm lying limply across the center console, her body beginning to freeze—and he screamed some more, and wept for what seemed like hours.

Once he had eventually gathered himself, he looked around, surmising his situation—and quickly determined that the entire car was buried beneath an untold amount of snow.

This was not good.

He had also noticed that, like Angela, he too was starting to freeze—had begun shivering all over uncontrollably, numbness creeping into his extremities.

Leaning forward, he had turned the key in the ignition —and was elated, incredulous, that the engine started!

First thing he then did was dropped it into reverse... but he couldn't operate the pedals, with one leg trapped (and broken), and the floorboard caved in to the point that he couldn't get his other foot to the gas pedal.

He had quickly realized that there would be no moving the car.

So instead, throwing it into park, he had cranked up the heat until he stopped shivering, felt the warmth returning to his hands and feet.

Then he had turned off the engine, to preserve fuel. Who knows how long he would be trapped here before somebody found him.

So he continued this routine on and off for the next several days. It was just enough to keep him from freezing to death, while Angela's body remained frozen.

But now, he was getting desperate.

Days had passed and he had not heard any sign of traffic on the highway above, and his car remained buried in snow. He knew that the only chance of rescue would come after the snow melted enough for the road to reopen, and for his car to be visible from above.

He'd tried the horn: nothing, deafening silence.

Surely, by now someone was aware that they hadn't shown up at the resort, and were missing? Surely Mom, Dad, the authorities, were looking for them by now?

Had to be.

So it was only a matter of time.

He just had to stay alive...

And now, the Jag's battery was dying, and the fuel gauge was showing the tank near empty. If he wasn't rescued soon, he would freeze to death.

And worst of all, he was getting dizzy and light-headed from lack of food. He had been able to eat a little snow scooped through the windshield (his electric side window was jammed shut), drink the dribbles that melted off when he ran the heat, enough to stave off dehydration... but he had nothing whatsoever to eat, and at this point was having trouble remaining conscious.

And he knew if he lost consciousness now, it would likely be for the last time.

He couldn't believe that after all the food they had at the wedding reception, they hadn't thought to bring any with them.

Or did they? Maybe Angela brought something he wasn't aware of?

Excited at the prospect, he wrenched his head around, peering as far as he could into the back seat, hoping to spy a covered dish, plastic-wrapped plate, Tupperware container, *something...*

It was an absolute wreck back there: boxes strewn everywhere, loose things thrown all about, glass items shattered, fragile goods damaged or destroyed in the accident.

Scouring the mess, he saw the crystal champaign glasses lying on the floorboard, most of them cracked or shattered; the shambles of the cutlery set, empty slotted wood block on the floor, wood-handled knives of every kind scattered everywhere; the scented candle set, still in the box, lying upside-down in front of the seat.

But he saw nothing in the way of food.

Turning back around, he sighed heavily in futility.

"I'm sorry, baby," he said softly, reaching down and

patting Angelas frozen, lifeless hand, still lying across the center console.

Suddenly, he knew he wasn't going to make it. He was going to starve to death. What a kicker: survive what should have been a fatal accident, only to starve and/or freeze to death under a foot of snow.

Laying his head back on the headrest, he closed his eyes for a moment, trying to think, unable to concentrate in his weakened, starving state. Then, when he opened his eyes, he was looking directly at the photo hanging from the rear-view mirror...

Christopher.

He simply couldn't allow himself to die. Christopher had already lost his mom, how would he ever manage if he lost his dad, too—only two years later?

I can't die, he thought. *I can't do that to him...*

A wave of dizziness and light-headedness engulfed him, but he willed himself to stay conscious.

How much longer could he survive? Long enough to be rescued? Best he could tell, the snow hadn't even started melting off of his vehicle yet...

Once again, he scoured the inside of the car, desperate for an idea...anything that might save him...

...save *Christopher*...

Then his eyes returned to Angela's arm, lying pale and frozen before him. Slowly turning to the back seat, his eyes came to rest on the hazard of knives lying all over the floorboard from the new cutlery set they had received as a wedding gift.

No...

Looking away, he again sighed heavily.

There's no other way...

He looked down at the gleaming wedding rings on her cold, lifeless finger.

No...

Again, he fought off a major fainting spell.

When the spinning stopped and his vision cleared—possibly for the last time—he again looked up at the photo of Christopher.

You have to...for Christopher...

That did it.

Heart sinking, he reached behind the seat and plucked the big carving knife out from under the pile, the others dropping back to the floor in a metallic rattle.

Again he placed his hand over Angela's, but this time he grasped it firmly, bringing the knife to her frozen arm with the other hand.

"I'm sorry, baby," he whispered.

"I'm so sorry...but it's the only way I'll survive."

Tears welling in his eyes, he began to slowly saw...

"No way!"
"Ohhhh!"
"Grohhhsssss!"

The reaction of the kids around fire was raucous, while Jackie just looked around at them, grinning ear to ear, silver tooth glinting in the firelight.

"You are one sick pup," Nick said, shaking his head in disbelief.

"Yeah...how could you even *think up* something like that?" Ryan asked harshly.

"I thought it was totally awesome!" Chaz commended, smiling, nodding his head in approval.

"I toldja I had a good one this week," Jackie reiterated. "I been working on it for a while."

"So the knife set was the wedding gift in the title," Nick said, figuring it out.

"No..." Casey corrected. "*Angela* was the wedding gift." Then she turned to Jackie. "Right?"

"That's right," Jackie concurred., nodding. Then he donned a concerned look. "It didn't upset you, did it?" he asked.

"Not really," she said, shrugging. "I mean, if she really loved him, she would *want* him to do that, if that's what he had to do to survive. So no, I'm not upset." Then she smiled devilishly at him. "*Disturbed* maybe, but not really *upset*...but Nick is right, you're a *sick pup!*"

At this the rest of the boys broke out laughing.

As their chuckling died down, she added: "On the other hand, I really liked the part about the spiritual connection between Steve and Christopher, the loving bond between father and son. That was pretty awesome."

A chorus of agreement issued from the others.

"And that poor dude," Nick added. "Imagine the odds, a great big buck tumbling down a cliff and jumping out onto the highway in front of him, right when he's coming around the bend!"

"It was luck," Jackie said. "*Bad* luck, but still luck. Just like the snowstorm hitting the town just as they left for the cabin was *bad* luck...but that someone gave them a kitchen knife set as a wedding gift was *good* luck...and that they chose that gift to take with them up to the cabin was even *better* luck...it was *all* luck, some good and some bad...so *now* do you guys see what I mean about luck?"

The rest of them nodded their heads in understanding.

Then Casey spoke up confidently:

"Well, even though I thought that *was* a pretty good story...I think *mine* might be even better!"

That got everyone's attention, and they turned to her.

"Be my guest," Jackie said, gesturing to her.

"Okay, here goes..."

With that she took a deep breath, exhaled, and paused for a moment, appearing to be gathering her thoughts. Then she looked back up at them.

"Mine's called *Jacob's Ladder*...see, there's this old man named Jacob who lives all alone because his wife had died unexpectedly. His house is up on a hill on the outskirts of town, but his mailbox is down the hill a ways, so he has to walk down there to get his mail...

Jacob's Ladder

by Casandra Wells

The last thing Jacob expected to see when he opened his mailbox was a package.

Bills, sure.

Junk mail, usually.

But a package?

He glanced at his watch: just after eleven. So too early for today's mail—no way Carl had been here yet, he never shows up before noon, usually much later—so it must've been delivered earlier in the week; hard to say exactly when, it had been a few days since he had ventured down the hill to check his mailbox.

Frowning, he slid the box out—surprisingly heavy, it was about the size of a shoebox, only a little wider, and slightly flatter, and felt solid—and eyed it top to bottom, thinking it was probably delivered to the wrong address, and now he was going to have to figure out how to get it to the right one. But he was surprised to find that it was indeed addressed to him, here at his home address—but who sent it? The return address simply read "HF Fulfillment Center," with just a department number listed underneath instead of a street address, followed by Albany, New York with a 12202 zip.

"Hmph," he grunted. *Now who in Sam Hill would be sending me a package,* he thought. *And from New York, no less?*

The old man stood there in his denim overalls and brown plaid flannel shirt, under the cover of countless trees steeped in birdsong, at the point on the hill where the old cracked and pitted one-lane asphalt road ended and his gravel drive began, wondering what it could be.

Turning the plain brown package over in his hands a few times, he suddenly remembered his upcoming birthday; but that was a couple of weeks off yet. He would be seventy-two (nothing at all to look forward to, even if he *expected* gifts, which he didn't). Because this year, he couldn't think of anyone who would be sending him a birthday present; by now most of his closest friends and family had already passed on, including his only son Ronnie, who'd died in a tragic motorcycle accident on the highway while in the prime of his youth, some thirty years ago.

So Jacob hadn't gotten any gifts by mail in years.

Decades, more like.

Flummoxed, he squeaked the rusty mailbox door shut and headed back up the hill toward his house, gravel and dead leaves crunching under his work boots as he trudged back up the drive.

After taking only a few steps, he heard a squeaking sound behind him, and turned to see the mailbox door hanging open again, swinging back and forth on its rusty hinge. He stopped, taking in the sight with sadness: the bent and corroded flag; the paint peeling off the box like curled white scabs, exposing the rusty wounds beneath; the old split and splintered wood post now leaning slightly to one side...

He barely even recognized the flowers anymore—now faded and camouflaged among the myriad rust spots—that his beloved wife Marge had so meticulously painted onto the sides of the plain metal box when it was brand-new, back when he'd moved his mailbox further down the hill from up top, where it was closer to his house, at the request of the Town Council.

•

One hot summer day many years ago, Carl Jenkins, the local mailman, got his mail truck stuck up there. The hill is steep and the drive loose gravel, and while trying to turn around after delivering Jacob's mail, he managed to drop a rear tire off the drive and into the runoff, and, try as he might, couldn't get out. And the longer he was stuck, the madder he got, and the madder he got, the more he floored it, and the more he floored it, the deeper the errant tire dug itself in.

As luck would have it, Jacob and Marge weren't home at the time, they had spent the day in town at the pitch-in barbecue picnic that their church holds every year. Marge had made a huge batch of her world-famous potato salad, as always refusing to divulge her secret ingredient to the many admirers who probed her for it (smoked paprika), and Jacob always enjoyed manning one of the many smokey outdoor grills, dishing up all manner of dogs, burgers, ribs, chicken—you name it, somebody brought it and Jacob threw it on, the barbecue sauce flowing generously.

There were games and prizes for the kids, horseback rides, and a hayride and huge bonfire in the evening, with roasted marshmallows and s'mores and ice cream and peach and apple pie and punch and iced tea and apple cider for all.

And, of course, the offering plate was passed around

toward the end of the day, and was generously laden with tithes from the pleasantly sated crowd.

So ends up, Carl had to call on the radio for a tow, and spent a good deal of his day sitting up there waiting, instead of getting his route finished so he could get down to *Beer-Thirty*, the local dive, and start the beer before five when it started filling up and getting noisy—or really more so he could get himself and his mail truck out of there before too many people showed up and saw him and started talking rumors. (On the other hand, the handful of regulars were no problem, they didn't much care if he showed up driving his mail truck and wearing his government-issued postal carrier uniform, they had their own problems to sort out as they upended their glasses).

But instead, he was stuck up on this stupid hill in the heat of the day and, being quite the rotund fellow, quickly got hot, sweaty, and thirsty as hell. And boy, was he was livid—you know how government workers can get when they're the least bit inconvenienced—so soon thereafter he launched a one-man campaign, petitioning the Town Council to make Jacob move his mailbox down the hill to the asphalt road, where he could access the box and do his damn job without "risking his life" having to drive all the way up that steep hill on that dangerous, unstable gravel drive...

Well apparently he was becoming quite a nuisance, because finally Earl and Hal, who headed the Council, came up to pay Jacob a visit, Hal's truck spitting rocks and dipping into potholes all the way up the hill. Jacob was out in the barn sharpening his chainsaw blade, and could hear the truck's ruckus from a good distance away, and so went out to meet it as it pulled up.

They had all grown up together, and after saying their hellos, Jacob invited them inside, where they calmly sat around the living room, drinking iced tea and smoking—Hal his pipe, Earl a cigar, and Jacob his usual hand-rolled cigarette. After a nice chat, everyone catching up with everyone, they asked Jacob if he wouldn't mind moving his mailbox down to the bottom of the hill—a matter of thirty yards, maybe less—if nothing else to shut Carl up and get him the hell off their backs about it.

Jacob said sure—we don't want ol' Carl to have an aneurysm.

They finished their tea and smokes over ancient memories, laughing together now and then, the way only old, lifelong friends can. They also talked guns for a bit—with Hal and Earl admiring Jacob's large collection of antique pieces mounted neatly on the brick wall above the fireplace, Jacob describing each one and its era in history.

Then they all shook hands, said their farewells, and parted company.

So that's how it happened. Jacob tore down his old mailbox, bought a new white metal one down at Stan's Hardware (Stan gave anyone over sixty a senior discount, so Jacob always went there first), cut a four-by-four post himself, and set up the new box down the hill, next to the drive just before the asphalt ended and the gravel began.

Perfect, he thought, because the drive widened a tad where it met the asphalt, offering more room for ol' Carl to get his truck in and out without much problem, no matter how fat his ass or inept his driving.

But before Marge let him install the new box, she insisted on hand-painted a smattering of pretty, colorful flowers on both sides of the plain white box, making it the most beautiful mailbox in town.

Or so she believed.

And at the time, he agreed; it probably was.

But that had been back when Marge was still alive...

•

Last summer, on a particularly hot and humid Saturday, while he was out in the driveway lying under his truck changing the oil, he'd gotten the phone call—that life-changing phone call that you dread getting more and more the older you get, because you know it's eventually coming, that it's getting closer with each passing day...

Earlier that day, leaving Jacob to his chores, Marge had gone to the craft bazaar at Washington Elementary— they held one every August, a critical fundraiser for the after-school programs they put on for the kids once school started in the fall—and, having volunteered to help with concessions like she did every year, she'd been scurrying about outside in the stifling heat and humidity, lugging a heavy tray loaded with cold soft drinks from tent to tent to tent, welcome refreshments for both the craftspeople selling their wares (all proceeds to be donated to the school, of course) and customers alike. And, being no spring chicken—having just turned 68, though she'd always been a wiry, energetic, active woman, even at that age—she'd apparently overexerted herself and collapsed in the grass on her way back to the school building to fetch another round.

With all the noise and hustle and bustle of the bazaar, apparently nobody noticed her for a while, until some kids started screaming when, while playing a game of tag, they stumbled onto her body lying in the grass over on the other side of the flower bed that encircled the base of the flagpole out in front of the school, a host of flies crawling and buzzing all over the drink-splattered tray and empty soda bottles and plastic cups that lay about her motionless head.

Apparently, she'd suffered a massive coronary.

Using their field defibrillator, the EMTs got her heart going again—barely—before rushing her off to the hospital.

She spent four days in a coma in the ICU, with Jacob never leaving her side. But she had never regained consciousness; the doctors said that maybe if they had found her a little sooner, things would've been different— but she had suffered severe brain damage from the lack of blood flow.

On the fourth long day, an exhausted Jacob stood beside his beloved wife's tiny, withered body—barely recognizable for all the tubes and wires and sensors and such running everywhere—holding her hand and softy whispering to her to please come back, to please make it, he didn't know what he would do without her, when suddenly he felt her gently squeeze his hand a single time —barely, but he *knew* he felt it—and a solitary tear left the corner of her eternally closed eye and trailed down her pale, wrinkled cheek just as the heart monitor flatlined with a soft, monotone alarm that he'd never since been able to forget, never been able to get it out of his head, it haunted his dreams to this day.

They all rushed in, of course. But it was over. He knew that before they'd flooded in, Marge had told him as much, with that single squeeze of her tiny hand.

So he quietly moved to the other side of the room and sat in one of the badly worn visitor chairs, achingly crushed, as the mob of clean white coats and blue scrubs scurried about and shouted to one another over her already vacated body.

•

Now, package in hand and with a heavy heart, Jacob sighed and returned to the mailbox, shut the door, pushed on it a few times to make sure it stayed closed this time, then trudged his way back up the hill, the birds silently flitting in the branches above as he went.

Up top, at the end of his drive, he stopped. Having just noticed the shoddy, deteriorated condition of his once brand-new and arguably most beautiful mailbox in town, he now noticed the similar condition of his house, his yard. Even his truck, which sat looking scornfully at him, having been neglected for much too long, both inside and out. Jacob hadn't bothered to change the oil this year, like he usually did. And he hadn't washed it in months. And one of the front tires was a little low, the slight lean giving the truck a forlorn-looking slump.

The adjacent yard was unkempt too, riddled with weeds and dandelions, and even the grass was getting out of hand, desperately in need of a long-overdue mowing. He didn't bother planting the flowerbed in front of the house this year either, instead leaving a dried bed of dirt, dead flowers from last year, and sprouting weeds among a scattering of old brittle leaves in its place. And the house behind it needed painting too—had needed it for years, really—but after losing Marge last summer, this summer he just couldn't muster the motivation, the desire, to tackle the job.

Or any of the rest of the chores, either.

Fact was, though he used to take care of all these things like clockwork—he just figured it was his job, and besides, he always believed in proper maintenance and quality craftsmanship, and for the most part enjoyed the work, the feeling of accomplishment, of a job well done— but these days he simply didn't give a damn anymore.

About any of it.

Ignoring the neglected eyesore that was once his and Marge's lovely home, he continued forward. Scuffing his way through the weeds and overgrown grass, he climbed the steps to the front porch and went inside, letting the old screen door *squeak!* and *bang!* shut behind him.

•

In the living room, he shoved the pile of unopened mail, the stack of old, tattered gun catalogs, a slew of empty coffee cups and drink glasses, and the butt-loaded ashtray to one side of the coffee table to make room, and set the package down, seating himself on the couch in the process.

That's when he noticed the company logo printed on the front of the box: bold, black, blockish, italicized letters HF, circumscribed by a blue ellipse, wider on the sides and thinner at the top, both of which were printed within a white silhouette of the state of New York. Frowning, he thought it looked vaguely familiar; like he should know that logo from somewhere...but he couldn't quite put his finger on it.

Leaning to one side, he dug in his right pants pocket and pulled out his pocketknife, unfolded it, leaned forward, and slit the top of the box open. A smattering of styrofoam peanuts tumbled out, and brushing aside the remaining ones in the box revealed a finely crafted wooden case beneath. Reaching in, he carefully slid the shiny case out. It was crafted from a dark hardwood—cherry, or maybe walnut, he wasn't quite sure—and as he turned it over in his hands, its richly lacquered surfaces gleamed under the faint overhead light, and reflected the occasionally glint of sunlight cast by the distant windows.

On the top, centered in the lid, a curved image—almost looked like a snake, in roughly the shape of a fancy letter "C"—was finely carved into the wood, and inlaid with what looked to be brass. Again, the shape of that emblem, or logo, whatever it was, looked vaguely familiar, but he still couldn't quite place it.

The entire bottom of the case was laminated with black felt, and it sat solidly and quietly when he placed it on the coffee table. A shiny brass latch adorned the front of the box, securing the lid.

He popped the latch, opened the lid—and gasped.

He could not believe what he was seeing.

There, lying before him, gleaming in the overhead light, nestled into a custom-formed black felt cradle within the wooden case, was a...

"First-generation Colt single action army revolver," he said aloud, almost in a whisper. His mind was blown as he surveyed the darkish brown, coppery hue of the old, worn, but highly polished metal body, the slightly yellowing real stag handles.

Then it occurred to him that the bronze-inlaid "snake" on the top of the case was the "C" from the Colt company logo. That's right; taken out of context, it's hard to place...but he knew he'd seen it somewhere before.

But where had this come from? He had wanted to add this exact gun to his collection for—

—his head jerked to the left, eyes locking on the stack of old gun catalogs he'd shoved aside to make room for the package—

"—at least a year," he muttered aloud, grabbing the stack from the table and slapping it down in his lap. Starting at the top, he lifted the top corner of each successive magazine, glancing at the issue stamps (they were published quarterly), until he found last year's spring issue. He yanked it out, and tossed the rest of the catalogs on the floor. And just before he opened it, he noticed the logo at the top: the same one that was printed on the front of the box, the HF standing for Hudson Firearms, located in Albany, New York. So that's what it was! He thought he'd recognized it...

Flipping through the magazine, he found it right away. He had stopped and looked at that page so often, the catalog practically fell open to the picture of the very gun that now sat on his table, gleaming within its hardwood case, which he had circled with a bright red marker in the catalog: Colt Single Action Army First Generation, Calvary Standard, Real Stag Grips...

He glanced over at the revolver in the box and quickly determined that yes, it was the Calvary Standard, with the 7.5" barrel, rather than the shorter 4.75" or 5.5" barrels of the Civilian and Artillery models.

"Well I'll be," he muttered to himself. He was totally perplexed. He knew he hadn't ordered it, much as he wanted it—it was listed in the catalog for $7,500...where would he get that kind of money?

Setting the catalog aside, he finally reached into the

case to extract the beautiful antique revolver, when he noticed an envelope stuck to the inside of the open lid, which was now lying back on the table behind the case.

Reaching past the gun, he instead retrieved the envelope. It was plain white, about the size of a—

"—birthday card?" he wondered allowed. Perhaps. But from who?

He opened the envelope, and sure enough, was greeted with a blue and yellow birthday card. On the front, in big, fancy silver script, were simply the words *"A dream..."*

He then opened to the inside:

> *"...for the man of my dreams!*
> *Happy birthday, Jacob!*
> *I love you!*
> *Love, Marge"*

For an instant, he was still bewildered. He just sat and stared at the card, trying to put the pieces together. How had she known? And how could she have possibly afforded this?

Then he noticed another folded paper in the bottom of the shipping box, that had been packed under the wooden case. He lifted it, and let it fall open: the order invoice.

For $7,500, plus tax.

Dated April of last year, with a requested ship date of June 1—last week.

Then it clicked:

First, he remembered telling her about the gun in the catalog—he'd circled it in red marker before showing it to her—and lamenting that if he didn't hurry and buy it, someone else would snatch it up, and he'd lose his chance. But he simply couldn't afford it...not at the time, anyway. Where the hell was he going to get $7,500? To spend on an antique gun, no less?

That had been late last spring...and the fateful school bazaar had been later, in August.

Then, he remembered that after the funeral, and all the legalities, the life insurance and such, he'd gone to the bank to close out Marge's savings account—and had been surprised that there was less than a hundred dollars in her account. He was certain she'd been saving for years. Where did it all go? *Who knows, with the way that woman can shop,* he'd thought at the time.

Perplexed, he took what little the young teller said there was, closed the account, and went home.

Now here it was, June of the following year, and his birthday was coming up in a couple weeks, and here it is, the gun from the catalog that he'd wanted so bad. So she knew it was time-sensitive—if she didn't buy it right away, she'd probably lose the chance—but Jacob's birthday wasn't until the following June. So she'd wiped out her savings account and ordered it ahead of time, with instructions to ship it just in time for his birthday. And, since it was a gift, they'd apparently had some sort of gift card option she must have used to create the custom birthday card.

Crafty woman, as he placed the card upright and open

on the table.

Then a wave of overwhelming grief and sadness came crashing down on him, and, unable to stave it off, he bent over, and buried his face in his hands.

Jacob wept.

He wept long and hard, until it seemed like he ran out of tears.

Then, still sniffling, he quietly rolled a cigarette, and sat back and smoked, occasionally looking around at his poor excuse for a home.

For the rest of the afternoon, he spent long stretches of time just staring out the window at the bright day, a brightness that just didn't stimulate him anymore.

Finally, he looked back down at the gift lying on the table before him.

Suddenly, *he knew.*

Snuffing the cigarette out in the ashtray, he rose from the couch and trod silently out to the front porch, letting the old screen door *squeak!* and *bang!* behind him. There he stopped for a moment, staring into the sky, as if beseeching the heavens. He knew she was up there somewhere, waiting for him. He could *feel* her presence, close and intimate, sure as if she were standing right next to him on their porch, softly holding his hand like she always did.

He turned and started toward the barn, his boots clopping hollowly across the wood porch before swishing through the tall grass then crunching across the gravel as he headed silently across the drive.

Under the ancient workbench, he tried one old wooden drawer, then the next, and finally a third before finding what he sought: a smattering of old, antique bullets rolling around loose in the drawer, which he had collected throughout his life just like the antique guns. Whenever he'd happened to come across one over the years, he'd tossed it in the drawer with the others, along with some old silver coins, and even a crumpled, faded two-dollar Confederate Note.

He rummaged through them.

He was pretty sure he had one in there somewhere...

•

Carl Jenkins was just tossing a slim stack of mail into the old man's mailbox when he heard a gunshot—distant, muffled—causing him to duck slightly and look around in wide-eyed fear, wondering if there were hunters in the area or something.

Turning the mail truck hard to the left, he gunned it, tires squealing, exhaust belching blue smoke, and sped back down the hill.

Behind him, the mailbox door hung open, squeaking as it swung back and forth on its rusty hinge...

With that Casey looked up almost apologetically, waiting for their response. But for a moment, all was quiet, just the crackling of the fire, while they all absorbed the ending.

"He killed himself," Chaz said matter-of-factly, as if he just figured it out.

"Man...you thought *my* story was sad, but yours, well..." Nick trailed off, looking away in wide-eyed disbelief.

"Jacob's ladder...as in ladder to heaven...sorta like stairway to heaven," Ryan said softly, getting the meaning.

"Zeppelin!" Nick interjected. "They're badass!"

"So...the gun was the ladder," Ryan continued softly. "And *she* sent it to him...wow...that's pretty *deep*."

"That's right," Casey confirmed. "And like I said before, *love* is the most important thing in life. Without love, life just wouldn't be worth living."

They all nodded in silence, nobody could dispute the truth of her statement.

"Wow...that was a great story," Jackie finally said.

And once again, he and Casey smiled at each other.

"It *was* pretty good..." Ryan agreed. "But I wanna know something: how do you know so much about guns? I mean, that all sounded pretty real to me."

A chorus of agreement from the others, all looking at her, waiting for explanation.

"My dad—I mean my *real* dad—really *did* collect them. He was totally into them, and taught me a lot about 'em. Showed me all kinds of stuff in the catalogues, explained all about those and the ones he actually owned. He has a big collection of antique guns...*had* a big collection, that is...but when he was killed in that hunting accident—which I don't think was because of the guns, I think it was because of the booze—then mom, in all her wisdom, got rid of all the guns, sold them all off for next to nothing, and now refuses to allow any guns in the house. But of course the booze stays. And good thing for her, because if she'da banned the booze instead, then dickhead woulda never stuck around in the first place, let alone long enough to get her to marry him."

"Gee, I'm really sorry to hear that about your dad," Jackie said sincerely.

The rest of the boys echoed the heartfelt sentiment.

"Thanks," Casey said, tearing up. "It's been hard...but it helps to have friends who understand."

"Well, I'm...I mean *we're* definitely your friends now," Nick said, smiling at her.

And again, they all chimed in, nodding and agreeing, even Ryan this time.

"Okay, so now we gotta vote on the best story," Jackie announced.

But just as he said it, deep thunder rumbled off in the distance.

"Holy shit!" Jackie exclaimed. "A storm's comin!"

"They didn't say anything about storms on the news," Nick said. "I specifically watched the forecast for the weekend, just in case. It was supposed to be sunny, hot, and humid...that's all they said."

"Probably a heat thunderstorm," Chaz said. "They brew up unexpectedly, usually in the evenings, and you can't predict 'em. Did you notice how the heat and humidity was getting worse all day? That's a sure sign."

A bright flash lit the dark sky to the west, followed by

another low rumble of thunder.

"Great, now what're we gonna do?" Ryan said, sounding exasperated. "We didn't bring tents or anything, and there's no shelter around here!"

"What about the raft?" Casey asked, looking around at the rest of them. "Can we use that somehow? For shelter?"

"Way too heavy, we'll never get it out the water," Chaz said, shaking his head.

"And 'sides, even if we *could* lift it, it's too big to move around in that little cove," Jackie added.

Just as he said that, rain began to spit—small, widely dispersed droplets pelting all around them, and emitting a soft sizzling sound from the surrounding woods.

Then, a mild gust kicked up, disturbing the trees around their camp, and causing the campfire to swoop and dance momentarily.

"Well, we better hurry up and think of something," Nick warned, "Cuz—"

But he was cut off by a blinding flash of lightening and deafening crack of thunder, very close to them now.

Another gust of wind raked the surrounding trees—but this time, it maintained, rather than dying back down, indicating that the storm was bearing down on them.

"The roof!" Chaz yelled, pointing at the piles of burned rubble behind them.

"What?" Jackie hollered back.

Another flash of lightening and burst of thunder, and the rain became more intense, turning into a light downpour.

They all looked at Chaz, waiting for his idea, as he glanced around at the surrounding woods, then up at the sky. Then he pointed at the pile of rubble where the shack once stood.

"There's two intact corner sections of the roof there in the pile!" he hollered over the now howling wind. "The storm—the wind—is coming from the west! So we grab those two roof sections, and take them over to those two big trees—"

—he pointed from the burned debris to two towering trees with thick tree trunks to the left of the rubble—

"—and lean them against the tree trunks, facing west!"

"Lean-tos!" Nick hollered, suddenly recognizing what Chaz was describing.

"Yeah!" Chaz confirmed. "We can use Jackie's rope to lash 'em down, then we weather the storm under them—"

—as if on cue, a monstrous lightening bolt flashed across the sky above them, ear-splitting thunder right behind—

"—and hopefully stay mostly dry!"

"I'll get the rope!" Jackie cried as he scrambled to his backpack.

The others jumped up and darted over to the shack. Nick and Casey began working one roof corner out of the debris, while Ryan and Chaz worked on the other.

Moving quickly, the four dragged the roof sections over to the two big trees Chaz had specified, and Jackie met them there with what was left of the spool of rope.

They stopped for a moment and looked up at all the flailing trees, trying to gauge the exact direction of the wind. It appeared to be practically due west.

Chaz turned directly into the wind, pointing both of his arms out in that direction. "That way!" he hollered.

Fighting the escalating wind, they turned the two roofing sections as close as they could to facing exactly into the wind—Ryan and Casey's segment lifting like a sail, the wind nearly pulling it from their grasp, but Jackie grabbed hold too and helped them regain control—and leaned them against the stout tree trunks.

"Lower!" Chaz cried, waving his hand up and down to indicate that they needed to come down toward the ground.

They pushed the shingled frames downward, until they rested against the trees about three feet off the ground, and extended outward to rest on the ground, one about five feet long and the other about six.

Using the firewood hatchet, Nick chopped two lengths of rope from the spool, and handed one to Jackie. Then Jackie, Casey, and Ryan worked at lashing the larger roofing section securely to the tree, wrapping the rope around and around the charred ends of the roof supports that protruded out from under the wood shingles, while Nick and Chaz secured the other, slightly smaller one, in the same manner.

Just as Casey ducked underneath the lean-to she'd helped secure, the rain began to pour.

Jackie's eyes widened with realization. "Our backpacks!" he yelled at the others through the rain.

Leaving Casey under the lean-to, the four boys raced back to the campfire—which was by now extinguished, the last few lingering streams of smoke rising weakly upwards—grabbed their backpacks, yanked up their bedrolls, and scurried back to the lean-tos, diving underneath them just as the downpour intensified.

Chaz and Nick took the shorter of the two lean-tos, while Jackie, Casey, and Ryan took the longer, all of them shoving their backpacks into the lowest corners of the structures where the roof met the ground, then spreading their bedrolls out over the rocky earth, creating makeshift padded floors.

The two groups of kids faced each other from about ten feet apart, the distance between the two huge trees.

Taking full advantage of this sudden, unexpected situation, Casey whispered "I'm cold!" to Jackie as she wriggled herself up tight against him, and he just smiled.

They all lay on their bellies smiling at one another through the rain that poured like a curtain between them. It hammered above them against the old wood shingles of their lean-tos, but most of it ran harmlessly off to the ground.

Aside from getting a little wet as they scurried about in the rain, they were now staying dry, at least for the most part. Nick leaned over and punched Chaz happily on the shoulder.

"Great idea, Chaz! One of your best!"

The others agreed, but Chaz didn't look so cheery. Instead, he was looking up and around at the treetops above them, worry on his face.

"Let's just hope that neither of these trees gets struck by lightening!" he cautioned, his eyes huge as he looked around at them them all through his thick, now rain-spotted glasses.

With that their smiles also turned to worrisome looks as

they also turned upward to the treetops above, watching with trepidation as the storm raged all around them.

•

Turns out, neither of those trees—or any other tree in the area, for that matter—were struck my lightening that night. And what's more, the kids had managed to stay relatively dry through the night, even though the storm had raged on for hours, dumping rain non-stop over the area like a waterfall.

But finally, in the wee hours of the morning, the storm had moved off to the east, having given the town of Hope and the surrounding woods, fields, and untamed wilderness a good soaking before it went.

Then, at least for a few hours before daybreak, the kids had finally fallen asleep to the peaceful and tranquil sound of fresh rainwater dripping from the myriad leaves and branches that surrounded them on all sides.

Casey began to wake to the soft melody of morning birdsong, and, eyes still closed, yawned, stretched, and went to wrap her arm once again around Jackie—but sat up with a start when she realized he wasn't there. Blinking in the morning sunlight, she glanced around. Ryan slept soundly on her other side, and Nick was still slumbering in the other lean-to, but both Jackie and Chaz were nowhere to be seen.

Then she heard their voices, floating to her from what sounded like over near the campfire site, so she scrambled out of the lean-to and headed that way.

The two had gathered all the supplies together and packed them up, preparing to leave. As she approached them, Chaz was looking at his watch while pressing a series of buttons on the side, and Jackie had his back to her. She snuck up behind him, slid her arms under his, and wrapped them around body, resting her chin on his shoulder.

"Hey, you," she greeted softly in his ear.

Jackie wrapped his own arms around hers, and squeezed. "Hey," he whispered back.

Chaz finished whatever he was doing with his watch, and looked up at them.

"We should wake Ryan and Nick up...we'll need to leave soon if we wanna make it back in time. Plus, we don't even know what time it really is, since my watch apparently stopped working for a while down in the tunnel yesterday. Best I can figure is to add thirty minutes, so I've reset it, but who knows."

"So it didn't go back to the right time after we came out?"

"Nope. We were down there at least forty minutes, there and back—but according to my watch, it was more like ten. "

"That's weird," Casey said.

Chaz shrugged. "I guess being so far underground, once we got down in the solid rock part of the tunnel, the magnetic field changed, or was blocked or something—messed up my compass and my watch."

"Well, anyway, we know it's still early, and we got all day," Jackie said, shrugging.

"Yeah, but remember," Chaz explained, pushing his glasses back up on his nose. "Goin' back, we'll be paddlin' upstream, against the current. It'll take longer to go back than it took to get here—a *lot* longer."

"Oh yeah, that's right," Jackie agreed, nodding his head.

Just then Nick walked up from behind them. When he saw him coming, Jackie released Casey and turned to meet him a short distance away. As he walked, he dug into his pocket and produced the Zippo.

"Look, Nick—I'm sorry I took your lighter during the game. It 's not fair, it's yours and you should have it back."

With that, he held the lighter out to Nick, and couldn't help noticing Nick glancing over his shoulder at Casey behind him, then back at Jackie.

"And I'm sorry about Casey," he added...I can tell you like her, and I never expected her to like me. It just happened."

Nick looked from Jackie's sincere eyes down to the lighter he was still holding out to him.

"You won it fair and square," he shrugged. "I'll just have to win it back next week," he said with a grin.

Then, with one last glance over his shoulder at the girl:

"You won 'em *both* fair and square," he added with a wink, then turned quickly and headed back to start packing.

As he walked quietly away, Casey and Chaz approached Jackie from behind.

"What was that about?" she asked, curious.

"We were just discussing next week's blackjack game. He hopes to win his lighter back."

With that he held up the Zippo, glistening in the sunlight.

"I don't blame him, it's a cool lighter," she said admirably.

"Yep," he agreed. "Genuine Zippo."

But he said nothing more as he pocketed the lighter.

"I'll go wake up Ryan," Casey volunteered.

"Well, we gotta get our bedrolls anyway," Jackie said, taking her by the hand and pulling her along, bounding and giggling.

Chaz followed wordlessly, pushing a series of buttons on his watch with tiny beeps.

•

"Whoa," Nick said as they all stood on the bank in the cove, staring disconcertedly at the raft. The water in the cove had risen considerably, lifting the raft at least a foot higher than it had been when they left it, and it was now bobbing and undulating noticeably from a disruptive turbulence entering the cove from the entrance off the creek.

"It musta rained a *lot* last night," Ryan said. "Look how much the creek rose!"

"And judgin' by the way it's rockin', I'd say the creek is running a lot faster than it was yesterday," Chaz speculated.

"This is really gonna suck," Nick said. "Tryin' to paddle upstream the whole way back, in this current? And with only two oars?"

Jackie thought about this for a moment, then got an idea, and turned to Chaz.

"Think we can make two more oars outta some boards from those roof sections we used for the lean-tos?"

Chaz nodded at this. "That, or we might be able to find a coupla usable boards buried in all that burned rubble. Either way, I think we should be able to find somethin' we can use for oars, sure."

With that, they all turned and headed back to the camp area. Before long, they had secured two additional boards to use for oars, one from the charred remains of the shack, and one from the longer of the two roofing sections they'd used as lean-tos. Chaz marked the hand grips like he had the others, and Nick quickly sawed the notches out, along with lopping off the charred ends.

Then, they boarded the raft, and under Jackie's direction, secured all of their gear to the center of the deck, lashed down tightly with the remaining rope criss-crossed over and over.

Using his oar, Nick shoved them away from the bank, and the raft began drifting back toward the entrance to the cove, which was covered by multiple drenched and drooping tree branches, concealing the creek from full view—but as they approached it, they could hear the sound of rushing water.

"Sounds like the creek is really moving," Ryan said cautiously.

"Storm surge...all that rain last night, it's swelled up and rushing," Jackie said. "We'll need to be really careful once we get out there."

"No shit," Nick said. "It'll take all four of us rowin' like crazy to go back upstream, in *this* heavy current."

"But you guys can do it, right? Get us back?" Casey asked, fear rising in her voice.

"I think so," Jackie reassured her. "With all four of us rowing, we should be able to."

For a moment they paused in silence under the hanging

branches, just inside the mouth of the cove, before it exited out to the creek. The raft was bobbing pretty good now, the turbulence from the rushing creek spreading into the cove.

Chaz had been quiet, seemingly contemplating something. Then he looked around at the others. "I think if we keep the raft sideways," he explained, "it'll be easier to row upstream. The fronts of the barrels are flat, so they'll cause more resistance. Keeping the raft sideways, like it is now, will put the sides of the barrels against the water instead—they're rounded, so should cause less resistance."

They nodded at this, understanding.

"So if the front of the raft is already perpendicular to the creek," Jackie said, "then this left side—"

—he waved his hand along that side of the raft—

"—will be pointing upstream."

"So I should stay here," Nick added, standing on the back of the raft, "cuz this'll be left side of the raft when we get out on the creek."

"Yes," Jackie concurred. "Ryan, why don't you take this side with Nick, and I'll take the other side—"

—he stepped forward to the front as Ryan moved back to the rear—

"—which will be on the right once we're on the creek, and Chaz—"

"And I'll take starboard side with you," Chaz interrupted, moving to the front of the raft to stand alongside Jackie. "That puts Nick and Ryan port side."

"And where do you want *me?*" Casey asked, looking at

Jackie with big, admiring eyes.

Jackie pointed to the left side of the raft. "You take the—

—he looked over at Chaz for help—

"Bow," Chaz said. "The front is the bow."

"—the bow," Jackie directed, smiling. "You can be our lookout."

"*Lookout?*" she repeated, incredulous. "Just cuz I'm a girl? Screw that, that's so *lame!* I wanna *help*—give me something to *do*. Something *important.*"

"Here," Chaz said, prompting both Casey and Jackie to look over at him. Kneeling, he began digging through the pile of backpacks that were tied down in the middle of the raft, found his own, opened a side flap—and once again produced his camo binoculars. He handed them up to Casey, strap dangling.

"The lookout *is* important," Jackie said, improvising now, thanks to Chaz's quick thinking. "It's your job to make sure we don't hit any submerged rocks, or floating logs, or any other debris that might be coming at us in this strong current. The binoculars will help you spot any hazards while they're still far enough away so we can avoid 'em."

"Cool!" Casey said, smiling as she took the binoculars, throwing the strap over her head and around her neck as she stepped over to the left side of the raft. Putting them to her eyes, she scoped around, trying them out. Then, dropping them and turning back to the boys, she smiled hugely: "You can count on me! I'll make a *great* lookout!"

Turning slightly, Jackie smiled and winked at Chaz, who

smiled back wryly.

Then Nick spoke up: "And I can step to the back—"

"—stern," Chaz corrected—

"—stern," Nick repeated, "And act as the rudder, if we need to steer the raft from behind once in a while."

"Good thinking," Jackie commended, and Nick blushed and smiled over at Casey, who smiled back, a look of approval in her eyes.

Then Jackie continued: "Once we're out on the creek and headed upstream, that'll put me and Ryan at the front corners of the raft, and Chaz and Nick at the rear corners, which will sorta even out the rowing between both sides."

The raft had been rocking slightly while they were all shifting around and trading positions, but once they finished, it settled back into the rhythmic undulating caused by the turbulence creeping into the cove from the racing creek.

Now they turned to Jackie, awaiting further instructions.

"Okay," Jackie said. "All our gear is secured to the raft with rope, right?"

Nick stepped forward, leaned in, and yanked on several of the ropes running over all the mounded gear in the middle of the raft. They all held, stout and secure.

"Aye, aye, Cap'n!" he confirmed in his Popeye voice—which this time sounded more like a pirate than Popeye—and stepped back to his rowing position.

"So, when we push out there, we wanna keep the raft in this position—headin' upstream sideways, so the curved sides of the barrels are against the current for less resistance, like

Chaz said—and then we want to start rowin' to the left, headin' north 'till we go around the bend, then back west 'till we get back to the construction yard, where we'll dock."

The rest looked around at each other in understanding—except for Chaz, who had stepped to the front right corner of the raft and was bent over, hands on knees, looking at the front side of the barrel on that side.

"We got a problem," he announced, his voice sounding ominous.

He stood and turned to the others, pushing his glasses up on his nose. "I thought I noticed this corner of the raft seemed lower," he said. Then he turned and stepped back to the edge of the raft, bent over, and pointed at the end of the barrel.

The rest of them crossed the raft and crowded around him, looking over the edge to where he was pointing.

"Somewhere along the way, we lost the plug in the top side of this barrel. See? That three-inch hole just above the waterline? It's been taking on water, so now it's sitting lower than the others. I don't know how much more it'll take and still float."

"But it'll be on the side of the raft once we get out on the creek," Jackie pointed out. "So it shouldn't get much water in it, right?"

"Maybe," Chaz conceded. "Hard to say, really…depends on how much turbulence there is out there. But it might be okay."

"But we tested all those plugs before we even left the barn," Nick protested. "They were all rusted shut, weren't they?"

Chaz shrugged. "Yeah, I thought so anyway."

"No, Nick's right," Jackie agreed. "They were all rusted shut. We couldn't budge any of 'em."

"Can't we plug it with something?" Casey asked simply.

"Well, I suppose I could cover it with duct tape," Chaz said, "But I don't know how much it'll help. It might not even stay on, if it gets too wet. Plus the surface is so rusty, tape might not stick. But we can give it a shot."

With that he stepped over to the lashed supplies and began foraging for his backpack in the pile.

"Maybe it came loose when we raced the barrels down that hill," Ryan suggested. "You guys hit that log pretty hard… maybe it got knocked loose then…or even popped out, and nobody noticed."

"Doubt it," Nick objected. "I'm sure one of us woulda noticed that plug missing when we built the raft."

"Well, however it happened, it happened," Jackie said. "Alls we can do now is try to patch it up, and hope it holds 'til we get back."

They nodded in silent agreement as Chaz returned from his backpack with tape in hand, bent over the edge of raft, ripped three foot-long strips of duct tape from the roll and gently applied them to the front of the barrel, covering the hole then rubbing it all vigorously so it would stick to the rusty metal surface as well as possible. When he finished, he stood, turned to the others, and shrugged.

"For what it's worth."

"You guys raced down a hill on these barrels?" Casey said, smiling with excitement. "How cool was *that*?"

"Yeah, it was pretty fun, even though I *lost*," Chaz said as he returned the duct tape to his backpack..

"Okay, so *you* lost...but who *won*?" Casey asked, looking around at all of them, eyes sparkling.

Jackie smiled, and his silver tooth flashed.

"YOU!" Casey asked him, so impressed that her mouth hung open.

"Well, sorta," Jackie said, glancing at Nick, who was smiling back at him. "It was more like a tie between me and Nick, really. But we both crashed into this big log at the bottom of the hill, and ended up in a full drainage ditch, soaking wet."

At this, both Chaz and Ryan started cracking up—again.

Nick was chuckling, too. "Yeah, we got soaked."

"Took us all day to dry out," Jackie added, still smiling.

"You guys are so crazy," Casey said, smiling and shaking her head as she returned to her position along the left side of the raft.

"SPUH-LASSSHHH!!" Chaz cried, throwing his hands up in the air mimicking a huge splash of water, which sent both himself and Ryan back into gales of laughter.

At various levels of laughing and chuckling, the four boys dispersed to their respective rowing positions on the raft.

•

Chaz, stationed at the front right corner of the raft, slowly lifted the wet overhanging branches with his oar in preparation for their launch from the cove, for the first time exposing the swollen and raging creek ahead for all to see. He turned and looked wide-eyed at the others, his eyes once again appearing huge and insect-like through his thick glasses.

"Man, look at that," Ryan muttered nervously.

"Holy shit," Nick said.

"It's okay," Jackie reassured everyone. "It's only moving fast up here, close to the bank. Look out there, in the middle. It's moving a lot slower, and that's where we'll be."

They all peered out to the middle of the creek, and agreed: the water's movement appeared to be much slower out there, whereas it seemed to rushing much faster along the sides, closer to the banks.

"So everybody get ready," he continued. "Remember, we're already facing the right direction, we just go straight out, then continue to the left, upstream, but leave the raft turned this way, so the curved sides of the barrels will be in front when we head into the current."

The others nodded in understanding.

"Nick, you give us a shove from behind, and when we get out onto the creek, everyone paddle hard to get us past the faster current along the bank, and once we get out toward the middle, where it's slower, we'll shift and begin paddling upstream."

"Ay, ay, Cap'n," Nick answered in his Popeye (or pirate) voice, as he moved to the center rear of the raft and shoved the end of his oar down into the rocky bed of the cove and leaned heavily on it, ready to shove off on command.

"Okay, is everyone ready?" Jackie asked the crew.

Chaz and Ryan nodded in the affirmative, each of them

furrowing their brows, donning solemn looks in preparation for the rigorous chore ahead, like soldiers preparing to charge into battle.

Binoculars at the ready in one hand, Casey turned and gave Jackie a thumbs up with the other, than turned back.

"Okay, on the count of three...one...two.......THREE!"

On three, Nick shoved them forward with his oar as hard as he could, launching the raft out of the cove. As the front of the raft exited the cove, and both Chaz and Jackie had cleared the overhanging branches, Chaz let go of them and crouched into rowing position, oar at the ready.

As the raft glided forward, Ryan lifted the overhanging branches out of the way with his oar, a mix of rain and creek water dripping all over himself, Casey, and Nick as they slid underneath. Then, as soon as Nick had ducked under, Ryan let the wet branches drop and Nick returned to his position at the right rear corner, ready to start rowing.

Unfortunately, their entire plan collapsed as soon as the raft began clearing the cove and drifting out onto the creek.

First, the raging creek's current caught hold of the front barrels and began turning the raft to the right, heading downstream. Jackie and Chaz immediately began paddling like mad against the current, but to no avail. It was as if they didn't even have oars in the water, the raft was moving on its own, helplessly pushed along by the torrent.

"Paddle! Paddle!" Jackie cried, swinging his oar as hard and fast as he could, Chaz doing the same.

Then, as the rear of the raft exited the cove, Ryan and Nick began paddling madly as well, but the raft completed its turn to the right and began racing downstream with the current.

"No, no no!" Chaz hollered.

"Quick! Everyone to this side!" Jackie yelled over the raging creek, waving the others over to his side of the raft, which was now pointing downstream. "Turn this thing around!"

Yanking their oars from the water, Ryan and Nick bolted across to the leading side of the raft, positioning themselves between Chaz and Jackie, and the four of them shoved their oars into the rushing water and pushed sideways, trying to force the raft to turn back around.

Quickly seeing the futility of their efforts, Jackie had another idea. Yanking his oar from the water, he shifted to one side of the raft and plunged it back in. "Just paddle!" he yelled, pointing at both sides of the raft. "We don't need to turn it around, just reverse direction!"

With this, Chaz joined Jackie on that side of the raft, while Ryan and Nick hopped over to the opposite side, and they all began paddling ferociously against current, attempting to reverse the course of the raft—but still, there was no effect, the raging waters had them, and there was nothing they could do about it.

•

Suddenly, the rapids increased in intensity, rocking the raft violently up and down, making it difficult for the boys to remain upright as they desperately paddled.

Looking up and off to the side, Jackie saw the rocky faces begin to rise upward from the low, grassy banks, and he slowly stopped rowing and just stared up at them.

Seeing Jackie's transfixed look, Casey followed his eyes upward, to the rocky faces now enclosing them on both sides of the creek.

Then the other three stopped paddling and did the same.

"The canyon," Jackie muttered, his voice downed out by the sounds of the raging water. Then, at the top of his lungs, "THE CANYON!"

Everyone turned and looked at him, eyes wide in terror, awaiting instructions.

"What do we do?!" Ryan desperately hollered over the rushing waves.

"Everyone take a corner!" he shouted, "We can't fight the current, alls we can do is try to protect the raft! Use your oars to keep us from hitting anything! Nick, I need you here in front! You're the strongest!"

Understanding, the others darted about, each taking a corner of the raft, Nick shifting over to one front corner and Jackie taking the other, while Ryan and Chaz moved to the rear corners.

"What about me?" Casey yelled.

"Just hang on!" Jackie answered, pointing to the lashed supplies in the center of the raft. "And make sure we don't lose anything!"

As the raft began rocking, Casey leapt to the center and embraced the supplies with her arms, gripping the ropes on either side tightly with both hands.

Now the rock faces on either side rose sharply, and

boulders could be seen jutting out of the water up ahead.

"We're going in!" Jackie hollered, his voice shaky from the now wildly undulating raft. "Just try to keep away from the rocks!"

It was now impossible for the boys to remain standing, the raft was rocking and shifting so violently. In response, they dropped to their knees, their makeshift oars poking outward from each corner, teetering above the raging water.

Water was splashing all around them now, the spray soaking them so badly they had to constantly wipe it from their eyes, their faces, and push their drenched hair back so they could see.

"Oh, shit!" Nick yelled, spying the first boulder up ahead, which was coming directly at them, rising from the exact center of the creek, the raging water spilling to either side of it in white-foaming rapids.

He and Jackie shifted to the center of the raft, aiming their oars at the fast-approaching cold emotionless monster, as Chaz and Ryan watched from behind in desperation.

Nick's oar was the first to reach the boulder, making hard contact with an audible, sharp wooden *thunk!* and, as ensconced as he was in preparation, he was immediately shoved backward, falling first onto his rear, then his back, the oar pushing him across the deck of the raft, which was now covered in a thick sheen of water

Jackie's oar struck the rock in the next second, and he, too was thrown to the deck and pushed backward, both his and Nick's efforts barely altering the course of the raft at all, the undulating wooden craft careening toward the massive boulder unabated. As they all braced for impact, Nick and Jackie both slid back until they met Casey at the center of the raft—where their supplies were roped tautly to the deck—and the securely lashed stockpile abruptly halted their rearward progression, their oars pressing the two boys against the ropes to either side of the girl.

Just as the front edge of the raft was about to slam into the face of the rock, it came to a slow halt against the now rigid oars, then began rotating to the left and drifting around the right side of the boulder.

By now Chaz and Ryan had crossed over and joined in the effort with their oars, shoving them with all their strength into the monster rock, expediting the raft's rightward arc around it.

As Jackie and Nick regained their feet and doubled their efforts against the boulder, the raft suddenly broke free, cleared the boulder and left it behind, rocking and bobbing viciously as it continued its trek down the creek atop the raging rapids.

Without a word, the four boys also shifted to the right—which was now the leading edge of the raft—and kneeled, shoulder to shoulder, their oars jutting forward together, ready to repel the next obstruction in their path, while Casey took the opportunity to let go and quickly re-establish a better grip on the supply ropes.

Unfortunately, the next obstruction wasn't alone; directly ahead, not thirty feet away and closing rapidly, were not one b u t *two* smaller boulders jutting upward from the raging rapids, one rising a couple of feet from the surface, the other only about a foot, partially submerged on the far side. But they were only about six feet apart; there would be no way of missing them both, the raft was too wide to go between them, and they had neither the distance nor time to try to maneuver to either side of the twin sentinels.

Thinking quickly, Chaz hollered at the others: "To the right! To the right! Try to go over the short one on the side that's half-submerged!—"

—he pointed to the lower of the two rocks on the right, then down at the leading edge of the raft—

"—we have the curved sides of the barrels forward now, so we might be able to ride over that lower one without too much damage!"

Understanding, the others shifted on their knees to the left, aiming their oars at the taller of the two boulders.

Though the four of them, working their oars together, were able to stave off impact with the larger boulder, the raft again rotating to the left as it drifted around the rock, and for a moment it looked like they were going to clear the smaller boulder too—but as they drifted around it, instead of floating roughly over the submerged side as they'd hoped, the right leading barrel struck it hard, sounding like a small, hollow explosion, prompting Casey to let out a shrill scream. The violent impact knocked all four boys from their knees, rolling and scrabbling around on the deck, as the right corner of the raft exploded, several boards splintering upward, the barrel still lashed to them with bright blue nylon rope.

The entire right side of the raft then lifted violently upward as it scraped over the half-submerged rock, the boys all tumbling to the center, again piling onto Casey and the roped supplies. In the process, Chaz and Ryan lost grip of their oars, which began hydroplaning across deck, careening toward the right edge.

Seeing what was happening, Nick lashed out with one hand and secured one of the oars—but the other slid right off the deck and into the raging creek, heading downstream and out of reach before anyone else could react. In no time, it disappeared under the rapids.

Then, as quickly as it happened, it was over—the raft righted itself and continued somewhat smoothly downstream atop the foaming current, broken and splintered pieces of wood suddenly surfacing and drifting ahead.

"Damn! We lost an oar!" Nick shouted, as they all regained their feet and began moving back to the front of the raft, each shaking their heads and wiping water from their eyes and faces. This time, Casey stood and joined them—and, though she was now thoroughly soaked, her long blonde hair plastered back like smooth, shiny silk, her t-shirt clinging to her body like wet, translucent paint, easily revealing her emerging womanhood—the boys didn't seem to even notice this time, so focused and intent were they on their very survival.

"We still have the barrel!" Chaz hollered, pointing to the right front corner of the raft, which now splintered and broken, a gaping hole in the deck, frothy water splashing through. "It's still tied to the front frame board, which is still nailed in on the other end!" With this, he pointed to the left front corner of the raft, which was still intact. The other end of the framing board jutted outward under the jagged hole in the deck, the barrel still lashed tightly to it—but it was obviously damaged, much of it crumpled, the front side completely caved in.

"But I lost my oar!" Ryan hollered.

Seeing more boulders up ahead, Jackie responded quickly: "Chaz, you and Ryan move to the center, and man your oar together! Me and Nick will flank you on each side!"

With this, Nick tossed the salvaged oar back to Chaz, Ryan joined him, and they all took their positions at the front of the broken, now lightly undulating raft, their three oars jutting out side-by-side over the roiling surface of the creek. But this time, Casey stepped up and joined Jackie, sharing his oar, locking eyes with him ever so briefly, a smile on her lips. He smiled back at her, nodding slightly—then they both turned and crouched together, awaiting the next obstacle.

For a while, the waves calmed a little, the raft settling enough that the kids could all remain on their feet. And though there were several other boulders jutting up from the creek, they happened to glide harmlessly past each of them, all three oars pointing at the threat and following it as they bobbed past, just in case.

But up ahead, the walls of the canyon suddenly closed inward, creating a narrower point where the creek swelled up and poured through, raging down the greater incline on the other side. They could already hear the roaring rapids on the downward side, even though they remained out of view.

Jackie thought he knew what was coming up ahead. To confirm his suspicions, he looked upward, scouring the tops of the rocky cliffs to either side of the upcoming rapids—and sure enough, he spotted the thick wood posts anchored into the rock hundreds of feet above, two poking out on each side of the creek, from this far below looking the size of mere pencils: all that remained of the old rope bridge that long ago spanned the creek at the narrowest point.

To Jackie and the rest of the kids, the rope bridge—*Old Rope*, the locals had called it—and the dangerous rapids that exploded just beyond this, the narrowest point of the canyon, then progressing as the altitude suddenly dropped, the falling creek water raging all the way down Silver Hills until the downward grade ended and the creek turned back to the east, in the process spilling over its banks on the back side of Black Woods to create Blackwater Swamp—were mere folklore. However, though none of them had ever seen the bridge or witnessed the rapids—they'd all been mere toddlers, not even in kindergarten yet, when a local man had taken it upon himself to take an axe to the thick, stout ropes, hacking down the bridge, and getting himself killed in the process (or so the story went)—they had no reason to doubt it. All the adults in town talked about it, especially since that Baker kid had vanished years ago when he tried to cross the unstable bridge during a raging storm.

Jackie pointed up at the cliffs above. "That's where the rope bridge used to cross! It's the narrowest point in the canyon—and the worst rapids start on the other side!"

The rest of them looked up to where he was pointing, and saw the tiny wooden posts jutting from the rocky precipice—then they turned back to Jackie, eyes wide with fear.

•

Suddenly, the raft began rising noticeably as the raging creek water heaved upward, being forced through the narrower point between the canyon walls where the old rope bridge had once swayed high above.

"Everyone get ready!" Jackie hollered. "This is the worst part—but if we can make it through the rapids to the bottom of the hill, we'll be alright! It'll be over!"

The rest of the boys looked ominously at each other, knowing what that meant: assuming they made it through the rapids in one piece, they'd be landing smack-dab in the middle of Blackwater Swamp. Not only had they been warned to stay away from there—as all the kids in town had been warned—because it was unsanitary, full of fifth and disease and all manner of parasites and bacteria—but it was also rumored to be haunted, being in the back of Black Woods, which nobody disputed was *definitely* haunted.

In fact, a few years back, a local businessman had even sighted some sort of strange creature in there—or so he claimed—that had stalked him while he was fishing in the swamp, having ventured in with his boat after he'd had no luck nearby in the creek. He couldn't describe it, of course—said he'd not seen the actual beast, had only heard it and saw the bushes and tree branches moving as it lumbered toward him—but most everyone believed him, because it scared the living daylights out of him. People who knew him said you could see the genuine terror in his eyes as he described the incident. And, to this day, he still avoids talking talk about it...

...but on the other hand, that weekend he supposedly put a hunting party together and the heavily-armed group went back into Black Woods and Blackwater Swamp looking for the beast, but eventually returned empty-handed.

But still. It was real enough to make believers out of most everyone in town, the history of which was rife with similar folklore—and, of course, all those mysterious disappearances over the years...

So now, though nobody admitted it, their faces all told: none of them were all that eager to land in Blackwater Swamp, even if it meant making it through the rapids.

Nevertheless, the kids braced themselves on their knees, oars jutting out ahead of them, as the raft crested the swell, sending a tickle of weightlessness through their stomachs as it rose, plateaued for a moment, then pointed downward and heaved forward, surfing the beast like a rolling ocean wave.

They all screamed like kids riding a roller coaster as they rode the upended raft quickly downward before plunging into the water as the creek leveled slightly after the initial drop. The broken corner of the raft went clean under, the entire craft tilting ominously to that side and knocking the kids from their knees in the process, sending them rolling before the front of the raft then exploded violently upward, throwing them all once again onto the supply pile that was lashed tightly to the center of the deck.

But at least this time, they had all managed to hang on to their oars.

But then the raft suddenly righted itself, and began roughly riding the rapids down the hill. The kids quickly recovered, swiping the water from their faces, and scurried on hands and knees back to the front of the raft, dragging their oars along with them, then resumed their original configuration, a tight row of five determined kids, thrusting their three stout oars outward, ready for battle.

They all saw it at the same time.

Ahead: boulders...*big* boulders...*countless* big boulders, scattered throughout the violent, splashing creek before them.

And worse, the right front corner of the raft was listing badly. The damaged barrel was sinking, the broken frame and deck on that side now riding along the surface of the creek, occasionally even bobbing under.

"We're never gonna make it!" Ryan screamed in panic over the splashing waves.

"Just brace yourself!" Nick hollered back. "Get your oar into position! We can do this—just don't let the raft hit the rocks!"

Encouraged, Ryan took on a determined look, and adjusted his stance accordingly.

Chaz, who was sharing his oar, did the same.

The boulders were approaching fast.

But then, Jackie saw a way out, up ahead...

"Hey—look!" he shouted at the others, pointing at the

cluster of approaching boulders, the first huge boulder coming in fast. The others first turned and looked at him, then out ahead where he was pointing.

"After that first big boulder, if you look down across the whole length of the creek ahead, all the way to the bottom—there's a clear path, right down the middle of them, like a pattern! See it?"

Nick was the first to confirm this, hollering over the ruckus: "I see it! It sort of zig-zags, but if we stay in that clear part…"

"Yes!" Ryan exclaimed. "I see it too! Right down the middle, after that first big boulder!"

Chaz and Casey both nodded, seeing the pattern too.

"So all we have to do is get past the first boulder," Jackie yelled, "Then just try to keep the raft in the middle of the creek, ride it between the rest of them all the way to the bottom!"

They all nodded in understanding, but they were out of time—the lead boulder was upon them.

As they rocketed toward it, on their knees, oars at the ready, Jackie commanded: "And….NOW!!"

Together, they thrust their oars into the face of the rock, more prepared this time to be shoved backward from the force, braced against it, determined. As they did so, they all let out a scream of attack, like a group rebel yell.

All three oars struck the boulder hard and in succession with a loud *wha-wha-whack!*, and, though they all remained firmly ensconced on their knees, they were again shoved backward together, their knees hydroplaning on the saturated deck boards. But they at least managed to slow the raft's plunging speed noticeably, and, like before, once they had all been shoved against the ropes behind them, the oars stabilized, and the raft slowed to a momentary, rocking stop, waves splashing along both sides—then began a slow drift to the right, circling the boulder rather than careening into it.

At first, it looked like they'd cleared the biggest hurdle—but as they rotated around the mammoth rock, a second, smaller boulder materialized directly behind, and thus hidden by, the first.

And by the time they saw it, it was too late.

Pivoting against the oars, the raft swung around violently as the raging creek pushed it past the first massive boulder, and before any of them could move to reposition their oars against the one behind it, the already broken and crippled corner of the raft slammed into it, this time tearing the barrel—along with much of the frame to which is was lashed—completely off, sending more broken wood and boards exploding into the air above them as the entire front of the raft heaved upward against the boulder, sending the kids sprawling and again grasping for the supply ropes. The raft then slapped roughly back down on the creek and continued swiftly downstream toward the many boulders strewn ahead, the rogue barrel drifting away ahead of them.

As the kids watched in despair, the barrel finally sank in the rapids, pulling the few broken boards that remained roped to it down with it, until it all disappeared beneath the black, roiling murk.

By now the broken and mangled corner of the raft was entirely submerged, and the left rear barrel—the one with the missing plug, the duct tape now long gone—was also sinking, the deck now only about six inches above the water. Between the two, the raft was listing badly to the left.

"Shift to the right, for balance!" Chaz yelled.

Crawling forward from the supply pile, they positioned themselves toward the right corner of the raft, which helped balance it out, the broken and sinking left corner rising a little in response.

"Okay, now we just gotta stay in the middle of the creek!" Jackie yelled. "Use the oars to guide it, from the corners, if we can! If we can stay inside the open path, we should be able to get all the way down the rest of the way without hitting any more rocks!"

At this, they spread out to the remaining three still-floating corners of the raft, Casey and Jackie taking the right front, Ryan and Chaz the left rear, and Nick manning the right rear. He shoved his oar into the water, and began guiding the raft best he could from behind, like a rudder. Seeing this, Chaz and Ryan did the same, while Jackie and Casey kept their oar facing outward to ward off any oncoming obstacles if need be.

Fortunately, they had guessed correctly; from that point on, by managing to stay roughly in the middle of the creek, they were able to navigate through the rest of the boulders without much incident. With Nick, Chaz, and Ryan guiding the raft with their oars from behind, they rocked and weaved another mile or so downstream on the rapids, meandering back and forth slightly to stay between the rocks and boulders, flanked on both sides by the high granite walls Hope Creek Canyon.

And for a while, it worked; but then…

The creek had finally settled slightly, the raft gently undulated as they were swept downstream. While it was relatively calm, Casey took the opportunity to leave Jackie to the oar and peer ahead with the binoculars—then she gasped, dropped them from her eyes, and turned and looked at the others wide-eyed.

"What's wrong?" Jackie asked.

"I'm not sure," she said, turning and squinting into the distance, then back. "I can't see it from here, but through the binoculars, up ahead it looks like the creek just…*disappears*."

"What? Disappears? Let me see." Still holding the oar, Jackie took the binoculars in one hand and peered ahead for a moment, then lowered them and turned to look at the others, who were looking at him expectantly. He shrugged. "She's right. It's weird. It's like the creek just ends."

Nick was also peering ahead from the rear of the raft, one hand up shading his eyes, and noticed trees were now visible way off in the distance. Looking to either side, he also noticed that the towering canyon walls were now receding, dropping in altitude. Then his eyes widened in realization.

"Oh, no!" he cried.

They all turned to him, Chaz asking "What?"

"We're coming to the end of the canyon. See the woods down below?" He pointed at the thick blanket of trees in the distance, and they all turned to look where he was pointing, then nodded and muttered in agreement.

"That's where the creek comes out of the canyon and spills into Blackwater Swamp, before it turns back east!"

"Yeah, so?" Jackie asked.

As the boys were looking ahead at what Nick was pointing out, Casey retrieved the binoculars from Jackie and was again peering through them.

"Well, if that's where the creek pours out of the canyon and into Blackwater Swamp," Nick continued, "and from a distance it looks like the creek just ends there, or disappears, then what it probably is, is a—"

"Waterfall!" Casey announced, saying the word exactly in unison with Chaz as she dropped the binoculars and looked around at them in horror. "It's a waterfall!"

With that, Jackie grabbed the binoculars and looked again, then lowered them and turned to the others, also wide-eyed. "She's right! It's a waterfall!"

"And we're headed right for it!" Nick said.

"Oh my God!" Ryan cried in futility, dropping his face into his hands and collapsing to his knees next to Chaz. Then, through his hands, somewhat muffled: "Now what are we gonna do?"

In desperation, Jackie brought the binoculars back up and scanned the entire width of the falls, from bank to bank, as the raft dipped and rocked toward it, looking for…something.

Anything.

Left, right, left…

"We're running out of time!" Nick yelled from behind. "We

gotta do something, before it's too late!"

Jackie continued scouring ahead...right, left, right—than a jerk back to the left. For a long moment, Jackie froze, peering off to the left of the falls. Then, without taking his eyes from the binoculars, pointed with one finger. "There!" he hollered, prompting the others to look where he was pointing.

"What, that rock?" Casey asked, bewildered. She was referring to a large boulder protruding several feet above the creek, off to the left, maybe ten or fifteen feet before the waterfall dropoff.

Jackie lowered the binoculars and turned to her. "Yes!" he hollered. Then, turning to the others: "That rock, and that side of the creek, near the bank!"

As the others looked in that direction, he continued, still pointing over to that side of the falls: "The waterfall doesn't go all the way across! Over by the bank, where the cliff wall ends, part of the creek separates and continues into the woods! See?"

They all peered across the creek where he was pointing, off to the left of the falls.

"You're right, I see it!" Nick yelled, now also pointing. "The creek splits right there, most of it goes over the falls, but part of it runs off into the woods!"

"And if we can push off that rock," Jackie explained, now pointing to the huge boulder, "maybe we can force the raft over into the other fork, and avoid the waterfall!"

Nothing more needed to be said, they scrambled to the still-floating front half of the raft and raised their oars, bracing for impact.

As luck would have it, the raft drifted left toward the boulder as they rapidly approached, and they kept their oars pointed at the behemoth stone, the raft closing in fast.

"On the count of three!" Jackie yelled above not only the splashing of the rapids, but the roar of the waterfall they could now hear.

Twenty feet...

Fifteen feet...

"One!"

Ten feet...

"Two!"

Five feet...

"THREE!!"

With that, they shoved the ends of the oar into the face of the boulder, once again emitting a group rebel yell as they gave it all they had.

And it worked.

They met the boulder at just enough of an angle to jar the raft to the left, the rear barrels turning toward the rock wall on that side. Then, as they rounded the stone and started to pass it, Jackie screamed "PUSH!!"

The group continued screaming as they shoved off the boulder with all their collective strength, pushing the raft toward the left end of the falls. Now it was a toss-up; they were moving toward the narrow side-fork of the creek that trailed off into the woods, at about the same rate that they were drifting toward the waterfall.

They watched in silent anticipation, turning first to the left side where the creek forked, then to the edge of the waterfall ahead. It quickly became evident they weren't going to make it to the fork-off, but were going to plummet down the waterfall just short of the split.

"We aren't gonna make it, are we?" Ryan wondered aloud.

Jackie just slowly shook his head.

With that, Ryan threw his arms into the air, threw his head back, and screamed at the sky, "Save us, Lord! Don't let us go over the waterfall and drown!"

Chaz and Nick just looked at each other in horror.

Casey put both her arms around Jackie and laid her head on his shoulder, bracing for the falls.

Then they all began backing away from the submerged side of the raft, which had become the leading edge when they turned around the boulder.

As their sideways travel slowed, and they instead began fast approaching the edge of the waterfall, Nick noticed a submerged boulder on the very precipice of the drop-off, just under the surface of the creek. Yanking his oar up over his head, he ran to the front of the raft, sloshing through the several inches of boarding water and, just before they reached the falls, plunged the oar into the water in front of the raft, wedging it against the submerged rock. Yelling with the effort, he then yanked it sideways, and began pulling it with all his might, trying to force the raft around to the left of it. He did manage to stop their forward progression for just a moment, but was unable to swing the raft around. For a brief instant, the raft stopped, and they seemed to be floating there on the edge, their plummet down the falls to certain death below momentarily stalled.

Realizing what Nick was doing, Jackie leapt forward and joined him, grabbing the oar and helping pull it back, attempting to pry the raft to the left, toward the fork in the creek, to which they were oh so close.

Then, the rest dropped the other oars and joined in.

With yet another collective rebel yell, they heaved on the oar as hard as they could...

...and it worked! The raft slowly backed away from the waterfall, and began again moving to the left, in the direction of the fork.

As the raft drifted, Nick spied another underwater boulder between the first one and the fork they were trying to reach. Yanking the oar up out of the water—and out of everyone else's hands—he turned and jammed the oar between the raft and the second rock, and started the whole prying motion again, the others grabbing hold and helping.

This time, they were able to coax the raft entirely away from the waterfall, and into the narrow portion of the creek that split away and headed into the woods.

Suddenly, the rapids ended, and the raft simply drifted calmly and quietly into the cover of the woods, the roar of the waterfall diminishing in the distance. This fork of the creek was much narrower than the other, only about thirty feet across, and densely shrouded by the woods. As the raft floated away from the roaring falls and into the quiet forest, the kids all collapsed to their knees on the deck, exhausted and relieved.

"Praise be to Jesus!" Ryan shouted, as Nick and Chaz bumped fists, and Casey grasped Jackie's hand and squeezed, and they turned and smiled at each other.

Then, Chaz began looking around them, and above at the thickening canopy of trees. They had left the towering canyon walls behind, and were now flanked by dark, peaceful woods, the creek itself calm and quiet as if it was being cautious as it traveled through the darkening forest.

Seeing Chaz examining their surroundings, Jackie asked:

"Are we where I think we are?"

"I think so," Chaz replied, nodding. Then Chaz and Jackie said in unison:

"Black Woods!"

With this Ryan's eyes widened, and Nick began looking around, fear on his face. "No shit?" he said, almost to himself.

"Are you sure?" Casey asked.

"If we'da gone down the waterfall, I think somewhere right after that is where the creek turns to the east and spills out of its banks into Blackwater Swamp," Chaz speculated. "The waves from the falls must be why it spills out at the turn, and Black Woods is always flooded there...that's what makes Blackwater Swamp."

"But we didn't go down the falls," Nick said. "So we're not gonna end up in Blackwater Swamp. So—"

—he then leaned forward, peering ahead into the deepening, ominous woods—

"—where does *this* go?"

"Good question," Jackie said.

"Yea, though I walk through the valley of the shadow of death, I will fear no evil, for thou art with me, thy rod and thy staff they comfort me..." Ryan began muttering to himself, now sitting with his legs crossed and head bowed in prayer.

Everyone just looked at him for a moment, and Chaz rolled his eyes at Nick, while Casey and Jackie smiled at each other, and Jackie shrugged, as if conveying, *can't hurt...*

Chaz pulled his compass from his pocket, turned it a few times while scrutinizing the dial, then looked up at the others. "We're going more southeast now, instead of due south like the main creek. Best guess is we're on the south side of Silver Hills, but we're not all the way down at the bottom yet. We're somewhere in Black Woods, yes, but up a ways on the hill from Blackwater Swamp. Maybe this part of the creek goes into the swamp at another spot, like further back in the woods somewhere, once it reaches the bottom of the hill."

The others looked around at each other, silently nodding in speculative agreement.

"It's getting really dark in here," Casey said, concern in her voice as she looked up and around at the thickening canopy above.

"Yeah, that's why it's called Black Woods," Nick said knowledgeably, smiling at her. Then he turned to Jackie. "So what do we do?"

Jackie shrugged. "Only thing I can figger is we ride the creek the rest of the way down, see where it comes out at."

"Why don't we just dock here?" Ryan pleaded. "I mean,

how long is this thing gonna even float—"

—he waved his hand toward the right edge of the raft, which was now completely underwater—

"—we could just dock the raft and *walk* back to town...just head west."

"I don't think that's a good idea," Jackie said. "We don't even know where we are, and we'd be walking blind in these woods."

"Jackie's right," Nick agreed. "If we stay on the raft, it could take us at least down to the swamp, which is closer to town. Or, we could even go through the swamp and take the creek east, till we see the next sign of civilization. Wouldn't be far from there, just around the bend and east a ways, we'll probably see a ranch or farm or road or something in no time after that."

While Nick spoke, Chaz was walking the perimeter of the raft, inspecting the barrels, the frame, assessing the damage.

"I think we should cut this other barrel loose," he concluded to the others, pointing down at the front corner of the raft that was now submerged.

"What??" Ryan cried, suddenly yanking his head up from his prayers, incredulous. "Cut the barrel loose? If we do that, won't we sink?"

"It's full of water—that's the one with the missing plug, and the tape didn't hold in the rapids—so it isn't floating anymore. In fact, it's heavy, and pulling that corner of the raft underwater. If we cut it loose, get rid of the extra weight, the wood frame and deck would actually float better, I think."

"Good idea," Jackie agreed. "Who has a knife handy?"

Chaz pulled his multi-tool out of his pocket and unfolded the blade, but it was too small. Nick, on the other hand, pulled a hunting knife from his pocket, and unfolded a serrated blade at least three times the size of Chaz's.

Eyes wide, they all moved aside as Nick crossed over to the submerged corner of the raft, slopping his way through the creek water. Bending, he sawed through the blue rope quickly and easily, first on one side of the corner of the frame, then on the other.

After a few cuts, the barrel fell away—and took the entire front frame board with it, plunging into the depths of the murky creek and disappearing.

Still kneeling, he turned to the others.

"Looks like that barrel was all that was holding that part of the frame on," he said apologetically.

And with the frame board gone, the entire right side of the raft sank even further into the creek. Nick hurried back to his feet and sloshed back onto the dry deck near center of the raft, where everyone else was standing as they watched.

"That's just great," Ryan said, shaking his head. "What do we do when it sinks?"

"It's not gonna sink," Jackie said.

The creek had narrowed considerably since they'd entered the woods on this fork, and Jackie pointed that out.

"And 'sides, it's so narrow here, even if the raft sank— which it won't—it's just a quick swim to the shore. Can't be more than ten, fifteen feet, in either direction. Then we walk back to town, just like you said before."

This seemed to calm Ryan down a bit, and he nodded quietly in acceptance.

"Maybe we should try to turn it around," Chaz suggested. "Use the oars to rotate it so the good barrels are in front, with the submerged side behind us. Probably take on less water that way."

With a chorus of agreement, they all shifted to the right side of the raft, with Nick, Jackie, and Ryan taking up the three remaining oars.

The five of them stood at the waterline of the submerged side of the raft, looking down at the surface of the creek as they pondered how to go about turning the raft around. All was quiet for a moment as they glided ever deeper into the forest, seemingly ominous birdsong intermixed with the odd sounds of countless other unknown and unseen woodland creatures wafting around them from behind.

"Maybe start at that corner—"

—Nick pointed to the far rear, destroyed corner—

"—and start rowing to the right? Rotate the other side to the front?"

Chaz nodded. "I think that'll work."

As those two shifted toward the rear of the raft, discussing their strategy, Casey noticed something strange, pointing up into into a tree on the bank as they drifted by.

"Hey, look at that," she said, and Jackie and Ryan, standing to either side of her, looked up to where she pointed. An entire flock of small birds were sitting silently in the tree, myriad little silhouettes all over, looking almost like so much fruit on the branches.

"Sparrows again?" Jackie said softly, remembering the same weird incident he saw in the woods right before he fell into that first tunnel.

"Looks like it," Casey agreed. "But weird how they're just sitting there, not moving, not singing, not making a sound."

"That *is* weird," Jack Concurred.

"Listen...Casey..." Ryan interrupted from behind, and she turned and looked back questioningly.

"I just wanted to say—"

—he paused, shrugging, an apologetic look on his face—

"—just wanted to say, I'm glad you came. You've been a big help through all of this, starting with helping us build the raft, and I'm sorry that at the beginning—Friday night, when we first met you—I said I didn't want—"

—and that's when the raft suddenly upended and turned violently before plummeting through a massive hole in the ground along the left bank, as that side of the creek first whirl-pooled then poured down into the unknown depths, the kids' surprised screams becoming muffled as they went under.

●

They fell.

Twenty feet...

Thirty feet...

Forty feet...

The raft led the way, pointing straight down, the kids ejected from the deck and following behind, tumbling and screaming in mid-air downward in near total darkness.

Then, with a quick series of splashes, the first one big—and accompanied by the unmistakable sound of cracking and splintering wood, the raft suffering further damage as it struck the water—immediately followed by five smaller ones as the the kids plunged one-by-one into a deep pool of water.

In the darkness, each of them could be heard re-surfacing and gasping for air, but none of them could see the others, or the raft. The splashing water, and the sounds they uttered as they resurfaced, all echoed back to them and then echoed again back and forth all around them with a nearly dizzying reverb effect.

They were apparently in an underground cave, which was also apparently filled with water like an isolated pond. The sloppy waterfall pouring through the hole far above gushed into the pond behind them, pushing them and the raft further into the cave and away from the point of entry.

Once they'd drifted far enough from the showering creek water that they could hear over the ruckus, Jackie began shouting:

"Is everyone okay?" he hollered over the splashes, gasps and coughs of the others, his voice echoing all around.

"I'm okay!" Nick hollered from nearby, though Jackie couldn't see him.

Casey had landed right next to Jackie, and spoke up when he called out, "I'm okay!"

"Me too!" Chaz called out.

"Yes! I'm okay!" Ryan hollered into the darkness.

Once all the echoing faded away, Jackie called out into the blackness, "Can anyone feel the raft? Or does anyone at least know where it is?"

They all began splashing about, trying to locate the raft.

"Here it is!" Nick hollered, his hand bumping the wooden side of the craft as he flailed about himself in the darkness. He grabbed hold of it and pulled himself to it. "Over here! Follow my voice!"

One by one, the rest of them dog-paddled toward Nick's voice, each of them finding purchase on the side of the raft and hoisting themselves up onto the deck in the darkness.

"Hey, I'm starting to be able to see," Casey said to the others, her voice elevated with excitement. "My eyes must be adjusting to the dark."

"She's right, I can see a little now, too," Ryan agreed.

"Me too," Nick joined in.

As they each chimed in, their shapes began materializing to each other as they huddled in a circle on the deck of the now lightly undulating raft. They peered around them in total silence, but could see nothing of the cave, nor hear anything but the distant splashing of the waterfall behind them, along with intermittent dripping sounds all around them.

The hole in the top of the cave, through which they'd fallen, was now just a glint of grayness far above and behind them, what little sunlight that managed to penetrate the thick canopy of trees above now diminished with distance—but there was just enough light coming through to keep the cave from being completely black.

But then Casey noticed something else: another source of light, from the other side of the cave…and lifted the binoculars to her eyes.

Simultaneously, Chaz and Jackie pulled their flashlights from their pockets and flicked them on, surveying the raft.

"Looks like our supplies stayed in place," Jackie said as he tugged on random ropes, all still taut.

"Maybe, but the raft took a lot more damage," Chaz said in response from the front of the raft, where he stood ankle-deep in water, shining his light down on the dark surface. "This side is further under water, and about a third of the deck is under now. If it sinks much further, the supplies will start to go under, too—"

—he then trudged wetly across the deck to the back of the raft and bent over, shining the light first on one corner, then along the side of the raft, then on the other corner. Standing, he turned back to the others—

"—and we lost the other barrel on this side. That section of the frame board must've broken off when it hit the water, and took that barrel off with it. Who knows where it is now, it probably sank like the others. So now we're down to just one barrel—"

—he turned and pointed his light at the other corner, then turned back to them—

"—and that one looks like it's probably taking on water, too, it's sitting pretty low."

"There!" Casey suddenly cried, pointing ahead as she peered through the binoculars. Nobody had noticed that she'd broken from the group and was scouting ahead—toward the distant source of light—as they were surveying the condition of the raft.

Turning and peering into the darkness, the rest of them could just make out a blazing bright patch of whiteness in the distant blackness, maybe a hundred yards or so away.

She then lowered the binoculars, unlooped the strap from around her neck, and offered them to Jackie. "That must be the cave opening way down there, the sunlight shining through. I mean, the creek's gotta go somewhere, right? Else the cave would fill up."

Jackie put the binoculars to his eyes. "I bet it comes out in Blackwater swamp," he said as he lowered them and looped the strap around his neck.

"So we just gotta row down there to the cave opening," Ryan said.

"We better hurry," Chaz warned, pointing his light down at the encroaching water. "Water's almost to the supplies already. The raft is definitely sinking."

"Wait—the oars!" Nick suddenly realized. "Where are all the oars?"

With that, both Nick and Ryan pulled out their flashlights too, and the boys scampered around the wobbling raft, shining their lights all about, scouring the water for their oars.

There were none to be seen.

"Great," Nick huffed.

"Look," Jackie explained calmly. "If the creek water comes in from up there—"

—he pointed his flashlight at the now distant glow of the opening in the ceiling of the cave, from which the glistening waterfall emanated—

"—and goes out down there—"

—he turned and pointed his flashlight into the darkness ahead, indicating the bright cave opening in the distance—

"—then alls we gotta do is float on the current, like we are. It'll take us right there. Where else are we gonna go?"

"*If* we make it that far," Chaz again warned. "I'm tellin' ya, the raft is—"

—but he was cut off by a deep, guttural growl that emanated from somewhere in the darkness nearby, the echoes bouncing all around them, making it difficult to discern the direction from which it originated.

Seized with fear, they stopped and silently looked around at each other with widened eyes.

"What the hell was *that?*" Nick whispered.

"Now *that* sounded like a monster!" Casey murmured, recalling their debate about the rumbling sound they heard in the tunnels under the burned-down shack.

"Or a *demon,*" Ryan corrected with a mutter.

"Something's definitely in here with us!" Jackie whispered back to Nick.

With that, they began shining their flashlights around, the beams of light whipping in all directions, mostly disappearing into the darkness before ever landing upon anything solid.

"Shit, I can't even see the cave walls from here," Nick noted.

Now Chaz was peering ahead, in the direction of the

distant sunlit opening. His eyes then followed along what had to be the cave wall from there, though it was too dark and too distant to actually see, the beam of his flashlight didn't reach that far. He turned to the others.

"That opening down there *has* to be at the bottom of Silver Hills, where the creek comes out of the canyon and Blackwater Swamp starts," he surmised. "So this entire side of the cave to our left must be the outside wall. That means the right side—"

"—he shined his light into the depths of the darkness on the other side of the raft, to no avail, prompting the others to turn and peer into the blackness with him—

"—goes back into the hill itself. Who knows how deep it goes, but I bet that's where the tunnel we saw yesterday leads, into this cave somewhere over on that other side."

"That would probably explain why we smelled water in the tunnel," Nick said.

"Yes," Chaz agreed, nodding.

"So whatever just growled is probably deeper in the cave, cuz it came from that side somewhere," Jackie concluded, shining his light around, also to no avail, it was just too dark and the walls too distant to do any good. "So maybe it came here through the tunnels above?"

"Could be," Chaz said.

"What kind of animal do you think it is?" Casey turned and asked the others. "Like maybe a bear or something?"

"I don't think there's any bears around here," Nick said. "In fact, I don't think there are *any* big animals in this area. Maybe coyotes, but that's about it."

"That wasn't any coyote," Ryan protested. "And if there aren't any big animals in this area, then it *has* to be—"

—another deep growl interrupted him—this one shorter, and definitely coming from the depths of the cave to their right—and was followed by a distant *splash!* —

"Oh shit, it's coming after us!" Ryan cried.

"Keep your voice down!" Jackie hissed at him, then continued in a low whisper. "There's no way any animal could even know we're here—we're so far away from that side of the cave, our lights won't even shine that far. So how could it see us? I doubt it could smell us from that far, either, specially since this whole cave smells like damp, moldy rock and muddy creek water. So if we just stay quiet, and keep moving toward the opening down there, we should be fine. It'll never know we're here."

As the others nodded in agreement, Chaz shined his light on the pile of backpacks lashed down in the middle of the raft. The water was now lapping up onto the edge of the pile, the entire front side of the deck now submerged. The kids stood in a semi-circle around the back side, facing one another over the heap of packs. Chaz then directed his light to the higher of the two back corners, revealing the final remaining barrel was now halfway underwater too.

"We're sinking pretty quick," he said. "At this rate, we won't make it all the way to that exit before she goes under. We're gonna have to find a way to move faster."

"Sinking?!" Ryan cried, immediately berated by a *sshhhhhhhh!* from Jackie. "That's just great," he said, lowering his voice to a near whisper. "There's something in here with us, that can obviously swim just fine—an animal, or creature, or monster, or demon or whatever the hell it is—and now we're *sinking, too?*"

"Somebody's gonna hafta paddle," Nick said.

"Paddle? With *what?*" Ryan asked, shaking his head and raising his hands to his sides in futility. "In case you're not keeping up with current events pal, we lost all the oars in the fall, remember?"

"Well..." Nick trailed off and looked to the side, down at the edge of the raft, then back, concern on his face.

"By hand," Jackie finished for him, and Nick looked back at Jackie and quietly nodded.

"By *hand?* Are you *crazy?*" Ryan asked, incredulous. "No way I'm sticking my arm down into that water! You heard it— that thing, whatever it is—just dove in! It could bite our arms right off!"

"I'll do it," Casey said strongly, immediately stepping to one side of the raft, just behind the sunken portion of the deck, and dropping down to her belly. Then, inching herself all the way to the edge of the raft, she dunk one arm down into the black water, and began paddling.

After standing and watching her for a moment, the boys looked at each other, and without a word, Jackie, Nick, and Chaz dispersed to both sides of the raft, pocketing their flashlights before laying down and pitching in, Jackie joining Casey on that side and Nick and Chaz positioning themselves opposite.

"You guys are all crazy, Ryan said, shaking his head. "*I'm* sure as hell not sticking *my* arm down in the water," he said defiantly. "I'd kinda like to keep my arm attached, thank you very much. In fact, I'd kinda like to *stay alive.*"

"Fine, you can be the guide," Jackie said, handing the binoculars up with one hand. "Make sure we stay on course to the exit."

"Yeah!" Ryan said enthusiastically, obviously relieved as he snatched up the binoculars. "I'll be the guide!" With that, he looped the strap around his neck, and shimmied himself up onto the pile of backpacks, elevating himself so he could see up ahead a little better.

The others began paddling, each of them lying on their stomachs with one arm in the water, stroking. Progress was slow—but definitely faster than when they were just floating on the weak current.

Suddenly, Ryan had an idea. Dropping the binoculars, he jumped down and began searching the pile for his own backpack. Finally finding it, he unzipped the top, rummaged around inside for a moment, and pulled out his bible.

Turning back toward the front, he shimmied back up onto the pile, sat, and began flipping through the pages, glancing at each sticky-note with his flashlight and then moving on, obviously looking for something specific. Finally, he seemed to have found what he was looking for. He read silently for a moment, nodded his head in approval, then stood up, bible held in front of him in one hand, flashlight illuminating the page with the other. He cleared his throat.

"Psalm twenty-three," he said quietly, before going on:

"The Lord is my shepherd, I shall not want. He makes me lie down in green pastures; He leads me beside quiet waters. He restores my soul; He guides me in the paths of righteousness, for His name's sake."

But he stopped abruptly, interrupted by the distant sound of splashing water, another deep, guttural growl, followed by another splash, this one considerably closer.

At this, the others yanked their arms from the water and began shining their flashlights about, trying to spot whatever it was they had heard.

Then suddenly, in a loud, booming voice, Ryan began shouting into the depths of the cave: "Yea, though I walk through the valley of the shadow of death, I fear no evil! For You are with me! Your rod and your staff, they comfort me!" Now he was swinging his arms in the air for emphasis, waving the book around and throwing flashlight beam into great arcs in the darkness.

Alarmed, Jackie tried to warn him: "Ryan!" he hissed. "Shut the fuck up! You're gonna get us all—"

—but he was interrupted by a massive impact under him, something slamming into the bottom of the raft and lifting it from the water with a booming splash.

The kids screamed as that side of the raft shot into the air, each gripping the sides of the deck with all their strength to keep from being thrown overboard as the raft was upended, nearly turned over.

All of them but Ryan, that is.

Bible and flashlight flying into the air, he was catapulted off the raft and into the darkness, screaming the entire way, until he was heard landing in the water some distance away with a *splash!*

The raft hung in the air sideways, balanced there for just a moment, then came crashing back down hard, the kids still screaming like they were on an amusement park ride.

A thick blanket of water came splashing down on them as the frame of the raft slammed down onto the surface, then went under, then came back up again just in time to catch the vertical wave it created on impact. Now, instead of screaming, they were all coughing and choking as the water receded, pouring from the deck back into the black lake.

Nick was the first to recover. "Ryan!" he called out, climbing to his feet and darting to the edge of the raft, yanking his light out, flicking it on, and shining it all across the still rippling water.

He saw nothing.

"Ryan!" he called again, louder this time, as the others came over and joined him, Jackie and Chaz adding their flashlight beams to the attempt, as all four of them began shouting Ryan's name, the shouts echoing back from various distances, sounding like an entire crowd calling his name.

Still, nothing.

Just as they were about to give up, looking horrified at one another, they heard Ryan's voice way off in the distance, somewhere behind them.

"Help!"

His voice sounded garbled and weak, full of water, shouted between gasps and coughs. They could hear him splashing about in the distance, and they rushed to the rear corner of the raft and again started calling his name and shining the flashlights about. But apparently he was too far away, farther than their tiny lights could penetrate in the cave's near total darkness.

Then, suddenly, he cried out: "I see it! I *see* it! It's...It's..."

But his words were cut off by the boy's high-pitched, blood-curdling scream, joined by another deep, roaring growl, all terminated by another *splash!*....and then silence.

Again they all began frantically shouting Ryan's name into the darkness, desperately shining their lights all over, in the direction they'd heard his voice in the darkness...but after a few minutes, futility set in.

They knew.

Then Casey broke down and started crying, scared out of her wits. Jackie's eyes were also welling up, as the reality of his friend's demise set in.

"We gotta get the fuck outta here," Nick said boldly.

Chaz shined his light around the deck of the raft, all of which was now covered with a thin sheen of water.

"That last barrel has taken on too much water," he said, pointing his light at that corner of the raft. "It's sinking, and pulling the raft down with it. We need to cut it loose."

With that, Nick wasted no time extracting his knife, hopping over to that corner of the raft, and going to work on the ropes.

"We gotta keep quiet," Jackie whispered to the others as Nick worked to free the sinking barrel. "It came after Ryan because he was talking loud, making noise. Probably alerted it to us, and it attacked."

"And the lights," Chaz added. "Probably should kill those, too, in case they attract it."

As the ropes let go, Nick pushed the full barrel away from the raft, and it silently sank into the murky depths. It worked; relieved of the weight, the back of the raft lifted back up out of the water. Now just the front half was submerged, like before.

"That should buy us some time," he said quietly as he stood, folding the knife and tucking it into his pocket. But then he stopped abruptly, shining his light down onto the water just beyond the edge of the raft. Dropping to his knees, he reached overboard for something.

"Shouldn't we go back for him?" Casey asked the others, still sobbing. "I mean, we can't just leave him."

"He's gone," Nick said matter-of-factly, approaching them from the back corner. "This was floating in the water."

He held up the waterlogged bible, which hung open at one of the many now sopping sticky notes. Turning it upward, he shined his light on it, and read out loud for a moment:

"Then I saw a beast coming up out of the sea, having ten horns and seven heads, and on his horns were ten diadems, and on his heads were blasphemous names. And the beast which I saw was like a leopard, and his feet were like those of a bear, and his mouth like the mouth of a lion…"

Then, with widened eyes, he looked up at the others, his

face pale with fright.

"The beast," Jackie whispered.

"It's from Revelation...the end times," Nick said, terrified.

Chaz rolled his eyes and sighed. "Guys, we gotta get a move on. And whatever's in this cave with us, is just some kind of wild animal. Maybe a bear or something, like Casey said before. It's not the beast from the bible, and this isn't the end of the world. We live in *Hope*, for crying out loud! Even if those stories in the bible were true, the beast isn't gonna come from this tiny little podunk town in the middle of nowhere, and the end of the world isn't gonna start here! So you all need to get a grip, and let's get the hell outta here before this fucking raft sinks! *Okay?"*

Turning, Nick tossed the soaked book back into the water, toward the back where they'd last heard Ryan's voice.

"God be with you, my friend," he spoke across the water. Then he turned to the others. "Amen."

The rest of them repeated the amen, as if this were Ryan's funeral, and Nick had just finished his eulogy. After a moment of silence, Jackie spoke up.

"Unfortunately, Ryan had the binoculars," he stated quietly. He then turned and peered ahead into the darkness. The bright opening in the wall was still at least seventy-five yards away. "We'll have to eyeball it from here. But like Chaz said, the current should take us right to it, we just need to expedite."

At this, Casey looked up and glared at him, wide eyes red and wet with tears. "You expect us to put our arms back down into the water?" she hissed. "With that...that *thing* down there somewhere? Are you *nuts?*"

"We don't have a choice," Chaz said quietly. Again, he pointed his flashlight around the sinking deck. "Cutting that barrel loose helped, but we're still sinking. The wood itself is getting waterlogged. It's just cheap pine, the kind they use for construction. It's very porous, and so it's filling up with water. It's only a matter of time before the whole thing goes under, especially with all our weight on it. So we gotta hurry, if we wanna make it out of the cave in time."

"And 'sides," Jackie added, "that thing, whatever it is, didn't bother us when our arms were in the water before—hell, it probably didn't even know we were here. It wasn't until Ryan started making that ruckus that it attacked—and it only took Ryan because he fell in the water, none of us were touched."

Nick and Chaz both nodded in agreement, and they all watched Casey, waiting in earnest for her approval.

Finally, she sighed and slowly made her way back to the side of the raft and began lying back down. "Okay," she said quietly. "But we better fucking make it quick."

"Lights out," Chaz reminded them, clicking off his light and pocketing it.

As the others positioned themselves to each side of the raft, they also clicked their lights out and pocketed them, then assumed their paddling positions. Warily, eyes darting about in the darkness, they each lowered their arms slowly into the black water and started paddling as gently as possible.

•

It wasn't long before they began once again hearing more

ominous splashing sounds, first in front, then beside, then behind, then in front again, and very close.

Like they were being stalked…

As the splashes continued, and sounded like they were getting closer with each pass, Nick finally stood and went to the supply pile, and started rummaging through it, looking for his backpack.

Once he located it, he opened it and pulled out the hatchet, holding it up before him.

"I *dare* that thing to attack us again," he announced in a threatening voice. "I'll cut the motherfucker to pieces!"

He then swung the hatch back and forth a few times, as if assailing an invisible beast, shouting "Ya! Ya! Ya!" as he did so. He then returned to his paddling position at the side of the raft, and, keeping hold of the hatchet with his right hand, went back to paddling with his left.

And, as if on cue, a massive *splash!* exploded right next to him, the water showering down on him as the beast's howling growl echoed throughout the cave. Nick's side of the raft lifted slightly with the turbulence, helping Nick to roll away and spring to his feet, hatchet raised and ready to strike, as the other kids screamed in horror. With his free hand, he slopped the water off his face and pushed his soaked hair back over the top of his head, then pulled his hunting knife from his front pocket, snapping it open with one thumb.

He then stepped forward.

"Nick, no!" Chaz yelled. "Get away from it!"

They could all just see the silhouette of the thing as it rose from the water before Nick…

…four feet…

…six feet…

…eight feet…!!!

Now the kids were all screaming again, including Nick. Nevertheless, he took another brave step forward, trembling all over with fear as he did so.

"Come and get it, asshole!" he screamed at the nearly indiscernible form towering before him in the darkness, holding the hatchet up in swinging position high over his shoulder, the knife forward at the ready.

As if actually responding to Nick's invitation, the beast roared deafeningly and lashed quickly out with multiple thick, wet, slippery tentacles, knocking the knife from Nick's hand and into the water and enwrapping the boy even as he swung the hatchet futilely with a valiant yell.

The others screamed as Nick was yanked violently off the raft, the dropped hatchet hitting the deck and bouncing into the water as the boy was lifted in the air, squirming and screaming, enwrapped in massive thick tentacles, before the beast grunted one last time and disappeared under the surface with another huge *splash!*, the wave of water raining down on the rest of the kids as the raft rocked in the turbulence for a moment, then settled again.

Chaz was the first one up, yanking out his flashlight and flicking it on. "Nick!" he yelled, starting to sob as he cast the light onto the roiling water where the beast had gone under with his best friend. "Nick!"

Jackie and Casey were both crying, too. Casey had gone into hysterics, muttering incoherently between sobs—

…oh my god…

sob

sob

…what are we gonna do…

sob

sob

…it's gonna kill us all…

—while Jackie held her, also sobbing himself.

"Nick!" Chaz yelled again, at the top of his lungs, shining his light all about the water's black surface.

"He's gone!" Jackie yelled at him. "Didn't you see that thing? What it did to Nick? No way he survived…even if he survived the attack, he's drowned by now!"

At this, Chaz slumped his shoulders and plopped down onto his butt with a tiny splash, as the entire deck was now slightly underwater. He then removed his glasses with one hand, and rubbed his eyes with the other, quietly sobbing.

Finally, Jackie recovered. Sobs tapering off, he stood and looked toward the tiny cave opening off in the distance. Then he turned to Chaz.

"Look, we're almost halfway there," he said calmly, quietly. "We just gotta keep going. We can make it, but only if we keep really *quiet*."

"You mean if we're fucking *lucky!*" Casey cried up at him. through her tears. She then pointed out over the water, into the darkness of the cave. "That thing is gonna keep attacking, and taking each one of us off this fucking piece of shit raft you idiots designed, even before the stupid thing sinks! Every time we even *try* to move, it's gonna come back, and it's gonna—"

"Keep your voice down!" Jackie hissed, and that shut her up. Instead, she buried her face in her hands and continued sobbing quietly.

Jackie turned back to Chaz. "We gotta keep going. We at least gotta *try*."

With that, Chaz's sobbing trailed off, and he nodded his head in silent agreement.

"You guys keep paddling toward the opening," he said as he trudged through the sheen of water on the deck to the pile of backpacks, flicking his flashlight on as he approached it. "I've got an idea for a weapon—a *real* weapon, not just a knife or hatchet—but it'll take me a few minutes to build it."

He then began untying the ropes around the backpacks and pulling them free.

As he did so, Jackie knelt down to Casey, whose sobbing seemed to have abated somewhat.

"Listen, we gotta keep going, okay? If we don't, that thing'll *definitely* get us. We can't just sit here and wait for it. If we try to keep moving toward the cave opening, at least we have a chance, right?"

Casey continued to look downward, as if contemplating this for a moment. Then, she began nodding her head.

"Good. And Chaz has an idea for a weapon. I don't know what it is, but he's pretty smart, pretty good at stuff like that. So maybe that'll help. But he needs a few minutes to make it.

Meantime, we need to keep paddling, get to that exit as fast as we can."

Without a word, Casey nodded, wiped the tears from her eyes, turned, laid down on the wet deck, lowered her arm into the water, and began paddling, quietly sniffling as she did so.

"I have to go over to the other side now," Jackie explained quietly. "It's just you and me now, there's nobody to paddle over there. But when Chaz is done, he can take over, and I'll come back over here with you, okay?"

Casey just nodded in the darkness, still sniffling, still paddling.

Jackie rose and slopped across the water-covered deck, then laid down on the other side and began paddling.

The first thing Chaz did after loosening the ropes is identify both Ryan's and Nick's backpacks—figuring his friends were, unfortunately, no longer going to need them—pulled them free of the pile, and set them down flat on the submerged deck, creating a dry surface on which he could work. He then pulled his own pack free, started unzipping and unsnapping various compartments, and one-by-one retrieved an array of items, which he laid out before him across the somewhat stable platform he'd created.

Off in the distance, a splash, and a grunt...but it sounded quite a ways away, only echoing to them, not really sounding threatening...at least not *yet*...

In mere minutes, Chaz had laid out an array of odd items: the small, green propane tank from the portable grill; the bundle of candles; the bundle of flares; the roll of duct tape;

the small roll of fishing line. He also pulled the small multi-tool from his pocket, and set it down with all the other stuff.

As Jackie paddled quietly with one arm, his head was turned as he watched Chaz with curiosity, wondering what he was up to. Occasionally he glanced over at Casey, who had finally stopped sobbing, and was just paddling, turned away from him and staring out over the water into the darkness.

Working quickly and quietly, Chaz pulled one of the long, white candles from the bundle, broke the bottom section off, about three inches long, and yanked out the wick. This he shoved and twisted into the threaded nozzle on the end of the propane tank, until it would go no further. Laying the tank down, he rose and sloshed to the most damaged corner of the raft, shining his light down into the water. The light beam zigging this way and that, he finally stopped near one edge, bent, and pried up a splinter of broken deck wood, about an inch thick and a foot long.

Returning to his makeshift workbench, he crouched back down to his knees, tore off a strip of duct tape from the roll, and taped one end of the wooden shank to the end of the propane tank, wrapping the tape around and around both the threaded spout and the short section of candle, securing that end of the stick, which protruded out eight or nine inches.

He then pulled a flare from the bundle, peeled off the tape and removed the ignition cap. Unwinding the fishing line, he wrapped it around and around the cap, extracted the knife from his multi-tool, and cut the line, leaving about a foot dangling from the cap. He then wrapped a strip of duct tape around the whole contraption, securing the line to the cap.

Turning the cap so the scratching surface was against the igniter button in the end of the flare, he pressed the other end into the end of the candle, pressed the flare into the scratching pad on the cap, then taped the flare in place, wrapping duct tape around the flare and the wooden stake that protruded from the propane tank. He held it up. The tension between the flare and the candle held the cap tightly in place, the fishing line dangling beneath.

Looking around, he located a metal ring on the end of one of his friend's backpack straps, opened his multi-tool pliers, and pried the ring open, removing it from the strap. After bending it back closed, he tied it onto the end of the dangling fishing line, looping it over and through and over and through before finally knotting it.

Again he held the whole thing up for inspection, the metal ring dangling a foot below the tank, candle, cap, and flare, all taped together in a gray jerry-rigged-looking mess. Noticing Jackie watching him with a questioning look, he smiled.

"Propane bomb," he said.

Jackie's eyes widened. He was impressed.

"How's it work?" he asked.

"Real simple. You open the valve at the base of the spout—"

—he pointed to the small knob sticking out of the base—

"—then pull the igniting cap out with the ringed line—"

—he motioned with a hard, downward yank, miming the removal of the cap—

"—the flare will light, and begin melting the candle that's

wedged in the nozzle, blocking the propane from escaping the tank. Might take a minute, maybe less, to melt through the wax, then—"

"Bammo," Jackie finished for him, prompting a smile and nod from Chaz.

"Yep. The only trick is, there's no way of knowing how long it'll take to melt the wax. You gotta light it, and watch it—and when it looks like it's about to melt through, throw it at the target...and then hope."

"Might work," Jackie said with hope, nodding his head.

"Let's just hope we don't need to use it," Casey said from the other side. Unbeknownst to the boys, she'd turned and been watching the demonstration.

Then Jackie had a thought. "So, say we use it against the... animal, beast, monster, whatever it is...we light it, wait for the wax to melt, then throw it at it—but it goes in the water. Won't the water extinguish the flare?"

"I think the flare will still burn underwater," Chaz said. "They're usually waterproof. But just in case, I should probably attach the bomb to some kind of floating device. Besides, the explosion will be bigger and stronger if it's above water...if it happens to explode underwater, I don't know..."

With that, he began searching around and over the packs with his flashlight. As he did so, another rumbling growl was heard, still distant—but closer than before. Jackie and Casey exchanged worried glances, but continued paddling. Jackie then looked forward. They were closer to the exit, but it was still pretty far away. He began to doubt whether they would make it, after all.

That's when he noticed the water he was laying in was getting deeper. The raft was indeed sinking, even with the last water-filled barrel cut loose.

Grabbing up Nick's backpack, Chaz opened the main section and yanked out the saw they'd used to cut wood for the raft, then turned the pack over and opened and emptied the last remnants of food, along with the now thawed ice packs, from the cooler section in the back. Working vigorously, he began sawing between the two sections. The saw was good and sharp, and began cutting through the material quickly.

"What are you doing?" Jackie asked, curious.

"This is the insulated part of the backpack, and it's lined with plastic walls inside," Chaz explained without looking up from his work. "I'm gonna separate it from the the rest of the pack, and seal the top shut. At that point, it'll basically be an empty, sealed plastic container."

"It'll float," Jackie said, nodding.

"I'll mount the bomb to it, so even if it lands in the water—hopefully near the...*thing*—it won't sink before it goes off."

"That's brilliant," Casey said from the other side.

Smiling, Chaz continued sawing.

But then a loud growl blasted them from the darkness, very close now. Water could be heard stirring, apparently disturbed by something...*big*.

"Better hurry with that thing," Jackie said, cautiously yanking his arm from the water. Casey also pulled her arm out, while Chaz doubled down on his efforts.

Once removed from the backpack, the cooler compartment was about fourteen inches square by four inches deep. In no time, Chaz had it sealed shut with duct tape. Then he cut a couple pieces of the blue nylon rope he'd untied from the supplies and secured the bomb to the makeshift float, tying it down tightly, front and rear.

By the time he finished, grunts, growls, and telltale splashes had become closer and more frequent, approaching from the cave side of the raft, the side where Casey lay.

Carrying the bomb in both hands, Chaz sloshed his way over to that side and stood just behind Casey's outstretched body, peering forward, ascertaining the distance to the cave entrance, which was still a good ways away.

"We're still floating toward the exit," he said quietly. "We should get there soon...but if that thing shows up before then, I'll let him have it with this—"

And that's when a tangle of monstrous tentacles burst from the black water just below Casey, seizing Chaz in a flurry of splashing water and thrusting him into the air, his glasses flying, his screams mixing with the screams of the others as they watched helplessly.

As Chaz was flung upward into a sweeping arc, entangled in thick, wet tentacles, the bomb flew from his hands and out into the darkness. He'd never even had a chance to pull the string, it all happened so fast.

Then he and the beast were gone, ending with another monstrous *splash!* sending the raft into wild undulations and again raining water down onto Jackie and Casey as they clung to the deck in horror.

Casey was still screaming, but Jackie darted across the raft and knelt beside her, clasping his hand over her mouth.

"Shhhhhhh," he hissed. "Stay down, and stay quiet."

She immediately stifled herself, nodding in understanding.

They stayed totally silent and perfectly still for a few moments, as the raft and the surrounding water settled. Finally, deciding the beast was gone—at least for now—Jackie released his hand from Casey's mouth.

Leaning closer, he whispered in her ear: "Every time someone stands up, or speaks above a whisper, that thing attacks. So we gotta stay down, stay quiet, and hope we make it to that exit."

Again, she nodded in understanding.

Slowly and quietly, Jackie pulled his flashlight from his pocket, flicked it on, and shined it out onto the water.

Terrified, Casey urgently shook her head no, implying that he was putting them in jeopardy. He raised his hand to comfort her.

"It's okay, It think it's gone, at least for now. I just wanna make a quick check for the bomb. I saw it fly outta Chaz's hands when he went up and over, before they went under, and it's supposed to be able to float…it might still be around here somewhere."

Crouching behind Casey at the edge of the raft, he slowly pivoted the flashlight beam over the top of the water, which was almost totally calm now.

And sure enough, there it was.

About twenty feet out, the bomb atop the plastic container, floating gently and quietly on the surface, like nothing had even happened.

"I see it," Jackie whispered, pointing out across the water.

Casey turned and looked, following the white beam, and saw it too. She nodded.

"How do we get it?" she whispered.

"Good question," Jackie responded with a shrug. He then stood, shining his light over the strewn pile of backpacks. "Maybe we can—"

He was interrupted by a long, purring, guttural growl, close by, flanking them, seemingly moving from one end of the raft to the other as it rumbled.

With this, Jackie ducked down and hurried back over to Casey, dropping to his knees beside her and killing his light.

Casey, afraid of being so close to the water, slowly sat up and shimmied back, away from the edge of the deck.

The two sat together in the rising water atop the deck, waiting, watching—but seeing nothing in the near total darkness.

Practically lying down on the deck now, Casey looked out at the cave entrance, closer but still too far. Then she had an idea, and turned to Jackie.

"I'm a pretty good swimmer," she said.

"What?" Jackie responded, perplexed.

"I took classes in school…was one of the best in my class, got all A's…was planning to try out for the swim team next year...we obviously aren't gonna make it, the raft is sinking, you said so yourself...so maybe you could try to distract the monster, and I could swim to the opening, then go for help."

"Help from *where?*" Jackie almost cried, but kept his voice down. "You'll end up somewhere in the middle of Blackwater Swamp. There's nothing around for miles."

"Better than dying in here, killed by that...*thing*."

"Forget it. You ain't swimmin' outta here. No way," Jackie said authoritatively, shaking his head in denial.

Casey heaved a sigh, nodding in sullen acceptance. Then, thinking about their predicament, she muttered, "You know, I don't know if I even *want* to get outta here anyway."

"What?" Jackie said, stunned. "Why not?"

"For the same reason I ended up here in the first place," she said, shrugging matter-of-factly. "Even if we get out, I've got no place to go... except back home...back to...*him*."

With that she gazed out across the murky water, and saw the bomb floating and bobbing in the distance, barely visible in the darkness, and she had an idea...and slowly stood up.

Then Jackie starting trying to talk some sense into her: "Well, being back home with your mom—even if you've got a dickhead for a stepdad—would be way better than—"

—and suddenly the beast slammed into the bottom of the raft, again lifting the entire side of the raft that they occupied into the air. As Jackie fell backward sprawling into the supplies behind him, he was astonished to see Casey use the upward momentum like a springboard—or more like a *diving* board—and launch herself into the air in a beautiful, graceful arc, up and over, then she raised her arms, pressed her palms together, and lowered her head to dive down like a missile into the water, disappearing beneath it with barely a splash.

"Casey!" he managed to holler before the raft came slamming back down onto the surface of the water, throwing him and the backpacks tumbling back toward the edge of the raft, two of them rolling off into the water before Jackie was just able to stop his own momentum right at the edge, the splashing water from the impact blinding him to whatever Casey was doing out there.

But then, silence. The water once again settled, and all seemed calm. Just the incessant dripping sounds all around, the sloshing of the raft, the distant echoes—all of which he'd become accustomed to since landing in this underground lake —but that was all.

Was it going after Casey?

And where did she go? What was she doing?

"What was she even *thinking?*" he muttered, shaking his head in confusion.

He was still clutching his flashlight, and, deciding it was safe for the moment, he flicked it on and shined it out where he'd seen Casey go under.

Nothing.

Scanning the light across the water, he came to the spot where he'd last seen the bomb floating.

Nothing there, either. The bomb was gone.

Shining the light all around the area, he didn't see Casey or the bomb anywhere.

"Pssst. Over here," he heard whispered from behind him.

Casey's voice.

Turning, he swung his light to the other side of the raft. It illuminated her face, blonde hair slicked back like wet silk, face wet and pretty like a fresh, dew-ladened flower.

She was holding the bomb.

He dashed over to that side of the raft, and she handed it up to him, then grasped the side of the raft with both hands.

As he turned away to set it down behind him, he thought he heard her whisper, *Jackie's ladder*.

Then he turned back to her.

"What?" he asked.

"Nothing," she said quietly.

Then he noticed she was pale and shivering—or more like shaking violently, all over.

"Looks like you're freezing!" he said, extending his hand. "Hurry...let's get you back up on the raft before—"

—but then a growl and a splash behind her cut him off.

Jackie pointed the light over her and into the darkness and saw it—for just a second, only ten feet away: a glowing yellow reptilian-type eye, reflecting his light back at him from within a gray-green, wet rubbery-looking socket, before disappearing back under the murky black water.

Eyes wide, he looked back down at Casey in desperation, pushing his hand even closer to her. "Quick, take my hand!"

Still grasping the edge of the raft with both hands, she ignored his outstretched hand, and instead lifted herself from the water, kissing him softly on the cheek.

"I love you," she whispered into his ear. Then, shivering violently and quickly losing color, she seemed to collapse, splashing back down.

And that was when he saw it, in the brief moment that she was balanced on the edge of the deck, kissing his cheek: her left leg was severed just below the knee, strands of skin and muscle and sinew hanging, dripping, the dark water below tinged a deep red.

"YOUR LEG!!" he yelled, eyes wide in horror—but he kept his hand outstretched.

As they looked silently into each other's eyes, a single tear streamed down her cheek.

Then the water behind her swirled and swelled and she was suddenly and violently yanked under, her screams first muffled and bubbling, then ceasing altogether as she vanished into the black water.

"CASEY!" Jackie screamed, thrusting his hand under the water in an attempt to grab her.

But it was too late; she was gone.

"NOOOOOOO!!!!!" he screamed at the water at the top of his lungs. He then stood and turned toward the depths of the cave. "NOOOOOOO!!!!"

He flung himself to the flooded deck with a splash, beating his fist and the flashlight over and over against the watery boards, angry and terrified and sad and...

...alone.

•

He lay on his back, water nearly to his ears now. He didn't

move, he didn't utter a sound. Tears streamed from his eyes, but he cried silently, even tried to stifle his intermittent sobbing. He kept seeing her face, over and over again in his mind, as she gazed into his eyes just before going under—and he would begin weeping all over again.

Time went by. He had no idea how long it had been, there was no way of telling. The raft drifted, he quietly sobbed, and he no longer much cared if he made it out of the cave or not.

Then, suddenly, he realized that quite a bit of time had gone by in which he'd not seen or heard any sign of the beast…*at all.*

And, it was lighter now inside the cave.

Noticeably lighter.

He lifted his head and listened.

Nothing.

He slowly, quietly, rolled over, and looked ahead.

The exit was right there, not thirty feet away!

Then he looked around at the raft. It no longer seemed to be sinking! Apparently, devoid of so much weight now, it seemed to be maintaining!

He sat up, slowly and quietly, and turned to the front of the raft, looking at the cave exit: a nearly perfectly curved arc of thick, moss-laden stone, some twenty feet or so in diameter, sunlight streaming in at a sharp angle. Squinting into the blinding brightness, he could just make out the trees beyond, and the dark water that pooled around their gnarled trunks.

Blackwater Swamp.

So they'd guessed right.

And he was going to make it!

Carefully, he switched on his flashlight, and shined it all around the cave behind him.

No sign of the beast.

He quietly rose to his hands and knees, and crawled over to the bomb, which sat in the middle of the raft where he'd discarded it after Casey handed it to him.

Picking it up under one arm, he turned and tried to crawl back to the side of the raft, so he could use it against the beast if it showed back up—but it was so wet, misshapen and awkward that it slipped out and bounced on the deck of the raft with a series of loud clumps.

Still crawling, he chased it down on his hands and knees and snatched it up before it made any more noise.

But as he feared, a deep growl emanated from behind him, a distance away, echoing around inside the cave.

Hurrying now, he stood with the bomb in both hands, and sloshed across the flooded deck to the side, where he crouched back down, and listened.

Another growl, long and guttural, still from behind him, but closer now.

Looking ahead, he was now less that twenty feet from the cave entrance.

"Come on, come ON!" he hissed, trying to urge the raft to move a little quicker. Then he turned back to the rear, watching and listening. This time, he heard nothing. All was quiet. To his delight, he could now hear distant birdsong wafting in from the woods outside.

He looked down at the makeshift bomb in his hands. It was still entirely intact, even after being thrown quite a distance and landing hard in the water, then floating, then Casey taking it underwater to the other side of the raft.

Seeing the ringed nylon line dangling underneath, he grabbed it and wrapped it around his hand, gripping it firmly.

"Even if you get me," he whispered into the cave behind him, "I'm taking your evil ass with me. No way this leaves my hands without going off."

Jaw set in firm determination, he turned back toward the entrance. It was now just over ten feet away, and he was gently approaching it.

He was going to make it.

He heaved a sigh of relief.

But suddenly the water exploded from underneath the raft, lifting the side on which he was crouching slowly out of the water, accompanied by the longest, loudest, most terrifying roar he had ever heard.

As the raft tilted upward, the collected water rushed off toward the other side, along with the last of the packs and cut segments of rope, all of it washing into the water.

Jackie managed to hang on, dropping his flashlight and finding purchase in the split of a broken board with his free hand, holding the bomb tightly under his other arm and scrabbling with his feet until they, too found cracks or holes in the splintered and mangled deck boards to dig into.

The raft continued to rise, the deck now facing outward right in front of the cave entrance, Jackie feeling the sunlight on his back as he clung to the broken boards on the surface on one side of the craft, the beast lifting the whole thing out of the water on the other, it's massive tentacles beginning to work their way around the edges, trying to reach him.

It roared again, and this time Jackie smelled its breath—like rotting worms and dead fish, a nauseating stench of stagnation and death.

The raft now seemed to balance for a moment, the beast's tentacles working around the sides and in the process holding the craft upright. As Jackie watched in horror, the tentacles slowly slid around the frame of the raft—but when they moved into the bright sunlight that was shining onto the raft from the cave entrance, they began transforming! Right before his eyes, they turned from wet, slippery-looking meaty gray-green tentacles—their smooth, shiny texture reminding him of a wetsuit—to thick, furry, dark-brown appendages, with huge black claws extending from the ends!

He thought he was going crazy, so he blinked hard, shook his head, and looked again. But there they were. Big, brown, hairy, clawed…hands? Feet? Paws? He wasn't sure what he was seeing.

Deciding that his feet were now secure enough to hold him up, he let go of the crack in the deck and jerked his hand down, twisted open the valve on top of the propane tank, then shifted the bomb from under his arm to his hand, gripping it by the horizontal wooden shank, then yanked hard on the fishing line that was wrapped around his other hand.

The ignition cap pulled free—but nothing happened. The

igniter didn't spark, the flare didn't light.

Maybe because it was wet?

He didn't know.

So he thought he'd try again.

Hands shaking and working quickly as the raft was slowly rising in the grip of the monster, he shoved the ignition cap back into place, once again wedging it between the wax candle butt and the flare's igniter button, then yanked it back out, even faster and harder this time.

Still nothing.

Just then, he felt a light breeze on his back, as a gust of wind whistled through the cave opening and bathed the entire raft in a wisp of coolness, the trees outside rustling crisply in the wind.

And suddenly he felt himself begin to rise quickly away from the surface of the water. Looking back up, he saw two huge, leathery wings emerge from behind the raft, the creature roaring again as they began flapping, shedding water is they freed themselves from the lake.

It was starting to fly, and taking him and the raft with it.

Glancing to either side, he saw that the huge, brown, furry, clawed paws had changed again—this time to black, leathery, scaly taloned feet, like those of a huge bird *(or dragon?)*, the leathery scales reminding him of the skin of a huge snake.

Wondering what, exactly, was now lifting him and the raft from the water, he saw a thin split in the deck boards within reach of his eyes, and stretch his neck up to peer through, if only for an instant. But all he saw on the other side was one huge, yellow, reptilian-like eye glaring back at him through the tiny crack—the very same eye he had seen in the water behind Casey—but this time he couldn't see what type of face or head the eye was set in.

He pulled away from the crack, confused.

How is this possible? What kind of animal can change from a tentacled sea-creature to a huge, furry, clawed mammal, then to a massive reptilian, bat-like (or dragon-like) flying beast?

Knowing that there WAS no such creature (except maybe in fairy tales or movies...or maybe the bible), he let go of the question and looked back down at the bomb, which still hung dead in his hand.

And then he noticed the raft was starting to drift away from the cave entrance, the huge wings flapping backward, the scaly talons gripping the sides of the raft as the beast lifted it up and started back into the cave.

It roared again, except this time it was more of a high-pitched screech, which echoed back to them from the depths of the cave.

Was this the end?

He had to think of something...

Then he had an idea—but he had to work fast, as the now winged creature was about to air-lift him and his raft back into the cave, where he'd likely never again see the light of day—or anything else, for that matter...

Digging furiously in his jeans pocket, he yanked out the Zippo lighter he'd won from Nick during their blackjack game the other night. Flicking it open, he thumbed the igniter wheel...once, twice, three times, and it caught!

The creature screeched again, blasting his ears, and began flapping even harder, and looking up, Jackie saw that he and the raft were rapidly drifting away from the cave entrance and deeper into the cave.

Looking back to the bomb, he held the lit lighter under the igniter button protruding from the end of the flare, just hoping it could be lit with a flame...he figured if it could be lit with a mere spark, then surely an actual flame could light it too...but he didn't know for sure.

Pressing his head against the deck of the raft, curling his toes to hang on for dear life as the raft rose higher into the air, he watched as the igniter button first began to glow orange from the lighter's flame, then it sparked...once, twice, just tiny sparks flying from the button, but producing no results. Then there were more sparks, and more, until finally! The flare burst into flame, which immediately began melting the wax in front of it, protruding from the propane tank's spout.

He smiled as the melting candle wax began dripping onto the water below, instantly solidifying and floating away in white splatters.

But was it soon enough? Would he even get a chance to use the bomb, before the beast yanked him from the raft and tore him limb from limb, or even ate him alive?

As he wondered this, he felt the sun on his back dissipate, felt the air begin to cool as he was carried bit by bit away from the entrance.

And the wax candle was only burned halfway through.

He stared at it, urging it on, wondering if he would make it out of this cave alive. There was no way of knowing, he could only hope he was that lucky.

Then he thought: how had things even come to this? Who could've possibly known, back when he and his friends were planning this fun rafting adventure—their last big shebang, their grande finale, on the last weekend of the summer before school started back up, no less—that in a few short days his friends would all be dead, and he would be looking into the face of death himself, at the hands (tentacles? claws?) of some unheard-of beast, with the unimaginable ability to shape-shift on-demand from a huge tentacled sea creature, to a giant clawed land-roving beast, to a massive, flying reptile?

Closing his eyes, he thought back to when this had all started, just a few days ago; he thought of his friends, and then of Casey...

...and suddenly, he remembered that first night in the woods, and how they'd all spelled out their life philosophies, what it takes to succeed in life—and realized their beliefs had all played out right here, in this cave, as they had faced this unknown creature and tried, in their various ways, to defeat it and survive.

Ryan, the first to be taken, had tried religion, praying to God and citing verses from the bible...

Nick, the next to die, had tried brute force, using his size, strength, hunting knife and hatchet...

Chaz, using his scientific knowledge, had crafted a bomb to use against the beast...

And here he was, the sole survivor, and it was only by sheer luck—just as he believed dictated life in every aspect—that he was still alive, and still had a chance, as tiny as it was, to defeat this evil monster and get out of this cave alive...the simple realization that until a few days ago, he didn't even *have* the Zippo lighter...

Now that's some life-saving luck, he thought.

Opening his eyes, he saw that the candle wax was now three-quarter burned through. Another deafening screech made him look back up, and he saw that they were now sailing quickly away from the mouth of the cave, the dragon-like creature's huge, shiny, black-scaled talons firmly gripping the raft on both sides as it them back into the cave.

Luck...so that would be his ticket home.

As always.

He lifted the bomb to his shoulders, preparing to toss it over the top of the raft and right into the lap of the beast... when he thought of Casey, and realized:

No, he was wrong.

It wasn't just luck.

If not for Casey, and her professed love for him, he wouldn't even have this bomb. It would still be floating in the water way back in the cave somewhere, and he'd have no chance of escaping this cave, the beast, and certain death.

So maybe she was right, after all...maybe love *was* the key to success and happiness in life...or at least a combination of love, and luck...

With that, he lifted the bomb up over his head, and took

one last look up at the wax barrier between the flare's hissing flame and the propane tank. It was very thin; he didn't have much time.

Then, another realization:

It wasn't just luck...and it wasn't just love...

Ryan's religion gave him the strength to face the beast, at least in his own way; and same with Nick, he had the courage to face the beast, and try to protect the rest of them from it. And, if not for Chaz's scientific prowess, the bomb now in his hands, about to be thrown at the beast, wouldn't even exist.

No, it was no single factor, none of their individual beliefs that had proven successful—but a combination of all of them that had brought him this far, and given him a chance to defeat this evil and survive to see another day...a chance to turn certain death into a fighting chance to live.

As he watched the last of the wax melt and drip away, he had one final thought: their blackjack game, back in the barn, before they started this strange and tragic journey...

First Ryan had a twenty-one, and thought he'd won...then Nick had one too, and thought it was a tie...then Chaz had a blackjack, and so thought he'd won...but then Jackie himself turned over a suited...

"BLACKJACK!!" he yelled at the top of his lungs as he tossed the bomb over the top edge of the raft, and, as it descended on the other side, pin-balling down between the raft and the beast, he grabbed hold of the broken deck boards with both hands, gripping them with all his strength, and hugged the surface of the raft with all his might, his eyes scrunched tightly closed, the side of his face pressed hard against the damp wood...

The propane tank exploded in a giant fireball, accompanied by the beast's piercing screech, which was nearly as loud as the explosion itself.

The raft was blown clear out of the cave, with Jackie still clinging to it, and began fragmenting in mid-air as it sailed through the tree branches above Blackwater Swamp.

Though the wooden deck boards shielded him from the worst of the explosion, he was not entirely protected, the boards splintering, the raft blowing apart into pieces, flames bursting through.

The sheer impact of the explosion and the flames that momentarily engulfed him, along with the shattering raft and scraggly tree branches beating, cutting, and breaking him as he sailed through the air with the rest of the debris, all served to injure him badly.

The one saving grace was that after the raft broke up, he was thrown away from the largest pieces and landed on his back in the water, a little less than a foot deep, splashing first then hydroplaning backward until he swept up onto the exposed muddy roots of a large tree.

As he lay their in intense pain, shock began setting in. He knew he was badly burned, and badly injured, his body cut and bleeding, bones broken.

But he was alive.

And he was out of the cave.

And the beast was...dead?

He could only hope.

As he drifted toward unconsciousness, he turned his head and looked at a large segment of the raft that was lying in the water a few feet away, still burning, bobbing gently.

On the deck's surface, wedged between two splintered and dislocated boards, was a huge, shiny black claw, and from it, sticking up into the air, was what looked like a massive brown hairy toe, curled and severed at the knuckle.

If the beast even *has* knuckles…

He didn't know.

He then looked upward at the bright, sunny, clear blue sky, the only cloud being the huge black plume of smoke now rising above the cave entrance behind him.

He smiled, his silver tooth flashing in the sunlight.

He'd made it.

But would he actually survive?

He didn't know that, either.

With that, he closed his eyes, and lost consciousness.

— Interlude —

Sheriff Collins was sitting at his desk hurrying through some delinquent paperwork that he should've done yesterday, when he stopped, looking strangely around the office.

Was that a tremor? he wondered.

He waited, but felt nothing more, then shrugged and turned back to his paperwork.

It wasn't long before the phones started ringing, which he thought was odd...*people don't usually call about a tremor.*

Turns out, reports of an explosion out on the east end of town—somewhere up in Silver Hills, it seemed—were flooding in, mostly from residents in or near The Flats.

Odd, it felt like a tremor, he thought. *Could an explosion up in Silver Hills be felt all the way here?* He doubted it...

Stepping outside, he could just see the dark plume of smoke rising above the south side of Silver Hills, he guessed in the area of the creek or Blackwater Swamp.

"I'll take the boat from the marina," he told the others as he headed out. "That's the closest and quickest way to Blackwater."

Lights and siren on, the sheriff gunned it out of the headquarters parking lot and down the street, heading as fast as he could to the marina.

Part III:
The Hunt

The Town of Hope
Blackwater Swamp
& Silver Hills Mine
August 1985

"I have to go back."

Jenny was just walking back into Winnie's dorm room from the bathroom. Barefoot, she wore only his black and red plaid flannel shirt, which hung nearly to her knees, and her panties underneath. She'd just washed up and re-done her makeup, and was in the process of pulling her dark brunette hair back into a ponytail as she re-emerged.

"What?" she said as she approached him from behind. He was sitting in the middle of the couch—shirtless and barefoot, his jeans still unbuttoned—leaning forward, elbows on his knees, enrapt with whatever he was watching on the old console TV that sat against the opposite wall, rabbit ears on top all askew.

Glancing up at the television screen, she saw it was the morning news.

"Back where? What happened?"

"Back home. I've gotta go back home, to Hope. And I've gotta go back *now*. I'm gonna book the next available flight."

"What are you talking about?" she asked, dropping her eyes from the TV and frowning down at him from behind.

Pointing the remote at the TV, he clicked it off, then stood and turned to her.

"Look, I shouldn't be here, I should be at home—"

But she was already shaking her head in disagreement, and cut him off:

"Winnie, we've been through this, over and over. It was an accident. Lots of people die on the highway during snowstorms—especially people who drive for a *living*, like your dad did. Yes, it's risky, but it's part of their job, and they know the hazards. And there's nothing wrong with you using his life insurance money to pay for college, to get an education, to better your life. It's what he would've wanted you to do. And in the long run, it'll be better for your mom, too. You'll be better able to take care of her—"

Now it was his turn to cut her off: "No, it's not that," he said, waving his hand in dismissal as he walked around the couch and over to the walk-in closet next to the bed on the other side of the room. "I'm talking about Tommy."

She rolled her eyes.

Tommy again. Jesus, is he ever gonna let that go? After all, they were just kids…

He pulled a suitcase from the back of the closet, tossed it on a recliner that sat next to the closet door, bent, clicked the latches, and opened it.

"Are you *serious?*" she said in an incredulous tone.

He stood and turned to her, his shoulder-length hair still hanging over his face. He brushed his hand quickly through it, pushing it back.

"It's back." His look was dead-serious.

"*What's* back?" she asked, slightly shaking her head, confused. Then her eyes widened when she got it. "You mean that beast...creature...monster...whatever it is that everyone thinks is haunting the woods—and that swamp?"

"That's right. In Black Woods and Blackwater Swamp, out on the outskirts of town."

She tried to keep a poker face, but her patience was wearing thin. She still didn't know whether or not to believe the weird stories he had told her about the strange things that supposedly happened during his childhood, growing up in that small, backward town of Hope. To her it all just sounded like rumors...folklore...old wive's tales...superstitions...or just plain lunacy.

Or perhaps *mass delusion?*

But on the other hand, after he had told her the stories, she *wanted* to believe him, as hard as it was—so she had checked the news archives at the university library, and verified for herself that his best friend Tommy had, in fact, disappeared the summer of 1975, when they were twelve, and Winnie was, in fact, the last one to see him alive—or to see him period, since no trace of his friend was never found, and so it is unknown to this day whether the missing boy is alive or dead.

So at least *that* part seemed to be true...

…but a *monster?* Come on.

Without waiting for a response, Winnie turned and re-entered the closet, yanking clothes off of hangers and tossing them out the door and into a haphazard heap on the open suitcase in the chair just outside the door.

She took a long breath, closing her eyes, trying to stay calm. Then she opened them, and spoke softly:

"Okay…so let's say there *is* something to the rumors—"

"They're NOT RUMORS!" he hollered from the closet, as he continued pulling clothes off hangers, not bothering to look in her direction as he did so.

"Okay, so say this…*thing*…this…this…*monster*…actually exists. What makes you think it's back?"

Then she recalled the news program he had been watching, and took a guess: "Wait—did you see something on the news?"

Exiting the closet, he tossed an armful of clothes onto the now buried suitcase. Stopping and sifting through the heap, he pulled a black long-sleeve t-shirt out and quickly pulled it on over his head, his hair again falling over his face, which he again pushed back with his hands as he looked up at her.

"Yes," he confirmed. Then he walked to the dresser next to the bed, opened the top drawer, and fished out a pair of crew socks. Sitting on the bed, he lifted a foot and started pulling one on.

"What?" she asked, concern now building in her voice as she approached him, arms crossed in compassion. "What happened? What did you see?"

"A big news story from back home. From Hope. There was

an explosion, somewhere out in Blackwater Swamp, near the south end of Black Woods. And there's an injured kid in the hospital."

She pondered this for a moment, but didn't see the connection, and frowned.

"What's that got to do with…with…(she hated to say it, but decided she must)…the *monster?*"

"Because it's been ten years…I've been waiting for something like this to happen, and it just did…but *this* time not just *one* kid disappeared, but *three.*"

Finished socking his feet, he grabbed his sneakers off the floor and tossed them onto the bed, then headed into the bathroom, where he began noisily collecting various toiletries for the trip.

"I'm still confused. *What's* been ten years? How does this…this…*explosion* or whatever, have anything to do with the stories about the monster? Why do you think you have to go back? And even if you did, what could you even *do* about any of it, anyway? And especially with classes about to start…you need to be *here,* not *there,* and besides, there's nothing you can do about whatever has happened there anyway."

"That's where you're wrong," he said as he brushed past her, carrying an armload of toiletries, which he unloaded onto the couch next to the suitcase. Returning to the bed, he sat to put on his shoes.

"Apparently, the plume of smoke could be seen from town —calls flooded into the sheriff's office, reports about a small, black "mushroom cloud" coming from somewhere on the other side of Silver Hills—and so the sheriff went to investigate, and found the kid hobbling around in the swamp like a zombie, incoherent with multiple injuries and burns. He told reporters that while he was rushing him to the hospital the kid kept mumbling something about some kind of monster before he lost consciousness."

Her eyes widened. *Could the stories be true after all?*

"No shit?" was all she could muster.

"And," he added, "he also mumbled something about his friends too. And when the sheriff contacted his parents, they confirmed the names of his best friends—Charlie Miller, Ryan Harris, and Nick Gardner—so the department made some calls, and turns out they're all missing. Once they put all the pieces together, they figured out that the kids spent the weekend together, and were supposedly gonna go to the carnival, and that they were all supposed to be back home last night. But nobody's seen them all weekend, and nobody seems to have seen any of them at the carnival, either Friday or Saturday. Now three of them are missing, and one of them is in the hospital, miraculously found alive in Blackwater Swamp after nearly being killed by some kind of explosion, and muttering about seeing a monster somewhere in there before he lost consciousness."

Stooping, he slipped his shoes on, and began tying them.

"I still don't see how you think you can help anything by going home now."

Finished with his laces, he sat up and looked at her.

"It's my fault Tommy's missing."

"No, it's not—"

But he cut her off: "I should've stopped him from going back up the hill and near Black Woods with that big storm coming, just to look for his stupid slingshot. I didn't try hard enough. I need to go back and find him...if he's still alive. But even if not, I need to *know* what happened to him."

He stood, went to the couch, and began haphazardly folding clothes and slapping them into the suitcase.

Following him, she asked, "You said something about it being ten years. What did you mean by that?"

"When we were kids, old man Wilson—he used to drive the ice cream truck in our neighborhood—told us that over the course of his life, seemed it was happening every nine or ten years, like clockwork."

"*What* was happening?"

"Kids were disappearing."

"Really? You never told me that..."

"There's lots of things I haven't told you. It's hard to talk about, since, you know, everyone just thinks I'm a loon... including *you*."

"Well, if it helps any, I don't think you're a loon...*most* of the time, anyway," she finished with a smirk.

Ignoring her remark, he went on: "Anyway, it's been ten years since Tommy disappeared. And this time, *three* kids went missing, just like Tommy did. I can't live with that, without trying to do whatever I can about it, any more than I can live with Tommy disappearing, and I didn't do whatever I could to prevent it back then either."

"But what can you *possibly* do?" she asked sternly, getting irate, throwing her hands out to the side in futility.

He began shoving toiletries into various interior pockets of the suitcase, zipping and snapping them closed as he did.

"This time, it's different. One of the kids survived, and was found. And from what the sheriff reported, he's an eyewitness to the monster, and that it lives somewhere in Black Woods or Blackwater Swamp. And if that's so, that also makes him the *first* eyewitness…at least the first one to live to tell about it."

"Okay…so what do you plan to do?"

Winnie slapped the suitcase shut and snapped both the latches closed, then lifted it from the couch by the handle.

"I'm gonna go pay him a visit. Talk to him. Find out what he knows, what he saw. Maybe he even knows where that thing *lives*."

She sighed exasperatedly, shook her head in disagreement.

"Yeah…and *then* what?"

"Then maybe I'll be able to hunt it down—and maybe even find Tommy in the process, or at least figure out what happened to him, once and for all."

She pondered all this for a few moments, seeming to finally get it, nodding her head slightly in approval.

"Okay…I guess I understand."

With that she turned and walked over to the bed, and, keeping her back to him, peeled off his shirt, tossed it on the bed, then began snatching her own clothes up off the floor.

"Don't worry, I'll be back before classes start," he said.

Still turned, she clipped her bra on, then pulled her jeans

on one leg at a time, turning to him as she zipped them up.

"You promise?"

"Well, no...if there's a chance I can find Tommy, then that's what I'm gonna do, no matter how long it takes. That's the priority. I've been waiting ten years to do something about what happened, and now's my chance. But if nothing surfaces while I'm there, and it's all just a dead end, like before, then yes...I promise, I'll be back in time for classes. And you'll be the first to know, either way."

She nodded just before pulling her sweater on over her head, then shaking her ponytail loose in back. She stooped and picked up her shoes, then stood and looked him in the eyes.

"Okay. But promise me you'll keep in touch, you'll keep me posted, Winston Milhouse."

"Absolutely. I'll call whenever I get a chance. Now let's get you outta here before the dorm dad starts making his morning rounds, finds out you spent the night, and I end up spending the day in his office getting reprimanded."

"Or getting expelled," she said, grinning.

"Or getting expelled, he echoed, grinning back.

"But even so, ya gotta admit, it was worth it, no?" With that she ran her hands up and down, gesturing to herself, as if putting her entire body on display.

Smiling ear-to-ear, he again said, "Absolutely."

"Good answer," she said, smiling and nodding. "Now let's get you to the airport."

•

The taxi dropped Winnie off at Town Square in downtown

Hope, in front of *The Cobblestone Inn*, a small motel near Grande Festival Plaza, where he checked in.

On the flight down, he had decided to stay there instead of at home because he knew that if he stopped at home first, his mother would talk him out of doing what he needed to do—or try her best to talk him out of it, anyway—and he didn't want to chance that.

Once he secured a small room and tossed his suitcase on the bed, he locked the door and headed out, hoofing it to the south end of Town Square, where the new *Hope Springs Eternal* hospital stood, the modern eight-story slate gray steel-and-concrete monstrosity striped with nearly opaque dark tinted windows looking somewhat out of place in the otherwise quaint little town.

The automatic doors whooshed open as he approached the entrance, and stepping from the hot, humid outdoors into the cool, dry air conditioning of the lobby felt like he was traveling between two completely different worlds.

He strolled quickly through the waiting area to the front desk, then patiently waited for the woman to get off the phone, and when she quietly set the receiver in the cradle she looked up at him expectantly, but didn't say anything. Attractive black woman, probably mid- to late-thirties, a little heavy-set, but very pretty.

He glanced at her name badge: Olivia.

"Hi, Olivia...I'm here to see Jackson Higgins? Young boy, brought in yesterday?"

"Yes, Jackie was admitted yesterday. Some pretty serious

injuries, but nothing life-threatening. He's in stable condition, but while he's under sedation, we try to keep visitation minimal, preferably only family members."

"That's okay," Winnie said with a slight nod, also catching the boy's informal name. "I'm Jackie's...brother."

Olivia laughed out loud at this, causing a few people in the waiting area to look over for a moment, then turn back down to their magazines or up to the TV mounted on the wall, the sound muted.

"His *brother*, eh?" She chuckled again, shaking her head. Boy, you must really be anxious to see him!"

"I am," Winnie replied, unsure of what the big deal was.

She then eyeballed him suspiciously.

"Who are you *really?*"

He didn't know how she knew he was lying, but he decided to come clean. Mostly, anyway.

"Okay...my name is Winston Milhouse. I grew up here in town—in The Flats, down on the other side of the railroad tracks—but I've been out of state at college the last few years. My mom still lives here, has her whole life. I heard about what happened on the news, and came straight home to visit Jackie.

"Wait...Winston Milhouse? That name sounds vaguely familiar..."

"Yeah, probably because I was in all the local papers ten years ago, when my best friend Tommy Baker disappeared up near Black Woods. You probably remember me as Winnie."

"That's right!" The woman snapped, making the connection. "Winnie...I remember now...there was a big search for Tommy, but they never found him...and you were the last one to see him alive, right?"

Winnie just nodded silently, again saddened by the memory.

"That must've been really hard."

"It still is."

"Believe me, I know exactly how you feel."

Winnie just frowned at her, unsure of what she meant by that. Then, she seemed to quickly change the subject.

"So anyway, what do you want with Jackie?

"Well, I'm still hoping to find out what happened to Tommy all those years ago, and...well, Jackie might know something, since the same thing might have just happened to his friends, the three who are now missing."

"Four now. There was a young girl, not acquainted with those four boys. Possibly a runaway, but nobody knows, she hasn't been seen all weekend either, which y'ask me, is quite a coincidence."

"I agree. Which makes it even more important that I talk to Jackie, see if he knows something that will help me find the... well, you know. Whatever's doing this."

"I see," she said, then leaned forward and lowered her voice, eyes wide. "So do you think there's something to the rumors? The stories...that there's—"

—she glanced around, making sure nobody was listening, then back to him—

"—something out there? In Black Woods?"

"Well, I *believe* there is, but don't know for sure. That's what

I came back to find out."

"Well, I *believe* there's something out there, too," the woman said. Then she quickly looked around again, before continuing, lowering her voice even further: "Because the same thing happened to my cousin Trish, years before it happened to your friend Tommy…one day she just vanished."

"Really?" Winnie asked, taken aback.

"Yep. Almost thirty years ago. Nineteen fifty-seven, when me and Trish were just kids."

"What happened?"

"Well, like you, we both lived in The Flats. Her family lived up on the north side, off of Homestretch. We lived in the southern part, across from that big open field in the corner, by that old road that runs next to the woods along Sliver Hills."

"I know that field," Winnie concurred. "We used to play baseball there when we were kids."

"That's the one," she said, nodding in affirmation. "So one summer morning Trish came down to my house, and brought her new Frisbee—they'd just come out that year, and were the hottest thing going—"

—she gave him devilish grin—

"—well, except for Elvis maybe—"

—then back to a serious tone—

"—anyway, she'd got this new fluorescent pink Frisbee for her birthday and we took it across the street to the field to throw it. We were listening to Elvis on the radio, I remember because sometimes the station—I don't recall the name, but it was out of Denver—didn't come in very well, but luckily that day we got great reception, even at that distance, it was such a beautiful, clear day, not a cloud in the sky…in fact, there was a big, bright full moon the night before, I remember that like it was yesterday…

Liv, Trish, & Elvis
Summer 1957

"We can set the radio here," Liv said, pointing to a knee-high boulder ensconced in the edge of the field, just a little way off the road.

Trish agreed, and they positioned the Sony TR-63 radio on the rock facing the field, then turned it to KDC, the top-40 station out of Denver, Colorado (it was far away and they couldn't always get it, but on a clear day like today it came in fairly well…and the station played a lot of Elvis, and that's all they wanted to hear, so KDC was their best bet).

As luck would have it, as they positioned themselves a distance apart in the field and began tossing the Frisbee back and forth, the station played a "two-for-Tuesday" of Elvis, starting with *Too Much* and closing with *Teddy Bear*.

"I hope they play *All Shook Up*, soon…that would be perfect!" Trish said as she tossed the fluorescent pink disc to Liv. Just as Liv went to catch it, a breeze picked it up slightly, almost making her miss. But fortunately, using what her dad called her "cat-like reflexes", she adjusted at the last second and still caught it.

"I know!" Liv agreed. "I wish they played nothing *but* Elvis… that would be even…perfecter!"

They both giggled at the word as Liv returned the Frisbee to Trish, but it banked to the right and even running and reaching, she missed it this time.

"Sorry, my bad," Liv admitted.

This went on for the balance of the morning, until finally, to the girls' delight, the radio kicked up with *All Shook Up*, and they ran over to the boulder to listen to their favorite song and take a rest from all the running and throwing.

But as soon as the lyrics began, they threw themselves in, dancing and singing along:

a well I bless my soul
what's wrong with me?
I'm itchin' like a man on a fuzzy tree
my friends say I'm actin' wild as a bug
I'm in love
I'm all shook up
mm-mm…mm…yeah, yeah…yeah
well my hands are shaky
and my knees are weak
I can't seem to stand on my own two feet
who do you thank when you have such luck?
I'm in love
I'm all shook up

But just then, Liv's mother stepped out on the porch across the street and called to them.

"Trisha, your mom just called, she wants you to come home for lunch!"

"Okay Mom, soon as this song is over!" Liv called back.

The two girls commenced singing and dancing around the

radio until the song ended and a commercial came on for some new powdered drink mix called *Tang*, at which time Liv picked up the radio and switched it off, and they headed back across the street to Liv's house.

When they reached the porch, Trish said, ""Maybe I can come back tomorrow, and we can do it again!"

"I hope so, that was fun!"

"I'll ask my mom, and call you if I can come over."

"Okay."

With that, Liv opened the screen door to go inside, while Trish turned toward the road to walk home, shiny new Frisbee in hand.

Then Liv stopped in the doorway and, holding the screen door open, turned and half-sang, half-shouted to Trish: "I'm all shook up, wooh!"

Smiling, Trish turned back for a moment and giggled, then pretended to throw the frisbee at her cousin, who ducked behind the screen door for cover, but Trish held on to it and turned to walk home, hollering, "Made ya duck!" behind her.

Smiling, Liv watched as her cousin and best friend began skipping down the road, singing something (probably Elvis), but she couldn't hear what it was. As her voice faded into the distance, Liv's gaze traveled upward to a large tree standing on the far side of the road, and marveled at what she saw: an entire flock of small birds—sparrows?—sitting among the branches, just sitting there, not moving, not making a sound.

Weird, she thought.

"Liv, lunch is ready!" came her mother's voice from back in

the kitchen, and she immediately forgot the birds and stepped back inside, letting the screen door *squeak!* and *bang!* behind her as she skipped back toward the kitchen.

"Except Trish never made it home that day," Olivia said, eyes welling up. "She was never seen again...she just... *vanished*. No body, no nothing. Just like your friend Tommy, years later. Search parties came up empty. Not a clue. They did eventually find her Frisbee though, lying in the tall weeds between that road and the woods. But no sign of my poor cousin Trish."

Winnie let out a low whistle. "That's terrible," he muttered, empathetic. "But why would she walk home alone on that old road along the woods on the outskirts of The Flats, instead of taking a safer route through the neighborhood?"

"Oh sure, she could get home from my house walking the streets through the neighborhood, but that was the long way— a lot of zig-zagging and criss-crossing, if she stayed on the sidewalks—but it was a lot faster if she just took that old side road straight up north to Homestretch, then a quick jaunt west over to her house. Heck, we'd both walked it so many times, it never even occurred to us that it could be dangerous. But I was a little older, and should've known better. Especially shouldn't've let her walk it alone. Sometimes I feel like what happened to her is *my* fault, instead of that...that...whatever it is that's out there..."

"Believe me, I know exactly how you feel," Winnie said, and they locked eyes in complete understanding.

Finally she broke eye contact, looking down at her desk and sighing heavily, as if mulling something over in her head. Then she looked back up at him.

"Look, I'm not supposed to do this, but since I understand what you've been through, and if you think talking to Jackie will help you find that...that—

—she shook her head, unable to come up with a word—

—and finally get rid of it, end it, kill it, whatever you need to do to stop the evil that's been plaguing this town all these years, then I'm willing to help you, even if I get in trouble—heck, even if it costs me my job—because if you succeed, I'll be forever in your debt...as will the entire town."

"That's my plan," Winnie said confidently.

"Then I'll give you fifteen minutes with Jackie, but not a minute more. He's probably still under anyway, with all the meds, so what's the harm? But I'm about to go on break, and I'm gonna come up and check on you, so you better behave yourself. And I mean it—I'm kicking you out in fifteen minutes. His parents just left to go get a bite to eat, and I don't wanna risk them showing back up while you're there, who knows how they'd take it, some stranger in the room with Jackie...especially with them being under so much stress already."

Then she paused, having a thought. She reached over and snatched up the directory from beside her on the desk, flipped a couple pages back, ran her finger down one column, stopped on a line, and muttered "Ellie Johnson, that's right."

Then up to him: "If anyone comes in while you're there, tell them you must have the wrong room, you were looking for Ellie Johnson."

"Ellie Johnson?" Winnie asked, somewhat perplexed.

"Yes. She was in that room for a week or so before Jackie, but she was discharged Saturday night. Jackie came in on Sunday, and after the ER we moved him there. It'll look like an honest mistake."

"Ellie Johnson...got it," Winnie repeated carefully, as they grinned mischievously at each other. "And thank you, I appreciate it," he said sincerely.

She relayed the proper floor and room number to him, and he thanked her again and headed eagerly across the lobby to the elevator.

•

It didn't take long for Winnie to realize how Olivia had known he wasn't Jackie's brother, why in fact she had laughed out loud when he had lied that he was. All he had to do was enter the room and see Jackie in his bed, and he shook his head and sighed, suddenly embarrassed, thankful there was nobody in the room to see him blush.

Standing quietly at the side of his bed, Winnie wondered what to do next. He scanned across the various machines and monitors that surrounded the kid, a few of them softly beeping and blinking, with myriad tubes and wires running back and forth to the boy.

He appeared to have multiple burns or other injuries, just like Winnie had seen reported on the news, with various bandages all over, and a cast on his left arm. Off to the side, on a small rolling table next to the bed, sat a discarded food tray. On it, a plastic plate holding a cold, uneaten breakfast of scrambled eggs and toast that looked like maybe it had been picked at, but that was it. White plastic spoon and fork, a small carton of milk, and a limp, browning banana peel sitting atop a thin stack of paper napkins.

He turned back to the boy.

"Hello? Jackie? Do you hear me?" he uttered, not much louder than a whisper.

Nothing.

Machines beeping and whirring.

Jackie breathing softly.

Winnie sighed again. He really wanted to talk to the boy, but how could he, if he was unconscious?

He looked at his watch. Four minutes had already passed, just with the time he'd spent in the elevator then roaming the hallways looking for the right room.

"Only eleven more minutes," he whispered, looking forlornly down at the sleeping child.

Just then, the boy stirred a little—his sheets rasping with the movement of his legs as he stretched in his sleep—and Winnie watched excitedly, thinking he might be waking up.

But then, he again went silent and still.

"Come on, wake up," he urged in a whisper.

Nothing.

After a few more silent moments, he heard the door open behind him. He turned to see Olivia entering, a styrofoam cup of coffee in her hand.

"Told you he's sedated…been out all day," she said quietly, looking past him at the boy.

"Yeah, I was hoping to talk to him. So far, no such luck."

She looked at her watch.

"You've got ten minutes. I'm gonna step out and use the restroom. But when I get back, you gotta leave."

"Yes ma'am."

She turned and padded quietly out, the door closing softly behind her.

Looking back down at the boy, futility set in. He wasn't going to be able to talk to the kid, find out what he knew, what had happened and where, and this whole trip would be for nothing. Besides, did he *really* think he would actually find Tommy? Or even find out what happened to him? After all these years?

He waited in silence for a few more long minutes, but still no stir from the boy.

Sighing heavily, and somewhat angry now, he turned abruptly to leave—and his hand struck a corner of the meal tray that protruded beyond the rolling table top, knocking it and the dishes to the floor with a clattering ruckus .

"Shit!" he muttered, stooping to snatch it all up off the floor, nervously glancing up at the door as he did so. Nobody came to see what the ruckus was, thankfully. Crouching beside the bed, he returned the items piece by piece up to the rolling table, then used the napkins to scoop up what he could of the scrambled eggs from the white linoleum floor.

When he finished and stood, he nearly jumped when he

saw that the boy's eyes were wide open and he was looking right at him.

"Jackie?" he said.

"Who are you?" The boy slurred, frowning slightly.

Winnie glanced down at his watch. Four minutes, give or take. He needed to talk fast.

"Jackie, my name is Winnie. I used to live here in town. I heard about what happened to you and your friends, and the same thing happened to me and a friend of mine a long time ago, so I came to town to see if I could help. If you can tell me what happened, I'm gonna go try to find the monster that did this to you, and hopefully get rid of it once and for all. And I hope to find your friends, too."

"They're dead," he mumbled matter-of-factly.

Hearing this, Winnie's heart sank.

"Are you sure? Maybe—"

"I seen the monster kill 'em, down in the cave."

"Cave? There's a cave?" Winnie said, incredulous.

"Yeah, and underground tunnels, too," Jackie added.

Another glance at his watch: three minutes…

"I'm really sorry about your friends, Jackie. But if you can tell me what happened, and where, I'll do my best to find that monster and kill it. Your friends deserve that, don't they? *You* deserve it."

"Okay."

Winnie's heart jumped at the word.

In a slow, slurred voice, Jackie began rattling off his story in bits in pieces, starting with the raft. Winnie listened, asking a few quick questions here and there for clarification, especially about the cave, which he'd never heard of before. For the most part, he was able to follow the boy's general story of what had happened. And he was pretty sure he knew where the kids had been, because he remembered boating on the creek with Tommy when they were kids, and that old shack in the woods that they had explored. And he knew where the rapids were, where Hope Creek headed down Silver Hills and into Blackwater Swamp, and that's where the boy said part of the creek branched off into the woods and apparently created an unknown waterfall into a hidden cave somewhere deep within Silver Hills.

But then, as the boy began to describe the monster in the cave that had killed his friends, some sort of slimy sea-creature with giant tentacles and yellow eyes—

"—at first anyway, but then it changed," he slurred—

—but then he began drifting in and out of consciousness.

"C'mon, stay with me, Jackie," Winnie urged softly. "The monster changed? Changed how? I need to know exactly what it looks like, how big it is, how it acts, what it did to them, anything you can tell me so I'll know what I'm up against."

With one final effort, Jackie was able to relay bits and pieces about how he could see the distant cave opening in the swamp and was trying to maneuver the raft toward it, trying to escape, but the monster caught up with him—

"—and…and—"

—but then came another pause, during which he closed his eyes—but this time, they remained closed.

"And what?" Winnie urged. "Jackie? C'mon Jackie," he was nudging him gently. "I need to know where the mouth of that cave is, so I can find it! At least get me close! And what about the tunnels? And how did the monster change? And the explosion—what was *that? What the hell happened??*"

But his prodding was to no avail. The boy's eyes remained closed as he slipped back into sleep—or unconsciousness? Either way, his head fell to one side, mouth agape. The kid was out cold.

So that was it. Winnie would get no more info out of him.

Sighing heavily, he whispered a *thank you* to the boy, then turned to leave—and was halfway to the door when Olivia returned, opening the door before him, and so they left together, Winnie thanking her gratefully as they strolled to the elevator.

Down in the lobby, as they exited the elevator into the lobby and started parting ways—Olivia walking toward the reception desk, Winnie toward the front doors—she stopped and spoke up:

"Mr. Milhouse?"

He stopped and turned back to her.

"You go and find that thing, whatever it is, and you make sure you kill it, once and for all...for Jackie...for your friend Tommy...for my cousin Trish...for *all* of us."

"That's the plan," he said, smiling resolutely.

Smiling back, she winked and bid him good luck, then turned and continued toward the desk.

Out on the sidewalk in front of the hospital, he glanced

around, got his bearings, then headed east.

Next stop: Hank's Hobbies & Sporting Gear...

•

He couldn't believe that old bell still tinkled above the door when he pushed into Hank's. It made him smile, brought back fond memories of his youth.

The two men standing behind the counter—one older with gray hair and goatee on the left side near the phone, the other around the corner to the right, tan, buff, and clean-cut, with a short dark crew cut, thinning a little on top—looked up and gawked at him.

"Well I'll be damned if it ain't Winnie Milhouse!" Hank exclaimed from the left, while the man to the right continued to stare, but then broke into a smile of recognition upon hearing his name.

Winnie turned and approached Hank, reaching across the counter to shake his hand.

"Hank, all these years, and you haven't changed a bit!"

Hank slapped his protruding gut with both hands. "Still a little too much beer over the years—but ya know what they say: it all turns to dick after midnight!"

The three of them laughed. Then Hank motioned toward the other man.

"I believe you've met my boy, Joey?"

"Winnie," he said mildly, nodding. "Been a long time."

"No shit...*you're Joey?* I'da never recognized you!"

Winnie walked over to shake his hand over the counter.

"Joey got onto a health kick a few years ago...quit smoking, no drinking or drugs, healthy food and works out like a madman," Hank explained, obviously proud.

His grip was like iron, his arm rippling with muscle and impressive vascularity as he extended it over the counter to accept Winnie's hand.

"Wow, lookin' good!" Winnie complimented. "Big change from what I remember, back when you were in high school… definitely for the better!"

"Not just me," Joey countered. "I even got the ol' man to stop smoking too!" He jerked his head in Hank's direction. "Still working on the diet and exercise part, though." With that, he flashed a quick wink at Hank, smiling.

"That'll be the day!" Hank proclaimed. "I'm not into rabbit food—and hell if I'm givin' up the beer! And I get plenty of exercise, with you on my back all day!"

They all laughed.

"Boy got tall, didn't he Joey?" Hank said, both of them looking at Winnie, who was now a couple inches taller than both of them.

"I was gonna say," Joey responded. "And lost the glasses, too. Hate to say it, but the kid grew up kinda handsome."

"Contacts," Winnie said. "And I'm not so sure about the handsome part." With that, he pushed his hair back with one hand, a habit he didn't even notice anymore.

"Well, at least you've still got all your hair," Joey admired. "Looks like I got dad's bald gene."

While he rubbed his hand over his dark, thinning crew cut, Winnie looked over at Hank and for the first time noticed he was totally bald on top now, his scalp a dark tan like the rest of him. However, the gray sides were still pulled back into a ponytail, just like Winnie remembered from ten years ago.

"Sorry, kid—I gave you my good looks, brains, and charming personality, but unfortunately the hair loss comes with it...package deal!"

Another round of chuckling.

"So, what brings you into this ol' hole-in-the-wall?" Hank asked Winnie, once their chuckling died down.

•

Winnie relayed the sketchy story that he'd been able to get from Jackie, including some kind of creature with yellow eyes, to which Hank nodded and said, "I heard about the explosion, and that the sheriff found that kid badly injured in the swamp, and took him to the hospital. But I never heard what happened, seems nobody knows anything yet—and they sure as hell didn't say anything about a monster!"

Winnie then explained that he planned to go hunt that beast down and kill it, and had come to Hank's to purchase a gun—rifle, shotgun, something, wasn't sure, was hoping Hank could guide him on that—but Hank had a better idea.

"I'll go with you. No need to buy one, I've got plenty of guns at home...if that kid is right, and that thing is some kind of sea creature, living in that underground lake— "

"—or swamp creature!" Joey cut in, prompting Hank to turn and glare at him—

"—there's no such thing as swamp creatures dumbass, you've been watching too many stupid B-flicks", then he turned back to Winnie—

"—then a couple of rifles should suffice…and, I have all the supplies we'll need, and a boat. Two actually, we "adopted" that old rowboat you and Tommy told Joey about so many years ago, that you kept stashed under that pier."

"No shit, I forgot all about that thing"

Hank went on: "Sounds like that cave opening he told you about is probably in the back part of Blackwater Swamp somewhere, on the south side of Silver Hills. We can take Hope Creek and go in from the south, and hopefully find the cave that way, instead of risking that hidden waterfall they fell through up top, I don't know how we'd manage something like that anyway. Joey can stay here and watch the shop—"

"Aw dad, why should I have to stay here?" Joey protested. "I wanna go huntin' with you guys. It sounds so exciting! Besides, we won't be busy here, we're always dead the first half of the week!"

Hank turned sternly to Joey. "You owe me big time for bailin' your ass out and covering your shifts for a whole week last month when you hurt yourself showin' off at the gym. Time to pay up."

"Oh, alright…whatever."

Hank turned back to Winnie.

"Besides, I don't want you goin' out there by yourself. It's too dangerous, and I'm guessing you don't have much experience handling a gun, either. It's a lot different than that Wrist Wrockets you boys used to hunt with. You go out there and find that thing, come face-to-face with it, and don't know how to handle your weapon, how do you plan to fight it? Harsh language?"

Winnie agreed; in fact, he thought going out there with Hank was a great idea.

"You stayin' at your mom's house?" Hank asked. I can pick you up—"

But Winnie waved him off.

"No way. She doesn't even know I'm in town yet. If I went there first, I know she'd try to stop me—beg, plead, cry—and she'd probably succeed. So I think it's better I do this first, I'm scared enough as it is, don't need to risk being talked out of it."

"Wise man," Hank said, nodding in understanding.

"I'll swing by to see her after we—well, *if* we find that thing, whatever it is...and hopefully kill it."

"So where you stayin'? Or did you just get into town?"

"I'm staying around the corner at the Cobblestone Inn. Didn't bring much though, a few changes of clothes is all. Hoping to be back on campus by the weekend. Classes start next week, I need to start getting ready. And I promised Jenny I'd be back in time."

"Ooooh, Jeh-niiieee!" Joey cooed, grinning ear-to-ear. "Little Winnie's all growed up and got hisself a hot college girl now!"

"Joey, nice to see you're still an asshole," Winnie said with a smile. "I guess some things never change!"

"Yeah, he still has his moments," Hank added, without looking at his son.

"Ouch!" Joey said, chuckling. He then turned and grabbed a white cloth towel and spray bottle from a shelf behind him, then began spraying the glass countertop and wiping it down, pretending to mind his own business.

Winnie turned back to Hank, who continued:

"Well, I got all the gear we'll need at my place, and we can take my truck. Go pack what you think you'll need for a couple days. Let me finish up a few things here, and then I'll pick you up and we'll head to my place from there. Load up with supplies, hook up the boat, then head down to the creek south of town."

He glanced down at his watch, then out the glass doors at the sky, gauging the time and nodding.

"We should reach Blackwater before nightfall. We'll set up camp across the creek, then go look for that cave in the morning, first light."

"Sounds good," Winnie agreed, nodding excitedly.

•

The weather was predicted to be clear and calm overnight, so they decided they probably wouldn't need a tent. Just a couple of sleeping bags and backpacks, some camping supplies, food and drinks, and of course a variety of guns. Without a tent, it was all much more manageable. Walking back and forth, Hank produced all the supplies from inside a storage shed in his back yard, with each trip handing the stuff to Winnie, who then staged it around Hank's truck in preparation for loading.

Once it was all loaded into the truck, Hank jerked his head toward the back of the house and simply said "C'mon," with his patented smirk. Smiling with curiosity Winnie followed

Hank as he walked briskly to the house, trotted up the wood steps and through the back door—the spring-loaded screen door swinging and slamming shut behind them with a *squeak* and *bang!*—then through the linoleum-floored kitchen, around the corner through the carpeted living room then down a short hallway, and into a back room, which appeared to Winnie to be a study of some sort: hardwood floor, desk, bookshelves.

Winnie watched as Hank traversed the room to a tall steel safe in the back corner next to a storage closet, and began turning the dial on the front.

One he had the gun safe open, he waved Winnie over, and handed him a rifle.

"Remington 700," he said. "I think you can handle this, with a little practice."

Winnie carefully accepted the gun, looking it admirably up and down before nervously slinging it over his shoulder. Then his eyes widened as he watched Hank produce a big firearm that looked to him like some sort of machine gun: All black, with a raised site above the pistol grip and a long magazine extending several inches from under the barrel.

Winnie let out a low whistle. "What's that, a machine gun?" he said in awe, his voice almost cracking.

"M16," Hank announced.

"I've never seen a gun like that—other than in the movies, anyway," Winnie said. "Where would you even *buy* something like that?"

"Military issue," Hank said matter-of-factly. "And it beats the hell outta the M14, its predecessor. Lighter, faster firing rate, and a 30-round magazine, as opposed to just 20 with the M14. Lots of guys said they had problems with it jamming, but I found that with a little tender love and kindness—like I do with all my outdoor equipment, especially for hunting or fishing—it works just fine. You just gotta take proper care of it. In fact, I took such good care of her, unlike most the other guys in my platoon, I carved my initials into the stock, so nobody would get any funny ideas, or keep them from getting mixed up somehow."

With that he held the stock out to Winnie, and looking down he saw the HS meticulously carved into the heavy composite resin, in such fine craftsmanship it almost looked like it was stamped in there during the manufacturing process. Then he looked back up at Hank.

"So you *were* in the military...me and Tommy always thought so, because of your tattoo," Winnie said, pointing to the spread-winged eagle on his forearm, nestled among the many other tattoos.

"Army," Hank said. "Infantry. Or more specifically, EOD specialist."

"EOD?" Winnie asked.

"Explosive Ordnance Disposal."

"So you're an explosives expert?"

"That's what they tell me," Hank said with a wink.

"Wow...did you see any action?" Winnie asked.

Hank donned a strained look on his face, a slight grimace.

"I suppose...does Vietnam count?."

Winnie let out a low whistle.

"Wow…I never knew you were in Vietnam," he said almost apologetically.

"Not many people do," Hank said. "I don't talk much about it. Try to avoid it, mostly…it was a dark time in my life…I'd rather forget about it."

Winnie caught the implication, his eyes widening again.

"Did you kill anyone?"

Hank just nodded, looking down at the floor.

"Unfortunately, yes," he said quietly. "Viet Cong. But I don't know how many…couldn't see much in the jungle… especially *at night*."

Then he looked back up.

"But at least one, that I know of. Probably a few. Maybe a *lot*. And unfortunately, *they* killed a lot of *us*, too. Most of my platoon, actually."

"I'm sorry, Hank. I didn't know you went through that. It's difficult to even imagine. What was it like?—"

—but he immediately caught himself, and quickly raised a halting hand—

"—no, never mind, sorry, I know you don't want to talk about it, so forget I asked."

With that Hank looked down at the big rifle cradled in his arms for a moment, apparently considering something, then back up.

"No, it's okay. See, I have a mantra, when it comes to hunting: always know who you're hunting with. Lots of bad things can happen out there, between the testosterone, the guns, the poor visibility, the camo gear, and especially the booze. And if you don't know enough about the guy you're hunting with—what type of man he is, his temperament, his attitude, how he handles his firearms—and his alcohol, for that matter—his shooting accuracy, how he tracks, how and where he tends to hide when he spots...it can get dangerous... for *both* of you.

"Makes sense," Winnie said, nodding.

"And I know plenty about you...hell, I've known you since you were a kid. Watched you grow up over the years. And I doubt there's much more to know, seeing as you've never been hunting or even handled a rifle before, right?

"That's right."

"But *you* know next to nothing about *me*. And with what we're about to do, you deserve to know as much about me as possible, for your own safety if nothing else. Or even to back out, once you hear my story, it might scare you away. But either way, you've earned it, simply by being willing to go back out there—maybe even risk your life—to not only avenge Tommy, but to rid the entire town of this evil that's been plaguing us all for decades. That makes you a hero in my book. And so you should know as much about me as possible, before you take that kind of risk. So I think you should hear my story, that I've kept to myself all these years. And besides, I've been thinking about that lately, that it might do me good to talk about it, get it all out in the open, and off my chest. Like a confession. So fact is, we'll both benefit."

"Hank, you don't have to tell me anything you don't want to," Winnie reiterated, shaking his head. "No worries."

"I could use a cup of coffee before we leave," Hank said. "You drink coffee?"

"Of course," Winnie said, smiling. "I'd never get through some of those boring classes without it."

With that they headed back to the kitchen, Hank poured two cups, then looked up at Winnie.

"Cream or sugar?"

"Black."

"My kinda guy!"

He handed one over, and they sat down across from each other at Hank's old wooden dining table.

Then Hank looked down at the table and went completely silent, apparently thinking it all through. After nearly a minute of dead silence—just the clock on the wall ticking, to Winnie seeming louder and louder as he waited—Hank finally looked back up, and let go a long sigh.

"Okay, here goes," he started.

"I was part of the 4th Infantry Division," he began. We shipped in on the east coast, the II Corps region, put in at Quy Nhon. Then my company was helicoptered inland to the Central Highlands, near Dak To, where we were ordered to proceed on foot to carry out a "search and destroy" mission. We split up by platoons, and my platoon was to head north. The monsoon season was coming on, and brass didn't want us getting caught up in the heavy rain out in the jungle, so all four platoons were to meet up again in ten days at hill 875—"

"—wait, hill 875?" Winnie asked, perplexed.

"Intelligence had identified all of the hills in the country, and numbered them on the maps according to their height in meters. So, hill 875 was simply 875 meters high, that's all."

"I see," Winnie said as he nodded in understanding, then Hank continued.

"—so we were to meet up with the other platoons in 10 days at hill 875, at which time we would be helicoptered back to base at Quy Nhon for a quick rest before receiving new orders...

Private Henry Stevens
U.S. Army, 4th Infantry Division
Central Highlands, Vietnam
Summer 1966

It was hot and humid, and they were fighting all sorts of flying insects, especially mosquitos.

The platoon had started out with 40 men, under the command of Lieutenant Pearce, but had already lost nearly half their number, not only to the regular ambushes by the Viet Cong—who would attack out of nowhere then vanish back into the jungle like ghosts—but also from landmines, *caltrops* and *pungi*, and even bites from poisonous snakes, as had happened with Cox, their radio operator. During an enemy attack, he had crouched into some thick brush to try to call in air support—which was typically impossible, or at best ineffective, due to the double- and triple-layered canopy of the jungle, the aircraft simply couldn't see their location or that of the enemy from the air—and in mid-sentence was bitten by a red-tailed bamboo pit viper, which he never saw, as the leaf-green snake was well camouflaged in the foliage. Shortly thereafter he starting having difficulty breathing, then progressed into convulsive shock and died. Fischer, the medic, was powerless to do anything; bullet wounds, burns and other injuries, even illnesses, sure—he even had chloroquine for malaria—but he had nothing at hand for treating venomous snake bites.

Seeking a replacement among the ranks, a soldier—Private Henry Stevens—was said to have some radio experience from his high school electronics class, so he was handed the equipment and was now the new RTO—

"—Never mind that the radio I built in high school never worked," Hank said, smiling across at Winnie. "I always sucked at electronics, just wasn't my bag. But *they* didn't know that—and at that point probably didn't much care either, so I was selected." He shrugged. "I didn't mind. I mean yeah, I was the EOD too, but there really wasn't much for me to do in the jungle, as far as that goes. At least being RTO gave me something to do, other than get shot at, like a sitting duck—"

—so now the platoon was down to around 20 men or so, many of whom were sick or injured, not to mention hungry, with their rations running out, as well as exhausted, having to constantly battle their way through elephant grass, thick vines —many heavy with thorns—and dense bamboo stands, some towering as high as 15 or 20 feet.

But at least they were approaching the end of their mission, with hill 875 dimly visible ahead on the horizon, and they were all anxious to reach it by morning and get out of this God-forsaken hell-hole.

But then, unexpectedly, the jungle broke and they were looking at an expansive rice paddy, with a small village just visible in the distance on the other side, the huts set in a close cluster between the paddy and the jungle behind them.

Staying just inside the tree line, they crouched in the brush as the lieutenant had Sergeant Turner lay out the map on the ground at the base of a tree.

"You sure it's not on there?" Pearce asked after some quick consultation.

"Nope," he confirmed. Then he tapped the map. "Here's hill 875—"

—he pointed off into the distance at the faded hill, then back to the map—

"—and we crossed this river yesterday—"

—he ran his finger along a squiggly blue line—

"—so that puts us right about here, give or take—"

—again, he tapped the map, a location between the hill marked 875 and the blue squiggly line—

"—and as you can see, it's all jungle, there's no indication of a rice field, a farm, a village…nothing."

"So it looks like Intel didn't know this was here," Pearce speculated.

"Apparently not."

"But do you suppose the Viet Cong know about it?"

"Probably."

Part III: The Hunt

They decided to keep under cover of the jungle and go around. Too dangerous exposing themselves crossing a paddy this size in broad daylight, plus there's always the possibility of booby traps and landmines.

Going around, they stopped just inside the tree line when they reached the clearing, maybe 100 feet from the huts.

Nearly an hour of observation—even with binoculars—didn't reveal much. A few elderly women, most of them wearing their conical *nón lás*, and that was it. Most likely South Vietnamese, but it was nearly impossible to spot NVA soldiers or VC guerrillas if they were dressed in civvies and mingling among the locals. On the other hand, there were no men or young women to be seen, and the old women seemed to be congregating at one particular hut, with smoke or steam trailing out around it...and it smelled like home cooking. And an old water buffalo stood out front, lashed to a wooden cart, docily nibbling at the wild grass which sprouted here and there from the dirt.

"Looks safe," Turner suggested, shrugging.

"Well, we have a mission to carry out," Pearce said. "We'll have to go in, see if we find any VC or NVA, and if so, we take 'em out."

Pearce turned to the men.

"Stevens, you're with me. And the rest of you—"

—he waved his hand over the soldiers to his right—

"—at the ready, and follow me, we'll go to the main hut, see if we can get any intel from those women."

At the command, the soldiers brought up their weapons

and moved together behind the Lieutenant.

Then Pearce turned back to Turner.

"Turner, you take the rest of the men around—"

—he waved his hand over and around to the left, between the paddy and the village—

"—start on the east end of the village, and do a clearing sweep to the west, toward us at that main hut. Hopefully by then we'll have an idea what the situation is, and can determine our next course of action."

"Yessir," Turner responded. Then he motioned to the group of soldiers to his left, and they brought their weapons up and moved in behind him.

"And keep it *quiet*," Pearce reminded as Turner and his men moved out. Then he turned to his men.

"Everyone keep your eyes peeled," he warned. "I know It looks harmless, but you never know what we'll run into."

They all nodded in understanding, then quietly followed the Lieutenant out of the tree line and cautiously across the clearing, everyone looking everywhere as they approached the main hut.

As they neared, one of the women inside came to the doorway, stopped in her tracks with wide eyes when she saw them, then turned and darted back inside, shouting alarmed Vietnamese to the others.

Then three women reappeared in the door just as Henry and the lieutenant reached it, flanked by the rest of the soldiers. Pearce directed the men to keep a lookout as he spoke to the women, and they all turned and created a semi-circle sentry around the door.

"—Needless to say, we didn't get much "intel" from them," Hank explained to Winnie, shaking his head and taking a sip of coffee. "They didn't speak any English, and mostly didn't speak to us at all. The woman who seemed to be in charge, the few times she DID speak, just kept barking at us in Vietnamese, we couldn't understand a word of it, and the others remained silent, not a peep—"

Finally, frustrated, Pearce motioned curiously to the big pot sitting behind the women on a makeshift stove made of clay bricks with a rusty steel grate on top, the fire underneath boiling it, filling the hut with steam.

"Smells wonderful," Henry muttered as the woman led them inside and back to the pot, lifted the lid using a thick cloth as a hot pad, then stepped back as the lieutenant peered in.

"Rice," he said matter-of-factly. Then he turned to Henry. "A huge pot full of rice."

Pearce nodded in thanks to the woman and stepped back as she picked up a bamboo rod and gently stirred the rice a few times, then replaced the lid.

"You know," Henry started. "We're all pretty hungry, and rations are low…and that's an awful lot of rice…"

"My thoughts exactly," Pearce said. "But for a different reason. Let's step outside."

Just as they stepped outside, Turner and his men were approaching from the east, and Pearce waved his men toward them, and they all met in the alley between the huts.

"Anything?" Pearce asked.

"No sir. All clear. Everything's empty, we didn't see anyone else at all. Seems those little old ladies in there are the only ones here."

"So, no men—young or old—and no children either."

"No sir."

Then the lieutenant turned to Henry.

"That great big pot of rice in there, that you were just about drooling over?"

Henry nodded.

"Well, don't you think that's an awful lot of rice for just a few old women? I doubt any of em's over a hundred pounds. And seventy if they're a day."

"It does seem odd," Henry agreed.

Pearce turned back to Turner. "And why do you suppose there are no men here? Young or old?"

Turner shrugged. "Out fighting the war?"

"Probably. But no way of knowing for who. The RVN...the PAVN...the VC...could be any of 'em."

Turner just nodded in understanding.

"And this neck of the woods, my money's on the VC," Pearce continued. "Those bastards are rounding up all the able-bodied villagers they can find and forcing them into military service."

"I've heard about that," Turner agreed. "*Re-education*, I think they call it."

"Well, I say it's more like *brainwashing*," Pearce corrected before continuing: "My next question is, why do you suppose there's no children around? Call it a farm, call it a village, you'd think there'd be kids running around. At least a few."

Henry and Turner just nodded in agreement, and Pearce continued:

"So I think all that rice is for more than just those old ladies. There must be kids here…somewhere."

"Hiding?" Turner suggested. They'd all heard that the Vietnamese sometimes hid their children in underground bunkers if the fighting reached their village.

"Exactly. And why do you suppose they'd be hiding the kids right now?"

Turner's eyes widened in sudden understanding. "Probably because they know—"

—but he was cut off when the entire jungle behind the huts suddenly erupted into gunfire. It was like the tree line itself exploded: rifles, machine guns, mortars, rocket launchers… and the ruckus deafening.

Pearce was one of the first ones hit, multiple bullets striking him all over—head, neck, chest—and he dropped to the ground without another word.

The soldiers all began yelling and ducking and taking cover wherever they could as a hail of bullets ripped through everything and random explosions rocked the area, sporadically returning fire in the general direction of the assault, but they could see nothing beyond the jungle tree line. It was pure chaos, and they were dropping like flies, grossly out-numbered and caught off-guard.

As soon as the mayhem started, the water buffalo began screeching and kicking in sheer terror, quickly breaking itself loose from the old wooden cart and splashing out across the rice paddy, bawling as it ran until it was out of earshot.

Taking advantage, Henry dove under the now vacated cart and rolled to the other side, then sat behind it with his back to the large wood-spoked wheel as he began wrestling the radio out of his pack in a desperate attempt to call in air support.

But before he could even begin to operate the thing, something exploded on the other side of the cart—a grenade, a mortar shell, a rocket, undetermined—blowing him and the cart up into the air and across the dirt clearing, landing several yards away and tumbling on the hardened ground, the cart shattering into pieces and Henry unconscious before he even hit the ground.

"—I woke up in the back of a truck," he said, giving Winnie a serious look. "Some kind of small box truck, almost like a paddy wagon. Completely dark inside, with just one small window in the back door. Must've been middle of the night, when I looked out it was almost completely dark, I could barely see anything, with apparently just enough moonlight— I'm guessing, since I couldn't see the sky through that tiny window—that I could just see dense lines of trees, probably the jungle, crowding both sides of the road. The ride was slow and rocking, the truck rattling and squeaking, like we were on a dirt road full of bumps and potholes, that's about all I could tell...and seeing that it was nighttime, I guessed I'd probably been out for hours—so hard tellin' where we were at that point, we could've been anywhere. And they'd taken everything from me—my radio and weapon obviously, my ID, tags, everything from my pockets, all of it. Even my socks and boots. I was barefoot, with just my pants and shirt, which were pretty torn up from my..."flight" and "hard landing" I suppose you could call it—"

—he made air quotes to accentuate the terms—

"—and, I was racked with pain...but I sat and carefully examined myself by feel from head to toe, and didn't detect any major injuries, just lots of bumps, bruises, cuts and scrapes, some light bleeding. Everything hurt, like I'd had the shit kicked outta me...but nothing seemed broken or life-threatening."

"Wow, I had no idea you were a P.O.W. in Vietnam," Winnie said sympathetically. "I've never even *heard* anything like that about you."

"Like I said, I don't talk about it," Hank assured. "It's not something I even want to *remember*, much less *ruminate* about —which is probably what I'd do if I started talking about it."

Winnie just nodded in understanding, and Hank continued:

"Eventually we stopped, and a few armed VC yanked the back door open, grabbed me, pulled me out, and started pushing and shoving me around the truck and toward a couple of huts sitting in a clearing off the road, a fire out front with a few more armed men sitting around it..."

They stopped a short distance from the fire, the two groups of men exchanging words that Henry couldn't understand, then they continued shoving him beyond the front of the truck and toward the tree line, angrily barking Vietnamese at him.

It got darker the farther they traveled from the fire, and Henry began fearing for his life, thinking they were taking him into the jungle to execute him.

But after about thirty yards, they stopped just in front of the tree line, and he could just see in the moonlight a bamboo grate on the ground before them, next to a chest-high mound of rocks and dirt. As they approached, a man materialized from the darkness, sitting against a tree between the grate and the jungle, an old bolt-action rifle cradled in his lap. Henry hadn't even seen him there as they approached in the darkness, and was surprised when he stood, dropped his rifle to his side, then greeted the others. As they spoke, one of the guards took the man's rifle and handed him what appeared to be an automatic—though Henry couldn't see the make or model in the darkness—prompting the man to smile and speak rapidly —which he guessed was some kind of profuse thank you.

After taking a moment to admire the weapon up and down, smiling ear-to-ear, finally he slung it then turned and walked to the closest corner of the grate. Bending, he lifted it—and turns out it was a door covering a big square pit dug in the ground, the resultant rocks and dirt piled into the mound next to the hole, which the guard had to skirt in order to reach and operate the gate.

About the time Henry figured out what he was seeing, he

was shoved hard from behind, sending him off-balance to the pit, then half-jumping, half-falling into it. Fortunately he landed on his feet, stumbling and striking the far dirt wall pretty hard, but was not injured by the 8-foot drop (at least no more than he already was from the ambush and subsequent explosion back in the village). Plus, as he staggered toward the wall, he felt hands grabbing him from behind, slowing his stumble.

The guard who opened the grate above dropped it shut with a hollow *bang!*, then paused for a moment, looking down at them. Hawking roughly, he leaned and spit through the grate, causing the men to dodge the spinning gob, after which the man above smiled, amused—and showing a few missing teeth—then vanished from their view as he presumably resumed his post at the tree.

In the darkness of the pit, Henry could just make out two other men, who had grabbed him as he landed, softening his fall. He started to speak, but one of them immediately put his finger to his lips, silently shaking his head, the other holding his hands up in warning. Then the first man dropped his hand and leaned in to Henry's ear, whispering, barely audible:

"They won't let us talk to each other…if they hear us, we get punished…the daily interrogations are bad enough, we don't need even more beatings on top of that."

Then the man stepped back, an inquiring look on his bruised and filthy face, and Henry nodded in understanding.

Standing tightly together, they whispered their names to each other and shook hands. Paul and Gary were both army, but from different companies that Henry was not familiar with, so they were nobody he knew...but fellow soldiers.

And none of them knew where they were being held, they had all been transported blindly for considerable time before arriving here. But the others told Henry that they suspected they were near a river, if you listened closely you could hear the drone of running water off in the distance, possibly even a waterfall. They went silent for a moment while Henry listened, and yes, he could just hear the unmistakable hiss of rushing water—or, like they suggested, maybe a distant waterfall—that sounded like it was coming from somewhere deep in the jungle or beyond.

Sitting down in a tight circle, they used a combination of lip-reading, hand signals, and light whispering to clue Henry in to how it worked, what to expect.

They were interrogated daily, and with each passing day the beatings had progressed. They'd both been in the hole for several days now—and both admitted they'd lost track of exactly how many, though Paul said he had been there a couple days before Gary arrived—and even in the darkness, Henry could see they were in pretty bad shape. Worse for the wear, as they say. And they were essentially being starved to boot, saying they were given a bowl of some kind of rice gruel and a cup of water per day, the water dirty and sometimes even greenish, and the gruel often included bugs, usually still alive and feisty.

There was an old wooden bucket in one corner, swarming with flies, with a pile of broad leaves and palm fronds lying next to it. Every couple days, the guards would force one of them to carry it up out of the pit and dump it beyond the tree line. There was no way to clean it out or even rinse it, so it got worse over time, but at least it got emptied, and they didn't have to squat on the floor of the pit or sleep in their own piss.

And it frightened Henry considerably when they informed him that he would probably be first in line for interrogation tomorrow morning, being "new blood". Then they advised him to try to get some sleep, even though sunrise was just a few hours away, because this would probably be his last chance, since after interrogation they were usually in too much pain to sleep much. And with monsoon season fast approaching, once the rain started, that would be a whole-nother problem.

If they survived until then, that is…

Needless to say, Henry didn't sleep that night.

At daybreak, the others awoke, and as the morning sun rose, Henry was better able to see just how bad they looked: not just filthy dirty, but bruises and swelling and dried blood, on their faces, head and neck, even on their arms, legs, and feet. Cringing, he thought they both looked like they had somehow survived a terrible car wreck.

Once there was enough sunlight shining in the pit, Henry began scouring the walls, walking around and around, looking for a way out, or perhaps just trying to better determine their situation. But the walls were solid, dirt and rock, with no roots, no crevices, no rocks jutting out, no fingerholds whatsoever.

Sighing heavily, he turned and leaned into one corner, as the other two soldiers glanced at each other, then shook their heads at him, silently conveying the futility of his effort.

Been there, done that.

There was no way out—other than up through the grate, as Paul indicated by pointing upward, then shook his head and mouthed the word *guard*.

And suddenly, as if on cue, the grate above was yanked open, and a crude bamboo ladder was dropped into the pit. As an armed soldier climbed down, others above pointed their guns down at them for cover.

And his new comrades were right: the guard pointed his weapon at Henry, then motioned up the ladder. Henry glanced over at the other two, and they just gave him helpless looks.

Without a word, he began climbing the ladder, the guard climbing up close behind, one hand on the ladder and one hand keeping his rifle pointed at the back of Henry's head.

Once he was out of the pit, the ladder was hauled back up, the grate was again dropped with a *bang!*, and Henry and the guards all vanished from view.

"They had one guy—seemed to be an officer of some sort, but it's hard to tell with the Viet Cong, they didn't typically dress in military uniforms, they looked more like a hardcore street gang—who could speak some broken English. Not much, but enough that I could tell what they wanted: Intel. Locations, numbers of troops, military hardware, anything that would help them fight the Americans. But all they got from me—from any of us, according to what the others told me—was name, rank, serial." He shrugged, took a sip of coffee, swallowed. "Besides, I didn't know anything anyway.

They don't tell us grunts anything, for exactly this reason. In case somebody breaks. So I gave them nothing, and in return they gave me some really good beatings. Suffice it to say, I know what the butt-end of a rifle looks like…up close."

"Jesus, Hank," Winnie sighed over his coffee. "It must've been horrific. I can't even imagine."

"It was a fucking nightmare," Hank confirmed. "To this day, I can't believe I survived, that I'm able to sit here today and describe it to you."

"So how *did* you survive?" Winnie asked.

"Well, I'm getting to that part," he said with a grin…

Henry's first interrogation round was lighter than he had expected, just some moderate abuse, which only slightly exacerbated the pain of his previous injuries. Just a couple of hours: he didn't talk, they beat him, he still didn't talk, they beat him some more, until the officer got frustrated and ordered him taken back to the pit.

Like the others had warned, with each passing day the beatings became longer and more severe, until finally Paul was brought back unconscious and covered in blood. The next day, the same with Gary. And Henry knew he was next.

"Fortunately, I lost consciousness early on," he said, taking another sip of his coffee. "A blow to the back of the head that I never saw coming. I woke up in the pit that night, dizzy and racked with pain. The others propped me up and poured their own daily rations of water down my throat, and I slowly came to. And man, did everything hurt."

Winnie just sat staring at him, rapt, unable to even drink his coffee at that point.

"But after that, things got worse."

"Worse?!" Winnie barked, eyes wide. "How the hell could it get any worse!?"

"The next morning, they took Paul again. He'd been getting the worst of it, having been there the longest. Except...they never brought him back..."

Henry and Gary just stared at each other across the pit with terrified eyes when they heard Paul screaming off in the distance. That was the first time any of them had screamed— at least loud enough to be heard in the pit—and it went on and on, intermittently, with short periods of silence between, until finally, they heard what they had always feared they eventually hear: a single gunshot.

And Paul was never returned to the pit.

They knew damn well what had happened.

The next morning, as usual, the ladder was dropped down, one guard above holding the grate open while another guard descended into the pit. Using his rifle, he motioned for Gary to go up the ladder.

Gary and Henry exchanged horrified glances, both knowing what was probably going to happen: the same thing that happened to Paul.

And with just that slight delay, the guard began barking Vietnamese and jabbing Gary in the back with his rifle.

Limping, Gary approached the ladder, then began slowly ascending, the guard climbing up behind—but when he got about halfway up, Henry couldn't take it anymore, and began yelling: "Take me! Don't take him, take me!" and started pulling Gary and the guard back down the ladder, offering himself up instead.

"I'll go! Take me! Let him rest, he's injured!"

The guard on the ladder began yelling at him over his shoulder and batting him away with one arm, Gary was hollering for him to stop, it's okay, it doesn't matter anymore, it's over, and the guard above was yelling at him, too. The scene was chaotic, with everybody yelling at the same time, but nobody listening.

But Henry kept at it, until finally the guard above kicked a big rock over the lip of the pit with his foot, and it came careening down at him, a cloud of dirt and pebbles following. About the size of a flattened bowling ball—and just as heavy— it came close to landing right on his head—probably would have cracked his skull, maybe even killed him—but at the last second he ducked, and it slammed into his shoulder instead, knocking him to the ground. It then tumbled to the corner of the pit and struck the wooden bucket just hard enough to knock it over, the raw sewage spilling out, sparking an angry buzzing protest from a cloud of swarming flies.

As the guard up top continued to yell down at him, the other guard hurried Gary up the ladder, and once again the gate was dropped shut with a *bang!,* and they all vanished from view as Henry writhed on the ground grimacing and clutching his shoulder and neck in pain.

He laid there for a long time, futility setting in. And then, about the time he started needing to pee, he heard Gary start screaming in the distance, along with muffled, barely audible shouting in Vietnamese. He clamped his hands over his ears, and began sobbing.

But eventually, he couldn't put it off any longer, he needed to urinate, so he dragged himself up and over to the bucket, uprighting it, again sending the flies into a tizzy.

When he'd finished, he stared down at the rock, now lying flat on the ground, and decided maybe it would make a good seat...a hard one, yes—but at least he wouldn't have to sit in the half-dirt, half-mud floor of the pit. So he lifted the rock and carried it across the pit to the other wall, dropped it flat on the ground, and collapsed onto it with a sigh. Yes...it may be a little hard on his butt, but it was definitely the better option. He was looking forward to the seat of his pants drying out for the first time in days.

As the summer heat set in, he dozed, stirring now and then when Gary's intermittent screaming from above penetrated his subconscious...until the inevitable distant gunshot awoke him with a start.

For the rest of the afternoon, he watched above for any sign of them returning with Gary, but as he feared, dusk was now setting, and they never did.

And he knew he was next.

I gotta get outta here, he thought in desperation. *Before tomorrow morning...somehow.*

He jumped up and, once again walking in circles, scoured the walls for...*something...anything...some way out...I HAVE to find a way...my life depends on it...*

After several laps around the pit, feeling the walls, poking, scraping, trying to come up with an idea, he returned to the rock and collapsed on it, sulking.

He knew he was going to die, just like the others. Probably tomorrow. And if not tomorrow, then soon after...nobody could survive these conditions, this treatment, for long.

In fact, he began to think that dying tomorrow—quick and painless, a shot to the head—was actually the best option, all things considered.

Then he suddenly sat bolt upright, remembering something that hadn't occurred to him earlier.

The rock.

He shimmied off the rock and onto the ground, then picked it up to inspect it, turning it over this way and that in his hands. It was about the size of a frisbee, except about 3" thick and very heavy. But, flipping it up to view the back edge, his memory was correct: at some point the rock had split— whether from natural pressure or elements over the eons underground, or during the hole-digging process, he had no way of knowing—and one end was broken off, so the whole rock tapered down to a sharp edge.

Like a huge stone axe head...

And as he realized what he was looking at, thunder rumbled off in the distance.

A storm was approaching.

And, grinning in the growing darkness, he had an idea…

…the rock was his ticket out of there.

"I waited until nightfall," he explained. "Then decided to perform a test: I began hollering for the guard, louder and louder, until he showed up looking down at me, gun at the ready, and I pointed to the shit bucket in the corner and said it needed to be emptied. Obviously annoyed, he slung his weapon, unbuttoned his fly, and started pissing down through the grate, intentionally trying to hit me, making me dance all around dodging the stream, then laughed and walked away as he buttoned back up. But the joke was on him—I just needed to verify that they actually posted a guard at night, we had no way of knowing for sure, they only took us out and brought us back during the day. I needed to to be sure what I would be up against, and so now I knew."

Winnie just sighed and rubbed his eyes, as if he was getting exhausted just listening to Hank's story. Then he returned his attention to Hank across the table, taking a gulp of coffee.

"Recalling what I'd see up top when they'd taken me back and forth, I knew the guard usually posted up by that big tree to the right, probably for the shade, and that the big mound of dirt and rocks that came from digging the hole was to the left, the jungle's tree line beyond both. So I figured I should exit the pit from the side closest to the mound, so I could go around behind it and approach the guard from his right flank, maybe even a little behind his peripheral."

"Wait," Winnie said, shaking his head. "You were deep in

the jungle somewhere, with no idea where, and it was the middle of the night. How did you even know where to go? How to get out of there?" Winnie held his hands out in a gesture of incredulity.

"Remember the waterfall I told you about? We could hear it, just barely, off in the distance. So that meant there was a river over there somewhere. And if there was a river, then there were three possibilities: it either went straight south, or to the southwest, or to the southeast. So I figured once I was out, I would work my way through the jungle toward that waterfall, then follow the river...if it went straight south, it would take me back into South Vietnam, where chances were pretty good I would run into some friendlies. If it went southwest, it would probably take me across the border into Thailand. And if it went to the southeast, it should run to the east coast, where the U.S. Navy was patrolling in order to cut off supplies from the north—Operation Market Time, I think it was called—so if I survived long enough without getting caught then I'd probably end up in one of those three scenarios, and might actually be rescued."

"Wow...that's a lot of ifs," Winnie said, shaking his head.

"Yes it was...but what was gonna happen the next day probably wasn't an *if*, more like a *when*. So I decided the *ifs* sounded better..."

Henry couldn't believe his luck as the storm neared, the intermittent thunder growing louder. The timing was fairly consistent too: a flash of lightening, a second of silence, then the boom of thunder.

And even the strengthening wind was welcome, as the blowing trees helped mask any subtle noises he might be making as he worked.

With each flash of lightning, Henry timed the thunder, and with each boom, he chopped the sharp edge of the rock into the wall, starting about two feet from the floor. Swing by swing —boom by boom—he axed an elongated hole into the hardened dirt wall.

Then another one, two feet above that, and the final one two more feet above that, which was just above his head.

Stepping back, he admired his makeshift ladder. Nodding in approval, he set the rock down quietly, then trained his ears overhead, straining to hear any sounds from the guard above.

Nothing.

Taking a deep breath and letting it out quietly, he reached up and gripped the top hole with both hands, and stepped up into the bottom hole with one foot, lifting himself from the floor of the pit. There he again waited for a moment, again listening, and again heard nothing…a soft roll of thunder, a gust of wind in the trees above.

In no time he was at the top, easing up the bamboo grate, peering out with his eyes just above the ground. He was right, the guard was sitting against that tree, rifle lying across his lap. Turning a little further to the right, he saw, maybe a hundred feet away, the other men were sitting around the campfire, and the building behind them where the interrogations took place was mostly dark, just a dim yellow light emanating from one side window. But the fire was casting just enough light to dimly illuminate the guard resting up against the tree, at least well enough that Henry could assess the situation. He looked from the other men, talking and laughing and tipping bottles, back to the man just 20 feet from him.

Then he noticed the man was not moving. At all.

Is he asleep? Henry wondered. He was leaning against the tree with his head lowered, a wide-brimmed hat hiding his eyes, so it was impossible to tell. Scanning the scene, he saw that the guard had one hand resting on the gun in his lap, but the other held a glass bottle, gripping it by the long neck— looked like a booze bottle—and even from that distance he could see that it was nearly empty.

"I thought it was probably *ruou de* (he pronounced it "roo-uh-day), a liquor they distilled from rice. Sorta like what we would call moonshine here," Hank explained.

"So he was drunk," Winnie surmised.

"Maybe," Hank said cautiously. "But I had no way of being sure. I was just gonna have to stick to the plan, and hope I didn't alert the others..."

As quietly as he could, Henry dragged himself over the edge of the pit, hugging the ground, the lowered the gate gently with his foot. Then he belly-crawled around behind the rock pile until he was fairly sure he was out of view, then waited there for a moment, holding his breath and listening.

There was a distant flash of lightening, and when the

thunder stopped rolling, he could still hear the men around the fire chattering in the distance, but he heard nothing from the guard just on the other side of the mound.

As the wind picked up, he slowly leaned to his left and peered around the mound, only to see the man still lying propped against the tree, head down, bottle in hand. He hadn't moved a bit.

Glancing around, he selected a softball-sized rock, heavy and jagged, then slowly stood, but staying crouched as low as he could. He looked once more at the others, but they were still unaware of anything unusual. Slowly, he made a wide girth from the rock pile to the guard's right flank, approaching him in what he hoped was just behind his peripheral.

When he was within just a few feet, slightly behind the man, a flash of lightening made him stop in his tracks: the momentary brilliant white light cast by lightening revealed the initials HS carved into the stock of the gun now lying across the guard's lap.

A burst of anger coursed throughout him.

"Let's just say I relieved him of my weapon," he said, with a little smirk. "Then I leaned his body back against the tree, and covered what was left of his skull with his hat. But then another bright flash of lightening lit up the entire area—I felt like I was in a spotlight—and I dove back behind the mound, and just laid there on the rocks, looking up at the sky and waiting for the inevitable: alarmed and angry shouts in Vietnamese, a dozen boots running in my direction, maybe intermittent gunfire."

"Did they see you?" Winnie asked, terrified.

"Apparently not," Hank said. "If they were all drinking that...*moonshine*...too, then they probably had no sense of what was happening a hundred feet away or so...especially since they had a guard posted."

"So what'd you do then?" Winnie asked, relieved.

"Well, you won't believe this, but laying their waiting, eyes to the dark sky... I fell asleep."

"What??"

"I guess I was just exhausted. Starving, dehydrated, beat to within an inch of my life, the emotional stress of my comrades being murdered and knowing I was next, digging my way outta that hole, taking out the guard, all of it. After all that, I was laying there on the rocks in the dark, looking at the sky, praying to God that the others hadn't noticed me, and must have just fallen asleep...or maybe more accurately, passed out...but not for very long I don't think, just a few minutes, maybe ten at the most..."

He awoke to darkness, with no idea how long he was out.

He was racked all over with pain, especially where that big rock had landed on his shoulder and knocked him down.

He sensed nothing—other than a gentle rumbling, which he seemed to feel more than hear—but then it was gone.

Laying alone among the rocks, he felt utterly exhausted, not sure he could move, much less stand up.

Everything hurt.

He felt like he was dying.

But he knew if he was going to make it out of there alive, he had to get up.

The thought seemed impossible.

But then he barely heard it: a distant splashing sound.

The waterfall.

He could see nothing in the darkness, but he could hear that waterfall.

Just walk toward the waterfall…

He struggled to sit up, grunting so loudly that he almost screamed, intense pain shooting all over his body.

He sat still for a moment, panting and waiting for the pain to subside, or at least become bearable.

Finally, wincing and gritting his teeth, he forced himself slowly to his feet…

…and staggered toward the wonderful sound of that distant waterfall…

"I got pretty worried when it started raining shortly after I headed into the jungle," Hank said, a disconcerted look on his face. "Once the rain started, I figured the others would pack up and head inside, and when the pit guard didn't move, they'd get suspicious and check it out and discover he was dead and I was gone. So they wouldn't be far behind."

"Well obviously they didn't catch you," Winnie said with a relieved smile.

"Nope. I traveled as fast as I could—at least for the condition I was in, and remember I was barefoot too, working my way through a thick, untamed jungle—but the river was closer than I'd anticipated, so again, I got pretty lucky. And even more luck: the waterfall we were hearing—which was really more like rapids, tumbling down maybe a twenty-foot rock incline—was to the north of where I stumbled out of the jungle, but I needed to go south, so didn't have to traverse the falls…and, downstream just a bit there was a footbridge where I crossed over and continued south, putting the thirty or forty feet of swift river between me and any pursuers, if they were after me. And even more luck: the storm continued moving away behind me to the north, and before long I was out from under it, which made travel a lot easier. But I never heard or saw anyone behind me. Maybe they all passed out from the booze. Or maybe they didn't care enough about me to chase me down in the storm…especially if they were gonna execute me the next day anyway. Save them the effort, the bullet, the body to dispose. Or maybe they figured I'd die anyway, out there in the jungle, since I was nearly dead already—"

—he shrugged—

"— I don't know. "

Winnie let out a low whistle. "So how long were you out there?"

"A few days. Just like in the pit, after a while I started losing track. Soon my feet were shredded, but all I could think about was to keep moving. At some point I ripped off my sleeves and wrapped my feet best I could, that helped a little. And I only moved at night, keeping to the river banks, under cover of the tree line, couldn't risk being seen in daylight.

Drank river water—and man, did that give me the shits, but it kept me alive—"

—he winked and grinned—

"—and ate what I could catch: small rodents, frogs, a fish now and then, a little vegetation if it didn't look, smell, or taste like it might be poisonous. All hand-caught, I didn't dare fire my gun, draw attention to myself from who knows where. And my calculation was correct: the river flowed southeast, and I eventually made it to the east coast, where I was picked up by the good ol' United States Navy."

With that, he drained the last of his coffee, and plunked the empty mug down on the table in finale.

"Well, hallelujah!" Winnie exclaimed.

"So short story long, to answer your question, *that's* how I survived. And I learned shortly thereafter that nobody else in my platoon did. Just me."

Hank then donned a sad look, gazing down at the mug in front of him. Then back up at Winnie.

"Which is another reason I don't like to talk about it. It doesn't seem fair, for me alone to make it out, while nobody else did. I mean, a lot of those guys were way better soldiers than I was."

"Well, I for one am glad you made it," Winnie said, trying to be encouraging. "And I'm sure your family, friends, and pretty much everyone else in town is, too."

With that, Winnie finished his coffee, set the mug on the table, and smiled at Hank.

"Well, I appreciate that," Hank responded. Then, smiling

devilishly, and with that twinkle back in his eye: "So now that you know my story, do you still wanna do this? Or did I scare you off?"

"No way!" Winnie almost shouted. "I'm definitely still in!"

"Okay, but fair warning: I didn't give up then, and I ain't gonna give up now. I plan to find that thing, whatever and wherever it is, and put an end to it, once and for all...if it's the last damn thing that I do!"

"Absolutely!" Winnie agreed, nodding. "And I'm honored to be your wingman on that mission!"

"Okay...but we better get a move on," Hank said. "It ain't gettin' any earlier."

With that, they stood from the table and slung their rifles.

Winnie followed Hank across the kitchen to the back door, where Hank stopped and swung the heavy wooden door away from the back wall, revealing a coat rack with a shelf above. Hanging next to a couple of coats was a leather holster containing a pistol, which Hank lifted from the hook. He then reached up to the shelf and lifted off a sawed-off shotgun. When he turned back to Winnie, he noticed the young man gawking, eyes wide.

So first, he held up the shotgun.

"For close encounters—"

—he pumped the shotgun with a metalic *chuh-chuh!* —

"And for backup—"

—lowering the shotgun, he held up the holster, revealing a sizable pistol—

"Nine millimeter...should stop just about anything at close

range, if all else fails."

Winnie simply nodded in silent agreement.

Then Hank turned, swung the outer screen door open, and headed outside and down the steps.

Winnie followed, closing both doors behind them.

They spent some time out on the back forty, Hank showing Winnie how to load and fire a Remington 700 bolt-action rifle, which Winnie picked up fairly quickly.

Soon they returned to the truck and gear, and set about systematically loading it all, Hank directing Winnie what to put where, having done this many times over the years.

Once everything was loaded, they hooked up the boat—a small outboard fishing rig nestled onto an old rusty trailer.

Then they hopped in, and headed south.

"Once we get south of town," Hank nearly had to shout over the loud, smoky engine of the old Ford, "we'll put the boat in the creek—there's a perfect spot under the railroad tracks, I use it all the time when I fish down there—then cruise back upstream toward Blackwater. Once we're close, we'll stop for the night, then head into the swamp in the morning, see if we can find that cave."

Suddenly, Winnie was glad he hadn't tried to head down there by himself. What was he thinking?

Now having a better idea of exactly what he was in for, he was damn glad to have Hank around.

I probably wouldn't last two days out there by myself...

•

After cutting through town, the railroad tracks continued

south for a few miles before swooping to the east, where it eventually crossed the southern branch of Hope Creek southeast of town.

Hank headed west across town, then took County Road 200 south until they crossed the railroad tracks down near Edgewood, then continued south, the road slicing through heavy woods. A few miles further south, he turned left on an old farm road that— though marked by a faded street sign on a crooked rusty post as CR 800 S—barely seemed an actual road; in some places the old asphalt had deteriorated so badly it was not much more than a couple of tire tracks worn into either side of a dirt and rock trail, infested with weeds and wild grass—and, of course, countless chuckholes, all still full of muddy water from the downpour over the weekend.

On this poor excuse for a road, they bumped and rocked for several miles, the old boat trailer behind them rattling loudly in protest. The racket was so bad that Winnie wondered if the trailer would stay in one piece long enough for them to get there—wherever *there* was…

As they traveled along for several miles, he lost himself in the passing lush green crop fields, occasionally interspersed with unkempt wild fields that spread to the south nearly as far as the eye could see, and couldn't help but remember all the times he and Tommy went hunting with their wrist-wrockets in that field up on the other side of Old Rope, near Black Woods; and then the truck would pass through a wooded area, reminding Winnie of the countless times he and Tommy rode their bikes together on those old country roads, or explored the woods, or took that beat-up rowboat down the creek, the woods crowding in on both sides; and then, every once in a while, they drove past a small farmhouse that reminded him of the Baker's farmhouse, where he'd visited Tommy many times—at least until his dad's drinking started getting out of hand, when both the boys avoided spending any time there if possible.

It just didn't seem normal now, traveling through all this scenic countryside without Tommy at his side.

And though in his mind he had ample doubt, deep down in his heart he hoped that his best friend was still alive, and that Winnie was finally going to find him and bring him home.

Somehow...

Winnie was jerked from his reverie when Hank swerved left into a nearly hidden offshoot that headed downhill, the truck and trailer bouncing down a narrow dirt path flanked by heavy foliage that beat the sides of the truck mercilessly.

Finally, about halfway down the incline, Winnie could see Hope Creek ahead, it's sun-struck water glistening here and there through the thick tree branches.

As they approached the bank of the creek, an old rusty trestle suddenly loomed above the trees on the left, almost out of nowhere. Winnie guessed that the railroad tracks must turn east, running parallel to the old county road before crossing Hope Creek here, where it turns back to the south from its southeast heading upon leaving Hope.

"The road doesn't go across," Hank said, as if reading Winnie's mind. "It dead-ends at the creek, then starts up again on the other side. Probably not enough traffic—if there's any at all this far out—to warrant the cost of putting in a bridge. Good thing, though—that's how I found this nifty little hidden outlet down to the creek, and've been using it ever since. One day when I was heading back to town after running down to Gainesville to pick up some truck parts, I tried taking 800 west thinking it might connect with a north-south road to town and I could get back home quicker than going all the way around, but it dead-ended here at the creek. And it's so narrow here, I had to put it in reverse and back up to get turned around— and voilà! A nice little hidden path magically appeared before me. Curious, I checked it out—and discovered the best fishing spot in the county!"

The truck now sat idling on a flat rocky area under the trestle, and, looking around, Winnie could why it was probably such a great fishing spot: it was essentially a cove, secluded all around by heavily wooded banks, and shaded not only by the trestle but also by a thick canopy of trees, and it was cool, calm, and serene. To each side of the clearing, thick foliage on the banks huddled right up to the edge of the water, and on the opposite wooded bank, many tree branches actually hung into the surface of the calm pool that collected in the wider opening under the trestle before the creek narrowed again as it headed south.

The actual creek, which was still running a little full from the heavy rain Saturday night, could just be heard in the distance, somewhere beyond the thick stand of trees encircling the cove.

"Wow," was all Winnie could muster; he mostly just smiled and nodded in agreement.

•

The clearing was just wide enough for Hank to turn the truck around and back the boat trailer down the embankment, stopping just short of the water's edge. He killed the engine, and they hopped out and begin loading their supplies.

"All these years, I've never seen anyone else down here," Hank said, smiling, as they traversed back and forth over the rocky clearing, transferring the camping and hunting gear from the back of the truck to the boat. "I've left the truck and trailer here for the entire weekend sometimes, while I was out hunting or fishing, and nobody's ever bothered it, far as I can tell. I put a hitch lock on it, just in case—but when I get back, everything's always still just sitting here, exactly as I left it, seemingly untouched."

"So all the fish down here are yours for the taking," Winnie said with a sly grin.

"You betcha!"

After retrieving the last two items—the holstered handgun and the sawed-off shotgun—from behind the seat, Hank cranked up the window, locked the door, slammed it shut, then headed around the front of the truck to do the same with the passenger door. Pocketing the keys, he shuffled down toward Winnie, who was waiting patiently near the boat.

Hank stowed the guns under one of the boat seats, then began releasing the harnesses on one side of the trailer. Winnie pitched in on the other side, then together they backed the boat off the trailer and gently lowered it into the creek, the old rusty rollers squealing the entire length of the hull.

As the boat drifted slowly out onto the calm water under the trestle, they hopped in on either side, and Hank turned to start the outboard motor.

•

Though the creek was running a little heavier than normal from the weekend rain, the motorboat handled it smoothly, Hank expertly guiding it out of the quiet cove and out into the main current, then upstream, heading back north toward Blackwater on the south side of Silver Hills.

It had turned out to be an unseasonably pleasant day, the weekend storm having ushered cooler, dryer air in behind it. The sun blazed in a cloudless, deep blue sky, a light breeze keeping the heat at bay. All along the bank, the trees seemed to be airing out their tired branches, leaves rustling, with countless birds—seen and unseen—singing happily along.

The scene was beautiful, picture-perfect; worthy of gracing the front of a postcard.

As the creek widened, the current calmed considerably, and Hank was able to set the outboard to a low idle and still make good progress. As a result, the loud motor quieted substantially, and with one hand guiding the tiller handle, he relaxed and turned back to Winnie.

"Say, you remember when you and Tommy found that old shack back in Black Woods, and came to the store and told my boy Joey about it?"

This unexpected recollection snatched Winnie's attention;

he hadn't thought about that for years...

"Of course," Winnie said, his curiosity piqued.

"Well, I don't know if you knew this, but I took a few of my hunting friends—Big John, Chet from down at the club, Frank next door, a few other guys, don't know if you know any of 'em, like Don Emerson—"

"I remember Don," Winnie interrupted. "Fireman, right?"

"Fire *chief* actually. Been with the department for years, as long as I can remember. Anyway, we all went out there the next day to find that shack, and whatever it was you thought you heard in there."

"No shit?" Winnie said, genuinely surprised. He'd never heard any more about it at the time—but then, Tommy's disappearance had dominated his life and was the talk of the town for weeks after that, so in a way he wasn't surprised he hadn't heard any more about that old shack.

"First, we found that old boat the two of you used to "borrow"—

—with this, he used slow, sarcastic air quotes—

"—under that old half-overgrown pier...matter of fact, I've still got it, stored in the outbuilding on the back forty. Still floats, far as I know."

"Really? Did you ever find out who it belonged to?"

"Nope. I checked with the owners of nearest house, but they didn't claim it. But they did say they'd bought the place way back in the thirties from an old retired guy who moved to Florida—name of Richard, or Richards, I think they said—and thought maybe the boat had been his. But they didn't care one way or the other, said take it if I want it, they had no use for it, so I did. Never know when you might need a backup boat—even if it is just a rowboat…as long as it floats, why not?"

"Damn," Winnie muttered, when it suddenly dawned on him that he and Tommy could've just as easily kept the boat for themselves, if they'd only known it didn't belong to anyone…wouldn't that have been *awesome*?

"And you might like to know that we *did* find that shack back in the woods, along with what you heard in there."

"Really? What was it?!" Winnie was so excited he sat up.

Hank chuckled. "Actually, it was *who*, not *what*. Turns out what you boys heard inside the shack was that Walsh kid… Jimmy Walsh? The kid that got caught smokin pot at school, and got kicked off the varsity football team? He was so afraid of the hidin' he was gonna get from his ol' man—who was on the school board you know, so imagine his embarrassment, his own son, and besides that, the man always was a hothead, throwing a fit over every little thing—that he ran away from home, and was livin' in that shack. Who knows how he found it, just sheer luck I guess, he said he'd been wondering around lost in the woods for days. Anyway, he was strung out, hungry, and scared, so it was pretty easy to convince him to go home and face the music, that his parents were more worried sick than angry, and would be happy to see him. And Frank even volunteered to go with him, play referee in case his ol' man got out of hand."

"Wow, that's awesome! I'm glad to hear he's okay…alive. Back then, we all thought he'd been…well, like Tommy…"

"Nope. Made it home, safe and sound. And the ol' man pulled some strings—and some of us guys had a talk with the football coach, too—and he wasn't kicked off the team after all. Just on probation, keep his shit straight for the rest of the season or he's gone. And he did. In fact, I heard he scored a football scholarship to a big-ten college. You believe that shit?"

They both laughed, shaking their heads at the irony.

"Anyway, that damn shack was about to collapse, was even swaying in the wind that day, and we didn't want anyone else risking their neck hanging out in that death trap, so we got the gas can from the boat, doused it and set it on fire, burned it to the ground."

"What?!" Winnie nearly shouted. "You tryin' to start a forest fire or what?!"

"Nah, Don kept it under strict control. He knew exactly what he was doing, it was actually pretty impressive to watch him doing what he does. A fire expert if there ever was one."

"Fire chief, that's right," Winnie said, nodding his head.

"Shack collapsed in on itself like a controlled demolition, there was never any threat of the fire spreading to the surrounding woods. The whole thing went down in less than an hour."

"So what do you think it was? The shack, I mean."

Hank shrugged. "Hard tellin'. Might've been built by a trapper or hunter, a pioneer, long ago, back before the town was even settled. Who knows."

"And the tunnel? That's what I always wondered about."

He shrugged again. "I don't know, might've started out as a

shit-hole or something. A garbage area. Then maybe rain washed it out over the years, or some kind of animal dug it out, made it its den or burrow. There's just no way of knowing for sure."

That got Winnie remembering...*animal...or monster?*

"Speaking of animals, what about your hunt? Did you ever find the beast, or monster, or whatever it is? See anything?"

Hank sighed. "Nope. Nothing. We went pretty deep into Black Woods from the shack, followed the creek all the way up to where we could see the rapids heading back downhill...but never saw a damned thing. Didn't even *hear* anything unusual, no signs of something hiding nearby, or stalking us—like I suspected in Blackwater that one day—nothin'. And once it started getting dark, we headed back."

Now Winnie sighed heavily.

"Well, I sure hope we at least see *something* this time...I'm tired of feeling like I'm crazy...and of everyone else thinking I'm crazy. Even *Tommy* thought I was crazy."

"I sure wish we'da known about that cave back then," Hank said. "That's gonna be the ticket, I think. Where it's been hiding all these years."

Winnie just nodded, a look of determination on his face.

With that they grew quiet, both probably trying to imagine what they would find, what would happen, what they would do, once they found that cave...

...and maybe some kind of monster?

●

It took them the rest of the afternoon to motor upstream.

The breeze eventually died off, allowing the heat to intensify, which also increased the humidity from the moisture rising off the creek water, and more than once they had each wiped the sweat from their foreheads, exposing sweat stains building under their arms.

The sun was setting as they rounded a bend, Hank looking down at his compass and saying softly, "It should be right about—

—and suddenly Blackwater Swamp materialized ahead, with the thickly wooded Sliver Hills looming behind, at this hour melding into a black silhouette set against a deepening purple night sky.

"Thar she blows," Hank said, folding the compass and cutting the motor.

In the sudden silence, the myriad chirps, rasps, and croaks of countless insects, river-dwelling critters, and woodland creatures was suddenly much more audible, saturating the air all around them.

Winnie looked up at the darkening sky, then down at his watch: it was just after eight. He looked up at Hank.

"How much daylight do you suppose we have left?" he asked, concerned about setting up camp before it got dark.

"Not much," Hank answered. "Let's find a place to dock along the far bank over there—"

—he pointed across the creek at the wooded embankment to the southwest—

"—then hopefully we can find a decent clearing in there somewhere, where we can set up camp right quick. Pretty sure

I've seen a few open spots back in there before."

As Hank slid an oar out of its keeper, Winnie again looked at his watch, again concerned, and now he was getting even more nervous, as the nighttime symphony produced by the millions of strange and unseen creatures all around them seemed to intensify.

•

Thanks to Hank's expert outdoorsmanship, they were able to quickly find an apt docking spot, locate a reasonable clearing just inside the woods above the riverbank, gather some firewood, and set up a makeshift camp, all just before a thick darkness fell.

It didn't take long for Hank to get the fire going, since he was smart enough to bring a box of matches. Winnie felt fortunate—and again, like an idiot—because he never even *thought* of bringing matches...*or even a lighter...duh.*

They ate in silence in front of a small fire, hot dogs and beans prepared with astonishing speed and efficiency by Hank. As he wolfed it down—suddenly aware that he'd missed lunch in his urgency to get home and begin his hunt—Winnie thought he'd never tasted such a fine meal in a long, long time..

As the night set in it became almost palpable, but fortunately a light breeze kicked back up, which not only cut the humidity somewhat, but also seemed to settle the woodland creatures a bit, softening the constant buzzing din considerably, making it almost unnoticeable after a while.

After finishing their meal, they settled into their sleeping bags, preparing to call it a night.

Before sliding into his bag, Winnie took a small plastic case from his pocket and carefully plucked out each of his contacts, storing them with a tiny *snap!* as he closed the case and returned it to his pocket. Then he eased himself into the sleeping bag.

"Time's like this I'd sure love to have a smoke," Hank said, a longing in his voice.

"How long has it been? Since you quit?"

"Oh, I lost track…a few years, anyway."

"Congrats. Keep it up!"

Hank just grinned, but Winnie could tell that behind that smile, he was still wishing for a cigarette.

After a few minutes of silence, both watching as the softly crackling fire began to die down, Hank suddenly spoke up.

"Hey, I wanted to ask you…I mean, if you're up to it, and I understand if you'd rather not talk about it…but I've always wondered what happened to your dad? I heard the news of course, but not much in the way of details…if you don't mind me askin', that is…I knew him a little, mostly seen him around town for years, and I can't help but wonder what happened…"

"No, it's fine," Winnie responded. "It was a long time ago. It's gotten easier to talk about."

"Well, all I know is it was an accident on the highway…I knew he was a truck driver…"

"Yes. On the I-95, just south of Boston. Ice. Winter storm."

"No shit…I hadn't heard that."

"Thing of it is, he was almost to his stop for the night, in

Boston. Earlier that evening he'd stopped in Canton for dinner, a little cafe near the Canton Shopping Center, and supposedly the waitress there cautioned him about driving in such bad weather, that maybe he should stay the night, wait for the winter storm to blow through...

Interstate 95,
South of Boston
Winter 1978

It was a quaint little family cafe, nestled into the corner of Washington and Bolivar. He'd been there before, he was sure of it—but he couldn't remember when. Some years ago, he guessed. So many towns, so many years, so many little diners like this. The ol' gray matter just wasn't what it used to be...

He'd planned to stop for the night further north, in Boston—in fact, already had a motel reservation—but he'd also heard on the radio that the weather was turning, and fast. Cold front coming through—northerner, courtesy of Canada.

And, trying to save time, he'd skipped lunch, and so now he was starving.

Inside, there was a TV on the wall behind the bar, which was showing constant weather updates. As he ate, he watched intently, trying to ascertain whether he should stop here for the night, or continue on to Boston as planned.

"Looks like it's gonna get pretty bad," the waitress said, noticing his attention was fixed on the TV while she re-filled his iced tea.

"Yeah, if I'm gonna make it up to Boston tonight, I better get a move on."

Her eyes widened. "You ain't *drivin'* in this crap, are you?" she asked, incredulous. "They're talkin' up to a foot of snow!"

"Yep. That's what I do. And don't worry, I've seen much worse in my day. I'll be okay."

With that, they both looked back to the TV, where the meteorologist was waving his arms, animating the cold front barreling down from the north, bringing blizzard conditions.

"Maybe you better just stay here in Canton tonight. There's a Holiday Inn Express right around the corner, nice place from what I hear. They even have continental breakfast."

"Thanks, but the weather guy's sayin' the storm won't hit Boston proper for another hour yet. Say it's fifteen, twenty miles tops, here to the north side—I'll make it in plenty of time before the main storm gets there. And besides, I gotta make this fuel delivery first thing in the morning, I'll never make it on time if I'm still hangin' around here come sunup, specially in a foot of snow—"

—he winked at her—

"—much as I like the company."

She smiled warmly at the compliment.

Finished, he stood, fished his wallet out of his back pocket, opened it, plucked out a twenty, and tossed it onto the table.

"I'll be right back with your change," she said as she plucked up the bill and turned toward the register.

"Keep it," he said, smiling at her as he donned his hat.

With that she stopped, turned back, and nodded in appreciation. "Thank you kindly, sir," a genuine smile lighting up her face. "And you be careful out there."

"You bet."

Tipping his hat to her, he turned and headed out.

•

The thick storm clouds brought with them a premature twilight, turning to full dark before he even made it to the south side of Boston. And worse, the South 95 loop was crowded with rush-hour traffic, people trying to get home from work before the winter snowstorm came crashing down on them.

It was raining, difficult to see the road, and getting windy, his truck shaking and rattling, pulling at the wheel with each gust. But still, as he'd told the waitress at the diner: he'd seen much worse in his day, and had little doubt he'd make it to the north side in plenty of time before the full storm arrived and started dumping snow.

But then, the South 95 & Highway 1 interchange was backed up with traffic, costing him some valuable time. So once he got clear of that mess, he hit the gas, wanting to make up for lost time.

"It's just rain," he muttered under his breath. "Y'all act like it's a blizzard already."

Finally, the traffic thinned considerably, and he open her up, rain pelting the windshield even harder with his increased speed.

But unbeknownst to him, the bridge over Washington Street had iced up, the cold wet pavement freezing atop the elevated girders turned rigid with the wind. The "black ice" had caused a multi-vehicle pileup on the bridge, and by the time he noticed the traffic ahead was stopped, it was too late. He locked up his breaks, but his momentum kept him skating on the ice as if he'd never touched the pedal, and he was careening toward a cluster of stopped vehicles that had all tangled with one another in the right two lanes. He had just enough time to glimpse a few people standing around the cars, and some people still inside them, and knew that he was about to kill some of them, his load of fuel now essentially a sliding bomb.

He cranked the steering wheel to the left, trying to get around them and into the left lane that was still clear, but again, no response from the truck, he continued sliding right toward them. One of the women near the closest car turned and looked up at him as he approached, her face glowing from his headlights.

They seemed to lock eyes, both of them knowing what was about to happen, but both also being helpless to do anything about it.

"Dear Jesus," he whispered, helpless, anticipating the coming impact.

But at the last moment before impact, his tires caught a dry patch of pavement, and the cab lurched to the left and around the stopped vehicles, which in turn swung the tank out quickly behind the cab on the ice, and he could feel the truck jackknifing.

He let go the breaks for a second, then reapplied them, trying to stabilize the slide. The truck straightened in response, but now he was sliding sideways toward the outer guardrail.

He cranked the wheel to the right, but to no avail, the ice

had him once more, and before he even knew what was happening, the truck struck the guardrail full force, tilted sideways over it, then flipped upside down as it fell from the bridge, plummeting silently through some fifty feet of empty air before bursting into a massive flaming explosion upon impact with the pavement below...

"He died instantly," Winnie added, then chuckled cynically. "I've always thought that was weird, they kept telling me that, as if it would make me feel better somehow: 'he died instantly.' I was just a kid. My dad was dead. My mom was alone. And now we were broke too, without Dad to support us. My entire world had just collapsed—but somehow, knowing that he had *died instantly*, instead of suffering there on the road, or for a while in the hospital or something, would somehow help make me feel better...well, it didn't."

"I'm sorry," Hank said softly.

"What *does* help though, is knowing that he sacrificed his own life to save the lives of others. Complete strangers even. I mean, he could've slammed into their cars and got his truck stopped, but probably would've killed a few of them in the process. He chose instead to do whatever he could to avoid them, and it cost him his life. But that's the kind of man my dad was. And knowing *that* about him helps me deal with what happened to him."

With that, Winnie turned back to the fire, letting out a long, sad sigh.

"I only hope I can hold a candle to him some day," he

added softly.

"Well, I think that coming here to face this thing—whatever it is—and to get answers about your friend Tommy, proves that heroes run in the family. It's in your blood. You don't have to worry about holding a candle to your dad, you *are* his candle. His flame, his spirit, is living on in you. The way *I* see it, anyway."

Tears were welling in Winnie's eyes, but he smiled at Hank's words. They felt wonderful to hear. He'd always wondered if he would, or even *could*, live up to his ol' man. Probably not—but maybe one day he can at least vindicate himself for his cowardly loss of Tommy…

After a few silent minutes, Winnie pulled himself together, and looked back up at Hank.

"Okay, so that's my story. Now I wanna know yours."

"My story? What story?" Hank asked, perplexed.

"About your wife. Joey's mom. All anyone knows is that she's not around anymore, and nobody seems to know why, or what happened. Joey refuses to talk about it. At least not to me and Tommy—"

—he shrugged—

"—so we've always wondered."

"I see. Well, I don't like to talk about it either, but I suppose it's only fair—you spilled your guts, now it's my turn to spill mine. Quid pro quo."

But Winnie shook his head and held his hand out. "No, you don't have to if you don't want to. I'm just curious, and thought maybe if you didn't mind…but don't worry about it if you don't—"

"No, it's fine, I don't mind. And it's real simple, too—"

—now it was his turn to shrug—

"—Mary took a bottle of pills one day while I was at the shop and Joey was at school."

"Jesus, Hank, I had no idea...I'm sorry," Winnie sincerely expressed.

"Well, like you said about your old man, it was a long time ago, and over the years it's gotten easier to deal with. The thing that bothers me most about it is, that morning—the morning of that fateful day—well, it seemed like a normal morning, like any other morning, other than she was acting a little strange, but I blew it off, suspected her meds—she had really bad mood swings before she started on the meds, and sometimes even with them—and I went to work at the shop, like, no big deal...but I shoulda been paying better attention, I shoulda known something wasn't right..."

The Stevens Household
Fall 1963

"You're not gonna have any breakfast?" Hank asked as Mary set a steaming plate of bacon, eggs, and toast in front of him, another in front of and Joey's chair, but didn't set one down for herself, and he didn't see any more plates over by the stove.

"Not today," she said, turning away and returning to the stove. "I'm not really hungry."

Just then Joey entered from the hallway.

"Hey, kiddo," Hank greeted as the boy slid his chair out, sat down, then immediately grabbed the glass of orange juice and gulped some down.

Then he put the glass down with a clunk, picked up a fork, but stopped and looked up at his dad. "Can I stay home from school today?" he said, grinning ear to ear.

Hank sighed and chuckled.

"Are we gonna go through this every morning?"

Joey began cutting a fried egg, yolk running out as if trying to escape. "Until you say yes," he muttered, still smiling.

"Fat chance!" Hank replied, chuckling. Then he turned back to Mary: "Hey, you got yoga today? How's that been going? I know you've been looking for something to do during the day, too much time on your hands. Has it been helping?"

She turned back to him, skillet in one hand, spatula in the other. "Yeah, a little I suppose…but I'm not going today."

"Really? Why not?"

"Just don't really feel like it."

"Are you feeling okay? First no breakfast, and now you're blowing off yoga too?"

"Maybe a little tired, that's all."

Then Hank had a thought.

"You been remembering to take your pills, right? We've been through this before, you always get depressed when you forget to take them."

"No, I've been taking them. But they're not miracle drugs, I still get tired sometimes, and just need time to myself, to recharge."

"Well, okay. I hope you get to feeling better. And as always, call me at the shop if you need anything."

"Yep."

With that, she turned and began cleaning up the counter and stove of breakfast paraphernalia, and Hank noticed she seemed to be moving rather slowly.

Hank could only hope that she was being truthful, that she really was taking her pills…

"But apparently, she wasn't. Instead, she was hiding them, hoarding them, waiting for the right time—or maybe the right mood—whatever, who knows what goes through people's minds when they're suicidal, right? But that day, I went to work as usual, and Joey went to school as usual, and Mary took a hot bath as usual, which she likes to do when she feels down…but this time, she swallowed all the pills she'd been saving, washed them down with her favorite wine…and emptied most of the bottle before she lost consciousness. Joey found her when he got home from school. He was devastated…Christ, the kid was only eight!"

"Hank, I'm really sorry…that must've been really hard…for both you and Joey…" Winnie muttered.

"Hard for me, yes," Hank agreed. "But even harder on Joey. In fact, he's always blamed *me* for it."

"Blamed *you*? How the hell was it *your* fault?" Winnie asked, incredulous.

"Well, the simple reason is, he thinks I should've known something was wrong, and stayed home with her until we got to the bottom of it, helped her deal…or maybe took her back in to see her therapist…*something*…instead of just going to work and pretending everything was okay."

"But there's no way you could've known," Winnie said. "I mean, she didn't, you couldn't've—"

"But that's not all of it," Hank interrupted. The *real* issue, to Joey anyway, is more complicated: *why the hell was she so depressed in the first place?* That's what he thinks is my fault. And, since she didn't leave any kind of a note, didn't tell anyone, just…checked out…then all he's got to go on is his gut, his speculations…and since the two of them were close, it obviously wasn't *him*…so that leaves *me*. And I was always working at the shop, always out hunting or fishing, not paying enough attention to her, attending to her needs. He says it was all me me me. And once he got old enough to tell me so, he did. Quite loudly, I might add. Then he left. Hasn't been back. Got his own place. And ever since, our relationship has been… difficult, to say the least."

At this Winnie furrowed his brow, again perplexed.

"But he was at the shop today…you guys work together, right? You seemed to get along okay…"

"We do, on a surface level. But more like co-workers, not like father and son. He's really distant when it comes to his personal life, doesn't talk to me about anything, especially what happened with Mary. It hurts sometimes, but that's the way it is, I just try to get used to it. Like we're estranged, in a way. In fact, sometimes I think it would be better for us to be *completely* estranged, than to have deal with the pain of seeing him all the time, being around him at the shop, when he's always so distant, acting almost like a stranger, or at best a co-worker, instead of like family."

"Don't say that!" Winnie hissed, taking Hank aback. "You're lucky Joey is still alive! My dad is gone, and gone forever! I'll never, *ever* be able to reconnect with him, to say all the things I wish I could say to him—*should've* said to him—or just to hug him and tell him I love him…and now it's too late! But *your* son is still alive, and you should make every effort to reconcile with him while you can! Because one day, it *will* be too late, and you'll be sorry, trust me I know! And if reconciliation isn't possible—if he refuses—then at least appreciate what you *do* have with him! At least you have *something*!" Then Winnie looked down into the fire, again tears welling up, and said quietly: "I've got nothin'…"

Hank was quiet for a long time, then he said softly: "You're right. I guess I just needed to hear that, someone just needed to knock me upside the head, knock some goddamn sense into this thick skull of mine. Thank you for that. When I get back home, I'll talk to Joey. Try to, anyway. See if he'll listen. I'll *definitely* listen, if I can convince him to talk to me. Not sure how I'll do it, but I'll sure as hell try."

With that, both men went silent, both just gazing into the dwindling fire, each lost in their own thoughts, or perhaps their own guilty memories.

•

Eventually, Winnie leaned back on his sleeping bag, and that's when he noticed the huge full moon in the night sky, nestled among millions of stars.

"Wow," he said, impressed.

Hank looked over at him, a questioning look on his face.

Winnie jerked his chin toward the sky.

"Full moon, he said. "Might be the biggest I've seen."

Hank looked up, and nodded in agreement.

"Yeah, but you shoulda seen it last year about this time. It was even bigger. They were callin' it a *super moon*," he said.

"That's right," Winnie said softly, as if recalling something. "The lunar precession…"

Turning back to Winnie, Hank asked: "Lunar what?"

"Lunar precession. We learned about it in astronomy class at school last year."

"Astronomy?" Hank asked incredulously. "Ain't that like the Zodiac, and planets aligning, and fortune telling and shit? You're tellin' me they teach that crap in *college* now?"

Winnie chucked. "No, that's *astrology*, where people believe that celestial movement and planetary positions influence people and events, the kinda stuff I like to call *hocus-pocus*. *Astronomy*, on the other hand, is the actual *science* of celestial movement."

"Ah," Hank said, nodding. In understanding. "So what's this lunar procession?"

*"Pre*cession, not *pro*cession. See, the moon's orbit scribes an ellipse around the earth, but that ellipse isn't stationary, it rotates too, only in a reverse direction. Plus there's the rotation of the earth to factor in. So take one point in the ellipse, then take a full lunar orbit—the moon travels the ellipse and

returns to that same point on the ellipse—that point will be slightly behind, or *precedes*, its original location above earth by just a little. Long story short, in order for the same point in the moon's orbit—say, the closest point, or super moon—to reach the exact same spot above the earth—like, say, right above Hope—takes approximately nine years. And last year was the first time since 1975, nine years ago. That's why it looked so huge. It wasn't just a super moon—the closest point in the current orbit, which happens about once a month, somewhere over the earth—but it was the nine-year super moon, when that closest point happened to be directly above Hope again."

Hank was impressed.

"Wow, I didn't know that…just goes to show ya, you learn somethin' every day, huh?"

"Most people these days aren't aware of it, but historically, it's been a major mythological event in many cultures and religions. The ancient Egyptians…the Greeks…it's mentioned in Norse mythology…the Inca, the Aztecs, and the Maya too… it's even symbolized in the famous Mayan calendar. They all believed, in one way or another, that the lunar cycle influenced people, animals, the weather, the crop yield, the economy, and even potentially, war. It was usually equated with bad luck or evil, because the moon is often considered the God of night or darkness."

"In other words, astrology," Hank said with a grin.

"Essentially, yes," Winnie agreed. "But in modern times, there's still some similar beliefs, only based on long-term data. Like the Juglar Wave, or Cycle, a nine-year economic cycle identified in the 19th century by French statistician Clément Juglar, with some people believing that the moon's increased gravitational pull and resultant electromagnetic fluctuations may cause people to become depressed or emotionally unstable and act more conservatively or even pessimistically, causing market downturns. And more recently, an eight-plus-year cycle of global rainfall has been identified, which some are linking to the lunar precession. So there are some convincing correlations...but whether they're coincidence or not is anyone's call."

"No shit," Hank said, amazed. "So last year was it, huh? The nine-year super moon?"

"Yep. Unfortunately I missed it, was still on campus out of state, and didn't even see the normal full moon from there because I was indoors studying. But I heard about it later—and learned about the lunar precession the following semester—and wished I'da been here to see it."

"Gotta admit, it was amazing," Hank said. Then he winked. "Maybe next time."

"Maybe," Winnie said, smiling. Then he thought about it for a minute, but shook his head and shrugged.

"What?" Hank asked, noticing him grappling with something.

"You know, I was about to say that maybe the lunar precession has some correlation with all the strange sightings and mysterious disappearances that have happened over the years, like whatever happened to Jackie's friends that went missing this weekend. And Tommy back in '75. After all, they say it also affects animals, and Jackie says he saw some kind of big animal...called it a monster, but it sounded to me like some sort of sea creature, but that *changed* somehow...and it's rumored that some kind of animal, or creature, or beast—*something*—is involved in all of those other disappearances, too, that supposedly lives in Black Woods."

Hank nodded in agreement, and Winnie continued:

"But on the other hand, the super moon only happens in the same place—in this case, above Hope—every nine years, but now it's been *ten* years since...well, you know, Tommy vanished...so it doesn't add up...so never mind, forget I said anything—"

—he shrugged—

"—guess I'm just grasping for straws..."

At this, Hank donned a troubled look, took a deep breath and blew it out long and hard, then gave Winnie a look like he was stressed about something.

Winnie noticed, and waited, but Hank said nothing, he just turned away.

After a moment of silence, he asked Hank: "What?"

"I don't know how to tell you this—"

—but then he stopped and shook his head almost imperceptibly, apparently changing his mind—

—but I probably shouldn't. I'd just be feeding into your little astrology hocus-pocus theory, and getting you needlessly worked up, and frankly, that's probably not a good idea right before we head into that cave tomorrow. We got no idea what we'll find in there, could get dangerous, so we gotta be sharp and on our toes, thinking clearly, no fuckups…last thing you need is unnecessary distraction, your mind preoccupied with crazy ideas."

"C'mon, Hank, I'm not a twelve-year-old kid anymore. I can handle it. I've handled Tommy's tragic disappearance all these years, without going crazy—"

—he paused, and grinned—

"—though I suppose that might be debatable, especially if you asked Jenny—"

"—but still…out with it! What's on your mind?"

Hank gazed into the fire and silently pondered his thoughts for a moment, while Winnie just waited. Again he sighed and exhaled under the pressure of the decision. Then he looked back at Winnie.

"Okay. But promise me you won't read too much into it. When we head in tomorrow, let's just go with what me know —the facts, reality—and leave the hypothesizing for afterward, when we're out of danger and have the luxury of post-hunt analysis…okay?"

"You got it," Winnie said solemnly, nodding in the affirmative.

"The thing is," Hank paused, easing in. "There was an incident last year…so if your nine-year lunar cycle theory holds, then that one *does* fit the cycle. Doesn't explain what just happened to those kids this weekend, though."

"Last year?"

"Up at Silver Hills Campgrounds. Last summer. Six people —three couples—five were found dead, all mutilated, apparently by some type of wild animal, the sixth evidently carried off, she was never found. Many think it was probably a bear, but there aren't many bears in this area, and besides, a bear might attack a human—like to defend her cubs or something—but attacking and killing *six people?* And then carrying one of them off? That's unheard of. Anyway, the old campgrounds maintenance guy—name of Ed White as I recall —was the last to see them alive that evening, but later found them all slaughtered, their mutilated bodies strewn around the campsite."

"No shit? I hadn't heard anything about that."

"Oddly, there wasn't a lot of publicity. I think the story was quashed. Dallas Armstrong—the hotel billionaire?—"

—Winnie nodded in recognition—

"—owns the campgrounds, probably has connections all over the country, and I'm sure in government and law enforcement too, big political donor—not to mention access to plenty of hush money—and if word got out of the massacre up there, Silver Hills Campgrounds would go out of business, nobody would set foot in the place. So I'm thinkin' he got the story buried. But even so, he couldn't stop the locals from hearing and talking about it, which they did, but mostly under their breath or whispered in back rooms, the whole incident scared people to even *think* about, much less discuss."

Then he thought for a moment, and frowned. "So you didn't hear about it? Not even from your mom? I'm sure she probably heard…at least the rumors, they were rampant for a while there."

"I rarely watch the news at college, too busy with classes and school work...plus, I've been taking summer classes and haven't been coming home even for the summer...it was just blind luck that I happened to turn on the TV yesterday while I was waiting for Jenny to get done in the bathroom, and saw the story about Jackie and the other kids. And I imagine mom would shelter me from that type of news anyway, thinking it would just distract me from my school work...or worse, intensify my memories about Tommy..."

"Well, I suppose from your mother's perspective, that's understandable," Hank said, nodding.

"Anyway, so what happened?"

"From what I've heard, there were three couples camping that night, had the whole place to themselves. A storm blew through and knocked out the power, so the maintenance guy was called in to check out the generator, that's when he spoke with the group while they were sitting around the campfire..."

Silver Hills
Campground Massacre
Spring 1984

Stacie had to pee—*bad*—but it was awful dark out there, and she hated using the "latrine" (which in her mind was simply a euphemism for *disgusting campground toilet*), even during the day...let alone at *night*.

Yuck.

Besides, it was way over on the other side of the dark campground somewhere, the night was getting cold, and she was nice and warm sitting here cuddling with Brad in front of the campfire…and she still had nearly half a Corona to finish.

Might as well wait.

Maybe after I finish my beer…

"To good friends!" Josh suddenly proclaimed from across the campfire, raising his beer toward the others.

A smattering of acknowledgments emanated from around the group, as the three couples raised bottles of various hue in the general direction of the fire that burned in the center of their makeshift log circle. Clinking sounds pierced the darkness from all around as they toasted one another, then the crackling of the campfire and the incessant ratcheting of countless crickets took over as everyone drank in the silence of the superficial ceremony.

Stacie seized the opportunity to quickly gulp down the last of her beer, and, empty bottle in hand, she turned and peered into the darkness behind Brad, attempting to locate the latrine. Tonight there was no moon to help diffuse the darkness; the sky was still veiled with swollen clouds from the storm that had blown through earlier that evening—which was disappointing, there was supposed to be a super moon that night, and they all had looked forward to witnessing the rare event.

And worse, what had been at best scant electrical lighting around the campgrounds had blinked out during the storm—an apparent power outage—shrouding the entire camp with increasing darkness as the evening wore on. But upon discussing it, they had all agreed that they shouldn't be overly concerned; after all, they were supposed to be *camping*, which in the strictest sense means no electricity or other modern conveniences—so they would just have to make do, and they had all agreed that they were good with that.

In fact, the sudden lack of electricity had added a bit of challenge, an edgy atmosphere of excitement, to their camping experience: suddenly, they really were *roughing it.*

The guys were all noticeably excited at the prospect, starting a big campfire in the center of the log circle (fortunately the rack of pre-cut firewood was tarped over, and stayed dry though the storm), and loading a big ice chest full of beer from the tiny cabin refrigerators, which were now dead due to the power outage—but the girls were a tad more reserved, though cautiously receptive.

Mostly, the girls agreed that at least it had stopped raining…for now, anyway.

So with what little electric light there had been now extinguished, Stacie squinted into the blackness, trying in vain to locate the tiny restroom structure off in the distance.

Somewhere back there, just past the cabins…behind the last two I think…

Fireflies blinked everywhere, a mild distraction as her eyes darted about the distant edges of the camp. She peered into the darkness as far as the flickering golden glow of the campfire would allow, but the tiny structure eluded her, hiding in the shadows back there somewhere.

Damn.

Turning back, she hoped her friends didn't notice that she was squirming…but the din of talking and laughing had returned to the group, and nobody seemed to be paying any attention to her.

"This place is great," Dan suddenly announced from his side of the fire, his girlfriend Mindy cuddled against him. "And these cabins are *actually* old—not simulated to look retro or antiquated, but seems they were actually *real* cabins once, a long time ago."

"They were," Josh confirmed.

They all turned to him.

"Now that you mention it, this place actually has an interesting history," Josh continued.

"Oh?" Dan said, intrigued.

"It started out as a mining camp, built back in the thirties. The miners lived here while they worked in a sliver mine up in these hills somewhere. But just a few years later, the mine was mysteriously closed down and abandoned. So this became a ghost town—or ghost *camp*."

"Ooooooooh" Dan moaned like a stereotypical ghost, grabbing Mindy abruptly around her ribs, causing her to jump. "So it's not just a *cool* camp, but a *ghost* camp! And how cool is *that?*"

"Knock it off," his girlfriend muttered, pushing his hands away, annoyed. "You startled me...and no, I *don't* think ghosts are *cool.*"

Looking up, she noticed they were all looking at her, as if trying to determine whether she was serious or joking.

"Well, I don't," she said defensively, shrugging. While quiet snickering floated around her circle of friends, she turned her gaze to the campfire, ignoring them.

"Then, it became a hippie commune," Josh continued. "Back in the early sixties, a bunch of hippies moved in—squatters, essentially—who wanted to isolate themselves from mainstream society...get out of the rat-race...you know—live in peace and tranquility, one with nature, sex, drugs and rock-n-roll, that sort of thing."

They all looked at each other in amazement—along with a certain level of understanding, signified by their quiet nods.

"But the commune only lasted a few years...one by one the hippies left for better opportunities, or to get married, or whatever reason hippies find for leaving their commune."

"Prolly ran out of weed!" Brad joked, scoring laughter from around the campfire. But their laughter was suddenly disrupted when something popped loudly in the fire with a *pow!*, sending a host of tiny yellow sparks floating into the air while the fire crackled loudly for a moment.

Everyone watched as the sparks gently faded away—along with their laughter—into the night sky...then turned their attention back to Josh, who continued:

"Eventually, only one couple remained—the couple who'd started the commune in the first place—and then sometime in 1966, they seemed to just up and vanish...some friends came up to visit them but they weren't here, and there were no signs of anyone having been here for a while...and the couple hasn't been seen since, never turned up anywhere else, nobody seems to know where they went or what became of them. So this place was once again abandoned—again, a ghost camp—

and it sat vacant for years, slowly being reclaimed by nature... at least until Dallas Armstrong bought it, along with this land along the hillside."

"Wait a sec—Dallas Armstrong? The millionaire real estate tycoon?" Dan asked, a hint of incredulity in his voice.

Josh nodded in confirmation. "Yes. Dallas Armstrong, the *billionaire* tycoon," he corrected. "Owns a few hotels here in town, and a lot more across the country. And big ones, too—like in Vegas...L.A....New York."

He looked around at the group for a reaction to this news, and smiled as impressed profanities and low whistles were expressed.

Then Roe—Josh's girlfriend—suddenly piped up:

"Wow—I sure would like to meet *that* guy," she purred suggestively, while Mindy giggled at her from across the campfire.

"Oh, I bet you would, *Rowena*," Josh returned sarcastically. "And you'd probably be in luck—rumor has it he's into mindless bimbos!"

The others laughed and cringed at the jab.

"You're such a jerk!" she barked, slapping his shoulder in mock offense while the rest of them laughed. Then, donning a dramatic pout like a child, she leaned affectionately against him...but then, dropping the pout, she looked up at him and said softly but sternly: "And I've told you a million times not to call me that...it's *Roe*."

Apparently ignoring her, Josh just put his arm around her and continued:

"Anyway, he bought up all this land, and turned the old mining camp—turned ghost camp, then hippy commune, then abandoned—into this wonderful wilderness retreat now known as *Silver Hills Campgrounds*." As he spoke, he waved his beer in a wide arc that encompassed all the land around them.

"He left most of the natural rustic look, though—these old cabins, for instance." He looked over at Dan and nodded in acknowledgement, and Dan nodded back.

Everyone else turned to take another quick look at the cabins off in the distance, with a newfound appreciation.

Stacie looked too, an excuse to once again scope for the latrine, but she still couldn't see it.

"And these big ol' trees."

He comically threw his head back to look up and around, waving his bottle at the huge, overhanging branches behind him, which launched out from massive oaks that rose like ancient towers throughout the camp.

The rest of the group took the opportunity to tilt their bottles back and drink while they were looking up anyway. Silently, their eyes darted around, taking in all the trees that they really hadn't noticed before now. Huge, old trees—like right out of a fantasy book or movie.

"But he also added a few amenities." Josh changed his tone to one of less awe and more sensibility, and everone looked back to him.

"Like electric power, for one. Back in the day, the silver camp didn't have it…nor did the hippie commune."

"No *electricity?* You mean, like, no power *at all?*" Roe was shocked. "Man, would that SUCK! What the HELL were they thinking?" With a look of total bewilderment on her face, she looked around the group for support, shaking her head in disbelief. The group chimed in with mumbled agreements and disapprovals, then Josh continued:

"He just added very basic power—a generator, with two single wires strung atop those wooden utility poles—"

—he motioned with his bottle toward the poles running down the hill and disappearing into the darkness—

"—just enough power for a few lights, small refrigerators in the cabins, a water pump for running water—sinks, toilets, showers—so the guests don't have to totally *rough it* while they're here…but close."

"Gee, that was awful *nice* of him to add toilets with running water," Mindy remarked with mild sarcasm. "Like, I mean, can you even *imagine* taking a shit in the *woods?*"

"Oh my god, just shoot me now!" Roe shouted, laughing at the prospect. She was joined by chuckles from the rest of the group.

"I know, right?" Mindy answered. She then took a swig from her beer, wiped her mouth with the back of her hand, and leaned back into Dan's arm, turning her attention back to Josh as he continued:

"Armstrong thought he could make a go of the rustic theme and serene wilderness setting. The camp is completely secluded from the stresses and problems of everyday life in the city; there's no traffic, no phones—there's the one phone line in the office, and that's it—no TV, no annoying neighbors, no loud music, no barking dogs, no *nothing*. Just woods, nature, fresh air, peace and quiet, and just enough amenities to make it a little more comfortable for the guests, but that's it. And it looks like he was right—because this place is booked solid, every weekend for the rest of the year."

At this, impressed comments once again traveling around the group. But then, amazed (and a tad suspicious) at Josh's knowledge of the camp, Brad piped up:

"Hey—and how the hell do you know so much about this place, anyway?"

With a clownish face, Josh held up a glossy, folded pamphlet before him, and barked, "Brochure!"

They all burst into laughter, and someone threw a bottle cap at him. Josh ducked slightly, laughing with them, then tossed the brochure into the fire. They grew quiet as they watched the paper blacken, curl, and burst into flames.

Stacie was still gazing into the fire when she suddenly smelled the unmistakable aroma of marijuana. Glancing around, she came to rest on Josh and Roe, sitting opposite the campfire from her, and in the dim light of the dwindling flames she could just see them passing something back and forth, and figured that was the source—and hoped they would pass if around.

But *man*, she had to *pee*…

Then, the smell of lime.

She looked down: Brad was holding a fresh Corona before her. Water from the ice chest was still dripping from the bottle, and a huge wedge of lime protruded from the longneck.

She looked up at him, surprised.

"You look like you could use another one," he said, giving her an encouraging nudge with the bottle.

She smiled slightly and took it without comment, dropping her empty bottle between her legs into the wet grass and dandelions that skirted the base of the old dead log they were sitting on. It thumped, rolled a little, and stopped against the warm, cracked timber.

"Shit—somebody's coming," Josh said quietly, just loud enough for the others to hear but no more. He immediately tossed his joint into the fire, then quickly fetched his pack of cigarettes from his shirt pocket, tapped one out, lit it, and exhaled strongly, blowing the smoke around, trying to mask the telltale herbal aroma of weed.

The others looked at Josh with wide-eyed astonishment (probably more shocked at him throwing a perfectly good joint into the fire than at the warning he had just muttered under his breath). In response to the silent inquisition, he jerked his chin in the direction of the narrow one-lane access road that led up the hill to the camp. In unison, they all turned in that direction.

A short distance away, the dark silhouette of a man was walking up the gravel road wielding a flashlight. The small, dancing beam of white light pierced the darkness, zigzagging this way and that, briefly illuminating random patches of weeds and the occasional tree that bordered the road, all of which glistened in the light, still wet from the rainstorm earlier.

The intruder's gait was steady, purposeful—and he was headed right toward them!

"Who can *that* be?" Roe whispered from the other side of the circle.

Josh shrugged. "Not sure," he whispered back. "We're supposed to be the only campers up here this weekend, I reserved the whole camp just for us." He then glanced around at all his friends. "Just stay cool, everyone."

Well, they had no problem *staying cool.* Most of them were too scared to move anyway. Out of the corner of her eye, Stacie saw Brad take a quick swig from his bottle, heard him swallow nervously. But that was all.

They waited in tense silence as the stranger approached, the beam of light growing in size and brightness.

As the man drew nearer, brief reflections of light from the collected rain puddles revealed that his boots were wet and muddy—but that was all they could see of the daunting figure moving toward them..

When his crunching footsteps came within earshot, the man finally materialized behind the flashlight. He wore a long raincoat, boots, and an Aussie-style hat.

"Is that Indiana Jones?" Brad asked, stifling a nervous snicker, while Stacie elbowed him to shut up.

"Whaddo we do?" Mindy asked in a barely audible, panicked whisper.

"Shhhhh…" Josh hissed, putting his finger to his lips, then camouflaging the move by taking the cigarette from them and blowing smoke.

As the man neared, he left the road, trudged through the unkempt grass toward them, and stopped just short of the circle of riveted campers. His face was mostly hidden in the shadow of his hat, and the flickering light from the fire gave him a spooky, shape-shifting quality. He peered around the group, taking them in one by one.

They all waited quietly, unknowing. Even the crickets had gone silent, as if they somehow knew something bad was about to happen. Far off in the distance, thunder rumbled across the sky, and faded quickly. Then the only sound was the soft crackling of the fire.

Now Stacie *really* had to pee…

"It was a cave-in," the man said.

At this, they all looked around at each other, confused.

"What?" Josh asked.

"On the way up here, I overheard y'all talking about the old silver mining camp this place use to be," he said. "The camp brochure mentions that, yes, but what it doesn't mention is that a lot of miners died—couple dozen of 'em, or so the story goes —in a cave-in. Back in thirty-nine. That's why the mine was abandoned."

"No shit?" Dan blurted, while the rest of them uttered softly:

wow
no way
a cave-in
damn

"And you would be…?" Josh now asked the stranger, in a slightly suspicious tone.

The man tipped his hat. "Name's Edwin White…but y'all can just call me Ed, same's everyone else."

"And, Mr. White…Ed…what are you doing up here, and sneaking up on us like that? We thought we were the only ones staying here tonight."

"Maintenance. They shoulda toldja at the office when you checked in that I'd be around now and then. I handle all the maintenance on these grounds. Jules—she's the cleaning lady —was down at the office when the power went out during that storm—a noisy one, wasn't it?—and gave me a call. So I came in to check things out. Seems the generator kicked out, not sure why—but thought I'd check in with you folks first, make sure everything's okay before I head down to the generator."

"So this place really runs on a generator?" Brad asked, incredulous.

"Yessir. Propane. In a utility shed down around behind the office building—"

—he turned and pointed down the hill, where the utility poles carrying the power line disappeared into the darkness, then back—

"—I suppose it could be outta propane is all, but I just checked it a few days ago, and the gauge showed about half, so there shoulda been plenty—"

—he shrugged—

"—so I don't know. Could be any number of things. So if y'all are okay for now, you can just sit tight while I head back down the hill and get to work on it, see if I can get the lights back on."

With that they looked around at each other, shrugging and nodding and chiming into a chorus of

we're fine
no problem
yeah, fine
everything's cool

"Good. Then y'all have a fun—and by the way, I don't mind if y'all wanna burn somethin' other than tobacco—"

—he looked around at them and winked—

"—so don't worry, far as I'm concerned, I didn't see or smell nothin...y'all have a good time, that's what you're here for, right?"

As they all agreed, smiling at each other, the man turned to leave. But after only a few steps, Josh called after him:

"Sir...?"

The man stopped in the darkness, looking back at Josh expectantly.

"You say the silver mine caved in? Killed some miners? And that's why it was abandoned?"

"That's right."

"Could you tell us about that? How did it happen? Or do you know?"

As the others turned from Josh to Ed, now also with expectant looks on their faces, the man turned and walked back a few steps toward them, and stepped into the glow of the campfire.

"Well, I don't see why not," he said, looking around at them. "Generator's waited this long, I reckon it can wait a little longer."

Then he spotted the cooler off to one side, between Brad

and Dan.

"You got any extra?" he asked, jerking his chin in the direction of the cooler. "A man can get a tad thirsty tellin' stories around a campfire." Then he smiled big and friendly.

Everyone chuckled as Brad turned and opened the cooler.

"Of course…what's your poison?"

"Oh, I'm a simple man…got anything simple?"

"Of course…from one beer lover to another," Dan said as he pulled a brown bottle from the cooler, dripping wet. Using the bottle opener on the side of the cooler, he popped the cap off and handed it to Brad, who handed it up to Ed.

"Strohs," he said with a smile, and tipped it back for a lengthy swig.

"Ahhhh….he exhaled afterward, still smiling, then wiped his mouth with his sleeve.

"Pull up a log." Josh motioned with his own beer at the vacant log lying at Ed's feet. "Plenty of room."

"Don't mind if I do," he said, stepping over the log and sitting down.

"Anyone else?" Dan asked, holding up another dripping bottle and glancing around the campfire.

"I'll take one." It was Roe. Dan popped the cap off and handed it around to Josh, who handed it to Roe.

Everyone else said they were good.

Ed took another swig, and the group grew quiet, waiting.

Again wiping his mouth with his sleeve, he began:

"Like I said, it was the spring of thirty-nine. It'd rained hard that spring, damn near flooded the mine, at best turned much of the floor to mud. And, story goes, there'd been some… *vibrations*—though some said it was tremors. Fearing the integrity of the mine, some of the miners confronted their bosses about it. But the owner—man by the name of Doyle, if I recall correctly—of course managed to convince them that everything was fine, and that digging was to continue.

"Now, the mine entrance was up there on the north side of Silver Hills—"

—he motioned his bottle into the woods behind them somewhere, and they all turned to look, but then turned back when they couldn't see anything—

—and they all nodded, a few taking swigs—

"—but the deeper the mining tunnel went into the hill— unbeknownst to them mind you—the closer they got to the existing cave system."

"Cave system?" Josh asked, curious. "There's caves in Silver Hills?"

"Yessir. Supposedly, there's another entrance—a hidden cave I'm told—somewhere on the south side."

"Wait—there's supposedly a swamp on the south side of Silver Hills," Josh interjected. At least that's what the maps showed, when I was checking this place out."

"Blackwater Swamp," he acknowledged with a nod. "But rumor has it, somewhere deep within that swamp there's a hidden cave…and that it's connected to an entire system of tunnels and caverns that run deep inside Silver Hills."

Again, a chorus of muttering around the fire:

wow

no shit
I didn't know that
caves, huh? Cool!

"Anyway, they'd struck a big vein of silver, and the owner was all excited about it, was pushing them to keep digging… but then, just as quick as they'd found it, they lost it again, it just seemed to run out…"

Silver Hills
Silver Mine Cave-in
Spring 1939

John Doyle sat in a plastic folding chair at an aluminum-framed rectangular folding table inside a large army-green tent posted in a clearing just outside the mine entrance, it's front opening facing the tracks. That way the ore cars exiting the mine, each of which was rated to carry up to a ton of ore when fully loaded—and he made damn sure that each one was— would pass right in front of him, for easy counting.

Clenching an unlit pipe in the side of his mouth, he was engrossed in the study of multiple maps and papers that were strewn before him on the table: geographic surveys, topographical maps, a rough hand-drawn diagram of the mine they were digging, along with tallies of the silver ore they'd thus far extracted, future projections, the going rate, the bids he'd received from buyers. Plus, a little accounting: profit/loss statements, business expenses, and of course worker payroll.

The rich silver vein they'd struck earlier that month had been paying off nicely, and at the moment he was projecting how much money he would pull in by end of month, if things continued as they were. And once last night's rain had finally let up (he was getting worried there for a minute, watching the storm's downpour from his cabin in camp), he had no reason to think they wouldn't—except for the mild tremors they'd felt in the area over the last couple of days, that is; but so far today, everything had been calm, and he now felt confident that any threat of stronger, actually damaging tremors—or even an all-out earthquake—had passed.

Fingers crossed, anyway…

And besides, shutting down the mine over such unfounded paranoia would be entirely too costly at this juncture, and therefore out of the question. That morning some of the men had expressed concern, but he'd quickly placated them with a promise of bonuses, to be paid at the end of the week on top of their standard pay, along with passing along an entirely fabricated report from the USGS that the tremors had ended with no more expected, and that had shut them up and got them back to work.

Easy peasy.

Now he smiled, seeing that the numbers were adding up nicely, and—

"Sir?"

Doyle looked up, agitated that his concentration had been broken. It was Danny, the youngest lad on the crew. Filthy black head to toe, sweat streaks running down the sides of his flushed face, boots caked with mud, he stood in the entrance of the tent, the open flap shuttering in the breeze behind him.

"What is it?"

"Foreman needs to see you."

"Sure. Send him in."

At this, the young man fidgeted, looking uncomfortable.

"Is there a problem Dan?"

"Well...he needs to see you down in the mine."

Doyle just stared at him, incredulous.

"Down in the mine."

"Yessir."

"Now what could Mr. Harvey possibly need me to come down in the mine for?"

"Well..." he hesitated. Then, looking sheepishly down, he murmured: "Seems we've lost the vein, sir."

Doyle's pipe fell to the table with a clatter.

•

"When did you lose it?" Doyle asked Mike Harvey, the crew foreman.

He, Harvey, and a handful of crewmen were standing at the end of the tunnel, their collective helmet lanterns illuminating the blank stone wall before them.

"At least twenty feet back," Harvey said, jerking his head in the direction of the tunnel behind them. "There at the end of the tracks. We were going along great, then it just...stopped."

"Silver veins don't just stop," Doyle said rather curtly.

"Well, this one did. We kept going though, figuring we'd eventually pick it back up. But so far, nothing."

"And the detectors?"

"Nothing. Not a peep."

"So it must've turned."

"Could be. But that's why I called you down. If we change course, start a new tunnel in a different direction…well, that'd be your call, not mine. So I need to know what you want us to do. If we keep digging, what direction?"

With that, Doyle walked back down the tunnel to end of the tracks, the point that Harvey indicated the vein had stopped. The crewmen lifted their shovels and pickaxes and followed, a gaggle of beams from their headlamps bouncing and turning every which way in the dark tunnel. Though most of the rain-induced flooding had finally dried up, the tunnel floor was still muddy, and their boots stuck a little with each step, emitting a chorus of wet sucking and slapping sounds as they walked.

They stopped at the end of the tracks and watched as Doyle looked closely at the walls, the ceiling between the timber beams, shining his flashlight all over the rough stone. Then he looked at Harvey.

"Got any idea? A hunch? Seems after years of mining, you'd've learned something about the nature of these things."

Harvey nodded. "Well, I can tell ya I've never seen a vein turn back on itself."

"Meaning what, exactly?"

"Well, if the vein turned inward from this wall—"

—he placed his hand on the wall before them—

"—then it would be heading back more or less in the direction of the entrance. So it'd essentially be turning back on itself. And I ain't never seen a vein do that."

"So you think it would've turned the other way—"

—Doyle pointed across the narrow tunnel to the opposite stone wall—

"—continuing away from the entrance?"

"If it's turned at all. Could've just stopped. Never know. Unusual, but I seen it now and then over the years. But if it did turn—my money's on that direction, yes. Away from the entrance, continuing deeper into the mountain."

With that, Doyle crossed the tracks, shining his light on the far wall as he approached. First he looked up and down, then, shrugging after not seeing anything of note, he reached up and placed his hand on the stone wall before him—and stopped with a jerk, coming to attention.

"Now that's odd. Harvey, come check this out."

Harvey crossed the tunnel, the men following close behind, the chorus of headlamps now illuminating the entire wall before them.

"What up?" Harvey asked.

His hand still on the wall, Doyle said, "I might be imagining things, but I'd swear this wall feels…warmer. Or at least not as dead-cold."

With that he quickly trotted back across the tunnel, placed his hand on the other wall for a moment, then came back and once again felt the wall before them.

"I'll be damned if it doesn't feel a tad warmer."

Harvey stepped up to the wall and placed his hand against the stone, silent and intent on how it felt. Then he mimicked Doyle, walking quickly over to the other side, feeling the opposite wall, then coming back and feeling this wall again.

"You may be right. Hard to say for sure, though."

"If so, what could that mean?"

"I don't know. More porous rock? Greater dirt content? Maybe even water—from all that rain last night?" He shrugged. "Have to be something that could transmit surface heat more effectively than just solid stone."

"Like…silver?" Doyle ventured, a twinkle in his eye.

Harvey shrugged. "Could be, I suppose. After all, minerals do conduct heat better than stone."

"Gentlemen, I think we just found our new tunnel," Doyle said, looking around at the crewmen and grinning ear-to-ear as he eagerly patted the stone wall with his hand.

The men all nodded in agreement.

Then Harvey called to Henson, the powder guy:

"Henson, we got any Giant powder left?

"Yessir," Henson answered. Box is gettin' low, but there's few sticks left."

Harvey and Doyle just looked at each other and nodded in agreement.

"Bring it up, we'll start with that," Harvey ordered, while Doyle headed confidently down the tunnel...

"And that was how they ended up finding the cave," Ed said, tipping back the bottle, the campfire reflecting off the dark glass as he did so.

"Wait—I thought you said there was a cave-in," Josh objected.

"That was later. When they blasted the opposite wall to

start the digging, the explosion opened a hole into the cave and tunnel system. Apparently, that's why that wall felt a little warmer—because there was warmer air inside the cave on the other side."

"Okay, I'll buy that," Brad said, the rest of them nodding.

"Now we come to the part about the cave-in," the man promised, then took a swig before continuing…

"A cave?" Doyle said, looking incredulous at Harvey, who was standing in the tent entrance, dirty work helmet in hand.

"Yep. I didn't go very far in, but from what little I could see, looks like there's tunnels running from it, too. Might be a whole cave network inside the mountain. Wanted to come get you before we went any further, see what you think, what you want us to do next."

•

The entire crew had come to see the cave, as word had spread quickly throughout the mine about the unusual discovery. As Harvey and Doyle approached, dozens of men stood at the breach, leaning on their shovels and pickaxes, shining their headlamps and flashlights inside, but remaining in the mine tunnel as directed by their foreman while he went to fetch the boss.

"So this might explain the warmer rock," Harvey said as he motioned toward the hole they'd blasted open, about as high as a standard doorway, but more rounded. "Warmer air on the other side, in the cave."

"I'll be damned," Doyle muttered under his breath as he

shined his flashlight inside. "And is that water I smell?"

"I believe it is," Harvey confirmed. "Might be an underground creek, or even a pond."

"But no silver vein."

"Not yet. The first blast broke through to the cave. All we did after that was wait for your directions…see if you want us to investigate."

"Well, I don't know—"

Just then a low rumbling sound traveled through the tunnel toward them, and as soon as it reached them, the entire tunnel began to tremble.

Doyle and Harvey looked wide-eyed at each other.

"Is that—?" Doyle started, but was cut off when the earthquake shook them all to the floor, the walls cracking, rock crumbling from above, timber struts splintering and tumbling.

Then the rumbling intensified, and the tunnel floor itself began to split and crack—until it, too, gave way and collapsed into some type of cavern beneath, taking the entire crew of writhing men, tools, supplies, everything with it, down into the dark unknown depths, and within moments their terrified screams could no longer be heard.

"None of the miners were ever seen again, including Doyle, the owner. With the quake, the mine had become too unstable to risk any sort of search or rescue. So they were all presumed dead, their bodies still buried down in that collapsed mine somewhere."

With that, the old man leaned back and finished his beer,

then set the bottle down in the grass between his legs.

"Sounds like an old wives' tale, or folklore to me," Josh said, skeptical. "Pretty convenient none of the miners were ever found. Anyone could make up any story they wanted, with no proof needed."

The rest of the group tentatively agreed, nodding and shrugging around the fire, considering Josh's point at least a possibility.

"Could be," Ed agreed, standing. "But my ol' man was friends with many of those miners, and that's what he says happened. He told me about it countless times when I was a kid, which I thought at the time was because it was an exciting and scary story—but later realized he was probably just trying to scare me, to dissuade me from going out looking for that mine."

"Did you?" Dan asked. "Look for the mine?"

Everyone looked from Dan to Ed, waiting.

Ed just smiled, but didn't answer the question.

"Well, I suppose I should get down to that generator, see what's up."

With that he turned to leave as the group all looked around at each other in disbelief, but then he stopped short after just a few steps and looked over his shoulder.

"And about that last hippie couple…they didn't just *vanish*, as the brochure states…there was blood. *Human* blood. *Lots* of it. But their bodies were ever found. So it's true that nobody knows what happened to them…but maybe not quite true that they simply *vanished*."

This solicited a slew of remarks around the campfire:

blood?
no way
what happened to them?
creepy

With that, Ed turned and walked away into the darkness, leaving the group to once again glance around at each other in wide-eyed awe.

"Sounds like this camp is bad luck," Dan muttered.

"No shit," Mindy concurred.

"Sorry guys, Josh apologized. "I had no idea when I booked the place. Like he said, the sales brochure never mentions any of that."

"I can't imagine why not," Brad said, smirking, and the others looked at him. "I mean, it would probably be great for business: a spooky campground haunted by the ghosts of dozens of long-lost miners buried alive in a 1930s cave-in… and that's not all! You also get a creepy, bloody double-murder and mysterious disappearance to boot!"

They chuckled nervously at the sarcastic remark before silence descended on the group and they returned to quietly sipping their beers and staring into the fire, thinking about all the old man had told them.

Finally, Stacie couldn't hold off any longer. Her bladder was about to bust.

"Guys, I gotta use the restroom," she announced, standing and stretching. Then she turned to look across the dark campgrounds, trying to spot the tiny structure.

Noticing how she was peering into the darkness, Brad asked: "You know where it is, right? Back behind the last two cabins." With that, he turned and pointed in the general direction behind the cabins.

"I think I see it," she said, nodding.

As she crossed her arms and walked briskly away, Brad turned back to the group.

"I'm next," Roe said.

Then there was a smattering of others around the fire calling out their successive turns to use the latrine next, after Stacie returned.

•

It was really dark in there. Pitch black. No electricity, no moonlight, no nothing. Deciding to chance it, she reached over next to the door and flicked the light switch on, hoping—but as she suspected, nothing.

Damn generator…

So, eyes opened wide, Stacie felt her way inside, sliding along the wall, groping in the darkness, maneuvering around the sink, then stepping across to about where she though she remembered the stall being. She missed the door by a foot or so, bumping into the outside corner of the stall, then side-stepped to the door and felt her way inside. She felt silly closing the stall door and sliding the latch in the total darkness, but…why not? Better safe than sorry.

Groping, she finally found the seat; but it was ice-cold, making her hesitate.

Just get it over with, she thought.

Turning and dropping her jeans and panties in one quick movement, she sat, grimacing in the darkness...it was like sitting on ice. But that seemed to help things along, and she quickly emptied her bladder.

It was while she was pulling her jeans up in the darkness that the distant screaming started. Not knowing what what going on—were her friends playing a joke on her? Probably— but the horrific sound prompted her to quickly button and zip her jeans, and grapple for the door latch in front of her in the darkness, sliding it roughly open with a loud *clack!*

The distant screaming continued as she exited the stall, but it seemed it was fewer voices now. Good. Some of her friends probably realized the joke wasn't really funny—in fact, is was downright *mean*—and stopped.

"Drink another one," she whispered as she left the latrine.

But when she got halfway back to the campfire, she stopped in her tracks.

The distance, and darkness, made it difficult to discern, but best she could tell, her friends were all lying on the ground, spread out a short distance from the campfire...bloody and mutilated and...

...dead?

When she screamed—an all out, horrified screech—a tall, massive, hairy beast turned quickly and looked in her direction, seemingly yellow eyes reflecting the flames.

Standing on the far side of the strewn bodies, cloaked in shadows, she'd mistaken it for one of the many trees that bordered the clearing.

Seeing it turn and look at her caused her to cut her scream short, clasping her hands tightly to her mouth, eyes wide with horror.

The beast dropped the limp, bloody corpse that it had been clutching—smaller, maybe Roe?—and began running toward her, emitting a guttural roar.

Stacie screamed again as she turned and ran back toward the latrine as fast as her legs could carry her.

Inside, she bolted into the stall, slammed the door shut, and latched it. She then covered her mouth with both hands, attempting to stifle her terrified sobs and panicked breathing.

In a matter of moments, she heard the thing slowly enter the latrine in the darkness. She held her breath and remained completely motionless. She could hear it treading slowly around inside the latrine, investigating. Had it seen her come in here? Hopefully not, and it would be on its way when it didn't find her.

Then she realized the stall walls didn't go all the way to the floor, there was a foot or so gap between the wall and the floor. As quietly as she could, she braced both hands against the stall walls on either side of the toilet, and stepped first one foot, then the other onto the toilet seat, lifting herself up above that wall opening so the creature couldn't see her feet, even as dark as it was in there, but who knows.

It began shuffling around the stall. She could smell it now, a wild, musky animal smell, and could hear its heavy breathing. Starting on one side, it walked the perimeter, turning the corner, passing the door, continuing around the other side, stopping to...*sniff the air?*...every foot or so.

She closed her eyes, praying that it would not sense her in there and would instead leave the latrine and look for her elsewhere.

But just then, the lights flickered on. Three small bulbs hanging from the ceiling, above the sink, the urinal, and the stall. And when the lights came on, she saw its feet on the other side of the wall, through the gap at the bottom. It was huge, with massive claws—more like talons, and *black* at that —and covered with course, brown hair, which was streaked and splattered with fresh, dripping blood.

No longer able to stifle her horror, she screamed.

Roaring, it began tearing at the stall wall, the thin pressboard shaking and cracking and splintering while Stacie screamed and screamed and screamed...

"...and according to the maintenance guy, one of the girl's blood was splattered all over the restroom, and the stall was torn to pieces, thinks she might've been hiding from the animal in there, but it found her. But nobody's sure, since she was never found. No sign of her or her body, even after days of searching. And no sign of whatever it was that attacked and killed the rest of them, either. So to this day, nobody knows."

With that, Hank shrugged.

Winnie let out a low whistle. "No shit. That's horrible. I can't even imagine...by the way, were the victims anyone we know? From here in town?"

"Nah, they were campers in from out of state. Nobody knew

any of them."

"So what do they *think* it was? Did the maintenance guy see anything?"

"No, he said he was working on the propane generator, trying to get it going again, and, it was kicking on and off, which was really loud inside the utility shed, and he didn't hear a thing. Once it was going strong and he was confident it was good for the night, he went back up to the camp to let them know—and found the scene. He was the one that called the police. But they never found whoever—or *whatever*—did it, and like I said never found that one girl's body either. White was never a suspect, they figured it was some kind of animal that did it. Something *big*."

"So what the hell kind of animal slaughters six people, leaves five of them behind and carries one of them off?" Winnie wondered aloud.

Hank paused for a moment, a grave look on his face.

"Maybe some kind of creature that lives in the caves under Black Woods?"

At this, Winnie just looked at him across the fire, and their eyes locked.

•

Hank was up at sunrise, fire-brewing the best coffee Winnie had ever tasted. Afterward they broke camp, packed everything up, boarded, and Hank tooled the boat toward Blackwater swamp.

Once they exited the creek proper, maneuvering between the thickening brush and overhanging trees and floating into the calm, shallow waters of the swamp, Winnie pulled out his contacts case and reinserted them, blinking a few times as they settled in, then Hank killed the engine and slid the oars out, keeping one and handing the other to Winnie.

"This is where I come in here sometimes when I'm fishing," Hank said softly. "We can row in a ways before it gets too shallow, then dock the boat and see if we can find that cave. Have any idea where it is? Did the kid tell you anything?"

"Unfortunately, he didn't say anything about the cave location down here in the swamp," Winnie lamented. "Just that there's an entrance up on the hill, a waterfall from the creek."

"Well, according to the sheriff's press conference, some kind of explosion blew Jackie through a bunch of trees, but he landed in shallow water, which probably saved his life. So that must've been right on the edge of the swamp, before it turns to dry land but not out where it's so deep he woulda drowned."

Winnie nodded. "That makes sense," he agreed.

"And since the cave must be hidden—seeing as apparently nobody's seen it or knows about it—then it must be deeper in the woods—"

—he pointed off to the west—

"—cuz I'm sure any cave close to the creek would've been discovered by now. So I say we dock on the west side of the swamp, furthest from the creek, and head into the woods from there, see what we find."

"Sounds like a plan."

•

Back at the shop, Joey was grumbling to himself as he

walked sleepily up to the front door and turned the deadbolt to unlock it, then gave the string dangling from the adjacent neon OPEN sign a yank. The old tubes blinked and flashed for a moment before brightening to a solid violet color as the sign swung gently back and forth from the tiny suspension chains.

He always thought opening the store an hour earlier was pointless. Eight o'clock was fine. Why seven? They rarely ever had any customers that early, and, aside from maybe cleaning the glass counters or straightening something on the shelves, there wasn't much to do either, at least once the pre-stocked cash drawer was pulled from the safe and installed in the register.

Just unlock the door and turn on the sign.

But the old man had insisted, and Joey had relented…after all, he *was* the boss.

One of the many benefits of being the owner…

Shaking his head in futility, Joey walked back behind the counter in silence, expecting another boring day, starting with at least an hour or two of quiet solitude, the store empty this early as usual.

Shoulda brought a book…

Shrugging his shoulders, he picked up the blue spray bottle of glass cleaner and the white polishing towel, figured he'd clean the glass counters…again.

At least it was something to do.

The counter was L-shaped, and he always started at the far end and worked his way around to the cash register, which was on the other end in front of the office door. But he had only made it halfway—just to the corner before turning toward the register—when the tiny bell jingled above the front door.

Looking up, he stopped in his tracks, mouth agape. He couldn't believe who was standing there.

After a moment of the two looking at each other across the store, the young man in the doorway smiled and walked purposely up to the counter.

He spoke in a low tone, as if fearing someone would overhear, even though the store was completely empty at this early hour. Joey responded likewise, immediately grasping the gravity of the discussion. Their covert exchange went on for a few minutes, with the only audible segment—if anyone had been there to overhear it, that is—being Joey saying, "He still has it…"

A few more quiet exchanges, and they came to some kind of agreement. Then Joey went into the office, rummaged through some drawers in the old steel desk, and reappeared holding a ring of keys, which he slid into his front pocket as he walked across to the front door, locked the door, yanked the string to turn off the OPEN sign, then proceeded across the shop to the back door, the other man falling in behind him without a word.

They exited the store into the rear gravel lot, where the man had parked his truck next to Joey's car. Joey couldn't help but admire the big Ford F250 dually for a moment before he turned to lock the back door. Then they got into their respective vehicles and left the lot out the back way, Joey heading to Hank's house, the other man following.

•

After docking the boat at the edge of the swamp, Hank and Winnie pulled on some fishing boots, and, deciding to leave most the gear in the boat for now, they each just slung a rifle.

"You know, just in case," Hank said with a wink.

Turning, they slopped through the shallow standing water into the woods and, they hoped, toward dryer land.

But suddenly Hank stopped in his tracks, Winnie nearly running into him.

"Look at that," he said, pointing down at the water.

Winnie followed his arm and saw a charred piece of lumber, broken and splintered, bobbing in the tiny waves they were making.

"And there," Hank added, pointing over by a huge, gnarled tree ahead, swamp water pooled around its roots. There, half sunk in the water, lay a piece of something that had been built with lumber. A square corner, with crooked, broken boards jutting out in two opposing directions, much of it also charred.

"The raft," Winnie said.

"Or what's left of it," Hank concurred.

"Did the sheriff mention seeing anything besides the boy? Any other details, like the raft or the cave or anything? Or about the explosion?" Winnie asked as they looked all around for more evidence.

"Only that he found something strange, an object he couldn't identify, that he sent off to a lab for analysis—and that he couldn't say any more about it until they cleared it. As careful as he was with his words, and his refusal to answer any questions about it, well...sounded like probably the Feds," Hank relayed.

"And that was all? Just the one strange object? Out of all this debris?"

"He said his priority was to get the kid out of there and to the hospital as fast as possible, so he didn't take time to search the area, just grabbed the one thing he noticed on his way out."

"Maybe it had something to do with the explosion," Winnie guessed. "Jackie went back under before he could tell me anything about that. But the sheriff didn't give any indication what he thought this mystery object might be?"

"Not a word, not even a vague clue. Just...*something*."

"Well, I imagine there's lots of *somethings* in Black Woods, and Blackwater Swamp," Winnie said.

"C'mon, that cave's gotta be around here somewhere," Hank prodded, heading further into the woods, waving Winnie along.

It turned out to be an easy find, they just followed the random pickings of charred wood and debris that had scattered in an expanding pattern from the source, which led them through the swampy woods for a few minutes, until—

"Thar she blows," Hank said softly as they rounded an ancient tree and stood before a small, shallow creek that emanated from a large, moss-covered opening in the side of the hill, and flowed south into the woods until it vanished, the closest edge swirling and bubbling as it mixed with the swamp water.

"Where do you suppose it goes?" Winnie asked, peering into the woods.

"No idea," Hank said, shrugging. "Maybe it meets back up with the main branch somewhere down south," he speculated. "Or it might be the source of one of the countless little creeks that run all through this area. Who knows."

With that, they both turned to the cave opening. From where they stood, they could only see a little way inside—but they could tell it was wall-to-wall water, like an indoor pond.

"You thinkin' what I'm thinkin'?" Winnie asked

"Let's get the boat," Hank said matter-of-factly.

With that, they turned and headed excitedly back into the swamp, their boots splashing in the shallow water.

•

It took some work, but between the two of them, they managed to mostly drag/carry/maneuver the boat through the shallow swamp and thick woods to the cave. In order to lighten the load as much as possible, they removed the clamp-on outboard motor, and opted to leave much of their supplies behind, piled onto a half-submerged boulder to keep dry, and just bring the oars and what they absolutely needed for the cave—and, of course, the hunt. Along with their slung rifles, Hank strapped on the holster, and looped the shotgun over his opposite shoulder. Then he picked his satchel up off the log— brown leather, old, worn, obviously extremely used—and held it out to Winnie.

"What's that for?" Winnie asked, taking it by the strap.

"We're going hunting, aren't we?"

"Well, yeah," he agreed.

"Well, if there's anything I've learned, it's never to go hunting—or fishing, or even just hiking—without a way to carry back anything you might find while you're out there. Y'never know, you could find something interesting or useful —even valuable—then you got no way to haul it back with you. Or at a minimum, it's a pain in the ass. Happened to me a few times over the years, so now my motto is, don't leave home without it!"

Winnie nodded skeptically. "Whatever," he said in youthful resignation, slinging the bag over his free shoulder as they stooped, lifted the boat, and began trudging back to the cave.

•

As they approached the cave entrance, they could hear distant water splashing inside somewhere.

"Sounds like a waterfall…maybe the one the kid told you about, how they got into the cave in the first place."

"Probably," Winnie agreed. Then, as they left the edge of the woods, he happened to look up and noticed a flock of sparrows sitting in the branches of a towering oak, motionless, totally silent, seemingly watching them.

He shivered at the memory—but also scolded himself for believing that stupid myth when he was a kid.

C'mon, Winston, you're not a twelve-year-old kid anymore…

Eyes back forward, they entered the cave.

On the right side of the entrance there was a raised, rocky plateau, the creek water running around it to exit the cave on the left. After setting the boat down, Hank retrieved two long flashlights from under a seat, handing one to Winnie. Then they picked their way up the incline and looked inside.

The raised area ran along the inside wall for 20 or 30 feet, running outward 10 or 15 feet.

Venturing in across the rocky plateau, they immediately spotted the distant waterfall, about a hundred yards to the northeast, plunging down through the ceiling of the dave, bright beams of sunlight streaming down around it like a heavenly scene.

Shining their lights all around, they saw nothing else but complete and utter darkness.

"This thing is huge," Hank said, amazed, shining his light all around and above. A moment later his voice echoed softly back from the distant blackness.

"You know, this might be all there is, just a big cave," he surmised. "You say that kid said the thing he saw was slimy with tentacles, like a sea-creature? Maybe it lives right here, in this hidden pond…which is almost more like a *lake*, actually."

With that he aimed his light down into the water, as if looking for the sea creature. But it was too murky, the light barely penetrated past the surface, much like the cave itself.

"Well, he *did* say there were underground tunnels…but then, he was pretty drugged up and barely conscious, so who knows. But remember the campground massacre you told me about last night? Not to mention the nurse at the hospital, who told me her cousin disappeared on her way back home when they were kids. And, of course, Tommy…those all happened on dry land, nowhere near this or any other lake. If anything, they were near the woods."

Hank looked back at him.

"Good point," he nodded. "But maybe there's actually more than one...*creature*...maybe there's a *few* different types of animals living in Black Woods or Blackwater Swamp, and we've just been attributing all of the mysterious attacks and disappearances to *one* unknown beast all this time."

That was when Winnie recalled that Jackie had mentioned that the swamp-creature had *changed* somehow...but decided to keep it to himself, at least for now.

"Maybe," was all he allowed.

"This plateau will make a perfect launch point for the boat," Hank surmised, looking around at the natural platform on which they stood.

"It's almost like an actual landing deck," Winnie agreed.

With that, they turned and headed back to the boat.

After carrying it up over the plateau then easing it into the water in the cave, they carefully stepped into the gently rocking craft. Once seated, they relieved themselves of their long guns and the satchel. Hank then retrieved the flashlight from Winnie and explained:

"Well, if there really *are* tunnels like the kid said, then they'd *have* to be deeper in."

"Makes sense," Winnie agreed.

"So I say we head straight north—"

—he pointed behind him, out across the water—

"—and hopefully, we'll be able to see something further in with these Maglights. They're the strongest lights I've got. The plan is to find someplace on the other side where we can dock the boat, then we can explore the rest of the cave on foot—along with any tunnels we happen to find."

Picking up an oar, Winnie nodded.

"Sounds like a plan."

With that, Hank turned around, positioned the flashlights at the front of the boat, shining forward like headlights, then looked at his Casio G-Shock LCD outdoor sports watch.

"Eight thirty-five," he said aloud, looking back at Winnie. "If we track the time, we can approximate distance."

Winnie nodded again.

Then Hank retrieved the other oar and they started rowing, the boat quietly drifting into the darkness of the cave.

•

Before long the far wall of the cave drifted into the flashlight beams, and soon they arrived there—and to their amazement, a rock ledge protruded just above the water line, running along the back of the cave to an opening in the stone wall, about 7 or 8 feet in diameter: a tunnel!

Hank tied the boat, looping the rope several times around a large rock. Retrieving their guns and the bag, they stepped up onto the ledge. It was just wide enough for them to traverse to the tunnel in single file..

They stood at the tunnel opening, pointing their lights inside. But like the cave itself, the lights vanished into the darkness, they couldn't see far enough to discern anything.

Hank dropped his rifle off his shoulder, holding it at the ready with one hand, the Maglight in the other. He turned and looked at Winnie, who did the same.

"Ready?" he said, eyes twinkling, excitement in his voice.

"As I'll ever be," Winnie said, not so excited.

"Okay then...let's see what we got."

With that he turned and stepped into the tunnel, Winnie following behind.

●

The tunnel walls were solid stone, damp, and the floor was sparsely strewn with rocks of various size, but was mostly solid stone as well.

They traveled straight north for quite some distance before the tunnel seemed to begin turning in random directions. At the first turn, Hank stopped, slung his rifle, dug a fat chalk stick from one of his cargo pockets, and marked a large white X on the wall.

"Good thinking," Winnie said, nodding in approval.

"I figure it's better than leaving a popcorn trail," Hank responded with a smile and a wink.

They continued on for quite some time, marking turn after turn, venturing deeper and deeper, without seeing or hearing anything unusual. Then they came to a "Y" intersection, the tunnel splitting off both to the left and the right. They stepped through and shone their lights into both tunnels, but couldn't see anything either way.

"We need to keep going north, if we can," Hank said, fishing his compass out of his pocket and clicking it open. "If we're gonna find that...*thing*...we gotta penetrate its home, which must be further in, or I think we'da probably seen somethin' by now."

"Right," Winnie agreed, nodding.

"Now, that's weird," Hank said, looking at his compass.

"What?" Winnie asked, looking down at it too.

Shining his light on it, Hank turned it this way and that, watching the needle. Then he himself turned in all directions, eyeing the compass as he did so.

"Weird," he said again, holding it out under his flashlight, for Winnie to see.

Winnie watched as the needle spun quickly around in one direction, slowed, stopped, then spun around in the opposite direction, slowing and stopping again before repeating the strange gyration.

"It just keeps spinning," Hank said. It's supposed to point to magnetic north, but it's just spinning round and round...I've never seen anything like that before."

"Like there's some kind of strange magnetic field screwing it up," Winnie reasoned.

That got Hank thinking...then he said bluntly, "Magma."

"What?" Winnie said, perplexed.

"Magma. The Yellowstone volcano is a just few hundred miles from here, right?"

"Right."

"Well, they say there's magma veins running for hundreds of miles from the Yellowstone caldera, deep underground. If that's true, then we could be above a magma vein right now, and as deep as these tunnels are, we've gotten close enough that it's affecting the magnetic field, screwing up the compass."

"I suppose," Winnie tentatively agreed. But—"

—and just then, they heard a deep rumble in the distance.

"Was that some kind of animal?" Winnie said, eyes wide.

"Coulda been. But I think it sounded like a tremor, or some kind of vibration in these tunnels."

"Tremor?!" Winnie almost shouted. "Shouldn't we get the hell outta here then, before a tremor, or even an earthquake, buries us alive!?"

"I've lived here my whole life, and never heard of an earthquake here. It coulda been anything. Hell, wind blowing through the tunnels. Or, as you say, some kind of animal. The cold rock walls shifting as the day warms up. Or maybe even the magma veins below us, if they're really there. But I don't think it's anything to worry about. So don't worry, we're not gonna get buried alive."

Winnie just sighed heavily as he pondered Hank's suggestions.

"We need to keep going. My compass is useless, but my gut says we should turn left, to keep heading the right direction."

Winnie thought for a moment, about all the turns they made since entering the tunnel, then nodded in agreement.

"I think you're right," he finally said.

"Left it is," Hank said as he chalked a big X on the floor in the middle of the intersection before they turned left and proceeded.

It was probably another half hour of twists and turns and chalking Xs before they had their first unusual find.

The were walking straight, lights pointed ahead, when

Winnie happened to sweep his light to the side and saw it, stopping him in his tracks.

"Hank, check this out."

Hank stopped, backtracked to Winnie, then shone his light together with Winnie's, illuminating a pile of bones lying at the base of the wall.

They walked over, shining their lights on it.

"Definitely human," Hank said.

"Damn," Winnie said softly.

"And based on the size, I'd say it was a man. And based on the decomposition, I'd say it's old. Like, *real* old. Probably been in here decades, if not centuries," Hank guessed.

With that, he bent down, and picked up the skull.

"What happened to you?" he asked quietly, turning it over in his hands. Then he stood and held it out to Winnie.

"No thanks," Winnie said, hands (rifle and flashlight) raised in rejection.

"Put it in the satchel," Hank directed.

"Why?"

"We can have it analyzed when we get back. Find out how old it is, where he was from, maybe even how he got here and how he died. What, are you afraid you might learn something, college boy?"

Slinging his rifle, Winnie sighed and held the satchel open, and Hank dropped it in with a thump.

Then they moved on.

Not long after that, they came to another Y split, and Hank, after confirming his compass was still haywire, dug back in his pocket and pulled out a silver dollar.

"We'll do this one the scientific way," he said, smiling.

Winnie shined his light on Hank's hand as he flipped the coin into the air, caught it, then slapped it down on the back of his other arm.

"Call it," he said, not looking up.

"Heads we go right, tails left," Winnie blurted out.

Hank lifted his hand from the coin, and Winnie's light showed tails.

"Left it is, again," he said.

After stopping to chalk an X on the floor, he proceeded into the left tunnel, Winnie following.

Again, multiple twists and turns over a period of time, when they once again came across a pile of old bones. Again Hank retrieved the skull, silently handing it to Winnie, who stashed it in the bag, this time without protest.

Moving on, they continued navigating the dark tunnel, seeing nothing.

"Seems to be getting colder," Hank observed.

"I was just about to say that myself," Winnie concurred.

It was another uneventful hour or so when they both stopped in their tracks, flashlights illuminating another "Y" split just ahead of them. And there on the floor in the middle of the intersecting tunnels: a big, white X.

"What the fuck?" Hank whispered, perplexed.

"There's no way," Winnie said, shaking his head.

Hank dug out his compass, opened it, shined his light on it, shook his head, uttered a *fuck!* under his breath, then slapped it shut and stuffed it back in his pocket.

"Still screwy?" Winnie asked.

"Yep. Worthless."

Just then, another distant rumble, only this one sounding a bit closer.

"I could *swear* I felt *that* one through my shoes," Winnie said in a warning tone of voice.

"Me too," Hank concurred. "And to think we've been walking in a big circle all this time…it's been what, a couple hours—"

—he lifted his Casio and pushed the backlight button—

"—Sonofa*bitch!*" he exclaimed, saying it like one word.

Winnie just stared at him, waiting for an explanation.

Hank looked up. "Wouldn't you say we've been in these tunnels now for a couple of hours?"

"At least an hour, maybe two, yes," Winnie nodded.

Angling his arm, Hank turned his wristwatch toward Winnie, and pointed at it with his other hand.

Winnie could see the digital numbers: 9:08.

"My watch says it's only been a little over half an hour," Hank said, incredulous.

"No way," Winnie rejected. "It's been way longer than that." Then a thought: "Dead battery?"

"No, I installed a new one a few days ago," he said. "And it always lasts for months, I've never had an issue before."

"So the weird magnetic field that's fucking up your compass is fucking up your watch too?" Winnie speculated.

"Well, the compass I can sorta understand, because it's a

mechanical device...but I've never heard of a mild magnetic field fluctuation screwing up electronics. So it's probably something else."

"Like what?" Winnie asked. "Radiation or something?"

Hank's eyes suddenly widened.

"Wow, I never thought of that," he said, wiping the sweat from his forehead with the back of his arm.

"Shit," Winnie said softly.

Shining his light around at all the various tunnel options, Hank thought for a moment, then turned to Winnie.

"Okay. We know going left just took us in a big circle. And we're feeling some kind of tremors, or hearing a very big animal growling, or something...and we're fucking around in some sort of magnetic field flux that's got our devices screwed up, so we have no idea how long it's been or how far in we've come—or in what direction, for that matter. So I'd say at this point, we need to head back to the boat, get outta this cave, then regroup and figure out what to do next."

"I second that," Winnie agreed strongly.

"So we just follow the Xs back, only take right turns this time," Hank said, as he started toward the right tunnel on the other side of the X.

But Winnie grabbed his arm, stopping him in his tracks.

"That's the wrong way," he said. Then, pointing down the other tunnel: "We need to go left."

"But we turned left coming in," Hank refuted. "So shouldn't we turn right to go back?"

Standing in the intersection, they pointed their lights in all directions, trying to determine which way was which.

"The mark is in the middle of the intersection, there's no way of telling which way we came from the first time, and with all the twists and turns since, no way of knowing up from down, right from left," Hank said.

"If we assume we traveled in a big circle like you said, then we would still turn left, like we did coming in, because we're back to facing that same direction, but now we're on the opposite side of the ex," Winnie reasoned. "On the other hand, if we were coming back the way we came—facing the opposite direction, and on the other side of the ex—then yes, we would turn right."

Hank thought about this, then slowly nodded.

"I see what you're saying…I think you're right."

And again, a loud rumble sounded behind them, echoing in all directions.

Looking ominously at each other, they turned and headed down the left tunnel, quickening their pace.

Roughly half an hour later, they approached the first "Y" intersection that they had traversed earlier, spotting the X scrawled on the floor and hurrying toward it, relief sweeping over them. They quickly turned left again, eagerly heading down the final tunnel toward the boat and their escape.

•

Something was wrong.

At least an hour had passed since taking the last turn, and still no cave, no boat. In fact, not even the *smell* of water nearby, which permeated the air inside the tunnel when they started out.

"I don't like this," Hank finally said, stopping and shining his light first ahead, then behind them.

"Seems like it's taking way too long," Winnie agreed. "We've been walking this tunnel considerably longer than it took us to walk it coming in."

"My thoughts exactly," Hank said. "And we've been going mostly straight. No turns, like coming in."

"And no Xs," Winnie whispered, frighted at the prospect.

Just to be sure, Hank pulled his compass from his pocket, checked it along with his watch with his flashlight, Winnie watching in hopeful anticipation.

"Still fucked up," Hank said, sighing while he futilely pocketed the compass.

"Well, at least it looks like we're not just going in a big circle this time," Winnie smiled painfully.

After thinking for a moment, Hank posited:

"Okay, we've come this far, mostly in a straight line. And we haven't found what we're looking for...and the rumbling seems to have stopped, which could mean we're moving away from the deepest of the tunnels."

"Okay," Winnie said cautiously.

"And I don't think we're getting any kind of radiation, or we'd probably be starting to feel sick by now." He shrugged. "I feel fine."

"Me too," Winnie concurred.

"So I say we continue for a while. Say, another half hour? If we don't see anything or reach the cave, we'll turn around and go back. It's pretty much a straight shot, we'll get back to the intersection and figure out what we did wrong, go from there."

"Sounds like a plan," Winnie nodded.

With that they pointed their flashlights into the darkness ahead, pausing for a moment, then reluctantly continued on.

About fifteen minutes later they both noticed that it seemed to be getting warmer.

"So we might be reaching the end after all," Hank said optimistically.

Then they stopped in their tracks, pointing their flashlights around, having entered some sort of internal cave or cavern.

"Well, we definitely didn't see *this* before," Hank said.

"Yeah, we *must've* turned the wrong way at that last split-off," Winnie agreed.

Though their flashlight beams mostly vanished into the darkness, they could just see the far wall in the distance, along with what appeared to be a tunnel opening, about the size of a standard doorway, with rocks and rubble strewn it.

"While we're here, might as well see where that goes," Hank suggested.

Winnie shrugged. "We've come this far, might as well check it out. Then we can head back."

They walked together across the cavern, to the hole in the wall on the other side.

Hank quickly scanned his light along the inside of the hole, and along the debris at the bottom.

"This looks dug," he said.

"Definitely not natural," Winnie concurred.

Then Hank shone his flashlight into the other side.

"Damn," he said softly.

"What is it?" Winnie asked, but Hank was already stepping through, so he followed him.

On the other side of the hole, they stood together on a narrow precipice before a massive opening in the cave floor. Shining their lights down, they could see a huge pile of rocks, dirt, massive slabs of stone, and all manner of debris maybe 20 feet below them.

"Looks like some sort of cave-in," Winnie observed.

"Used to be a mine!" Hank said excitedly.

Winnie looked up, and Hank had his light trained across the gaping hole, illuminating a tunnel on the far side that had partially collapsed, big support timbers fallen and broken, and a pair of steel tracks could just be seen jutting out from under the rocks and debris.

"Seems I vaguely remember a story about an old mining cave-in, back in the day," Hank said. "I think my ol' man's pop used to talk about it. Silver, I think."

Winnie shook his head surprisingly and shrugged. "First I've heard of it."

"I remember now…Grandpa said a bunch of the miners were killed—he actually knew some of them—and the mine was abandoned."

"Wow," Winnie whispered, again shaking his head.

Hank returned his light to the debris below, swinging it this way and that, inspecting the damage. It looked like the cave-in started on the track side, so the pile of rocks and debris and broken stone slabs was inclined from the bottom up toward the narrow ledge where the two were perched.

"I think we can climb down this incline," he said, pointing down the steep embankment of rocky rubble.

"What?" Winnie said, shocked. "Are you *nuts?*"

Hank looked back at him, with that smirk and twinkle in his eye again.

"Did you not hear me? I just said it was a *silver* mine…so who knows what we could find down there…and we have the satchel—something like this is exactly why I brought it!"

Winnie just gave him an annoyed face, and sighed.

"I thought you said you'd never heard of an earthquake here?" he said, implying the worst.

"We don't know it was caused by an earthquake," Hank refuted. Then he shrugged. "Could've been anything!"

But Winnie was shaking his head.

"Come on, we gotta go check it out!" Hank said, smiling. "We can't just leave it—then spend the rest of our lives wondering! At least *I* can't."

Then Hank just waited, his eyes gleaming.

Winnie sighed again, apparently relenting…again.

"Okay," he said. "We climb down, rummage around for a bit, see if we find anything…then we get out and head back."

"Deal!" Hank said.

"And while we're down there, if there's another one of those tremors we've been feeling, I'm out *right now.*"

"Absolutely."

With that, they unslung their guns and leaned them both

together against the cave wall.

•

After carefully picking their way down the embankment, they stood on top of the main pile of rubble, shining their flashlights around. Stone slabs, rocks and boulder, dirt, an array of dirty and broken digging tools...and disturbingly, a few miner's helmets.

As they scuttled down off the pile, Winnie called Hank's attention to a skeletal hand, barely visible in the debris, his light trained on it just long enough for Hank to acknowledge and shake his head in dismay, then they continued to the cave floor, again shining their lights around. Hank stopped his light on something over against the cave wall, and walked over to it. Winnie followed. Hanks beam of light revealed a pile of random bones, seemingly collected there.

"These look like they were *put* there, not like someone died there...you know, someone landed there, or crawled there and died after the cave-in. And it looks like the bones of more than one person."

"Definitely look collected...but by *what?*" Winnie asked. He couldn't help but recall a similar pile of bones that he and Tommy had found in the tunnel under that shack so many years ago.

And then he saw it.

Buried under the pile of bones, almost hidden from view, save a gleaming pit of metal reflecting their light beams— could it be?

Without a word, Winnie bent down, dug his hand under

the bones, and pulled out...

...a wrist-wrocket slingshot. Dusty, bent, decayed—but definitely silver, meaning definitely Tommy's.

Winnie let out a wail, hugging it to his chest.

Hank tried to console him, put his arm around him.

"I'm sorry, Winnie. Tommy was a good kid. But that's why we're here, right? Revenge for Tommy—and all the others? I know there's no easy way to deal with this, but we need to stay focused on the mission. For Tommy."

Sobbing, Winnie shook his head in agreement.

"Goodbye, Tommy," he mumbled, tossing the wrist-wrocket back onto the pile. "I'm sorry I didn't stop you. I've never forgiven myself for letting you down."

"Let's go," Hank whispered. He then began scouring the area with his flashlight, and stopped with his beam aimed to their left—into darkness, as far as he could see. Sniffing, Winnie joined Hank's beam with his own, to no avail.

And that's when they realized that they were not merely in another cavern, but actually in another *tunnel*, that stretched off into the darkness ahead. Behind them, the tunnel was completely sealed off by the avalanche from above, giving it the initial impression of a cave.

"Well I'll be damned," Hank said, shining his light into the distance, revealing nothing but blackness. "They were digging right above an existing tunnel, and didn't even know it—until the top tunnel collapsed into this lower one. And I wonder where this one goes?" With that he turned back to Winnie, grinning.

"Don't even think about it," Winnie warned, wiping away the last of his tears.

"Come on, we said we'd go a half hour before turning around to go back, but it was only like 15 minutes before we found that cavern, and then this cave-in. So the way I see it, you owe me at *least* 15 more minutes, right?"

"You sure have a strange way of seeing things," Winnie said, smiling slightly now, to his own chagrin.

"Yeah, old age does that to ya," Hank said with a wink.

"So what about your little silver hunt?" Winnie prodded.

Hank shined his light around the pile of rubble, the debris scattered everywhere, the half-buried tools, the bones, then shook his head and shrugged his shoulders.

"I don't see any sign of any silver—or *anything* of any value, for that matter—so I think we're done here," he said. "So we might as well continue on, see what's in that tunnel."

"If you say so," Winnie responded.

"That's my boy," Hank said, elated.

They both again trained their lights into the darkness of the tunnel, but could see nothing.

"Well, there's no way of telling time down here," Winnie said, "but let's say we go down this last tunnel for about 15 minutes, give or take, and if we don't find anything, we turn around and go back the way we came."

"You got it," Hank said.

With that they ventured into the darkness.

•

It was impossible to tell how long they'd been walking,

examining the new tunnel with their flashlights and finding essentially nothing, but Winnie was beginning to suspect it had been longer than 15 minutes, when Hank mentioned it was feeling warmer, and Winnie agreed—and right then they came upon yet another pile of rubble, completely blocking the tunnel ahead.

They could go no further.

Winnie had to hide his relief.

While they shined their lights up and down the pile, Hank began sniffing the air.

"Smell that? It smells odd, but vaguely familiar…can't quite place it though."

Winnie raised his nose in the air and sniffed around.

"Sulfur?"

Then Hank's light rested on something on the ground, and he walked over and snatched it up, then held it up for Winnie to see. Looked like a small metal canister of some kind, about the size of a thick hockey puck, with a large, barely legible "No. 8" printed on the worn label.

"Number eight blasting caps," Hank said, tossing it to the ground. "We used those in the Army, for detonation. So you were close when you said sulphur—but it's gunpowder. *Spent* powder. Dynamite. I thought I recognized it, but it's been a long time. I almost forgot that smell."

With that, they trained their lights back up toward the top of the heap.

"So you're saying someone blasted something above, causing this cave-in?"

"Looks like it. And by the lingering odor, I'd say it was recent. Probably within the last year or two."

Then Hank again began sniffing the air.

"It's not just warmer here," he said. "It also smells like *fresh* air, like from outside. I bet there's a cave or tunnel entrance somewhere up there."

"Which somebody must have blasted, and caved it in...but who...and why?"

Hank shrugged. "Maybe it was the mine entrance? That old abandoned silver mine? But that was decades ago, doesn't explain something this recent."

"Weird," Winnie said.

Then Hank released a heavy sigh.

"Well, looks like the tour's over, boys and girls."

"Hallelujah," Winnie said under his breath.

And as if on cue, another rumble emanated from within the mountain somewhere, tiny bits of dust and scale raining down around them.

"That's our cue," Winnie said nervously. "Time to go!"

"I'm with you," Hank agreed, and they turned and hurried back down the tunnel.

•

After scrabbling back up the rubble pile, retrieving their guns, and slipping through the narrow stone "doorway" back into the cavern, Hank happened to notice some more bones off to the right, against the wall. He hurried over, aiming his light down on them.

"Another skeleton," he said as Winnie approached.

"Smaller, maybe female."

He picked up the skull and handed it over to Winnie.

"One more for the road," he said with a grin.

Winnie dropped it into the satchel, zipped it shut, shouldered it, and they turned toward the far tunnel to leave the cavern.

But again, the entire cavern rumbled and shook, this time nearly knocking them to the ground, with dust, pebbles, and even sizable rocks tumbling down around them.

Once it finished, they quickly darted into the tunnel to finally exit the mountain.

•

Eventually they reached the big chalk X on the floor at the last 3-way split, and figured out that they had made the wrong turn there, which took them to the cavern and collapsed mining tunnel.

This time, they made sure to take the right tunnel, heading back to the original cave where they had started.

Now they felt relieved, recognizing the twists and turns with all of the chalk Xs Hank had left. And before long, they spotted the original entrance from the cave where they had started, up ahead after the last turn, along with the hiss of the distant waterfall beyond.

"I can't believe we've been in here this long, and gone through all those tunnels—two different levels, even—and never saw any sign of a beast, or creature, or even a large animal, whatever we thought we'd find," Winnie lamented.

"Well, I would say that pile of random bones was definitely

evidence of something living in here," Hank corrected. "For one thing, I highly doubt that Tommy carried his slingshot all the way in there on his own. Plus, there's the individual skeletons…we don't know if they merely died, or something killed them."

With that they stepped through the cave opening and turned onto the narrow precipice toward the boat.

"Yeah, but you'd think—

—but Winnie was cut off when two huge tentacles swiped him off the ledge, the rifle and satchel arching up and over him, following him into the water, his scream cut off as he went under.

His flashlight clattered to the stone ledge, spun a bit, then came to a stop with the beam shining on the beast, which had apparently just climbed onto the ledge from the water when Hank and Winnie turned the corner from the tunnel and ran right into it.

The beast then turned toward Hank. Between his own flashlight and Winnie's shining from below, he could see it was huge, wet, and slimy, greenish-gray with almost glowing yellow eyes and countless massive tentacles. And oddly, the end of one of its tentacles was missing, torn off maybe a third of the way down its length, and oozing a thick black fluid, streaks running down toward it's massive body.

As Hank tried to yank the shotgun from his shoulder with his free hand, the creature again lashed out, knocking him violently down, the shotgun clattering across the rock ledge and disappearing into the water.

Now on his back with his M16 pinned beneath him, he began wrestling with the pistol, trying desperately to free it from the holster around his waist, keeping his light trained on the creature as it approached him. But it was already too close! So to buy more time, he crab-walked quickly backward into the tunnel.

Finally, the pistol came free, and he pointed it and the flashlight up at the tunnel opening, waiting for the beast to appear from around the corner.

And it did, a moment later—but what Hank now saw stunned him so badly that he didn't fire his gun right away, trying to understand what he was seeing:

Instead of a big, slimy, tentacled sea creature, what stepped into the tunnel before him was a tall, brown, hairy beast, like a cross between an ape and a human, and close to seven foot tall, with fierce yellow eyes. Long, sharp, black claws extended from both its hands and feet—with one toe missing, like it had been torn from his foot, the end of his foot tattered and soaked in black...blood?—

—in that instant, Hank's memory flashed back to the animal that had stalked him so many years ago when he was fishing in Blackwater Swamp: the one glimpse he'd gotten was of a large, brown-haired beast, which he guessed could be a bear, but he never really saw it...could it be?—

—and it started toward him and he began to squeeze the trigger and—

—Pow! Pow!...Pow! Pow!...Pow Pow!—

—gunshots rang out in quick succession from the cave somewhere behind the monster.

The creature began shrieking—a sound unlike anything Hank had ever heard, in a lifetime of hunting—and turned back toward the cave, exposing multiple bullet wounds in its back oozing thick black fluid.

Then it was gone, and Hank heard more shots and men hollering, all echoing within the cave, and he quickly regained his feet and ran out of the tunnel to see what was going on.

Two men sat in a small rowboat a few yards from the stone ledge, firing rifles one after the other at the beast, which continued shrieking and jerking backward with each bullet strike. On the front of the boat, a big portable floodlight was directed forward, bathing the entire cave wall, stone ledge, and tunnel opening in a bright bluish-white light.

Just as Hank raised his pistol to the creature's head, essentially point blank now, the creature screamed and rushed past him, spinning him into the wall just as he pulled the trigger, the report deafening and echoing in the cave. Before he could aim and fire again, the beast dove into the dark water with a massive splash.

Thinking quickly, Hank snatched up Winnie's flashlight and pointed it down into the water with one hand, aiming his pistol with the other. Nothing for a moment, then he saw movement as the thing swam away under the surface—but even through the murky water, he could see that it was not the tall, brown-haired beast, but the gray tentacled creature that had initially attacked them. For a moment he just stared at it, once again perplexed, but then quickly snapped out of it and pulled the trigger.

He fired a few times, but it was already too far away and too deep, and, realizing it was pointless, he stopped just as the dim figure vanished into the depths.

As Winnie hauled himself into their tied boat, the other boat approached, and Hank couldn't believe his eyes.

Joey, and a second young man he didn't recognize, with rifles, sitting in the old rowboat the he had scavenged from under that half-sunk abandoned dock on Hope Creek so many years ago!

As they rowed toward the ledge, Joey reached out and plucked the satchel from the surface of the water, where it was bobbing and weaving, but hadn't yet sunk. Then he looked up at Hank.

"What the hell *was* that?" he shouted across the water.

"I have no idea. But there seemed to be two different creatures—a tentacled sea creature of some kind, and a big, hairy beast…almost like a Bigfoot."

Then Hank looked over at Winnie. "You okay?"

Winnie was looking at his arm, which now sported two huge red welts, like wide whip marks. And, they looked to be bruising around the edges.

"Other than my arm hurting like hell, I think I'm okay," he said, rubbing his shoulder.

Then Hank looked back at Joey, amazement on his face.

"And what the hell are *you* doing here? And how did you even *find* us?"

With that, Winnie looked up, and his eyes widened in disbelief. "Will?" he hollered in recognition. He hadn't seen Tommy's older brother in nearly ten years, ever since he ran off after his father died, shortly after Tommy had disappeared.

"Will?" Hank said in disbelief, now recognizing the young man in the boat with his son.

"He showed up at the store first thing this morning, and believe it or not, he had the same plan you two had…to hunt down the beast."

"I saw the news report about the kids this weekend…and it's been a burden on me all these years, ever since Tommy… you know…went missing. So I finally decided to come back and end this thing once and for all. Stopped into the shop for a hunting rifle and some supplies, and ran into Joey."

"When he told me his plan, I offered to join him, and maybe we could meet up with you and make it a party. So we went to your place and got the extra boat and some hunting rifles—and by the way, you should probably lock your gun safe when you leave the house—and fortunately, you left a pretty obvious trail. I new you were coming to the swamp, I knew where you usually fished there, so we tried that spot first, and sure enough, found your gear, but no boat—so it was pretty easy to figure out you took the boat to the cave, once we found it by following the debris from the explosion—probably like you did, too—and discovered this damn near lake inside."

Now the rowboat had reached the ledge next to Hank's boat, and Joey reached out, handing the sopping wet satchel over to Winnie.

"What's in that?" he asked.

"Don't ask," Winnie replied.

"Souvenirs!" Hank shouted with a grin.

"I'd like to strongly suggest we get the fuck outta here before that...*thing*...comes back," Winnie said sarcastically. "I mean, how many times did you guys shoot it, and it didn't go down? Who knows if we can even kill it with just these rifles. So howzabout we load up the boats and skedaddle, while we still can?"

"Absolutely," Hank agreed. He holstered his pistol, trotted over to pick up Winnie's flashlight, then back over to the boat, where he untied it before stepping in, discarding his flashlight and handing the other to Winnie, while Joey and Will began paddling, turning their boat around.

They paddled quickly across the pond/lake to the stone plateau near the cave entrance, hearing and seeing nothing of the beast(s) along the way.

Once at the plateau, they all stepped out of the boats, and were just about to begin pulling them up onto the rocks to carry them out of the cave, when a distant rumbling started from deep within the cave, likely from the tunnels.

"There's that rumbling again," Winnie said. "I'm sure glad we're outta there."

Except the rumbling didn't stop; instead it intensified, and seemed to be approaching across the cave, causing the smooth water to begin sloshing.

"It's a big one!" Hank hollered. "Everyone head for the woods, we can come back for the gear when it's safe!"

But as soon as they began running—Winnie and Hank leading the way, followed by Will, then Joey—the tremor advanced to a full-blown earthquake, shaking the ground with such force they all began to weave, stumble, and fall as they tried to make it to the cave entrance. First dust, pebbles, and rocks started falling from the cave ceiling above, but they quickly turned to big rocks, boulders, and slabs of stone crashing down all around them.

The entire cave was collapsing!

Winnie made it out, then turned his light back around, watching Hank approaching—but then Joey fell down behind Will, rolling around, trying to regain his feet but he just kept stumbling and falling.

Hank turned back and saw his son flailing.

"Joey!" he called, racing back into the collapsing cave.

Will emerged from the cave just as Hank passed him going back in, swerving with the quake and dodging the falling rocks. Upon reaching Joey, he looped his arms under his son's armpits and yanked him to his feet, then held his shoulders as he guided/pushed him toward the cave entrance, with Winnie and Will gesturing wildly and hollering their encouragement.

About halfway to the entrance, Hank gave Joey a final shove, causing him to stumble the rest of the way out, barely dodging the falling rubble. Then Hank turned and staggered, lurching and weaving on the shaking ground, back to the boats, which were rocking with the waves.

"What the hell are you *doing?*" Winnie yelled. "Get the fuck outta there!"

Joey made it out and turned to stand with the others, watching Hank in amazement.

"Dad!" he cried.

But just as Hank turned back toward them, the loaded satchel in hand, the entrance to the cave began to crack, crumble, and collapse from the quake.

"Come on!" Joey screamed, waving his arm in "let's go" motion, while the other two simply watched in horror.

The entrance began coming down in sheets, forcing them all to retreat further into the swamp, barely escaping the falling rock.

From there they watched as Hank approached the entrance —now barely visible through the avalanche—but was struck by a large falling rock, hitting his shoulder and knocking him to the ground. He rolled and writhed for a moment, then tried to regain his feet, but the ground was shaking too violently, he just kept falling back down.

"Dad!" Joey screamed again. *"Dad!"*

Looking up from where he lay, he grabbed the shoulder strap of the satchel, and with one mighty heave, flung it across the plateau and through the cave entrance. It landed in the swamp with a splash, between where the others stood and the collapsing entrance, having miraculously avoided the hail of falling rocks and debris.

Then the entrance collapsed completely, again forcing the others back even further, where they watched as the entire hillside came crashing down, sealing the entire mouth of the cave from view.

"Nooooooo!!!" Joey screamed, then started running back toward the cave, but Will and Winnie grabbed him, holding him back.

"Let me go!" he yelled. "He's still in there!"

"He's gone!" Winnie yelled on one side.

"You can't help him! There's nothing you can do!" Will yelled from his other side.

As Joey collapsed to his knees in the shallow swamp water, the quake began to subside.

Within a minute, all was calm again.

And, standing below that towering oak tree at the edge of the woods, Winnie looked up and couldn't help noticing: the sparrows were gone.

— Interlude —

He awoke to darkness, with no idea how long he was out.

He was racked all over with pain, especially where that big rock had landed on his shoulder and knocked him down.

He sensed nothing—other than a gentle rumbling, which he seemed to feel more than hear—but then it was gone.

Laying alone among the rocks, he felt utterly exhausted, not sure he could move, much less stand up.

Everything hurt.

He felt like he was dying.

But he knew if he was going to make it out of there alive, he had to get up.

The thought seemed impossible.

But then he barely heard it: a distant splashing sound.

The waterfall.

He could see nothing in the darkness, but he could hear that waterfall.

Just walk toward the waterfall…

He struggled to sit up, grunting so loudly that he almost screamed, intense pain shooting all over his body.

He sat still for a moment, panting and waiting for the pain to subside, or at least become bearable.

Finally, wincing and gritting his teeth, he forced himself slowly to his feet…

…and staggered toward the wonderful sound of that distant waterfall…

Epilogue

The next couple of days were chaotic, Winnie living in a veritable whirlwind: police interrogations, filling out seemingly endless forms and reports, dodging obnoxious and annoying reporters everywhere he went.

He also had to turn over the satchel, which was quickly ushered into a back room somewhere and he hadn't seen it since, or even heard what became of it. He asked, but was stonewalled.

"Don't you worry about that, son. Just be glad you're still alive. Your little tote bag is in good hands. We'll get it back to you once everything is processed."

"Processed", he thought skeptically, wondering what they *really* meant...

As soon as he could, he checked out of *The Cobblestone Inn*, and was now staying at his mother's house. As soon as she heard he was in town, she'd insisted, and he'd relented. In the beginning he hadn't wanted her to worry, but now she was worrying anyway—and besides, her nondescript shack in The Flats would probably offer him a little more privacy than a tiny motel smack in the middle of town.

And it appeared to work. By Thursday, things seemed to be calming down, and he had booked a flight back to school the following Saturday.

He was sitting in a recliner in the living room, going over all the horrific events in his mind while trying to outrun the black dogs of depression, when the phone rang.

His mother answered it in the kitchen.

He couldn't make out her distant conversation, but she ended with "Yes, he's right here," and she appeared in the kitchen doorway to tell him the phone was for him.

"Jenny?" he assumed, hauling himself with some effort out of the big chair and walking tiredly to the kitchen. "I already gave her my flight information, that I'll be there tomorrow."

"No, it's someone named Joey," she said.

As he approached, she picked the receiver up from the kitchen counter and handed it to him.

"Hello?"

"Winnie? Hey, it's Joey Stevens."

"Hey Joey. Listen, I'm really sorry about your dad."

"Well, you don't have to be," Joey said. "That's why I'm calling. Dad's alive! I just saw him at the hospital!"

Winnie couldn't didn't believe his own ears.

"Hank's alive?! That's great! But how…I mean…*how?*"

"I don't have the details yet, but he wanted me to call you

and Will and let you both know. All I know so far is he said he got out through the mine entrance—wherever *that* is—but that was as he was leaving in a hurry and that he'd fill me in later."

"Leaving?" Winnie asked, confused. "Leaving where? You mean the hospital?"

"Yeah, he was pretty banged up, but nothing too serious. Bruises, some stitches, they checked him over yesterday, kept him overnight just to be safe, then released him this morning. I went to pick him up, but by the time I got there he had other plans, and took off."

"Took off," Winnie said, incredulous.

"Well, turns out there's this reporter guy from the *Times* in town, he showed up at the hospital wanting to interview the kid...Jason?"

"Jackie," Winnie corrected.

"Jackie, that's right. But they wouldn't let him, said it was family only. So he started asking around the lobby if anyone could recommend a guide to take them to the cave site, and just so happens Hank came through on his way out and overheard him. So they took off pretty quick to head back to the cave, Hank just hollered back at me to call you guys and let you know he's okay, and he would fill us all in when he gets back."

"No shit," Winnie said. "He's going right back out there. Is he trying to get himself killed?"

"More like trying to get that beast killed, I think. But you know Dad, always up for an adventure."

"You can say that again. He's been that way ever since I've known him, since I was a little kid."

"Yep. Me too," Joey concurred.

"Well, unfortunately," Winnie conveyed, "I'm flying back to school on Saturday. Flight's already booked, 316 at eight in the morning."

"Hmmm...." Joey said, thinking. "Tell you what, if he gets back before then, I'll have him contact you, fill you in."

"I'd appreciate that," Winnie said.

"Sure thing. Besides you deserving to know Dad's alive, I also wanted to thank you."

"Thank *me*? For what?"

"When Dad called me from the hospital, we talked some. He told me about the little heart-to-heart you gave him when you were camping outside Blackwater that night, and how he really wants to try to work things out between us. And for that I thank you."

"Well, I didn't do much, it was all Hank. And besides, it takes two to tango, so unless you're willing to work things out too, I'm not sure how much good my little pep talk was."

"That's the other thing," Joey said. "He saved my life—as shitty as I've treated him all these years, even blaming him for what Mom did—that sonofabitch saved my life anyway. He would've made it outta that cave free and clear, but he came back for me...was willing to sacrifice his own life to save mine. And for that, I'm willing to give it a go, see if we can patch things up. I can see now that I've been wrong about him all these years."

After they said their goodbyes and Winnie hung up the phone, he turned and smiled at his mother, feeling better at that moment than he had in a long, long time.

•

Sitting at the airport, Winnie couldn't stop looking at his watch every five minutes.

It was still an hour before his flight, and he was so eager to get back to see Jenny, he couldn't sit still.

And he needed to pee.

When he emerged from the restroom, Hank and another man were standing in the seating area, looking around.

"Hank!" Winnie greeted, walking eagerly back.

Hank turned and smiled at him as he approached, and they shook hands.

Winnie was taken aback how beat up he looked.

"No offense, but you look like you must've pissed off Mohammed Ali. Damn...you sure you're okay?"

The other man laughed.

"Son, I don't think I could've put it any better," Hank said. "I *feel* like I pissed off Mohammed Ali! But don't worry, it's all just flesh wounds, nothing broken or damaged beyond repair—"

—then his famous smile and wink—

"—luckily, the biggest rock landed on my thick skull—

—he rapped solidly on the top of his head—

"—which of course didn't hurt me...but you shoulda seen that rock shatter!"

They all chuckled at that.

Then Hank turned to the man next to him.

"Walt, this is Winston Milhouse, or Winnie."

"Winnie, meet Walt, a journalist with the *Times.*"

They shook hands.

"I believe I've heard of you," Winnie said.

"Probably. Over the years I've been with all the big ones, at one time or another."

Then Winnie looked at Hank.

"So, Joey must've relayed my flight info to you. He said if you got back in time he'd have you contact me, fill me in on everything. Of course, I expected a phone call—but this is way better!"

"What we have to tell you, a phone call won't do," Hank said. "Let's have a seat."

They all sat down, Winnie moving his carry-on off one chair and beside his own, then looking eagerly back and forth between the two.

"Okay, before you start, I need to know: how the *hell* did you get out of that cave alive?" Winnie asked, incredulous.

"Damn near didn't make it, my man. Got pretty banged up, as you can see, but I survived the cave-in. Barely. One big rock knocked me down and out for a bit. And when I came to—no idea how long I was out—I couldn't see shit, it was so dark in the cave—but I could hear that waterfall in the distance, and knew if I walked toward that, I'd find the boats. And sure enough, they were right where we'd left them. And fortunately, my flashlight was in one of them, so I paddled it across the cave, hobbled through all those tunnels, and eventually made my way to that mine cave-in. Remember the tools we saw? I went down there to grab a pickaxe and shovel, and while I was at it I found a busted-up wood box of dynamite sticks. They were mostly smashed and torn and useless, but I found ONE in the very bottom that seemed to still be intact. So I took that and the tools to the mine entrance in the back—you know, the one that'd been dynamited?—and we were right, that *was* fresh air we were smelling in there. As banged up as I was, I managed to climb up on the rubble pile, and found a crevice at the top just big enough to slide that stick of dynamite in. I fashioned a makeshift fuse using a match stick, lit it, shoved it as far as I could into that hole, then hurried down the pile and across the cave as far as I could get. But turns out, the dynamite wasn't in very good shape—might've gotten wet, or was just old, or maybe the matchstick fuse didn't work so well, who knows—so the blast wasn't very strong. But it did the trick, dislodged the biggest rocks and debris from the top of pile, and I was able dig the rest of the way through the entrance from there. Had to move some pretty heavy shit, and it took me all night, but I finally managed to get out."

"That's awesome!" Winnie exclaimed. "I'm so glad you made it out alive!"

"Me too," Hank said with that devilish grin.

"So, you're not gonna believe what happened next," Hank teased.

Winnie just waited in eager anticipation.

"Middle of the night, I finally got through that caved-in mine entrance, then started weaving my way blindly through the woods—not only in the dark, but I had no idea where I was, either. But just sheer dumb luck, I stumbled out into a clearing…Silver Hills Campgrounds, to be exact!"

"No way!" Winnie exclaimed. "How lucky can you get?"

"And that's not all: the camp was vacant, except for the maintenance guy…"

"Don't even tell me it was Ed White," Winnie said, shaking his head in disbelief.

"That it was," Hank said matter-of-factly. "Ol man White gave me a lift to the hospital in his truck—a long drive, it was damn near daybreak when we got there—so we had a nice little conversation along the way."

"I can't wait to hear *this*," Winnie said.

"So he told me about the silver mine collapse. Said it happened in the spring of 1939—and that summer was the first attack, or disappearance, to be reported in this area. A young girl, by the name of—"

"Charlotte...Wilson, I'm guessing?" Winnie finished.

"That's right," Hank said, surprised. You already knew?"

"Charlie was Wilson's daughter—you know, the old ice cream truck driver?—"

"The one they found hanging from Old Rope years ago? Got it in his head to cut it down, and got himself killed in the process? Yeah, I knew him, but I didn't know Charlotte was his daughter."

"Yeah, he told me and Tommy about her disappearance one day when we were buying ice cream from him…and ironically, that same day, Tommy disappeared. And both incidents happened near Black Woods, across the creek on the other side of Old Rope…probably why he decided to cut it down."

"Makes sense," Hank said, nodding. Then he continued:

"Okay, so she disappeared in 1939. If we jump forward in 9-year increments as per your super moon theory, that brings us up to last year, 1984, the attack at Silver Hills Campground, five dead and one girl missing."

"Yes, with Ed White as an eye-witness."

"Yep. So, guess what else happened in 1984, shortly after the campground attack?"

Winnie just shrugged and shook his head.

"Many people suspected that an animal of some kind—like maybe a bear, or a mountain lion, or something like that—might've come from the abandoned mine...after all, the entrance is back in the woods a ways from the campground, but close enough to fit the theory—and now I know first-hand how close it is—but besides that, that also wasn't the first such incident; turns out that in 1966, a squatter couple that was living in the old mining camp vanished, and reports were there was blood everywhere, but no bodies."

"The hippies," Winnie added, suddenly remembering.

"You already know about them?" Hank asked.

"Wilson also told me and Tommy bout a couple that vanished in the sixties, camping up in the hills. I'd totally forgotten about that."

"Yes, many people referred to them as hippies, and they were apparently attacked or killed and subsequently vanished from that camp back in 1966, making last year's massacre actually the *second* attack in that same area, with the common denominator being that old mine entrance hidden in the adjacent woods. So the morning after that second attack, they dynamited the mine entrance closed. Problem solved."

"So that's why we smelled gunpowder when we found the rubble in the tunnel, and like you said, it was probably recent—in fact, it was just last year," Winnie said.

"Exactly," Hank confirmed.

"Then another nine years later—1975—Tommy," Winnie lamented.

"Unfortunately, yes," Hank said sadly.

Then Winnies eye's widened. "Wait a sec—Olivia, the nurse at the hospital, told me her cousin Trish vanished the summer of 1957...so 18 years after Charlotte, and 9 years before that couple at Silver Hills Campground, which was also 9 years before Tommy...so the 9-year lunar cycle theory still works, we just don't know anything about 1948," Winnie surmised.

"That's right," Hank agreed.

Then Winnie had a thought, a distant memory, and said softly, "Nicky", nodding his head.

It fit.

"What was that? Hank asked.

"Wilson also told us about a kid named Nicky—I don't remember his last name—that vanished back in the forties. Went across Old Rope to the Black Woods side, and that's the last his friend—or anyone, for that matter—ever saw of him. Wilson had a theory—which I admit sounded crazy at the time —that all those mysterious disappearances seemed to be happening about once every decade."

"Well, your super moon theory is every nine years, right? So he was close. I mean, once every nine years sure would seem like once every decade."

Winnie nodded in agreement, then frowned.

"But still...*this* year's attack doesn't fit," Winnie reiterated.

"Well, I have a theory about that," Hank posited. "Think about it...when we found the dynamited mine entrance, we were in the *lower* tunnel, which we'd climbed down to from the collapsed mine tunnel *above*. But when they dynamited the cave entrance, it collapsed into the tunnel below, just like the first cave-in did back in '39. "

"Okay...." Winnie said, not really following.

"Well, let's say the creature, or creatures, were living in the lower tunnels, maybe even for eons. The mining company was digging above, having no idea they were right above an existing tunnel. And they unexpectedly broke through the wall into that cavern we found, which eventually leads out to the main cave. But when the mine collapsed—into the tunnels below—that opened the cave—and the mine tunnel itself—to the creatures, allowing them to exit the tunnel system into Blackwater to the south, and Silver Hills to the north. So that summer, they took their first victim form the Silver Hills side: Charlotte."

"So how does that explain this year's attack?" Winnie asked, shrugging.

"Well, here's what I speculate: what if the next morning right after the attack, the beast was still in the cave system somewhere, maybe took the missing girl in there, when they TNT'd the mine entrance, collapsing the upper mine tunnel into the lower creature tunnel...thereby trapping the beast in the upper cave system? So now it's stuck there, in that cave, and can't get back to it's home tunnel system…and this past weekend those kids just happened to ride their raft down that waterfall in there and land right on top of it?"

Winnie thought about that for a moment, but was skeptical.

"I suppose that could be…sound's like a stretch, though."

"Well, while you chew on that theory for a while, there's more you should know," Hank said.

Winnie looked at his watch: half hour to go.

"Looks like my time's getting short, so shoot," he said.

"Okay, so after I got poked, prodded, and stitched up at the hospital, next morning I called Joey to come pick me up, and went to the lobby to wait. That's when I met Walt. He was in town to investigate the mysterious explosion, and was asking around for someone to take him—like a guide of sorts—to Blackwater Swamp and the cave site.

"I heard about the explosion and the missing kids on the wire Sunday," Walt explained, "And was already making arrangements to fly out here to investigate, when news of the cave-in and Hank's apparent demise followed, then I definitely wanted to get here as soon as possible. So first, I tried to visit Jackie in the hospital, get his story, but they wouldn't let me in, saying family visitation only, and they even asked Derek to leave the building—"

—with this, Winnie frowned in confusion, and looked to Hank for clarification—

"—His cameraman," Hank said—

—and Winnie nodded and turned back to Walt—

"So I started asking around in the lobby for someone who could take me to the cave site, and what do ya know, the supposedly dead Hank Stevens was right there, in the flesh! I couldn't believe it!"

"And of course I was itchin' to get back out there, so I offered to take them," Hank continued. "I'm pretty banged up, but I'm definitely not done with our business out there."

"All Joey told me was that you were okay, and you and "a reporter from the *Times*" were going back out to the cave."

"That's right…we rented a boat and went back to the same place in Blackwater where you and I started the first time," Hank said. "Since it was smooth sailing all the way from the Marina, we arrived mid-day on Thursday."

"But we couldn't get in," Walt said.

"That's right," Hank concurred. "The entire area was taped off and blockaded, with guards posted, like coast guard or Feds or something in law enforcement or military-looking boats, blocking anyone from entering Blackwater."

"Really?" Winnie asked, eyes wide.

"In fact, two of the guards boarded our boat, confiscated all of Derek's film, warned us in no uncertain terms not to take any more photos or videos, then advised us to just turn around and go back the way we came."

"Move along, nothing to see here," Winnie said softly.

"Yep, exactly," Hank agreed.

"Well, turns out Hank knew another way in," Walt said, "So we went around a bend in the creek, and found a spot to dock. Then we hiked a little ways through the woods and made it to the edge of the swamp, were we could see the cave entrance, maybe a hundred feet or so away," Walt said.

"Here's where it gets real interesting," Hank said. "There were several pieces of heavy equipment at the cave-in site: bulldozers, cranes, earthmovers, you name it, along with a couple of military Hummers—we figured they must've helicoptered the stuff in there, Chinooks or something—that'd started removing the big boulders and rubble from the cave entrance. And, there were several armed guards standing around the perimeter—again, what looked like probably Feds. And while we were checking out the scene, we felt at least two more short, mild tremors. Aftershocks, I'm guessing."

"But then we noticed a black helicopter circling pretty low overhead, so we got the hell outta there," Walt said.

"They're opening it back up," Winnie said, understanding.

"They're opening it back up," Walt and Hank said in unison.

"Jinx, y'owe me a coke," Hand said, winking at Walt.

"Wow," was all Winnie could muster.

"But it doesn't end there, there's still more," Hank said.

At this point Winnie was nearly overwhelmed.

"Okaaaay…," he said cautiously, bracing himself.

Hank grinned, and got that twinkle in his eye.

"I think I'll let Walt take it from here," he said, nodding at the journalist to his left.

Winnie turned to Walt, all ears.

"Okay, I've spent years in investigative journalism, and like I said, I've worked for all the big publications. As a result, I've procured contacts on the *inside*. *Lots* of contacts. Informants, whistleblowers…in government, in the military, in law enforcement, within multi-national corporations, you name it. So whenever I'm on a case, I can usually pull some strings and get some inside information. Comes with the job."

"Right…" Winnie followed, nodding.

"So that's what I did after we saw what was going on at the cave, indicating that for *some* reason, the Feds have taken a mighty keen interest in your…*creature*, if you will.

"At this point I would say *creatures*," Hank interjected.

"Well at any rate," Walt continued, "Yesterday I tracked down the skulls you guys collected in the tunnels and turned over to authorities at the station. Ends up they were sent to a government lab for analysis, a lab where I just happen to have one of those helpful contacts."

"What lab?" Winnie asked, curious.

"Well, I can't tell you that. Yet, anyway. And it's quite possible that even if I *did* tell you, then I'd have to kill you."

He paused for a moment, letting the uncomfortable silence sink in, then he smiled and winked, and the other two chuckled nervously.

"Anyway, here's the thing: there were three skulls, right? Well, analysis showed one was female, from North America, recently deceased, probably local."

Winnie looked at Hank.

"The girl from last year's massacre?" he asked.

"Probably. The skeleton we found in that cavern before the collapsed mine definitely looked female, judging by the size."

"But the other two were male," Walt continued. "And much

older, like centuries old: one was from Australia, and one was from Africa."

Winnie let out a low whistle. "So, they came from different countries."

"Not just different countries, son—different *continents*."

But it didn't quite sink in, what they were telling him, so Hank clarified:

"So in other words, those tunnels must be connected, all around the world...they even traverse the oceans somehow... like *under* them."

Winnie's eyes widened in sudden understanding.

"So they're not just here," Winnie said quietly.

"It's doubtful," Walt speculated. "They're probably all over the world, living underground in caves and tunnels."

"And who knows how many of them there are," Winnie added. "I mean, for years, we all thought there was just one animal or creature of some kind living somewhere in Black Woods and/or Blackwater Swamp. But as of Tuesday, we came to suspect there were *two different* creatures, one living in the cave lake and one living in the tunnels. But now it sounds like there could be multitudes, living underground, in caves, or in lakes, around the world?"

"Looks like it," Hank agreed.

"And that brings us to the really juicy part," Walt said.

Winnie looked up cautiously, like *what more can there be?*

"Remember that mysterious 'something' that Sheriff Collins said he'd found in the swamp with Jackie, and sent off to a lab, and was all hush-hush about?" Hank asked.

Winnie turned to him. "Yes…" he said slowly, a questioning look on his face.

"It was sent to a top-secret government lab," Walt said. "Again, I can't divulge what lab or where, suffice it to say somewhere in Utah—and again, I know people there too."

"So what was it?" Winnie prodded. "Do they know?"

Both Walt and Hank chuckled.

"Here's what's unbelievable," Walt said. "Turns out, the 'mysterious something' was some sort of hairy appendage, with a big black claw protruding from one end. Like from a bear maybe, but much bigger than your average bear."

"Wow…a hairy, clawed toe from some kind of huge creature?" Winnie said excitedly.

"Yes…specifically, the same one we shot in the cave," Hank answered. "I got a pretty close look at it, and noticed its foot was ragged and bleeding…like it was missing a toe."

"Wow," was again all that Winnie could muster, it was all so overwhelming to think about.

"But that's still not all," Hank said.

Winnie just stared with a look of concern on his face.

"It was caked in mud, so they decide to clean it up," Walt continued, "So they submerged it in a tank of cleaning solution —mostly water, with cleaning/sanitizing agents added—but then the lab tech turned away to write something on his clipboard, and when he turned back around, the hairy clawed toe was gone."

"Gone?!" Winnie nearly shouted.

"Yep. And in it's place was the tip of a tentacle, complete

with suction cups and everything. A green/gray color with black spots, different than any species we're aware of."

"As you can image, the guy was amazed, and quickly reached in and pulled the tentacle out of the tank to take a closer look...and right before his eyes, it began changing again...turning brown, growing a black claw, and hair..."

"No way!" Winnie gasped. "It changed from a sea creature's tentacle to some kind of mammalian clawed toe?" Then, turning to Hank: "So what we saw in the cave wasn't two different creatures, but one, that...that...*shape shifted*?"

"Looks that way...and once Walt told me about that, I remembered that the sea creature that attacked you was also missing the end of one tentacle. And they *both* had these intense yellow reptilian-looking eyes. In all the excitement, I never put the two together, the missing tentacle then the missing toe, the matching yellow eyes. Until now, anyway."

"No shit," Winnie whispered, shaking his head in disbelief.

But there's still more," Hank said, donning a serious look.

Winnie stared back at Walt, mouth agape in disbelief.

"So then the tech put the now wet hairy clawed toe on a table in front of a fan to dry it quicker, and again went to document things, or maybe to call his boss, and this time when he turned around—the hairy clawed toe was gone, and instead it was some sort of gray, leathery—maybe even *scaly*, he wasn't sure—toe with a big black talon protruding from it. Like from some kind of huge bird of prey—almost like something from prehistoric times."

Winnie just looked down, shaking his head, unable to wrap

his brain around it. But then, remembering, he looked quickly back up.

"At the hospital, Jackie said the creature he saw had tentacles and yellow eyes...but then he said that was just at first, but then it *changed* somehow...but he went back under before he could elaborate."

"Well, that certainly fits the *modus operandi*," Hank agreed. "So he must've witnessed it shape-shift, from the sea creature to one of the others."

"Or both," Winnie suggested.

"And like Hank said, that theory matches what the tech witnessed in the lab: one piece changing into three different forms—from tentacle, to hairy mammal toe, to talon."

"And speaking of that...*appendage*...what are they gonna do with it?" Winnie asked.

"Well, we don't know," Walt said. "Apparently when he reported the events, a crew in hazmat suits and dark tinted face shields suddenly showed up and relieve him of the...*specimen*... and wouldn't answer any of his questions. So at this point, nobody knows where it is or what they're planning to do with it. At least nobody *I* know, knows. Yet, anyway."

"So, a huge beast that can change from a big sea creature, to a towering land mammal, to a huge flying bird of prey, at will. Living underground, in tunnels and caves—and maybe even underwater—and as far as we know, all around the world?"

"That pretty much sums it up," Hank said.

"What in the holy hell," Winnie said, exasperated. "If that's true, how in the world do we not already know about them?"

"It's quite possible we already do," Walt said. "And have for centuries."

"What?" Winnie gasped, again incredulous.

"I mean, think about it," Walt continued. "This could explain the strange sightings people have been reporting throughout history—like Bigfoot, Sasquatch, the Mogollon Monster, the Ireland Shapeshifter, the Fouke Monster, Chupacabra, and so many others...and maybe even the mysterious water monsters or giant sea creatures reported by sailors crossing the ocean in sailing ships back in the day, or even others like Nessie. And don't forget gargoyles, and chimera—they date back to biblical times, and even earlier in Greek mythology."

"I've never even heard of half of those," Winnie protested.

"Well believe me, they exist—in people's minds, anyway. People around the world have been reporting supposed sightings of all sorts of mysterious, unexplained creatures since...well, forever. Maybe all this time, it's been these underground, "shape-shifting" (he used air quotes when he said it) creatures that you and Hank just discovered down in those tunnels this week."

"And, since there's apparently a flying version of these things too, that might even explain some of the UFO and aliens sightings that have been reported in more recent times," Hank added. Then he clarified: "Not so much the "flying saucers", I'm thinking more of the literal "unidentified flying objects" that could be just about anything, but continue to be unexplained."

Winnie thought about all this for a long moment, fully absorbing the theory.

Then he said: "Okay, let's say all this is true: that these creatures are living in a vast global network of underground caves and tunnels, or in underground lakes, or even under the oceans, and *have* been since the beginning of time; and we're thinking they emerge every nine years—we're hypothesizing it's during a super moon, based on the lunar precession, which always falls on different dates in different locations around the world—to feed, or round up food to take back to their...I don't know, hive, pack, clan, or whatever; and what's more, they can physically change to adapt to any geographic conditions or environment—be it land, water, or air...do I have that right?"

Hank shrugged. "Well, obviously, it's all theoretical at this point. But it's a theory worth considering. At least *I* think so."

"It's a good theory," Winnie said. "But now that I think about it, if it's all true, I think there may be even more to it."

Hank and Walt looked at each other with surprise, then back at Winnie, eagerly waiting.

Winnie paused for a moment, looking down, gathering his thoughts. Then he looked back up at them.

"Do you suppose the creatures could have dug the tunnels? That they don't just happen to live in them, but dug them themselves, created a network of tunnels around the world, working on them since the beginning of time, and that's their world? Always has been?"

"Well, there's a thought," Hank said. "I suppose they could've dug a huge network of underground tunnels over thousands of years—no different than us building cities up here on the surface over thousands of years, eventually spreading around the world."

"Makes sense," Walt agreed.

"Well, the reason I ask," Winnie continued, "Is because I thought I noticed something during the time we were in the tunnels…and now that I think it all over, I think I'm right."

"Oh?" Hank said, curious.

"It's about the tremors. When we first went into the tunnels, the tremors were light…but the longer we stayed, and the further in we went, the stronger they became…almost like a warning…and then, when we fought that creature and wounded it and it escaped back into the water—maybe even into an underwater tunnel that we don't know about—a full-on earthquake was triggered, forcing us to get out."

"Wait…are you saying you think the *creatures* could've been causing those tremors?" Hank asked, incredulous. "Controlling them, and even causing the *earthquake* somehow?"

Winnie just shrugged. "As you say, it's just a theory. But one worth considering. At least *I* think so."

Winnie smiled at his clever comeback.

Hank and Walt just turned and looked at each other, eyebrows raised.

Then the intercom came on, announcing flight 316 was boarding at gate B.

"That's me," Winnie said, standing and shouldering his carry-on bag. "Guess the party's over, huh?"

"I'm sure we'll be talking again soon," Hank said, standing from his chair. "I know where you live, remember?" he said with a wink and smile.

"And I'm sure I'll be scrounging up more information as things progress," Walt said. "I'll be sure to keep in touch with Hank, and he can convey anything I find out to you. After all, if the Feds have decided to reopen that cave, and look for that— or *those*—creatures…well, then this isn't over, by any means."

With that, he extended his hand, Winnie shook it.

"It was a pleasure meeting you," Walt said politely.

"Likewise," Winnie returned.

"Have a safe flight back," Hank said, patting Winnie on the shoulder. "And say hi to that girl of yours for me. I hope to meet her someday!"

"Jenny," Winnie said, smiling. "I'll be sure tell her. And she wants to meet you someday, too. I've told her a lot of good things about you."

"None of it's true!" Hank protested, and they all chuckled.

With that, they turned and separated, Winnie toward the gate area and Hank and Walt toward the exit.

●

A line had formed at the gate, scores of passengers handing boarding passes to the attendants at the podium, and while Winnie was waiting in line his attention was drawn to a nearby TV that was hanging from a ceiling mount, showing a national news program.

He looked up briefly, but then turned away so he could keep an eye on the moving line in front of him.

But then when he heard the news anchor utter the word "tremors", he did a double take, looking back up and listening more intently:

"*Scientists still can't explain the tremors, which have been reported in every major city around the world, all on the same day—which the USGS has reported to have occurred over the course of the day this past Thursday. And, also according to the USGS, such a phenomenon has never been recorded once since their inception in 1879, or over 100 years ago. And they're particularly concerned about the major tremor recorded under Yellowstone National Park, and are watching that area closely. We'll keep you apprised as we learn more, as this is a breaking story...again, simultaneous tremors were reported all around the world on Thursday...*"

Winnie turned away, deeply concerned about what he'd just heard—especially after everything he'd just discussed with Hank and Walt.

He handed over his boarding pass and entered the airliner, stowing his bag in the overhead compartment before flopping himself into his seat, exhausted.

Sitting in silence, he heard Walt's voice echo in his head:

...this isn't over, by any means.

No..., he thought, laying his head back on the head rest and closing his eyes.

This isn't the end...not by a long shot...

With that thought, he turned and looked out the window at his home town of Hope, then up toward the horizon and the world beyond, his next thought very unsettling:

In fact, this is only the beginning...

Also by Rand Eastwood:

Rand Eastwood | Author
Author & Blogger • Artist & Craftsman
randeastwood.com

Rolling The Bones
12 Tales of Life, Death, Loss, & Redemption
amazon.com/rolling-bones-tales-death-redemption/
dp/0692716203

Woodlands Press
on Amazon
amazon.com/author/randeastwood

OUSIA Magazine
The Essence of Truth, Wisdom, & Being
Reason • Philosophy • Lifestyle • Culture
ousiamagazine.com

Lifeology Store
Unique & Exclusive Gifts
lifeologystore.com

Typology Mugs
Because Everyone is Unique
lifeologystore.com/collections/typology-mugs

Compass Bookstore
Explore a World of Great Reads
bookshop.org/shop/compassbookstore

EVOLVE: Toward Autarchy
on Substack
Individualism • Consensualism • Free Markets • Stewardship
towardautarchy.substack.com